PENGUIN CLASSICS

THE TENANT OF WILDFELL HALL

ANNE BRONTË, who was born in 1820, was brought up in the Yorkshire village of Haworth where her father was curate. She was educated at home and, as a child, she invented with her sister Emily the imaginary world of Gondal, for which she wrote copious chronicles and poems. She held two positions as governess, with the Inghams at Blake Hall and, from 1840–45, with the Robinson family at Thorp Green. As a religious lyric poet, Anne Brontë's hymns and lyrics rank with those of Cowper. Her first novel *Agnes Grey* (1847), published under the pseudonym Acton Bell, is in the tradition of fictional spiritual autobiography, written with conciseness, integrity and irony. *The Tenant of Wildfell Hall* (1848) is a powerful feminist testament, attacking the marriage laws, double standards of sexual morality and the education of men and women. Anne Brontë died at Scarborough in 1849. She was the youngest of the Brontë sisters, whose extraordinary gifts are only now receiving just appraisal.

DR STEVIE DAVIES lectured in English Literature at Manchester University from 1971 to 1984. She left to become a full-time novelist and literary critic. Her novel, *Boy Blue*, published in 1987, won the Fawcett Society Book Prize in 1989, and was followed by *Primavera* (1990), *Arms and the Girl* (1992) and *Closing the Book* (1994). She has published eleven critical books, the most recent being *John Donne* (1994), *Emily Brontë: Heretic* (1994) and *Henry Vaughan* (1995). She has written three books in the Penguin Critical Studies series: *To the Lighthouse, Twelfth Night* and *The Taming of the Shrew*. She is currently Senior Research Fellow at Roehampton Institute.

ANNE BRONTË

The Tenant of Wildfell Hall

Edited with an Introduction and Notes by
STEVIE DAVIES

PENGUIN BOOKS

PENGUIN BOOKS

Published by the Penguin Group
Penguin Books Ltd, 27 Wrights Lane, London w8 5tz, England
Penguin Putnam Inc., 375 Hudson Street, New York, New York 10014, USA
Penguin Books Australia Ltd, Ringwood, Victoria, Australia
Penguin Books Canada Ltd, 10 Alcorn Avenue, Toronto, Ontario, Canada m4v 3b2
Penguin Books (NZ) Ltd, 182–190 Wairau Road, Auckland 10, New Zealand

Penguin Books Ltd, Registered Offices: Harmondsworth, Middlesex, England

First published 1848
This edition first published 1996
5 7 9 10 8 6 4

Editorial matter copyright © Stevie Davies, 1996
All rights reserved

The moral right of the editor has been asserted

Set in 10/12.5pt Janson Monotype
Typeset by Datix International Limited, Bungay, Suffolk
Printed in England by Clays Ltd, St Ives plc

CONTENTS

INTRODUCTION

'Sick of mankind and their disgusting ways,' scribbled Anne Brontë in pencil at the back of her Prayer Book.[1] In her 1845 diary paper, she wrote of having undergone 'unpleasant and undreamt-of experiences of human nature'[2] at Thorp Green, where she had been working as governess for five years. Anne had seen at close quarters her brother's degeneration and disgrace; the hypocrisy, affectation and abuse of privilege of the gentry class. She had been bereaved; had understood that she would probably never marry and have the baby she craved; had felt her faith severely tested by desperate periods of religious doubt. *The Tenant of Wildfell Hall* was the testament of this sombre vision. Reviewers reacted with fascinated shock to this 'coarse' and 'brutal' work, in which élite males degenerate into addicts and libertines.[3] Charles Kingsley criticized the work as atonal, 'tortured by a defective chord, in which one false note perpetually recurs'.[4] The defective chord might be called the key of 'H',[5] in which a system of characters – Huntingdon, Hargrave, Hattersley, echoed by Halford and Helen, and, in 'G', Grimsby, at Grassdale – riot against human decency. The 'H' characters are more than men behaving badly – drinking, gaming, abusing their wives (and servants, and dogs), squandering fortunes, fornicating – they are hell-bent souls recklessly playing away the hope of heaven, within a patriarchal system that licenses the soulless pleasures of 'gentlemen'. The cosmic and the domestic occupy the same page; and the realism of the telling coexists with a quality resonant of medieval morality drama and *Dr Faustus*. In *Wildfell Hall*, moral disease has become a norm.

Charlotte Brontë, who had always for complex reasons babied Anne, failing to recognize her strength of character and originality, wished *Wildfell Hall* had never been written. She recoiled with hot pangs of shock from the account of ugly facts which brought to mind the shattering disintegration of their brother: '*Wildfell Hall* it hardly seems to me desirable to preserve,' she wrote betrayingly to her publisher. 'The choice of subject in that work is a mistake',[6] and she said the same to the public in her 'Biographical Notice' of Ellis and Acton Bell. The book was morbid, Charlotte said, the work of 'a sensitive, reserved, and dejected nature' which, having been confronted at close quarters by 'talents misused and faculties abused', felt conscientiously bound to warn others about the dangers, although she 'hated her work'.[7] Yet Anne Brontë was and remained a child of Gondal, the land of the imagination she founded with Emily in her childhood – a grown-up child, of course, a rational, realistic, pensive, radically Christian woman. If she had put away childish things, she was still the same person who had acted the characters of seducers, adulterers, warriors, hell-raisers, outlaws and who, though her heart was no longer in the play, had into her mid-twenties improvised with Emily a cast of Gondal characters, all the way to York and back: 'And during our excursion we were, Ronald Macalgin, Henry Angora, Juliet Angusteena . . . escaping from the palaces of instruction to join the Royalists', wrote Emily in her diary paper of 1845.[8] Echoes of Gondal combined with addictive childhood reading of Moore's life of Byron, with its account of wild Regency womanizing, gaming, shooting, carousing, and those more recondite pleasures of sacrilege exemplified in dressing as monks and drinking from 'a human skull filled with burgundy'.[9] Hence, surely, the bold and free dialogue in the diary section of *The Tenant of Wildfell Hall*; the quality of language caught warm, slangy and sharp from the speaker's mouth. The scintillating sex-appeal of Arthur Huntingdon and the voluptuous physique of Annabella Wilmot may well be relics of Gondal. Wit, humour and irony, as well as tender passages and lyrical scene-making, are essential to the telling. It is impossible to credit Charlotte's statement that the author 'hated her work'.

*

The title of Anne Brontë's second novel relates a person to a place – but her surname, Helen 'Graham' is an assumed name and the place, the derelict moorland mansion, does not belong to her. Helen therefore is inscrutable to the northern community amongst whom she has sought sanctuary, and exists on their margins as a focus of rumour, gossip, speculation and suspicion. Neither does she wish to be known. She hides behind her pseudonym and buries herself as far off the map as she can retire. The first of the two narrators, Gilbert Markham, is a member of that community, a young farmer with hints of a culture beyond agriculture, whose ownership of the 'paternal acres' roots him to the earth, to primogeniture and settled custom. Helen's 'real' name, we later discover, is Helen 'Huntingdon' – but she can only be accounted nominally married to her degenerate husband, for 'my higher and better self is indeed unmarried' (p. 243), and besides, when a woman has been handed round for the use of anyone who will have her, how far can she count as the offerer's wife: '"I value her so highly, that any one among you, that can fancy her, may have her and welcome"' (p. 355)? When Helen leaves her husband and chooses an incognito, she homes to her mother's maiden name (p. 388) to which she feels she has some claim, and returns to the ruined home of her own childhood where Rachel, her servant, said 'she had often walked with me in her arms, and little thought to come again so many years after' (p. 391). The 'tenant' therefore has a vestigial title to her adopted name and the refuge she leases. But this belonging is known neither to the reader nor to the tattling community, which registers her not as a returnee but as an unknown quantity, bringing in alien values. Into the old-fashioned provincial world retires a strong-minded independent woman, who earns her living as an artist, eloquent, forceful, anomalous. Dispossessed and displaced, she becomes a mysterious object of fascination both to the community and the narrator.

Anne Brontë's novel is a powerful and disputatious sister-novel to Emily Brontë's *Wuthering Heights*. The very initials of the place – 'W.H.' – and those of the system of 'H' characters (playing on the Heights series, Hindley, Heathcliff, Hareton) spell out this kinship. In both novels, the moorland house is dynastic and the locus of desire and curiosity. But neither uncanny presences, violent usurpation nor extremes of possessive hatred and need haunt Anne's hall as they do Emily's. 'Wild' and on the 'fells', just off the edge of the community, where culture meets nature, 'the superannuated mansion of the Elizabethan era' has already made progress in resolving issues of patrimony by crumbling uninhabitably back into the heath. Human beings have abandoned the place as too wuthering – 'only shielded from the war of wind and weather by a group of Scotch firs, themselves half blighted with storms' (pp. 22–3). The phrasing echoes *Wuthering Heights*: 'the excessive slant of a few, stunted firs at the end of the house; and ... a range of gaunt thorns all stretching their limbs one way, as if craving alms of the sun' (Chapter 1). Perhaps both houses derive from a common *Ur*-hall in Gondal. Emily's utilitarian Romanticism is answered by Anne's picturesque rationalism. Whereas Wuthering Heights is a working farm run by hardy, spartan people, the hall of Anne's novel is the decayed relic of an outworn patrician class, whose armorial bearings dominate the church but whose pretensions are mocked by the recrudescence of mansion into moor. Her ruin is a folly. Its garden displays the heraldic pretensions of a grotesquely deformed topiary sprouting back into the wilderness of nature: 'the old boxwood swan, that sat beside the scraper, had lost its neck and half its body' and laurel castellations, warrior and lion guarding the gateway 'had sprouted into such fantastic shapes as resembled nothing in heaven or earth' (p. 23). The overgrown garden of Anne's hall mocks the vanity of human wishes, a late-flowering instance of eighteenth-century Enlightenment consciousness in an author who, following Ecclesiastes and Dr Johnson's *The Vanity of Human Wishes*, had written a poem entitled 'Vanitas Vanitatum':

> Should wealth or fame our life employ,
> Death comes our labour to destroy,
> To snatch th'untasted cup away,
> For which we toiled so many a day.
>
> (32–5)

Anne Brontë's garden of vanity comments on the fabrications of human architecture and that arboricultural boastfulness which cultivated nature (boxwood, laurel) into an art-work in imitation of nature (swan, lion) appropriated to the self-glorifying iconography of 'great' families, only to be overrun by the profusely scathing energies of nature. Anne Brontë's ancient hall demystifies Gothic. Her ruined house is not haunted. It is simply dilapidated, damp and unwelcoming.

Helen Graham is a transient. At her married home, Grassdale, she was numbered, we later discover, amongst goods and chattels. Anne Brontë brings into full focus the expropriated, estranged nature of women's lives. Helen can call neither her home nor her name her own. *Wildfell Hall* is a feminist manifesto of revolutionary power and intelligence. Helen 'Graham' or 'Huntingdon' or 'Lawrence' stands as an image of unaccommodated woman, in a landscape of biblical texts as well as moorlands and pasture, in which we plainly see that the daughter of woman has nowhere to lay her head. Paradoxically, her destabilizing inheritance is contradicted by her exceptional strength and stability as a person, with a core of impregnable self-esteem, far more steadfast in herself than the volatile male narrator, plodding through his acres, through whose eyes we first approach and experience her. The dispossessed Helen is transgressive: a challenge both to the narrator and the narrator's community. She lives alone. She earns her own living; keeps her own counsel and tells the definitive version of her own story.

The reader views not only the narrator's word-picture of Wildfell Hall but, in a chapter entitled 'The Studio', the figure of a woman with easel and oils (the prerogative of the male artist) painting her own picture of Wildfell Hall 'as seen at early morning from the field below, rising in dark relief against a sky of clear silvery blue ... very elegantly and artistically handled' (p. 46). Anne Brontë's portrait of the artist as a fee-earning young woman trebly trespasses on the domain of the masculine: female artists dabbled in water-colours or sketched decoratively in pencil or pen and ink; 'ladies' did not engage in trade; and, besides, the tools of her trade in this case count as stolen. The artist's materials noted by Markham on entry are formally the property of her husband – a point Anne Brontë concisely makes in Chapter 40 when Huntingdon burns her materials – 'the oil and turpentine sent hissing and roaring up the chimney' (p. 365) and has the easel, canvas, stretcher and half-finished picture carted off for a larger conflagration. Then he laughs in her face. For what's hers is his; but what's his is not hers. Hence, Helen must sell her pictures under false names: 'Fernley Manor, Cumberland, instead of Wildfell Hall' (p. 47). Names, for the author who wrote pseud-onymously as 'Acton Bell' rather than Anne Brontë, to protect herself from the unjust criticism meted out to women authors, were a place of hiding to the woman who wished to publish her fiction without publicizing herself. The Parsonage at Haworth, on the threshold where the village community met the wild fells, was a retreat in which to be securely oneself. The fugitive heroine covers for an anomalous author at odds with the male-dominated society in and against which she had formed her vagrant personal truth.

Wildfell Hall is told by two narrators, in two literary forms (Markham's letters framing Helen's diary), concerned with two periods of time (the beginning and end of the 1820s), in two keys. Beginning in the minor key of romantic-domestic social comedy, it moves back in time to the major key of tragic irony in Helen's inset diary, succeeded by further letters by Gilbert encapsulating a cluster of new letters from Helen. Both frame and core narratives are spiritual testaments in the tradition of Puritan spiritual autobiography – Richardson's epistolary novels on the one hand, Bunyan and the Puritan conversion narratives and spiritual journals on the other. But the outer, epistolary, witness, is subordinate to and changed by the inner diary witness, and though spatially his account encompasses hers, spiritually hers dominates, rebukes and transforms his. The central diary represents an individual's authoritative personal witness to the fruit of traumatizing and chastening experience, 'experience' being a key-word. Appropriating themes from Richardson's *Pamela* and more especially *Clarissa* (the sexual pursuit by a libertine of a virtuous woman under family pressure to accept an obnoxious suitor), Anne Brontë transfers what in Richardson was shown in letters into the private testimony of the diary: things outward and visible are converted to confessions inward and spiritual. Richardson has his heroine write giddily to her friend:

And then the secret pleasure intruded itself, to be able to reclaim such a man to the paths of virtue and honour: to be a *secondary* means, if I were to be his, of saving him, and preventing the mischiefs so enterprising a creature might otherwise be guilty of, if he be such a one. (Letter 40, p. 183)

Anne Brontë's Helen writes, to herself:

there is a secret something – an inward instinct that assures me I am right. There is essential goodness in him – and what delight to unfold it! If he has wandered, what bliss to recall him! If he is now exposed to the baneful influence of corrupting and wicked companions, what glory to deliver him from them! – Oh! if I could but believe that Heaven has designed me for this! (pp. 152–3)

For Richardson's rapist, Lovelace, Clarissa is 'that angel of a woman' who never falls from grace but, like a greater Eve, endures her 1,500-page trial of virtue (p. 430) transcendently. The male author turns his heroine face-outwards so that we can all enjoy her. The transactions of Helen's diary are soliloquistic, moving from naïve self-delusion to the recognition that 'I am no angel' (p. 267). Though Arthur Huntingdon echoes Lovelace's assumed name of 'Huntingford' (*Clarissa*, p. 417) and has some of his qualities of Godforsaken levity, Lovelace's predatory sexuality is realized in the vulpine Hargrave, a more minor character. For the nineteenth-century woman author, the question of chastity is secondary to problems of integrity, truthfulness, affection, motherhood, livelihood. The framing letters in *Wildfell Hall* communicate outwards to an imagined reader (Halford) and to ourselves as readers how 'the old Adam' may be charged and changed by the private words of a compulsive truth-seeker and truth-teller. Helen's words build on the Word, and the seriousness of her attempt to account for her life stands in contrast to the mindless 'small talk' of Markham's community: '"I was wearied to death with small-talk,"' she tells him – '"nothing wears me out like that. I cannot imagine how they *can* go on as they do."' Gilbert cannot help 'smiling at the serious depth of her wonderment'

(p. 85).[10] Anne Brontë's novel is profoundly concerned for the integrity of the word: it examines the abuse of language in the small talk of women, the big talk of men, in prattle, insult, gossip, curses and the bearing of false witness both through lies and self-delusion. *Wildfell Hall* searches toward a communication which will be communion: 'the unity of accordant thoughts and feelings, and truly loving, sympathizing hearts and souls' (p. 485).

The opening section (Chapters 1–15) reveals Gilbert Markham as first cousin to Emily Brontë's Lockwood – an unreliable narrator, fundamentally a decent man in a novel not rich in human decency especially amongst males, but with a little of the oaf, a little of the cad. Subject to swerves of feeling, he is sometimes silly and imperceptive, often kind, generous, sympathetic, and willing to grow in spirit – that is, if such growth will turn Helen into Helen Markham. Flouncing and exploding, manipulative and irresponsible, he rises to displays of prodigious learning ('So we talked about painting, poetry, and music, theology, geology, and philosophy ...' (p. 73)), and sinks to peevish sulks or twaddling conferences with his irritating brother Fergus. Markham's tenderness for animals and children would have spoken eloquently for him in Anne's book. As he falls in love with Helen, he and the community fall out of love with one another. The stranger, with her outlandish values, provokes and threatens parish norms as endorsed by the comic vicar, Reverend Millward, who regards Helen's attempt to immunize her son against alcohol as '"criminal, I should say – criminal!" ... "contrary to Scripture and to reason to teach a child to look with contempt and disgust upon the blessings of Providence"' (pp. 42–3). Markham's mother amiably but vacuously polices the community's patriarchal values in the home, where she ensures that her elder son is nicely spoilt, fed, fussed, and endorses the scandalous rumours circulating about the stranger at Wildfell, for '"I always thought there was something odd about her. – You see what it is for women to affect to be different from other people"' (p. 89). Social comedy after the manner of Jane Austen characterizes Markham's letters but they also incorporate glimpses of another, emotionally and intellectually ampler world, as the text rises in a chapter entitled 'A Controversy' to the style of a novel of ideas. In a powerfully argued Miltonic debate about experience, choice and temptation, Helen contests the segregated education of male and female, with its over-protection of girls and over-exposure of boys.

The intimation of worlds beyond the insular tea-party world of innuendo and rumour recurs in the view of the sea in Chapter 7, 'The Excursion', which kindles the haughty and sombre Helen into 'a smile of exalted, glad intelligence as her eye met mine' (p. 65). Anne Brontë recaptures the magic of her own sea-visits to Scarborough which would call her back as she was dying: it was her version of the 'oceanic feeling' which Emily Brontë associated with the moors. After Anne's death, Charlotte was to remember her in large vistas: 'the distant prospects were Anne's delight, and when I look round, she is in the blue tints, the pale mists, the waves and shadows of the horizon'.[11] The woman artist at the cliff-edge who 'plied her solitary task' recalls Anne Brontë's pencil-sketch of a young girl looking out to sea in valediction or welcome, towards a sun that is rising or setting. But even here the low style is held, as the callow, magnetized lover–narrator hovers round the artist, aspersing plain women, 'grumbling', wheedling, sulking. Later, in a spasm of jealous rage, Markham astoundingly beats her supposed lover, Lawrence, delivering 'a powerful blow', for which, even with the advantage of twenty years' mature consideration, he does not know whether to claim 'credit' or 'blame'. Then he leaves him for dead. Later he uncouthly apologizes. The unstable tone of this episode repelled reviewers, who felt, like E. P. Whipple in the *North American Review* that Markham 'would serve as the ruffian of any other novelist' but 'seems to be a favourite with the author'.[12] It was generally assumed that Acton and Ellis Bell were one person, 'violent', 'coarse' and 'brutal'. *Wildfell Hall* fails to comprehend its twin narrators as does *Wuthering Heights* in its system of 'Chinese box' encapsulations.[13] Markham's character constantly flies asunder, and whether the author or the character cannot hold him together is at times unclear. Maybe Anne felt men did not really make sense, a suspicion that has occurred to women before and since. As Charlotte Brontë wrote to Miss Wooler, 'You ask me if I do not think men are strange beings. I do indeed – and I think too that the mode of bringing them up is strange.'[14]

Any flaw in design is not fatal. In some respects the instability vitalizes the link between the inner and major plot told by Helen's diary and the outer domesticated realism: for the males of *Wildfell Hall* are unstable. Ironically, they are what men have conventionally called women: *varium et mutabile semper*. Branwell Brontë, himself driven by violent rages, directionless impulses, hypersensitive outbursts, wrote of his *alter ego*, Charles Wentworth, 'as to fixed detail of character, he had none'.[15] Markham describes himself indulgently as 'a little bit spoiled by my mother and sister, and some other ladies of my acquaintance' (p. 36). 'Spoiled' men are the tragic centre of the novel. Huntingdon is so totally spoiled that he can never grow up; Markham emerges from the narcissism that makes his judgements shallow (his preference for the silly and mean Eliza, his dismissiveness of the 'nonentity', plain Mary Millward). The infantile basis of the conditioned male psyche is humorously explored in the figure of Huntingdon, jealous of his own baby as a competitor for mother's attentions ('"That's more, in one minute, lavished on that little senseless, thankless oyster, than you have given me these three weeks past"' (p. 242)), for Arthur is also '"a little selfish, senseless, sensualist"', from cradle-days petted and privileged, and the novel asks: what if babies ruled the world?

It answers: they already do.

Reviewers, largely themselves male, naturally took exception to this depiction of males as either infantile or depraved. *Sharpe's London Magazine* was shocked at the portrayal of women as 'superior in every quality, moral and intellectual, to all the men', who 'appear at once coarse, brutal, and contemptibly weak, at once disgusting and ridiculous'.[16] The *Literary World* pointed out that all that was good or attractive about Acton Bell's male characters 'is or might be womanish'.[17] The author had searched the males of her acquaintance for signs of a higher nature: she had not found it conspicuous in a range of men from the lovable but unreliable William Weightman, to violently authoritarian men like her employer Joshua Ingham of

Blake Hall, and especially Branwell and his drinking cronies. Indulged as the only boy in a family of six, Branwell was a temperamental being who would 'drive his first through the panel of a door' to find relief from his powerful feelings: warm-hearted and void of purpose, he drifted into the arms of the fraternity of debauch. Anne Brontë, herself an educator, analysed the lack of sense and reason amongst males as the consequence of a value-system based on the worship of machismo. '"By G—d he drinks like a man"', was a compliment Lord Byron had proudly reported of himself.[18] To hold your liquor was accounted then as now a sign of virility. Anne Brontë's analysis, linking the mild case of Markham with the terminal case of Huntingdon, also bonds the debate in the opening section with the demonstration in the diary account, where the men pass round their needful alcohol like a baby's bottle, stupefying themselves and creating mayhem for the women to clear up. At Linden-Car, the community expresses its view, through derision, that for a woman to guard and guide her son is to turn him into '"the veriest milksop that ever was sopped"', '"you'll spoil his spirit, and make a mere Miss Nancy of him"' (pp. 31, 33). Helen's diary, the testimony of experience, ironizes this prejudice, for the fraternity of the bottle is revealed as the real milksops, a gang of soaks who urge one another on to '"seize the bottle and suck away"' (p. 193), in a perpetual uproar, like children bereft of supervision. They remain in the equivalent of a ruffianly childhood, running amok, fighting, throwing things, cursing for effect, shamelessly baring their addled brains to public view. Huntingdon is in effect hardly literate: he unlearns the art of letter-writing and fails to compute his finances. Grimsby, who prides himself on his capacity to '"take three times as much as they have tonight"', cannot tell a saucer from a cup for the purposes of pouring cream, and mistakes the sugar-basin for a slop-bowl (p. 275). All are at the stage of resourceless children requiring the stimulation of amusements, their sole occupations being gaming and hunting. Helen's letters quoted in the final part of Markham's narrative conclude the demonstration with a final terrifying proof of the construction of '"the veriest milksop that ever was sopped"' by male upbringing and privilege, in the pathetic death of Huntingdon, utterly dependent, helpless, clinging to 'mother'. For he has no soul to call his own.

Helen's diary builds a case against the marriage laws of Anne Brontë's day, in the light of this disastrous acculturation of males. Several years after the publication of *Wildfell Hall*, the case of Mrs Norton focused the deep injustice of the marriage laws.[19] Her husband brought legal actions against her on the grounds of adultery with Lord Melbourne. When she was proved innocent, he deprived her of her children, refused her maintenance, and claimed what she had earned for herself by writing pamphlets, all of which he could legitimately do, since a married woman was feme covert, having no legal existence in her own right and hence no right to own property (being herself property), save in the form of the 'settlements' of statute law. As the popular summary had it, 'Husband and wife are one person under the law, and that person is the husband'. Anne Brontë's novel is in part a polemic against these abuses of reason and human rights. Helen has no redress against her husband's raids on decency. She cannot obtain a divorce when his adultery with Annabella, and later with 'Miss Myers', the 'governess', is detected; though as a male and a peer, Annabella's husband can. She has no legal right to the pen in her hand, the diary in which she writes, her paints and canvases, her pictures, or the earnings from those pictures; nor can she call her son her own, but must steal him from the house in which they belong. It is important to recognize that the tenant of Wildfell Hall lives outside the law; is an outlaw. The uncontrollable 'baby' has legal right of control over the self-commanding woman.

These themes extend the logic of Anne Brontë's 'governess' story, *Agnes Grey*, which examined the education of young males at the stage where they bond with other males in contempt of women. Uncle Robson applauds the sadism of young Tom, as 'with fiendish glee' he salivates over the pleasure of torturing and dismembering baby birds:

'Well, you *are* a good un! . . . Damme, but the lad has some spunk in him too! Curse me, if ever I saw a nobler little scoundrel than that! He's beyond petticoat government already: by G—, he defies mother, granny, governess,

and all! Ha, ha, ha! Never mind, Tom, I'll get you another brood tomorrow.'
(Chapter 5)

Agnes's mercy-killing is seen as a sin against the God-given right of
a human boy to mutilate a 'soulless brute'. But who is the soulless
brute: human boy or helpless animal? If Anne's first novel taught its
reader to reassess the doctrine of 'spunk' and to inquire what was
meant by 'nobility' when applied to male behaviour, it also brought
into relief the trampling of 'petticoat government' over which the
male establishment straddles, gun in hand, mimed by the fledgeling
male 'with his legs wide apart, his hands thrust into his breeches-
pockets' in 'an ecstasy of delight' – a posture at once ludicrous,
shameful and dismaying. Since maternal values were equated with
nurture, tenderness, restraint and reason, such 'petticoat government'
would also be Christian government. *Wildfell Hall* takes this analysis
a step further. The males swagger with their guns. Their sports are
blood-sports. In a horrifying image, the amorous Huntingdon ambles
over to Annabella and Helen 'all spattered and splashed as he was,
and stained with the blood of his prey' (p. 161). For the female of our
own species is also the object of male 'sport' and the stain Huntingdon
wears will widen to include some of Helen's life's blood. His 'friend'
Hargrave soon joins the hunt for prey by subjecting Helen to a
campaign of what would today be called sexual harassment. The
phallic gun of the sportsmen dominates the novel (Markham too
shoots game on his estate) and the shooters time their year according
to the hunting calendar: '"Are you too busy making love ..."',
Helen's uncle joshes Huntingdon, '"to make war with the pheasants?
– First of October remember!"' (p. 185). Anne and Emily had kept a
pet pheasant along with the geese in the outhouse: in her 1834 diary
paper, Emily had noted: 'I fed Rainbow, Diamond, Snowflake, Jasper
phaesant' [sic].[20] Branwell killed pheasants and grouse on the moors
and painted himself with his unarmed sisters in a now lost portrait
called 'The Gun Group', weapon raised, dead birds displayed on the
table before them. As Hargrave seeks to compromise his wife,
Hattersley is outside the door, 'busy with his ramrod and his gun'
(p. 358), ready to accompany his friends in a pheasant-kill, and

shortly discharges against Helen 'a volley of the vilest and grossest abuse' at the thought that she is engaged in an adulterous liaison. Having rammed the charge down into the barrel of one gun, the sportsman turns in legitimized violence against his wife, whose defences are the pen, the mind, and the palette-knife of her trade turned outwards (p. 358). Yet these are potent defences, and Helen does not go the way of Lucrece and Clarissa.

The power to make this feminist statement derived from Anne Brontë's Christian belief: she represents a development of radical Protestantism which insists on the right and duty of the individual to interpret the Scriptures for herself in the light of the Spirit's promptings, and to make known her understanding. The Authorized Version of the Bible is warp and weft of the discourse of *Wildfell Hall*, both as a code of belief and behaviour and as a sacred poem, a polyphony of voices, speaking not only of the comfort and admonition of the Gospels, especially Jesus' parables (Dives and Lazarus, the house built on sand, the sower, the talents, the grain of mustard seed) but in prophetic condemnation of social evils (the 'vanity' motif of Ecclesiastes and the Book of Proverbs) and the mourning voice of affliction and exile (Lamentations, Job, the Psalms). The strong-minded woman author gives the flabby-minded male narrator initially only a casual and shallow understanding of Scripture: he quotes speciously and spends his time in church ogling the beautiful stranger. Later, having read the diary and under the influence of Helen's passionate spirituality, he will be caught up unawares into her vision of eternity, and, awed into serious appraisal of the Christian vision for the first time in his life, will be alarmed at the glaring prospect, not of hell but of heaven: '"But can *you*, Helen, contemplate with delight this prospect of losing me in a sea of glory?"' (p. 405). The commonplace mind (and Gilbert claims to be no more than an ordinary, shabby, wanting man) is shocked and baffled by a mind like Helen's – and her author's – to which the Absolute is literally real. The voice of the diary is rich and deep with biblical allusion, strenuously expressing the depths of Helen's clarifying suffering and dark enlightenment, in the aftermath of her giddy, tragic marriage-choice. Anne Brontë's Protestant vision encompassed awareness of the depravity to which fallen people could sink, along with a refusal of the doctrine of hell, which she believed incompatible with a God of Love. Helen's debate with her pious but untender aunt concerning the destination of the 'reprobate' (Chapter 20) trades conflicting biblical texts. Here Anne Brontë plays out on the page the agonizing personal conflict which in an illness of 1837 had brought to her bedside the Moravian minister, James La Trobe, to lead her to a belief in universal salvation – a conflict which occupies many of her lyric poems, with their sense of unworthiness and their yearning tenderness towards Jesus:

> I cannot say my faith is strong,
> I dare not hope my love is great;
> But strength and love to Thee belong,
> O, do not leave me desolate.

Anne's lyric poems, which she called 'pillars of witness'[21] recorded a hope without which she felt her spirit would fail her that 'Even the wicked shall at last / Be fitted for the skies' ('A Word to the Calvinists', 37–8). It was a desperate issue, always a source of introspective conflict, to which she accorded the status of 'hope', never a dogmatic certainty; and *Wildfell Hall* articulates that conflict, not its resolution. Anne Brontë had been subject to periods of religious doubt when, like Branwell, she wondered if God existed at all; and, if he did, could he care for her? Her austere quatrains wrestle with doubt. Branwell too had wrestled and been thrown. Then he had run away:

> 'Tis something far more dread
> Which haunts me in my dying bed!
> I have lost – long lost – my trust in Thee!
> I cannot hope that Thou wilt hear
> The unrepentant sinner's prayer!
> So, whither must my spirit flee
> For succour through Eternity?
>
> ('Harriet' (2))

Wildfell Hall attempts to encounter the terrors which were the converse of Branwell's self-consciously Byronic defiance of heaven. Huntingdon, more trivial and worldly than Branwell, becomes a shallow Faustus in his ending: '"But death *will* come – it is coming now – fast, fast! – and – Oh, if I *could* believe there was nothing after!" … "I *can't* repent; I only fear."' (p. 445). After his death, Helen clings to her hope that her husband's soul 'is not lost, and God, who hateth nothing that He hath made, *will* bless it in the end"' (p. 447). It is necessary for a secular reader to appreciate that Anne Brontë took her faith with literality: if God was real, he was real not nominally, hypothetically or on Sundays, but in the here-and-now of every day, in an urgent sense. But people do not see him; the material world is mistaken for reality, while the air throngs with transparent agencies of light and the legion shadows of evil. They do not hear their own casual blasphemies blackening their tongues and turning all their speeches into self-damning ironies. The drama of the 'diary' narrative uncovers the eternal implications of casual deeds and conventional language, especially the language of profane love. '"Sweet angel, I adore you!"', says Huntingdon, manipulating Helen with exploitative demands and familiar touching of her body; but her aunt interrupts, 'And I left him, muttering maledictions against his evil angel' (p. 147). Rescued from the attentions of the unappealing Mr Wilmot, she feels 'It was like turning from some purgatorial fiend to an angel of light, come to announce that the season of torment was past' (p. 146). But the season of torment is just beginning, and the bright-haired, beautiful young man is racing his fellow reprobates down the road to hell – and winning.

If *Wildfell Hall* is a dissenting sister of *Wuthering Heights*, it is also spiritual kin to Charlotte Brontë's *Jane Eyre*. Sharing the passionate truth to self of Charlotte's novel and with something of the mutinous energy of Jane's 'I', which begets itself in the reader who shares her journey, the 'diary' section of *Wildfell Hall* (Chapters 16–44) also represents its territories as landscapes of the mind, viewed in the light of eternity. Jane makes Bunyanesque linear passage from one emblematic resting-place and tempting-place to another – from Gateshead, through Lowood, Thornfield, Whitcross, to Moor End, whence, having acquired an independent inheritance and the romantic equivalent of the Puritan 'call', she circles back via the destroyed Thornfield, the site of Rochester's atonement, to sanctuary at Ferndene. But Helen's journey, from Staningley to Grassdale, escaping to Wildfell, only to return via Grassdale to Staningley, ultimate sole heir to both, is viewed both retrospectively and prospectively from the way-stage of Wildfell. The 'progress' is therefore not as clearly marked. The struggling, implicated quality of human life is more evident in *Wildfell Hall* as Helen is tainted by the corruption she cannot escape: 'I HATE him! The word stares me in the face like a guilty confession, but it is true: I hate him – I hate him!' (p. 308); 'Instead of being humbled and purified by my afflictions, I feel that they are turning my nature into gall' (p. 313). Grassdale bears a weight of symbolic meaning comparable with the pilgrim's sojourns in *Jane Eyre*: at first it is a fool's paradise, then a false paradise. Lush and tender descriptions of its natural beauty are blighted not only by the loneliness of Huntingdon's absence but by the lurking of a snake in the grass, Hargrave, a cold comment upon the intemperately warm-hearted attempt to master Jane by Rochester. Insinuating himself into Helen's good graces in a scene of wistfully Edenic beauty, Hargrave resembles Milton's Satan's slyly ingratiating approaches to Eve in *Paradise Lost*. The sense of paradisal innocence is conveyed by a tenderly observed scene of play between mother, nurse and child in the grace of a 'sweet, warm evening' in the park:

I was standing with Rachel beside the water, amusing the laughing baby in her arms with a twig of willow laden with golden catkins, when greatly to my surprise, he entered the park, mounted on his costly black hunter, and crossed over the grass to meet me. (pp. 246–7)

This sinister figure again penetrates the lyrical scene of Helen kneeling before her baby, 'having gathered a handful of bluebells and wild roses ... and presenting them, one by one, to the grasp of his tiny fingers' (p. 250). Hargrave, the dark mounted figure on the 'costly black hunter' hunts Helen with sexual threat which culminates in the chess-game of Chapter 33, so reminiscent of the chess-scene in Middleton's tragedy, *Women Beware Women*.[22] Grassdale represents a paradise already lost in the moment of enjoyment: Helen must substitute for its idyll the Miltonic 'paradise within thee, happier far' (XII. 587) in her flight from its bounds. The house becomes a hell on earth, and the repeated 'hell' chimes with Helen's name. Her sufferings culminate in the detection of Huntingdon and his mistress in sexual play in the shrubbery, where Helen's husband swears '"by all that's sacred"' that he no longer loves his wife (p. 303). In this moment of absolute affliction, the prose deepens to a throbbing biblical intensity reminiscent of *Jane Eyre*: in the extremity of need is vouchsafed a breathing of grace and the fellowship of the creation in a vision of the stars: 'I knew their God was mine, and He was strong to save and swift to hear' (p. 303).

One of the novel's triumphs is to make Arthur Huntingdon not a fiend incarnate but an immature, boyish figure, with real gaiety, some warmth and charm, who feels as deep a tenderness for his wife as he knows how to feel. Possessive and despotic in his initial affection for Helen, he lavishes affectionate attention on her, and craves total attention in return. Jealous of all that distracts her from him ('when he sees me occupied with a book, he won't let me rest till I close it' (p. 208), Huntingdon has no inner resources and hence is easily bored, filling the time when Helen runs out of amusements for him by 'lolling' beside her on the sofa trying to arouse her jealousy by spinning tales of former amours. Their honeymoon is a bizarre scamper round Europe, which is no novelty to him and whose fascinations he begrudges to his wife 'in as much as it proved that I could take delight in anything disconnected with himself' (p. 203). Objecting to her religious devotion, he explains that '"it is enough to make one jealous of one's Maker – which is very wrong, you know; so don't excite such wicked passions again, for my soul's sake"' (p. 204). Helen's locking of her door against her spouse is a memorable act of feminist defiance; it is also an episode in a banal household row, which reflects credit on neither party. The next morning Huntingdon seethes with malign sulks; it rains; he yawns, fidgets, drinks, bangs doors and strikes the cocker spaniel off 'with a smart blow'. The dog retreats and, when its master wants to pet it again, cleaves to Helen and will not come. 'Enraged at this, his master snatched up a heavy book and hurled it at his head' (p. 212). Helen lets it out. Such minor fracas are proleptic. Helen will love; be abused; recoil in anger and hurt; and, for her recoil (interpreted as rejection) be rejected; then she will reject in earnest. The particular quarrel is resolved within the chapter, in which the tension is broken by her yielding to his not very abject penitence and caresses. But it sets up a pattern of deterioration which is mercilessly inexorable, for Helen's very character in its forthrightness and integrity have the ironic effect of alienating her husband. The narrative moves in a rhythm of mounting misery with pauses and reprieves; chapters end on upbeats of hope or downbeats of apprehension as skilfully managed dynamic scenes of quarrel are played out, in which both manoeuvre for advantage. 'What shall I do with the serious part of myself?' ends Chapter 22 ominously. 'I trust we shall be happy yet,' Chapter 24 falteringly concludes.

Long before Helen has consciously recognized her bad bargain, the reader has understood that there is nothing to Arthur Huntingdon. It is not that he is an intrinsically evil person. He is a brat. The centre is painfully hollow. Even Huntingdon seems conscious of this absence of something vital in his human make-up: gentle when ill after his first major debauch, he turns thankfully to Helen, as though her resources could serve for them both. A real pathos surrounds him. But he must fill his emptiness with excitement and intrigue, and in the measure that Helen withdraws from this compulsion, she helps to empty him further, so that he must have more gratification. He pours drink into himself; fills his house with the roaring fraternity; courts that fine animal, Annabella; abuses Helen. Helen's tenderness is hard to kill; its durability is expressed when she sees a letter in Hargrave's hand, 'with Arthur's still beloved hand on the address' (p. 251). The author does not allow us to forget how sexually attractive and childishly appealing Huntingdon is: how puzzled (when he can be bothered to think) by the circumstances he is creating. But Huntingdon's behaviour is not an isolated instance; it belongs to a social norm for élite males. In the confraternity, Anne Brontë studies the dynamics of group mentality, the mutual reinforcement of male 'club' behaviour. The melancholy and Byronic Lord Lowborough's betrayal to drink, drugs and suicidal despair, taunted with unmanliness by his 'friends' and his adulterous wife; Hattersley's abuse of his 'invitingly meek and mim' wife, the timorous Milicent; the cynicism of Hargrave's sexual approaches and Grimsby's squalid antics represent a group code which not only legitimates but authorizes infantilism as a norm. Hattersley is redeemed; Hargrave repelled; Lowborough divorces, to begin a new life: only Huntingdon is entirely destitute of hope. Anne Brontë focuses the nihilism attendant on terminal weakness and self-indulgence; spoilt in this life, he is spoilt for the next world. We smile at his Branwellian antics in church, perusing his Prayer Book upside down, adopting a 'puritanical air of mock solemnity': '"I'll come home sighing like a furnace, and full of the savour and unction of dear Mr Blatant's discourse –"' (p. 174). Branwell too had monkeyed about in his pew and had a running joke about how 'two fireballs' (brandy with egg) make the tippler 'a brand plucked from the burning'[23] – Wesley's favourite text for his own conversion. Branwell too had been spoilt, and lost. As his friend Grundy put it, 'he was just a man moving in a mist who lost his way'.[24] The reality of such loss and such burning are borne out in Huntingdon's death-scene, an evasion of 'repentance' by one who has misplaced his soul and now, in extreme need, cannot lay claim to it: '"I'm not going to die yet. – I can't and won't."' He clings to the person who has kept hers ('"Helen, you *must* save me!"') and tries to grapple her down into the grave with him, to answer for him. His last words are '"Don't leave me!"' (pp. 441–7). He dies, indeed, without being weaned.

Helen's testament is a story of double temptation and double failure: Huntingdon's and her own. The diary throws the mature woman of 1828 back to her susceptible, needy and spirited girlhood at the beginning of the decade, the pert niece of a severe aunt whose anxious piety is counter-productive in provoking mischievous answers. When Aunt Maxwell points out the horror of finding your husband '"a worthless reprobate, or even an impractical fool"', Helen flightily wonders, '"But what are all the poor fools and reprobates to do, aunt?"' and mentions the danger of depopulation (p. 132). The levity in Helen is evidently fair game for Huntingdon's sparkling flightiness: but Helen is a complex, deep, and deepening character. The notion she boasts of 'saving' her irresponsible spouse – a favourite female myth of the mid-nineteenth century – is exposed as rash arrogance, the tragic flaw of pride which brings her falling headlong. It unleashes in Huntingdon a Nemesis whose black taunts she has herself invited: '"Yes, *now*, my immaculate angel ..."' (p. 441). Helen's diary plots her downward course into disillusion, hurt, rage, moral petrification and embitterment. To her alarm, she begins to adapt to the debased norms of Grassdale,

till I am familiarized with vice and almost a partaker in his sins. Things that formerly shocked and disgusted me now seem only natural ... Fool that I was to dream that I had strength and purity enough to save myself and him! (p. 262)

Her temper sours; her tongue lashes out, for 'I am no angel' (p. 267). Helen wrestles not only against her husband but against herself, for her own soul. The two climaxes of action come in Chapter 33, the anguished scene in the shrubbery in which she comes face to face with her husband's adultery; and Chapter 40, the centre of violation, in which Huntingdon rakes through her diary, discovers her savings and has her paintings burned, a spiritual rape. Huntingdon's early proposal to '"Let me have its bowels then"', as he eviscerates her portfolio, and rifles the contents (p. 160), proleptically foreshadows the vandalizing of Helen's inner and private world and the destruction of her means of subsistence.

Helen's life is centred in her child, the second Arthur Huntingdon – bidding fair to become a second edition of the first as the father and his peers '"make a man of him"' by teaching him 'to tipple wine like papa, to swear like Mr Hattersley, and to have his own way like a man' (p. 350). Cursing his mother as Heathcliff teaches Hareton to curse his family, 'the infant profligate' (p. 351) terrifies Helen with the success of the experiment to alienate him from her loving, principled education, reconstituting him in the image of the patriarchy which has in turn reproduced and authorized its damaged pattern in father and son from generation to generation. Shocking as this perversion is, Anne Brontë presents it as an extreme version of a norm familiar to all of us, current in phrases such as 'like a man', 'make a man of him', 'manly', which by this stage in the narrative have a chilling effect on the reader. Meanwhile, Helen recognizes her own unfitness to mother Arthur under this pressure: 'I am too grave to minister to his amusements' (p. 325) and play with him as he needs, for she is neurotically given to detecting the father's pernicious influence in the son's innocent high spirits. Ironically, Helen is reproducing the repressive demeanour of the aunt against whom she had rebelled. Faced with the choice between a depressed mother and 'joyous, amusing, ever-indulgent papa', the child naturally gravitates toward the fun and games. Any normal child would do the same. The cycle begins again.

If marriage to Gilbert Markham is not felt by the reader to be the ideal union of souls to which a young woman might aspire, Gilbert is presented as honourable in intention, ordinary, solid, open to reason. Helen will keep him in order. Transposed from farming into landed opulence, he will certainly do more good than harm, and the book seems disposed to settle for common decency as a rather rare commodity in the marriage-market of the time. In such competition, Gilbert's price is above rubies. It seems significant that Helen has to come down a class to find him. Contemporary reviewers tended to point out that such rakes as populate the central story were not a feature of contemporary Victorian life. The raunchy bucks of the Regency have not 'been tolerated for many years, within the pale of civilized society'.[25] But the author of this historical novel insists in her Preface that this is 'the truth': 'I know that such characters do exist' (p. 4). She had lived in books but, at Thorp Green, she had seen at first hand the behaviour of the gentry and aristocracy (Branwell liked to boast that the Robinson family was collateral to a Marquis and a Member of Parliament); Anne's employer would remarry to become Lady Scott. She could say 'I know' because she had lived through a momentous equivalent of the events transcribed in *Wildfell Hall* and had tasted the disgrace of a beloved brother, sharing his disintegration as if she were (as indeed a sister is, in a literal sense) 'one flesh'.

She dated her Preface 22 July 1848. Branwell was at home, in advanced stages of addiction. Six days later, Charlotte wrote that his 'constitution is shattered'; 'he sleeps all day' and is 'awake all night'. Two months later, on 24 September, he was dead. Eight months later, the twenty-nine-year-old author of *The Tenant of Wildfell Hall* followed him, making a self-commanding Christian death of awesome control and determination: 'Take courage, Charlotte; take courage.'[26]

NOTES

(Abbreviations are explained on p. 491.)

1. See Edward Chitham, *The Poems of Anne Brontë* (Macmillan, 1979), Appendix III.

2. No manuscript is available. The diary paper's first transcribed publication is in Clement Shorter's *Charlotte Brontë and her Circle* (Hodder & Stoughton, 1891), pp. 152–3.

3. See the reviews assembled by Miriam Allott in *CH*, pp. 254–73.

4. Charles Kingsley, 'Recent Novels', *Fraser's Magazine* 39 (April 1849), p. 273. Kingsley, in a conspicuously intelligent review, which however is tense with self-contradiction, defines *Wuthering Heights* as a disharmonious defiance of musical key, which he regrets on Christian humanist grounds which serve to point up both Anne Brontë's technical protomodernism and her post-humanist analysis of human nature.

5. Characters' names in *Wuthering Heights* and *Wildfell Hall* tend to cluster under identical initials, especially 'H' and 'L': the latter novel consciously echoes *Wuthering Heights* in its system of 'H' characters, designating (chiefly but not exclusively) the libertine males. In *Wuthering Heights* the 'H' characters are Hindley, Heathcliff and Hareton; in *Wildfell Hall*, Huntingdon, Hattersley, Halford, Hargrave, Helen. This coding sets up a kind of inde-terminacy and identity-loss amongst the fraternal 'club' which turns Helen's life into hell (a recurrent word). Characters also group under other letters, a tendency which is also seen in the lists of fragments which have survived from the Gondal saga. I also posit a vestigial influence from the 'H' and 'L' names in Richardson's *Clarissa*, which incorporates a similarly cryptic pattern-ing of namings and shares several names in common with *Wildfell Hall*, attached to the theme of pathological libertinism.

6. Charlotte Brontë, letter of 15 September 1850, to W. S. Williams.

7. 'Biographical Notice of Ellis and Acton Bell', as reprinted from the second edition (1850) in the edition of *Wuthering Heights* by Ian Jack (OUP, 1981), pp. 362–3.

8. Emily Brontë's diary paper of 1845, *SHLL*, Vol. II, pp. 49–51.

9. Thomas Moore, *The Letters and Journals of Lord Byron; with Notices of his Life* (Chatto & Windus, 1830), p. 136.

10. For this theme, see Jan B. Gordon, 'Gossip, Diary, Letter, Text: Anne Brontë's Narrative Tenant and the Problematic of the Gothic Sequel', *English Literary History*, 51, 4 (Winter 1984), pp. 719–45; Elizabeth Langland, *Anne Brontë: The Other One* (Macmillan, 1989), pp. 120–23.

11. Charlotte Brontë, letter to James Taylor, *SHLL*, Vol. III, p. 138.

12. E. P. Whipple, 'Novels of the Season', *North American Review*, 141 (October 1848), in *CH*, p. 262.

13. On Emily Brontë's narrative mode in *Wuthering Heights*, see J. Hillis Miller, *Fiction and Repetition: Seven English Novels* (Harvard University Press, 1982).

14. Charlotte Brontë, letter of 30 January 1846, to Miss Wooler, in *The Brontës, Life and Letters*, ed. Clement Shorter (Hodder & Stoughton, 1908), Vol. I, p. 315.

15. Branwell Brontë, *History of Angria* (1836). See Winifred Gérin, *Branwell Brontë* (Nelson, 1961), p. 99. Huntingdon is in no sense a 'portrait' of Branwell: rather, Branwell's decline gave Anne Brontë insight into the processes she describes in *Wildfell Hall*.

16. Unsigned review in *Sharpe's London Magazine* 7 (August 1848), in *CH*, p. 265.

17. Unsigned review in the *Literary World* (12 August 1848), in *CH*, p. 259.

18. Thomas Moore, *Byron*, p. 277.

19. See 'The Non-existence of Women', *North British Review* (August 1855); Caroline Cornwallis, 'The Property of Married Women', *Westminster Review* 10 (October 1856). The first Married Women's Property Act was not passed until 1882.

20. 1834 diary paper, Brontë Parsonage Museum.

21. In *Agnes Grey*, Ch. 17: 'pillars of witness set up, in travelling through the vale of life, to mark particular occurrences'.

22. See Inga-Stina Ewbank, '*The Tenant of Wildfell Hall* and *Women Beware Women*', *Notes and Queries* 10 (1963), pp. 449–50.

23. In *And The Weary Are At Rest*, quoted with comments by Winifred Gérin, *Branwell Brontë*, pp. 257.

24. F. H. Grundy, *Pictures of the Past* (1879): see Gérin's moving remarks on this in *Branwell Brontë*, p. 301.

25. Unsigned review, *Examiner* (29 July 1848), p. 256.

26. Ellen Nussey's account to Mrs Gaskell, *SHLL*, Vol. II, p. 336.

TEXTUAL NOTE

No manuscript of *The Tenant of Wildfell Hall* has survived. It seems likely that the first draft of the novel was composed during the period of the Brontë sisters' 'workshops' in the second half of 1846, when *Jane Eyre* was being projected and (in Edward Chitham's view: *Life*, pp. 139–40) *Wuthering Heights* may have been undergoing revision. It is safe to hypothesize that the first draft of *Wildfell Hall* was completed on 10 June 1847, the date which is given at the conclusion of the narrator Markham's correspondence with Halford. After November 1847 (when Anne had finished correcting the proofs of *Agnes Grey*), she may have redrafted and fair-copied the new novel, which she offered to her original publisher, T. C. Newby, who had bound her to an option on a second novel. Newby published *The Tenant of Wildfell Hall* at the end of June 1848, in a three-volume edition by 'Acton Bell' costing £1. 11s. 6d. In July it was published by Harper Brothers in New York, in a one-volume edition (and additionally in two paperback parts). However, Newby had sold *Wildfell Hall* to the American publisher under false pretences as the work of 'Currer Bell', Charlotte's pseudonym, in order to cash in on the sensational success of *Jane Eyre*. As Charlotte Brontë wrote, 'Acton Bell's publisher is a shuffling scamp' (Letter to Mary Taylor, 4 September 1848, *SHLL*, p. 251). She complained that the proof-corrections of *Wuthering Heights* and *Agnes Grey* were ignored by his printer, and lamented Newby's technical negligence as well as his lack of probity.

Newby published what he called, and the 'Bells' accepted (CB Letter to W. S. Williams, September 1848, *SHLL*, Vol. II, p. 255), a 'second edition' in London, in August 1848, but this is better described as a second issue, consisting of unsold sheets of the first London edition, together with a Preface by the author dated 22 July 1848, which Charlotte (who deplored Anne's second novel) described as 'sensible' (ibid., p. 255). Textual variations between these two issues are minor but have been considered by the present editor in making editorial judgements.

A cheap edition was issued in 1854 by Thomas Hodgson in the *Parlour Library* series, priced one shilling and sixpence. This corrupt text, which is highly expurgated, would become the basis for most subsequent British editions. It is worthless to the modern editor.

The text reproduced here, which is based on the Newby 'first edition' in the Bodleian Library, incorporates the Bodleian copy of the 'second edition' Preface. Hargreaves's belief that the New York edition 'if set from Newby proofs, may preserve a few authorial features that differ from the final Newby version' (p. 19) admits of some doubt. The 'Author's Own Copy' of the first edition, held by Princeton University Library, contains thirty-four pencilled revisions in Volume II, which may be Anne Brontë's own, and which are worth taking into account. However, not only is the volume's provenance problematic but these corrections are puzzling in their mingling of sensible revisions with the introduction of fresh errors together with the retention of old errors.

Anne Brontë's handwriting was habitually neat and legible. The errors and inconsistencies in the first edition in spelling, punctuation and use of capitals may therefore be the result of compositorial interference whether conscious or unconscious; the practice of an apprentice reading aloud to the compositor; together with the possible eccentricity of Anne Brontë's own usage. Careless reading seems to have turned 'earnest supplication' into 'earnest application' (p. 303); 'exclamation' into 'explanation' (p. 305), 'gambolling' into 'gambling' (p. 51), 'might' into 'mite' (p. 381). The present edition draws attention to such errors, and judicious amendment has been made in the text.

The vexed question of Anne Brontë's eccentric punctuation, involving inconsistent use of the comma, both in excess and defect; heavy informal use of the dash; and heavy formal use of the semicolon is addressed in the present text as a complex issue. It is possible, as Hargreaves believes, that some of the variation reflects the influence of different compositors in typesetting. My assessment, however, is that the curious mingling of informalizing punctuation with what we would see as overly formal punctuation (even acknowledging the more formal standard practice of the times) represents a conflict germane to the author herself. The free use of dashes, as rhythmic devices to indicate impromptu speech or thought, was a device favoured by all three Brontë sisters, especially in dialogue and expressive narrative, as giving a breathing immediacy to language. It would be natural to expect such voice-prints in the informal discourse of fictionalized letters and diary, as representing written language at its most intimate and spontaneous – and of course *The Tenant of Wildfell Hall* is an epistolary novel with inset diary. It should also be recalled that Anne and Emily Brontë had improvised orally in composing their Gondal narratives, thus generating the facility for bravura speech and the feeling for exponential development of narrative. This narrowing of the gap between spoken (or thought) and printed words is, however, contradicted in Anne Brontë by the classicizing influence of her 'Enlightenment' rationalism, which strives towards the greatest precision and control.

These two influences produce a schismatic struggle on the page which may be viewed through the contradictory notations of a punctuation striving at once toward expressiveness and toward balance and reason. Hence I have taken care not to over-correct passages where, for instance, dashes are accompanied by commas or semicolons, and where commas are absent, e.g., before a name or title in the vocative ('"You are mistaken there ma'am"'', '"you must see her Gilbert"' (p. 16), or in impetuous utterances ('"I won't I tell you"' (p. 61) or slangy emphasis ('no not a sketch'), even where this is followed by what we would see as over-punctuation ('no not a sketch, – a full and faithful account'). Epistolary discourse is in itself quite enough to justify usage fluctuating between formality and informality. Hence a degree of inconsistency should be tolerated rather than eliminated. In, for instance, Chapter 35, when Helen exclaims 'God, only, knows how often I shall need it [self-command] in this rough, dark road that lies before me' (p. 316), the commas around 'only' are allowed to remain as minute breathing-pauses, substituting for italics, to indicate that God *only* can penetrate the nil visibility in Helen's world. Nor have I deleted commas before vocatives, where these are supplied, since the formality they imply may be intended, in a rhetorical rhythm that moves freely (if sometimes confusingly) between high and low styles.

Commas have however been deleted between a complex subject and its verb and inserted where only half of a pair of commas occurs around an adverb in the first edition; and I have removed supernumerary commas attendant on a parenthesis, or resituated the second of the two – for the reason that, in these cases, *Wildfell Hall*'s anomalous punctuation is either redundant or obscuring. I have on occasion allowed an intrusive comma after 'perhaps' to stand, as this is an observable feature of northern usage even today, and may have represented Anne Brontë's own idiolect, placing emphasis on the doubt conveyed in the 'perhaps'; likewise, commas after 'because' are not invariably eliminated (see Chapter 15, n. 1). The principle of minimal interference allows the editor to represent a genuine tension within Anne Brontë's mind and expression. This tension is often in the form of the struggle of hypotaxis against parataxis. It is frequently found in long, formless sentences (see Chapter 25, n. 5), whose complex grammar of hypotaxis is strung paratactically upon dashes representing the mind in ferment, rhapsody or wandering (the Romantic impulse), bearing the broken chains of heavier and more securely formal punctuation (the 'Enlightenment' impulse). Notes draw attention to the more notable of such stylistic features.

Spelling has generally been regularized and normalized in accordance with Penguin house style, except where Anne Brontë's characteristic inconsistencies cause no problem in comprehension. Single quotation marks are used for the first edition's double quotation marks; full stops after 'Mr' and 'Mrs' are omitted; italicization has been retained. The latter is essential to the emotional forcefulness and immediacy of Anne Brontë's style, and is another form held in common with the authors of *Jane Eyre* and *Wuthering Heights*, working with the dashes to suggest the rhythms of minds freely and intensely expressing themselves. The following spellings are now obsolete or obsolescent and have been amended accordingly in the text: blythe (blithe), canvass (canvas), chesnut (chestnut), controul (control), dyed (died), exstatic (ecstatic), illude (elude), irradicate (eradicate), expence (expense), phrensy (frenzy), gulph (gulf), gingling (jingling), P jacket (pea-jacket), pretensious (pretentious), recompence (recompense), referrible (referable), skreen (screen), secresy (secrecy), shew (show), snoose (snooze), teaze (tease), tremour (tremor), vengibly (vengeably (see Chapter 13, n. 2)), villan (villain), visiter (visitor), wo (woe). Words with prefix 'in-' or 'im-' (e.g., incased, ingaged, imbowered) have been amended where appropriate to 'en-' or 'em-' in accordance with modern usage.

THE TENANT

OF

WILDFELL HALL.

BY

ACTON BELL.

IN THREE VOLUMES.

VOL. I.

LONDON:
T. C. NEWBY, PUBLISHER,
72, MORTIMER STREET, CAVENDISH SQUARE.
1848.

Facsimile title page of the first edition of *The Tenant of Wildfell Hall*

PREFACE TO THE SECOND
EDITION

While I acknowledge the success of the present work[1] to have been greater than I anticipated, and the praises it has elicited from a few kind critics to have been greater than it deserved, I must also admit that from some other quarters it has been censured[2] with an asperity which I was as little prepared to expect, and which my judgment, as well as my feelings, assures me is more bitter than just. It is scarcely the province of an author to refute the arguments of his censors and vindicate his own productions, but I may be allowed to make here a few observations with which I would have prefaced the first edition had I foreseen the necessity of such precautions against the misapprehensions of those who would read it with a prejudiced mind or be content to judge it by a hasty glance.

My object in writing the following pages, was not simply to amuse the Reader, neither was it to gratify my own taste, nor yet to ingratiate myself with the Press and the Public: I wished to tell the truth, for truth always conveys its own moral to those who are able to receive it. But as the priceless treasure too frequently hides at the bottom of a well, it needs some courage to dive for it, especially as he that does so will be likely to incur more scorn and obloquy for the mud and water into which he has ventured to plunge, than thanks for the jewel he procures; as, in like manner, she who undertakes the cleansing of a careless bachelor's apartment will be liable to more abuse for the dust she raises, than commendation for the clearance she effects.[3] Let it not be imagined, however, that I consider myself competent to reform the errors and abuses of society, but only that I would fain contribute my humble quota towards so good an aim, and if I can gain the public ear at all, I would rather whisper a few wholesome truths therein than much soft nonsense.

As the story of 'Agnes Grey' was accused of extravagant over-colouring[4] in those very parts that were carefully copied from the life, with a most scrupulous avoidance of all exaggeration, so, in the present work, I find myself censured for depicting *con amore*, with 'a morbid love of the coarse, if not of the brutal,'[5] those scenes which, I will venture to say, have not been more painful for the most fastidious of my critics to read, than they were for me to describe. I may have gone too far, in which case I shall be careful not to trouble myself or my readers in the same way again; but when we have to do with vice and vicious characters, I maintain it is better to depict them as they really are than as they would wish to appear. To represent a bad thing in its least offensive light is doubtless the most agreeable course for a writer of fiction to pursue; but is it the most honest, or the safest? Is it better to reveal the snares and pitfalls of life to the young and thoughtless traveller, or to cover them with branches and flowers? O Reader! if there were less of this delicate concealment of facts – this whispering 'Peace, peace,' when there is no peace[6] – there would be less of sin and misery to the young of both sexes who are left to wring their bitter knowledge from experience.

I would not be understood to suppose that the proceedings of the unhappy scapegrace with his few profligate companions I have here introduced are a specimen of the common practices of society: the case is an extreme one, as I trusted none would fail to perceive; but I know that such characters do exist, and if I have warned one rash youth from following in their steps, or prevented one thoughtless girl from falling into the very natural error of my heroine, the book has not been written in vain. But, at the same time, if any honest reader shall have derived more pain than pleasure from its perusal, and have closed the last volume with a disagreeable impression on his mind, I humbly crave his pardon, for such was far from my intention; and I will endeavour to do better another time, for I love to give innocent pleasure. Yet, be it understood, I shall not limit my ambition to this, – or even to producing 'a perfect work of art:' time and talents so spent, I should consider wasted and misapplied. Such humble talents[7] as God has given me I will endeavour to put to their greatest use; if I am able to amuse I will try to benefit too; and when I feel it my duty to speak an unpalatable truth, with the help of God, I *will* speak it, though it be to the prejudice of my name and to the detriment of my reader's immediate pleasure as well as my own.

One word more, and I have done. Respecting the author's identity,[8] I would have it to be distinctly understood that Acton Bell is neither Currer nor Ellis Bell, and therefore, let not his faults be attributed to them. As to whether the name be real or fictitious, it cannot greatly signify to those who know him only by his works. As little, I should think, can it matter whether the writer so designated is a man, or a woman as one or two of my critics profess to have discovered. I take the imputation in good part, as a compliment to the just delineation of my female characters; and though I am bound to attribute much of the severity of my censors to this suspicion, I make no effort to refute it, because, in my own mind, I am satisfied that if a book is a good one, it is so whatever the sex of the author may be. All novels are or should be written for both men and women to read, and I am at a loss to conceive how a man should permit himself to write anything that would be really disgraceful to a woman, or why a woman should be censured for writing anything that would be proper and becoming for a man.

July 22nd, 1848.

VOLUME I

TO J. HALFORD, ESQ.[1]

Dear Halford,

When we were together last, you gave me a very particular and interesting account of the most remarkable occurrences of your early life, previous to our acquaintance; and then you requested a return of confidence from me. Not being in a story-telling humour at the time, I declined, under the plea of having nothing to tell, and the like shuffling excuses, which were regarded as wholly inadmissible by you; for though you instantly turned the conversation, it was with the air of an uncomplaining, but deeply injured man, and your face was overshadowed with a cloud which darkened it to the end of our interview, and, for what I know, darkens it still; for your letters have, ever since, been distinguished by a certain dignified, semi-melancholy stiffness and reserve, that would have been very affecting, if my conscience had accused me of deserving it.

Are you not ashamed, old boy – at your age, and when we have known each other so intimately and so long, and when I have already given you so many proofs of frankness and confidence, and never resented your comparative closeness and taciturnity? – But there it is, I suppose; you are not naturally communicative, and you thought you had done great things, and given an unparalleled proof of friendly confidence on that memorable occasion – which, doubtless, you have sworn shall be the last of the kind, – and you deemed that the smallest return I could make for so mighty a favour would be to follow your example without a moment's hesitation. –

Well! – I did not take up my pen to reproach you, nor to defend myself, nor to apologize for past offences, but, if possible, to atone for them.

It is a soaking, rainy day, the family are absent on a visit, I am alone in my library, and have been looking over certain musty old letters and papers, and musing on past times; so that I am now in a very proper frame of mind for amusing you with an old world story; – and, having withdrawn my well-roasted feet from the hobs, wheeled round to the table, and indited the above lines to my crusty old friend, I am about to give him a sketch – no not a sketch, – a full and faithful account of certain circumstances connected with the most important event of my life – previous to my acquaintance with Jack Halford at least; – and when you have read it, charge me with ingratitude and unfriendly reserve if you can.

I know you like a long story, and are as great a stickler for particularities and circumstantial details as my grandmother, so I will not spare you: my own patience and leisure shall be my only limits.

Among the letters and papers I spoke of, there is a certain faded old journal of mine, which I mention by way of assurance that I have not my memory alone – tenacious as it is – to depend upon; in order that your credulity may not be too severely taxed in following me through the minute details of my narrative. – To begin then, at once, with Chapter First, – for it shall be a tale of many chapters. –

CHAPTER I

A DISCOVERY

You must go back with me to the autumn of 1827.

My father, as you know, was a sort of gentleman farmer in —shire; and I, by his express desire, succeeded him in the same quiet occupation, not very willingly, for ambition urged me to higher aims, and self-conceit assured me that, in disregarding its voice, I was burying my talent in the earth, and hiding my light under a bushel.[1] My mother had done her utmost to persuade me that I was capable of great achievements; but my father, who thought ambition was the surest road to ruin, and change but another word for destruction, would listen to no scheme for bettering either my own condition, or that of my fellow mortals. He assured me it was all rubbish, and exhorted me, with his dying breath, to continue in the good old way, to follow his steps, and those of his father before him, and let my highest ambition be, to walk honestly through the world, looking neither to the right hand nor to the left,[2] and to transmit the paternal acres to my children in, at least, as flourishing a condition as he left them to me.

'Well! – an honest and industrious farmer is one of the most useful members of society; and if I devote my talents to the cultivation of my farm, and the improvement of agriculture in general, I shall thereby benefit, not only my own immediate connections and dependants, but in some degree, mankind at large: – hence I shall not have lived in vain.'

With such reflections as these, I was endeavouring to console myself, as I plodded home from the fields, one cold, damp, cloudy evening towards the close of October. But the gleam of a bright red fire through the parlour window had more effect in cheering my spirits, and rebuking my thankless repinings, than all the sage reflections and good resolutions I had forced my mind to frame; – for I was young then, remember – only four and twenty – and had not acquired half the rule over my own spirit, that I now possess – trifling as that may be.

However, that haven of bliss must not be entered till I had exchanged my miry boots, for a clean pair of shoes, and my rough surtout[3] for a respectable coat, and made myself generally presentable before decent society; for my mother, with all her kindness, was vastly particular on certain points.

In ascending to my room, I was met upon the stairs by a smart, pretty girl of nineteen, with a tidy, dumpy figure, a round face, bright, blooming cheeks, glossy, clustering curls, and little merry brown eyes. I need not tell you this was my sister Rose. She is, I know, a comely matron still, and, doubtless, no less lovely – in *your* eyes – than on the happy day you first beheld her. Nothing told me then, that she, a few years hence, would be the wife of one – entirely unknown to me as yet, but destined, hereafter, to become a closer friend than even herself, more intimate than that unmannerly lad of seventeen, by whom I was collared in the passage, on coming down, and wellnigh jerked off my equilibrium, and who, in correction for his impudence, received a resounding whack over the sconce, which, however, sustained no serious injury from the infliction; as, besides being more than commonly thick, it was protected by a redundant shock of short, reddish curls, that my mother called auburn.

On entering the parlour, we found that honoured lady seated in her arm chair at the fireside, working away at her knitting, according to her usual custom, when she had nothing else to do. She had swept the hearth, and made a bright blazing fire for our reception; the servant had just brought in the tea-tray; and Rose was producing the sugar-basin and tea-caddy, from the cupboard in the black, oak sideboard, that shone like polished ebony, in the cheerful parlour twilight.

'Well! here they both are,' cried my mother, looking round upon us without retarding the motion of her nimble fingers, and glittering needles. 'Now shut the door, and come to the fire, while Rose gets the tea ready; I'm sure you must be starved; – and tell me what you've been about all day; – I like to know what my children have been about.'

'I've been breaking in the grey colt – no easy business that – directing the ploughing of the last wheat stubble – for the ploughboy has not the sense to direct himself – and carrying out a plan for the extensive and efficient draining of the low meadow-lands.'

'That's my brave boy! – and Fergus – what have you been doing?'

'Badger-baiting.'

And here he proceeded to give a particular account of his sport, and the respective traits of prowess evinced by the badger and the dogs; my mother pretending to listen with deep attention, and watching his animated countenance with a degree of maternal admiration I thought highly disproportioned to its object.

'It's time you should be doing something else, Fergus,' said I, as soon as a momentary pause in his narration allowed me to get in a word.

'What *can* I do?' replied he, 'my mother won't let me go to sea or enter the army; and I'm determined to do nothing else – except make myself such a nuisance to you all, that you will be thankful to get rid of me, on any terms.'

Our parent soothingly stroked his stiff, short curls. He growled, and tried to look sulky, and then, we all took our seats at the table, in obedience to the thrice repeated summons of Rose.

'Now take your tea,' said she; 'and I'll tell you what *I've* been doing. I've been to call on the Wilsons; and it's a *thousand* pities you didn't go with me, Gilbert, for Eliza Millward was there!'

'Well! what of her?'

'Oh nothing! – I'm not going to tell you about her; – only that she's a nice, amusing little thing, when she is in a merry humour, and I shouldn't mind calling her –'

'Hush, hush, my dear! your brother has no such idea!' whispered my mother earnestly, holding up her finger.

'Well,' resumed Rose; 'I was going to tell you an important piece of news I heard there – I've been bursting with it ever since. You know it was reported a month ago, that somebody was going to take Wildfell Hall[4] – and – what do you think? It has actually been inhabited above a week! – and we never knew!'

'Impossible!' cried my mother.

'Preposterous!!!' shrieked Fergus.

'It has indeed! – and by a single lady!'

'Good gracious, my dear! The place is in ruins!'

'She has had two or three rooms made habitable; and there she lives, all alone – except an old woman for a servant!'

'Oh dear! that spoils it – I'd hoped she was a witch,' observed Fergus, while carving his inch-thick slice of bread and butter.

'Nonsense, Fergus! But isn't it strange mamma?'

'Strange! I can hardly believe it.'

'But you may believe it; for Jane Wilson has seen her. She went with her mother, who, of course, when she heard of a stranger being in the neighbourhood, would be on pins and needles till she had seen her and got all she could out of her. She is called Mrs Graham, and she is in mourning – not window's weeds, but slightish mourning – and she is quite young, they say, – not above five or six and twenty, – but *so* reserved! They tried all they could to find out who she was, and where she came from, and all about her, but neither Mrs Wilson, with her pertinacious and impertinent home thrusts, nor Miss Wilson, with her skilful manoeuvering, could manage to elicit a single satisfactory answer, or even a casual remark, or chance expression calculated to allay their curiosity, or throw the faintest ray of light upon her history, circumstances, or connections. Moreover, she was barely civil to them, and evidently better pleased to say "goodbye," than "how do you do." But Eliza Millward says her father intends to call upon her soon, to offer some pastoral advice, which he fears she needs, as, though she is known to have entered the neighbourhood early last week, she did not make her appearance at church on Sunday; and she – Eliza, that is – will beg to accompany him, and is sure *she* can succeed in wheedling something out of her – you know, Gilbert, *she* can do anything. And *we* should call some time, mamma; it's only proper, you know.'

'Of course, my dear. Poor thing! how lonely she must feel!'

'And pray be quick about it; and mind you bring me word how much sugar she puts in her tea, and what sort of caps and aprons she wears, and all about it; for I don't know how I can live till I know,' said Fergus, very gravely.

But if he intended the speech to be hailed as a master-stroke of wit, he signally failed, for nobody laughed. However, he was not much disconcerted at that; for when he had taken a mouthful of bread and butter, and was about to swallow a gulp of tea, the humour of the thing burst upon him with such irresistible force, that he was obliged to jump up from the table, and rush snorting and choking from the room; and a minute after, was heard screaming in fearful agony in the garden.

As for me, I was hungry, and contented myself with silently demolishing the tea, ham, and toast, while my mother and sister went on talking, and continued to discuss the apparent, or non-apparent circumstances, and probable or improbable history of the mysterious lady; but I must confess that, after my brother's misadventure, I once or twice raised the cup to my lips, and put it down again without daring to taste the contents, lest I should injure my dignity by a similar explosion.

The next day, my mother and Rose hastened to pay their compliments to the fair recluse; and came back but little wiser than they went; though my mother declared she did not regret the journey, for, if she had not gained much good, she flattered herself she had imparted some, and that was better: she had given some useful advice, which, she hoped, would not be thrown away; for Mrs Graham, though she said little to any purpose, and appeared somewhat self-opinionated, seemed not incapable of reflection, – though she did not know where she had been all her life, poor thing, for she betrayed a lamentable ignorance on certain points, and had not even the sense to be ashamed of it.

'On what points, mother?' asked I.

'On household matters, and all the little niceties of cookery, and such things, that every lady ought to be familiar with,[5] whether she be required to make a practical use of her knowledge or not. I gave her some useful pieces of information, however, and several excellent receipts, the value of which she evidently could not appreciate, for she begged I would not trouble myself, as she lived in such a plain, quiet way, that she was sure she should never make use of them. "No matter, my dear," said I; "it is what every respectable female ought to know; – and besides, though you are alone now, you will not be always so; you *have* been married, and probably – I might say almost certainly – will be again." "You are mistaken there ma'am," said she, almost haughtily; "I am certain I never shall." – But I told her *I* knew better.'

'Some romantic young widow, I suppose,' said I, 'come there to end her days in solitude, and mourn in secret for the dear departed – but it won't last long.'

'No, I think not,' observed Rose; 'for she didn't seem *very* disconsolate after all; and she's excessively pretty – handsome rather – you must see her Gilbert; you will call her a perfect beauty, though you could hardly pretend to discover a resemblance between her and Eliza Millward.'

'Well, I can imagine many faces more beautiful than Eliza's, though not more charming. I allow she has small claims to perfection; but then, I maintain that, if she were more perfect, she would be less interesting.'

'And so you prefer her faults to other people's perfections?'

'Just so – saving my mother's presence.'

'Oh, my dear Gilbert, what nonsense you talk! – I know you don't mean it; it's quite out of the question,' said my mother, getting up, and bustling out of the room, under pretence of household business, in order to escape the contradiction that was trembling on my tongue.

After that, Rose favoured me with further particulars respecting Mrs Graham. Her appearance, manners, and dress, and the very furniture of the room she inhabited, were all set before me, with rather more clearness and precision than I cared to see them; but, as I was not a very attentive listener, I could not repeat the description if I would.

The next day was Saturday; and, on Sunday, everybody wondered whether or not the fair unknown would profit by the vicar's remonstrance, and come to church. I confess, I looked with some interest myself towards the old family pew, appertaining to Wildfell Hall, where the faded crimson cushions and lining had been unpressed and unrenewed so many years, and the grim escutcheons,[6] with their lugubrious borders of rusty black cloth, frowned so sternly from the wall above.

And there I beheld a tall, ladylike figure, clad in black. Her face was towards me, and there was something in it, which, once seen, invited me to look again. Her hair was raven black, and disposed in long glossy ringlets, a style of coiffure rather unusual in those days, but always graceful and becoming; her complexion was clear and pale; her eyes I could not see, for being bent upon her prayer-book they were concealed by their drooping lids and long black lashes, but the brows above were expressive and well defined, the forehead was lofty and intellectual, the nose, a perfect aquiline, and the features in general, unexceptionable – only there was a slight hollowness about the cheeks and eyes, and the lips, though finely formed, were a little too thin, a little too firmly compressed, and had something about them that betokened, I thought, no very soft or amiable temper; and I said in my heart –

'I would rather admire you from this distance, fair lady, than be the partner of your home.'

Just then, she happened to raise her eyes, and they met mine; I did not choose to withdraw my gaze, and she turned again to her book, but with a momentary, indefinable expression of quiet scorn, that was inexpressibly provoking to me.

'She thinks me an impudent puppy,' thought I. 'Humph! – she shall change her mind before long, if I think it worthwhile.'

But then, it flashed upon me that these were very improper thoughts for a place of worship, and that my behaviour, on the present occasion, was anything but what it ought to be. Previous, however, to directing my mind to the service, I glanced round the church to see if anyone had been observing me; – but no, – all who were not attending to their prayer-books, were attending to the strange lady, – my good mother and sister among the rest, and Mrs Wilson and her daughter; and even Eliza Millward was slyly glancing from the corners of her eyes towards the object of general attraction. Then, she glanced at me, simpered a little, and blushed, – modestly looked at her prayer-book, and endeavoured to compose her features.

Here I was transgressing again; and this time I was made sensible of it by a sudden dig in the ribs, from the elbow of my pert brother. For the present, I could only resent the insult by pressing my foot upon his toes, deferring further vengeance till we got out of church.

Now, Halford, before I close this letter, I'll tell you who Eliza Millward was: she was the vicar's younger daughter, and a very engaging little creature, for whom I felt no small degree of partiality; – and she knew it, though I had never come to any direct explanation, and had no definite intention of so doing, for my mother, who maintained there was no one good enough for me, within twenty miles round, could not bear the thought of my marrying that insignificant little thing, who, in addition to her numerous other disqualifications, had not twenty pounds to call her own. Eliza's figure was at once slight and plump, her face small, and nearly as round as my sister's, – complexion, something similar to hers, but more delicate and less decidedly blooming, – nose, *retroussé*, – features, generally irregular; – and, altogether, she was rather charming than pretty. But her eyes – I must not forget those remarkable features, for therein her chief attraction lay – in outward aspect at least; – they were long and narrow in shape, the irids black, or very dark brown, the expression various, and ever changing, but always either preternaturally – I had almost said *diabolically* – wicked, or irresistibly bewitching – often both. Her voice was gentle and childish, her tread light and soft as that of a cat; – but her manners more frequently resembled those of a pretty, playful kitten, that is now pert and roguish, now timid and demure, according to its own sweet will.

Her sister, Mary, was several years older, several inches taller, and of a larger, coarser build – a plain, quiet, sensible girl, who had patiently nursed their mother, through her last long, tedious illness, and been the housekeeper, and family drudge, from thence to the present time. She was trusted and valued by her father, loved and courted by all dogs, cats, children, and poor people, and slighted and neglected by everybody else.

The Reverend Michael Millward himself was a tall, ponderous, elderly gentleman, who placed a shovel hat[7] above his large, square, massive-featured face, carried a stout walking stick in his hand, and encased his still powerful limbs in knee breeches and gaiters, – or black silk stockings on state occasions. He was a man of fixed principles, strong prejudices, and regular habits, – intolerant of dissent in any shape, acting under a firm conviction that *his* opinions were always right, and whoever differed from them must be either most deplorably ignorant, or wilfully blind.

In childhood, I had always been accustomed to regard him with a feeling of reverential awe – but lately, even now, surmounted, for, though he had a fatherly kindness for the well-behaved, he was a strict disciplinarian, and had often sternly reproved our juvenile failings and peccadillos; and moreover, in those days whenever he called upon our parents, we had to stand up before him, and say our catechism, or repeat 'How doth the little busy bee,'[8] or some other hymn, or – worse than all – be questioned about his last text and the heads of the discourse, which we never could remember. Sometimes, the worthy gentleman would reprove my mother for being over indulgent to her sons, with a reference to old Eli, or David and Absalom,[9] which was particularly galling to her feelings; and, very highly as she respected him, and all his sayings, I once heard her exclaim, 'I wish to goodness he had a son himself! He wouldn't be so ready with his advice to other people then; – he'd see what it *is* to have a couple of boys to keep in order.'

He had a laudable care for his own bodily health – kept very early hours, regularly took a walk before breakfast, was vastly particular about warm and dry clothing, had never been known to preach a sermon without previously swallowing a raw egg – albeit he was gifted with good lungs and a powerful voice, – and was, generally, extremely particular about what he ate and drank, though by no means abstemious, and having a mode of dietary peculiar to himself, – being a great despiser of tea and such slops, and a patron of malt liquors, bacon and eggs, ham, hung beef, and other strong meats, which agreed well enough with his digestive organs, and therefore were maintained by him to be good and wholesome for everybody, and confidently recommended to the most delicate convalescents or dyspeptics, who, if they failed to derive the promised benefit from his prescriptions, were told it was because they had not persevered, and if they complained of inconvenient results therefrom, were assured it was all fancy.[10]

I will just touch upon two other persons whom I have mentioned, and then bring this long letter to a close. These are Mrs Wilson and her daughter. The former was the widow of a substantial farmer, a narrow-minded, tattling old gossip, whose character is not worth describing. She had two sons, Robert, a rough countrified farmer, and Richard, a retiring, studious young man, who was studying the classics with the vicar's assistance, preparing for college, with a view to enter the church.

Their sister Jane was a young lady of some talents and more ambition. She had, at her own desire, received a regular boarding-school education, superior to what any member of the family had obtained before. She had taken the polish well, acquired considerable elegance of manners, quite lost her provincial accent, and could boast of more accomplishments than the vicar's daughters. She was considered a beauty besides; but never for a moment could she number me amongst her admirers. She was about six and twenty, rather tall and very slender; her hair was neither chestnut nor auburn, but a most decided, bright, light red; her complexion was remarkably fair and brilliant, her head small, neck long, chin well turned, but very short, lips thin and red, eyes clear hazel, quick and penetrating, but entirely destitute of poetry or feeling. She had, or might have had, many suitors in her own rank of life, but scornfully repulsed or rejected them all; for none but a gentleman could please her refined taste, and none but a rich one could satisfy her soaring ambition. One gentleman there was, from whom she had lately received some rather pointed attentions, and upon whose heart, name, and fortune, it was whispered, she had serious designs. This was Mr Lawrence, the young squire whose family had formerly occupied Wildfell Hall, but had deserted it, some fifteen years ago, for a more modern and commodious mansion in the neighbouring parish.

Now Halford, I bid you adieu for the present. This is the first instalment of my debt. If the coin suits you, tell me so, and I'll send you the rest at my leisure: if you would rather remain my creditor than stuff your purse with such ungainly heavy pieces, – tell me still, and I'll pardon your bad taste, and willingly keep the treasure to myself.

Yours immutably,
Gilbert Markham

CHAPTER 2

AN INTERVIEW

I perceive, with joy, my most valued friend, that the cloud of your displeasure has passed away; the light of your countenance[1] blesses me once more, and you desire the continuation of my story: therefore, without more ado, you shall have it.

I think the day I last mentioned, was a certain Sunday, the latest in the October of 1827. On the following Tuesday I was out with my dog and gun, in pursuit of such game as I could find within the territory of Linden-Car;[2] but finding none at all, I turned my arms against the hawks and carrion crows, whose depredations, as I suspected, had deprived me of better prey. To this end, I left the more frequented regions, the wooded valleys, the cornfields, and the meadow lands, and proceeded to mount the steep acclivity of Wildfell, the wildest and the loftiest eminence in our neighbour-hood,[3] where, as you ascend, the hedges, as well as the trees, become scanty and stunted, the former, at length, giving place to rough stone fences, partly greened over with ivy and moss, the latter to larches and Scotch fir-trees, or isolated blackthorns. The fields, being rough and stony and wholly unfit for the plough, were mostly devoted to the pasturing of sheep and cattle; the soil was thin and poor: bits of grey rock here and there peeped out from the grassy hillocks; bilberry plants and heather – relics of more savage wildness – grew under the walls; and in many of the enclosures, ragweeds and rushes usurped supremacy over the scanty herbage; – but these were not *my* property.

Near the top of this hill, about two miles from Linden-Car, stood Wildfell Hall, a superannuated mansion of the Elizabethan era,[4] built of dark grey stone, – venerable and picturesque to look at, but, doubtless, cold and gloomy enough to inhabit, with its thick stone mullions and little latticed panes, its time-eaten airholes, and its too lonely, too unsheltered situation, – only shielded from the war of wind and weather by a group of Scotch firs, themselves half blighted with storms, and looking as stern and gloomy as the Hall itself. Behind it lay a few desolate fields, and then, the brown heathclad summit of the hill; before it (enclosed by stone walls, and entered by an iron gate with large balls of grey granite – similar to those which decorated the roof and gables – surmounting the gateposts), was a garden, – once, stocked with such hardy plants and flowers as could best brook the soil and climate, and such trees and shrubs as could best endure the gardener's torturing shears, and most readily assume the shapes he chose to give them,[5] – now, having been left so many years, untilled and untrimmed, abandoned to the weeds and the grass, to the frost and the wind, the rain and the drought, it presented a very singular appearance indeed. The close green walls of privet, that had bordered the principal walk, were two thirds withered away, and the rest grown beyond all reasonable bounds; the old boxwood swan, that sat beside the scraper, had lost its neck and half its body; the castellated towers of laurel in the middle of the garden, the gigantic warrior that stood on one side of the gateway, and the lion that guarded the other, were sprouted into such fantastic shapes as resembled nothing either in heaven or earth, or in the waters under the earth;[6] but, to my young imagination, they presented all of them a goblinish appearance, that harmonized well with the ghostly legends[7] and dark traditions our old nurse had told us respecting the haunted hall and its departed occupants.

I had succeeded in killing a hawk and two crows when I came within sight of the mansion; and then, relinquishing further depredations, I sauntered on, to have a look at the old place, and see what changes had been wrought in it by its new inhabitant. I did not like to go quite to the front and stare in at the gate; but I paused beside the garden wall, and looked, and saw no change – except in one wing, where the broken windows and dilapidated roof had evidently been repaired, and where a thin wreath of smoke was curling up from the stack of chimneys.

While I thus stood, leaning on my gun, and looking up at the dark gables, sunk in an idle reverie, weaving a tissue of wayward fancies, in which old associations and the fair young hermit, now within those walls, bore a nearly equal part, I heard a slight rustling and scrambling just within the garden; and, glancing in the direction whence the sound proceeded, I beheld a tiny hand elevated above the wall: it clung to the topmost stone, and then another little hand was raised to take a firmer hold, and then appeared a small white forehead, surmounted with wreaths of light brown hair, with a pair of deep blue eyes beneath, and the upper portion of a diminutive ivory nose.[8]

The eyes did not notice me, but sparkled with glee on beholding Sancho, my beautiful black and white setter, that was coursing about the field with its muzzle to the ground. The little creature raised its face and called aloud to the dog. The good-natured animal paused, looked up, and wagged his tail, but made no further advances. The child, (a little boy, apparently about five years old) scrambled up to the top of the wall and called again and again; but finding this of no avail, apparently made up his mind, like Mahomet, to go to the mountain since the mountain would not come to him,[9] and attempted to get over; but a crabbed old cherry tree, that grew hard by, caught him by the frock[10] in one of its crooked scraggy arms that stretched over the wall. In attempting to disengage himself, his foot slipped, and down he tumbled — but not to the earth; — the tree still kept him suspended. There was a silent struggle, and then a piercing shriek; — but, in an instant, I had dropped my gun on the grass, and caught the little fellow in my arms.

I wiped his eyes with his frock, told him he was all right, and called Sancho to pacify him. He was just putting his little hand on the dog's neck and beginning to smile through his tears, when I heard, behind me, a click of the iron gate and a rustle of female garments, and lo! Mrs Graham darted upon me, — her neck uncovered, her black locks streaming in the wind.

'Give me the child!'

She said in a voice scarce louder than a whisper, but with a tone of startling vehemence, and, seizing the boy, she snatched him from me, as if some dire contamination were in my touch, and then stood with one hand firmly clasping his, the other on his shoulder, fixing upon me her large, luminous, dark eyes – pale, breathless, quivering with agitation.

'I was not harming the child madam,' said I, scarce knowing whether to be most astonished or displeased, 'he was tumbling off the wall there; and I was so fortunate as to catch him, while he hung suspended headlong from that tree, and prevent I know not what catastrophe.'

'I beg your pardon sir,' stammered she, – suddenly calming down, – the light of reason seeming to break upon her beclouded spirit and a faint blush mantling on her cheek – 'I did not know you; – and I thought' –

She stooped to kiss the child, and fondly clasped her arm round his neck.

'You thought I was going to kidnap your son, I suppose?'

She stroked his head with a half-embarrassed laugh, and replied, –

'I did not know he had attempted to climb the wall. – I have the pleasure of addressing Mr Markham, I believe?' she added somewhat abruptly.

I bowed, but ventured to ask how she knew me.

'Your sister called here, a few days ago, with Mrs Markham.'

'Is the resemblance so strong then?' I asked in some surprise, and not so greatly flattered at the idea as I ought to have been.

'There is a likeness about the eyes and complexion I think,' replied she, somewhat dubiously surveying my face; – 'and I think I saw you at church on Sunday.'

I smiled. – There was something either in that smile or the recollections it awakened that was particularly displeasing to her, for she suddenly assumed again that proud, chilly look that had so unspeakably roused my corruption[11] at church – a look of repellent scorn, so easily assumed, and so entirely without the least distortion of a single feature that, while there, it seemed like the natural expression of the face, and was the more provoking to me, because I could not think it affected.

'Good morning, Mr Markham,' said she; and, without another word or glance, she withdrew with her child into the garden; and I returned home, angry and dissatisfied – I could scarcely tell you why – and therefore will not attempt it.

I only stayed to put away my gun and powder-horn, and give some requisite directions to one of the farming-men, and then repaired to the vicarage, to solace my spirit and sooth my ruffled temper with the company and conversation of Eliza Millward.

I found her, as usual, busy with some piece of soft embroidery (the mania for Berlin wools[12] had not yet commenced), while her sister was seated at the chimney-corner, with the cat on her knee, mending a heap of stockings.

'Mary – Mary! put them away!' Eliza was hastily saying, just as I entered the room.

'Not I, indeed!' was the phlegmatic reply; and my appearance prevented further discussion.

'You're *so* unfortunate, Mr Markham!' observed the younger sister, with one of her arch, sidelong glances. 'Papa's just gone out into the parish, and not likely to be back for an hour!'

'Never mind; I can manage to spend a few minutes with his daughters, if they'll allow me,' said I, bringing a chair to the fire, and seating myself therein, without waiting to be asked.

'Well, if you'll be very good and amusing, we shan't object.'

'Let your permission be unconditional, pray; for I came not to give pleasure, but to seek it,' I answered.

However, I thought it but reasonable to make some slight exertion to render my company agreeable; and what little effort I made was apparently pretty successful, for Miss Eliza was never in a better humour. We seemed, indeed, to be mutually pleased with each other, and managed to maintain between us a cheerful and animated, though not very profound, conversation. It was little better than a tête-à-tête, for Miss Millward never opened her lips, except occasionally to correct some random assertion or exaggerated expression of her sister's, and once to ask her to pick up the ball of cotton, that had rolled under the table. I did this myself, however, as in duty bound.

'Thank you, Mr Markham,' said she, as I presented it to her. 'I would have picked it up myself; only I did not want to disturb the cat.'

'Mary, dear, *that* won't excuse you in Mr Markham's eyes,' said Eliza; 'he hates cats, I dare say, as cordially as he does old maids – like all other gentlemen – Don't you Mr Markham?'

'I believe it is natural for our unamiable sex, to dislike the creatures,' replied I; 'for you ladies lavish so many caresses upon them.'

'Bless them – little darlings!' cried she, in a sudden burst of enthusiasm, turning round and overwhelming her sister's pet with a shower of kisses.

'Don't Eliza!' said Miss Millward, somewhat gruffly, as she impatiently pushed her away.

But it was time for me to be going: make what haste I would, I should still be too late for tea; and my mother was the soul of order and punctuality.

My fair friend was evidently unwilling to bid me adieu. I tenderly squeezed her little hand at parting; and she repaid me with one of her softest smiles and most bewitching glances. I went home very happy, with a heart brimful of complacency for myself, and overflowing with love for Eliza.

CHAPTER 3

A CONTROVERSY

Two days after, Mrs Graham called at Linden-Car, contrary to the expectation of Rose, who entertained an idea that the mysterious occupant of Wildfell Hall would wholly disregard the common observances of civilized life, – in which opinion she was supported by the Wilsons, who testified that neither their call nor the Millwards' had been returned as yet. Now, however, the cause of that omission was explained, though not entirely to the satisfaction of Rose. Mrs Graham had brought her child with her, and on my mother's expressing surprise that he could walk so far, she replied, –

'It is a long walk for him; but I must have either taken him with me, or relinquished the visit altogether: for I never leave him alone; and I think, Mrs Markham, I must beg you to make my excuses to the Millwards and Mrs Wilson, when you see them, as I fear I cannot do myself the pleasure of calling upon them till my little Arthur is able to accompany me.'

'But you have a servant,' said Rose; 'could you not leave him with her?'

'She has her own occupations to attend to; and besides, she is too old to run after a child, and he is too mercurial to be tied to an elderly woman.'

'But you left him to come to church.'

'Yes, once; but I would not have left him for any other purpose; and I think, in future, I must contrive to bring him with me, or stay at home.'

'Is he so mischievous?' asked my mother, considerably shocked.

'No,' replied the lady, sadly smiling, as she stroked the wavy locks of her son, who was seated on a low stool at her feet, 'but he is my only treasure; and I am his only friend, so we don't like to be separated.'

'But my dear, I call that doting,' said my plain-spoken parent. 'You should try to suppress such foolish fondness, as well to save your son from ruin as yourself from ridicule.'

'*Ruin*, Mrs Markham?'[1]

'Yes; it is spoiling the child. Even at *his* age, he ought not to be always tied to his mother's apron string; he should learn to be ashamed of it.'

'Mrs Markham, I beg you will not say such things in *his* presence, at least. I trust my son will *never* be ashamed to love his mother!' said Mrs Graham, with a serious energy that startled the company.

My mother attempted to appease her by an explanation; but she seemed to think enough had been said on the subject, and abruptly turned the conversation.

'Just as I thought,' said I to myself: 'the lady's temper is none of the mildest, notwithstanding her sweet, pale face and lofty brow, where thought and suffering seem equally to have stamped their impress.'

All this time, I was seated at a table on the other side of the room, apparently immersed in the perusal of a volume of the 'Farmer's Magazine,'[2] which I happened to have been reading at the moment of our visitor's arrival; and, not choosing to be over civil, I had merely bowed as she entered, and continued my occupation as before.

In a little while, however, I was sensible that someone was approaching me, with a light, but slow and hesitating tread. It was little Arthur, irresistibly attracted by my dog Sancho, that was lying at my feet. On looking up, I beheld him standing about two yards off, with his clear blue eyes wistfully gazing on the dog, transfixed to the spot, not by fear of the animal, but by a timid disinclination to approach its master. A little encouragement, however, induced him to come forward. The child, though shy, was not sullen. In a minute he was kneeling on the carpet, with his arms round Sancho's neck, and in a minute or two more, the little fellow was seated on my knee, surveying with eager interest the various specimens of horses, cattle, pigs, and model farms portrayed in the volume before me. I glanced at his mother now and then, to see how she relished the new-sprung intimacy; and I saw, by the unquiet aspect of her eye, that for some reason or other, she was uneasy at the child's position.

'Arthur,' said she, at length, 'come here. You are troublesome to Mr Markham: he wishes to read.'

'By no means, Mrs Graham; pray let him stay. I am as much amused as he is,' pleaded I. But still, with hand and eye, she silently called him to her side.

'No, mamma,' said the child; 'let me look at these pictures first; and then I'll come, and tell you all about them.'

'We are going to have a small party on Monday, the fifth of November,' said my mother; 'and I hope you will not refuse to make one, Mrs Graham. You can bring your little boy with you, you know – I dare say we shall be able to amuse him; – and then you can make your own apologies to the Millwards and Wilsons, – they will all be here I expect.'

'Thank you, I never go to parties.'

'Oh! but this will be quite a family concern – early hours, and nobody here but ourselves, and just the Millwards and Wilsons, most of whom you already know, and Mr Lawrence, your landlord, whom you ought to make acquaintance with.'

'I do know something of him – but you must excuse me this time; for the evenings, now, are dark and damp, and Arthur, I fear, is too delicate to risk exposure to their influence with impunity. We must defer the enjoyment of your hospitality, till the return of longer days and warmer nights.'

Rose, now, at a hint from my mother, produced a decanter of wine, with accompaniments of glasses and cake, from the cupboard under the oak sideboard, and the refreshment was duly presented to the guests. They both partook of the cake, but obstinately refused the wine, in spite of their hostess's hospitable attempts to force it upon them. Arthur, especially shrank from the ruby nectar as if in terror and disgust, and was ready to cry when urged to take it.

'Never mind, Arthur,' said his mamma, 'Mrs Markham thinks it will do you good, as you were tired with your walk; but she will not oblige you to take it; – I dare say you will do very well without. He detests the very sight of wine,' she added, 'and the smell of it almost makes him sick. I have been accustomed to make him swallow a little wine or weak spirits-and-water, by way of medicine when he was sick, and, in fact, I have done what I could to make him hate them.'[3]

Everybody laughed, except the young widow and her son.

'Well, Mrs Graham,' said my mother, wiping the tears of merriment from her bright, blue eyes – 'well, you surprise me! I really gave you credit for having more sense – The poor child will be the veriest milksop that ever was sopped! Only think what a man you will make of him, if you persist in –'

'I think it a very excellent plan,' interrupted Mrs Graham with imperturbable gravity. 'By that means I hope to save him from one degrading vice at least. I wish I could render the incentives to every other equally innoxious in his case.'

'But by such means,' said I, 'you will never render him virtuous. – What is it that constitutes virtue, Mrs Graham?[4] Is it the circumstance of being able and willing to resist temptation; or that of having no temptations to resist? – Is he a strong man that overcomes great obstacles and performs surprising achievements, though by dint of great muscular exertion, and at the risk of some subsequent fatigue, or he that sits in his chair all day, with nothing to do more laborious than stirring the fire, and carrying his food to his mouth? If you would have your son to walk honourably through the world, you must not attempt to clear the stones from his path, but teach him to walk firmly over them – not insist upon leading him by the hand, but let him learn to go alone.'

'I will lead him by the hand, Mr Markham, till he has strength to go alone; and I will clear as many stones from his path as I can, and teach him to avoid the *rest* – or walk firmly over them, as you say; – for when I have done my utmost, in the way of clearance, there will still be plenty left to exercise all the agility, steadiness, and circumspection he will ever have. – It is all very well to talk about noble resistance, and trials of virtue; but for fifty – or five hundred men that have yielded to temptation, show me one that has had virtue to resist. And why should I take it for granted that my son will be one in a thousand? – and not rather prepare for the worst, and suppose he will be like his – like the rest of mankind, unless I take care to prevent it?'

'You are very complimentary to us all,' I observed.

'I know nothing about *you* – I speak of those I do know – and when I see the whole race of mankind (with a few rare exceptions) stumbling and blundering along the path of life, sinking into every pitfall, and breaking their shins over every impediment that lies in their way, shall I not use all the means in my power to ensure for him, a smoother and a safer passage?'

'Yes, but the surest means will be to endeavour to fortify him *against* temptation, not to remove it out of his way.'

'I will do both, Mr Markham. God knows he will have temptations enough to assail him, both from within and without, when I have done all I can to render vice as uninviting to him, as it is abominable in its own nature – I myself, have had, indeed, but few incentives to what the world calls vice, but yet, I have experienced temptations and trials of another kind, that have required, on many occasions, more watchfulness and firmness to resist, than I have hitherto been able to muster against them.[5] And this, I believe, is what most others would acknowledge, who are accustomed to reflection, and wishful to strive against their natural corruptions.'

'Yes,' said my mother, but half apprehending her drift; 'but you would not judge of a boy by yourself – and my dear Mrs Graham, let me warn you in good time against the error – the fatal error, I may call it – of taking that boy's education upon yourself. – Because you are clever, in some things, and well informed, you may fancy yourself equal to the task; but indeed you are not; and, if you persist in the attempt, believe me, you will bitterly repent it when the mischief is done.'

'I am to send him to school, I suppose, to learn to despise his mother's authority and affection!' said the lady, with a rather bitter smile.

'Oh, *no*! – But if you would have a boy to despise his mother, let her keep him at home, and spend her life in petting him up, and slaving to indulge his follies and caprices.'

'I perfectly agree with you Mrs Markham; but nothing can be further from my principles and practice than such criminal weakness as that.'

'Well, but you will treat him like a girl – you'll spoil his spirit, and make a mere Miss Nancy[6] of him – you will indeed, Mrs Graham, whatever you may think – But I'll get Mr Millward to talk to you about it:[7] – *he'll* tell you the consequences; – he'll set it before you as plain as the day; – and tell you what you ought to do, and all about it; – and, I don't doubt, he'll be able to convince you in a minute.'

'No occasion to trouble the vicar,' said Mrs Graham, glancing at me – I suppose I was smiling at my mother's unbounded confidence in that worthy gentleman – 'Mr Markham here thinks his powers of conviction at least equal to Mr Millward's. If I hear not him, neither should I be convinced though one arose from the dead,[8] he would tell you. – Well Mr Markham, you that maintain that a boy should not be shielded from evil, but sent out to battle against it, alone and unassisted – not taught to avoid the snares of life, but boldly to rush into them, or over them, as he may – to seek danger rather than shun it, and feed his virtue by temptation, – would you –'

'I beg your pardon, Mrs Graham – but you get on too fast. I have not yet said that a boy should be taught to rush into the snares of life, – or even wilfully to seek temptation for the sake of exercising his virtue by overcoming it; – I only say that it is better to arm and strengthen your hero, than to disarm and enfeeble the foe; – and if you were to rear an oak sapling in a hothouse, tending it carefully night and day, and shielding it from every breath of wind, you could not expect it to become a hardy tree, like that which has grown up on the mountain-side, exposed to all the action of the elements, and not even sheltered from the shock of the tempest.'

'Granted; – but would you use the same argument with regard to a girl?'[9]

'Certainly not.'

'No; you would have her to be tenderly and delicately nurtured, like a hot-house plant – taught to cling to others for direction and support, and guarded, as much as possible, from the very knowledge of evil. But will you be so good as to inform me, why you make this distinction? Is it that you think she *has* no virtue?'

'Assuredly not.'

'Well, but you affirm that virtue is only elicited by temptation; – and you think that a woman cannot be too little exposed to temptation, or too little acquainted with vice, or anything connected therewith – It *must* be, either, that you think she is essentially so vicious, or so feeble-minded that she *cannot* withstand temptation, – and though she may be pure and innocent as long as she is kept in ignorance and restraint, yet, being destitute of *real* virtue, to teach her how to sin is at once[10] to make her a sinner, and the greater her knowledge, the wider her liberty, the deeper will be her depravity, – whereas, in the nobler sex, there is a natural tendency to goodness, guarded by a superior fortitude, which, the more it is exercised by trials and dangers, is only the further developed –'

'Heaven forbid that I should think so!' I interrupted at last.

'Well then, it must be that you think they are *both* weak and prone to err, and the slightest error, the merest shadow of pollution will ruin the one, while the character of the other will be strengthened and embellished – his education properly finished by a little practical acquaintance with forbidden things. Such experience, to him, (to use a trite simile) will be like the storm to the oak, which, though it may scatter the leaves, and snap the smaller branches, serves but to rivet the roots, and to harden and condense the fibres of the tree. You would have us encourage our sons to prove all things by their own experience, while our daughters must not even profit by the experience of others. Now *I* would have both so to benefit by the experience of others, and the precepts of a higher authority, that they should know beforehand to refuse the evil and choose the good, and require no experimental proofs to teach them the evil of transgression. I would not send a poor girl into the world, unarmed against her foes, and ignorant of the snares that beset her path: nor would I watch and guard her, till, deprived of self-respect and self-reliance, she lost the power, or the will, to watch and guard herself; –

and as for my son – if I thought he would grow up to be what you call a man of the world – one that has "*seen life*," and glories in his experience, even though he should so far profit by it, as to sober down, at length, into a useful and respected member of society – I would rather that he died tomorrow! – rather a thousand times!' she earnestly repeated, pressing her darling to her side and kissing his forehead with intense affection. He had, already, left his new companion, and been standing for some time beside his mother's knee, looking up into her face, and listening in silent wonder to her incomprehensible discourse.[11]

'Well! you ladies must always have the last word, I suppose,' said I, observing her rise, and begin to take leave of my mother.

'You may have as many words as you please, – only I can't stay to hear them.'

'No; that is the way: you hear just as much of an argument as you please; and the rest may be spoken to the wind.'

'If you are anxious to say anything more on the subject,' replied she, as she shook hands with Rose, 'you must bring your sister to see me some fine day, and I'll listen, as patiently as you could wish, to whatever you please to say. I would rather be lectured by you than the vicar, because I should have less remorse in telling you, at the end of the discourse, that I preserve my own opinion precisely the same as at the beginning – as would be the case, I am persuaded, with regard to either logician.'

'Yes, of course,' replied I, determined to be as provoking as herself; 'for, when a lady does consent to listen to an argument against her own opinions, she is always predetermined to withstand it – to listen only with her bodily ears, keeping the mental organs resolutely closed against the strongest reasoning.'

'Good morning, Mr Markham,' said my fair antagonist with a pitying smile; and deigning no further rejoinder, she slightly bowed, and was about to withdraw; but her son, with childish impertinence, arrested her by exclaiming,

'Mamma, you have not shaken hands with Mr Markham!'

She laughingly turned round, and held out her hand. I gave it a spiteful squeeze; for I was annoyed at the continual injustice she had done me from the very dawn of our acquaintance. Without knowing anything about my real disposition and principles, she was evidently prejudiced against me, and seemed bent upon showing me that her opinions respecting me, on every particular, fell far below those I entertained of myself. I was naturally touchy, or, it would not have vexed me so much. Perhaps, too, I was a little bit spoiled by my mother and sister, and some other ladies of my acquaintance;[12] – and yet, I was by no means a fop – of that I am fully convinced, whether *you* are or not.

CHAPTER 4

THE PARTY

Our party, on the fifth of November, passed off very well in spite of Mrs Graham's refusal to grace it with her presence. Indeed, it is probable that, had she been there, there would have been less cordiality, freedom, and frolic amongst us than there was without her.

My mother, as usual, was cheerful and chatty, full of activity and good-nature, and only faulty in being too anxious to make her guests happy, thereby forcing several of them to do what their soul abhorred,[1] in the way of eating or drinking, sitting opposite the blazing fire, or talking when they would be silent. Nevertheless, they bore it very well, being all in their holiday humours.

Mr Millward was mighty in important dogmas and sententious jokes, pompous anecdotes and oracular discourses, dealt out for the edification of the whole assembly in general, and of the admiring Mrs Markham, the polite Mr Lawrence, the sedate Mary Millward, the quiet Richard Wilson, and the matter of fact Robert, in particular, – as being the most attentive listeners.

Mrs Wilson was more brilliant than ever, with her budgets of fresh news and old scandal, strung together with trivial questions and remarks, and oft repeated observations, uttered apparently for the sole purpose of denying a moment's rest to her inexhaustible organs of speech. She had brought her knitting with her, and it seemed as if her tongue had laid a wager with her fingers, to outdo them in swift and ceaseless motion.

Her daughter Jane was, of course, as graceful and elegant, as witty and seductive as she could possibly manage to be; for here were all the ladies to outshine, and all the gentlemen to charm, – and Mr Lawrence, especially, to capture and subdue. Her little arts to effect his subjugation were too subtle and impalpable to attract my observation; but I thought there was a certain *refined* affectation of superiority, and an ungenial self-consciousness about her, that negatived all her advantages, and after she was gone Rose interpreted to me her various looks, words, and actions with a mingled acuteness and asperity that made me wonder, equally, at the lady's artifice and my sister's penetration, and ask myself if she too had an eye to the squire – but never mind, Halford; she had not.

Richard Wilson, Jane's younger brother, sat in a corner, apparently good-tempered, but silent and shy, desirous to escape observation, but willing enough to listen and observe: and, although somewhat out of his element, he would have been happy enough in his own quiet way, if my mother could only have let him alone, but in her mistaken kindness, she would keep persecuting him with her attentions – pressing upon him all manner of viands, under the notion that he was too bashful to help himself, and obliging him to shout across the room his monosyllabic replies to the numerous questions and observations by which she vainly attempted to draw him into conversation.

Rose informed me that he never would have favoured us with his company, but for the importunities of his sister Jane, who was most anxious to show Mr Lawrence that she had at least one brother more gentlemanly and refined than Robert. That worthy individual she had been equally solicitous to keep away; but he affirmed that he saw no reason why he should not enjoy a crack[2] with Markham and the old lady (my mother was not old really), and bonny Miss Rose and the parson, as well as the best; – and he was in the right of it too. So he talked commonplace with my mother and Rose, and discussed parish affairs with the vicar, farming matters with me, and politics with us both.

Mary Millward was another mute, – not so much tormented with cruel kindness as Dick Wilson, because she had a certain short, decided way of answering and refusing, and was supposed to be rather sullen than diffident. However that might be, she certainly did not give much pleasure to the company; – nor did she appear to derive much from it. Eliza told me she had only come because her father insisted upon it, having taken it into his head that she devoted herself too exclusively to her household duties, to the neglect of such relaxations and innocent enjoyments as were proper to her age and sex. She seemed, to me, to be good-humoured enough on the whole. Once or twice she was provoked to laughter by the wit or the merriment of some favoured individual amongst us; and then I observed she sought the eye of Richard Wilson, who sat over against her. As he studied with her father, she had some acquaintance with him, in spite of the retiring habits of both, and I suppose there was a kind of fellow-feeling established between them.

My Eliza was charming beyond description, coquettish without affectation, and evidently more desirous to engage my attention than that of all the room besides. Her delight in having me near her, seated or standing by her side, whispering in her ear, or pressing her hand in the dance, was plainly legible in her glowing face and heaving bosom, however belied by saucy words and gestures. But I had better hold my tongue: if I boast of these things now, I shall have to blush hereafter.

To proceed then, with the various individuals of our party; Rose was simple and natural as usual, and full of mirth and vivacity.

Fergus was impertinent and absurd; but his impertinence and folly served to make others laugh, if they did not raise himself in their estimation.

And finally (for I omit myself), Mr Lawrence was gentlemanly and inoffensive to all, and polite to the vicar and the ladies, especially his hostess and her daughter, and Miss Wilson – misguided man; he had not the taste to prefer Eliza Millward. Mr Lawrence and I were on tolerably intimate terms. Essentially of reserved habits, and but seldom quitting the secluded place of his birth, where he had lived in solitary state since the death of his father, he had neither the opportunity nor the inclination for forming many acquaintances; and, of all he had ever known, I (judging by the results) was the companion most agreeable to his taste. I liked the man well enough, but he was too cold, and shy, and self-contained, to obtain my cordial sympathies. A spirit of candour and frankness, when wholly unaccompanied with coarseness, he admired in others, but he could not acquire it himself. His excessive reserve upon all his own concerns was, indeed, provoking and chilly enough; but I forgave it, from a conviction that it originated, less in pride and want of confidence in his friends, than in a certain morbid feeling of delicacy, and a peculiar diffidence, that he was sensible of, but wanted energy to overcome. His heart was like a sensitive plant, that opens for a moment in the sunshine, but curls up and shrinks into itself at the slightest touch of the finger, or the lightest breath of wind. And, upon the whole, our intimacy was rather a mutual predilection than a deep and solid friendship, such as has since arisen between myself and you, Halford, whom, in spite of your occasional crustiness, I can liken to nothing so well as an old coat, unimpeachable in texture, but easy and loose – that has conformed itself to the shape of the wearer, and which he may use as he pleases, without being bothered with the fear of spoiling it; – whereas Mr Lawrence was like a new garment, all very neat and trim to look at, but so tight in the elbows that you would fear to split the seams by the unrestricted motion of your arms, and so smooth and fine in surface that you scruple to expose it to a single drop of rain.

Soon after the arrival of the guests, my mother mentioned Mrs Graham, regretted she was not there to meet them, and explained to the Millwards and Wilsons the reasons she had given for neglecting to return their calls, hoping they would excuse her, as she was sure she did not mean to be uncivil, and would be glad to see them at any time; –

'But she is a very singular lady, Mr Lawrence,' added she; 'we don't know what to make of her – but I dare say you can tell us something about her; for she is your tenant, you know, – and she said she knew you a little.'

All eyes were turned to Mr Lawrence. I thought he looked unnecessarily confused at being so appealed to.

'I, Mrs Markham!' said he, 'you are mistaken – I don't – that is – I have seen her certainly; but I am the last person you should apply to for information respecting Mrs Graham.'

He then immediately turned to Rose, and asked her to favour the company with a song, or a tune on the piano.

'No,' said she; 'you must ask Miss Wilson: she outshines us all in singing, and music too.'

Miss Wilson demurred.

'*She'll* sing readily enough,' said Fergus, 'if you'll undertake to stand by her, Mr Lawrence, and turn over the leaves for her.'

'I shall be most happy to do so. Miss Wilson, will you allow me?'

She bridled her long neck and smiled, and suffered him to lead her to the instrument, where she played and sang, in her very best style, one piece after another; while he stood patiently by, leaning one hand on the back of her chair, and turning over the leaves of her book with the other. Perhaps, he was as much charmed with her performance as she was. It was all very fine in its way; but I cannot say that it moved me very deeply. There was plenty of skill and execution, but precious little feeling.

But we had not done with Mrs Graham yet.

'I don't take wine Mrs Markham,' said Mr Millward, upon the introduction of that beverage; 'I'll take a little of your home-brewed to anything else.'

Flattered at this compliment, my mother rang the bell, and a china jug of our best ale was presently brought, and set before the worthy gentleman who so well knew how to appreciate its excellencies.

'Now THIS is the thing!' cried he, pouring out a glass of the same in a long stream, skilfully directed from the jug to the tumbler, so as to produce much foam without spilling a drop; and, having surveyed it for a moment opposite the candle, he took a deep draught, and then smacked his lips, drew a long breath, and refilled his glass, my mother looking on with the greatest satisfaction.

'There's nothing like this Mrs Markham!' said he, 'I always maintain that there's nothing to compare with your home-brewed ale.'

'I'm sure I'm glad you like it, sir. I always look after the brewing myself, as well as the cheese and the butter – I like to have things well done, while we're about it.'

'*Quite right* Mrs Markham!'

'But then, Mr Millward, you don't think it *wrong* to take a little wine now and then – or a little spirits either?' said my mother, as she handed a smoking tumbler of gin and water to Mrs Wilson, who affirmed that wine sat heavy on her stomach, and whose son Robert was at that moment helping himself to a pretty stiff glass of the same.

'By no means!' replied the oracle with a Jove-like nod;[3] 'these things are all blessings and mercies, if we only knew how to make use of them.'

'But Mrs Graham doesn't think so. You shall just hear now, what she told us the other day – I *told* her I'd tell you.'

And my mother favoured the company with a particular account of that lady's mistaken ideas and conduct regarding the matter in hand, concluding with, 'Now don't you think it is wrong?'

'Wrong!' repeated the vicar, with more than common solemnity – 'criminal, I should say – criminal! – Not only is it making a fool of the boy, but it is despising the gifts of Providence, and teaching him to trample them under his feet.'

He then entered more fully into the question, and explained at large the folly and impiety of such a proceeding. My mother heard him with profoundest reverence; and even Mrs Wilson vouchsafed to rest her tongue for a moment, and listen in silence, while she complacently sipped her gin and water. Mr Lawrence sat with his elbow on the table, carelessly playing with his half-empty wine-glass, and covertly smiling to himself.

'But don't you think, Mr Millward,' suggested he, when at length that gentleman paused in his discourse, 'that when a child may be naturally prone to intemperance – by the fault of its parents or ancestors, for instance – some precautions are advisable?' (Now it was generally believed that Mr Lawrence's father had shortened his days by intemperance.)[4]

'Some precautions, it may be; but temperance, sir, is one thing, and abstinence another.'

'But I have heard that, with some persons, temperance – that is moderation – is almost impossible; and if abstinence be an evil (which some have doubted), no one will deny that excess is a greater. Some parents have entirely prohibited their children from tasting intoxicating liquors; but a parent's authority cannot last for ever: children are naturally prone to hanker after forbidden things; and a child, in such a case, would be likely to have a strong curiosity to taste, and try the effect of what has been so lauded and enjoyed by others, so strictly forbidden to himself – which curiosity would generally be gratified on the first convenient opportunity; and the restraint once broken, serious consequences might ensue. I don't pretend to be a judge of such matters, but it seems to me, that this plan of Mrs Graham's, as you describe it, Mrs Markham, extra-ordinary as it may be, is not without its advantages; for here you see, the child is delivered at once from temptation; he has no secret curiosity, no hankering desire; he is as well acquainted with the tempting liquors as he ever wishes to be; and is thoroughly disgusted with them without having suffered from their effects.'

'And is that right, sir? Have I not proven to you how wrong it is – how contrary to Scripture and to reason to teach a child to look with contempt and disgust upon the blessings of Providence, instead of to use them aright?'

'You may consider laudanum[5] a blessing of Providence, sir,' replied Mr Lawrence, smiling; 'and yet, you will allow that most of us had better abstain from it, even in moderation; but,' added he, 'I would not desire you to follow out my simile too closely – in witness whereof I finish my glass.'

'And take another I hope, Mr Lawrence,' said my mother, pushing the bottle towards him.

He politely declined, and pushing his chair a little away from the table, leant back towards me – I was seated a trifle behind, on the sofa beside Eliza Millward – and carelessly asked me if I knew Mrs Graham.

'I have met her once or twice,' I replied.

'What do you think of her?'

'I cannot say that I like her much. She is handsome – or rather I should say distinguished and interesting – in her appearance, but by no means amiable – a woman liable to take strong prejudices, I should fancy, and stick to them through thick and thin, twisting everything into conformity with her own preconceived opinions – too hard, too sharp, too bitter for my taste.'

He made no reply, but looked down and bit his lip and shortly after rose and sauntered up to Miss Wilson, as much repelled by me, I fancy, as attracted by her. I scarcely noticed it at the time, but afterwards, I was led to recall this and other trifling facts, of a similar nature, to my remembrance, when – but I must not anticipate.

We wound up the evening with dancing – our worthy pastor thinking it no scandal to be present on the occasion, though one of the village musicians was engaged to direct our evolutions[6] with his violin. But Mary Millward obstinately refused to join us; and so did Richard Wilson, though my mother earnestly entreated him to do so, and even offered to be his partner.

We managed very well without them, however. With a single set of quadrilles, and several country dances, we carried it on to a pretty late hour; and at length, having called upon our musician to strike up a waltz, I was just about to whirl Eliza round in that delightful dance, accompanied by Lawrence and Jane Wilson, and Fergus and Rose, when Mr Millward interposed with, –

'No, no, I don't allow that![7] Come it's time to be going now.'

'Oh, no, papa!' pleaded Eliza.

'High time my girl – high time! – Moderation in all things remember! That's the plan – "Let your moderation be known unto all men!"'[8]

But in revenge, I followed Eliza into the dimly lighted passage, where under pretence of helping her on with her shawl, I fear I must plead guilty to snatching a kiss behind her father's back, while he was enveloping his throat and chin in the folds of a mighty comforter. But alas! in turning round, there was my mother close beside me. The consequence was, that no sooner were the guests departed, than I was doomed to a very serious remonstrance, which unpleasantly checked the galloping course of my spirits, and made a disagreeable close to the evening.

'My dear Gilbert,' said she, 'I wish you wouldn't do so! You know how deeply I have your advantage at heart, how I love you and prize you above everything else in the world, and how much I long to see you well settled in life – and how bitterly it would grieve me to see you married to that girl – or any other in the neighbourhood. What you *see* in her I don't know. It isn't only the want of money that I think about – nothing of the kind – but there's neither beauty, nor cleverness, nor goodness, nor anything else that's desirable. If you knew your own value as I do, you wouldn't dream of it. Do wait awhile and see! If you bind yourself to her, you'll repent it all your life-time when you look round you and see how many better there are. Take my word for it, you will.'

'Well mother, do be quiet! – I hate to be lectured! – I'm not going to marry yet, I tell you; but – dear me! mayn't I enjoy myself at *all*?'

'Yes, my dear boy, but not in that way. Indeed you shouldn't do such things. You would be wronging the girl, if she were what she ought to be; but I assure you she is as artful a little hussy as anybody need wish to see; and you'll get entangled in her snares before you know where you are. And if you do marry her Gilbert, you'll break my heart – so there's an end of it.'

'Well, don't cry about it mother,' said I; for the tears were gushing from her eyes, 'there, let that kiss efface the one I gave Eliza; don't abuse her any more, and set your mind at rest; for I'll promise never to – that is, I'll promise to – to think twice before I take any important step you seriously disapprove of.'

So saying, I lighted my candle, and went to bed, considerably quenched in spirit.

CHAPTER 5

THE STUDIO

It was about the close of the month, that, yielding at length to the urgent importunities of Rose, I accompanied her in a visit to Wildfell Hall. To our surprise, we were ushered into a room where the first object that met the eye was a painter's easel,[1] with a table beside it covered with rolls of canvas, bottles of oil and varnish, palette, brushes, paints, etc. Leaning against the wall were several sketches in various stages of progression, and a few finished paintings – mostly of landscapes and figures.

'I must make you welcome to my studio, said Mrs Graham; 'there is no fire in the sitting room today, and it is rather too cold to show you into a place with an empty grate.'

And disengaging a couple of chairs from the artistical lumber that usurped them, she bid us be seated, and resumed her place beside the easel – not facing it exactly, but now and then glancing at the picture upon it while she conversed, and giving it an occasional touch with her brush, as if she found it impossible to wean her attention entirely from her occupation to fix it upon her guests. It was a view of Wildfell Hall, as seen at early morning from the field below, rising in dark relief against a sky of clear silvery blue, with a few red streaks on the horizon, faithfully drawn and coloured, and very elegantly and artistically handled.

'I see your heart is in your work, Mrs Graham,' observed I: 'I must beg you to go on with it; for if you suffer our presence to interrupt you, we shall be constrained to regard ourselves as unwelcome intruders.'

'Oh, no!' replied she, throwing her brush on to the table, as if startled into politeness. 'I am not so beset with visitors, but that I can readily spare a few minutes to the few that do favour me with their company.'

'You have almost completed your painting,' said I, approaching to observe it more closely, and surveying it with a greater degree of admiration and delight than I cared to express. 'A few more touches in the foreground will finish it I should think. – But why have you called it Fernley Manor, Cumberland, instead of Wildfell Hall, —shire?' I asked, alluding to the name she had traced in small characters at the bottom of the canvas.

But immediately I was sensible of having committed an act of impertinence in so doing; for she coloured and hesitated; but after a moment's pause, with a kind of desperate frankness, she replied, –

'Because I have friends – acquaintances at least – in the world, from whom I desire my present abode to be concealed; and as they might see the picture, and might possibly recognize the style in spite of the false initials I have put in the corner, I take the precaution to give a false name to the place also, in order to put them on a wrong scent, if they should attempt to trace me out by it.'

'Then you don't intend to keep the picture?' said I, anxious to say anything to change the subject.

'No; I cannot afford to paint for my own amusement.'

'Mamma sends all her pictures to London,' said Arthur; 'and somebody sells them for her there, and sends us the money.'

In looking round upon the other pieces, I remarked a pretty sketch of Lindenhope from the top of the hill; another view of the old hall, basking in the sunny haze of a quiet summer afternoon; and a simple but striking little picture of a child brooding with looks of silent, but deep and sorrowful regret, over a handful of withered flowers, with glimpses of dark low hills and autumnal fields behind it, and a dull beclouded sky above.

'You see there is a sad dearth of subjects,' observed the fair artist. 'I took the old hall once on a moonlight night, and I suppose I must take it again on a snowy winter's day, and then again on a dark cloudy evening; for I really have nothing else to paint. I have been told that you have a fine view of the sea somewhere in the neighbourhood – Is it true? – and is it within walking distance?'

'Yes, if you don't object to walking four miles, – or nearly so – little short of eight miles there and back – and over a somewhat rough, fatiguing road.'

'In what direction does it lie?'

I described the situation as well as I could, and was entering upon an explanation of the various roads, lanes, and fields to be traversed in order to reach it, the goings straight on, and turnings to the right, and the left, when she checked me with, –

'Oh, stop! – don't tell me now: I shall forget every word of your directions before I require them. I shall not think about going till next spring; and then, perhaps, I may trouble you. At present we have the winter before us, and –'

She suddenly paused, with a suppressed exclamation started up from her seat, and saying, 'Excuse me one moment,' hurried from the room, and shut the door behind her.

Curious to see what had startled her so, I looked towards the window, – for her eyes had been carelessly fixed upon it the moment before – and just beheld the skirts of a man's coat vanishing behind a large holly bush that stood between the window and the porch.

'It's Mamma's friend,' said Arthur.

Rose and I looked at each other.

'I don't know what to make of her, at all,' whispered Rose.

The child looked at her in grave surprise. She straightway began to talk to him on indifferent matters, while I amused myself with looking at the pictures. There was one in an obscure corner that I had not before observed. It was a little child, seated on the grass with its lap full of flowers. The tiny features and large, blue eyes, smiling through a shock of light brown curls, shaken over the forehead as it bent above its treasure, bore sufficient resemblance to those of the young gentleman before me, to proclaim it a portrait of Arthur Graham in his early infancy.

In taking this up to bring it to the light, I discovered another behind it, with its face to the wall. I ventured to take that up too. It was the portrait of a gentleman[2] in the full prime of youthful manhood – handsome enough, and not badly executed; but, if done by the same hand as the others, it was evidently some years before; for there was far more careful minuteness of detail, and less of that freshness of colouring and freedom of handling, that delighted and surprised me in them. Nevertheless, I surveyed it with considerable interest. There was a certain individuality in the features and expression that stamped it, at once, a successful likeness. The bright, blue eyes regarded the spectator with a kind of lurking drollery – you almost expected to see them wink; the lips – a little too voluptuously full – seemed ready to break into a smile; the warmly tinted cheeks were embellished with a luxuriant growth of reddish whiskers; while the bright chestnut hair, clustering in abundant, wavy curls, trespassed too much upon the forehead,[3] and seemed to intimate that the owner thereof was prouder of his beauty than his intellect – as perhaps, he had reason to be; – and yet he looked no fool.

I had not had the portrait in my hands two minutes before the fair artist returned.

'Only someone come about the pictures,' said she, in apology for her abrupt departure: 'I told him to wait.'

'I fear it will be considered an act of impertinence,' said I, 'to presume to look at a picture that the artist has turned to the wall; but may I ask' –

'It *is* an act of very great impertinence, sir; and therefore, I beg you will ask nothing about it, for your curiosity will not be gratified,' replied she, attempting to cover the tartness of her rebuke with a smile; – but I could see, by her flushed cheek and kindling eye, that she was seriously annoyed.

'I was only going to ask if you had painted it yourself,' said I, sulkily resigning the picture into her hands; for without a grain of ceremony, she took it from me; and quickly restoring it to the dark corner, with its face to the wall, placed the other against it as before, and then turned to me and laughed.

But I was in no humour for jesting. I carelessly turned to the window, and stood looking out upon the desolate garden, leaving her to talk to Rose for a minute or two; and then, telling my sister it was time to go, shook hands with the little gentleman, coolly bowed to the lady, and moved towards the door. But, having bid adieu to Rose, Mrs Graham presented her hand to me, saying, with a soft voice, and by no means a disagreeable smile, –

'Let not the sun go down upon your wrath,[4] Mr Markham. I'm sorry I offended you by my abruptness.'

When a lady condescends to apologize, there is no keeping one's anger of course; so we parted good friends for once; and *this* time, I squeezed her hand with a cordial, not a spiteful pressure.

CHAPTER 6

PROGRESSION

During the next four months, I did not enter Mrs Graham's house, nor she mine; but still, the ladies continued to talk about her, and still, our acquaintance continued, though slowly, to advance. As for their talk, I paid but little attention to that (when it related to the fair hermit, I mean), and the only information I derived from it, was that, one fine, frosty day, she had ventured to take her little boy as far as the vicarage, and that, unfortunately, nobody was at home but Miss Millward;[1] nevertheless, she had sat a long time, and, by all accounts, they had found a good deal to say to each other, and parted with a mutual desire to meet again. – But Mary liked children, and fond mammas like those who can duly appreciate their treasures.

But sometimes, I saw her myself, – not only when she came to church, but when she was out on the hills with her son, whether taking a long, purpose-like walk, or – on special fine days – leisurely rambling over the moor or the bleak pasture-lands surrounding the old hall, herself with a book in her hand, her son gambolling about her; and, on any of these occasions, when I caught sight of her in my solitary walks or rides, or while following my agricultural pursuits, I generally contrived to meet or overtake her; for I rather liked to see Mrs Graham, and to talk to her, and I decidedly liked to talk to her little companion, whom, when once the ice of his shyness was fairly broken, I found to be a very amiable, intelligent, and entertaining little fellow; and we soon became excellent friends – how much to the gratification of his mamma, I cannot undertake to say. I suspected at first, that she was desirous of throwing cold water on this growing intimacy – to quench, as it were, the kindling flame of our friendship – but discovering, at length, in spite of her prejudice against me, that I was perfectly harmless, and even well-intentioned, and that, between myself and my dog, her son derived a great deal of pleasure from the acquaintance, that he would not otherwise have known, she ceased to object, and even welcomed my coming with a smile.

As for Arthur, he would shout his welcome from afar, and run to meet me fifty yards from his mother's side. If I happened to be on horseback, he was sure to get a canter or a gallop; or, if there was one of the draught horses within an available distance, he was treated to a steady ride upon that, which served his turn almost as well; but his mother would always follow and trudge beside him – not so much, I believe, to ensure his safe conduct, as to see that I instilled no objectionable notions into his infant mind; for she was ever on the watch, and never would allow him to be taken out of her sight. What pleased her best of all was to see him romping and racing with Sancho, while I walked by her side – not, I fear, for love of my company (though I sometimes deluded myself with that idea), so much as for the delight she took in seeing her son thus happily engaged in the enjoyment of those active sports, so invigorating to his tender frame, yet so seldom exercised for want of playmates suited to his years; and, perhaps, her pleasure was sweetened, not a little, by the fact of my being with *her* instead of with *him*; and therefore incapable of doing him any injury directly or indirectly, designedly or otherwise – small thanks to her for that same.

But sometimes, I believe, she really had some little gratification in conversing with me; and one bright February morning, during twenty minutes' stroll along the moor, she laid aside her usual asperity and reserve, and fairly entered into conversation with me, discoursing with so much· eloquence, and depth of thought and feeling, on a subject, happily coinciding with my own ideas, and looking so beautiful withal, that I went home enchanted; and on the way (morally) started to find myself thinking that, after all, it would, perhaps, be better to spend one's days with such a woman than with Eliza Millward; – and then I (figuratively) blushed for my inconstancy.

On entering the parlour, I found Eliza there, with Rose and no one else. The surprise was not altogether so agreeable as it ought to have been. We chatted together a long time; but I found her rather frivolous, and even a little insipid, compared with the more mature and earnest Mrs Graham – Alas, for human constancy!

'However,' thought I, 'I ought not to marry Eliza since my mother so strongly objects to it, and I ought not to delude the girl with the idea that I intended to do so. Now, if this mood continue, I shall have less difficulty in emancipating my affections from her soft, yet unrelenting sway; and, though Mrs Graham might be equally objectionable, I may be permitted, like the doctors, to cure a greater evil by a less;[2] for I shall not fall seriously in love with the young widow, I think, – nor she with me – that's certain – but if I find a little pleasure in her society, I may surely be allowed to seek it; and if the star of her divinity be bright enough to dim the lustre of Eliza's, so much the better; but I scarcely can think it.'

And thereafter, I seldom suffered a fine day to pass without paying a visit to Wildfell, about the time my new acquaintance usually left her hermitage; but so frequently was I balked in my expectations of another interview, so changeable was she in her times of coming forth, and in her places of resort, so transient were the occasional glimpses I was able to obtain, that I felt half inclined to think she took as much pains to avoid my company, as I to seek hers; but this was too disagreeable a supposition to be entertained a moment after it could, conveniently, be dismissed.

One calm, clear afternoon, however, in March, as I was superintending the rolling of the meadow-land, and the repairing of a hedge in the valley, I saw Mrs Graham down by the brook, with a sketch-book in her hand, absorbed in the exercise of her favourite art, while Arthur was putting on the time with constructing dams and break-waters in the shallow, stony stream. I was rather in want of amusement, and so rare an opportunity was not to be neglected; so, leaving both meadow and hedge, I quickly repaired to the spot, – but not before Sancho, who, immediately upon perceiving his young friend, scoured at full gallop the intervening space, and pounced upon him with an impetuous mirth that precipitated the child almost into the middle of the beck; but, happily, the stones preserved him from any serious wetting, while their smoothness prevented his being too much hurt to laugh at the untoward event.

Mrs Graham was studying the distinctive characters of the different varieties of trees in their winter nakedness, and copying, with a spirited though delicate touch, their various ramifications. She did not talk much; but I stood and watched the progress of her pencil: it was a pleasure to behold it so dextrously guided by those fair and graceful fingers. But erelong their dexterity became impaired, they began to hesitate, to tremble slightly, and make false strokes, and then suddenly came to a pause, while their owner laughingly raised her face to mine, and told me that her sketch did not profit by my superintendence.

'Then,' said I, 'I'll talk to Arthur, till you've done.'

'I should like to have a ride, Mr Markham, if Mamma will let me,' said the child.

'What on, my boy?'

'I think there's a horse in that field,' replied he, pointing to where the strong black mare was pulling the roller.

'No, no, Arthur; it's too far,' objected his mother.

But I promised to bring him safe back, after a turn or two up and down the meadow; and when she looked at his eager face, she smiled and let him go. It was the first time she had even allowed me to take him so much as half a field's length from her side.

Enthroned upon his monstrous steed, and solemnly proceeding up and down the wide, steep field, he looked the very incarnation of quiet, gleeful satisfaction and delight. The rolling, however, was soon completed; but when I dismounted the gallant horseman, and restored him to his mother, she seemed rather displeased at my keeping him so long. She had shut up her sketch-book, and been, probably for some minutes, impatiently waiting his return.

It was now high time to go home, she said, and would have bid me good evening; but I was not going to leave her yet: I accompanied her half way up the hill. She became more sociable; and I was beginning to be very happy; but, on coming within sight of the grim old Hall, she stood still and turned towards me while she spoke, as if expecting I should go no further, that the conversation would end here, and I should now take leave and depart – as, indeed, it was time to do; for 'the clear, cold eve' was fast 'declining,'[3] the sun had set, and the gibbous moon[4] was visibly brightening in the pale grey sky; but a feeling almost of compassion rivetted me to the spot. It seemed hard to leave her to such a lonely, comfortless home. I looked up at it. Silent and grim it frowned before us. A faint, red light was gleaming from the lower windows of one wing; but all the other windows were in darkness, and many exhibited their black, cavernous gulfs, entirely destitute of glazing or frame work.

'Do you not find it a desolate place to live in?' said I, after a moment of silent contemplation.

'I do, sometimes,' replied she. 'On winter evenings, when Arthur is in bed, and I am sitting there alone, hearing the bleak wind moaning round me and howling through the ruinous old chambers, no books or occupations can repress the dismal thoughts and apprehensions that come crowding in – but it is folly to give way to such weakness I know – If Rachel is satisfied with such a life, why should not I? – Indeed I cannot be too thankful for such an asylum, while it is left me.'

The closing sentence was uttered in an undertone, as if spoken rather to herself than to me. She then bid me good evening and withdrew.

I had not proceeded many steps on my way homewards, when I perceived Mr Lawrence, on his pretty grey pony, coming up the rugged lane that crossed over the hill top. I went a little out of my way to speak to him; for we had not met for some time.

'Was that Mrs Graham you were speaking to just now?' said he, after the first few words of greeting had passed between us.

'Yes.'

'Humph! I thought so.' He looked contemplatively at his horse's mane, as if he had some serious cause of dissatisfaction with it, or something else.

'Well! what then?'

'Oh, nothing!' replied he. 'Only, I thought you disliked her,' he quietly added, curling his classic lip with a slightly sarcastic smile.

'Suppose I did; mayn't a man change his mind on further acquaintance?'

'Yes, of course,' returned he, nicely reducing an entanglement in the pony's redundant, hoary mane. Then suddenly turning to me, and fixing his shy, hazel eyes upon me with a steady penetrating gaze, he added, 'Then you *have* changed your mind?'

'I can't say that I have exactly. No; I think I hold the same opinion respecting her as before – but slightly ameliorated.'

'Oh.' He looked round for something else to talk about; and glancing up at the moon, made some remark upon the beauty of the evening, which I did not answer, as being irrelevant to the subject.

'Lawrence,' said I, calmly looking him in the face, 'are you in love with Mrs Graham?'

Instead of his being deeply offended at this, as I more than half expected he would, the first start of surprise, at the audacious question, was followed by a tittering laugh, as if he was highly amused at the idea.

'*I* in love with her!' repeated he. 'What makes you dream of such a thing?'

'From the interest you take in the progress of my acquaintance with the lady, and the changes of my opinion concerning her, I thought you might be jealous.'

He laughed again. 'Jealous! no – But I thought you were going to marry Eliza Millward.'

'You thought wrong then; I am not going to marry either one or the other – that I know of.'

'Then I think you'd better let them alone.'

'Are you going to marry Jane Wilson?'

He coloured, and played with the mane again, but answered, –

'No, I think not.'

'Then you had better let her alone.'

She won't let me alone – he might have said; but he only looked silly and said nothing for the space of half a minute, and then made another attempt to turn the conversation; and, this time, I let it pass; for he had borne enough: another word on the subject would have been like the last atom that breaks the camel's back.[5]

I was too late for tea; but my mother had kindly kept the tea-pot and muffin warm upon the hobs, and, though she scolded me a little, readily admitted my excuses; and when I complained of the flavour of the overdrawn tea, she poured the remainder into the slop-basin, and bade Rose put some fresh into the pot, and reboil the kettle, which offices were performed with great commotion, and certain remarkable comments.

'Well! – if it had been *me* now, I should have had no tea at all – If it had been Fergus, even, he would have had to put up with such as there was, and been told to be thankful, for it was far too good for him; but *you* – we can't do too much for you – It's always so – if there's anything particularly nice at table, Mamma winks and nods at me, to abstain from it, and if I don't attend to that, she whispers, "Don't eat so much of that, Rose, Gilbert will like it for his supper" – *I'm* nothing at all – in the parlour, it's "Come Rose, put away your things, and let's have the room nice and tidy against they come in; and keep up a good fire; Gilbert likes a cheerful fire." In the kitchen – "Make that pie a large one, Rose, I dare say the boys 'll be hungry; – and don't put so much pepper in, they'll not like it I'm sure" – or, "Rose, don't put so many spices in the pudding, Gilbert likes it plain," – or, "Mind you put plenty of currants in the cake, Fergus likes plenty." If I say, "Well Mamma, *I* don't," I'm told I ought not to think of myself – "You know Rose, in all household matters, we have only two things to consider, first, what's proper to be done, and secondly, what's most agreeable to the gentlemen of the house – anything will do for the ladies."'

'And very good doctrine too,' said my mother. 'Gilbert thinks so, I'm sure.'

'Very convenient doctrine, for us at all events,' said I; 'but if you would really study my pleasure, Mother, you must consider your own comfort and convenience a little more than you do – as for Rose, I have no doubt she'll take care of herself; and whenever she does make a sacrifice or perform a remarkable act of devotedness, she'll take good care to let me know the extent of it. But for *you*, I might sink into the grossest condition of self-indulgence and careless-ness about the wants of others, from the mere habit of being constantly cared for myself, and having all my wants anticipated or immediately supplied, while left in total ignorance of what is done for me, – if Rose did not enlighten me now and then; and I should receive all your kindness as a matter of course, and never know how much I owe you.'[6]

'Ah! and you never *will* know, Gilbert, till you're married. Then, when you've got some trifling, self-conceited girl like Eliza Millward, careless of everything but her own immediate pleasure and advantage, or some misguided, obstinate woman like Mrs Graham, ignorant of her principal duties, and clever only in what concerns her least to know – then, you'll find the difference.'

'It will do me good Mother; I was not sent into the world merely to exercise the good capacities and good feelings of others – was I? – but to exert my own towards them; and when I marry, I shall expect to find more pleasure in making my wife happy and comfortable, than in being made so by her: I would rather give than receive.'

'Oh! that's all nonsense, my dear – It's mere boy's talk that! You'll soon tire of petting and humouring your wife, be she ever so charming, and *then* comes the trial.'

'Well, then, we must bear one another's burdens.'

'Then, you must fall each into your proper place. You'll do your business, and she, if she's worthy of you, will do hers; but it's your business to please yourself, and hers to please you. I'm sure your poor, dear father was as good a husband as ever lived, and after the first six months or so were over, I should as soon have expected him to fly, as to put himself out of his way to pleasure me. He always said I was a good wife, and did my duty; and he always did his – bless him! – he was steady and punctual, seldom found fault without a reason, always did justice to my good dinners, and hardly ever spoiled my cookery by delay – and that's as much as any woman can expect of any man.'

Is it so Halford? Is that the extent of *your* domestic virtues; and does your happy wife exact no more?

CHAPTER 7

THE EXCURSION

Not many days after this, on a mild sunny morning – rather soft under foot; for the last fall of snow was only just wasted away, leaving yet a thin ridge, here and there, lingering on the fresh, green grass beneath the hedges; but beside them already, the young primroses were peeping from among their moist, dark foliage, and the lark above was singing of summer, and hope, and love, and every heavenly thing – I was out on the hill-side, enjoying these delights, and looking after the well-being of my young lambs and their mothers, when, on glancing round me, I beheld three persons ascending from the vale below. They were Eliza Millward, Fergus and Rose; so I crossed the field to meet them; and, being told they were going to Wildfell Hall, I declared myself willing to go with them, and offering my arm to Eliza, who readily accepted it in lieu of my brother's, told the latter he might go back, for I would accompany the ladies.

'I beg *your* pardon!' exclaimed he – 'It's the ladies that are accompanying me, not I them. You had all had a peep at this wonderful stranger, but me, and I could endure my wretched ignorance no longer – come what would, I must be satisfied; so I begged Rose to go with me to the Hall, and introduce me to her at once. She swore she would not, unless Miss Eliza would go too; so I ran to the vicarage and fetched her; and we've come hooked all the way, as fond as a pair of lovers – and now you've taken her from me; and you want to deprive me of my walk and my visit besides – Go back to your fields and your cattle, you lubberly fellow; you're not fit to associate with ladies and gentlemen, like us, that have nothing to do but to run snooking about[1] to our neighbours' houses, peeping into their private corners; and scenting out their secrets, and picking holes in their coats, when we don't find them ready made to our hands – you don't understand such refined sources of enjoyment.'

'Can't you both go?' suggested Eliza, disregarding the latter half of the speech.

'Yes, both to be sure!' cried Rose; 'the more the merrier – and I'm sure we shall want all the cheerfulness we can carry with us to that great, dark, gloomy room, with its narrow latticed windows, and its dismal old furniture – unless she shows us into her studio again.'

So we went all in a body; and the meagre old maidservant, that opened the door, ushered us into an apartment, such as Rose had described to me as the scene of her first introduction to Mrs Graham, a tolerably spacious and lofty room, but obscurely lighted by the old-fashioned windows, the ceiling, panels and chimney-piece of grim black oak – the latter elaborately, but not very tastefully carved, – with tables and chairs to match, an old bookcase on one side of the fireplace, stocked with a motley assemblage of books, and an elderly cabinet piano on the other.

The lady was seated in a stiff, high-backed arm chair, with a small, round table, containing a desk and a work basket on one side of her, and her little boy on the other, who stood leaning his elbow on her knee, and reading to her, with wonderful fluency,[2] from a small volume that lay in her lap; while she rested her hand on his shoulder, and abstractedly played with the long, wavy curls that fell on his ivory neck. They struck me as forming a pleasing contrast to all the surrounding objects; but of course their position was immediately changed on our entrance; I could only observe the picture during the few brief seconds that Rachel held the door for our admittance.

I do not think Mrs Graham was particularly delighted to see us: there was something indescribably chilly in her quiet, calm civility; but I did not talk much to her. Seating myself near the window, a little back from the circle, I called Arthur to me, and he and I, and Sancho, amused ourselves very pleasantly together, while the two young ladies baited his mother with small talk, and Fergus sat opposite, with his legs crossed, and his hands in his breeches pockets, leaning back in his chair, and staring now up at the ceiling, now straight forward at his hostess (in a manner that made me strongly inclined to kick him out of the room), now whistling *sotto voce* to himself a snatch of a favourite air, now interrupting the conversation, or filling up a pause (as the case might be) with some most impertinent question or remark. At one time it was –

'It amazes me, Mrs Graham, how you could choose such a dilapidated, ricketty old place as this to live in. If you couldn't afford to occupy the whole house, and have it mended up, why couldn't you take a neat little cottage?'

'Perhaps, I was too proud, Mr Fergus,' replied she, smiling; 'Perhaps I took a particular fancy for this romantic, old-fashioned place – but indeed, it has many advantages over a cottage – in the first place, you see, the rooms are larger and more airy; in the second place, the unoccupied apartments, which I don't pay for, may serve as lumber-rooms, if I have anything to put in them; and they are very useful for my little boy to run about in on rainy days when he can't go out; and then, there is the garden for him to play in, and for me to work in. You see I have effected some little improvement already,' continued she, turning to the window. 'There is a bed of young vegetables in that corner, and here are some snowdrops and primroses already in bloom – and there, too, is a yellow crocus just opening in the sunshine.'

'But then, how can you bear such a situation – your nearest neighbours two miles distant, and nobody looking in or passing by? – Rose would go stark mad in such a place. She can't put on life unless she sees half a dozen fresh gowns and bonnets a day – not to speak of the faces within; but you might sit watching at these windows all day long, and never see so much as an old woman carrying her eggs to market.'

'I am not sure the loneliness of the place was not one of its chief recommendations – I take no pleasure in watching people pass the windows; and I like to be quiet.'

'Oh! as good as to say, you wish we would all of us mind our own business, and let you alone.'

'No, I dislike an extensive acquaintance; but if I have a few friends, of course I am glad to see them occasionally. No one can be happy in eternal solitude. Therefore, Mr Fergus, if you choose to enter my house as a friend, I will make you welcome; if not, I must confess, I would rather you kept away.' She then turned and addressed some observation to Rose or Eliza.

'And, Mrs Graham,' said he again, five minutes after, 'we were disputing, as we came along, a question that you can readily decide for us, as it mainly regarded yourself – and indeed, we often hold discussions about you; for some of us have nothing better to do than to talk about our neighbours' concerns, and we, the indigenous plants of the soil, have known each other so long, and talked each other over so often, that we are quite sick of that game; so that a stranger coming amongst us makes an invaluable addition to our exhausted sources of amusement. Well, the question, or questions you are requested to solve –'

'Hold your tongue, Fergus!' cried Rose, in a fever of apprehension and wrath.

'I won't I tell you. The questions you are requested to solve are these: – First, concerning your birth, extraction, and previous residence. Some will have it that you are a foreigner, and some an Englishwoman; some a native of the north country, and some of the south; some say –'

'Well, Mr Fergus, I'll tell you. I'm an Englishwoman – and I don't see why anyone should doubt it – and I was born in the country neither in the extreme north nor south of our happy isle; and in the country I have chiefly passed my life, and now, I hope, you are satisfied; for I am not disposed to answer any more questions at present.'

'Except this. –'

'No, not one more!' laughed she, and instantly quitting her seat, she sought refuge at the window by which I was seated, and, in very desperation, to escape my brother's persecutions, endeavoured to draw me into conversation.

'Mr Markham,' said she, her rapid utterance and heightened colour too plainly evincing her disquietude; 'have you forgotten the fine sea view we were speaking of some time ago? I think I must trouble you, now, to tell me the nearest way to it; for if this beautiful weather continue, I shall, perhaps, be able to walk there, and take my sketch; I have exhausted every other subject for painting; and I long to see it.'

I was about to comply with her request; but Rose would not suffer me to proceed.

'Oh, don't tell her Gilbert!' cried she; 'she shall go with us. It's — Bay you are thinking about, I suppose, Mrs Graham. It is a very long walk, too far for you, and out of the question for Arthur. But we were thinking about making a picnic to see it, some fine day; and, if you will wait till the settled fine weather comes, I'm sure we shall all be delighted to have you amongst us.'

Poor Mrs Graham looked dismayed, and attempted to make excuses, but Rose, either compassionating her lonely life, or anxious to cultivate her acquaintance, was determined to have her; and every objection was overruled. She was told it would only be a small party, and all friends, and that the best view of all was from — Cliffs, full five miles distant.[3]

'Just a nice walk for the gentlemen,' continued Rose; 'but the ladies will drive and walk by turns; for we shall have our pony-carriage, which will be plenty large enough to contain little Arthur and three ladies, together with your sketching apparatus, and our provisions.'

So the proposal was finally acceded to; and, after some further discussion respecting the time and manner of the projected excursion, we rose, and took our leave.

But this was only March: a cold, wet April, and two weeks of May passed over before we could venture forth on our expedition with the reasonable hope of obtaining that pleasure we sought in pleasant prospects, cheerful society, fresh air, good cheer, and exercise, without the alloy of bad roads, cold winds, or threatening clouds. Then, on a glorious morning, we gathered our forces and set forth. The company consisted of Mrs and Master Graham, Mary and Eliza Millward, Jane and Richard Wilson, and Rose, Fergus, and Gilbert Markham.

...d been invited to join us, but, for some reason ...imself, had refused to give us his company. I had ...avour myself. When I did so, he hesitated, and asked ...going. Upon my naming Miss Wilson among the rest, he ...half inclined to go, but when I mentioned Mrs Graham, ...ing it might be a further inducement, it appeared to have a contrary effect, and he declined it altogether, and, to confess the truth, the decision was not displeasing to me, though I could scarcely tell you why.

It was about midday, when we reached the place of our destination. Mrs Graham walked all the way to the cliffs; and little Arthur walked the greater part of it too; for he was now much more hardy and active, than when he first entered the neighbourhood, and he did not like being in the carriage with strangers, while all his four friends, Mamma, and Sancho, and Mr Markham, and Miss Millward, were on foot, journeying far behind, or passing through distant fields and lanes.

I have a very pleasant recollection of that walk, along the hard, white, sunny road, shaded here and there with bright, green trees, and adorned with flowery banks and blossoming hedges of delicious fragrance; or through pleasant fields and lanes, all glorious in the sweet flowers, and brilliant verdure of delightful May. It was true, Eliza was not beside me; but she was with her friends in the pony-carriage, as happy, I trusted, as I was; and even when we pedestrians, having forsaken the highway for a short cut across the fields, beheld the little carriage far away, disappearing amid the green, embowering trees, I did not hate those trees for snatching the dear little bonnet and shawl from my sight, nor did I feel that all those intervening objects lay between my happiness and me; for, to confess the truth, I was too happy in the company of Mrs Graham, to regret the absence of Eliza Millward.

The former, it is true, was most provokingly unsociable at first – seemingly bent upon talking to no one but Mary Millward and Arthur. She and Mary journeyed along together, generally with the child between them; – but where the road permitted, I always walked on the other side of her, Richard Wilson taking the other side of Miss Millward, and Fergus roving here and there according to his fancy; and after a while, she became more friendly, and at length, I succeeded in securing her attention, almost entirely to myself – and then I was happy indeed; for whenever she did condescend to converse, I liked to listen. Where her opinions and sentiments tallied with mine, it was her extreme good sense, her exquisite taste and feeling, that delighted me; where they differed, it was still her uncompromising boldness in the avowal or defence of that difference – her earnestness and keenness that piqued my fancy: and even when she angered me by her unkind words or looks, and her uncharitable conclusions respecting me, it only made me the more dissatisfied with myself for having so unfavourably impressed her, and the more desirous to vindicate my character and disposition in her eyes, and if possible, to win her esteem.

At length our walk was ended. The increasing height and boldness of the hills had for some time intercepted the prospect; but, on gaining the summit of a steep acclivity, and looking downward, an opening lay before us – and the blue sea burst upon our sight![4] – deep violet blue – not deadly calm, but covered with glinting breakers – diminutive white specks twinkling on its bosom, and scarcely to be distinguished by the keenest vision, from the little sea-mews that sported above, their white wings glittering in the sunshine: only one or two vessels were visible; and those were far away.

I looked at my companion to see what she thought of this glorious scene. She said nothing: but she stood still, and fixed her eyes upon it with a gaze that assured me she was not disappointed. She had very fine eyes by the by – I don't know whether I've told you before, but they were full of soul, large, clear, and nearly black – not brown, but very dark grey. A cool, reviving breeze, blew from the sea – soft, pure, salubrious: it waved her drooping ringlets, and imparted a livelier colour to her usually too pallid lip and cheek. She felt its exhilarating influence, and so did I – I felt it tingling through my frame, but dared not give way to it while she remained so quiet. There was an aspect of subdued exhilaration in her face, that kindled into almost a smile of exalted, glad intelligence as her eye met mine. Never had she looked so lovely: never had my heart so warmly cleaved to her as now. Had we been left two minutes longer, standing there alone, I cannot answer for the consequences. Happily for my discretion, perhaps for my enjoyment during the remainder of the day, we were speedily summoned to the repast – a very respectable collation, which Rose, assisted by Miss Wilson and Eliza, who, having shared her seat in the carriage, had arrived with her a little before the rest, had set out upon an elevated platform overlooking the sea, and sheltered from the hot sun by a shelving rock and overhanging trees.

Mrs Graham seated herself at a distance from me. Eliza was my nearest neighbour. She exerted herself to be agreeable, in her gentle, unobtrusive way, and was, no doubt, as fascinating and charming as ever, if I could only have felt it. But soon, my heart began to warm towards her once again; and we were all very merry and happy together – as far as I could see – throughout the protracted, social meal.

When that was over, Rose summoned Fergus to help her to gather up the fragments, and the knives, dishes, etc., and restore them to the baskets; and Mrs Graham took her camp-stool and drawing materials; and having begged Miss Millward to take charge of her precious son, and strictly enjoined him not to wander from his new guardian's side, she left us and proceeded along the steep, stony hill, to a loftier, more precipitous eminence at some distance, whence a still finer prospect was to be had, where she preferred taking her sketch, though some of the ladies told her it was a frightful place, and advised her not to attempt it.

When she was gone, I felt as if there was to be no more fun – though it is difficult to say what she had contributed to the hilarity of the party. No jests, and little laughter had escaped her lips; but her smile had animated my mirth, a keen observation or a cheerful word from her had insensibly sharpened my wits, and thrown an interest over all that was done and said by the rest. Even my conversation with Eliza had been enlivened by her presence, though I knew it not; and now that she was gone, Eliza's playful nonsense ceased to amuse me – nay, grew wearisome to my soul, and I grew weary of amusing her: I felt myself drawn by an irresistible attraction to that distant point where the fair artist sat and plied her solitary task – and not long did I attempt to resist it: while my little neighbour was exchanging a few words with Miss Wilson, I rose and cannily slipped away. A few rapid strides, and a little, active clambering, soon brought me to the place where she was seated – a narrow ledge of rock at the very verge of the cliff which descended with a steep, precipitous slant, quite down to the rocky shore.

She did not hear me coming: the falling of my shadow across her paper, gave her an electric start;[5] and she looked hastily round – any other lady of my acquaintance would have screamed under such a sudden alarm.

'Oh! I didn't know it was you – Why did you startle me so?' said she, somewhat testily, 'I hate anybody to come upon me so unexpectedly.'

'Why, what did you take me for?' said I; 'if I had known you were so nervous, I would have been more cautious; but –'

'Well, never mind. What did you come for? are they all coming?'

'No; this little ledge could scarcely contain them all.'

'I'm glad, for I'm tired of talking.'

'Well then, I won't talk. I'll only sit and watch your drawing.'

'Oh, but you know I don't like that.'

'Then I'll content myself with admiring this magnificent prospect.'

She made no objection to this; and, for some time, sketched away in silence. But I could not help stealing a glance, now and then, from the splendid view at our feet to the elegant white hand that held the pencil, and the graceful neck and glossy raven curls that drooped over the paper.

'Now,' thought I, 'if I had but a pencil and a morsel of paper, I could make a lovelier sketch than hers, admitting I had the power to delineate faithfully what is before me.'

But though this satisfaction was denied me, I was very well content to sit beside her there, and say nothing.

'Are you there still, Mr Markham?' said she, at length, looking round upon me – for I was seated a little behind on a mossy projection of the cliff. – 'Why don't you go and amuse yourself with your friends?'

'Because I am tired of them, like you; and I shall have enough of them tomorrow – or at any time hence; but you, I may not have the pleasure of seeing again for I know not how long.'

'What was Arthur doing when you came away?'

'He was with Miss Millward where you left him – all right, but hoping mamma would not be long away. You didn't entrust him to me, by the by,' I grumbled, 'though I had the honour of a much longer acquaintance; but Miss Millward has the art of conciliating and amusing children,' I carelessly added, 'if she is good for nothing else.'

'Miss Millward has many estimable qualities,[6] which such as you cannot be expected to perceive or appreciate. Will you tell Arthur that I shall come in a few minutes?'

'If that be the case, I will wait, with your permission, till those few minutes are past; and then I can assist you to descend this difficult path.'

'Thank you – I always manage best, on such occasions, without assistance.'

'But, at least, I can carry your stool and sketchbook.'

She did not deny me this favour; but I was rather offended at her evident desire to be rid of me, and was beginning to repent of my pertinacity, when she somewhat appeased me by consulting my taste and judgment about some doubtful matter in her drawing. My opinion, happily, met her approbation, and the improvement I suggested was adopted without hesitation.

'I have often wished in vain,' said she, 'for another's judgment to appeal to when I could scarcely trust the direction of my own eye and head, they having been so long occupied with the contemplation of a single object, as to become almost incapable of forming a proper idea respecting it.'

'That,' replied I, 'is only one of many evils to which a solitary life exposes us.'

'True,' said she; and again we relapsed into silence.

About two minutes after, however, she declared her sketch completed and closed the book.

On returning to the scene of our repast, we found all the company had deserted it, with the exception of three – Mary Millward, Richard Wilson, and Arthur Graham. The younger gentleman lay fast asleep with his head pillowed on the lady's lap; the other was seated beside her with a pocket edition of some classic author in his hand. He never went anywhere without such a companion wherewith to improve his leisure moments: all time seemed lost that was not devoted to study, or exacted, by his physical nature, for the bare support of life. Even now, he could not abandon himself to the enjoyment of that pure air and balmy sunshine – that splendid prospect, and those soothing sounds, the music of the waves and of the soft wind in the sheltering trees above him – not even with a lady by his side (though not a very charming one, I will allow) – he must pull out his book, and make the most of his time while digesting his temperate meal, and reposing his weary limbs, unused to so much exercise.

Perhaps, however, he spared a. moment to exchange a word or a glance with his companion now and then – at any rate, she did not appear at all resentful of his conduct; for her homely features wore an expression of unusual cheerfulness and serenity, and she was studying his pale, thoughtful face with great complacency when we arrived.

The journey homeward was by no means so agreeable, to me, as the former part of the day; for now Mrs Graham was in the carriage, and Eliza Millward was the companion of my walk. She had observed my preference for the young widow, and evidently felt herself neglected. She did not manifest her chagrin by keen reproaches, bitter sarcasms, or pouting sullen silence – any or all of these I could easily have endured, or lightly laughed away; but she showed it by a kind of gentle melancholy, a mild, reproachful sadness that cut me to the heart. I tried to cheer her up, and apparently succeeded in some degree, before the walk was over; but in the very act my conscience reproved me, knowing, as I did, that, sooner or later, the tie must be broken, and this was only nourishing false hopes, and putting off the evil day.

When the pony-carriage had approached as near Wildfell Hall as the road would permit – unless, indeed, it proceeded up the long rough lane, which Mrs Graham would not allow – the young widow and her son alighted, relinquishing the driver's seat to Rose; and I persuaded Eliza to take the latter's place. Having put her comfortably in, bid her take care of the evening air, and wished her a kind goodnight, I felt considerably relieved, and hastened to offer my services to Mrs Graham to carry her apparatus up the fields, but she had already hung her camp-stool on her arm and taken her sketch-book in her hand; and insisted upon bidding me adieu then and there, with the rest of the company. But this time, she declined my proffered aid in so kind and friendly a manner, that I almost forgave her.

CHAPTER 8

THE PRESENT

Six weeks had passed away. It was a splendid morning about the close of June. Most of the hay was cut, but the last week had been very unfavourable; and now that fine weather was come at last, being determined to make the most of it, I had gathered all hands together into the hayfield, and was working away myself, in the midst of them, in my shirt sleeves, with a light, shady straw hat on my head, catching up armfuls of moist, reeking grass, and shaking it out to the four winds of heaven, at the head of a goodly file of servants and hirelings – intending so to labour, from morning to night, with as much zeal and assiduity as I could look for from any of them, as well to prosper the work by my own exertion as to animate the workers by my example – when, lo! my resolutions were overthrown in a moment, by the simple fact of my brother's running up to me and putting into my hand a small parcel, just arrived from London, which I had been for some time expecting. I tore off the cover, and disclosed an elegant and portable edition of 'Marmion.'[1]

'I guess, I know who that's for,' said Fergus, who stood looking on while I complacently examined the volume. 'That's for Miss Eliza, now.'

He pronounced this with a tone and look so prodigiously knowing, that I was glad to contradict him.

'You're wrong my lad,' said I; and taking up my coat, I deposited the book in one of its pockets, and then put it on (i.e., the coat). 'Now come here you idle dog, and make yourself useful for once,' I continued – 'Pull off your coat, and take my place in the field till I come back.'

'Till you come back? – and where are you going, pray?'

'No matter – *where* – the *when* is all that concerns you; – and I shall be back by dinner at least.'

'Oh ho! and I'm to labour away till .then, am I? – and to keep all these fellows hard at it besides – Well, well! I'll submit – for once in a way. – Come my lads, you must look sharp: *I*'m coming to help you now; – and woe be to that man, or woman either, that pauses for a moment amongst you – whether to stare about him, to scratch his head, or blow his nose – no pretext will serve – nothing but work, work, work in the sweat of your face,' – etc., etc.

Leaving him thus haranguing the people, more to their amusement than edification, I returned to the house, and having made some alteration in my toilet, hastened away to Wildfell Hall, with the book in my pocket; for it was destined for the shelves of Mrs Graham.

'What, then, had she and you got on so well together as to come to the giving and receiving of presents?' – Not precisely, old buck;[2] this was my first experiment in that line; and I was very anxious to see the result of it.

We had met several times since the — Bay excursion, and I had found she was not averse to my company, provided I confined my conversation to the discussion of abstract matters, or topics of common interest; – the moment I touched upon the sentimental or the complimentary, or made the slightest approach to tenderness in word or look, I was not only punished by an immediate change in her manner at the time, but doomed to find her more cold and distant, if not entirely inaccessible, when next I sought her company. This circumstance did not greatly disconcert me however, because I attributed it, not so much to any dislike of my person, as to some absolute resolution against a second marriage formed prior to the time of our acquaintance, whether from excess of affection for her late husband, or because she had had enough of him and the matrimonial state together. At first, indeed, she had seemed to take a pleasure in mortifying my vanity and crushing my presumption – relentlessly nipping off bud by bud as they ventured to appear; and then, I confess, I was deeply wounded, though, at the same time, stimulated to seek revenge; – but latterly, finding, beyond a doubt, that I was not that empty-headed coxcomb she had first supposed me, she had repulsed my modest advances in quite a different spirit. It was a kind of serious, almost sorrowful displeasure, which I soon learnt carefully to avoid awakening.

'Let me first establish my position as a friend,' thought I, – 'the patron and playfellow of her son, the sober, solid, plain-dealing friend of herself, and then, when I have made myself fairly necessary to her comfort and enjoyment in life (as I believe I can), we'll see what next may be effected.'

So we talked about painting, poetry, and music, theology, geology, and philosophy: once or twice I lent her a book, and once she lent me one in return: I met her in walks as often as I could; I came to her house as often as I dared. My first pretext for invading the sanctum was to bring Arthur a little waddling puppy of which Sancho was the father, and which delighted the child beyond expression, and, consequently, could not fail to please his mamma. My second was to bring him a book, which, knowing his mother's particularity, I had carefully selected, and which I submitted for her approbation before presenting it to him. Then, I brought her some plants for her garden, in my sister's name – having previously persuaded Rose to send them. Each of these times I enquired after the picture she was painting from the sketch taken on the cliff, and was admitted into the studio, and asked my opinion or advice respecting its progress.

My last visit had been to return the book she had lent me; and then it was that, in casually discussing the poetry of Sir Walter Scott, she had expressed a wish to see 'Marmion,' and I had conceived the presumptuous idea of making her a present of it, and, on my return home, instantly sent for the smart little volume I had this morning received. But an apology for invading the hermitage was still necessary; so I had furnished myself with a blue morocco collar for Arthur's little dog; and that being given and received, with much more joy and gratitude, on the part of the receiver, than the worth of the gift, or the selfish motive of the giver deserved, I ventured to ask Mrs Graham for one more look at the picture, if it was still there.

'Oh yes! come in,' said she (for I had met them in the garden). 'It is finished and framed, all ready for sending away; but give me your last opinion, and, if you can suggest any further improvement, it shall be – duly considered, at least.'

The picture was strikingly beautiful: it was the very scene itself, transferred as if by magic to the canvas; but I expressed my approbation in guarded terms, and few words, for fear of displeasing her. She, however, attentively watched my looks, and her artist's pride was gratified, no doubt, to read my heart-felt admiration in my eyes. But, while I gazed, I thought upon the book, and wondered how it was to be presented. My heart failed me; but I determined not to be such a fool as to come away without having made the attempt. It was useless waiting for an opportunity, and useless trying to concoct a speech for the occasion. The more plainly and naturally the thing was done, the better, I thought; so I just looked out of the window to screw up my courage, and then pulled out the book, turned round, and put it into her hand, with this short explanation.

'You were wishing to see "Marmion," Mrs Graham; and here it is, if you will be so kind as to take it.'

A momentary flush suffused her face – perhaps, a blush of sympathetic shame for such an awkward style of presentation: she gravely examined the volume on both sides; then silently turned over the leaves, knitting her brows the while, in serious cogitation; then closed the book, and, turning from it to me, quietly asked the price of it. – I felt the hot blood rush to my face.

'I'm sorry to offend you Mr Markham,' said she, 'but unless I pay for the book, I cannot take it.' And she laid it on the table.

'Why cannot you?'

'Because,' – she paused, and looked at the carpet.

'Why cannot you?' I repeated with a degree of irascibility that roused her to lift her eyes, and look me steadily in the face.

'Because I don't like to put myself under obligations that I can never repay – I *am* obliged to you already for your kindness to my son; but his grateful affection, and your own good feelings, must reward you for that.'

'Nonsense!' ejaculated I.

She turned her eyes on me again, with a look of quiet, grave surprise, that had the effect of a rebuke, whether intended for such or not.

'Then you won't take the book?' I asked, more mildly than I had yet spoken.

'I will gladly take it, if you will let me pay for it.'

I told her the exact price, and the cost of the carriage besides, in as calm a tone as I could command – for in fact, I was ready to weep with disappointment and vexation.

She produced her purse, and coolly counted out the money, but hesitated to put it into my hand. Attentively regarding me, in a tone of soothing softness she observed, –

'You think yourself insulted Mr Markham – I wish I could make you understand that – that I –'

'I do understand you, perfectly,' I said, 'You think that if you were to accept that trifle from me now, I should presume upon it hereafter; but you are mistaken: – if you will only oblige me by taking it, believe me, I shall build no hopes upon it, and consider this no precedent for future favours: – and it is nonsense to talk about putting yourself under obligations to *me* when you must know that in such a case the obligation is entirely on my side, – the favour on yours.'

'Well then I'll take you at your word,' she answered with a most angelic smile, returning the odious money to her purse – 'but *remember!*'

'I will remember – what I have said; – but do not you punish my presumption by withdrawing your friendship entirely from me, – or expect me to atone for it by being *more* distant than before,' said I, extending my hand to take leave, for I was too much excited to remain.

'Well then! let us be as we were,' replied she, frankly placing her hand in mine; and while I held it there, I had much difficulty to refrain from pressing it to my lips; – but that would be suicidal madness: I had been bold enough already, and this premature offering had well-nigh given the death-blow to my hopes.

It was with an agitated burning heart and brain that I hurried homewards, regardless of that scorching noonday sun – forgetful of everything but her I had just left – regretting nothing but her impenetrability, and my own precipitancy and want of tact – fearing nothing but her hateful resolution, and my inability to overcome it – hoping nothing – but halt, – I will not bore you with my conflicting hopes and fears – my serious cogitations and resolves.

CHAPTER 9

A SNAKE IN THE GRASS

Though my affections might now be said to be fairly weaned from Eliza Millward, I did not yet entirely relinquish my visits to the vicarage, because I wanted, as it were, to let her down easy; without raising much sorrow, or incurring much resentment, – or making myself the talk of the parish; and besides, if I had wholly kept away, the vicar, who looked upon my visits as paid chiefly, if not entirely, to himself, would have felt himself decidedly affronted by the neglect. But when I called there the day after my interview with Mrs Graham, he happened to be from home – a circumstance by no means so agreeable to me now as it had been on former occasions. Miss Millward was there, it is true, but she, of course, would be little better than a nonentity. However, I resolved to make my visit a short one, and to talk to Eliza in a brotherly, friendly sort of way, such as our long acquaintance might warrant me in assuming, and which, I thought, could neither give offence nor serve to encourage false hopes.

It was never my custom to talk about Mrs Graham either to her or anyone else; but I had not been seated three minutes, before she brought that lady on to the carpet herself, in a rather remarkable manner.

'Oh, Mr Markham!' said she, with a shocked expression and voice subdued almost to a whisper – 'what do you think of these shocking reports about Mrs Graham? – can you encourage us to disbelieve them?'

'What reports?'

'Ah, now! *you* know!' she slyly smiled and shook her head.

'I know nothing about them – What in the world do you mean, Eliza?'

'Oh, don't ask *me*! – *I* can't explain it.' She took up the cambric handkerchief which she had been beautifying with a deep lace border, and began to be very busy.

'What is it, Miss Millward? what does she mean?' said I, appealing to her sister, who seemed to be absorbed in the hemming of a large, coarse sheet.

'I don't know,' replied she. – 'Some idle slander, somebody has been inventing, I suppose. I never heard it till Eliza told me, the other day, – but if all the parish dinned it in my ears, I shouldn't believe a word of it – I know Mrs Graham too well!'

'Quite right Miss Millward! – and so do I – whatever it may be.'

'Well!' observed Eliza with a gentle sigh – 'It's well to have such a comfortable assurance regarding the worth of those we love. – I only wish you may not find your confidence misplaced.'

And she raised her face, and gave me such a look of sorrowful tenderness as might have melted my heart, but within those eyes there lurked a something that I did not like; and I wondered how I ever could have admired them: her sister's honest face and small grey optics appeared far more agreeable; – but I was out of temper with Eliza, at that moment, for her insinuations against Mrs Graham – which were false, I was certain, whether she knew it or not.

I said nothing more on the subject, however, at the time, and but little on any other; for, finding I could not well recover my equanimity, I presently rose and took leave, excusing myself under the plea of business at the farm; – and to the farm I went – not troubling my mind one whit about the possible truth of these mysterious reports, but only wondering what they were, by whom originated, and on what foundations raised, – and how they could the most effectually be silenced or disproved.

A few days after this, we had another of our quiet little parties, to which the usual company of friends and neighbours had been invited, and Mrs Graham among the number. She could not now absent herself under the plea of dark evenings or inclement weather, and, greatly to my relief, she came. Without her I should have found the whole affair an intolerable bore; but the moment of her arrival brought new life to the house; and though I must not neglect the other guests for her, or expect to engross much of her attention and conversation to myself alone, I anticipated an evening of no common enjoyment.

Mr Lawrence came too. He did not arrive till some time after the rest were assembled. I was curious to see how he would comport himself to Mrs Graham. A slight bow was all that passed between them on his entrance; and, having politely greeted the other members of the company, he seated himself quite aloof from the young widow, between my mother and Rose.

'Did you ever see such art!' whispered Eliza, who was my nearest neighbour. 'Would you not say they were perfect strangers?'

'Almost; – but what then?'

'What then! – why you can't pretend to be ignorant?'

'Ignorant of *what*?' demanded I, so sharply that she started and replied. –

'Oh, hush! don't speak so loud.'

'Well, tell me then,' I answered in a lower tone; 'what is it you mean? I hate enigmas.'

'Well you know, I don't vouch for the truth of it – indeed, far from it – but haven't you heard –'

'I've heard *nothing*, except from you.'

'You must be wilfully deaf then; for anyone will tell you that – but I shall only anger you by repeating it, I see; so I had better hold my tongue.'

She closed her lips and folded her hands before her with an air of injured meekness.

'If you had wished not to anger me, you should have held your tongue from the beginning; or else spoken out plainly and honestly all you had to say.'

She turned aside her face, pulled out her handkerchief, rose, and went to the window, where she stood for some time, evidently dissolved in tears. I was astounded, provoked, ashamed – not so much for my harshness as for her childish weakness. However, no one seemed to notice her, and shortly after, we were summoned to the tea-table: in those parts it was customary to sit to the table at tea-time, on all occasions, and make a meal of it; for we dined early. On taking my seat, I had Rose on one side of me, and an empty chair on the other.

'May I sit by you?' said a soft voice at my elbow.

'If you like,' was the reply; and Eliza slipped into the vacant chair; then looking up in my face with a half sad, half playful smile, she whispered –

'You're so stern, Gilbert.'

I handed down her tea with a slightly contemptuous smile, and said nothing, for I had nothing to say.

'What have I done to offend you?' said she, more plaintively. 'I wish I knew.'

'Come, take your tea Eliza, and don't be foolish,' responded I, handing her the sugar and cream.

Just then, there arose a slight commotion on the other side of me, occasioned by Miss Wilson's coming to negotiate an exchange of seats with Rose.

'Will you be so good as to exchange places with me, Miss Markham?' said she, 'for I don't like to sit by Mrs Graham. If your mamma thinks proper to invite such persons to her house, she cannot object to her daughter's keeping company with them.'

This latter clause was added in a sort of soliloquy when Rose was gone; but I was not polite enough to let it pass:

'Will you be so good as to tell me what you mean, Miss Wilson?' said I.

The question startled her a little, but not much.

'Why Mr Markham,' replied she coolly, having quickly recovered her self-possession, 'it surprises me rather that Mrs Markham should invite such a person as Mrs Graham to her house; but, perhaps, she is not aware that the lady's character is considered scarcely respectable.'

'She is not, nor am I; and therefore, you would oblige me by explaining your meaning a little further.'

'This is scarcely the time or the place for such explanations; but I think you can hardly be so ignorant as you pretend: you must know her as well as I do.'

'I think I do, perhaps a little better; and therefore, if you will inform me what you have heard, or imagined, against her, I shall, perhaps, be able to set you right.'

'Can you tell me, then, who was her husband; or if she ever had any?'

Indignation kept me silent. At such a time and place I could not trust myself to answer.

'Have you never observed,' said Eliza, 'what a striking likeness there is between that child of hers and –'

'And whom?' demanded Miss Wilson, with an air of cold, but keen severity.

Eliza was startled: the timidly spoken suggestion had been intended for my ear alone.

'Oh, I beg your pardon!' pleaded she, 'I may be mistaken – perhaps I *was* mistaken.' But she accompanied the words with a sly glance of derision directed to me from the corner of her disingenuous eye.

'There's no need to ask *my* pardon,' replied her friend; 'but I see no one here that at all resembles that child, except his mother; and when you hear ill-natured reports, Miss Eliza, I will thank you – that is, I think you will do well to refrain from repeating them. I presume the person you allude to is Mr Lawrence; but I think I can assure you that your suspicions, in that respect, are utterly misplaced; and if he has any particular connection with the lady at all (which no one has a right to assert), at least, he has (what cannot be said of some others), sufficient sense of propriety to withhold him from acknowledging anything more than a bowing acquaintance in the presence of respectable persons – he was evidently both surprised and annoyed to find her here.'

'Go it!' cried Fergus, who sat on the other side of Eliza, and was the only individual who shared that side of the table with us; 'go it like bricks!¹ mind you don't leave her one stone upon another.'²

Miss Wilson drew herself up with a look of freezing scorn, but said nothing. Eliza would have replied, but I interrupted her by saying as calmly as I could, though in a tone which betrayed, no doubt, some little of what I felt within, –

'We have had enough of this subject: if we can only speak to slander our betters, let us hold our tongues.'

'I think you'd better,' observed Fergus; 'and so does our good parson: he has been addressing the company in his richest vein all the while, and eyeing you, from time to time, with looks of stern distaste, while you sat there, irreverently whispering and muttering together; and once he paused in the middle of a story – or a sermon, I don't know which, and fixed his eyes upon you, Gilbert, as much as to say – "When Mr Markham has done flirting with those two ladies I will proceed!"'

What more was said at the tea-table I cannot tell; nor how I found patience to sit till the meal was over. I remember, however, that I swallowed with difficulty the remainder of the tea that was in my cup, and ate nothing; and that the first thing I did was to stare at Arthur Graham, who sat beside his mother on the opposite side of the table, and the second to stare at Mr Lawrence, who sat below; and, first, it struck me that there *was* a likeness; but, on further contemplation, I concluded it was only in imagination. Both, it is true, had more delicate features and smaller bones than commonly fall to the lot of individuals of the rougher sex, and Lawrence's complexion was pale and clear, and Arthur's delicately fair; but Arthur's tiny, somewhat snubby nose could never become so long and straight as Mr Lawrence's, and the outline of his face, though not full enough to be round, and too finely converging to the small, dimpled chin to be square, could never be drawn out to the long oval of the other's; while the child's hair was evidently of a lighter, warmer tint than the elder gentleman's had ever been, and his large, clear, blue eyes, though prematurely serious at times, were utterly dissimilar to the shy hazel eyes of Mr Lawrence, whence the sensitive soul looked so distrustfully forth, as ever ready to retire within, from the offences of a too rude, too uncongenial world. Wretch that I was to harbour that detestable idea for a moment! Did I not know Mrs Graham? Had I not seen her, conversed with her time after time? Was I not certain that she, in intellect, in purity and elevation of soul, was immeasurably superior to any of her detractors; that she was, in fact, the noblest, the most adorable, of her sex I had ever beheld, or even imagined to exist? Yes, and I would say with Mary Millward (sensible girl as she was), that if all the parish, aye, or all the world should din these horrible lies in my ears, I would not believe them; for I knew her better than they.

Meantime, my brain was on fire with indignation, and my heart seemed ready to burst from its prison with conflicting passions. I regarded my two fair neighbours with a feeling of abhorrence and loathing I scarcely endeavoured to conceal: I was rallied from several quarters for my abstraction and ungallant neglect of the ladies; but I cared little for that: all I cared about, besides that one grand subject of my thoughts, was to see the cups travel up to the tea-tray, and not come down again. I thought Mr Millward never *would* cease telling us that he was no tea-drinker, and that it was highly injurious to keep loading the stomach with slops to the exclusion of more wholesome sustenance, and so give himself time to finish his fourth cup.

At length it was over; and I rose and left the table and the guests, without a word of apology – I could endure their company no longer. I rushed out to cool my brain in the balmy evening air, and to compose my mind, or indulge my passionate thoughts in the solitude of the garden.

To avoid being seen from the windows, I went down a quiet, little avenue, that skirted one side of the enclosure, at the bottom of which was a seat embowered in roses and honeysuckles. Here I sat down to think over the virtues and wrongs of the lady of Wildfell Hall; but I had not been so occupied two minutes, before voices and laughter, and glimpses of moving objects through the trees, informed me that the whole company had turned out to take an airing in the garden too. However, I nestled up in a corner of the bower, and hoped to retain possession of it, secure alike from observation and intrusion. But no – confound it – there was someone coming down the avenue! Why couldn't they enjoy the flowers and sunshine of the open garden, and leave that sunless nook to me, and the gnats and midges?

But peeping through my fragrant screen of interwoven branches to discover who the intruders were (for a murmur of voices told me it was more than one), my vexation instantly subsided, and far other feelings agitated my still unquiet soul; for there was Mrs Graham, slowly moving down the walk with Arthur by her side, and no one else. Why were they alone? Had the poison of detracting tongues already spread through all; and had they all turned their backs upon her? I now recollected having seen Mrs Wilson, in the early part of the evening, edging her chair close up to my mother, and bending forward, evidently in the delivery of some important, confidential intelligence; and from the incessant wagging of her head, the frequent distortions of her wrinkled physiognomy, and the winking and malicious twinkle of her little ugly eyes, I judged it was some spicy piece of scandal that engaged her powers; and from the cautious privacy of the communication, I supposed some person then present was the luckless object of her calumnies; and from all these tokens, together with my mother's looks and gestures of mingled horror and incredulity, I now concluded that object to have been Mrs Graham. I did not emerge from my place of concealment, till she had nearly reached the bottom of the walk, lest my appearance should drive her away; and when I did step forward, she stood still and seemed inclined to turn back as it was.[3]

'Oh, don't let us disturb you Mr Markham!' said she. 'We came here to seek retirement ourselves; not to intrude on your seclusion.'

'I am no hermit, Mrs Graham – though I own it looks rather like it, to absent myself in this uncourteous fashion from my guests.'

'I feared you were unwell,' said she with a look of real concern.

'I was rather, but it's over now. Do sit here a little, and rest, and tell me how you like this arbour,' said I, and, lifting Arthur by the shoulders, I planted him in the middle of the seat by way of securing his mamma, who, acknowledging it to be a tempting place of refuge, threw herself back in one corner, while I took possession of the other.

But that word 'refuge' disturbed me. Had their unkindness then really driven her to seek for peace in solitude?

'Why have they left you alone?' I asked.

'It is I who have left them,' was the smiling rejoinder. 'I was wearied to death with small-talk – nothing wears me out like that. I cannot imagine how they *can* go on as they do.'

I could not help smiling at the serious depth of her wonderment.

'Is it that they think it a *duty* to be continually talking,' pursued she; 'and so never pause to think, but fill up with aimless trifles and vain repetitions, when subjects of real interest fail to present themselves? – or do they really take pleasure in such discourse?'

'Very likely they do,' said I: 'their shallow minds can hold no great ideas, and their light heads are carried away by trivialities, that would not move a better furnished skull; – and their only alternative to such discourse, is to plunge over head and ears[4] into the slough of scandal – which is their chief delight.'

'Not all of them surely?' cried the lady, astonished at the bitterness of my remark.

'No, certainly; I exonerate my sister from such degraded tastes – and my mother too, if you included *her* in your animadversions.'

'I meant no animadversions against anyone, and certainly intended no disrespectful allusions to your mother. I have known some sensible persons great adepts in that style of conversation, when circumstances impelled them to it; but it is a gift I cannot boast the possession of. I kept up my attention, on this occasion, as long as I could, but when my powers were exhausted, I stole away, to seek a few minutes' repose in this quiet walk. I hate talking where there is no exchange of ideas or sentiments, and no good given or received.'[5]

'Well,' said I, 'if ever I trouble you with my loquacity, tell me so at once, and I promise not to be offended; for I possess the faculty of enjoying the company of those I – of my friends as well in silence as in conversation.'

'I don't quite believe you; but if it were so, you would exactly suit me for a companion.'

'I am all you wish, then, in other respects?'

'No, I don't mean that. How beautiful those little clusters of foliage look, where the sun comes through behind them!' said she, on purpose to change the subject.

And they did look beautiful, where at intervals the level rays of the sun, penetrating the thickness of trees and shrubs on the opposite side of the path before us, relieved their dusky verdure by displaying patches of semitransparent leaves of resplendent golden green.

'I almost wish I were not a painter,' observed my companion.

'Why so? one would think at such a time you would most exult in your privilege of being able to imitate the various brilliant and delightful touches of nature.'

'No; for instead of delivering myself up to the full enjoyment of them as others do, I am always troubling my head about how I could produce the same effect upon canvas; and as that can never be done, it is mere vanity and vexation of spirit.'[6]

'Perhaps you cannot do it to satisfy yourself, but you may and do succeed in delighting others with the result of your endeavours.'

'Well, after all I should not complain: perhaps few people gain their livelihood with so much pleasure in their toil as I do.[7] Here is someone coming.'

She seemed vexed at the interruption.

'It is only Mr Lawrence and Miss Wilson,' said I, 'coming to enjoy a quiet stroll. They will not disturb us.'

I could not quite decipher the expression of her face; but I was satisfied there was no jealousy therein. What business had I to look for it?

'What sort of a person is Miss Wilson?' she asked.

'She is elegant and accomplished above the generality of her birth and station; and some say she is ladylike and agreeable.'

'I thought her somewhat frigid, and rather supercilious in her manner today.'

'Very likely she might be so to you. She has possibly taken a prejudice against you, for I think she regards you in the light of a rival.'

'Me? Impossible Mr Markham!' said she, evidently astonished and annoyed.

'Well, I know nothing about it,' returned I, rather doggedly; for I thought her annoyance was chiefly against myself.

The pair had now approached within a few paces of us. Our arbour was set snugly back in a corner, before which the avenue, at its termination, turned off into the more airy walk along the bottom of the garden. As they approached this, I saw, by the aspect of Jane Wilson, that she was directing her companion's attention to us; and, as well by her cold, sarcastic smile, as by the few isolated words of her discourse that reached me, I knew full well that she was impressing him with the idea that we were strongly attached to each other. I noticed that he coloured up to the temples, gave us one furtive glance in passing, and walked on, looking grave, but seemingly offering no reply to her remarks.

It was true, then, that he *had* some designs upon Mrs Graham; and, were they honourable, he would not be so anxious to conceal them. *She* was blameless, of course, but he was detestable beyond all count.

While these thoughts flashed through my mind, my companion abruptly rose, and calling her son, said they would now go in quest of the company, and departed up the avenue. Doubtless she had heard or guessed something of Miss Wilson's remarks, and therefore, it was natural enough she should choose to continue the tête-à-tête no longer, especially as at that moment my cheeks were burning with indignation against my former friend, the token of which she might mistake for a blush of stupid embarrassment. For this I owed Miss Wilson yet another grudge; and still the more I thought upon her conduct, the more I hated her.

It was late in the evening before I joined the company. I found Mrs Graham already equipped for departure, and taking leave of the rest, who were now returned to the house. I offered – nay, begged to accompany her home. Mr Lawrence was standing by at the time, conversing with someone else. He did not look at us, but, on hearing my earnest request, he paused in the middle of a sentence to listen for her reply, and went on, with a look of quiet satisfaction, ·the moment he found it was to be a denial.

A denial it was, decided, though not unkind. She could not be persuaded to think there was danger for herself or her child in traversing those lonely lanes and fields without attendance. It was daylight still, and she should meet no one; or if she did, the people were quiet and harmless, she was well assured. In fact, she would not hear of anyone's putting himself out of the way to accompany her, though Fergus vouchsafed to offer his services, in case they should be more acceptable than mine, and my mother begged she might send one of the farming-men to escort her.

When she was gone, the rest was all a blank, or worse. Lawrence attempted to draw me into conversation, but I snubbed him, and went to another part of the room. Shortly after, the party broke up, and he himself took leave. When he came to me, I was blind to his extended hand, and deaf to his goodnight till he repeated it a second time; and then, to get rid of him, I muttered an inarticulate reply accompanied by a sulky nod.

'What is the matter Markham?' whispered he.

I replied by a wrathful and contemptuous stare.

'Are you angry because Mrs Graham would not let you go home with her?' he asked with a faint smile that nearly exasperated me beyond control.

But, swallowing down all fiercer answers, I merely demanded, –

'What business is it of yours?'

'Why, none,' replied he, with provoking quietness; 'only,' and here he raised his eyes to my face, and spoke with unusual solemnity, 'only let me tell you, Markham, that if you have any designs in that quarter they will certainly fail; and it grieves me to see you cherishing false hopes, and wasting your strength in useless efforts, for –'

'Hypocrite!' I exclaimed, and he held his breath, and looked very blank, turned white about the gills, and went away without another word.

I had wounded him to the quick; and I was glad of it.

CHAPTER 10

A CONTRACT AND A QUARREL

When all were gone, I learned that the vile slander had indeed been circulated throughout the company, in the very presence of the victim. Rose, however, vowed she did not and would not believe it, and my mother made the same declaration, though not, I fear, with the same amount of real, unwavering incredulity. It seemed to dwell continually on her mind, and she kept irritating me from time to time by such expressions as – 'Dear, dear, who would have thought it! – Well! I always thought there was something odd about her. – You see what it is for women to affect to be different to other people.' And once it was, –

'I misdoubted that appearance of mystery from the very first – I *thought* there would no good come of it; but this is a sad, sad business to be sure!'

'Why mother, you said you didn't believe these tales,' said Fergus.

'No more I do, my dear; but then, you know, there must be some foundation.'

'The foundation is in the wickedness and falsehood of the world,' said I, 'and in the fact that Mr Lawrence has been seen to go that way once or twice of an evening – and the village gossips say he goes to pay his addresses to the strange lady, and the scandalmongers have greedily seized the rumour, to make it the basis of their own infernal structure.'

'Well, but Gilbert, there must be something in her *manner* to countenance such reports.'

'Did *you* see anything in her manner?'

'No, certainly; but then you know, I always said there was something strange about her.'

I believe it was on that very evening that I ventured on another invasion of Wildfell Hall. From the time of our party, which was upwards of a week ago, I had been making daily efforts to meet its mistress in her walks; and, always disappointed (she must have managed it so on purpose), had nightly kept revolving in my mind some pretext for another call. At length, I concluded that the separation could be endured no longer, (by this time, you will see I was pretty far gone); and, taking from the book case an old volume that I thought she might be interested in, though, from its unsightly and somewhat dilapidated condition, I had not yet ventured to offer it for her perusal, I hastened away, – but not without sundry misgivings as to how she would receive me, or how I could summon courage to present myself with so slight an excuse. But perhaps I might see her in the field or the garden, and then there would be no great difficulty: it was the formal knocking at the door, with the prospect of being gravely ushered in, by Rachel, to the presence of a surprised, uncordial mistress, that so greatly disturbed me.

My wish, however, was not gratified. Mrs Graham herself was not to be seen; but there was Arthur playing with his frolicsome little dog in the garden. I looked over the gate and called him to me. He wanted me to come in; but I told him I could not without his mother's leave.

'I'll go and ask her,' said the child.

'No, no, Arthur, you mustn't do that, – but if she's not engaged, just ask her to come here a minute: tell her I want to speak to her.'

He ran to perform my bidding, and quickly returned with his mother. How lovely she looked with her dark ringlets streaming in the light summer breeze, her fair cheek slightly flushed, and her countenance radiant with smiles! – Dear Arthur! what did I not owe to you for this and every other happy meeting? – Through him, I was at once delivered from all formality, and terror, and constraint. In love affairs, there is no mediator like a merry, simple-hearted child – ever ready to cement divided hearts, to span the unfriendly gulf of custom, to melt the ice of cold reserve, and overthrow the separating walls of dread formality and pride.

'Well, Mr Markham, what is it?' said the young mother, accosting me with a pleasant smile.

'I want you to look at this book, and, if you please, to take it, and peruse it at your leisure. I make no apology for calling you out on such a lovely evening though it *be* for a matter of no greater importance.'

'Tell him to come in, mamma,' said Arthur.

'Would you like to come in?' asked the lady.

'Yes; I should like to see your improvements in the garden.'

'And how your sister's roots have prospered in my charge,' added she, as she opened the gate.

And we sauntered through the garden, and talked of the flowers, the trees, and the book, – and then of other things. The evening was kind and genial, and so was my companion. By degrees, I waxed more warm and tender than, perhaps, I had ever been before; but still, I said nothing tangible, and she attempted no repulse; until, in passing a moss rose-tree that I had brought her some weeks since, in my sister's name, she plucked a beautiful half open bud and bade me give it to Rose.

'May I not keep it myself?' I asked.

'No; but here is another for you.'

Instead of taking it quietly, I likewise took the hand that offered it, and looked into her face. She let me hold it for a moment, and I saw a flash of ecstatic brilliance in her eye, a glow of glad excitement on her face – I thought my hour of victory was come – but instantly, a painful recollection seemed to flash upon her; a cloud of anguish darkened her brow; a marble paleness blanched her cheek and lip; there seemed a moment of inward conflict, – and with a sudden effort, she withdrew her hand, and retreated a step or two back.

'Now Mr Markham,' said she, with a kind of desperate calmness, 'I must tell you plainly, that I cannot do with this. I like your company, because I am alone here, and your conversation pleases me more than that of any other person; but if you cannot be content to regard me as a friend – a plain, cold, motherly, or sisterly friend, I must beg you to leave me now, and let me alone hereafter – in fact, we must be strangers for the future.'

'I will, then – be your friend, – or brother, or anything you wish, if you will only let me continue to see you; but tell me why I cannot be anything more?'

There was a perplexed and thoughtful pause.

'Is it in consequence of some rash vow?'

'It is something of the kind,' she answered; – 'some day I may tell you, but at present you had better leave me; and never, Gilbert, put me to the painful necessity of repeating what I have just now said to you!' – she earnestly added, giving me her hand in serious kindness. How sweet, how musical my own name sounded in her mouth!

'I will not,' I replied. 'But you pardon *this* offence?'

'On condition that you never repeat it.'

'And may I come to see you now and then?'

'Perhaps, – occasionally; provided you never abuse the privilege.'

'I make no empty promises, but you shall see.'

'The moment you do, our intimacy is at an end, that's all.'

'And will you always call me Gilbert? – it sounds more sisterly, and it will serve to remind me of our contract.'

She smiled, and once more bid me go, – and, at length, I judged it prudent to obey; and she re-entered the house, and I went down the hill. But as I went, the tramp of horses' hoofs fell on my ear, and broke the stillness of the dewy evening; and, looking towards the lane, I saw a solitary equestrian coming up. Inclining to dusk as it was, I knew him at a glance: it was Mr Lawrence on his grey pony. I flew across the field – leaped the stone fence – and then walked down the lane to meet him. On seeing me, he suddenly drew in his little steed, and seemed inclined to turn back, but on second thought, apparently judged it better to continue his course as before. He accosted me with a slight bow, and, edging close to the wall, endeavoured to pass on – but I was not so minded: seizing his horse by the bridle, I exclaimed; –

'Now Lawrence, I will have this mystery explained! Tell me where you are going, and what you mean to do – at once, and distinctly!'

'Will you take your hand off the bridle?' said he, quietly; – 'you're hurting my pony's mouth.'

'You and your pony be —'

'What makes you so coarse and brutal, Markham? I'm quite ashamed of you.'

'You answer my questions – before you leave this spot! I *will* know what you mean by this perfidious duplicity?'

'I shall answer *no* questions till you let go the bridle, – if you stand till morning.'

'Now then,' said I, unclosing my hand, but still standing before him.

'Ask me some other time, when you can speak like a gentleman,' returned he, and he made an effort to pass me again; but I quickly recaptured the pony, scarce less astonished than its master at such uncivil usage.

'Really Mr Markham, this is *too* much!' said the latter. 'Can I not go to see my tenant on matters of business, without being assaulted in this manner by –'

'This is no time for business sir! – I'll tell you, now, what I think of your conduct.'

'You'd better defer your opinion to a more convenient season,' interrupted he in a low tone – 'here's the vicar.'

And in truth, the vicar was just behind me, plodding homeward from some remote corner of his parish. I immediately released the squire; and he went on his way, saluting Mr Millward as he passed.

'What, quarrelling Markham?' cried the latter, addressing himself to me, – 'and about that young widow I don't doubt,' he added, reproachfully shaking his head. 'But let me tell you young man,' (here he put his face into mine with an important, confidential air), 'she's not worth it!' and he confirmed the assertion by a solemn nod.

'MR MILLWARD!' I exclaimed, in a tone of wrathful menace that made the reverend gentleman look round – aghast – astounded at such unwonted insolence, and stare me in the face, with a look that plainly said: 'What, this to me!' But I was too indignant to apologize, or to speak another word to him: I turned away, and hastened homewards, descending with rapid strides the steep, rough lane, and leaving him to follow as he pleased.

CHAPTER II

THE VICAR AGAIN

You must suppose about three weeks passed over. Mrs Graham and I were now established friends – or brother and sister, as we rather chose to consider ourselves. She called me Gilbert, by my express desire, and I called her Helen, for I had seen that name written in her books. I seldom attempted to see her above twice a week; and still I made our meetings appear the result of accident as often as I could – for I found it necessary to be extremely careful – and, altogether, I behaved with such exceeding propriety that she never had occasion to reprove me once. Yet I could not but perceive that she was at times unhappy and dissatisfied with herself – or her position, and truly I myself was not quite contented with the latter: this assumption of brotherly nonchalance was very hard to sustain, and I often felt myself a most confounded hypocrite with it all; I saw too, or rather I felt, that, in spite of herself, 'I was not indifferent to her,'[1] as the novel heroes modestly express it, and while I thankfully enjoyed my present good fortune, I could not fail to wish and hope for something better in future; but of course, I kept such dreams entirely to myself.

'Where are you going Gilbert?' said Rose, one evening, shortly after tea, when I had been busy with the farm all day.

'To take a walk,' was the reply.

'Do you always brush your hat so carefully, and do your hair so nicely, and put on such smart new gloves when you take a walk?'

'Not always.'

'You're going to Wildfell Hall, aren't you?'

'What makes you think so?'

'Because you look as if you were – but I wish you wouldn't go so often.'

'Nonsense child! I don't go once in six weeks – what do you mean?'

'Well, but if I were you, I wouldn't have so much to do with Mrs Graham.'

'Why Rose, are you, too, giving in to the prevailing opinion?'

'No,' returned she, hesitatingly – 'but I've heard so much about her lately, both at the Wilsons and the vicarage; – and besides, mamma says, if she were a proper person, she would not be living there by herself[2] – and don't you remember last winter, Gilbert, all that about the false name to the picture; and how she explained it – saying she had friends or acquaintances from whom she wished her present residence to be concealed, and that she was afraid of their tracing her out; – and then, how suddenly she started up and left the room when that person came – whom she took good care not to let us catch a glimpse of, and who Arthur, with such an air of mystery, told us was his mamma's friend?'

'Yes Rose, I remember it all; and I can forgive your uncharitable conclusions; for perhaps, if I did not know her myself, I should put all these things together, and believe the same as you do; but thank God, I do know her; and I should be unworthy the name of a man, if I could believe anything that was said against her, unless I heard it from her own lips. – I should as soon believe such things of you Rose.'

'Oh, Gilbert!'

'Well, do you think I *could* believe anything of the kind, – whatever the Wilsons and Millwards dared to whisper?'

'I should hope *not* indeed!'

'And why not? – Because I know you – Well, and I know her just as well.'

'Oh, no! you know nothing of her former life; and last year at this time, you did not know that such a person existed.'

'No matter. There is such a thing as looking through a person's eyes into the heart, and learning more of the height, and breadth, and depth of another's soul in one hour, than it might take you a life time to discover, if he or she were not disposed to reveal it, – or if you had not the sense to understand it.'

'Then you *are* going to see her this evening?'

'To be sure I am!'

'But what would mamma say, Gilbert?'

'Mamma needn't know.'

'But she must know some time, if you go on.'

'Go on! – there's no going on in the matter – Mrs Graham and I are two friends – and will be; and no man breathing shall hinder it, – or has a right to interfere between us.'

'But if you knew how they talk, you would be more careful – for her sake as well as for your own. Jane Wilson thinks your visits to the old hall but another proof of her depravity –'

'Confound Jane Wilson!'

'And Eliza Millward is quite grieved about you.'

'I hope she is.'

'But I wouldn't if I were you.'

'Wouldn't what? – How do they know that I go there?'

'There's nothing hid from them: they spy out everything.'

'O, I never thought of this! – And so they dare to turn my friendship into food for further scandal against her! – That proves the falsehood of their other lies, at all events, if any proof were wanting. – Mind you contradict them Rose, whenever you can.'

'But they don't speak openly to me about such things: it is only by hints and innuendoes, and by what I hear others say, that I know what they think.'

'Well then, I won't go today, as it's getting latish. But oh, deuce take their cursed envenomed tongues!' I muttered in the bitterness of my soul.[3]

And just at that moment, the vicar entered the room: we had been too much absorbed in our conversation to observe his knock. After his customary, cheerful and fatherly greeting of Rose, who was rather a favourite with the old gentleman, he turned somewhat sternly to me: –

'Well sir!' said he, 'you're quite a stranger. It is – let – me – see,' he continued slowly, as he deposited his ponderous bulk in the arm chair that Rose officiously brought towards him, 'it is just – six – weeks – by my reckoning, since you darkened – my – door!' He spoke it with emphasis, and struck his stick on the floor.

'Is it sir?' said I.

'Aye! It is so!' He added an affirmatory nod, and continued to gaze upon me with a kind of irate solemnity, holding his substantial stick between his knees, with his hands clasped upon its head.

'I have been busy,' I said, for an apology was evidently demanded.

'Busy!' repeated he derisively.

'Yes; you know I've been getting in my hay; and now the harvest is beginning.'

'Humph!'

Just then my mother came in, and created a diversion in my favour, by her loquacious and animated welcome of the reverend guest. She regretted deeply that he had not come a little earlier, in time for tea, but offered to have some immediately prepared, if he would do her the favour to partake of it.

'Not any for me, I thank you,' replied he; 'I shall be at home in a few minutes.'

'Oh, but do stay and take a little! it will be ready in five minutes.'

But he rejected the offer, with a majestic wave of the hand.

'I'll tell you what I'll take, Mrs Markham,' said he: 'I'll take a glass of your excellent ale.'

'With pleasure!' cried my mother, proceeding with alacrity to pull the bell and order the favoured beverage.

'I thought,' continued he, 'I'd just look in upon you as I passed, and taste your home-brewed ale. I've been to call on Mrs Graham.'

'Have you indeed?'

He nodded gravely, and added with awful emphasis –

'I thought it incumbent upon me to do so.'

'Really!' ejaculated my mother.

'Why so, Mr Millward?' asked I. He looked at me with some severity, and, turning again to my mother, repeated –

'I thought it incumbent upon me!' and struck his stick on the floor again. My mother sat opposite, an awe-struck but admiring auditor.

'"Mrs Graham," said I,' he continued shaking his head as he

spoke, '"these are terrible reports!" "What sir?" says she, affecting to be ignorant of my meaning. "It is my – duty – as – your pastor," said I, "to tell you both everything that I myself see reprehensible in your conduct, and all I have reason to suspect and what others tell me concerning you." – So I told her!'

'You did sir?' cried I, starting from my seat, and striking my fist on the table. He merely glanced towards me, and continued – addressing his hostess; –

'It was a painful duty, Mrs Markham – but I told her!'

'And how did she take it?' asked my mother.

'Hardened, I fear – hardened!' he replied, with a despondent shake of the head; 'and at the same time, there was a strong display of unchastened, misdirected passions. She turned white in the face, and drew her breath through her teeth in a savage sort of way; – but she offered no extenuation or defence; and with a kind of shameless calmness – shocking indeed to witness, in one so young – as good as told me that my remonstrance was unavailing, and my pastoral advice quite thrown away upon her – nay, that my very *presence* was displeasing while I spoke such things. And I withdrew at length, too plainly seeing that nothing could be done – and sadly grieved to find her case so hopeless. But I am fully determined, Mrs Markham, that *my* daughters – shall – not – consort with her. Do you adopt the same resolution with regard to yours! – As for your sons – as for *you*, young man,' he continued, sternly turning to me.

'As for ME, sir,' – I began, but checked by some impediment in my utterance, and finding that my whole frame trembled with fury, I said no more – but took the wiser part of snatching up my hat and bolting from the room, slamming the door behind me, with a bang that shook the house to its foundations, and made my mother scream – and gave a momentary relief to my excited feelings.

The next minute saw me hurrying with rapid strides in the direction of Wildfell Hall – to what intent or purpose I could scarcely tell, but I must be moving somewhere, and no other goal would do – I must see her too, and speak to her – that was certain, but what to say or how to act, I had no definite idea. Such stormy thoughts – so many different resolutions crowded in upon me, that my mind was little better than a chaos of conflicting passions.

CHAPTER 12

A TÊTE-À-TÊTE AND A DISCOVERY

In little more than twenty minutes, the journey was accomplished. I paused at the gate to wipe my streaming forehead, and recover my breath and some degree of composure. Already the rapid walking had somewhat mitigated my excitement; and with a firm and steady tread, I paced the garden walk. In passing the inhabited wing of the building, I caught a sight of Mrs Graham, through the open window, slowly pacing up and down her lonely room.

She seemed agitated, and even dismayed, at my arrival, as if she thought I too was coming to accuse her. I had entered her presence intending to condole with her upon the wickedness of the world, and help her to abuse the vicar and his vile informants, but now I felt positively ashamed to mention the subject, and determined not to refer to it, unless she led the way.

'I am come at an unseasonable hour,' said I, assuming a cheerfulness I did not feel, in order to reassure her; 'but I won't stay many minutes.'

She smiled upon me, faintly it is true, but most kindly – I had almost said thankfully, as her apprehensions were removed.

'How dismal you are, Helen! Why have you no fire?' I said, looking round on the gloomy apartment.

'It is summer yet,' she replied.

'But *we always* have a fire in the evenings – if we can bear it; – and you, especially require one in this cold house and dreary room.'

'You should have come a little sooner, and I would have had one lighted for you; but it is not worthwhile now – you won't stay many minutes you say, and Arthur is gone to bed.'

'But I have a fancy for a fire, nevertheless. Will you order one, if I ring?'

'Why Gilbert, you don't *look* cold!' said she, smilingly regarding my face, which no doubt seemed warm enough.

'No,' replied I, 'but I want to see you comfortable before I go.'

'Me comfortable!' repeated she, with a bitter laugh, as if there were something amusingly absurd in the idea. 'It suits me better as it is,' she added in a tone of mournful resignation.

But, determined to have my own way, I pulled the bell.

'There now, Helen!' I said, as the approaching steps of Rachel were heard in answer to the summons. There was nothing for it but to turn round and desire the maid to light the fire.

I owe Rachel a grudge to this day for the look she cast upon me ere she departed on her mission – the sour, suspicious, inquisitorial look that plainly demanded, 'what are *you* here for, I wonder?' Her mistress did not fail to notice it, and a shade of uneasiness darkened her brow.

'You must not stay long Gilbert,' said she, when the door was closed upon us.

'I'm not going to,' said I, somewhat testily, though without a grain of anger in my heart against anyone but the meddling old woman. 'But Helen, I've something to say to you before I go.'

'What is it?'

'No, not now – I don't know yet precisely what it is – or how to say it,' replied I, with more truth than wisdom; and then, fearing lest she should turn me out of the house, I began talking about indifferent matters in order to gain time. Meanwhile Rachel came in to kindle the fire, which was soon effected by thrusting a red-hot poker between the bars of the grate, where the fuel was already disposed for ignition. She honoured me with another of her hard, inhospitable looks in departing, but, little moved thereby, I went on talking; and, setting a chair for Mrs Graham on one side of the hearth and one for myself on the other, I ventured to sit down, though half suspecting she would rather see me go.

In a little while we both relapsed into silence, and continued for several minutes gazing abstractedly into the fire – she intent upon her own sad thoughts, and I reflecting how delightful it would be to be seated thus beside her with no other presence to restrain our intercourse – not even that of Arthur, our mutual friend, without whom we had never met before – if only I could venture to speak my mind, and disburden my full heart of the feelings that had so long oppressed it, and which it now struggled to retain, with an effort that it seemed impossible to continue much longer, – and revolving the pros and cons for opening my heart to her there and then, and imploring a return of affection, the permission to regard her thenceforth as my own, and the right and the power to defend her from the calumnies of malicious tongues. On the one hand, I felt a newborn confidence in my powers of persuasion – a strong conviction that my own fervour of spirit would grant me eloquence – that my very determination – the absolute necessity for succeeding, that I felt – must win me what I sought; while on the other, I feared to lose the ground I had already gained with so much toil and skill, and destroy all future hope by one rash effort, when time and patience might have won success. It was like setting my life upon the cast of a die; and yet, I was ready to resolve upon the attempt. At any rate I would entreat the explanation she had half promised to give me before: I would demand the reason of this hateful barrier, this mysterious impediment to my happiness and, as I trusted, to her own.

But while I considered in what manner I could best frame my request, my companion wakened from her reverie with a scarcely audible sigh, and looking towards the window where the blood-red harvest moon, just rising over one of the grim, fantastic evergreens, was shining in upon us, said, –

'Gilbert, it is getting late.'

'I see,' said I. 'You want me to go, I suppose.'

'I think you ought. If my kind neighbours get to know of this visit – as no doubt they will – they will not turn it much to my advantage.'

It was with what the vicar would doubtless have called a savage sort of a smile that she said this.

'Let them turn it as they will,' said I. 'What are their thoughts to you or me, so long as we are satisfied with ourselves – and each other. Let them go to the deuce with their vile constructions, and their lying inventions!'

This outburst brought a flush of colour to her face.

'You have heard, then, what they say of me?'

'I heard some detestable falsehoods; but none but fools would credit them for a moment, Helen, so don't let them trouble you.'

'I did not think Mr Millward a fool, and he believes it all; but however little you may value the opinions of those about you – however little you may esteem them as individuals, it is not pleasant to be looked upon as a liar and a hypocrite, to be thought to practise what you abhor, and to encourage the vices you would discountenance, to find your good intentions frustrated, and your hands crippled by your supposed unworthiness, and to bring disgrace on the principles you profess.'

'True; and if I, by my thoughtlessness and selfish disregard to appearances, have at all assisted to expose you to these evils, let me entreat you not only to pardon me, but to enable me to make reparation; authorize me to clear your name from every imputation: give me the right to identify your honour with my own, and to defend your reputation as more precious than my life!'

'Are you hero enough to unite yourself to one whom you know to be suspected and despised by all around you, and identify your interests and your honour with hers? Think! it is a serious thing.'

'I should be proud to do it Helen! – most happy – delighted beyond expression! – and if that be all the obstacle to our union, it is demolished, and you must – you shall be mine!'

And starting from my seat in a frenzy of ardour, I seized her hand and would have pressed it to my lips, but she as suddenly caught it away, exclaiming in the bitterness of intense affliction: –

'No, no, it is not all!'

'What is it then? You promised I should know some time, and –'

'You shall know some time – but not now – my head aches terribly,' she said, pressing her hand to her forehead, 'and I must have some repose – and surely, I have had misery enough today!' she added, almost wildly.

'But it could not harm you to tell it,' I persisted: 'it would ease your mind; and I should then know how to comfort you.'

She shook her head despondingly. 'If you knew all, you, too, would blame me – perhaps even more than I deserve – though I have cruelly wronged you,' she added in a low murmur, as if she mused aloud.

'*You*, Helen? Impossible!'

'Yes, not willingly; for I did not know the strength and depth of your attachment – I thought – at least endeavoured to think your regard for me was as cold and fraternal as you professed it to be.'

'Or as yours?'

'Or as mine – ought to have been – of such a light and selfish, superficial nature that –'

'*There*, indeed, you wronged me.'

'I know I did; and sometimes, I suspected it then; but I thought, upon the whole, there could be no great harm in leaving your fancies and your hopes to dream themselves to nothing – or flutter away to some more fitting object, while your friendly sympathies remained with me; but if I had known the depth of your regard, the generous disinterested affection you seem to feel –'

'*Seem*, Helen?'

'That you *do* feel, then, I would have acted differently.'

'How? You *could* not have given me less encouragement, or treated me with greater severity than you did! And if you think you have wronged me by giving me your friendship, and occasionally admitting me to the enjoyment of your company and conversation, when all hopes of closer intimacy were vain – as indeed you always gave me to understand – if you think you have wronged me by this, you are mistaken; for such favours, in themselves alone, are not only delightful to my heart, but purifying, exalting, ennobling to my soul; and I would rather have your friendship than the love of any other woman in the world!'

Little comforted by this, she clasped her hands upon her knee, and glancing upward, seemed, in silent anguish, to implore divine assistance; then turning to me, she calmly said –

'Tomorrow, if you meet me on the moor about midday, I will tell you all you seek to know; and perhaps you will then see the necessity of discontinuing our intimacy – if, indeed, you do not willingly resign me as one no longer worthy of regard.'

'I can safely answer no, to that: you cannot have such grave confessions to make – you must be trying my faith, Helen.'

'No, no, no,' she earnestly repeated – 'I wish it were so! Thank Heaven;' she added, 'I have no great crime to confess; but I have more than you will like to hear, or, perhaps, can readily excuse, – and more than I can tell you now; so let me entreat you to leave me!'

'I will; but answer me this one question first; – do you love me?'

'I will not answer it!'

'Then I will conclude you do; and so goodnight.'

She turned from me to hide the emotion she could not quite control; but I took her hand and fervently kissed it.

'Gilbert, *do* leave me!' she cried, in a tone of such thrilling anguish that I felt it would be cruel to disobey.

But I gave one look back before I closed the door, and saw her leaning forward on the table, with her hands pressed against her eyes, sobbing convulsively; yet I withdrew in silence. I felt that to obtrude my consolations on her then would only serve to aggravate her sufferings.

To tell you all the questionings and conjectures – the fears, and hopes, and wild emotions that jostled and chased each other through my mind as I descended the hill, would almost fill a volume in itself. But before I was half way down a sentiment of strong sympathy for her I had left behind me had displaced all other feelings, and seemed imperatively to draw me back: I began to think, 'Why am I hurrying so fast in this direction? Can I find comfort or consolation – peace, certainty, contentment, all – or anything that I want at home? and can I leave all perturbation, sorrow and anxiety behind me there?'

And I turned round to look at the old Hall. There was little besides the chimneys visible above my contracted horizon. I walked back to get a better view of it. When it rose in sight, I stood still a moment to look, and then continued moving towards the gloomy object of attraction. Something called me nearer – nearer still – and why not, pray? Might I not find more benefit in the contemplation of that venerable pile with the full moon in the cloudless heaven shining so calmly above it – with that warm yellow lustre peculiar to an August night – and the mistress of my soul within, than in returning to my home where all comparatively was light, and life, and cheerfulness, and therefore inimical to me in my present frame of mind, – and the more so that its inmates all were more or less imbued with that detestable belief the very *thought* of which made my blood boil in my veins – and how could I endure to hear it openly declared – or cautiously insinuated – which was worse? – I had had trouble enough already, with some babbling fiend that would keep whispering in my ear, 'It may be true,' till I had shouted aloud, 'It is false! I defy you to make me suppose it!'

I could see the red firelight dimly gleaming from her parlour window. I went up to the garden wall, and stood leaning over it, with my eyes fixed upon the lattice, wondering what she was doing, thinking, or suffering now, and wishing I could speak to her but one word, or even catch one glimpse of her, before I went.

I had not thus looked, and wished, and wondered long, before I vaulted over the barrier, unable to resist the temptation of taking one glance through the window, just to see if she were more composed than when we parted; – and if I found her still in deep distress, perhaps I might venture to attempt a word of comfort – to utter one of the many things I should have said before, instead of aggravating her sufferings by my stupid impetuosity. I looked. Her chair was vacant: so was the room. But at that moment someone opened the outer door, and a voice – *her* voice – said, –

'Come out – I want to see the moon, and breathe the evening air: they will do me good – if anything will.'

Here, then, were she and Rachel coming to take a walk in the garden. I wished myself safe back over the wall. I stood, however, in the shadow of the tall holly bush, which, standing between the window and the porch, at present screened me from observation, but did not prevent me from seeing two figures come forth into the moonlight; Mrs Graham followed by another – *not* Rachel, but a young man, slender and rather tall. Oh heavens, how my temples throbbed! Intense anxiety darkened my sight; but I thought – yes, and the voice confirmed it – it was Mr Lawrence.

'You should not let it worry you so much, Helen,' said he; 'I will be more cautious in future; and in time –'

I did not hear the rest of the sentence; for he walked close beside her and spoke so gently that I could not catch the words. My heart was splitting with hatred; but I listened intently for her reply. I heard it plainly enough.

'But I must leave this place, Frederick,' she said – 'I never can be happy here, – nor anywhere else, indeed,' she added, with a mirthless laugh, – 'but I cannot rest here.'

'But where could you find a better place?' replied he, – 'so secluded – so near me, if you think anything of that.'

'Yes,' interrupted she, 'it is all I could wish, if they could only have left me alone.'

'But wherever you go, Helen, there will be the same sources of annoyance. I cannot consent to lose you: I must go with you, or come to you; and there are meddling fools elsewhere, as well as here.'

While thus conversing, they had sauntered slowly past me, down the walk, and I heard no more of their discourse; but I saw him put his arm round her waist, while she lovingly rested her hand on his shoulder; – and then, a tremulous darkness obscured my sight, my heart sickened and my head burned like fire, I half rushed, half staggered from the spot where horror had kept me rooted, and leaped or tumbled over the wall – I hardly know which – but I know that, afterwards, like a passionate child, I dashed myself on the ground and lay there in a paroxysm of anger and despair – how long, I cannot undertake to say; but it must have been a considerable time; for when, having partially relieved myself by a torrent of tears,[1] and looked up at the moon, shining so calmly and carelessly on, as little influenced by my misery as I was by its peaceful radiance, and earnestly prayed for death or forgetfulness, I had risen and journeyed homewards – little regarding the way, but carried instinctively by my feet to the door – I found it bolted against me, and everyone in bed except my mother, who hastened to answer my impatient knocking, and received me with a shower of questions and rebukes.

'Oh, Gilbert, how *could* you do so? Where *have* you been? Do come in and take your supper – I've got it all ready, though you don't deserve it, for keeping me in such a fright, after the strange

manner you left the house this evening. Mr Millward was quite –
Bless the boy! how ill he looks! Oh, gracious! what is the matter?'

'Nothing, nothing – give me a candle.'

'But won't you take some supper?'

'No, I want to go to bed,' said I, taking a candle and lighting it at
the one she held in her hand.

'Oh, Gilbert, how you tremble!' exclaimed my anxious parent.
'How white you look! – Do tell me what it is? Has anything
happened?'

'It's nothing!' cried I, ready to stamp with vexation because the
candle would not light. Then, suppressing my irritation, I added,
'I've been walking too fast, that's all. Goodnight,' and marched off to
bed, regardless of the 'Walking too fast! where have you been?' that
was called after me from below.

My mother followed me to the very door of my room with her
questionings and advice concerning my health and my conduct; but I
implored her to let me alone till morning; and she withdrew, and at
length, I had the satisfaction to hear her close her own door. There
was no sleep for me however, that night, as I thought; and instead of
attempting to solicit it, I employed myself in rapidly pacing the
chamber – having first removed my boots lest my mother should
hear me. But the boards creaked, and she was watchful. I had not
walked above a quarter of an hour before she was at the door again.

'Gilbert, why are you not in bed – you said you wanted to go?'

'Confound it! I'm going,' said I.

'But why are you so long about it? you must have something on
your mind –'

'For heaven's sake, let me alone, and get to bed yourself!'

'Can it be that Mrs Graham that distresses you so?'

'No, no, I tell you – It's nothing!'

'I wish to goodness it mayn't!' murmured she with a sigh, as she
returned to her own apartment, while I threw myself on the bed,
feeling most undutifully disaffected towards her for having deprived
me of what seemed the only shadow of a consolation that remained,
and chained me to that wretched couch of thorns.

Never did I endure so long, so miserable a night as that. And yet, it was not wholly sleepless: towards morning my distracting thoughts began to lose all pretensions to coherency, and shape themselves into confused and feverish dreams, and, at length, there followed an interval of unconscious slumber. But then the dawn of bitter recollection that succeeded – the waking to find life a blank, and worse than a blank – teeming with torment and misery – not a mere barren wilderness, but full of thorns and briars – to find myself deceived, duped, hopeless, my affections trampled upon, my angel not an angel, and my friend a fiend incarnate[2] – it was worse than if I had not slept at all.

It was a dull, gloomy morning, the weather had changed like my prospects, and the rain was pattering against the window. I rose nevertheless, and went out; not to look after the farm, though that would serve as my excuse, but to cool my brain, and regain, if possible, a sufficient degree of composure to meet the family at the morning meal without exciting inconvenient remarks. If I got a wetting, that, in conjunction with a pretended over-exertion before breakfast, might excuse my sudden loss of appetite; and if a cold ensued, the severer the better, it would help to account for the sullen moods and moping melancholy likely to cloud my brow for long enough.

CHAPTER 13

A RETURN TO DUTY

'My dear Gilbert! I wish you *would* try to be a little more amiable,' said my mother, one morning after some display of unjustifiable ill-humour on my part. 'You say there is nothing the matter with you, and nothing has happened to grieve you, and yet, I never *saw* anyone so altered as you within these last few days: you haven't a good word for anybody – friends and strangers, equals and inferiors – it's all the same. I do wish you'd try to check it.'

'Check what?'

'Why your strange temper. You don't know *how* it spoils you. I'm sure a finer disposition than yours, by nature, could not be, if you'd let it have fair play; so you've no excuse *that* way.'

While she thus remonstrated, I took up a book, and laying it open on the table before me, pretended to be deeply absorbed in its perusal; for I was equally unable to justify myself, and unwilling to acknowledge my errors; and I wished to have nothing to say on the matter. But my excellent parent went on lecturing, and then came to coaxing, and began to stroke my hair; and I was getting to feel quite a good boy, but my mischievous brother who was idling about the room, revived my corruption by suddenly calling out: –

'Don't touch him mother! he'll bite! He's a very tiger in human form. *I've* given him up, for my part – fairly disowned him – cast him off, root and branch. It's as much as my life is worth to come within six yards of him. The other day he nearly fractured my skull for singing a pretty, inoffensive love song, on purpose to amuse him.'

'Oh, Gilbert! how could you?' exclaimed my mother.

'I told you to hold your noise first, you know Fergus,' said I.

'Yes, but when I assured you it was no trouble, and went on with the next verse, thinking you might like it better, you clutched me by the shoulder and dashed me away, right against the wall there, with such force, that I thought I had bitten my tongue in two, and expected to see the place plastered with my brains; and when I put my hand to my head and found my skull not broken, I thought it was a miracle and no mistake. But poor fellow!' added he, with a sentimental sigh – 'his heart's broken – that's the truth of it – and his head's –'

'Will you be silent NOW?' cried I, starting up, and eyeing the fellow so fiercely that my mother, thinking I meant to inflict some grievous bodily injury, laid her hand on my arm, and besought me to let him alone, and he walked leisurely out, with his hands in his pockets, singing provokingly – 'Shall I because a woman's fair,' etc.[1]

'I'm not going to defile my fingers with him,' said I, in answer to the maternal intercession. 'I wouldn't touch him with the tongs.'

I now recollected that I had business with Robert Wilson, concerning the purchase of a certain field adjoining my farm – a business I had been putting off from day to day; for I had no interest in anything now; and besides, I was misanthropically inclined, and, moreover, had a particular objection to meeting Jane Wilson or her mother; for though I had too good reason, now, to credit their reports concerning Mrs Graham, I did not like *them* a bit the better for it – or Eliza Millward either – and the thought of meeting them was the more repugnant to me, that I could not, now, defy their seeming calumnies and triumph in my own convictions as before. But today, I determined to make an effort to return to my duty. Though I found no pleasure in it, it would be less irksome than idleness – at all events it would be more profitable. If life promised no enjoyment within my vocation, at least it offered no allurements out of it; and henceforth, I would put my shoulder to the wheel and toil away, like any poor drudge of a cart-horse that was fairly broken in to its labour, and plod through life, not wholly useless if not agreeable, and uncomplaining if not contented with my lot.

Thus resolving, with a kind of sullen resignation, if such a term may be allowed, I wended my way to Ryecote Farm, scarcely expecting to find its owner within at this time of day, but hoping to learn in what part of the premises he was most likely to be found.

Absent he was, but expected home in a few minutes; and I was desired to step into the parlour and wait. Mrs Wilson was busy in the kitchen, but the room was not empty; and I scarcely checked an involuntary recoil as I entered it; for there sat Miss Wilson chattering with Eliza Millward. However, I determined to be cool and civil. Eliza seemed to have made the same resolution on her part. We had not met since the evening of the tea party; but there was no visible emotion either of pleasure or pain, no attempt at pathos, no display of injured pride: she was cool in temper, civil in demeanour. There was even an ease and cheerfulness about her air and manner that I made no pretension to; but there was a depth of malice in her too expressive eye, that plainly told me I was not forgiven; for, though she no longer hoped to win me to herself, she still hated her rival, and evidently delighted to wreak her spite on me. On the other hand, Miss Wilson was as affable and courteous as heart could wish, and though I was in no very conversable humour myself, the two ladies between them managed to keep up a pretty continuous fire of small talk. But Eliza took advantage of the first convenient pause to ask if I had lately seen Mrs Graham, in a tone of merely casual enquiry, but with a sidelong glance – intended to be playfully mischievous – really, brimful and running over with malice.

'Not lately,' I replied, in a careless tone, but sternly repelling her odious glances with my eyes; for I was vexed to feel the colour mounting to my forehead, despite my strenuous efforts to appear unmoved.

'What! are you beginning to tire already? I thought so noble a creature would have power to attach you for a year at least!'

'I would rather not speak of her now.'

'Ah! then you are convinced at last, of your mistake – you have at length discovered that your divinity is not quite the immaculate –'

'I desired you not to speak of her, Miss Eliza.'

'Oh, I beg your pardon! I perceive Cupid's arrows have been too sharp for you: the wounds being more than skin-deep, are not yet healed and bleed afresh at every mention of the loved one's name.'

'Say rather,' interposed Miss Wilson, 'that Mr Markham feels that name is unworthy to be mentioned in the presence of right-minded females. I wonder Eliza, you should think of referring to that unfortunate person – you might know the mention of her would be anything but agreeable to anyone here present.'

How could this be borne? I rose and was about to clap my hat upon my head and burst away, in wrathful indignation, from the house; but recollecting – just in time to save my dignity – the folly of such a proceeding, and how it would only give my fair tormentors a merry laugh at my expense, for the sake of one I acknowledged in my own heart to be unworthy of the slightest sacrifice – though the ghost of my former reverence and love so hung about me still, that I could not bear to hear her name aspersed by others – I merely walked to the window, and having spent a few seconds in vengeably[2] biting my lips, and sternly repressing the passionate heavings of my chest, I observed to Miss Wilson, that I could see nothing of her brother, and added that as my time was precious, it would perhaps be better to call again tomorrow, at some time when I should be sure to find him at home.

'Oh no!' said she, 'if you wait a minute, he will be sure to come; for he has business at L—' (that was our market town) 'and will require a little refreshment before he goes.'

I submitted accordingly, with the best grace I could; and happily, I had not long to wait. Mr Wilson soon arrived, and, indisposed for business as I was at that moment, and little as I cared for the field or its owner, I forced my attention to the matter in hand, with very creditable determination, and quickly concluded the bargain – perhaps more to the thrifty farmer's satisfaction, than he cared to acknowledge. Then, leaving him to the discussion of his substantial 'refreshment,' I gladly quitted the house, and went to look after my reapers.

Leaving them busy at work on the side of the valley, I ascended the hill, intending to visit a cornfield in the more elevated regions, and see when it would be ripe for the sickle. But I did *not* visit it that day; for, as I approached, I beheld at no great distance Mrs Graham and her son coming down in the opposite direction. They saw me;

and Arthur, already, was running to meet me; but I immediately turned back and walked steadily homeward; for I had fully determined never to encounter his mother again; and regardless of the shrill voice in my ear, calling upon me to 'wait a moment,' I pursued the even tenor of my way; and he soon relinquished the pursuit as hopeless, or was called away by his mother. At all events, when I looked back, five minutes after, not a trace of either was to be seen.

This incident agitated and disturbed me most unaccountably – unless you would account for it by saying that Cupid's arrows not only had been too sharp for me, but they were barbed and deeply rooted, and I had not yet been able to wrench them from my heart. However that be, I was rendered doubly miserable for the remainder of the day.

CHAPTER 14

AN ASSAULT

Next morning, I bethought me, I, too, had business at L—; so I mounted my horse and set forth on the expedition, soon after breakfast. It was a dull, drizzly day; but that was no matter: it was all the more suitable to my frame of mind. It was likely to be a lonely journey; for it was no market-day, and the road I traversed was little frequented at any other time; but that suited me all the better too.

As I trotted along, however, chewing the cud of – *bitter* fancies,[1] I heard another horse at no great distance behind me; but I never conjectured who the rider might be – or troubled my head about him, till on slackening my pace to ascend a gentle acclivity – or rather suffering my horse to slacken its pace into a lazy walk; for, lost in my own reflections, I was letting it jog on as leisurely as it thought proper – I lost ground, and my fellow traveller overtook me. He accosted me by name; for it was no stranger – it was Mr Lawrence! Instinctively the fingers of my whip-hand tingled, and grasped their charge with convulsive energy; but I restrained the impulse, and answering his salutation with a nod, attempted to push on; but he pushed on beside me and began to talk about the weather and the crops. I gave the briefest possible answers to his queries and observations, and fell back. He fell back too, and asked if my horse was lame. I replied, with a *look* – at which he placidly smiled.

I was as much astonished as exasperated at this singular pertinacity and imperturbable assurance on his part. I had thought the circumstances of our last meeting would have left such an impression on his mind as to render him cold and distant ever after: instead of that he appeared not only to have forgotten all former offences, but to be impenetrable to all present incivilities. Formerly, the slightest hint, or mere fancied coldness in tone or glance, had sufficed to repulse him: now, positive rudeness could not drive him away. Had he heard of my disappointment; and was he come to witness the result, and triumph in my despair? I grasped my whip with more determined energy than before – but still forbore to raise it, and rode on in silence, waiting for some more tangible cause of offence, before I opened the floodgates of my soul, and poured out the dammed up fury that was foaming and swelling within.

'Markham,' said he, in his usual quiet tone, 'why do you quarrel with your friends, because you have been disappointed in one quarter? You have found your hopes defeated; but how am *I* to blame for it? I warned you beforehand, you know, but you would not –'

He said no more; for, impelled by some fiend at my elbow, I had seized my whip by the small end, and – swift and sudden as a flash of lightning – brought the other down upon his head. It was not without a feeling of savage satisfaction[2] that I beheld the instant, deadly pallor that overspread his face, and the few red drops that trickled down his forehead, while he reeled a moment in his saddle, and then fell backward to the ground. The pony, surprised to be so strangely relieved of its burden, started and capered, and kicked a little, and then made use of its freedom to go and crop the grass of the hedge bank; while its master lay as still and silent as a corpse. Had I killed him? – an icy hand seemed to grasp my heart and check its pulsation, as I bent over him, gazing with breathless intensity upon the ghastly, upturned face. But no; he moved his eyelids and uttered a slight groan. I breathed again – he was only stunned by the fall. It served him right – it would teach him better manners in future. Should I help him to his horse? No. For any other combination of offences I would; but his were too unpardonable. He might mount it himself, if he liked – in a while: already he was beginning to stir and look about him – and there it was for him, quietly browsing on the road-side.

So with a muttered execration, I left the fellow to his fate, and clapping spurs to my own horse, galloped away, excited by a combination of feelings it would not be easy to analyze; and perhaps, if I did so, the result would not be very creditable to my disposition; for I am not sure that a species of exultation in what I had done was not one principal concomitant.

Shortly, however, the effervescence began to abate, and not many minutes elapsed before I had turned and gone back to look after the fate of my victim. It was no generous impulse – no kind relentings that led me to this – nor even the fear of what might be the consequences to myself, if I finished my assault upon the squire by leaving him thus neglected, and exposed to further injury; it was, simply, the voice of conscience; and I took great credit to myself for attending so promptly to its dictates – and judging the merit of the deed by the sacrifice it cost, I was not far wrong.

Mr Lawrence and his pony had both altered their positions, in some degree. The pony had wandered eight or ten yards farther away; and he had managed, somehow, to remove himself from the middle of the road: I found him seated in a recumbent position on the bank, – looking very white and sickly still, and holding his cambric handkerchief (now more red than white) to his head. It must have been a powerful blow; but half the credit – or the blame of it (which you please) must be attributed to the whip, which was garnished with a massive horse's head of plated metal. The grass, being sodden with rain, afforded the young gentleman a rather inhospitable couch; his clothes were considerably bemired; and his hat was rolling in the mud, on the other side of the road. But his thoughts seemed chiefly bent upon his pony, on which he was wistfully gazing – half in helpless anxiety, and half in hopeless abandonment to his fate.

I dismounted, however, and having fastened my own animal to the nearest tree, first picked up his hat, intending to clap it on his head; but either he considered his head unfit for a hat, or the hat, in its present condition, unfit for his head; for, shrinking away the one, he took the other from my hand, and scornfully cast it aside.

'It's good enough for *you*,' I muttered.

My next good office was to catch his pony and bring it to him, which was soon accomplished; for the beast was quiet enough in the main, and only winced and flirted a trifle, till I got a hold of the bridle, – but then, I must see him in the saddle.

'Here, you fellow – scoundrel – dog – give me your hand, and I'll help you to mount.'

No; he turned from me in disgust. I attempted to take him by the arm. He shrank away as if there had been contamination in my touch.

'What, you won't? Well! you may sit there till doomsday, for what I care. But I suppose you don't want to lose all the blood in your body – I'll just condescend to bind that up for you.'

'Let me alone, if you please.'

'Humph! with all my heart. You may go to the d—l if you choose – and say I sent you.'

But before I abandoned him to his fate, I flung his pony's bridle over a stake in the hedge, and threw him my handkerchief, as his own was now saturated with blood. He took it and cast it back to me, in abhorrence and contempt, with all the strength he could muster. It wanted but this to fill the measure of his offences. With execrations not loud but deep,[3] I left him to live or die as he could, well satisfied that I had done *my* duty in attempting to save him – but forgetting how I had erred in bringing him into such a condition, and how insultingly my after-services had been offered – and sullenly prepared to meet the consequences if he should choose to say I had attempted to murder him, – which I thought not unlikely, as it seemed probable he was actuated by some such spiteful motives in so perseveringly refusing my assistance.

Having remounted my horse, I just looked back to see how he was getting on, before I rode away. He had risen from the ground, and, grasping his pony's mane, was attempting to resume his seat in the saddle; but scarcely had he put his foot in the stirrup, when a sickness or dizziness seemed to overpower him: he leant forward a moment, with his head drooped on the animal's back, and then made one more effort, which proving ineffectual, he sank back on to the bank, where I left him, reposing his head on the oozy turf, and, to all appearance, as calmly reclining as if he had been taking his rest on the sofa at home.[4]

I ought to have helped him in spite of himself – to have bound up the wound he was unable to stanch, and insisted upon getting him on to his horse and seeing him safe home; but, besides my bitter indignation against himself, there was the question what to say to his servants, – and what to my own family. Either I should have to acknowledge the deed, which would set me down as a madman, unless I acknowledged the motive too – and that seemed impossible, – or I must get up a lie, which seemed equally out of the question – especially as Mr Lawrence would probably reveal the whole truth, and thereby bring me to tenfold disgrace, – unless I were villain enough, presuming on the absence of witnesses, to persist in my own version of the case, and make him out a still greater scoundrel than he was. No; he had only received a cut above the temple, and perhaps a few bruises from the fall, or the hoofs of his own pony: that could not kill him if he lay there half the day; and, if he could not help himself, surely someone would be coming by: it would be impossible that a whole day should pass and no one traverse the road but ourselves. As for what he might choose to say hereafter, I would take my chance about it: if he told lies, I would contradict him; if he told the truth, I would bear it as I best could. I was not *obliged* to enter into explanations, further than I thought proper. Perhaps, he might choose to be silent on the subject, for fear of raising enquiries as to the cause of the quarrel, and drawing the public attention to his connection with Mrs Graham, which, whether for her sake or his own, he seemed so very desirous to conceal.

Thus reasoning, I trotted away to the town, where I duly transacted my business, and performed various little commissions for my mother and Rose, with very laudable exactitude, considering the different circumstances of the case. In returning home, I was troubled with sundry misgivings about the unfortunate Lawrence. The question, what if I should find him lying, still on the damp earth, fairly dying of cold and exhaustion – or already stark and chill? – thrust itself most unpleasantly upon my mind, and the appalling possibility pictured itself with painful vividness to my imagination as I approached the spot where I had left him. But no; thank Heaven, both man and horse were gone, and nothing was left to witness against me but two objects – unpleasant enough in themselves, to be sure, and presenting a very ugly, not to say murderous, appearance – in one place, the hat saturated with rain and coated with mud, indented and broken above the brim by that villainous whip-handle; in another, the crimson handkerchief, soaking in a deeply tinctured pool of water – for much rain had fallen in the interim.

Bad news fly fast: it was hardly four o'clock when I got home, but my mother gravely accosted me with –

'Oh, Gilbert! – *Such* an accident! Rose has been shopping in the village, and she's heard that Mr Lawrence has been thrown from his horse and brought home dying!'

This shocked me a trifle, as you may suppose; but I was comforted to hear that he had frightfully fractured his skull and broken a leg; for, assured of the falsehood of this, I trusted the rest of the story was equally exaggerated; and when I heard my mother and sister so feelingly deploring his condition, I had considerable difficulty in preventing myself from telling them the real extent of the injuries, as far as I knew them.

'You must go and see him tomorrow,' said my mother.

'Or today,' suggested Rose: 'there's plenty of time; and you can have the pony, if your horse is tired. Won't you Gilbert – as soon as you've had something to eat?'

'No, no – How can we tell that it isn't all a false report? It's highly im—'

'Oh, I'm sure it isn't; for the village is all alive about it; and I saw two people that had seen others that had seen the man that found him. That sounds far-fetched; but it isn't so, when you think of it.'

'Well, but Lawrence is a good rider; it is not likely he would fall from his horse at all; and if he did, it is highly improbable he should break his bones in that way. It must be a gross exaggeration at least.'

'No, but the horse kicked him – or something.'

'What, his quiet little pony?'

'How do you know it was that?'

'He seldom rides any other.'

'At any rate,' said my mother, 'you will call tomorrow. Whether it be true or false, exaggerated or otherwise, we shall like to know how he is.'

'Fergus may go.'

'Why not you?'

'He has more time: I am busy just now.'

'Oh! but Gilbert, how can you be so composed about it? You won't mind business, for an hour or two, in a case of this sort – when your friend is at the point of death!'

'He is *not*, I tell you!'

'For anything you know, he *may* be: you can't tell till you have seen him. – At all events, he must have met with some terrible accident, and you ought to see him: he'll take it very unkind of you if you don't.'

'Confound it! I can't. He and I have not been on good terms, of late.'

'O my *dear* boy! Surely, surely, you are not so unforgiving as to carry your little differences to such a length as –'

'Little differences, indeed!' I muttered.

'Well, but only remember the occasion! Think how –'

'Well, well, don't bother me now – I'll see about it,' I replied.

And my seeing about it was to send Fergus next morning, with my mother's compliments, to make the requisite enquiries; for, of course, my going was out of the question – or sending a message, either. He brought back intelligence that the young squire was laid up with the complicated evils of a broken head and certain contusions (occasioned by a fall – of which he did not trouble himself to relate the particulars – and the subsequent misconduct of his horse), and a severe cold, the consequence of lying on the wet ground in the rain; but there were no broken bones, and no immediate prospects of dissolution.

It was evident then, that, for Mrs Graham's sake, it was not his intention to criminate me.

CHAPTER 15

AN ENCOUNTER AND ITS CONSEQUENCES

That day was rainy like its predecessor; but towards evening it began to clear up a little, and the next morning was fair and promising. I was out on the hill with the reapers. A light wind swept over the corn; and all nature laughed in the sunshine. The lark was rejoicing among the silvery floating clouds. The late rain had so sweetly freshened and cleared the air, and washed the sky, and left such glittering gems on branch and blade, that not even the farmers could have the heart to blame it. But no ray of sunshine could reach my heart, no breeze could freshen it; nothing could fill the void my faith, and hope, and joy in Helen Graham had left, or drive away the keen regrets, and bitter dregs of lingering love that still oppressed it.

While I stood, with folded arms, abstractedly gazing on the undulating swell of the corn not yet disturbed by the reapers, something gently pulled my skirts, and a small voice, no longer welcome to my ears, aroused me with the startling words: –

'Mr Markham, mamma wants you.'

'Wants *me*, Arthur?'

'Yes. Why do you look so queer?' said he, half laughing, half frightened at the unexpected aspect of my face in suddenly turning towards him – 'and why have you kept so long away? – Come! – Won't you come?'

'I'm busy just now,' I replied, scarce knowing what to answer.

He looked up in childish bewilderment; but before I could speak again, the lady herself was at my side.

'Gilbert, I *must* speak with you!' said she in a tone of suppressed vehemence.

I looked at her pale cheek and glittering eye, but answered nothing.

'Only for a moment,' pleaded she. 'Just step aside into this other field,' she glanced at the reapers, some of whom were directing looks of impertinent curiosity towards her – 'I won't keep you a minute.'

I accompanied her through the gap.

'Arthur, darling, run and gather those bluebells,'[1] said she, pointing to some that were gleaming, at some distance, under the hedge along which we walked. The child hesitated, as if unwilling to quit my side. 'Go, love!' repeated she more urgently, and in a tone which, though not unkind, demanded prompt obedience, and obtained it.

'Well, Mrs Graham?' said I, calmly and coldly; for, though I saw she was miserable, and pitied her, I felt glad to have it in my power to torment her.

She fixed her eyes upon me with a look that pierced me to the heart; – and yet, it made me smile.

'I don't ask the reason of this change, Gilbert,' said she with bitter calmness. – 'I know it too well; but though I could see myself suspected and condemned by everyone else, and bear it with calmness, I cannot endure it from you – Why did you not come to hear my explanation on the day I appointed to give it?'

'Because, I happened, in the interim, to learn all you would have told me, – and a trifle more I imagine.'[2]

'Impossible, for I would have told you all!' cried she, passionately – 'But I won't now, for I see you are not worthy of it!'

And her pale lips quivered with agitation.

'Why not, may I ask?'

She repelled my mocking smile with a glance of scornful indignation.

'Because, you never understood me, or you would not soon have listened to my traducers – my confidence would be misplaced in you – you are not the man I thought you – Go! I won't care *what* you think of me!'

She turned away, and I went; for I thought that would torment her as much as anything; and I believe I was right; for, looking back a minute after, I saw her turn half round, as if hoping or expecting to find me still beside her; and then she stood still, and cast one look behind. It was a look less expressive of anger than of bitter anguish and despair; but I immediately assumed an aspect of indifference, and affected to be gazing carelessly round me, and I suppose she went on; for after lingering awhile to see if she would come back or call, I ventured one more glance, and saw her a good way off, moving rapidly up the field with little Arthur running by her side and apparently talking as he went; but she kept her face averted from him, as if to hide some uncontrollable emotion. And I returned to my business.

But I soon began to regret my precipitancy in leaving her so soon. It was evident she loved me – probably, she was tired of Mr Lawrence, and wished to exchange him for me; and if I had loved and reverenced her less to begin with, the preference might have gratified and amused me; but now, the contrast between her outward seeming and her inward mind, as I supposed, – between my former and my present opinion of her, was so harrowing – so distressing to my feelings, that it swallowed up every lighter consideration.

But still, I was curious to know what sort of an explanation she would have given me, – or would give now, if I pressed her for it – how much she would confess, and how she would endeavour to excuse herself. I longed to know what to despise, and what to admire in her, how much to pity, and how much to hate; – and, what was more, I *would* know. I would see her once more, and fairly satisfy myself in what light to regard her, before we parted. Lost to me she was, for ever, of course; but still, I could not bear to think that we had parted, for the last time, with so much unkindness and misery on both sides. That last look of hers had sunk into my heart; I could not forget it – But what a fool I was! – Had she not deceived me, injured me – blighted my happiness for life? 'Well I'll see her, however,' was my concluding resolve, – 'but not today: today and tonight, she may think upon her sins, and be as miserable as she will: tomorrow, I will see her once again, and know something more about her. The interview may be serviceable to her, or it may not. – At any rate, it will give a breath of excitement to the life she has doomed to stagnation, and may calm with certainty some agitating thoughts.'

I did go on the morrow; but not till towards evening, after the business of the day was concluded, that is between six and seven; and the westering sun was gleaming redly on the old hall, and flaming in the latticed windows, as I reached it, imparting to the place a cheerfulness not its own. I need not dilate upon the feelings with which I approached the shrine of my former divinity – that spot teeming with a thousand delightful recollections and glorious dreams – all darkened now, by one disastrous truth.

Rachel admitted me into the parlour, and went to call her mistress, for she was not there; but there was her desk left open on the little round table beside the high-backed chair, with a book laid upon it. Her limited but choice collection of books was almost as familiar to me as my own; but this volume I had not seen before. I took it up. It was Sir Humphrey Davy's 'Last days of a Philosopher,'[3] and on the first leaf was written, – 'Frederick Lawrence.' I closed the book, but kept it in my hand, and stood facing the door, with my back to the fireplace, calmly waiting her arrival; for I did not doubt she would come. And soon I heard her step in the hall. My heart was beginning to throb, but I checked it with an internal rebuke, and maintained my composure – outwardly, at least. She entered, calm, pale, collected.

'To what am I indebted for this favour, Mr Markham?' said she, with such severe but quiet dignity as almost disconcerted me; but I answered with a smile, and impudently enough: –

'Well, I am come to hear your explanation.'

'I told you I would not give it,' said she. 'I said you were unworthy of my confidence.'

'Oh, very well,' replied I, moving to the door.

'Stay a moment,' said she. 'This is the last time I shall see you: don't go just yet.'

I remained, awaiting her further commands.

'Tell me,' resumed she, 'on what grounds you believe these things against me; who told you; and what did they say?'

I paused a moment. She met my eye as unflinchingly as if her bosom had been steeled with conscious innocence. She was resolved to know the worst, and determined to dare it too.

'I can crush that bold spirit,' thought I. But while I secretly exulted in my power, I felt disposed to dally with my victim like a cat. Showing her the book that I still held in my hand, and pointing to the name on the fly leaf, but fixing my eye upon her face, I asked, –

'Do you know that gentleman?'

'Of course I do,' replied she; and a sudden flush suffused her features – whether of shame or anger I could not tell: it rather resembled the latter. 'What next sir?'

'How long is it since you saw him?'

'Who gave you the right to catechise me, on this or any other subject?'

'Oh, no one! – it's quite at your option whether to answer or not. – And now, let me ask – have you heard what has lately befallen this friend of yours? – because, if you have not –'

'I will not be insulted Mr Markham!' cried she almost infuriated at my manner – 'So you had better leave the house at once, if you came only for that.'

'I did not come to insult you: I came to hear your explanation.'

'And I tell you I won't give it!' retorted she, pacing the room in a state of strong excitement, with her hands clasped tightly together, breathing short, and flashing fires of indignation from her eyes. 'I will not condescend to explain myself to one that can make a jest of such horrible suspicions, and be so easily led to entertain them.'

'I do not make a jest of them, Mrs Graham,' returned I, dropping at once my tone of taunting sarcasm. 'I heartily wish I could find them a jesting matter! And as to being easily led to suspect, God only knows what a blind, incredulous fool I have hitherto been, perseveringly shutting my eyes and stopping my ears against everything that threatened to shake my confidence in you, till proof itself confounded my infatuation!'

'What proof, sir?'

'Well, I'll tell you. You remember that evening when I was here last?'

'I do.'

'Even then, you dropped some hints that might have opened the eyes of a wiser man; but they had no such effect upon me: I went on trusting and believing, hoping against hope, and adoring where I could not comprehend – It so happened, however, that after I had left you, I turned back – drawn by pure depth of sympathy, and ardour of affection – not daring to intrude my presence openly upon you, but unable to resist the temptation of catching one glimpse through the window, just to see how you were; for I had left you apparently in great affliction, and I partly blamed my own want of forbearance and discretion as the cause of it. If I did wrong, love alone was my incentive, and the punishment was severe enough; for it was just as I had reached that tree, that you came out into the garden with your friend. Not choosing to show myself, under the circumstances, I stood still, in the shadow, till you had both passed by.'

'And how much of our conversation did you hear?'

'I heard quite enough, Helen. And it was well for me that I did hear it; for nothing less could have cured my infatuation. I always said and thought, that I would never believe a word against you, unless I heard it from your own lips. All the hints and affirmations of others I treated as malignant, baseless slanders; your own self-accusations I believed to be over-strained; and all that seemed unaccountable in your position, I trusted that you could account for if you chose.'

Mrs Graham had discontinued her walk. She leant against one end of the chimney-piece, opposite that near which I was standing, with her chin resting on her closed hand, her eyes – no longer burning with anger, but gleaming with restless excitement – sometimes glancing at me while I spoke, then coursing the opposite wall, or fixed upon the carpet.

'You should have come to me, after all,' said she, 'and heard what I had to say in my own justification. It was ungenerous and wrong to withdraw yourself so secretly and suddenly, immediately after such ardent protestations of attachment, without ever assigning a reason for the change. You should have told me all – no matter *how* bitterly – It would have been better than this silence.'

'To what end should I have done so? – You could not have enlightened me farther, on the subject which alone concerned me; nor could you have made me discredit the evidence of my senses. I desired our intimacy to be discontinued at once, as you yourself had acknowledged would probably be the case if I knew all; but I did not wish to upbraid you, – though (as you also acknowledged) you had deeply wronged me – Yes; you have done me an injury you can never repair – or any other either – you have blighted the freshness and promise of youth, and made my life a wilderness! I might live a hundred years, but I could never recover from the effects of this withering blow – and never forget it! Hereafter – You smile Mrs Graham,' said I, suddenly stopping short, checked in my passionate declamation by unutterable feelings to behold her actually *smiling* at the picture of the ruin she had wrought.

'Did I?' replied she, looking seriously up, 'I was not aware of it. If I did, it was not for pleasure at the thought of the harm I had done you. – Heaven knows I have had torment enough at the bare possibility of that! – it was for joy to find that you had some depth of soul and feeling after all, and to hope that I had not been utterly mistaken in your worth. But smiles and tears are so alike with me; they are neither of them confined to any particular feelings: I often cry when I am happy, and smile when I am sad.'

She looked at me again, and seemed to expect a reply; but I continued silent.

'Would you be *very* glad,' resumed she, 'to find that you were mistaken in your conclusions?'

'How can you ask it, Helen?'

'I don't say I can clear myself altogether,' said she, speaking low and fast, while her heart beat visibly and her bosom heaved with excitement, – 'but would you be glad to discover I was better than you think me?'

'Anything, that could, in the least degree, tend to restore my former opinion of you, to excuse the regard I still feel for you, and alleviate the pangs of unutterable regret that accompany it, would be only too gladly – too eagerly received!'

Her cheeks burned and her whole frame trembled, now, with

excess of agitation. She did not speak, but flew to her desk, and, snatching thence what seemed a thick album or manuscript volume, hastily tore away a few leaves from the end,[4] and thrust the rest into my hand, saying, 'You needn't read it all; but take it home with you,' – and hurried from the room. But when I had left the house, and was proceeding down the walk, she opened the window and called me back. It was only to say, –

'Bring it back when you have read it; and don't breathe a word of what it tells you to any living being – I trust to your honour.'

Before I could answer, she had closed the casement and turned away. I saw her cast herself back in the old oak chair, and cover her face with her hands. Her feelings had been wrought to a pitch that rendered it necessary to seek relief in tears.

Panting with eagerness, and struggling to suppress my hopes, I hurried home, and rushed upstairs to my room, – having first provided myself with a candle, though it was scarcely twilight yet, – then, shut and bolted the door, determined to tolerate no interruption, and sitting down before the table, opened out my prize and delivered myself up to its perusal – first, hastily turning over the leaves and snatching a sentence here and there, and then, setting myself steadily to read it through.

I have it now before me; and though you could not, of course, peruse it with half the interest that I did, I know you would not be satisfied with an abbreviation of its contents and you shall have the whole, save, perhaps, a few passages here and there of merely temporal interest to the writer, or such as would serve to encumber the story rather than elucidate it. It begins somewhat abruptly, thus – but we will reserve its commencement for another chapter, and call it, –

CHAPTER 16

THE WARNINGS OF EXPERIENCE

June 1st, 1821.[1] – We have just returned to Staningley – that is, we returned some days ago, and I am not yet settled, and feel as if I never should be. We left town sooner than was intended, in consequence of my uncle's indisposition – I wonder what would have been the result if we had stayed the full time. I am quite ashamed of my new-sprung distaste for country life. All my former occupations seem so tedious and dull, my former amusements so insipid and unprofitable. I cannot enjoy my music, because there is no one to hear it. I cannot enjoy my walks, because there is no one to meet. I cannot enjoy my books, because they have not power to arrest my attention: my head is so haunted with the recollections of the last few weeks that I cannot attend to them. My drawing suits me best, for I can draw and think at the same time; and if my productions cannot now be seen by anyone but myself and those who do not care about them, they, possibly, may be, hereafter. But then, there is one face I am always trying to paint or to sketch, and always without success; and that vexes me. As for the owner of that face, I cannot get him out of my mind – and, indeed, I never try. I wonder whether he ever thinks of me; and I wonder whether I shall ever see him again. And then might follow a train of other wonderments – questions for time and fate to answer, concluding with: – supposing all the rest be answered in the affirmative, I wonder whether I shall ever repent it – as my aunt would tell me I should, if she knew what I was thinking about. How distinctly I remember our conversation that evening before our departure for town, when we were sitting together over the fire, my uncle having gone to bed with a slight attack of the gout.

'Helen,' said she, after a thoughtful silence, 'do you ever think about marriage?'

'Yes aunt, often.'

'And do you ever contemplate the possibility of being married yourself, or engaged, before the season is over?'

'Sometimes; but I don't think it at all likely that I *ever* shall.'

'Why so?'

'Because I imagine there must be only a very, very few men in the world, that I should like to marry; and of those few, it is ten to one I may never be acquainted with one; or if I should, it is twenty to one, he may not happen to be single, or to take a fancy to me.'

'That is no argument at all. It may be very true – and I hope *is* true, that there are very few men whom you could choose to marry, of yourself – It is not, indeed, to be supposed that you would *wish* to marry *any* one, till you were asked:[2] a girl's affections should never be won unsought. But when they *are* sought – when the citadel of the heart is fairly besieged, it is apt to surrender sooner than the owner is aware of, and often against her better judgment, and in opposition to all her preconceived ideas of what she could have loved, unless she be extremely careful and discreet. Now I want to warn you, Helen, of these things, and to exhort you to be watchful and circumspect from the very commencement of your career, and not to suffer your heart to be stolen from you by the first foolish or unprincipled person that covets the possession of it. – You know, my dear, you are only just eighteen; there is plenty of time before you, and neither your uncle nor I are in any hurry to get you off our hands; and, I may venture to say, there will be no lack of suitors; for you can boast a good family, a pretty considerable fortune and expectations, and, I may as well tell you likewise – for if I don't others will – that you have a fair share of beauty, besides – and I hope you may never have cause to regret it! –'

'I hope not, aunt; but why should you fear it?'

'Because, my dear, beauty is that quality which, next to money, is generally the most attractive to the worst kinds of men; and, there-fore, it is likely to entail a great deal of trouble on the possessor.'

'Have *you* been troubled in that way, aunt?'

'No, Helen,' said she, with reproachful gravity, 'but I know many that have; and some, through carelessness, have been the wretched victims of deceit; and some, through weakness, have fallen into snares and temptations terrible to relate.'

'Well, I shall be neither careless nor weak.'

'Remember Peter, Helen! Don't boast, but *watch*.[3] Keep a guard over your eyes and ears as the inlets of your heart, and over your lips as the outlet, lest they betray you in a moment of unwariness. Receive, coldly and dispassionately, every attention, till you have ascertained and duly considered the worth of the aspirant; and let your affections be consequent upon approbation alone. First study; then approve; then love. Let your eyes be blind to all external attractions, your ears deaf to all the fascinations of flattery and light discourse. – These are nothing – and worse than nothing – snares and wiles of the tempter, to lure the thoughtless to their own destruction. Principle is the first thing, after all; and next to that, good sense, respectability, and moderate wealth. If you should marry the handsomest, and most accomplished and superficially agreeable man in the world, you little know the misery that would overwhelm you, if, after all, you should find him to be a worthless reprobate,[4] or even an impracticable fool.'

'But what are all the poor fools and reprobates to do, aunt? If everybody followed your advice the world would soon come to an end.'

'Never fear, my dear! the male fools and reprobates will never want for partners while there are so many of the other sex to match them; but do *you* follow my advice. And this is no subject for jesting, Helen, I am sorry to see you treat the matter in that light way. Believe me, *matrimony is a serious thing.*' And she spoke it *so* seriously that one might have fancied she had known it to her cost; but I asked no more impertinent questions, and merely answered, –

'I know it is; and I know there is truth and sense in what you say; but you need not fear me, for I not only should think it *wrong* to marry a man that was deficient in sense or in principle, but I should never be *tempted* to do it; for I could not like him, if he were ever so handsome and ever so charming in other respects; I should hate him

– despise him – pity him – anything but love him. My affections not only *ought* to be founded on approbation, but they will and must be so: for without approving I cannot love. It is needless to say I ought to be able to respect and honour the man I marry as *well* as love him, for I cannot love him without. So set your mind at rest.'

'I hope it may be so,' answered she.

'I *know* it *is* so,' persisted I.

'You have not been tried yet, Helen: we can but hope,' said she, in her cold, cautious way.

I was vexed at her incredulity; but I am not sure her doubts were entirely without sagacity; I fear I have found it much easier to remember her advice than to profit by it – Indeed, I have sometimes been led to question the soundness of her doctrines on those subjects. Her counsels may be good, as far as they go – in the main points, at least; – but there are some things she has overlooked in her calculations. I wonder if *she* was ever in love.

I commenced my career – or my first campaign, as my uncle calls it – kindling with bright hopes and fancies – chiefly raised by this conversation – and full of confidence in my own discretion. At first, I was delighted with the novelty and excitement of our London life; but, soon, I began to weary of its mingled turbulence and constraint, and sigh for the freshness and freedom of home. My new acquaintances, both male and female, disappointed my expectations, and vexed and depressed me by turns; for I soon grew tired of studying their peculiarities, and laughing at their foibles – particularly as I was obliged to keep my criticisms to myself, for my aunt would not hear them – and they – the ladies especially – appeared so provokingly mindless, and heartless, and artificial. The gentlemen seemed better, but perhaps it was because I knew them less, perhaps, because they flattered me; but I did not fall in love with any of them, and if their attentions pleased me one moment, they provoked me the next, because they put me out of humour with myself, by revealing my vanity and making me fear I was becoming like some of the ladies I so heartily despised.

There was one elderly gentleman that annoyed me very much; a rich old friend of my uncle's who, I believe, thought I could not do better than marry him; but, besides being old, he was ugly and disagreeable, – and wicked, I am sure, though my aunt scolded me for saying so; but she allowed he was no saint. And there was another, less hateful, but still *more* tiresome, because she favoured him, and was always thrusting him upon me, and sounding his praises in my ears, Mr Boarham, by name,[5] Bore'em as I prefer spelling it, for a terrible bore he was: I shudder still, at the remembrance of his voice, drone, drone, drone, in my ear, while he sat beside me, prosing away by the half-hour together, and beguiling himself with the notion that he was improving my mind by useful information, or, impressing his dogmas upon me, and reforming my errors of judgment, or perhaps, that he was talking down to my level, and amusing me with entertaining discourse. Yet he was a decent man enough, in the main, I dare say; and if he had kept his distance, I never would have hated him. As it was, it was almost impossible to help it; for he not only bothered me with the infliction of his own presence, but he kept me from the enjoyment of more agreeable society.

One night, however, at a ball, he had been more than usually tormenting, and my patience was quite exhausted. – It appeared as if the whole evening was fated to be insupportable: I had just had one dance with an empty-headed coxcomb, and then Mr Boarham had come upon me, and seemed determined to cling to me for the rest of the night. He never danced himself, and there he sat, poking his head in my face, and impressing all beholders with the idea that he was a confirmed, acknowledged lover; my aunt looking complacently on, all the time, and wishing him God-speed. In vain I attempted to drive him away by giving a loose to my exasperated feelings, even to positive rudeness: nothing could convince him that his presence was disagreeable. Sullen silence was taken for rapt attention, and gave him greater room to talk; sharp answers were received as smart sallies of girlish vivacity, that only required an indulgent rebuke; and flat contradictions were but as oil to the flames, calling forth new strains of argument to support his dogmas, and bringing down upon me endless floods of reasoning to overwhelm me with conviction.

But there was one present who seemed to have a better appreciation of my frame of mind. A gentleman stood by, who had been watching our conference for some time, evidently much amused at my companion's remorseless pertinacity and my manifest annoyance, and laughing to himself at the asperity and uncompromising spirit of my replies. At length, however, he withdrew, and went to the lady of the house, apparently for the purpose of asking an introduction to me, for, shortly after, they both came up, and she introduced him as Mr Huntingdon, the son of a late friend of my uncle's. He asked me to dance. I gladly consented, of course; and he was my companion during the remainder of my stay, which was not long, for my aunt, as usual, insisted upon an early departure.

I was sorry to go, for I had found my new acquaintance a very lively and entertaining companion. There was a certain graceful ease and freedom about all he said and did, that gave a sense of repose and expansion to the mind, after so much constraint and formality as I had been doomed to suffer. There might be, it is true, a little too much careless boldness in his manner and address, but I was in so good a humour, and so grateful for my late deliverance from Mr Boarham, that it did not anger me.

'Well, Helen, how do you like Mr Boarham now?' said my aunt, as we took our seats in the carriage and drove away.

'Worse than ever,' I replied.

She looked displeased but said no more on that subject.

'Who was the gentleman you danced with last,' resumed she, after a pause – 'that was so officious in helping you on with your shawl?'

'He was not officious at all, aunt: he never *attempted* to help me, till he saw Mr Boarham coming to do so; and then he stepped laughingly forward and said, "Come I'll preserve you from that infliction." '

'Who was it, I ask?' said she, with frigid gravity.

'It was Mr Huntingdon, the son of uncle's old friend.'

'I have heard your uncle speak of young Mr Huntingdon. I've heard him say, "He's a fine lad, that young Huntingdon, but a bit wildish I fancy." So I'd have you beware.'

'What does "a bit wildish" mean?' I enquired.

'It means destitute of principle, and prone to every vice that is common to youth.'

'But I've heard uncle say he was a sad wild fellow himself, when he was young.'

She sternly shook her head.

'He was jesting then, I suppose,' said I, 'and here he was speaking at random – at least, I cannot believe there is any harm in those laughing blue eyes.'

'False reasoning, Helen!' said she with a sigh.

'Well, we ought to be charitable, you know, aunt – besides, I don't think it *is* false: I am an excellent physiognomist,[6] and I always judge of people's characters by their looks – not by whether they are handsome or ugly, but by the general cast of the countenance. For instance, I should know by your countenance that you were not of a cheerful, sanguine disposition; and I should know by Mr Wilmot's[7] that he was a worthless old reprobate, and by Mr Boarham's that he was not an agreeable companion, and by Mr Huntingdon's that he was neither a fool nor a knave, though, possibly, neither a sage nor a saint – but that is no matter to me, as I am not likely to meet him again – unless as an occasional partner in the ballroom.'

It was not so, however, for I met him again next morning. He came to call upon my uncle, apologizing for not having done so before, by saying he was only lately returned from the continent, and had not heard, till the previous night, of my uncle's arrival in town; and after that, I often met him; sometimes in public, sometimes at home; for he was very assiduous in paying his respects to his old friend, who did not, however, consider himself greatly obliged by the attention.

'I wonder what the deuce the lad means by coming so often,' he would say, – 'can *you* tell; Helen? – Hey? He wants none o'my company, nor I his – that's certain.'

'I wish you'd tell him so, then,' said my aunt.

'Why, what for? If I don't want him, somebody does mayhap (winking at me). Besides, he's a pretty tidy fortune, Peggy, you know – not such a catch as Wilmot, but then Helen won't hear of that match; for, somehow, these old chaps don't go down with the girls –

with *all* their money – and their experience to boot. I'll bet anything she'd rather have this young fellow without a penny, than Wilmot with his house full of gold – Wouldn't you Nell?'

'Yes uncle; but that's not saying much for Mr Huntingdon, for I'd rather be an old maid and a pauper, than Mrs Wilmot.'

'And Mrs Huntingdon? What would you rather be than Mrs Huntingdon? eh?'

'I'll tell you when I've considered the matter.'

'Ah! it needs consideration then – But come now – would you rather be an old maid – let alone the pauper?'

'I can't tell till I'm asked.'

And I left the room immediately, to escape further examination. But five minutes after, in looking from my window, I beheld Mr Boarham coming up to the door. I waited nearly half an hour in uncomfortable suspense, expecting every minute to be called, and vainly longing to hear him go. Then, footsteps were heard on the stairs, and my aunt entered the room with a solemn countenance, and closed the door behind her.

'Here is Mr Boarham, Helen,' said she. 'He wishes to see you.'

'Oh, aunt! Can't you tell him I'm indisposed? – I'm sure I am – to see *him*.'

'Nonsense, my dear! this is no trifling matter. He is come on a very important errand – to ask your hand in marriage, of your uncle and me.'

'I hope my uncle and you told him it was not in your power to give it. What right had he to ask *any* one before me?'

'Helen!'

'What did my uncle say?'

'He said he would not interfere in the matter; if you liked to accept Mr Boarham's obliging offer, you –'

'Did he say obliging offer?'

'No; he said if you liked to take him you might; and if not, you might please yourself.'

'He said right; and what did you say?'

'It is no matter what I said. What will *you* say? – that is the question. He is now waiting to ask you himself; but consider well before you go; and if you intend to refuse him, give me your reasons.'

'I *shall* refuse him, of course, but you must tell me how, for I want to be civil and yet decided – and when I've got rid of him, I'll give you my reasons afterwards.'

'But stay Helen; sit down a little, and compose yourself. Mr Boarham is in no particular hurry, for he has little doubt of your acceptance; and I want to speak with you. Tell me, my dear, what are your objections to him? Do you deny that he is an upright, honourable man?'

'No.'

'Do you deny that he is a sensible, sober, respectable?'

'No; he may be all this, but –'

'*But* Helen! How many such men do you expect to meet with in the world? Upright, honourable, sensible, sober, respectable! – Is *this* such an everyday character, that you should reject the possessor of such noble qualities, without a moment's hesitation? – Yes, *noble* I may call them; for, think of the full meaning of each, and how many inestimable virtues they include (and I might add many more to the list), and consider that all this is laid at your feet: it is in your power to secure this inestimable blessing for life – a worthy and excellent husband, who loves you tenderly, but not too fondly so as to blind him to your faults, and will be your guide throughout life's pilgrimage, and your partner in eternal bliss! Think how –'

'But I hate him, aunt,' said I, interrupting this unusual flow of eloquence.

'Hate him, Helen! Is this a Christian spirit? – *you hate him?* – and he so good a man!'

'I don't hate him as a man, but as a husband. As a man, I love him so much, that I wish him a better wife than I – one as good as himself, or better – if you think that possible – provided, she could like him; – but I never could, and therefore –'

'But why not? What objection do you find?'

'Firstly, he is, at least, forty years old – considerably more I should think, and I am but eighteen: secondly, he is narrow-minded and bigoted in the extreme; thirdly, his tastes and feelings are wholly dissimilar to mine; fourthly, his looks, voice, and manner are particularly displeasing to me; and finally, I have an aversion to his whole person that I never can surmount.'

'Then you ought to surmount it! And please to compare him for a moment with Mr Huntingdon, and, good looks apart (which contribute nothing to the merit of the man, or to the happiness of married life, and which you have so often professed to hold in light esteem), tell me which is the better man.'

'I have no doubt Mr Huntingdon is a much better man than you think him, – but we are not talking about him, now, but about Mr Boarham; and as I would rather grow, live and die in single blessedness[8] than be his wife, it is but right that I should tell him so at once, and put him out of suspense – so let me go.'

'But don't give him a flat denial; he has no idea of such a thing, and it would offend him greatly: say you have no thoughts of matrimony, at present –'

'But I *have* thoughts of it.'

'Or that you desire a further acquaintance.'

'But I don't desire a further acquaintance – quite the contrary.'

And without waiting for further admonitions, I left the room, and went to seek Mr Boarham. He was walking up and down the drawing room, humming snatches of tunes, and nibbling the end of his cane.

'My dear young lady,' said he, bowing and smirking with great complacency. 'I have your kind guardian's permission –'

'I know, sir,' said I, wishing to shorten the scene as much as possible, 'and I am greatly obliged for your preference, but must beg to decline the honour you wish to confer; for, I think, we were not made for each other – as you yourself would shortly discover if the experiment were tried.'

My aunt was right: it was quite evident he had had little doubt of my acceptance, and no idea of a positive denial. He was amazed – astounded at such an answer, but too incredulous to be much offended; and after a little humming and hawing, he returned to the attack.

'I know, my dear, that there exists a considerable disparity between us in years, in temperament, and perhaps some other things, but let me assure you, I shall not be severe to mark the faults and foibles of a young and ardent nature such as yours, and while I acknowledge them to myself, and even rebuke them with all a father's care, believe me, no youthful lover could be more tenderly indulgent towards the object of his affections, than I to you; and, on the other hand, let me hope that my more experienced years and graver habits of reflection will be no disparagement in your eyes, as I shall endeavour to make them all conducive to your happiness. Come now! What do you say? – Let us have no young lady's affectations and caprices, but speak out at once!'

'I will, but only to repeat what I said before, that I am certain we were not made for each other.'

'You really think so?'

'I do.'

'But you don't know me – you wish for a further acquaintance – a longer time to –'

'No, I don't. I know you as well as I ever shall, and better than you know me, or you would never dream of uniting yourself to one so incongruous – so utterly unsuitable to you in every way.'

'But my dear young lady, I don't look for perfection, I can excuse –'

'Thank you, Mr Boarham, but I won't trespass upon your goodness. You may save your indulgence and consideration for some more worthy object, that won't tax them so heavily.'

'But let me beg you to consult your aunt; that excellent lady, I am sure, will –'

'I have consulted her; and I know her wishes coincide with yours; but in such important matters, I take the liberty of judging for myself; and no persuasions can alter my inclinations, or induce me to believe that such a step would be conducive to my happiness, or yours – and I wonder that a man of your experience and discretion should think of choosing such a wife.'

'Ah, well!' said he – 'I have sometimes wondered at that myself. I have sometimes said to myself, "Now Boarham, what is this you're after? Take care man – look before you leap! This is a sweet, bewitching creature, but remember, the brightest attractions to the lover too often prove the husband's greatest torments!" – I assure you my choice has not been made without much reasoning and reflection. The seeming imprudence of the match has cost me many an anxious thought by day, and many a sleepless hour by night; but at length, I satisfied myself, that it was not, in very deed, imprudent. I saw my sweet girl was not without her faults, but of these, her youth, I trusted, was not one, but rather an earnest of virtues yet unblown – a strong ground of presumption that her little defects of temper, and errors of judgment, opinion, or manner were not irremediable, but might easily be removed or mitigated by the patient efforts of a watchful and judicious adviser, and where I failed to enlighten and control, I thought I might safely undertake to pardon, for the sake of her many excellencies. Therefore, my dearest girl, since *I* am satisfied, why should *you* object – on my account, at least.'

'But to tell you the truth Mr Boarham, it is on my own account I principally object; so let us – drop the subject,' I would have said, 'for it is worse than useless to pursue it any farther,' but he pertinaciously interrupted me with –

'But why so? I would love you, cherish you, protect you, etc., etc.'

I shall not trouble myself to put down all that passed between us. Suffice it to say, that I found him very troublesome, and very hard to convince that I really meant what I said, and really *was* so obstinate and blind to my own interests, that there was no shadow of a chance that either he or my aunt would ever be able to overcome my objections. Indeed, I am not sure that I succeeded after all, though wearied with his so pertinaciously returning to the same point and repeating the same arguments over and over again, forcing me to reiterate the same replies, I at length turned short and sharp upon him, and my last words were –

'I tell you plainly, that it cannot be. No consideration can induce me to marry against my inclinations. I respect you – at least, I would respect you, if you would behave like a sensible man – but I cannot love you, and never could – and the more you talk the farther you repel me; so pray don't say any more about it.'

Whereupon, he wished me a good morning and withdrew, disconcerted and offended, no doubt; but surely it was not my fault.

CHAPTER 17

FURTHER WARNINGS

The next day, I accompanied my uncle and aunt to a dinner party at Mr Wilmot's. He had two ladies staying with him, his niece Annabella, a fine dashing girl, or rather young woman, of some five and twenty, too great a flirt to be married, according to her own assertion, but greatly admired by the gentlemen, who universally pronounced her a splendid woman, – and her gentle cousin Milicent Hargrave, who had taken a violent fancy to me, mistaking me for something vastly better than I was. And I in return, was very fond of her – I should entirely exclude poor Milicent in my general animadversions against the ladies of my acquaintance. But it was not on her account, or her cousin's, that I have mentioned the party: it was for the sake of another of Mr Wilmot's guests, to wit Mr Huntingdon. I have good reason to remember his presence there, for this was the last time I saw him.

He did not sit near me at dinner; for it was his fate to hand in a capacious old dowager, and mine to be handed in by Mr Grimsby, a friend of his, but a man I very greatly disliked: there was a sinister cast in his countenance, and a mixture of lurking ferocity and fulsome insincerity in his demeanour, that I could not away with.[1] What a tiresome custom that is, by the by – one among the many sources of factitious annoyance of this ultra-civilized life. If the gentlemen *must* lead the ladies into the dining-room, why cannot they take those they like best?

I am not sure, however, that Mr Huntingdon would have taken me, if he *had* been at liberty to make his own selection. It is quite possible he might have chosen Miss Wilmot; for she seemed bent upon engrossing his attention to herself, and he seemed nothing loath to pay the homage she demanded. I thought so, at least, when I saw how they talked and laughed, and glanced across the table, to the neglect and evident umbrage of their respective neighbours – and afterwards, as the gentlemen joined us in the drawing-room, when she, immediately upon his entrance, loudly called upon him to be the arbiter of a dispute between herself and another lady, and he answered the summons with alacrity, and decided the question without a moment's hesitation in her favour – though, to my thinking, she was obviously in the wrong – and then stood chatting familiarly with her and a group of other ladies; while I sat with Milicent Hargrave, at the opposite end of the room, looking over the latter's drawings and aiding her with my critical observations and advice, at her particular desire. But in spite of my efforts to remain composed, my attention wandered from the drawings to the merry group, and against my better judgment my wrath rose, and doubtless, my countenance lowered; for Milicent, observing that I must be tired of her daubs and scratches, begged I would join the company now, and defer the examination of the remainder to another opportunity. But while I was assuring her that I had no wish to join them, and was not tired, Mr Huntingdon himself came up to the little round table at which we sat.

'Are these yours?' said he, carelessly taking up one of the drawings.

'No, they are Miss Hargrave's.'

'Oh! well, let's have a look at them.'[2]

And, regardless of Miss Hargrave's protestations, that they were not worth looking at, he drew a chair to my side, and receiving the drawings, one by one from my hand, successively scanned them over, and threw them on the table, but said not a word about them, though he was talking all the time. I don't know what Milicent Hargrave thought of such conduct, but *I* found his conversation extremely interesting, though as I afterwards discovered, when I came to analyze it, it was chiefly confined to quizzing[3] the different members of the company present; and albeit he made some clever remarks, and some excessively droll ones, I do not think the whole would appear anything very particular, if written here, without the adventitious aids of look, and tone, and gesture, and that ineffable but indefinite charm, which cast a halo over all he did and said, and which would have made it a delight to look in his face, and hear the music of his voice, if he had been talking positive nonsense – and which, moreover, made me feel so bitter against my aunt when she put a stop to this enjoyment, by coming composedly forward, under pretence of wishing to see the drawings, that she cared and knew nothing about, and while making believe to examine them, addressing herself to Mr Huntingdon, with one of her coldest and most repellent aspects, and beginning a series of the most commonplace and formidably formal questions and observations, on purpose to wrest his attention from me – on purpose to vex me, as I thought: and having now looked through the portfolio, I left them to their tête-à-tête, and seated myself on a sofa, quite apart from the company – never thinking how strange such conduct would appear, but merely to indulge, at first, the vexation of the moment, and subsequently to enjoy my private thoughts.

But I was not left long alone, for Mr Wilmot, of all men the least welcome, took advantage of my isolated position to come and plant himself beside me. I had flattered myself that I had so effectually repulsed his advances on all former occasions, that I had nothing more to apprehend from his unfortunate predilection; but it seems I was mistaken: so great was his confidence, either in his wealth or his remaining powers of attraction, and so firm his conviction of feminine weakness, that he thought himself warranted to return to the siege, which he did with renovated ardour, enkindled by the quantity of wine he had drunk – a circumstance that rendered him infinitely the more disgusting; but greatly as I abhorred him at that moment, I did not like to treat him with rudeness, as I was now his guest and had just been enjoying his hospitality; and I was no hand at a polite but determined rejection, nor would it have greatly availed me if I had; for he was too coarse-minded to take any repulse that was not as plain and positive as his own effrontery. The consequence was, that he waxed more fulsomely tender, and more repulsively warm, and I was driven to the very verge of desperation, and about to say, I know not what, when I felt my hand that hung over the arm of the sofa, suddenly taken by another and gently but fervently pressed. Instinctively, I guessed who it was, and on looking up, was less surprised than delighted, to see Mr Huntingdon smiling upon me. It was like turning from some purgatorial fiend to an angel of light,[4] come to announce that the season of torment was past.

'Helen,' said he, (he frequently called me Helen, and I never resented the freedom), 'I want you to look at this picture: Mr Wilmot will excuse you a moment, I'm sure.'

I rose with alacrity. He drew my arm within his, and led me across the room to a splendid painting of Vandyke's[5] that I had noticed before, but not sufficiently examined. After a moment of silent contemplation, I was beginning to comment on its beauties and peculiarities, when, playfully pressing the hand he still retained within his arm, he interrupted me with –

'Never mind the picture, it was not for that I brought you here; it was to get you away from that scoundrelly old profligate yonder, who is looking as if he would like to challenge me for the affront.'

'I am very much obliged to you,' said I. 'This is twice you have delivered me from such unpleasant companionship.'

'Don't be too thankful,' he answered: 'it is not all kindness to you; it is partly from a feeling of spite to your tormentors that makes me delighted to do the old fellows a bad turn, though I don't think I have any great reason to dread them as rivals – Have I Helen?'

'You know I detest them both.'

'And me?'

'I have no reason to detest *you*.'

'But what are your sentiments towards me? – Helen – Speak! – How do you regard me?'[6]

And again he pressed my hand; but I feared there was more of conscious power than tenderness in his demeanour, and I felt he had no right to extort a confession of attachment from me when he had made no correspondent avowal himself, and knew not what to answer. At last I said –

'How do *you* regard *me*?'

'Sweet angel, I adore you! I —'

'Helen, I want you a moment,' said the distinct, low voice of my aunt, close beside us. And I left him, muttering maledictions against his evil angel.[7]

'Well aunt, what is it? What do you want?' said I, following her to the embrasure of the window.

'I want you to join the company, when you are fit to be seen,' returned she, severely regarding me; 'but please to stay here a little till that shocking colour[8] is somewhat abated, and your eyes have recovered something of their natural expression. I should be ashamed for anyone to see you in your present state.'

Of course, such a remark had no effect in reducing the 'shocking colour;' on the contrary, I felt my face glow with redoubled fires kindled by a complication of emotions, of which indignant, swelling anger was the chief. I offered no reply, however, but pushed aside the curtain and looked into the night — or rather, into the lamplit square.

'Was Mr Huntingdon proposing to you, Helen?' enquired my too watchful relative.

'No.'

'What was he saying then? I heard something very like it.'

'I don't know what he would have said, if you hadn't interrupted him.'

'And would you have accepted him, Helen, if he had proposed?'

'Of course not — without consulting uncle and you.'

'Oh! I'm glad, my dear, you have so much prudence left. Well now,' she added, after a moment's pause, 'you have made yourself conspicuous enough for one evening. The ladies are directing enquiring glances towards us at this moment, I see. I shall join them. Do you come too, when you are sufficiently composed to appear as usual.'

'I am so now.'

'Speak gently then; and don't look so malicious,' said my calm, but provoking aunt. 'We shall return home shortly, and then,' she added with solemn significance, 'I have much to say to you.'

So I went home prepared for a formidable lecture. Little was said by either party in the carriage during our short transit homewards; but when I had entered my room and thrown myself into an easy chair to reflect on the events of the day, my aunt followed me thither, and having dismissed Rachel, who was carefully stowing away my ornaments, closed the door; and placing a chair beside me, or rather at right angles with mine, sat down. With due deference I offered her my more commodious seat. She declined it, and thus opened the conference:

'Do you remember, Helen, our conversation the night but one before we left Staningley?'

'Yes aunt.'

'And do you remember how I warned you against letting your heart be stolen from you by those unworthy of its possession; and fixing your affections where approbation did not go before, and where reason and judgment withheld their sanction?'

'Yes, but *my* reason –'

'Pardon me – and do you remember assuring me that there was no occasion for uneasiness on your account; for you should never be *tempted* to marry a man who was deficient in sense or principle, however handsome or charming in other respects he might be, for you could not love him, you should hate – despise – pity – anything but love him – were not those your words?'

'Yes, but –'

'And did you not say that your affection *must* be founded on approbation; and that unless you could approve and honour and respect, you could not love?'

'Yes, but I do approve and honour, and respect –'

'How so, my dear? is Mr Huntingdon a good man?'

'He is a much better man than you think him.'

'That is nothing to the purpose. Is he a *good* man?'

'Yes – in some respects. He has a good disposition.'

'Is he a man of *principle*?'

'Perhaps not, exactly; but it is only for want of thought: if he had someone to advise him, and remind him of what is right –'[9]

'He would soon learn, you think – and you yourself would willingly undertake to be his teacher? But, my dear, he is, I believe, full ten years older than you – how is it that you are so beforehand in moral acquirements?'

'Thanks to you, aunt, I have been well brought up, and had good examples always before me, which he, most likely, has not; – and besides, he is of a sanguine temperament, and a gay, thoughtless temper, and I am naturally inclined to reflection.'

'Well, now you have made him out to be deficient in both sense and principle, by your own confession –'

'Then, my sense and my principle are at his service!'

'That sounds presumptuous, Helen! Do you think you have enough for both; and do you imagine your merry, thoughtless profligate would allow himself to be guided by a young girl like you?'

'No; I should not wish to guide him; but I think I might have influence sufficient to save him from some errors, and I should think my life well spent in the effort to preserve so noble a nature from destruction. He always listens attentively now, when I speak seriously to him, (and I often venture to reprove his random way of talking), and sometimes he says that if he had me always by his side he should never do or say a wicked thing, and that a little daily talk with me would make him quite a saint. It may be partly jest and partly flattery, but still –'

'But still you think it may be truth?'

'If I do think there is any mixture of truth in it, it is not from confidence in my own powers, but in *his* natural goodness. – And you have no right to call him a profligate, aunt; he is nothing of the kind.'

'Who told you so, my dear? What was that story about his intrigue with a married lady – Lady who was it – Miss Wilmot herself was telling you the other day?'

'It was false – false!' I cried. 'I don't believe a word of it.'

'You think, then, that he is a virtuous, well-conducted young man?'

'I know nothing positive respecting his character. I only know that I have heard nothing definitive against it – nothing that could be proved, at least; and till people can prove their slanderous accusations, I will not believe them. And I know this, that if he has committed errors, they are only such as are common to youth, and such as nobody thinks anything about; for I see that everybody likes him, and all the mammas smile upon him, and their daughters – and Miss Wilmot herself, are only too glad to attract his attention.'

'Helen, the world *may* look upon such offences as venial; a few unprincipled mothers *may* be anxious to catch a young man of fortune without reference to his character; and thoughtless girls *may* be glad to win the smiles of so handsome a gentleman, without seeking to penetrate beyond the surface; but *you*, I trusted were better informed than to see with their eyes, and judge with their perverted judgment. I did not think *you* would call these venial errors!'

'Nor do I, aunt; but if I hate the sins I love the sinner,[10] and would do much for his salvation, even supposing your suspicions to be mainly true – which I do not and will not believe.'

'Well my dear, ask your uncle what sort of company he keeps, and if he is not banded with a set of loose, profligate young men, whom he calls his friends – his jolly companions, and whose chief delight is to wallow in vice, and vie with each other who can run fastest and farthest down the headlong road,[11] to the place prepared for the devil and his angels.'[12]

'Then, I will save him from them.'

'Oh, Helen, Helen! you little know the misery of uniting your fortunes to such a man!'

'I have such confidence in him, aunt, notwithstanding all you say, that I would willingly risk my happiness for the chance of securing his. I will leave better men to those who only consider their own advantage. If he has done amiss, I shall consider my life well spent in saving him from the consequences of his early errors, and striving to recall him to the path of virtue[13] – God grant me success!'

Here the conversation ended, for at this juncture, my uncle's voice was heard, from his chamber, loudly calling upon my aunt to come to bed. He was in a bad humour that night; for his gout was worse. It had been gradually increasing upon him ever since we came to town; and my aunt took advantage of the circumstance, next morning, to persuade him to return to the country immediately, without waiting for the close of the season. His physician supported and enforced her arguments; and contrary to her usual habits, she so hurried the preparations for removal (as much for my sake as my uncle's, I think), that in a very few days we departed; and I saw no more of Mr Huntingdon. My aunt flatters herself I shall soon forget him – perhaps she thinks I have forgotten him already, for I never mention his name; and she may continue to think so, till we meet again, – if ever that should be. I wonder if it will.

CHAPTER 18

THE MINIATURE

August 25th. – I am now quite settled down to my usual routine of steady occupations and quiet amusements – tolerably contented and cheerful, but still looking forward to spring with the hope of returning to town, not for its gaieties and dissipations, but for the chance of meeting Mr Huntingdon once again; for still, he is always in my thoughts and in my dreams. In all my employments, whatever I do, or see, or hear has an ultimate reference to him; whatever skill or knowledge I acquire is some day to be turned to his advantage or amusement; whatever new beauties in nature or art I discover, are to be depicted to meet his eye, or stored in my memory to be told him at some future period. This, at least, is the hope that I cherish, the fancy that lights me on my lonely way. It may be only an *ignis fatuus*, after all, but it can do no harm to follow it with my eyes and rejoice in its lustre, as long as it does not lure me from the path I ought to keep; and I think it will not, for I have thought deeply on my aunt's advice, and I see clearly, now, the folly of throwing myself away on one that is unworthy of all the love I have to give, and incapable of responding to the best and deepest feelings of my inmost heart – *so* clearly that even if I should see him again, and if he should remember me and love me still (which, alas! is too little probable, considering how he is situated, and by whom surrounded), and if he should ask me to marry him, – I am determined not to consent until I know for certain whether my aunt's opinion of him or mine is nearest the truth; for if mine is altogether wrong, it is not he that I love; it is a creature of my own imagination. But I think it is not wrong – no, no – there is a secret something – an inward instinct that assures me I am right. There *is* essential goodness in him; – and what delight to unfold it! If he has wandered, what bliss to recall him! If he is now exposed to the baneful influence of corrupting and wicked companions, what glory to deliver him from them! – Oh! if I could but believe that Heaven has designed me for this!

* * *

Today is the first of September; but my uncle has ordered the gamekeeper to spare the partridges[1] till the gentleman come. 'What gentlemen?' I asked when I heard it – a small party he had invited to shoot. His friend Mr Wilmot was one, and my aunt's friend Mr Boarham another. This struck me as terrible news, at the moment, but all regret and apprehension vanished like a dream when I heard that Mr Huntingdon was actually to be a third! My aunt is greatly against his coming, of course: she earnestly endeavoured to dissuade my uncle from asking him; but he, laughing at her objections, told her it was no use talking for the mischief was already done: he had invited Huntingdon and his friend Lord Lowborough before we left London, and nothing now remained but to fix the day for their coming. So he is safe, and I am sure of seeing him. I cannot express my joy – I find it very difficult to conceal it from my aunt; but I don't wish to trouble her with my feelings till I know whether I ought to indulge them or not. If I find it my absolute duty to suppress them, they shall trouble no one but myself; and if I can really feel myself justified in indulging this attachment, I can dare anything, even the anger and grief of my best friend, for its object – surely, I shall soon know. But they are not coming till about the middle of the month.

We are to have two lady visitors also: Mr Wilmot is to bring his niece and her cousin Milicent. I suppose, my aunt thinks the latter will benefit me by her society and the salutary example of her gentle deportment, and lowly and tractable spirit; and the former, I suspect she intends as a species of counter-attraction to win Mr Huntingdon's attention from me. I don't thank her for this; but I shall be glad of Milicent's company: she is a sweet, good girl, and I wish I were like her – *more* like her, at least, than I am.

* * *

19th. They are come. They came the day before yesterday. The gentlemen are all gone out to shoot, and the ladies are with my aunt, at work,[2] in the drawing-room. I have retired to the library, for I am very unhappy, and I want to be alone. Books cannot divert me; so, having opened my desk, I will try what may be done by detailing the cause of my uneasiness. This paper will serve instead of a confidential friend into whose ear I might pour forth the overflowings of my heart. It will not sympathize with my distresses, but then, it will not laugh at them, and, if I keep it close, it cannot tell again; so it is, perhaps, the best friend I could have for the purpose.

First, let me speak of his arrival – how I sat at my window and watched for nearly two hours, before his carriage entered the park gates – for they all came before him, – and how deeply I was disappointed at every arrival, because it was not his. First came Mr Wilmot and the ladies. When Milicent had got into her room, I quitted my post a few minutes, to look in upon her and have a little private conversation, for she was now my intimate friend, several long epistles having passed between us since our parting. On returning to my window, I beheld another carriage at the door. Was it his? No; it was Mr Boarham's plain, dark chariot;[3] and there stood he upon the steps, carefully superintending the dislodging of his various boxes and packages. What a collection! one would have thought he projected a visit of six months at least. A considerable time after, came Lord Lowborough in his barouche.[4] Is he one of the profligate friends, I wonder? I should think not; for no one could call *him* a jolly companion, I'm sure, – and besides, he appears too sober and gentlemanly in his demeanour, to merit such suspicions. He is a tall, thin, gloomy looking man, apparently between thirty and forty, and of a somewhat sickly, careworn aspect.

At last, Mr Huntingdon's light phaeton[5] came bowling merrily up the lawn. I had but a transient glimpse of him, for the moment it stopped, he sprang out over the side on to the portico steps, and disappeared into the house.

I now submitted to be dressed for dinner – a duty which Rachel had been urging upon me for the last twenty minutes; and when that important business was completed, I repaired to the drawing-room where I found Mr and Miss Wilmot, and Milicent Hargrave already assembled. Shortly after, Lord Lowborough entered, and then Mr Boarham, who seemed quite willing to forget and forgive my former conduct, and to hope that a little conciliation and steady perseverance on his part might yet succeed in bringing me to reason. While I stood at the window, conversing with Milicent, he came up to me, and was beginning to talk in nearly his usual strain, when Mr Huntingdon entered the room.

'How will he greet me, I wonder?' said my bounding heart; and instead of advancing to meet him, I turned to the window to hide or subdue my emotion. But having saluted his host and hostess, and the rest of the company, he came to me, ardently squeezed my hand, and murmured he was glad to see me once again. At that moment dinner was announced, my aunt desired him to take Miss Hargrave into the dining-room, and odious Mr Wilmot, with unspeakable grimaces, offered his arm to me; and I was condemned to sit between himself and Mr Boarham. But afterwards, when we were all again assembled in the drawing-room, I was indemnified for so much suffering by a few delightful minutes of conversation with Mr Huntingdon.

In the course of the evening, Miss Wilmot was called upon to sing and play for the amusement of the company, and I to exhibit my drawings, and, though he likes music, and she is an accomplished musician, I think I am right in affirming that he paid more attention to my drawings than to her music.

So far, so good; – but, hearing him pronounce, *sotto voce*, but with peculiar emphasis concerning one of the pieces, 'THIS is better than all!' – I looked up, curious to see which it was, and, to my horror, beheld him complacently gazing at the *back* of the picture – it was his own face that I had sketched there and forgotten to rub out! To make matters worse, in the agony of the moment, I attempted to snatch it from his hand; – but he prevented me, and, exclaiming, 'No – by George, I'll keep it!' placed it against his waistcoat, and buttoned his coat upon it with a delighted chuckle.

Then, drawing a candle close to his elbow, he gathered all the drawings to himself, as well what he had seen as the others, and muttering, 'I must look at *both* sides now,' he eagerly commenced an examination which I watched, at first, with tolerable composure, in the confidence that his vanity would not be gratified by any further discoveries; for, though I must plead guilty to having disfigured the backs of several with abortive attempts to delineate that too fascinating physiognomy, I was sure that, with that one unfortunate exception, I had carefully obliterated all such witnesses of my infatuation. But the pencil frequently leaves an impression upon cardboard that no amount of rubbing can efface. Such, it seems, was the case with most of these; and I confess I trembled when I saw him holding them so close to the candle, and poring so intently over the seeming blanks; but still, I trusted he would not be able to make out these dim traces to his own satisfaction. I was mistaken however – having ended his scrutiny, he quietly remarked, –

'I perceive, the backs of young ladies' drawings, like the postscripts of their letters,[6] are the most important and interesting part of the concern.'

Then, leaning back in his chair, he reflected a few minutes in silence, complacently smiling to himself, and, while I was concocting some cutting speech wherewith to check his gratification, he rose, and passing over to where Annabella Wilmot sat vehemently coquetting with Lord Lowborough, seated himself on the sofa beside her, and attached himself to her for the rest of the evening.

'So then!' thought I – 'he despises me, because he knows I love him.'

And the reflection made me so miserable I knew not what to do. Milicent came and began to admire my drawings and make remarks upon them; but I could not talk to her – I could talk to no one; and upon the introduction of tea, I took advantage of the open door and the slight diversion caused by its entrance, to slip out – for I was sure I could not take any – and take refuge in the library. My aunt sent Thomas in quest of me, to ask if I were not coming to tea; but I bade him say I should not take any tonight; and happily she was too much occupied with her guests to make any further enquiries at the time.

As most of the company had travelled far that day, they retired early to rest; and, having heard them all, as I thought, go upstairs, I ventured out, to get my candlestick from the drawing-room sideboard. But Mr Huntingdon had lingered behind the rest: he was just at the foot of the stairs when I opened the door; and, hearing my step in the hall – though I could hardly hear it myself – he instantly turned back.

'Helen, is that you?' said he, 'why did you run away from us?'

'Goodnight, Mr Huntingdon,' said I, coldly, not choosing to answer the question. And I turned away to enter the drawing-room.

'But you'll shake hands, won't you?' said he, placing himself in the doorway before me. And he seized my hand, and held it much against my will.

'Let me go, Mr Huntingdon!' said I – 'I want to get a candle.'

'The candle will keep,' returned he.

I made a desperate effort to free my hand from his grasp.

'Why are you in such a hurry to leave me, Helen?' he said, with a smile of the most provoking self-sufficiency – 'you don't hate me, you *know*.'

'Yes, I do – at this moment.'

'Not you! It is Annabella Wilmot you hate, not me.'

'I have nothing to do with Annabella Wilmot,' said I, burning with indignation.

'But *I* have, you know,' returned he, with peculiar emphasis.

'That is nothing to me sir!' I retorted.

'*Is* it nothing to you, Helen? – Will you swear it? – Will you?'

'No, I won't, Mr Huntingdon! and I *will* go!' cried I, not knowing whether to laugh or to cry, or to break out into a tempest of fury.

'Go then, you vixen!' he said; but the instant he released my hand, he had the audacity to put his arm round my neck and kiss me.[7]

Trembling with anger and agitation – and I don't know what besides – I broke away, and got my candle and rushed upstairs to my room. He would not have done so but for that hateful picture! And there he had it still in his possession, an eternal monument to his pride and my humiliation!

It was but little sleep I got that night; and in the morning I rose perplexed and troubled with the thought of meeting him at breakfast. I knew not how it was to be done; an assumption of dignified, cold indifference would hardly do after what he knew of my devotion – to his face, at least. Yet something must be done to check his presumption – I would not submit to be tyrannized over by those bright, laughing eyes. And accordingly, I received his cheerful morning salutation as calmly and coldly as my aunt could have wished, and defeated with brief answers his one or two attempts to draw me into conversation; while I comported myself with unusual cheerfulness and complaisance towards every other member of the party, especially Annabella Wilmot, and even her uncle and Mr Boarham were treated with an extra amount of civility on the occasion, not from any motives of coquetry, but just to show him that my particular coolness and reserve arose from no general ill-humour or depression of spirits.

He was not, however, to be repelled by such acting as this. He did not talk much to me, but when he did speak, it was with a degree of freedom and openness – and *kindliness* too – that plainly seemed to intimate he knew his words were music to my ears; and when his looks met mine, it was with a smile – presumptuous it might be – but oh, so sweet, so bright, so genial, that I could not possibly retain my anger; every vestige of displeasure soon melted away beneath it, like morning clouds before the summer sun.

Soon after breakfast all the gentlemen save one, with boyish eagerness, set out on their expedition against the hapless partridges; my uncle and Mr Wilmot on their shooting ponies, Mr Huntingdon and Lord Lowborough on their legs; the one exception being Mr Boarham, who, in consideration of the rain that had fallen during the night, thought it prudent to remain behind a little, and join them in a while, when the sun had dried the grass. And he favoured us all with a long and minute disquisition upon the evils and dangers attendant upon damp feet, delivered with the most imperturbable gravity, amid the jeers and laughter of Mr Huntingdon and my uncle, who, leaving the prudent sportsman to entertain the ladies with his medical discussions, sallied forth with their guns, bending their steps to the stables first, to have a look at the horses, and let out the dogs.

Not desirous of sharing Mr Boarham's company for the whole of the morning, I betook myself to the library; and there brought forth my easel, and began to paint. The easel and the painting apparatus would serve as an excuse for abandoning the drawing-room, if my aunt should come to complain of the desertion; and besides, I wanted to finish the picture. It was one I had taken great pains with, and I intended it to be my masterpiece, though it was somewhat presumptuous in the design. By the bright azure of the sky, and by the warm and brilliant lights, and deep, long shadows, I had endeavoured to convey the idea of a sunny morning. I had ventured to give more of the bright verdure of spring or early summer to the grass and foliage, than is commonly attempted in painting. The scene represented was an open glade in a wood. A group of dark Scotch firs was introduced in the middle distance to relieve the prevailing freshness of the rest; but in the foreground, were part of the gnarled trunk and of the spreading boughs of a large forest tree, whose foliage was of a brilliant golden green – not golden from autumnal mellowness, but from the sunshine, and the very immaturity of the scarce expanded leaves. Upon this bough, that stood out in bold relief against the sombre firs, were seated an amorous pair of turtle doves, whose soft sad coloured plumage afforded a contrast of another nature; and beneath it, a young girl was kneeling on the daisy-spangled turf, with head thrown back and masses of fair hair falling on her shoulders, her hands clasped, lips parted, and eyes intently gazing upward in pleased, yet earnest contemplation of those feathered lovers – too deeply absorbed in each other to notice her.[8]

I had scarcely settled to my work – which, however, wanted but a few touches to the finishing – when the sportsmen passed the window on their return from the stables. It was partly open, and Mr Huntingdon must have seen me as he went by, for in half a minute he came back, and, setting his gun against the wall, threw up the sash, and sprang in, and set himself before my picture.

'Very pretty, i'faith!' said he, after attentively regarding it for a few seconds – 'and a very fitting study for a young lady – Spring just opening into summer – morning just approaching noon – girlhood just ripening into womanhood – and hope just verging on fruition. She's a sweet creature! but why didn't you make her black hair?'

'I thought light hair would suit her better. You see I have made her blue-eyed, and plump, and fair and rosy.'

'Upon my word – a very Hebe![9] I should fall in love with her, if I hadn't the artist before me. Sweet innocent! she's thinking there will come a time when she will be wooed and won like that pretty hen-dove, by as fond and fervent a lover; and she's thinking how pleasant it will be, and how tender and faithful he will find her.'

'And perhaps,' suggested I, 'how tender and faithful she shall find him.'

'Perhaps – for there is no limit to the wild extravagance of hope's imaginings, at such an age.'

'Do you call that, then, one of her wild, extravagant delusions?'

'No; my heart tells me it is not. I might have thought so once, but now, I say, give me the girl I love, and I will swear eternal constancy to her and her alone, through summer and winter, through youth and age, and life and death! if age and death must come.'

He spoke this in such serious earnest that my heart bounded with delight; but the minute after he changed his tone, and asked, with a significant smile, if I had 'any more portraits.'

'No,' replied I, reddening with confusion and wrath. But my portfolio was on the table; he took it up, and coolly sat down to examine its contents.

'Mr Huntingdon, those are my unfinished sketches,' cried I, 'and I never let anyone see them.'

And I placed my hand on the portfolio to wrest it from him; but he maintained his hold, assuring me that he 'liked unfinished sketches of all things.'

'But I hate them to be seen,' returned I. 'I can't let you have it, indeed!'

'Let me have its bowels then,'[10] said he; and just as I wrenched the portfolio from his hand, he deftly abstracted the greater part of its contents, and after turning them over a moment, he cried out, —

'Bless my stars, here's another!' and slipped a small oval of ivory paper[11] into his waistcoat pocket – a complete miniature portrait, that I had sketched with such tolerable success, as to be induced to colour it with great pains and care. But I was determined he should not keep it.

'Mr Huntingdon,' cried I, 'I *insist* upon having that back! It is mine, and you have no *right* to take it. Give it me, directly – I'll never forgive you, if you don't!'

But the more vehemently I insisted, the more he aggravated my distress by his insulting, gleeful laugh. At length, however, he restored it to me, saying –

'Well, well, since you value it so much, I'll not deprive you of it.'

To show him how I valued it, I tore it in two, and threw it into the fire. He was not prepared for this. His merriment suddenly ceasing, he stared in mute amazement at the consuming treasure; and then, with a careless 'Humph! I'll go and shoot now,' he turned on his heel, and vacated the apartment by the window as he came, and, setting on his hat with an air, took up his gun and walked away, whistling as he went – and leaving me not too much agitated to finish my picture; for I was glad, at the moment, that I had vexed him.

When I returned to the drawing-room, I found Mr Boarham had ventured to follow his comrades to the field; and shortly after lunch, to which they did not think of returning, I volunteered to accompany the ladies in a walk, and show Annabella and Milicent the beauties of the country. We took a long ramble and re-entered the park just as the sportsmen were returning from their expedition. Toil-spent and travel-stained, the main body of them crossed over the grass to avoid us; but Mr Huntingdon, all spattered and splashed as he was, and stained with the blood of his prey[12] – to the no small offence of my aunt's strict sense of propriety – came out of his way to meet us, with cheerful smiles and words for all but me, and, placing himself between Annabella Wilmot and myself, walked up the road and began to relate the various exploits and disasters of the day, in a manner that would have convulsed me with laughter, if I had been on good terms with him; but he addressed himself entirely to Annabella, and I, of course, left all the laughter and all the badinage to her, and, affecting the utmost indifference to whatever passed between them, walked along a few paces apart, and looking every way but theirs; while my aunt and Milicent went before, linked arm in arm, and gravely discoursing together. At length, Mr Huntingdon turned to me, and, addressing me in a confidential whisper, said –

'Helen, why did you burn my picture?'

'Because, I wished to destroy it,' I answered, with an asperity it is useless now to lament.

'Oh, very good!' was the reply, 'if *you* don't value me, I must turn to somebody that will.'

I thought it was partly in jest – a half playful mixture of mock resignation and pretended indifference; but immediately he resumed his place beside Miss Wilmot, and from that hour to this – during all that evening, and all the next day, and the next, and the next, and all this morning (the 22nd), he has never given me one kind word or one pleasant look – never spoken to me, but from pure necessity – never glanced towards me, but with a cold, unfriendly look I thought him quite incapable of assuming.

My aunt observes the change, and though she has not enquired the cause or made any remark to me on the subject, I see it gives her pleasure. Miss Wilmot observes it too, and triumphantly ascribes it to her own superior charms and blandishments; but I am truly miserable – more so than I like to acknowledge to myself. Pride refuses to aid me. It has brought me into the scrape, and will not help me out of it.

He meant no harm – it was only his joyous, playful spirit; and I, by my acrimonious resentment – so serious, so disproportioned to the offence – have so wounded his feelings – so deeply offended him, that I fear he will never forgive me – and all for a mere jest! He thinks I dislike him, – and he must continue to think so. I must lose him for ever; and Annabella may win him, and triumph as she will.

But it is not my loss, nor her triumph, that I deplore so greatly as the wreck of my fond hopes for his advantage, and her unworthiness of his affection, and the injury he will do himself by trusting his happiness to her. *She* does not love him: she thinks only of herself. She cannot appreciate the good that is in him: she will neither see it, nor value it, nor cherish it. She will neither deplore his faults nor attempt their amendment, but rather aggravate them by her own. And I doubt whether she will not deceive him after all: I see she is playing double between him and Lord Lowborough, and while she amuses herself with the lively Huntingdon, she tries her utmost to enslave his moody friend; and should she succeed in bringing both to her feet, the fascinating commoner will have but little chance against the lordly peer. If he observes her artful by-play, it gives him no uneasiness, but rather adds new zest to his diversion by opposing a stimulating check to his otherwise too easy conquest.

Messrs Wilmot and Boarham have severally taken occasion by his neglect of me to renew their advances; and if I were like Annabella and some others, I should take advantage of their perseverance to endeavour to pique him into a revival of affection; but, justice and honesty apart, I could not *bear* to do it; I am annoyed enough by their present persecutions without encouraging them farther; – and even if I did, it would have precious little effect upon him. He sees me suffering under the condescending attentions and prosaic dis-courses of the one, and the repulsive obtrusions of the other, without so much as a shadow of commiseration for me, or resentment against my tormentors. He never could have loved me, or he would not have resigned me so willingly, and he would not go on talking to everybody else so cheerfully as he does – laughing and jesting with Lord Lowborough and my uncle, teasing Milicent Hargrave, and flirting with Annabella Wilmot – as if nothing were on his mind. Oh, why can't I hate him?[13] I must be infatuated, or I should *scorn* to regret him as I do! But I must rally all the powers I have remaining, and try to tear him from my heart. There goes the dinner bell – and here comes my aunt to scold me for sitting here at my desk all day, instead of staying with the company – I wish the company were – gone.

CHAPTER 19

AN INCIDENT

Twenty-second. Night – What have I done? and what will be the end of it? I cannot calmly reflect upon it; I cannot sleep. I must have recourse to my diary again; I will commit it to paper tonight, and see what I shall think of it tomorrow.

I went down to dinner resolving to be cheerful and well-conducted, and kept my resolution very creditably, considering how my head ached, and how internally wretched I felt – I don't know what is come over me of late; my very energies both mental and physical must be strangely impaired, or I should not have acted so weakly in many respects, as I have done; – but I have not been well this last day or two: I suppose it is with sleeping and eating so little, and thinking so much, and being so continually out of humour. But to return: I was exerting myself to sing and play for the amusement, and at the request of my aunt and Milicent, before the gentlemen came into the drawing-room (Miss Wilmot never likes to waste her musical efforts on ladies' ears alone): Milicent had asked for a little Scotch song, and I was just in the middle of it when they entered. The first thing Mr Huntingdon did was to walk up to Annabella: –

'Now, Miss Wilmot, won't *you* give us some music tonight?' said he. 'Do now! I know you will, when I tell you that I have been hungering and thirsting all day, for the sound of your voice. Come! the piano's vacant.'

It was; for I had quitted it immediately upon hearing his petition. Had I been endowed with a proper degree of self-possession, I should have turned to the lady myself, and cheerfully joined my entreaties to his; whereby I should have disappointed his expectations, if the affront had been purposely given, or made him sensible of the wrong, if it had only arisen from thoughtlessness; but I felt it too deeply to do anything but rise from the music-stool, and throw myself back on the sofa, suppressing with difficulty the audible expression of the bitterness I felt within. I knew Annabella's musical talents were superior to mine, but that was no reason why I should be treated as a perfect nonentity. The time and the manner of his asking her appeared like a gratuitous insult to me; and I could have wept with pure vexation.

Meantime, she exultantly seated herself at the piano, and favoured him with two of his favourite songs, in such superior style that even I soon lost my anger in admiration, and listened with a sort of gloomy pleasure to the skilful modulations of her full-toned and powerful voice, so judiciously aided by her rounded and spirited touch; and while my ears drank in the sound, my eyes rested on the face of her principal auditor, and derived an equal or superior delight from the contemplation of his speaking countenance, as he stood beside her – that eye and brow lighted up with keen enthusiasm, and that sweet smile passing and appearing like gleams of sunshine on an April day. No wonder he should hunger and thirst to hear her sing. I now forgave him, from my heart, his reckless slight of me, and I felt ashamed at my pettish resentment of such a trifle – ashamed too of those bitter envious pangs that gnawed my inmost heart, in spite of all this admiration and delight.

'There now!' said she, playfully running her fingers over the keys, when she had concluded the second song. 'What shall I give you next?'

But in saying this, she looked back at Lord Lowborough, who was standing a little behind, leaning against the back of a chair – an attentive listener, too, experiencing, to judge by his countenance, much the same feelings of mingled pleasure and sadness as I did. But the look she gave him, plainly said, 'Do you choose for me now: I have done enough for him, and will gladly exert myself to gratify you;' and thus encouraged, his lordship came forward, and turning over the music, presently set before her a little song that I had noticed before, and read more than once, with an interest arising from the circumstance of my connecting it in my mind with the reigning tyrant of my thoughts. And now with my nerves already excited and half unstrung, I could not hear those words so sweetly warbled forth, without some symptoms of emotion I was not able to suppress. Tears rose unbidden to my eyes, and I buried my face in the sofa-pillow that they might flow unseen while I listened. The air was simple, sweet, and sad; it is still running in my head, – and so are the words: –

> 'Farewell to thee![1] but not farewell
>   To all my fondest thoughts of thee:
> Within my heart they still shall dwell;
>   And they shall cheer and comfort me.
>
> O, beautiful, and full of grace!
>   If thou hadst never met mine eye,
> I had not dreamed a living face
>   Could fancied charms so far outvie.
>
> If I may ne'er behold again
>   That form and face, so dear to me,
> Nor hear thy voice, still would I fain
>   Preserve, for aye, their memory.
>
> That voice, the magic of whose tone
>   Can wake an echo in my breast,
> Creating feelings that, alone,
>   Can make my tranced spirit blest.
>
> That laughing eye, whose sunny beam
>   My memory would not cherish less; –
> And oh, that smile! whose joyous gleam
>   No mortal language[2] can express.
>
> Adieu! but let me cherish, still,
>   The hope with which I cannot part.
> Contempt may wound, and coldness chill,
>   But still it lingers in my heart.

> And who can tell but Heaven, at last,
>> May answer all my thousand prayers,
> And bid the future pay the past
>> With joy for anguish, smiles for tears?'

When it ceased, I longed for nothing so much as to be out of the room. The sofa was not far from the door, but I did not dare to raise my head, for I knew Mr Huntingdon was standing near me, and I knew by the sound of his voice, as he spoke in answer to some remark of Lord Lowborough's, that his face was turned towards me. Perhaps, a half suppressed sob had caught his ear, and caused him to look round – Heaven forbid! But, with a violent effort, I checked all further signs of weakness, dried my tears, and, when I thought he had turned away again, rose, and instantly left the apartment, taking refuge in my favourite resort, the library.

There was no light there but the faint red glow of the neglected fire; – but I did not want a light; I only wanted to indulge my thoughts, unnoticed and undisturbed; and, sitting down on a low stool before the easy chair, I sunk my head upon its cushioned seat, and thought, and thought, until the tears gushed out again, and I wept like any child. Presently, however, the door was gently opened and someone entered the room. I trusted it was only a servant, and did not stir. The door was closed again – but I was not alone: a hand gently touched my shoulder, and a voice said, softly –

'Helen, what is the matter?'

I could not answer at the moment.

'You must and shall tell me,' was added more vehemently, and the speaker threw himself on his knees, beside me on the rug, and forcibly possessed himself of my hand; but I hastily caught it away, and replied –

'It is nothing to you, Mr Huntingdon.'

'Are you sure it is nothing to me?' he returned, 'can you swear that you were not thinking of me while you wept?'

This was unendurable. I made an effort to rise, but he was kneeling on my dress.

'Tell me,' continued he – 'I want to know, – because, if you were,

I have something to say to you, – and if not, I'll go.'

'Go then!' I cried; but, fearing he would obey too well, and never come again, I hastily added – 'Or say what you have to say, and have done with it!'

'But which?' said he – 'for I shall only say it if you really were thinking of me. So tell me, Helen.'

'You're excessively impertinent, Mr Huntingdon!'

'Not at all – too pertinent, you mean – so you won't tell me? – Well, I'll spare your woman's pride, and, construing your silence into "Yes," I'll take it for granted that I *was* the subject of your thoughts, and the cause of your affliction –'

'Indeed, sir –'

'If you deny it, I won't tell you my secret,' threatened he; and I did not interrupt him again – or even attempt to repulse him, though he had taken my hand once more, and half embraced me with his other arm – I was scarcely conscious of it, at the time.

'It is this,' resumed he: 'that Annabella Wilmot, in comparison with you, is like a flaunting peony compared with a sweet, wild rosebud gemmed with dew – and I love you to distraction! – Now, tell me if that intelligence gives you any pleasure. – Silence again? That means yes – Then let me add, that I cannot live without you, and if you answer, No, to this last question, you will drive me mad – Will you bestow yourself upon me? – you will!' he cried, nearly squeezing me to death in his arms.

'No, no!' I exclaimed, struggling to free myself from him – 'you must ask my uncle and aunt.'

'They won't refuse me, if you don't.'

'I'm not so sure of that – my aunt dislikes you.'

'But *you* don't, Helen – say you love me, and I'll go.'

'I wish you *would* go!' I replied.

'I will, this instant, – if you'll only say you love me.'

'You know I do,' I answered. And again he caught me in his arms, and smothered me with kisses.

At that moment, my aunt opened wide the door, and stood before us, candle in hand, in shocked and horrified amazement, gazing alternately at Mr Huntingdon and me – for we had both started up, and now stood wide enough asunder. But *his* confusion was only for a moment. Rallying in an instant, with the most enviable assurance, he began –

'I beg ten thousand pardons, Mrs Maxwell! Don't be too severe upon me. I've been asking your sweet niece to take me for better, for worse; and she, like a good girl, informs me she cannot think of it without her uncle's and aunt's consent. So let me implore you not to condemn me to eternal wretchedness: if *you* favour my cause, I am safe; for Mr Maxwell, I am certain, can refuse you nothing.'

'We will talk of this tomorrow, sir,' said my aunt, coldly. 'It is a subject that demands mature and serious deliberation. At present, you had better return to the drawing-room.'

'But meantime,' pleaded he, 'let me commend my cause to your most indulgent –'

'No indulgence for you, Mr Huntingdon, must come between me and the consideration of my niece's happiness.'

'Ah, true! I know she is an angel, and I am a presumptuous dog to dream of possessing such a treasure; but, nevertheless, I would sooner die than relinquish her in favour of the best man that ever went to heaven – and as for her happiness, I would sacrifice my body and soul –'[3]

'Body and *soul* Mr Huntingdon – sacrifice your *soul*?'

'Well, I would lay down life –'

'You would not be required to lay it down.'

'I would spend it, then – devote my life – and all its powers to the promotion and preservation –'

'Another time, sir, we will talk of this – and I should have felt disposed to judge more favourably of your pretensions, if you too had chosen another time and place, and – let me add – another *manner* for your declaration.'

'Why, you see, Mrs Maxwell,' he began –

'Pardon me, sir,' said she, with dignity – 'The company are enquiring for you in the other room.' And she turned to me.

'Then *you* must plead for me, Helen,' said he, and at length withdrew.

'You had better retire to your room, Helen,' said my aunt, gravely. 'I will discuss this matter with you, too, tomorrow.'

'Don't be angry, aunt,' said I.

'My dear, I am not angry,' she replied: 'I am *surprised*. If it is true that you told him you could not accept his offer without our consent –'

'It *is* true,' interrupted I.

'Then how could you permit –'

'I couldn't help it, aunt,' I cried, bursting into tears. They were not altogether the tears of sorrow, or of fear for her displeasure, but rather the outbreak of the general tumultuous excitement of my feelings. But my good aunt was touched at my agitation. In a softer tone, she repeated her recommendation to retire, and gently kissing my forehead, bade me goodnight, and put her candle in my hand; and I went; – but my brain worked so, I could not think of sleeping. I feel calmer now that I have written all this; and I will go to bed, and try to win tired nature's sweet restorer.[4]

END OF VOLUME I

VOLUME II

CHAPTER 20

PERSISTENCE

September 24th. – In the morning I rose, light and cheerful, nay, intensely happy. The hovering cloud cast over me by my aunt's views, and by the fear of not obtaining her consent, was lost in the bright effulgence of my own hopes, and the too delightful consciousness of requited love. It was a splendid morning; and I went out to envoy it, in a quiet ramble in company with my own blissful thoughts. The dew was on the grass, and ten thousand gossamers were waving in the breeze; the happy redbreast was pouring out its little soul in song, and my heart overflowed with silent hymns of gratitude and praise to Heaven.

But I had not wandered far before my solitude was interrupted by the only person that could have disturbed my musings, at that moment, without being looked upon as an unwelcome intruder: Mr Huntingdon came suddenly upon me. So unexpected was the apparition, that I might have thought it the creation of an over-excited imagination, had the sense of sight alone borne witness to his presence; but immediately I felt his strong arm round my waist and his warm kiss on my cheek, while his keen and gleeful salutation, 'My own Helen!', was ringing in my ear.

'Nor yours yet,' said I, hastily swerving aside from this too presumptuous greeting – 'remember my guardians. You will not easily attain my aunt's consent. Don't you see she is prejudiced against you?'

'I do, dearest; and you must tell me why, that I may best know how to combat her objections. I suppose she thinks I am a prodigal,' pursued he, observing that I was unwilling to reply, 'and concludes that I shall have but little worldly goods wherewith to endow my better half? If so, you must tell her that my property is mostly entailed, and I cannot get rid of it. There may be a few mortgages on the rest – a few trifling debts and encumbrances here and there, but nothing to speak of; and though I acknowledge I am not so rich as I might be – or have been – still, I think, we could manage pretty comfortably on what's left. My father, you know, was something of a miser, and in his latter days especially, saw no pleasure in life but to amass riches; and so it is no wonder that his son should make it his chief delight to spend them, which was accordingly the case, until my acquaintance with you, dear Helen, taught me other views and nobler aims. And the very idea of having you to care for under my roof would force me to moderate my expenses and live like a Christian – not to speak of all the prudence and virtue you would instil into my mind by your wise counsels and sweet, attractive goodness.'

'But it is not that,' said I, 'it is not money my aunt thinks about. She knows better than to value worldly wealth above its price.'

'What is it then?'

'She wishes me to – to marry none but a really good man.'

'What, a man of "decided piety?"[1] – ahem! – Well, come, I'll manage that too! It's Sunday today, isn't it? I'll go to church morning, afternoon, and evening, and comport myself in such a godly sort that she shall regard me with admiration and sisterly love, as a brand plucked from the burning.[2] I'll come home sighing like a furnace, and full of the savour and unction of dear Mr Blatant's discourse –'

'Mr Leighton,' said I, dryly.

'Is Mr Leighton a "sweet preacher," Helen – a "dear, delightful, heavenly-minded man"?'[3]

'He is a *good* man, Mr Huntingdon. I wish I could say half as much for you.'

'Oh, I forgot, you are a saint, too. I crave your pardon, dearest – but don't call me Mr Huntingdon, my name is Arthur.'

'I'll call you nothing – for I'll have nothing at all to do with you, if you talk in that way any more. If you really mean to deceive my aunt as you say, you are very wicked; and if not, you are very wrong to jest on such a subject.'

'I stand corrected,' said he, concluding his laugh with a sorrowful sigh. 'Now,' resumed he, after a momentary pause, 'let us talk about something else. And come nearer to me, Helen, and take my arm; and then I'll let you alone. I can't be quiet while I see you walking there.'

I complied; but said we must soon return to the house.

'No one will be down to breakfast yet, for long enough,' he answered. 'You spoke of your guardians just now, Helen, but is not your father still living?'

'Yes, but I always look upon my uncle and aunt as my guardians, for they are so, in deed, though not in name. My father has entirely given me up to their care. I have never seen him since dear mamma died when I was a very little girl, and my aunt, at her request, offered to take charge of me, and took me away to Staningley, where I have remained ever since; and I don't think he would object to anything for me, that she thought proper to sanction.'

'But would he sanction anything to which she thought proper to object?'

'No, I don't think he cares enough about me.'[4]

'He is very much to blame – but he doesn't know what an angel he has for his daughter – which is all the better for me, as, if he did, he would not be willing to part with such a treasure.'

'And Mr Huntingdon,' said I. 'I suppose you *know* I am not an heiress?'

He protested he had never given it a thought, and begged I would not disturb his present enjoyment by the mention of such uninteresting subjects. I was glad of this proof of disinterested affection; for Annabella Wilmot is the probable heiress to all her uncle's wealth, in addition to her late father's property, which she has already in possession.

I now insisted upon retracing our steps to the house; but we walked slowly, and went on talking as we proceeded. I need not repeat all we said: let me rather refer to what passed between my aunt and me, after breakfast, when Mr Huntingdon called my uncle aside, no doubt to make his proposals, and she beckoned me into another room, where she once more commenced a solemn remonstrance which, however, entirely failed to convince me that her view of the case was preferable to my own.

'You judge him uncharitably, aunt, I know,' said I. 'His very friends are not half so bad as you represent them. There is Walter Hargrave, Milicent's brother, for one: he is but a little lower than the angels,[5] if half she says of him is true. She is continually talking to me about him, and lauding his many virtues to the skies.'

'You will form a very inadequate estimate of a man's character,' replied she, 'if you judge by what a fond sister says of him. The worst of them generally know how to hide their misdeeds from their sisters' eyes, and their mothers' too.'

'And there is Lord Lowborough,' continued I, 'quite a decent man.'

'Who told you so? Lord Lowborough is a *desperate* man. He has dissipated his fortune in gambling and other things, and is now seeking an heiress to retrieve it. I told Miss Wilmot so; but you're all alike: she haughtily answered she was very much obliged to me, but she believed *she* knew when a man was seeking her for her fortune, and when for herself; she flattered herself she had had experience enough in those matters, to be justified in trusting to her own judgment – and as for his lordship's lack of fortune, she cared nothing about that, as she hoped her own would suffice for both; and as for his wildness, she supposed he was no worse than others – besides he was reformed now. – Yes, they can all play the hypocrite when they want to take in a fond, misguided woman!'

'Well, I think he's about as good as she is,' said I. 'But when Mr Huntingdon is married, he won't have many opportunities of consorting with his bachelor friends; – and the worse they are, the more I long to deliver him from them.'

'To be sure, my dear; and the worse *he* is, I suppose, the more you long to deliver him from himself.'

'Yes, provided he is not incorrigible – that is, the more I long to deliver him from his faults – to give him an opportunity of shaking off the adventitious evil got from contact with others worse than himself, and shining out in the unclouded light of his own genuine goodness – to do my utmost to help his better self against his worse, and make him what he would have been if he had not, from the beginning, had a bad, selfish, miserly father, who to gratify his own sordid passions, restricted him in the most innocent enjoyments of childhood and youth, and so disgusted him with every kind of restraint; – and a foolish mother who indulged him to the top of his bent, deceiving her husband for him, and doing her utmost to encourage those germs of folly and vice it was her duty to suppress, – and then, such a set of companions as you represent his friends to be –'

'Poor man!' said she, sarcastically, 'his kind have greatly wronged him!'

'They have!' cried I – 'and they shall wrong him no more – his wife shall undo what his mother did!'[6]

'Well!' said she, after a short pause. 'I must say, Helen, I thought better of your judgment than this – and your taste too. How you can love such a man I cannot tell, or what pleasure you can find in his company; for "What fellowship hath light with darkness; or he that believeth with an infidel?"'[7]

'He is not an infidel; – and I am not light, and he is not darkness, his worst and only vice is thoughtlessness.'

'And thoughtlessness,' pursued my aunt, 'may lead to every crime, and will but poorly excuse our errors in the sight of God. Mr Huntingdon, I suppose, is not without the common faculties of men: he is not so light-headed as to be irresponsible: his Maker has endowed him with reason and conscience as well as the rest of us; the Scriptures are open to him as well as to others; – and "If he hear not them, neither will he hear though one rose from the dead."[8] And, remember, Helen,' continued she solemnly, '"The wicked shall be turned into hell, and they that *forget* God!"[9] And suppose, even, that he should continue to love you, and you him, and that you should pass through life together with tolerable comfort, – how will it be in the end, when you see yourselves parted for ever;[10] you, perhaps, taken into eternal bliss, and he cast into the lake that burneth with unquenchable fire[11] – there forever to –'

'Not for ever,'[12] I exclaimed, '"only till he has paid the uttermost farthing;"[13] for "If any man's work abide not the fire, he shall suffer loss, yet himself shall be saved, but so as by fire,"[14] and He that "is able to subdue all things to Himself, will have all men to be saved,"[15] and "will in the fulness of time, gather together in one all things in Christ Jesus, who tasted death for every man, and in whom God will reconcile all things to himself, whether they be things in earth or things in heaven."'[16]

'Oh, Helen! where did you learn all this?'

'In the Bible, aunt. I have searched it through, and found nearly thirty passages, all tending to support the same theory.'

'And is *that* the use you make of your Bible? And did you find no passages tending to prove the danger and the falsity of such a belief?'

'No: I found, indeed, some passages that, taken by themselves, might seem contradict that opinion; but they will all bear a different construction to that which is commonly given, and in most the only difficulty is in the word which we translate "everlasting" or "eternal:" I don't know the Greek, but I believe it strictly means for ages, and might signify either "endless" or "long-enduring."[17] And as for the danger of the belief, I would not publish it abroad, if I thought any poor wretch would be likely to presume upon it to his own destruction, but it is a glorious thought to cherish in one's own heart,[18] and I would not part with it for all the world can give!'

Here our conference ended, for it was now high time to prepare for church. Everyone attended the morning service, except my uncle, who hardly ever goes, and Mr Wilmot, who stayed at home with him to enjoy a quiet game of cribbage. In the afternoon Miss Wilmot and Lord Lowborough likewise excused themselves from attending; but Mr Huntingdon vouchsafed to accompany us again. Whether it was to ingratiate himself with my aunt I cannot tell, but, if so, he certainly should have behaved better. I must confess, I did not like his conduct during service at all. Holding his prayer-book upside down, or open at any place but the right, he did nothing but stare about him, unless he happened to catch my aunt's eye or mine, and then he would drop his own on his book, with a puritanical air of mock solemnity that would have been ludicrous, if it had not been too provoking.[19] Once, during the sermon, after attentively regarding Mr Leighton for a few minutes, he suddenly produced his gold pencil case and snatched up a Bible. Perceiving that I observed the movement, he whispered he was going to make a note of the sermon; but instead of that – as I sat next him I could not help seeing that he was making a caricature of the preacher,[20] giving to the respectable, pious, elderly gentleman, the air and aspect of a most absurd old hypocrite. And yet, upon his return, he talked to my aunt about the sermon with a degree of modest, serious discrimination that tempted me to believe he had really attended and profited by the discourse.

Just before dinner my uncle called me into the library for the discussion of a very important matter, which was dismissed in few words.

'Now Nell,' said he, 'This young Huntingdon has been asking for you: what must I say about it? Your aunt would answer "No" – but what say you?'

'I say yes, uncle,' replied I, without a moment's hesitation; for I had thoroughly made up my mind on the subject.

'Very good!' cried he. 'Now that's a good honest answer – wonderful for a girl! – Well, I'll write to your father tomorrow. He's sure to give his consent; so you may look on the matter as settled. You'd have done a deal better if you'd taken Wilmot, I can tell you; but that you won't believe. At your time of life, it's love that rules the roast:[21] at mine, it's solid, serviceable gold. I suppose now, you'd never dream of looking into the state of your husband's finances, or troubling your head about settlements, or anything of that sort?'

'I don't think I should.'

'Well, be thankful, then, that you've wiser heads to think for you. I haven't had time, yet, to examine thoroughly into this young rascal's affairs, but I see that a great part of his father's fine property has been squandered away; – but still, I think there's a pretty fair share of it left, and a little careful nursing may make a handsome thing of it yet; and then we must persuade your father to give you a decent fortune, as he has only one besides yourself to care for; – and, if you behave well, who knows but what I may be induced to remember you in my will?' continued he, putting his finger to his nose, with a knowing wink.

'Thanks uncle, for that and all your kindness,' replied I.

'Well, and I questioned this young spark on the matter of settlements,' continued he; 'and he seemed disposed to be generous enough on that point –'

'I knew he would!' said I. 'But pray don't trouble your head – or his, or mine about that; for all I have will be his, and all he has will be mine; and what more could either of us require?' And I was about to make my exit, but he called me back.

'Stop, stop!' cried he – 'We haven't mentioned the time yet. When must it be? Your aunt would put it off till the Lord knows when, but he is anxious to be bound as soon as may be: he won't hear of waiting beyond next month; and you, I guess, will be of the same mind, so –'

'Not at all, uncle; on the contrary, I should like to wait till after Christmas, at least.'

'Oh! pooh, pooh! never tell me that tale – I know better,' cried he; and he persisted in his incredulity. Nevertheless, it is quite true. I am in no hurry at all. How can I be, when I think of the momentous change that awaits me, and of all I have to leave? It is happiness enough, to know that we *are* to be united; and that he really loves me, and I may love *him* as devotedly, and think of him as often as I please. However, I insisted upon consulting my aunt about the *time* of the wedding, for I determined her counsels should not be utterly disregarded; and no conclusions on that particular are come to yet.

CHAPTER 21

OPINIONS

October 1st – All is settled now. My father has given his consent, and the time is fixed for Christmas, by a sort of compromise between the respective advocates for hurry and delay. Milicent Hargrave is to be one bridesmaid, and Annabella Wilmot the other – not that I am particularly fond of the latter, but she is an intimate of the family, and I have not another friend.

When I told Milicent of my engagement, she rather provoked me by her manner of taking it. After staring a moment in mute surprise, she said –

'Well Helen, I suppose I ought to congratulate you – and I *am* glad to see you so happy; but I did not think you would take him; and I can't help feeling surprised that you should like him so much.'

'Why so?'

'Because you are so superior to him in every way, and there's something so bold – and reckless about him – so, I don't know how – but I always feel a wish to get out of his way, when I see him approach.'

'You are timid, Milicent, but that's no fault of his.'

'And then his look,' continued she. 'People say he's handsome, and of course he is, but *I* don't *like* that kind of beauty; and I wonder that you should.'

'Why so, pray?'

'Well, you know, I think there's nothing noble or lofty in his appearance.'

'In fact, you wonder that I can like anyone so unlike the stilted heroes of romance? Well! give me my flesh and blood lover, and I'll leave all the Sir Herberts and Valentines[1] to you – if you can find them.'

'I don't want them,' said she. 'I'll be satisfied with flesh and blood too – only the spirit must shine through and predominate. But don't you think Mr Huntingdon's face is too red?'

'No!' cried I, indignantly. 'It is not red at all. There is just a pleasant glow – a healthy freshness in his complexion, the warm, pinky tint of the whole harmonizing with the deeper colour of the cheeks, exactly as it ought to do. I hate a man to be red and white, like a painted doll – or all sickly white, or smoky black, or cadaverous yellow!'

'Well, tastes differ – but *I* like pale or dark,' replied she. 'But, to tell you the truth Helen, I had been deluding myself with the hope that you would one day be my sister. I expected Walter would be introduced to you next season; and I thought you would like him, and was certain he would like you; and I flattered myself I should thus have the felicity of seeing the two persons I like best in the world – except mamma – united in one. He mayn't be exactly what you would call handsome, but he's far more distinguished-looking, and nicer and better than Mr Huntingdon; – and I'm sure you would say so, if you knew him.'

'Impossible, Milicent! You think so, because you're his sister; and, on that account, I'll forgive you; but nobody else should so disparage Arthur Huntingdon to me, with impunity.'

Miss Wilmot expressed her feelings on the subject, almost as openly.

'And so, Helen,' said she, coming up to me with a smile of no amiable import, 'you are to be Mrs Huntingdon, I suppose?'

'Yes,' replied I. 'Don't you envy me?'

'Oh, *dear*, no!' she exclaimed. 'I shall probably be Lady Lowborough some day, and then you know, dear, I shall be in a capacity to enquire, "Don't you envy *me*?" '

'Henceforth, I shall envy no one,' returned I.

'Indeed! Are you so happy then?' said she thoughtfully; and something very like a cloud of disappointment shadowed her face. 'And does he love you – I mean, does he idolize you as much as you do him?' she added, fixing her eyes upon me with ill-disguised anxiety for the reply.

'I don't want to be idolized,' I answered, 'but I am well assured that he *loves* me more than anybody else in the world – as I do him.'

'Exactly,' said she with a nod. 'I wish –' she paused.

'What do you wish?' asked I, annoyed at the vindictive expression of her countenance.

'I wish,' returned she, with a short laugh, 'that all the attractive points and desirable qualifications of the two gentlemen were united in one – that Lord Lowborough had Huntingdon's handsome face and good temper, and all his wit, and mirth and charm, or else that Huntingdon had Lowborough's pedigree, and title, and delightful old family seat, and I had him; and you might have the other and welcome.'

'Thank you, dear Annabella, I am better satisfied with things as they are, for my own part; and for you, I wish you were as well content with your intended, as I am with mine,' said I; and it was true enough; for, though vexed at first at her unamiable spirit, her frankness touched me, and the contrast between our situations was such, that I could well afford to pity her and wish her well.

Mr Huntingdon's acquaintances appear to be no better pleased with our approaching union than mine. This morning's post brought him letters from several of his friends, during the perusal of which, at the breakfast-table, he excited the attention of the company, by the singular variety of his grimaces. But he crushed them all into his pocket, with a private laugh, and said nothing till the meal was concluded. Then, while the company were hanging over the fire or loitering through the room, previous to settling to their various morning's avocations, he came and leant over the back of my chair, with his face in contact with my curls, and commencing with a quiet little kiss, poured forth the following complaints into my ear –

'Helen, you witch, do you know that you've entailed upon me the curses of all my friends? I wrote to them the other day, to tell them of my happy prospects, and now, instead of a bundle of congratulations, I've got a pocketful of bitter execrations and reproaches. There's not one kind wish for me, or one good word for you among them all. They say there'll be no more fun now, no more merry days and glorious nights – and all my fault – I am the first to break up the jovial band, and others, in pure despair, will follow my example. I was the very life and prop of the community, they do me the honour to say, and I have shamefully betrayed my trust –'

'You may join them again, if you like,' said I, somewhat piqued at the sorrowful tone of his discourse. 'I should be sorry to stand between any man – or body of men – and so much happiness; and perhaps I can manage to do without you, as well as your poor deserted friends.'

'Bless you! no,' murmured he. 'It's "all for love or the world well lost,"[2] with me. Let them go to — where they belong, to speak politely. But if you saw how they abuse me, Helen, you would love me all the more, for having ventured so much for your sake.'

He pulled out his crumpled letters. I thought he was going to show them to me, and told him I did not wish to see them.

'I'm not going to show them to you, love,' said he. 'They're hardly fit for a lady's eyes – the most part of them. But look here. This is Grimsby's scrawl – only three lines, the sulky dog! He doesn't say much, to be sure, but his very silence implies more than all the others' words, and the less he says, the more he thinks – G— d—n him! – I beg your pardon, dearest – and this is Hargrave's missive. He is particularly grieved at me, because, forsooth, he had fallen in love with you from his sister's reports, and meant to have married you himself, as soon as he had sown his wild oats.'

'I'm vastly obliged to him,' observed I.

'And so am I,' said he. 'And look at this. This is Hattersley's – every page stuffed full of railing accusations, bitter curses, and lamentable complaints, ending up with swearing that he'll get married himself in revenge: he'll throw himself away on the first old maid that chooses to set her cap at him, – as if *I* cared what he did with himself.'

'Well,' said I, 'if you do give up your intimacy with these men, I don't think you will have much cause to regret the loss of their society; for it's my belief they never did you much good.'

'Maybe not; but we'd a merry time of it, too, though mingled with sorrow and pain, as Lowborough knows to his cost – Ha, ha!' and while he was laughing at the recollection of Lowborough's troubles, my uncle came and clapped him on the shoulder.

'Come my lad!' said he. 'Are you too busy making love to my niece, to make war with the pheasants? – First of October remember! – Sun shines out – rain ceased – even Boarham's not afraid to venture in his waterproof boots; and Wilmot and I are going to beat you all. I declare, we old 'uns are the keenest sportsmen of the lot!'

'I'll show you what I can do today, however,' said my companion. 'I'll murder your birds by wholesale, just for keeping me away from better company than either you or them.'

And so saying he departed; and I saw no more of him till dinner. It seemed a weary time: I wonder what I shall do without him.

It is very true that the three elder gentlemen have proved themselves much keener sportsmen than the two younger ones; for both Lord Lowborough and Arthur Huntingdon have of late almost daily neglected the shooting excursions to accompany us in our various rides and rambles. But these merry times are fast drawing to a close. In less than a fortnight the party breaks up, much to my sorrow, for every day I enjoy it more and more – now that Messrs Boarham and Wilmot have ceased to tease me, and my aunt has ceased to lecture me, and I have ceased to be jealous of Annabella – and even to dislike her – and now that Mr Huntingdon is become *my* Arthur, and I may enjoy his society without restraint – What *shall* I do without him, I repeat?

CHAPTER 22

TRAITS OF FRIENDSHIP

October 5th. – My cup of sweets is not unmingled: it is dashed with a bitterness that I cannot hide from myself, disguise it as I will. I may try to persuade myself that the sweetness overpowers it; I may call it a pleasant aromatic flavour; but, say what I will, it is still there, and I cannot but taste it. I cannot shut my eyes to Arthur's faults; and the more I love him the more they trouble me. His very heart, that I trusted so, is, I fear, less warm and generous than I thought it. At least, he gave me a specimen of his character today, that seemed to merit a harder name than thoughtlessness. He and Lord Lowborough were accompanying Annabella and me in a long, delightful ride; he was riding by my side, us usual, and Annabella and Lord Lowborough were a little before us, the latter bending towards his companion as if in tender and confidential discourse.

'Those two will get the start of us, Helen, if we don't look sharp,' observed Huntingdon. 'They'll make a match of it, as sure as can be. That Lowborough's fairly besotted. But he'll find himself in a fix when he's got her, I doubt.'

'And she'll find *her*self in a fix when she's got *him*,' said I, 'if what I have heard of him is true.'

'Not a bit of it. She knows what she's about; but he, poor fool, deludes himself with the notion that she'll make him a good wife, and because she has amused[1] him with some rodomontade about despising rank and wealth in matters of love and marriage, he flatters himself that she's devotedly attached to him; that she will not refuse him for his poverty, and does not court him for his rank, but loves him for himself alone.'

'But is not *he* courting *her* for her fortune?'

'No, not he. That was the first attraction, certainly; but now, he has quite lost sight of it: it never enters his calculations, except merely as an essential without which, for the lady's own sake, he could not think of marrying her. No; he's fairly in love. He thought he never could be again, but he's in for it once more. He was to have been married before, some two or three years ago; but he lost his bride by losing his fortune. He got into a bad way among us in London: he had an unfortunate taste for gambling; and surely the fellow was born under an unlucky star, for he always lost thrice where he gained once. That's a mode of self-torment I never was much addicted to; when I spend my money I like to enjoy the full value of it: I see no fun in wasting it on thieves and blacklegs;[2] and as for *gaining* money, hitherto I have always had sufficient; it's time enough to be clutching for more, I think, when you begin to see the end of what you have. But I have sometimes frequented the gaming-houses just to watch the ongoings of those mad votaries of chance – a very interesting study, I assure you, Helen, and sometimes very diverting: I've had many a laugh at the boobies and bedlamites.[3] Lowborough was quite infatuated – not willingly, but of necessity, – he was always resolving to give it up, and always breaking his resolutions. Every venture was the "just once more:" if he gained a little, he hoped to gain a little more next time, and if he lost, it would not do to leave off at that juncture; he must go on till he had retrieved that last misfortune, at least: bad luck could not last for ever; and every lucky hit was looked upon as the dawn of better times, till experience proved the contrary. At length he grew desperate, and we were daily on the look out for a case of *felo-de-se*[4] – no great matter, some of us whispered, as his existence had ceased to be an acquisition to our club. At last, however, he came to a check. He made a large stake which he determined should be the last, whether he lost or won. He had often so determined before, to be sure, and as often broken his determination; and so it was this time. He lost; and while his antagonist smilingly swept away the stakes, he, turning chalky white, drew back in silence and wiped his forehead. I was present at the time; and while he stood with folded arms and eyes fixed on the ground, I knew well enough what was passing in his mind.

'"Is it to be the last, Lowborough?" said I, stepping up to him.

'"The last but ONE," he answered, with a grim smile; and then, rushing back to the table, he struck his hand upon it, and raising his voice high above all the confusion of jingling coins and muttered oaths and curses in the room, he swore a deep and solemn oath that, come what would, THIS trial *should* be the last, and imprecated unspeakable curses on his head, if ever he should shuffle a card or rattle a dice-box again. He then doubled his former stake, and challenged anyone present to play against him. Grimsby instantly presented himself. Lowborough glared fiercely at him, for Grimsby was almost as celebrated for his luck as *he* was for his ill-fortune. However, they fell to work. But Grimsby had much skill and little scruple, and whether he took advantage of the other's trembling, blinded eagerness to deal unfairly by him, I cannot undertake to say; but Lowborough lost again, and fell dead sick.

'"You'd better try once more," said Grimsby, leaning across the table. And then he winked at me.

'"I've nothing to try with," said the poor devil, with a ghastly smile.[5]

'"Oh, Huntingdon will lend you what you want," said the other.

'"No; you heard my oath," answered Lowborough, turning away in quiet despair. And I took him by the arm and led him out.

'"Is it to be the last, Lowborough?" I asked, when I got him into the street.

'"The last," he answered, somewhat against my expectation. And I took him home – that is, to our club[6] – for he was as submissive as a child, and plied him with brandy and water till he began to look rather brighter – rather more alive, at least.

'"Huntingdon, I'm ruined!" said he, taking the third glass from my hand – he had drunk the other in dead silence.

'"Not you!" said I. "You'll find a man can live without his money as merrily as a tortoise without its head, or a wasp without its body."

'"But I'm in debt," said he – "deep in debt! And I can never, *never* get out of it!"

'"Well, what of that? many a better man than you has lived and died in debt, and they can't put you in prison, you know, because you're a peer."[7] And I handed him his fourth tumbler.

'"But I hate to be in debt!" he shouted. "I wasn't born for it, and I cannot *bear* it!"

'"What can't be cured must be endured,"[8] said I, beginning to mix the fifth.

'"And then, I've lost my Caroline." And he began to snivel then, for the brandy had softened his heart.

'"No matter," I answered, "there are more Carolines in the world than one."

'"There's only one for me," he replied, with a dolorous sigh. "And if there were fifty more, who's to get them, I wonder, without money?"

'"Oh, somebody will take you for your title; and then you've your family estate yet; that's entailed, you know."

'"I wish to God I could sell it to pay my debts," he muttered.

'"And then," said Grimsby, who had just come in, "you can *try again*, you know. I *would* have one more chance if I were you. I'd never stop here."

'"I *won't*, I tell you!" shouted he. And he started up and left the room – walking rather unsteadily, for the liquor had got into his head. He was not so much used to it then, but after that, he took to it kindly to solace his cares.

'He kept his oath about gambling (not a little to the surprise of us all), though Grimsby did his utmost to tempt him to break it; but now he had got hold of another habit that bothered him nearly as much, for he soon discovered that the demon of drink was as black as the demon of play, and nearly as hard to get rid of – especially as his kind friends did all they could to second the promptings of his own insatiable cravings.'

'Then, they were demons themselves,'[9] cried I, unable to contain my indignation. 'And you, Mr Huntingdon, it seems, were the first to tempt him.'

'Well, what could we do?' replied he, deprecatingly – 'We meant it in kindness – we couldn't bear to see the poor fellow so miserable:

– and besides, he was such a damper upon us, sitting there, silent and glum, when he was under the threefold influence of the loss of his sweetheart, the loss of his fortune, and the reaction of the last night's debauch; whereas, when he had something in him, if he was not merry himself, he was an unfailing source of merriment to us. Even Grimsby could chuckle over his odd sayings: they delighted him far more than my merry jests or Hattersley's riotous mirth. But one evening, when we were sitting over our wine, after one of our club dinners, and had all been hearty together, – Lowborough giving us mad toasts, and hearing our wild songs and bearing a hand in the applause, if he did not help us to sing them himself, – he suddenly relapsed into silence, sinking his head on his hand, and never lifting his glass to his lips; – but this was nothing new; so we let him alone, and went on with our jollification, till, suddenly raising his head, he interrupted us in the middle of a roar of laughter, by exclaiming, –

'"Gentlemen, where is all this to end? – Will you just tell me *that* now? – Where is it all to end?"

'"In hell fire," growled Grimsby.

'"You've hit it – I thought so!" cried he. "Well then, I'll tell you what" – he rose.

'"A speech, a speech!" shouted we. "Hear, hear! Lowborough's going to give us a speech!"

'He waited calmly till the thunders of applause and jingling of glasses had ceased, and then proceeded, –

'"It's only this, gentlemen, – that I think we'd better go no farther. We'd better stop while we can."

'"Just so!" cried Hattersley –

> "Stop poor sinner, stop and think[10]
> Before you farther go,
> No longer sport upon the brink
> Of everlasting woe."

'"Exactly!" replied his lordship, with the utmost gravity. "And if *you* choose to visit the bottomless pit, I won't go with you – we must part company, for I swear I'll not move another step towards it! – What's this?" he said, taking up his glass of wine.

'"Taste it," suggested I.

'"This is hell broth!" he exclaimed. "I renounce it for ever!" And he threw it out into the middle of the table.

'"Fill again!" said I, handing him the bottle – "and let us drink to your renunciation."

'"It's rank poison," said he, grasping the bottle by the neck, "and I forswear it! I've given up gambling, and I'll give up this too." He was on the point of deliberately pouring the whole contents of the bottle on to the table, but Hargrave wrested it from him. "On you be the curse, then!" said he. And backing from the room, he shouted, "Farewell, ye tempters!" and vanished amid shouts of laughter and applause.

'We expected him back among us the next day; but to our surprise, the place remained vacant: we saw nothing of him for a whole week; and we really began to think he was going to keep his word. At last, one evening, when we were most of us assembled together again, he entered, silent and grim as a ghost, and would have quietly slipped into his usual seat at my elbow, but we all rose to welcome him, and several voices were raised to ask what he would have, and several hands were busy with bottle and glass to serve him; but I knew a smoking tumbler of brandy and water would comfort him best, and had nearly prepared it, when he peevishly pushed it away, saying,

'"Do let me alone, Huntingdon! Do be quiet, all of you! I'm not come to join you: I'm only come to be with you awhile, because I can't bear my own thoughts." And he folded his arms and leant back in his chair; so we let him be. But I left the glass by him; and after a while, Grimsby directed my attention towards it, by a significant wink; and, on turning my head, I saw it was drained to the bottom. He made me a sign to replenish, and quietly pushed up the bottle. I willingly complied; but Lowborough detected the pantomime, and, nettled at the intelligent grins that were passing between us, snatched the glass from my hand, dashed the contents of it in Grimsby's face, threw the empty tumbler at me, and then bolted from the room.'

'I hope he broke your head,' said I.

'No, love,' replied he, laughing immoderately at the recollection of the whole affair, 'he would have done so, – and perhaps spoilt my face, too, but providentially,[11] this forest of curls,' (taking off his hat and showing his luxuriant chestnut locks), 'saved my skull, and prevented the glass from breaking till it reached the table.

'After that,' he continued, 'Lowborough kept aloof from us a week or two longer. I used to meet him occasionally in the town; and then, as I was too good natured to resent his unmannerly conduct, and he bore no malice against me, – he was never unwilling to talk to me; on the contrary, he would cling to me and follow me anywhere, – but to the club, and the gaming-houses, and suchlike dangerous places of resort – he was so weary of his own moping, melancholy mind. At last, I got him to come in with me to the club, on condition that I would not tempt him to drink; and for some time, he continued to look in upon us pretty regularly of an evening, – still abstaining, with wonderful perseverance, from the "rank poison" he had so bravely forsworn. But some of our members protested against this conduct. They did not like to have him sitting there like a skeleton at a feast,[12] instead of contributing his quota to the general amusement, casting a cloud over all, and watching, with greedy eyes, every drop they carried to their lips, they vowed it was not fair; and some of them maintained that he should either be compelled to do as others did or expelled from the society, and swore that, next time he showed himself, they would tell him as much, and, if he did not take the warning, proceed to active measures. However, I befriended him on this occasion, and recommended them to let him be for a while, intimating that, with a little patience on our parts, he would soon come round again – But, to be sure, it *was* rather provoking; for though he refused to drink like an honest Christian, it was well known to me, that he kept a private bottle of laudanum about him, which he was continually soaking at – or rather, holding off and on with, abstaining one day and exceeding the next, just like the spirits.

'One night, however, during one of our orgies – one of our high festivals, I mean – he glided in, like the ghost in Macbeth,[13] and seated himself, as usual, a little back from the table, in the chair we always placed for "the spectre," whether it chose to fill it or not. I saw by his face that he was suffering from the effects of an overdose of his insidious comforter; but nobody spoke to him, and he spoke to nobody. A few sidelong glances, and a whispered observation that "the ghost was come," was all the notice he drew by his appearance, and we went on with our merry carousals as before, till he startled us all by suddenly drawing in his chair and leaning forward with his elbows on the table, and exclaiming with portentous solemnity, –

'"Well! it puzzles me what you can find to be so merry about. What *you* see in life I don't know – *I* see only the blackness of darkness and a fearful looking for of judgment and fiery indignation!"[14]

'All the company simultaneously pushed up their glasses to him, and I set them before him in a semicircle, and, tenderly patting him on the back, bid him drink and he would soon see as bright a prospect as any of us; but he pushed them back, muttering, –

'"Take them away! I won't taste it, I tell you – I won't – I won't!" So I handed them down again to the owners; but I saw that he followed them with a glare of hungry regret as they departed. Then, he clasped his hands before his eyes to shut out the sight, and two minutes after, lifted his head again, and said, in a hoarse but vehement whisper, –

'"And yet I must! Huntingdon, get me a glass!"

'"Take the bottle, man!" said I, thrusting the brandy-bottle into his hand – but stop, I'm telling too much,' muttered the narrator, startled at the look I turned upon him. 'But no matter,' he recklessly added, and thus continued his relation – 'In his desperate eagerness, he seized the bottle and sucked away, till he suddenly dropped from his chair, disappearing under the table amid a tempest of applause. The consequence of this imprudence was something like an apoplectic fit, followed by a rather severe brain fever –'[15]

'And what did you think of *yourself*, sir?' said I, quickly.

'Of course, I was very penitent,' he replied. 'I went to see him once or twice – nay, twice or thrice – or, by'r lady, some four times, – and when he got better, I tenderly brought him back to the fold.'[16]

'What do you mean?'

'I mean, I restored him to the bosom of the club, and, compassionating the feebleness of his health and extreme lowness of his spirits, I recommended him to "take a little wine for his stomach's sake,"[17] and, when he was sufficiently re-established, to embrace the *media-via, ni-jamais-ni-toujours*[18] plan – not to kill himself like a fool, and not to abstain like a ninny – in a word, to enjoy himself like a rational creature, and do as I did; – for don't think, Helen, that I'm a tippler; I'm nothing at all of the kind, and never was, and never shall be. I value my comfort far too much. I see that a man cannot give himself up to drinking without being miserable one half his days and mad the other; – besides, I like to enjoy my life at all sides and ends, which cannot be done by one that suffers himself to be the slave of a single propensity – and moreover, drinking spoils one's good looks,' he concluded, with a most conceited smile that ought to have provoked me more than it did.

'And did Lord Lowborough profit by your advice?' I asked.

'Why, yes, in a manner. For a while, he managed very well; indeed, he was a model of moderation and prudence – something too much so for the tastes of our wild community; – but, somehow, Lowborough had not the gift of moderation: if he stumbled a little to one side, he must go down before he could right himself: if he overshot the mark one night, the effects of it rendered him so miserable the next day that he must repeat the offence to mend it; and so on from day to day, till his clamorous conscience brought him to a stand. – And then, in his sober moments, he so bothered his friends with his remorse, and his terrors and woes, that they were obliged, in self-defence, to get him to drown his sorrows in wine, or any more potent beverage that came to hand; and when his first scruples of conscience were overcome, he would need no more persuading, he would often grow desperate, and be as great a blackguard as any of them could desire – but only to lament his own unutterable wickedness and degradation the more when the fit was over.

'At last, one day when he and I were alone together, after pondering awhile in one of his gloomy, abstracted moods, with his arms folded and his head sunk on his breast, – he suddenly woke up, and vehemently grasping my arm, said, –

'"Huntingdon, this won't do! I'm resolved to have done with it."

'"What, are you going to shoot yourself?" said I.

'"No; I'm going to reform."

'"Oh, *that's* nothing new! You've been going to reform these twelve months and more."

'"Yes, but you wouldn't let me; and I was such a fool I couldn't live without you. But now I see what it is that keeps me back, and what's wanted to save me; and I'd compass sea and land to get it – only I'm afraid there's no chance." And he sighed as if his heart would break.

'"What is it Lowborough?" said I, thinking he was fairly cracked at last.

'"A wife," he answered; "for I can't live alone, because my own mind distracts me, and I can't live with you, because you take the devil's part against me."

'"Who – I?"

'"Yes – all of you do, – and you more than any of them, you know. But if I could get a wife, with fortune enough to pay off my debts and set me straight in the world –"

'"To be sure," said I.

'"And sweetness and goodness enough," he continued, "to make home tolerable, and to reconcile me to myself, – I think I should do, yet. I shall never be in love again that's certain; but perhaps that would be no great matter, it would enable me to choose with my eyes open, – and I should make a good husband in spite of it; but could anyone be in love with *me*? – that's the question – With *your* good looks and powers of fascination," (he was pleased to say) "I might hope; but as it is, Huntingdon, do you think *any*body would take me – ruined and wretched as I am?"

'"Yes, certainly."

'"Who?"

'"Why, any neglected old maid, fast sinking in despair, would be delighted to –"

'"No, no," said he – "it must be somebody that I can love."

'"Why, you just said you never could be in love again?"

'"Well, love is not the word, – but somebody that I can like – I'll search all England through, at all events!" he cried, with a sudden burst of hope, or desperation. "Succeed or fail, it will be better than rushing headlong to destruction at that d—d club: so farewell to it and you. Whenever I meet you on honest ground or under a Christian roof, I shall be glad to see you; but never more shall you entice me to that *devil's den*!"

'This was shameful language, but I shook hands with him, and we parted. He kept his word; and from that time forward, he has been a pattern of propriety, as far as I can tell; but, till lately, I have not had very much to do with him. He occasionally sought my company but as frequently shrunk from it, fearing lest I should wile him back to destruction, and I found his not very entertaining, especially, as he sometimes attempted to awaken my conscience and draw me from the perdition he considered himself to have escaped; but when I did happen to meet him, I seldom failed to ask after the progress of his matrimonial efforts and researches, and, in general he could give me but a poor account. The mothers were repelled by his empty coffers and his reputation for gambling, and the daughters by his cloudy brow and melancholy temper, – besides, he didn't understand them; he wanted the spirit and assurance to carry his point.

'I left him at it when I went to the continent; and on my return, at the year's end, I found him still a disconsolate bachelor – though, certainly, looking somewhat less like an unblest exile from the tomb than before. The young ladies had ceased to be afraid of him, and were beginning to think him quite interesting; but the mammas were still unrelenting. It was about this time, Helen, that my good angel brought me into conjunction with you; and then I had eyes and ears for nobody else. But meantime, Lowborough became acquainted with our charming friend, Miss Wilmot – through the intervention of *his* good angel, no doubt he would tell you, though he did not dare to fix his hopes on one so courted and admired, till after they were brought into closer contact here at Staningley, and she, in the absence of her other admirers, indubitably courted his notice and held out every encouragement to his timid advances. Then indeed, he began to hope for a dawn of brighter days; and if for a while I darkened his prospects by standing between him and his sun – and so, nearly plunged him again into the abyss of despair – it only intensified his ardour and strengthened his hopes when I chose to abandon the field in the pursuit of a brighter treasure. In a word, as I told you, he is fairly besotted. At first, he could dimly perceive her faults, and they gave him considerable uneasiness; but now his passion and her art together have blinded him to everything but her perfections and his amazing good fortune. Last night, he came to me brimful of his new-found felicity:

'"Huntingdon, I am not a castaway!"[19] said he, seizing my hand and squeezing it like a vice. "There is happiness in store for me, yet – even in this life – she loves me!"

'"Indeed!" said I. "Has she told you so?"

'"No, but I can no longer doubt it. Do you not see how pointedly kind and affectionate she is? And she knows the utmost extent of my poverty, and cares nothing about it! She knows all the folly and all the wickedness of my former life, and is not afraid to trust me – and my rank and title are no allurements to her; for them, she utterly disregards. She is the most generous, high-minded being that can be conceived of. She will save me, body and soul, from destruction. Already, she has ennobled me in my own estimation, and made me three times better, wiser, greater than I was. Oh! if I had but known her before, how much degradation and misery I should have been spared! But what have I done to deserve so magnificent a creature?"

'And the cream of the jest,' continued Mr Huntingdon, laughing, 'is that the artful minx loves nothing about him, but his title and pedigree, and "that delightful old family seat."'

'How do you know?' said I.

'She told me so herself; she said, "as for the man himself, I thoroughly despise him; but then, I suppose, it is time to be making my choice, and if I waited for someone capable of eliciting my esteem and affection, I should have to pass my life in single blessedness, for I detest you all!" Ha, ha! I suspect she was wrong there; – but however, it is evident she has no love for *him*, poor fellow.'

'Then you ought to tell him so.'

'What, and spoil all her plans and prospects, poor girl? No, no:

that would be a breach of confidence, wouldn't it Helen? Ha, ha! Besides, it would break his heart.' And he laughed again.

'Well, Mr Huntingdon, I don't know what you see so amazingly diverting in the matter; *I* see nothing to laugh at.'

'I'm laughing at *you*, just now love,' said he, redoubling his cachinnations.

And, leaving him to enjoy his merriment alone, I touched Ruby with the whip, and cantered on to rejoin our companions; for we had been walking our horses all this time, and were consequently a long way behind. Arthur was soon at my side again; but, not disposed to talk to him, I broke into a gallop. He did the same: and we did not slacken our pace till we came up with Miss Wilmot and Lord Lowborough, which was within half a mile of the park gates. I avoided all further conversation with him, till we came to the end of our ride, when I meant to jump off my horse and vanish into the house, before he could offer his assistance; but while I was disengaging my habit from the crutch, he lifted me off, and held me by both hands, asserting that he would not let me go till I had forgiven him.

'I have nothing to forgive,' said I. 'You have not injured *me*.'

'No, darling – God forbid that I should! – but you are angry, because it was to me that Annabella confessed her lack of esteem for her lover.'

'No, Arthur, it is not *that* that displeases me: it is the whole system of your conduct towards your friend; and if you wish me to forget it, go, now, and tell him what sort of a woman it is, that he adores so madly, and on whom he has hung his hopes of future happiness.'

'I tell you, Helen, it would break his heart – it would be the death of him, – besides being a scandalous trick to poor Annabella. There is no help for him now; he is past praying for. Besides, she may keep up the deception to the end of the chapter; and then he will be just as happy in the illusion as if it were reality; or perhaps, he will only discover his mistake when he has ceased to love her; – and if not, it is much better that the truth should dawn gradually upon him. So now, my angel, I hope I have made out a clear case, and fully convinced you that I cannot make the atonement you require. What other requisition have you to make? Speak, and I will gladly obey.'

'I have none but this,' said I, as gravely as before; 'that, in future, you will never make a jest of the sufferings of others, and always use your influence with your friends for their own advantage against their evil propensities, instead of seconding their evil propensities against themselves.'

'I will do my utmost,' said he, 'to remember and perform the injunction of my angel monitress,' and after kissing both my gloved hands, he let me go.

When I entered my room, I was surprised to see Annabella Wilmot standing before my toilet-table, composedly surveying her features in the glass, with one hand flirting her gold-mounted whip,[20] and the other holding up her long habit.

'She certainly *is* a magnificent creature!' thought I, as I beheld that tall, finely developed figure, and the reflection of the handsome face in the mirror before me, with the glossy dark hair, slightly and not ungracefully disordered by the breezy ride, the rich brown complexion glowing with exercise, and the black eyes sparkling with unwonted brilliance. On perceiving me, she turned round exclaiming, with a laugh that savoured more of malice than of mirth, –

'Why Helen! what *have* you been doing so long? – I came to tell you my good fortune,' she continued, regardless of Rachel's presence. 'Lord Lowborough has proposed, and I have been graciously pleased to accept him. Don't you envy me, dear?'

'No, love,' said I – 'or him either,' I mentally added. 'And do you like him Annabella?'

'Like him! yes, to be sure – over head and ears in love!'

'Well, I hope you'll make him a good wife.'

'Thank you, my dear! And what besides do you hope?'

'I hope you will both love each other, and both be happy.'

'Thanks; – and I hope you will make a *very* good wife to Mr Huntingdon!' said she, with a queenly bow, and retired.

'Oh, Miss! how could you say so to her?' cried Rachel.

'Say what?' replied I.

'Why, that you hoped she would make him a good wife – I never heard such a thing!'

'Because, I do hope it – or rather, I wish it – she's almost past hope.'

'Well!' said she, 'I'm sure I hope he'll make *her* a good husband. They tell queer things about him downstairs. They were saying –'

'I know Rachel – I've heard all about him; but he's reformed now. And they have no business to tell tales about their masters.'

'No mum – or else, they *have* said some things about Mr Huntingdon too.'

'I won't hear them, Rachel; they tell lies.'

'Yes mum,' said she, quietly, as she went on arranging my hair.

'Do *you* believe them, Rachel?' I asked, after a short pause.

'No, miss, not all. You know when a lot of servants gets together, they like to talk about their betters; and some, for a bit of swagger, likes to make it appear as though they know more than they do, and to throw out hints and things, just to astonish the others. But I think, if I was you, Miss Helen, I'd look *very* well before I leaped. I do believe a young lady can't be too careful who she marries.'

'Of course not,' said I – 'but be quick, will you, Rachel? I want to be dressed.'

And indeed, I was anxious to be rid of the good woman, for I was in such a melancholy frame I could hardly keep the tears out of my eyes while she dressed me. It was not for Lord Lowborough – it was not for Annabella – it was not for myself – it was for Arthur Huntingdon that they rose.

* * *

13th. They are gone – and he is gone. We are to be parted for more than two months – above ten weeks! a long, long time to live and not to see him. But he has promised to write often, and made me promise to write still oftener, because he will be busy settling his affairs, and I shall have nothing better to do. Well, I think I shall always have plenty to say – But O! for the time when we shall be always together, and can exchange our thoughts without the intervention of these cold go-betweens, pen, ink, and paper!

* * *

22nd. I have had several letters from Arthur, already. They are not long, but passing sweet, and just like himself – full of ardent affection, and playful, lively humour; but – there is always a *but* in this imperfect world – and I do wish he would *sometimes* be serious. I cannot get him to write or speak in real, solid earnest. I don't much mind it *now*; but if it be always so, what shall I do with the serious part of myself?[21]

CHAPTER 23

FIRST WEEKS OF MATRIMONY

Feb. 18th, 1822. Early this morning, Arthur mounted his hunter and set off in high glee to meet the — hounds. He will be away all day; and so I will amuse myself with my neglected diary – if I can give that name to such an irregular composition. It is exactly four months since I opened it last.

I am married now, and settled down as Mrs Huntingdon of Grassdale Manor.[1] I have had eight weeks experience of matrimony. And do I regret the step I have taken? – No – though I must confess, in my secret heart, that Arthur is not what I thought him at first, and if I had known him in the beginning, as thoroughly as I do now, I probably never should have loved him, and if I had loved him first, and then made the discovery, I fear I should have thought it my duty not to have married him. To be sure, I might have known him, for everyone was willing enough to tell me about him, and he himself was no accomplished hypocrite, but I was wilfully blind, and now, instead of regretting that I did not discern his full character before I was indissolubly bound to him, I am *glad*; for it has saved me a great deal of battling with my conscience, and a great deal of consequent trouble and pain; and, whatever I *ought* to have done, my duty, now, is plainly to love him and to cleave to him;[2] and this just tallies with my inclination.

He is very fond of me – almost *too* fond. I could do with less caressing and more rationality: I should like to be less of a pet and more of a friend, if I might choose – but I won't complain of that: I am only afraid his affection loses in depth where it gains in ardour. I sometimes liken it to a fire of dry twigs and branches compared with one of solid coal, – very bright and hot, but if it should burn itself out and leave nothing but ashes behind, what shall I do? But it won't – it *shan't*, I am determined – and surely I have power to keep it alive. So let me dismiss *that* thought at once. But Arthur is selfish – I am constrained to acknowledge that; and, indeed, the admission gives me less pain than might be expected; for, since *I* love him so much, I can easily forgive him for loving himself: he likes to be pleased, and it is my delight to please him, – and when I regret this tendency of his, it is for his own sake, not for mine.

The first instance he gave was on the occasion of our bridal tour. He wanted to hurry it over, for all the continental scenes were already familiar to him: many had lost their interest in his eyes, and others had never had anything to lose. The consequence was, that, after a flying transit through part of France and part of Italy, I came back nearly as ignorant as I went, having made no acquaintance with persons and manners, and very little with things, – my head swarming with a motley confusion of objects and scenes – some, it is true, leaving a deeper and more pleasing impression than others, but these embittered by the recollection that my emotions had not been shared by my companion, but that, on the contrary, when I had expressed a particular interest in anything that I saw or desired to see, it had been displeasing to him in as much as it proved that I could take delight in anything disconnected with himself.

As for Paris, we only just touched at that, and he would not give me time to see one tenth of the beauties and interesting objects of Rome. He wanted to get me home, he said, to have me all to himself, and to see me safely installed as the mistress of Grassdale Manor, just as single-minded, as naïve, and piquante as I was; and, as if I had been some frail butterfly, he expressed himself fearful of rubbing the silver off my wings by bringing me into contact with society, especially that of Paris and Rome; and, moreover, he did not scruple to tell me that there were ladies in both places that would tear his eyes out if they happened to meet him with me.

Of course I was vexed at all this; but, still, it was less the disappointment to myself that annoyed me, than the disappointment *in him*, and the trouble I was at to frame excuses to my friends for having seen and observed so little, without imputing one particle of blame to my companion. But when we got home – to my new, delightful home – I was so happy and he was so kind that I freely forgave him all; – and I was beginning to think my lot *too* happy, and my husband actually too good for me, if not too good for this world, when, on the second Sunday after our arrival, he shocked and horrified me by another instance of his unreasonable exaction. We were walking home from the morning service – for it was a fine frosty day, and, as we are so near the church, I had requested the carriage should not be used: –

'Helen,' said he, with unusual gravity, 'I am not quite satisfied with you.'

I desired to know what was wrong.

'But will you promise to reform, if I tell you?'

'Yes, if I can – and without offending a higher authority.'

'Ah! there it is, you see – you don't love me with all your heart.'[3]

'I don't understand you, Arthur (at least, I hope I don't): pray tell me what I have done or said amiss?'

'It is nothing you have done or said; it is something that you *are*: you are too religious. Now I like a woman to be religious, and I think your piety one of your greatest charms, but then, like all other good things, it may be carried too far. To my thinking, a woman's religion ought not to lessen her devotion to her earthly lord. She should have enough to purify and etherialize her soul, but not enough to refine away her heart, and raise her above all human sympathies.'

'And am *I* above all human sympathies?' said I.

'No, darling; but you are making more progress towards that saintly condition than I like; for, all these two hours, I have been thinking of you and wanting to catch your eye, and you were so absorbed in your devotions that you had not even a glance to spare for me – I declare, it is enough to make one jealous of one's Maker – which is very wrong, you know; so don't excite such wicked passions again, for my soul's sake.'

'I will give my whole heart and soul to my Maker if I can,' I answered, 'and not one atom more of it to you than He allows.[4]

What are *you*, sir, that you should set yourself up as a god, and presume to dispute possession of my heart with Him to whom I owe all I have and all I am, every blessing I ever did or ever can enjoy – and yourself among the rest – if you *are* a blessing, which I am half inclined to doubt.'

'Don't be so hard upon me, Helen; and don't pinch my arm so, you're squeezing your fingers into the bone.'

'Arthur,' continued I, relaxing my hold of his arm, 'you don't love me half as much as I do you; and yet, if you loved me far less than you do, I would not complain, provided you loved your Maker more. I should *rejoice* to see you at any time, so deeply absorbed in your devotions that you had not a single thought to spare for me. But, indeed, I should lose nothing by the change, for the more you loved your God the more deep and pure and true would be your love to me.'

At this he only laughed, and kissed my hand, calling me a sweet enthusiast.[5] Then taking off his hat, he added –

'But look here, Helen – what can a man do with such a head as this?'

The head looked right enough, but when he placed my hand on the top of it, it sunk in a bed of curls, rather alarmingly low, especially in the middle.

'You see I was not made to be a saint,' said he, laughing. 'If God meant me to be religious, why didn't he give me a proper organ of veneration?'[6]

'You are like the servant,' I replied, 'who instead of employing his one talent in his master's service, restored it to him unimproved, alleging, as an excuse, that he knew him "to be a hard man, reaping where he had not sown and gathering where he had not strawed."[7] Of him, to whom less is given, less will be required; but our utmost exertions are required of us all. You are not without the capacity of veneration, and faith and hope, and conscience and reason, and every other requisite to a Christian's character, if you choose to employ them; but all our talents increase in the using, and every faculty, both good and bad, strengthens by exercise; therefore, if you choose to use the bad – or those which tend to evil till they become your masters and neglect the good till they dwindle away, you have only yourself to blame. But you *have* talents, Arthur – natural endowments, both of heart and mind, and temper such as many a better Christian would be glad to possess – if you would only employ them in God's service. I should never expect to see you a devotee, but it is quite possible to be a good Christian without ceasing to be a happy, merry-hearted man.'

'You speak like an oracle, Helen, and all you say is indisputably true; but listen here: I am hungry, and I see before me a good substantial dinner; I am told that, if I abstain from this today, I shall have a sumptuous feast tomorrow, consisting of all manner of dainties and delicacies. Now in the first place, I should be loath to wait till tomorrow, when I have the means of appeasing my hunger already before me; in the second place, the solid viands of today are more to my taste than the dainties that are promised me; in the third place, I don't *see* tomorrow's banquet, and how can I tell that it is not all a fable, got up by the greasy-faced fellow that is advising me to abstain, in order that he may have all the good victuals to himself? in the fourth place, this table must be spread for somebody, and, as Solomon says, "Who can eat, or who else can hasten hereunto more than I?"[8] and finally, with your leave, I'll sit down and satisfy my cravings of today, and leave tomorrow to shift for itself – who knows but what I may secure both this and that?'

'But you are not required to abstain from the substantial dinner of today; you are only advised to partake of these coarser viands in such moderation as not to incapacitate you from enjoying the choicer banquet of tomorrow. If, regardless of that counsel, you choose to make a beast of yourself now, and overeat and overdrink yourself till you turn the good victuals into poison, who is to blame if, hereafter, while you are suffering the torments of yesterday's gluttony and drunkenness, you see more temperate men sitting down to enjoy themselves at that splendid entertainment which you are unable to taste?'

'Most true my patron saint; but again, our friend Solomon says, – "There is nothing better for a man than to eat and to drink, and to be merry."'[9]

'And again,' returned I, 'he says, "Rejoice, O young man, in thy youth, and walk in the ways of thine heart and in the sight of thine eyes; but know thou that, for all these things, God will bring thee into judgment."'[10]

'Well but, Helen, I'm sure I've been very good these last few weeks. What have you seen amiss in me; and what would you have me to do?'

'Nothing – more than you do, Arthur: your actions are all right, so far; but I would have your thoughts changed; I would have you to fortify yourself against temptation, and not to call evil good, and good, evil; I should wish you to think more deeply, to look farther, and aim higher than you do.'

We now stood before our own door, and I said no more; but, with an ardent and tearful embrace, I left him, and went into the house, and upstairs to take off my bonnet and mantle. I wished to say nothing more on that subject at the time, lest I should disgust him with both it and me.

CHAPTER 24

FIRST QUARREL

March 25th. – Arthur is getting tired – not of me I trust, but of the idle, quiet life he leads – and no wonder, for he has so few sources of amusement; he never reads anything but newspapers and sporting magazines; and when he sees me occupied with a book, he won't let me rest till I close it. In fine weather he generally manages to get through the time pretty well: but on rainy days, of which we have had a good many of late, it is quite painful to witness his ennui. I do all I can to amuse him, but it is impossible to get him to feel interested in what I most like to talk about; while, on the other hand, he likes to talk about things that cannot interest me – or even that annoy me – and these please him the most of all; for his favourite amusement is to sit or loll beside me on the sofa and tell me stories of his former amours, always turning upon the ruin of some confiding girl or the cozening of some unsuspecting husband; and when I express my horror and indignation, he lays it all to the charge of jealousy, and laughs till the tears run down his cheeks. I used to fly into passions or melt into tears at first, but seeing that his delight increased in proportion to my anger and agitation, I have since endeavoured to suppress my feelings and receive his revelations in the silence of calm contempt; but still, he reads the inward struggle in my face, and misconstrues my bitterness of soul for his unworthiness into the pangs of wounded jealousy; and when he has sufficiently diverted himself with that, or fears my displeasure will become too serious for his comfort, he tries to kiss and soothe me into smiles again – never were his caresses so little welcome as then! This is *double* selfishness, displayed to me and to the victims of his former love. There are times when, with a momentary pang – a flash of wild dismay, I ask myself, 'Helen, what have you done?' But I rebuke the inward questioner, and repel the obtrusive thoughts that crowd upon me; for, were he ten times as sensual and impenetrable to good and lofty thoughts, I well know I have no right to complain. And I don't and won't complain. I do and will love him still; and I do not and will not regret that I have linked my fate with his.

April 4th. – We have had a downright quarrel. The particulars are as follows: – Arthur had told me, at different intervals, the whole story of his intrigue with Lady F—, which I would not believe before. It was some consolation, however, to find that, in this instance, the lady had been more to blame than he; for he was very young at the time, and she had decidedly made the first advances, if what he said was true. I hated her for it, for it seemed as if she had chiefly contributed to his corruption, and when he was beginning to talk about her the other day, I begged he would not mention her, for I detested the very sound of her name,

'Not because you loved her, Arthur, mind, but because she injured you, and deceived her husband, and was altogether a very abominable woman, whom you ought to be ashamed to mention.'

But he defended her by saying that she had a doting old husband, whom it was impossible to love.

'Then why did she marry him?' said I.

'For his money,' was the reply.

'Then that was another crime, and her solemn promise to love and honour him was another, that only increased the enormity of the last.'

'You are too severe upon the poor lady,' laughed he. 'But never mind, Helen, I don't care for her now; and I never loved any of them half as much as I do you; so you needn't fear to be forsaken like them.'

'If you had told me these things before, Arthur, I never should have given you the chance.'

'*Wouldn't* you, my darling!'

'Most certainly not!'

He laughed incredulously.

'I wish I could convince you of it now!' cried I, starting up from beside him; and for the first time in my life, and I hope the last, I wished I had not married him.

'Helen,' said he, more gravely, 'do you know that if I believed you now, I should be very angry? – but thank Heaven I don't. Though you stand there with your white face and flashing eyes, looking at me like a very tigress, I know the heart within you, perhaps a trifle better than you know it yourself.'

Without another word, I left the room, and locked myself up in my own chamber.[1] In about half an hour, he came to the door; and first he tried the handle, then he knocked.

'Won't you let me in, Helen?' said he.

'No; you have displeased me,' I replied, 'and I don't want to see your face or hear your voice again till the morning.'

He paused a moment, as if dumbfoundered[2] or uncertain how to answer such a speech, and then turned and walked away. This was only an hour after dinner: I knew he would find it very dull to sit alone all the evening; and this considerably softened my resentment, though it did not make me relent. I was determined to show him that my heart was not his slave, and I could live without him if I chose; and I sat down and wrote a long letter to my aunt – of course telling her nothing of all this. Soon after ten o'clock, I heard him come up again; but he passed my door and went straight to his own dressing-room, where he shut himself in for the night.

I was rather anxious to see how he would meet me in the morning, and not a little disappointed to behold him enter the breakfast-room with a careless smile.

'Are you cross still, Helen?' said he, approaching as if to salute me. I coldly turned to the table, and began to pour out the coffee, observing that he was rather late.

He uttered a low whistle and sauntered away to the window, where he stood for some minutes looking out upon the pleasing prospect of sullen, grey clouds, streaming rain, soaking lawn, and dripping, leafless trees – and muttering execrations on the weather, and then sat down to breakfast. While taking his coffee, he muttered it was 'd—d cold.'

'You should not have left it so long,' said I.

He made no answer, and the meal was concluded in silence. It was a relief to both when the letter-bag was brought in. It contained, upon examination, a newspaper and one or two letters for him, and a couple of letters for me, which he tossed across the table without a remark. One was from my brother, the other from Milicent Hargrave, who is now in London with her mother. His, I think, were business letters, and apparently not much to his mind, for he crushed them into his pocket with some muttered expletives, that I should have reproved him for at any other time. The paper, he set before him, and pretended to be deeply absorbed in its contents during the remainder of breakfast, and a considerable time after.

The reading and answering of my letters, and the direction of household concerns, afforded me ample employment for the morning; after lunch, I got my drawing, and from dinner till bed-time, I read. Meanwhile, poor Arthur was sadly at a loss for something to amuse him or to occupy his time. He wanted to appear as busy and as unconcerned as I did: had the weather at all permitted, he would doubtless have ordered his horse and set off to some distant region – no matter where – immediately after breakfast, and not returned till night; had there been a lady anywhere within reach, of any age between fifteen and forty-five, he would have sought revenge and found employment in getting up – or trying to get up – a desperate flirtation with her; but being, to my private satisfaction, entirely cut off from both these sources of diversion, his sufferings were truly deplorable. When he had done yawning over his paper and scribbling short answers to his shorter letters, he spent the remainder of the morning and the whole of the afternoon in fidgeting about from room to room, watching the clouds, cursing the rain, alternately petting, and teasing, and abusing his dogs, sometimes lounging on the sofa with a book that he could not force himself to read, and very often fixedly gazing at me, when he thought I did not perceive it, with the vain hope of detecting some traces of tears, or some tokens of remorseful anguish in my face. But I managed to preserve an undisturbed though grave serenity throughout the day. I was not really angry: I felt for him all the time, and longed to be reconciled;

but I determined he should make the first advances, or at least show some signs of an humble and contrite spirit, first; for, if I began, it would only minister to his self-conceit, increase his arrogance, and quite destroy the lesson I wanted to give him.

He made a long stay in the dining-room after dinner, and, I fear, took an unusual quantity of wine, but not enough to loosen his tongue; for when he came in and found me quietly occupied with my book, too busy to lift my head on his entrance, he merely murmured an expression of suppressed disapprobation, and, shutting the door with a bang, went and stretched himself at full length on the sofa, and composed himself to sleep. But his favourite cocker, Dash, that had been lying at my feet, took the liberty of jumping upon him and beginning to lick his face. He struck it off with a smart blow;[3] and the poor dog squeaked, and ran cowering back to me. When he woke up, about half an hour after, he called it to him again; but Dash only looked sheepish and wagged the tip of his tail. He called again, more sharply, but Dash only clung the closer to me, and licked my hand as if imploring protection. Enraged at this, his master snatched up a heavy book and hurled it at his head. The poor dog set up a piteous outcry and ran to the door. I let him out, and then quietly took up the book.

'Give that book to me,' said Arthur, in no very courteous tone. I gave it to him.

'Why did you let the dog out?' he asked. 'You knew I wanted him.'

'By what token?' I replied; 'by your throwing the book at him? but perhaps, it was intended for me?'

'No – but I see you've got a taste of it,' said he, looking at my hand, that had also been struck, and was rather severely grazed.

I returned to my reading; and he endeavoured to occupy himself in the same manner; but, in a little while, after several portentous yawns, he pronounced *his* book to be 'cursed trash,' and threw it on to the table. Then followed eight or ten minutes of silence, during the greater part of which, I believe, he was staring at me. At last his patience was tired out.

'What *is* that book, Helen?' he exclaimed.

I told him.

'Is it interesting?'

'Yes, very.'

'Humph!'

I went on reading – or pretending to read, at least – I cannot say there was much communication between my eyes and my brain; for, while the former ran over the pages, the latter was earnestly wondering when Arthur would speak next, and what he would say, and what I should answer. But he did not speak again till I rose to make the tea, and then it was only to say he should not take any. He continued lounging on the sofa, and alternately closing his eyes and looking at his watch and at me, till bed-time, when I rose, and took my candle and retired.

'Helen!' cried he, the moment I had left the room. I turned back, and stood awaiting his commands.

'What do you want, Arthur?' I said at length.

'Nothing,' replied he. 'Go!'

I went, but hearing him mutter something as I was closing the door, I turned again. It sounded very like 'confounded slut,' but I was quite willing it should be something else.

'Were you speaking Arthur?' I asked.

'No,' was the answer; and I shut the door and departed. I saw nothing more of him till the following morning at breakfast, when he came down a full hour after the usual time.

'You're very late,' was my morning's salutation.

'You needn't have waited for me,' was his; and he walked up to the window again. It was just such weather as yesterday.

'Oh, this confounded rain!' he muttered. But after studiously regarding it for a minute or two, a bright idea seemed to strike him, for he suddenly exclaimed, 'But I know what I'll do!' and then returned and took his seat at the table. The letter-bag was already there, waiting to be opened. He unlocked it and examined the contents, but said nothing about them.

'Is there anything for me?' I asked.

'No.'

He opened the newspaper and began to read.

'You'd better take your coffee,' suggested I; 'it will be cold again.'

'You may go,' said he, 'if you've done. I don't want you.'

I rose, and withdrew to the next room, wondering if we were to have another such miserable day as yesterday, and wishing intensely for an end of these mutually inflicted torments. Shortly after, I heard him ring the bell and give some orders about his wardrobe that sounded as if he meditated a long journey. He then sent for the coachman, and I heard something about the carriage and the horses, and London, and seven o'clock tomorrow morning, that startled and disturbed me not a little.

'I must not let him go to London, whatever comes of it,' said I to myself: 'he will run into all kinds of mischief, and I shall be the cause of it. But the question is, how am I to alter his purpose? – Well, I will wait awhile, and see if he mentions it.'

I waited most anxiously, from hour to hour; but not a word was spoken, on that or any other subject, to me. He whistled, and talked to his dogs, and wandered from room to room, much the same as on the previous day. At last I began to think I must introduce the subject myself, and was pondering how to bring it about, when John unwittingly came to my relief with the following message from the coachman.

'Please sir, Richard says one of the horses has got a very bad cold, and he thinks, sir, if you could make it convenient to go the day after tomorrow, instead of tomorrow, he could physic it today so as –'

'Confound his impudence!' interjected the master.

'Please sir, he says it would be a deal better if you could,' persisted John, 'for he hopes there'll be a change in the weather shortly, and he says it's not *likely*, when a horse is so bad with a cold, and physicked and all –'

'Devil take the horse!' cried the gentleman – 'Well, tell him I'll think about it,' he added, after a moment's reflection. He cast a searching glance at me, as the servant withdrew, expecting to see some token of deep astonishment and alarm; but, being previously prepared, I preserved an aspect of stoical indifference. His countenance fell as he met my steady gaze, and he turned away in very obvious disappointment, and walked up to the fireplace, where he stood in an attitude of undisguised dejection, leaning against the chimney-piece with his forehead sunk upon his arm.

'Where do you want to go, Arthur?' said I.

'To London,' replied he, gravely.

'What for?' I asked.

'Because I cannot be happy here.'

'Why not?'

'Because my wife doesn't love me.'

'She would love you with all her heart, if you deserved it.'

'What must I do to deserve it?'

This seemed humble and earnest enough; and I was so much affected, between sorrow and joy, that I was obliged to pause a few seconds before I could steady my voice to reply.

'If she gives you her heart,' said I, 'you must take it thankfully, and use it well, and not pull it in pieces, and laugh in her face, because she cannot snatch it away.'

He now turned round and stood facing me, with his back to the fire.

'Come then, Helen, are you going to be a good girl?'[4] said he.

This sounded rather too arrogant, and the smile that accompanied it did not please me. I therefore hesitated to reply. Perhaps, my former answer had implied too much: he had heard my voice falter, and might have seen me brush away a tear.

'Are you going to forgive me, Helen?' he resumed, more humbly.

'Are *you* penitent!' I replied, stepping up to him and smiling in his face.

'Heart-broken!' he answered, with a rueful countenance – yet with a merry smile just lurking within his eyes and about the corners of his mouth; but this could not repulse me, and I flew into his arms. He fervently embraced me and though I shed a torrent of tears, I think I never was happier in my life than at that moment.

'Then you won't go to London, Arthur?' I said, when the first transport of tears and kisses had subsided.

'No, love, – unless you will go with me.'

'I will, gladly,' I answered, 'if you think the change will amuse you, and if you will put off the journey till next week.'

He readily consented, but said there was no need of much preparation, as he should not be for staying long, for he did not wish me to be Londonized, and to lose my country freshness and originality by too much intercourse with the ladies of the world. I thought this folly; but I did not wish to contradict him now: I merely said that I was of very domestic habits, as he well knew, and had no particular wish to mingle with the world.

So we are to go to London on Monday, the day after tomorrow. It is now four days since the termination of our quarrel, and I'm sure it has done us both good: it has made me like Arthur a great deal better and made him behave a great deal better to me. He has never once attempted to annoy me, since, by the most distant allusion to Lady F— or any of those disagreeable reminiscences of his former life – I wish I could blot them from my memory, or else get him to regard such matters in the same light as I do. Well! it is something, however, to have made him see that they are not fit subjects for a conjugal jest. He may see farther sometime – I will put no limits to my hopes; and, in spite of my aunt's forebodings and my own unspoken fears, I trust we shall be happy yet.

CHAPTER 25

FIRST ABSENCE

On the eighth of April, we went to London; on the eighth of May I returned, in obedience to Arthur's wish: very much against my own, because I left him behind. If he had come with me, I should have been very glad to get home again, for he led me such a round of restless dissipation, while there, that, in that short space of time, I was quite tired out. He seemed bent upon displaying me to his friends and acquaintances in particular, and the public in general, on every possible occasion and to the greatest possible advantage. It was something to feel that he considered me a worthy object of pride; but I paid dear for the gratification, for in the first place, to please him, I had to violate my cherished predilections – my almost rooted principles in favour of a plain, dark, sober style of dress; I must sparkle in costly jewels and deck myself out like a painted butterfly, just as I had, long since, determined I would never do – and this was no trifling sacrifice; – in the second place, I was continually straining to satisfy his sanguine expectations and do honour to his choice, by my general conduct and deportment, and fearing to disappoint him by some awkward misdemeanour, or some trait of inexperienced ignorance about the customs of society, especially when I acted the part of hostess, which I was not unfrequently called upon to do; and in the third place, as I intimated before, I was wearied of the throng and bustle, the restless hurry and ceaseless change of a life so alien to all my previous habits. At last, he suddenly discovered that the London air did not agree with me, and I was languishing for my country home and must immediately return to Grassdale.

I laughingly assured him that the case was not so urgent as he appeared to think it, but I was quite willing to go home if he was. He replied that he should be obliged to remain a week or two longer, as he had business that required his presence.

'Then I will stay with you,' said I.

'But I can't do with you, Helen,' was his answer: 'as long as you stay, I shall attend to you and neglect my business.'

'But I won't let you,' I returned: 'now that I know you have business to attend to, I shall insist upon your attending to it, and letting me alone – and, to tell you the truth, I shall be glad of a little rest. I can take my rides and walks in the park as usual; and your business cannot occupy all your time; I shall see you at mealtimes and in the evenings, at least, and that will be better than being leagues away and never seeing you at all.'

'But my love, I cannot let you stay. How can I settle my affairs when I know that you are here, neglected –'

'I shall not feel myself neglected: while you are doing your duty, Arthur, I shall never complain of neglect. If you had told me, before, that you had anything to do, it would have been half done before this; and now you must make up for lost time by redoubled exertions. Tell me what it is; and I will be your taskmaster, instead of being a hindrance.'

'No, no,' persisted the impracticable creature; 'you *must* go home, Helen; I must have the satisfaction of knowing that you are safe and well, though far away. Don't I see that you are looking quite rakish?[1] – Your bright eyes are faded, and that tender, delicate bloom[2] has quite deserted your cheek.'

'That is only with too much gaiety and fatigue.'

'It is not, I tell you; it is the London air: you are pining for the fresh breezes of your country home – and you shall feel them, before you are two days older. And remember your situation, dearest Helen; on your health, you know, depends the health, if not the life of our future hope.'

'Then you really wish to get rid of me?'

'Positively, I do; and I will take you down myself to Grassdale, and then return. I shall not be absent above a week – or fortnight at most.'

'But if I must go, I will go alone: if you must stay, it is needless to waste your time in the journey there and back.'

But he did not like the idea of sending me alone.

'Why, what helpless creature do you take me for,' I replied, 'that you cannot trust me to go a hundred miles in our own carriage with our own footman and maid to attend me? If you come with me I shall assuredly keep you. But tell me, Arthur, what *is* this tiresome business; and why did you never mention it before?'

'It is only a little business with my lawyer,' said he; and he told me something about a piece of property he wanted to sell in order to pay off a part of the encumbrances on his estate; but either the account was a little confused or I was rather dull of comprehension, for I could not clearly understand how that should keep him in town a fortnight after me. Still less can I now comprehend how it should keep him a month – for it is nearly that time since I left him, and no signs of his return as yet. In every letter he promises to be with me in a few days, and every time deceives me – or deceives himself. His excuses are vague and insufficient. I cannot doubt that he is got among his former companions again – Oh, why did I leave him? I wish – I do intensely wish he would return!

June 29th. – No Arthur yet; and for many days I have been looking and longing in vain for a letter. His letters, when they come, are kind – if fair words and endearing epithets can give them a claim to the title – but very short, and full of trivial excuses and promises that I cannot trust; and yet how anxiously I look forward to them! how eagerly I open and devour one of those little, hastily scribbled returns for the three or four long letters, hitherto unanswered, he has had from me!

Oh, it is cruel to leave me so long alone! He knows I have no one but Rachel to speak to, for we have no neighbours here, except the Hargraves, whose residence I can dimly descry from these upper windows embosomed among those low, woody hills beyond the Dale. I was glad when I learnt that Milicent was so near us; and her company would be a soothing solace to me now, but she is still in town with her mother: there is no one at the grove but little Esther and her French governess, for Walter is always away. I saw that paragon of manly perfections in London: he seemed scarcely to merit the eulogiums of his mother and sister, though he certainly appeared more conversable and agreeable than Lord Lowborough, more candid and high-minded than Mr Grimsby, and more polished and gentlemanly than Mr Hattersley, Arthur's only other friend whom he judged fit to introduce to me – O Arthur, why won't you come! why won't you write to me at least! You talked about my health – how can you expect me to gather bloom and vigour here; pining in solitude and restless anxiety from day to day? – It would serve you right to come back and find my good looks entirely wasted away. I would beg my uncle and aunt, or my brother to come and see me, but I do not like to complain of my loneliness to them, – and indeed, loneliness is the least of my sufferings; but what is he doing – what is it that keeps him away? It is this ever-recurring question and the horrible suggestions it raises that distract me.

July 3rd. – My last bitter letter has wrung from him an answer at last, – and a rather longer one than usual; but still, I don't know what to make of it. He playfully abuses me for the gall and vinegar of my latest effusion, tells me I can have no conception of the multitudinous engagements that keep him away, but avers that, in spite of them all, he will assuredly be with me before the close of next week; though it is impossible for a man, so circumstanced as he is, to fix the precise day of his return: meantime, he exhorts me to the exercise of patience, 'that first of woman's virtues,'[3] and desires me to remember the saying, 'Absence makes the heart grow fonder,'[4] and comfort myself with the assurance that the longer he stays away, the better he shall love me when he returns; and till he does return, he begs I will continue to write to him constantly, for, though he is sometimes too idle and often too busy to answer my letters as they come, he likes to receive them daily, and if I fulfil my threat of punishing his seeming neglect by ceasing to write, he shall be so angry that he will do his utmost to forget me. He adds this piece of intelligence respecting poor Milicent Hargrave: –

'Your little friend Milicent is likely, before long, to follow your example, and take upon her the yoke of matrimony in conjunction with a friend of mine. Hattersley, you know, has not yet fulfilled his direful threat of throwing his precious person away on the first old maid that chose to evince a tenderness for him; but he still preserves a resolute determination to see himself a married man before the year is out: "Only," said he to me, "I must have somebody that will let me have my own way in everything – not like *your* wife, Huntingdon, she is a charming creature, but she looks as if she had a will of her own, and could play the vixen upon occasion," (I thought "you're right there, man," but I didn't say so.) "I must have some good, quiet soul that will let me just do what I like and go where I like, keep at home or stay away, without a word of reproach or complaint; for I can't do with being bothered." "Well," said I. "I know somebody that will suit you to a tee, if you don't care for money, and that's Hargrave's sister, Milicent." He desired to be introduced to her forthwith, for he said he had plenty of the needful himself – or should have, when his old governor[5] chose to quit the stage. So you see, Helen, I have managed pretty well, both for your friend and mine.'

Poor Milicent! But I cannot imagine she will ever be led to accept such a suitor – one so repugnant to all her ideas of a man to be honoured and loved.

5th. – Alas! I was mistaken. I have got a long letter from her this morning, telling me she is already engaged, and expects to be married before the close of the month.

'I hardly know what to say about it,' she writes, 'or what to think. To tell you the truth, Helen, I don't like the thought of it at all. If I *am* to be Mr Hattersley's wife, I must try to love him; and I do try with all my might; but I have made very little progress yet; and the worst symptom of the case is, that the further he is from me the better I like him: he frightens me with his abrupt manners and strange hectoring ways, and I dread the thought of marrying him. "Then why have you accepted him," you will ask; and I didn't know I had accepted him; but mamma tells me I have, and he seems to think so too. I certainly didn't mean to do so; but I did not like to give him a flat refusal for fear mamma should be grieved and angry, (for I knew she wished me to marry him) and I wanted to talk to her first about it, so I gave him what *I* thought was an evasive, half negative answer; but she says it was as good as an acceptance, and he would think me very capricious if I were to attempt to draw back – and indeed, I was so confused and frightened at the moment, I can hardly tell what I said. And next time I saw him, he accosted me in all confidence as his affianced bride, and immediately began to settle matters with mamma. I had not courage to contradict them then, and how can I do it now? I cannot: they would think me mad. Besides, mamma is so delighted with the idea of the match; she thinks she has managed so well for me; and I cannot bear to disappoint her. I do object sometimes, and tell her what I feel, but you don't know *how* she talks. Mr Hattersley, you know, is the son of a rich banker, and as Esther and I have no fortunes and Walter very little, our dear mamma is very anxious to see us all well married, that is, united to rich partners – it is not *my* idea of being well married, but she means it all for the best. She says when I am safe off her hands it will be such a relief to her mind; and she assures me it will be a good thing for the family as well as for me. Even Walter is pleased at the prospect, and when I confessed my reluctance·to him, he said it was all childish nonsense. Do *you* think it nonsense, Helen? I should not care if I could see any prospect of being able to love and admire him, but I can't. There is nothing about him to hang one's esteem and affection upon: he is so diametrically opposite to what I imagined my husband should be. Do write to me, and say all you can to encourage me. Don't attempt to dissuade me, for my fate is fixed: preparations for the important event are already going on around me; and don't say a word against Mr Hattersley, for I want to think well of him; and though I have spoken against him myself, it is for the last time: hereafter, I shall never permit myself to utter a word in his dispraise, however he may seem to deserve it; and whoever ventures to speak slightingly of the man I have promised to love, to honour, and obey, must expect my serious displeasure. After all, I think he is quite as good as Mr Huntingdon, if not better; and yet, you love *him*, and seem to be happy and contented; and perhaps I may manage as well. You must tell me, if you can, that Mr Hattersley is better than he seems – that he is upright, honourable, and open-hearted – in fact, a perfect diamond in the rough. He may be all this, but I don't know him – I know only the exterior and what I trust is the worst part of him.'

She concludes with 'Goodbye, dear Helen, I am waiting anxiously for your advice – but mind you let it be all on the right side.'

Alas! poor Milicent, what encouragement can I give you? – or what advice – except that it is better to make a bold stand now, though at the expense of disappointing and angering both mother and brother, and lover, than to devote your whole life, hereafter, to misery and vain regret?

Saturday, 13th. The week is over, and he is not come. All the sweet summer is passing away without one breath of pleasure to me or benefit to him. And I had all along been looking forward to this season with the fond, delusive hope that we should enjoy it so sweetly together; and that, with God's help and my exertions, it would be the means of elevating his mind, and refining his taste to a due appreciation of the salutary and pure delights of nature, and peace, and holy love. But now, – at evening, when I see the round, red sun sink quietly down behind those woody hills, leaving them sleeping in a warm, red, golden haze, I only think another lovely day is lost to him and me; – and at morning, when roused by the flutter and chirp of the sparrows, and the gleeful twitter of the swallows – all intent upon feeding their young, and full of life and joy in their own little frames – I open the window to inhale the balmy, soul-reviving air, and look out upon the lovely landscape, laughing in dew and sunshine, – I too often shame that glorious scene with tears of thankless misery, because *he* cannot feel its freshening influence; – and when I wander in the ancient woods, and meet the little wild-flowers smiling in my path, or sit in the shadow of our noble ash-trees by the waterside, with their branches gently swaying in the light summer breeze that murmurs through their feathery foliage – my ears full of that low music mingled with the dreamy hum of insects, my eyes abstractedly gazing on the glassy surface of the little lake before me, with the trees that crowd about its bank, some gracefully bending to kiss its waters, some rearing their stately heads high above, but stretching their wide arms over its margin, all faithfully mirrored far, far down in its glassy depth – though sometimes the images are partially broken by the sport of aquatic insects, and sometimes, for a moment, the whole is shivered into trembling fragments by a transient breeze that swept the surface too roughly, – still I have no pleasure; for the greater the happiness that nature sets before me, the more I lament that *he* is not here to taste it: the greater the bliss we might enjoy together, the more I feel our present wretchedness apart (yes, ours; he must be wretched, though he may not know it); and the more my senses are pleased, the more my heart is oppressed; for he keeps it with him confined amid the dust and smoke of London, – perhaps, shut up within the walls of his own abominable club.[6]

But most of all, at night, when I enter my lonely chamber, and look out upon the summer moon, 'sweet regent of the sky,'[7] floating above me in the 'black blue vault of heaven,'[8] shedding a flood of silver radiance over park, and wood, and water, so pure, so peaceful, so divine, – and think, 'Where is he now? – what is he doing at this moment? – wholly unconscious of this heavenly scene, – perhaps, revelling with his boon companions, perhaps –' God help me, it is too – *too* much!

23rd. Thank heaven, he is come at last! But how altered! – flushed and feverish, listless and languid, his beauty strangely diminished, his vigour and vivacity quite departed. I have not upbraided him by word or look; I have not even asked him what he has been doing. I have not the heart to do it, for I think he is ashamed of himself – he must be so indeed, – and such enquiries could not fail to be painful to both. My forbearance pleases him – touches him even, I am inclined to think. He says he is glad to be home again, and God knows how glad I am to get him back, even as he is. He lies on the sofa nearly all day long; and I play and sing to him for hours together. I write his letters for him, and get him everything he wants; and sometimes I read to him, and sometimes I talk, and sometimes only sit by him and soothe him with silent caresses. I know he does not deserve it; and I fear I am spoiling him; but this once, I will forgive him, freely and entirely – I will shame him into virtue if I can, and I will never let him leave me again.

He is pleased with my attentions – it may be, grateful for them.

He likes to have me near him; and, though he is peevish and testy with his servants and his dogs, he is gentle and kind to me. What he would be, if I did not so watchfully anticipate his wants, and so carefully avoid, or immediately desist from doing anything that has a tendency to irritate or disturb him, with however little reason, I cannot tell. How intensely I wish he were worthy of all this care! Last night as I sat beside him, with his head in my lap, passing my fingers through his beautiful curls, this thought made my eyes overflow with sorrowful tears – as it often does, – but this time, a tear fell on his face and made him look up. He smiled, but not insultingly.

'Dear Helen!' he said – 'why do you cry? you know that I love you' (and he pressed my hand to his feverish lips), 'and what more could you desire?'

'Only, Arthur, that you would love *yourself*, as truly and as faithfully as you are loved by me.'

'That would be hard indeed!' he replied, tenderly squeezing my hand.

I don't know whether he fully understood my meaning, but he smiled – thoughtfully and even sadly – a most unusual thing with him; – and then he closed his eyes and fell asleep, looking as careless and sinless as a child. As I watched that placid slumber, my heart swelled fuller than ever, and my tears flowed unrestrained.

August 24. Arthur is himself again, as lusty and reckless, as light of heart and head as ever, and as restless and hard to amuse as a spoilt child, – and almost as full of mischief too, especially when wet weather keeps him within doors. I wish he had something to do, some useful trade, or profession, or employment – anything to occupy his head or his hands for a few hours a day, and give him something besides his own pleasure to think about. If he would play the country gentleman, and attend to the farm – but that he knows nothing about, and won't give his mind to consider, – or if he would take up with some literary study, or learn to draw or to play – as he is so fond of music, I often try to persuade him to learn the piano, but he is far too idle for such an undertaking: he has no more idea of exerting himself to overcome obstacles than he has of restraining his natural appetites; and these two things are the ruin of him. I lay them both to the charge of his harsh yet careless father and his madly indulgent mother. If ever I am a mother I will zealously strive against this *crime* of over indulgence – I can hardly give it a milder name when I think of the evils it brings.

Happily, it will soon be the shooting season, and then, if the weather permit, he will find occupation enough in the pursuit and destruction of the partridges and pheasants: we have no grouse, or he might have been similarly occupied at this moment, instead of lying under the acacia tree pulling poor Dash's ears. But he says it is dull work shooting alone; he must have a friend or two to help him.

'Let them be tolerably decent then, Arthur,' said I – The word 'friend,' in his mouth makes me shudder: I know it was some of his 'friends' that induced him to stay behind me in London, and kept him away so long – indeed, from what he has unguardedly told me, or hinted from time to time, I cannot doubt that he frequently showed them my letters, to let them see how fondly his wife watched over his interests and how keenly she regretted his absence; and that they induced him to remain week after week, and to plunge into all manner of excesses to avoid being laughed at for a wife-ridden fool, and, perhaps, to show how far he could venture to go without danger of shaking the fond creature's devoted attachment. It is a hateful idea, but I cannot believe it is a false one.

'Well,' replied he, 'I thought of Lord Lowborough for one; but there is no possibility of getting him without his better half, our mutual friend Annabella; so we must ask them both. You're not afraid of her, are you Helen?' he asked, with a mischievous twinkle in his eyes.

'Of course not,' I answered: 'why should I? – And who besides?'

'Hargrave for one – he will be glad to come, though his own place is so near, for he has little enough land of his own to shoot over, and we can extend our depredations into it, if we like; – and he is thoroughly respectable, you know, Helen, quite a lady's man: – and I think, Grimsby for another: he's a decent, quiet fellow enough – you'll not object to Grimsby?'

'I hate him; but however, if you wish it, I'll try to endure his presence for a while.'

'All a prejudice Helen – a mere woman's antipathy.'

'No; I have solid grounds for my dislike. And is that all?'

'Why, yes, I think so. Hattersley will be too busy billing and cooing with his bride to have much time to spare for guns and dogs, at present,' he replied. – And that reminds me that I have had several letters from Milicent since her marriage, and that she either is or pretends to be quite reconciled to her lot. She professes to have discovered numberless virtues and perfections in her husband, some of which, I fear, less partial eyes would fail to distinguish, though they sought them carefully with tears;[9] and now that she is accustomed to his loud voice and abrupt, uncourteous manners, she affirms she finds no difficulty in loving him as a wife should do, and begs I will burn that letter wherein she spoke so unadvisedly against him. So that I trust she may yet be happy; but if she is, it will be entirely the reward of her own goodness of heart; for had she chosen to consider herself the victim of fate, or of her mother's worldly wisdom, she might have been thoroughly miserable; and, if, for duty's sake, she had not made every effort to love her husband, she would doubtless have hated him to the end of her days.

CHAPTER 26

THE GUESTS

Sept. 23rd. Our guests arrived about three weeks ago. Lord and Lady Lowborough have now been married above eight months; and I will do the lady the credit to say that her husband is quite an altered man: his looks, his spirits, and his temper are all perceptibly changed for the better since I last saw him. But there is room for improvement still. He is not always cheerful nor always contented, and she often complains of his ill-humour, which, however, of all persons, *she* ought to be the last to accuse him of, as he never displays it against her, except for such conduct as would provoke a saint. He adores her still, and would go to the world's end to please her. She knows her power, and she uses it too; but well knowing that to wheedle and coax is safer than to command, she judiciously tempers her despotism with flattery and blandishments enough to make him deem himself a favoured and a happy man. And yet, at times, a sombre shadow overclouds his brow even in her presence, but evidently the result of despondency rather than of ill-humour, and generally occasioned by some display of her ill-regulated temper or misguided mind – some wanton trampling upon his most cherished opinions – some reckless disregard of principle that makes him bitterly regret that she is not as good as she is charming and beloved. I pity him from my heart, for I know the misery of such regrets.

But she has another way of tormenting him, in which I am a fellow sufferer – or might be, if I chose to regard myself as such. This is by openly but not too glaringly coquetting with Mr Huntingdon, who is quite willing to be her partner in the game; but I don't care for it, because with him, I know there is nothing but personal vanity and a mischievous desire to excite my jealousy, and perhaps to torment his friend; and she, no doubt, is actuated by much the same motives; only there is more of malice and less of playfulness in *her* manoeuvres. It is obviously, therefore, my interest to disappoint them both, as far as I am concerned, by preserving a cheerful, undisturbed serenity throughout; and accordingly I endeavour to show the fullest confidence in my husband and the greatest indifference to the arts of my attractive guest. I have never reproached the former but once, and that was for laughing at Lord Lowborough's depressed and anxious countenance one evening, when they had both been particularly provoking; and then, indeed, I said a good deal on the subject, and rebuked him sternly enough; but he only laughed, and said –

'You can feel for him, Helen – can't you?'

'I can feel for anyone that is unjustly treated,' I replied, 'and I can feel for those that injure them too.'

'Why Helen, you are as jealous as he is!' cried he, laughing still more; and I found it impossible to convince him of his mistake. So from that time I have carefully refrained from any notice of the subject whatever, and left Lord Lowborough to take care of himself. He either has not the sense or the power to follow my example, though he does try to conceal his uneasiness as well as he can; but still, it will appear in his face, and his ill-humour will peep out at intervals, though not in the expression of open resentment – they never go far enough for that. But I confess I do feel jealous at times – most painfully, bitterly so – when she sings and plays to him, and he hangs over the instrument and dwells upon her voice with no affected interest; for then, I know he is really delighted, and I have no power to awaken similar fervour. I can amuse and please him with my simple songs, but not delight him thus.

I might retaliate if I chose, for Mr Hargrave is disposed to be very polite and attentive to me as his hostess – especially so when Arthur is the most neglectful, whether in mistaken compassion for me, or ambitious to show off his own good breeding by comparison with his friend's remissness, I cannot tell; but in either case, his civilities are highly distasteful to me. If Arthur is a little careless, of course it is unpleasant to have the fault exaggerated by contrast; and to be pitied as a neglected wife when I am not such, is an insult I can ill endure. But for hospitality's sake, I endeavour to suppress my impulse of scarcely reasonable resentment, and behave with decent civility to our guest, who, to give him his due, is by no means a disagreeable companion: he has good conversational powers and considerable information and taste, and talks about things that Arthur never could be brought to discuss, or to feel any interest in. But Arthur dislikes me to talk to him, and is visibly annoyed by his commonest acts of politeness; not that my husband has any unworthy suspicions of me – or of his friend either, as I believe – but he dislikes me to have any pleasure but in himself, any shadow of homage or kindness but such as he chooses to vouchsafe: he knows he is my sun, but when he chooses to withhold his light, he would have my sky to be all darkness; he cannot bear that I should have a moon to mitigate the deprivation.[1] This is unjust; and I am sometimes tempted to tease him accordingly; but I won't yield to the temptation: if he should carry his trifling with my feelings too far, I shall find some other means of checking him.

28th. – Yesterday we all went to the Grove, Mr Hargrave's much neglected home. His mother frequently asks us over that she may have the pleasure of her dear Walter's company; and this time she had invited us to a dinner party, and got together as many of the country gentry as were within reach to meet us. The entertainment was very well got up; but I could not help thinking about the cost of it all the time. I don't like Mrs Hargrave; she is a hard, pretentious, worldly-minded woman. She has money enough to live very comfortably, if she only knew how to use it judiciously, and had taught her son to do the same; but she is ever straining to keep up appearances, with that despicable pride that shuns the semblance of poverty as of a shameful crime. She grinds her dependants, pinches her servants, and deprives even her daughters and herself of the real comforts of life, because she will not consent to yield the palm in outward show to those who have three times her wealth, and, above all, because she is determined her cherished son shall be enabled to 'hold up his head with the highest gentleman in the land.' This same son, I imagine, is a man of expensive habits – no reckless spendthrift, and no abandoned sensualist, but one who likes to have 'everything handsome about him,'[2] and to go to 'a certain length in youthful indulgences – not so much to gratify his own tastes as to maintain his reputation as a man of fashion in the world, and a respectable fellow among his own lawless companions; while he is too selfish to consider how many comforts might be obtained for his fond mother and sisters with the money he thus wastes upon himself: as long as they can contrive to make a respectable appearance once a year when they come to town, he gives himself little concern about their private stintings and struggles at home. This is a harsh judgment to form of 'dear, noble-minded, generous-hearted Walter,' but I fear it is too just.

Mrs Hargrave's anxiety to make good matches for her daughters is partly the cause and partly the result of these errors: by making a figure in the world and showing them off to advantage, she hopes to obtain better chances for them; and by thus living beyond her legitimate means and lavishing so much on their brother, she renders them portionless, and makes them burdens on her hands. Poor Milicent, I fear, has already fallen a sacrifice to the manoeuvrings of this mistaken mother, who congratulates herself on having so satisfactorily discharged her maternal duty, and hopes to do as well for Esther. But Esther is a child as yet – a little merry romp of fourteen: as honest-hearted, and as guileless and simple as her sister, but with a fearless spirit of her own, that, I fancy, her mother will find some difficulty in bending to her purposes.

CHAPTER 27

A MISDEMEANOUR

October 9th. – While the gentlemen are ranging the woods and Lady Lowborough is busy writing her letters, I will return to my chronicle for the purpose of recording sayings and doings, the last of the kind I hope I shall ever have cause to describe.

It was on the night of the 4th, a little after tea, that Annabella had been singing and playing, with Arthur as usual at her side: she had ended her song, but still she sat at the instrument; and he stood leaning on the back of her chair, conversing in scarcely audible tones, with his face in very close proximity with hers. I looked at Lord Lowborough. He was at the other end of the room, talking with Messrs Hargrave and Grimsby; but I saw him dart towards his lady and his host a quick, impatient glance, expressive of intense disquietude, at which Grimsby smiled. Determined to interrupt the tête-à-tête, I rose, and, selecting a piece of music from the music-stand, stepped up to the piano, intending to ask the lady to play it; but I stood transfixed and speechless on seeing her seated there, listening with what seemed an exultant smile on her flushed face, to his soft murmurings, with her hand quietly surrendered to his clasp. The blood rushed first to my heart and then to my head – for there was more than this; almost at the moment of my approach, he cast a hurried glance over his shoulder towards the other occupants of the room, and then ardently pressed the unresisting hand to his lips. On raising his eyes he beheld me and dropped them again, confounded and dismayed. She saw me too, and confronted me with a look of hard defiance. I laid the music on the piano, and retired. I felt ill; but I did not leave the room: happily, it was getting late and could not be long before the company dispersed. I went to the fire and leant my head against the chimney-piece. In a minute or two, someone asked me if I felt unwell. I did not answer – indeed, at the time I knew not what was said – but I mechanically looked up, and saw Mr Hargrave standing beside me on the rug.

'Shall I get you a glass of wine?' said he.

'No, thank you,' I replied; and turning from him, I looked round. Lady Lowborough was beside her husband, bending over him as he sat, with her hand on his shoulder, softly talking and smiling in his face; and Arthur was at the table turning over a book of engravings. I seated myself in the nearest chair; and Mr Hargrave, finding his services were not desired, judiciously withdrew. Shortly after, the company broke up, and as the guests were retiring to their rooms, Arthur approached me, smiling with the utmost assurance.

'Are you *very* angry, Helen?' murmured he.

'This is no jest, Arthur,' said I seriously, but as calmly as I could – 'unless you think it a jest to lose my affection for ever.'

'What! so bitter?' he exclaimed, laughingly clasping my hand between both his; but I snatched it away, in indignation – almost in disgust, for he was obviously affected with wine.

'Then I must go down on my knees,' said he; and, kneeling before me with clasped hands uplifted in mock humiliation, he continued imploringly – 'Forgive me, Helen! – dear Helen forgive me, and I'll *never* do it again!' and, burying his face in his handkerchief, he affected to sob aloud.

Leaving him thus employed, I took my candle, and, slipping quietly from the room, hastened upstairs as fast as I could. But he soon discovered that I had left him, and rushing up after me, caught me in his arms, just as I had entered the chamber, and was about to shut the door in his face.

'No, no, by heaven, you shan't escape me so!' he cried. Then, alarmed at my agitation, he begged me not to put myself in such a passion, telling me I was white in the face, and should kill myself if I did so.

'Let me go then,' I murmured; and immediately he released me – and it was well he did, for I was really in a passion. I sunk into the easy-chair and endeavoured to compose myself, for I wanted to speak to him calmly. He stood beside me, but did not venture to touch me or to speak, for a few seconds; then, approaching a little nearer, he dropped on one knee – not in mock humility, but to bring himself nearer my level, and, leaning his hand on the arm of the chair, he began in a low voice –

'It is all nonsense, Helen – a jest, a mere nothing – not worth a thought. Will you *never* learn?' he continued more boldly, 'that you have nothing to fear from me? that I love you wholly and entirely? – or if,' he added with a lurking smile, 'I ever give a thought to another, you may well spare it, for those fancies are here and gone like a flash of lightning, while my love for you burns on steadily, and for ever like the sun. You little exorbitant tyrant, will not *that* –'

'Be quiet a moment, will you Arthur,' said I, 'and listen to me – and don't think I'm in a jealous fury: I am perfectly calm. Feel my hand.' And I gravely extended it towards him – but closed it upon his with an energy that seemed to disprove the assertion, and made him smile. 'You needn't smile, sir,' said I, still tightening my grasp, and looking steadfastly on him till he almost quailed before me. 'You may think it all very fine, Mr Huntingdon, to amuse yourself with rousing my jealousy; but take care you don't rouse my hate instead. And when you have once extinguished my love, you will find it no easy matter to kindle it again.'

'Well Helen, I won't repeat the offence. But I meant nothing by it, I assure you. I had taken too much wine, and I was scarcely myself, at the time.'

'You often take too much; – and that is another practice I detest.' He looked up astonished at my warmth. 'Yes,' I continued. 'I never mentioned it before, because I was ashamed to do so; but now I'll tell you that it distresses me, and may disgust me, if you go on and suffer the habit to grow upon you, as it will, if you don't check it in time. But the whole system of your conduct to Lady Lowborough, is not referable to wine; and this night you knew perfectly well what you were doing.'

'Well, I'm sorry for it,' replied he, with more of sulkiness than contrition: 'what more would you have?'

'You are sorry that I saw you, no doubt,' I answered coldly.

'If you had not seen me,' he muttered, fixing his eyes on the carpet, 'it would have done no harm.'

My heart felt ready to burst; but I resolutely swallowed back my emotion, and answered calmly. 'You think not?'

'No,' replied he, boldly. 'After all, what have I done? It's nothing – except as you choose to make it a subject of accusation and distress.'

'What would Lord Lowborough, your *friend* think, if he knew all? or what would you yourself think, if he or any other had acted the same part to me, throughout, as you have to Annabella?'

'I would blow his brains out.'

'Well then, Arthur, how can you call it nothing – an offence for which you would think yourself justified in blowing another man's brains out? Is it nothing to trifle with your friend's feelings and mine – to endeavour to steal a woman's affections from her husband – what he values more than his gold, and therefore what it is more dishonest to take? Are the marriage vows a jest; and is it nothing to make it your sport to break them, and to tempt another to do the same? Can I love a man that does such things, and coolly maintains it is nothing?'

'You are breaking your marriage vows yourself,'[1] said he, indignantly rising and pacing to and fro. 'You promised to honour and obey me, and now you attempt to hector over me, and threaten and accuse me and call me worse than a highwayman. If it were not for your situation Helen, I would not submit to it so tamely. I won't be dictated to by a woman, though she be my wife.'

'What will you do then? Will you go on till I hate you; and then accuse me of breaking my vows?'

He was silent a moment, and then replied,

'You never will hate me.' Returning and resuming his former position at my feet, he repeated more vehemently – 'You cannot hate me, as long as I love you.'

'But how can I believe that you love me, if you continue to act in this way? Just imagine yourself in my place: would *you* think I loved *you*, if *I* did so? Would you believe my protestations, and honour and trust me under such circumstances?'

'The cases are different,' he replied. 'It is a woman's nature to be constant – to love one and one only, blindly, tenderly, and for ever – bless them, dear creatures! and you above them all – but you must have some commiseration for us, Helen; you must give us a little more licence, for as Shakespeare has it –

> "However we do praise ourselves,
> Our fancies are more giddy and unfirm,
> More longing, wavering, sooner lost and won
> Than women's are."[2]

'Do you mean by that, that your fancies are lost to me, and won by Lady Lowborough?'

'No; Heaven is my witness that I think her mere dust and ashes in comparison with you, – and shall continue to think so, unless you drive me from you by too much severity. She is a daughter of earth; you are an angel of heaven; only be not too austere in your divinity, and remember that I am a poor, fallible mortal. Come now, Helen; won't you forgive me?' he said, gently taking my hand, and looking up with an innocent smile.

'If I do, you will repeat the offence.'

'I swear by –'

'Don't swear; I'll believe your word as well as your oath. I wish I could have confidence in either.'

'Try me then, Helen: only trust and pardon me this once, and you shall see! Come, I am in hell's torments till you speak the word.'

I did not speak it, but I put my hand on his shoulder and kissed his forehead, and then burst into tears. He embraced me tenderly; and we have been good friends ever since. He has been decently temperate at table, and well-conducted towards Lady Lowborough. The first day, he held himself aloof from her, as far as he could without any flagrant breach of hospitality: since that, he has been friendly and civil but nothing more – in my presence, at least, nor, I think, at any other time; for she seems haughty and displeased, and Lord Lowborough is manifestly more cheerful, and more cordial towards his host than before. But I shall be glad when they are gone, for I have so little love for Annabella that it is quite a task to be civil to her, and as she is the only woman here besides myself, we are necessarily thrown so much together. Next time Mrs Hargrave calls, I shall hail her advent as quite a relief. I have a good mind to ask Arthur's leave to invite the old lady to stay with us till our guests depart. I think I will. She will take it as a kind attention, and, though I have little relish for her society, she will be truly welcome as a third to stand between Lady Lowborough and me.

The first time the latter and I were alone together, after that unhappy evening, was an hour or two after breakfast on the following day, when the gentlemen were gone out after the usual time spent in the writing of letters, the reading of newspapers, and desultory conversation. We sat silent for two or three minutes. She was busy with her work and I was running over the columns of a paper from which I had extracted all the pith some twenty minutes before. It was a moment of painful embarrassment to me, and I thought it must be infinitely more so to her; but it seems I was mistaken. She was the first to speak; and, smiling with the coolest assurance, she began, –

'Your husband was merry last night, Helen: is he often so?'

My blood boiled in my face; but it was better she should seem to attribute his conduct to this than to anything else.

'No,' replied I, 'and never will be so again I trust.'

'You gave him a curtain lecture,[3] did you?'

'No; but I told him I disliked such conduct, and he promised me not to repeat it.'

'I *thought* he looked rather subdued this morning,' she continued; 'and you, Helen; you've been weeping I see – that's our grand resource, you know – but doesn't it make your eyes smart? – and do you always find it to answer?'

'I never cry for effect; nor can I conceive how anyone can.'

'Well, I don't know: I never had occasion to try it; – but I think if Lowborough were to commit such improprieties, I'd make *him* cry. I don't wonder at your being angry, for I'm sure I'd give my husband a lesson he would not soon forget for a lighter offence than that. But then he never *will* do anything of the kind; for I keep him in too good order for that.'

'Are you sure you don't arrogate too much of the credit to

yourself? Lord Lowborough was quite as remarkable for his abstemiousness for some time before you married him, as he is now, I have heard.'

'Oh, about the *wine* you mean – yes, he's safe enough for that. And as to looking askance to another woman – he's safe enough for that too, while I live, for he worships the very ground I tread on.'

'Indeed! and are you sure you deserve it?'

'Why, as to that, I can't say: you know we're all fallible creatures, Helen; we none of us deserve to be worshipped. But are *you* sure your darling Huntingdon deserves all the love you give to *him*?'

I knew not what to answer to this. I was burning with anger; but I suppressed all outward manifestations of it, and only bit my lip and pretended to arrange my work.

'At any rate,' resumed she, pursuing her advantage, 'you can console yourself with the assurance that *you* are worthy of all the love he gives to you.'

'You flatter me,' said I; 'but at least, I can try to be worthy of it.' And then I turned the conversation.

CHAPTER 28

PARENTAL FEELINGS

December 25th. – Last Christmas I was a bride, with a heart overflowing with present bliss, and full of ardent hopes for the future – though not unmingled with foreboding fears. Now I am a wife: my bliss is sobered, but not destroyed; my hopes diminished, but not departed; my fears increased but not yet thoroughly confirmed; – and, thank Heaven, I am a mother too. God has sent me a soul to educate for heaven, and given me a new and calmer bliss, and stronger hopes to comfort me. But where hope rises, fear *must* lurk behind, and when I clasp my little darling to my breast, or hang over his slumbers with unutterable delight, and a world of hope within my heart, one of two thoughts is ever at hand to check my swelling bliss; the one: 'He may be taken from me;'[1] the other: 'He may live to curse his own existence.'[2] In the first, I have this consolation: that the bud, though plucked, would not be withered, only transplanted to a fitter soil to ripen and blow beneath a brighter sun; and though I might not cherish and watch my child's unfolding intellect, he would be snatched away from all the suffering and sins of earth; and my understanding tells me this would be no great evil; but my heart shrinks from the contemplation of such a possibility, and whispers I could not bear to see him die, and relinquish to the cold and cruel grave this cherished form, now warm with tender life, flesh of my flesh and shrine of that pure spark[3] which it should be my life's sweet labour to keep unsullied from the world, – and ardently implores that heaven would spare him still, to be my comfort and my joy, and me to be his shield, instructor, friend – to guide him along the perilous path of youth, and train him to be God's servant while on earth, a blessed and honoured saint in heaven. But in the other case, if he should live to disappoint my hopes, and frustrate all my efforts – to be a slave of sin, the victim of vice and misery, a curse to others and himself – Eternal Father, if Thou beholdest such a life before him, tear him from me now in spite of all my anguish, and take him from my bosom to thine own, while he is yet a guileless, unpolluted lamb!

My little Arthur! there you lie in sweet, unconscious slumber, the tiny epitome of your father, but stainless yet as that pure snow, new-fallen from heaven – God shield thee from his errors! How will I watch and toil to guard thee from them! He wakes; his tiny arms are stretched towards me; his eyes unclose; they meet my gaze, but will not answer it. Little angel![4] you do not know me; you cannot think of me or love me yet; and yet how fervently my heart is knit to yours; how grateful I am for all the joy you give me! Would that your father could share it with me – that he could feel my love, my hope, and take an equal part in my resolves and projects for the future – nay, if he could but sympathize in half my views, and share one half my feelings, it would be indeed a blessing to both himself and me: it would elevate and purify his mind, and bind him closer to his home and me.

Perhaps, he will feel awakening interest and affection for his child as it grows older. At present, he is pleased with the acquisition, and hopes it will become a fine boy and a worthy heir; and that is nearly all I can say. At first, it was a thing to wonder and laugh at, not to touch: now, it is an object almost of indifference, except when his impatience is roused by its 'utter helplessness' and 'imperturbable stupidity' (as he calls it), or my too close attention to its wants. He frequently comes and sits beside me while I am busied with my maternal cares. I hoped at first it was for the pleasure of contemplating our priceless treasure; but I soon found it was only to enjoy my company, or escape the pains of solitude. He is kindly welcome of course, but the best compliment to a mother is to appreciate her little one. He shocked me very much on one occasion: it was about a fortnight after the birth of our son, and he was with me in the nursery. We had neither of us spoken for some time: I was lost in the contemplation of my nursling, and I thought he was similarly occupied – as far, at least, as I thought about him at all. But suddenly he startled me from my reverie by impatiently exclaiming, –

'Helen, I shall positively hate that little wretch, if you worship it so madly! You are absolutely infatuated about it.'[5]

I looked up in astonishment, to see if he could be in earnest.

'You have not a thought to spare for anything else,' he continued in the same strain: 'I may go or come, be present or absent, cheerful or sad; it's all the same to you. As long as you have that ugly little creature to dote upon, you care not a farthing what becomes of me.'

'It is false, Arthur; when you enter the room, it always doubles my happiness; when you are near me, the sense of your presence delights me, though I don't look at you; and when I think about our child, I please myself with the idea that you share my thoughts and feelings, though I don't speak them.'

'How the devil can I waste my thoughts and feelings on a little worthless idiot like that?'

'It is your own son Arthur, – or, if that consideration has no weight with you, it is mine; and you ought to respect my feelings.'

'Well, don't be cross; it was only a slip of the tongue,' pleaded he. 'The little fellow is well enough, only I can't worship him as you do.'

'You shall nurse him for me, as a punishment,' said I, rising to put my baby in its father's arms.

'No, don't, Helen – don't!' cried he, in real disquietude.

'I will: you'll love him better, when you feel the little creature in your arms.'

I deposited the precious burden in his hands, and retreated to the other side of the room, laughing at the ludicrous, half embarrassed air with which he sat, holding it at arm's length, and looking upon it as if it were some curious being of quite a different species to himself.

'Come, take it, Helen; take it,' he cried at length. 'I shall drop it, if you don't.'

Compassionating his distress – or rather the child's unsafe position – I relieved him of the charge.

'Kiss it, Arthur; do – you've never kissed it yet!' said I, kneeling and presenting it before him.

'I would rather kiss its mother,' replied he, embracing me. 'There now; won't that do as well?'

I resumed my seat in the easy chair, and gave my little one a shower of gentle kisses to make up for its other parent's refusal.

'There goes!' cried the jealous father. 'That's more, in one minute, lavished on that little senseless, thankless oyster, than you have given me these three weeks past.'

'Come here then, you insatiable monopolist, and you shall have as many as you like, incorrigible and undeserving as you are. – There now, won't that suffice? I have a good mind never to give you another till you have learnt to love my baby as a father should.'

'I like the little devil –'

'Arthur!'

'Well, the little angel – well enough,' and he pinched its delicate little nose to prove his affection, 'only I can't *love* it – what is there to love? It can't love me – or you either; it can't understand a single word you say to it, or feel one spark of gratitude for all your kindness. Wait till it can show some little affection for me, and then I'll see about loving it. At present it is nothing more than a little selfish, senseless sensualist, and if *you* see anything adorable in it, it's all very well – I only wonder how you can.'

'If you were less selfish yourself, Arthur, you would not regard it in that light.'

'Possibly not, love; but so it is: there's no help for it.'

CHAPTER 29

THE NEIGHBOUR

Dec. 25th, 1823. Another year is gone. My little Arthur lives and thrives. He is healthy but not robust, full of gentle playfulness and vivacity, already affectionate, and susceptible of passions and emotions it will be long ere he can find words to express. He has won his father's heart at last; and now my constant terror is, lest he should be ruined by that father's thoughtless indulgence. But I must beware of my own weakness too, for I never knew till now how strong are a parent's temptations to spoil an only child.

I have need of consolation in my son, for (to this silent paper I may confess it) I have but little in my husband. I love him still; and he loves me, in his own way – but oh, how different from the love I could have given, and once had hoped to receive! how little real sympathy there exists between us; how many of my thoughts and feelings are gloomily cloistered within my own mind; how much of my higher and better self is indeed unmarried – doomed either to harden and sour in the sunless shade of solitude, or to quite degenerate and fall away for lack of nutriment in this unwholesome soil! – But, I repeat, I have no right to complain: only let me state the truth – some of the truth at least, – and see hereafter, if any darker truths will blot these pages. We have now been full two years united – the 'romance' of our attachment must be worn away. Surely I have now got down to the lowest gradation in Arthur's affection, and discovered all the evils of his nature: if there be any further change, it must be for the better, as we become still more accustomed to each other: surely we shall find no lower depth than this. And, if so, I can bear it well – as well, at least, as I have borne it hitherto.

Arthur is not what is commonly called a *bad* man: he has many good qualities; but he is a man without self-restraint or lofty aspirations – a lover of pleasure, given up to animal enjoyments: he is not a bad husband, but his notions of matrimonial duties and comforts are not my notions. Judging from appearances, his idea of a wife is a thing to love one devotedly and to stay at home – to wait upon her husband, and amuse him and minister to his comfort in every possible way, while he chooses to stay with her; and, when he is absent, to attend to his interests, domestic or otherwise, and patiently wait his return; no matter how he may be occupied in the meantime.

Early in spring, he announced his intention of going to London: his affairs there demanded his attendance, he said, and he could refuse it no longer. He expressed his regret at having to leave me, but hoped I would amuse myself with the baby till he returned.

'But why leave me?' I said. 'I can go with you: I can be ready at any time.'

'You would not take that child to town?'

'Yes – why not?'

The thing was absurd: the air of the town would be certain to disagree with him, and with me as a nurse; the late hours and London habits would not suit me under such circumstances; and altogether he assured me that it would be excessively troublesome, injurious, and unsafe. I overruled his objections as well as I could, for I trembled at the thought of his going alone, and would sacrifice almost anything for myself, much even for my child, to prevent it; but at length he told me, plainly, and somewhat testily, that he could not do with me: he was worn out with the baby's restless nights,[1] and must have some repose. I proposed separate apartments; but it would not do.

'The truth is, Arthur,' I said at last, 'you are weary of my company, and determined not to have me with you. You might as well have said so at once.'

He denied it; but I immediately left the room, and flew to the nursery to hide my feelings, if I could not soothe them, there.

I was too much hurt to express any further dissatisfaction with his plans, or at all to refer to the subject again, except for the necessary arrangements concerning his departure and the conduct of affairs during his absence, – till the day before he went, when I earnestly exhorted him to take care of himself and keep out of the way of temptation. He laughed at my anxiety, but assured me there was no cause for it, and promised to attend to my advice.

'I suppose it is no use asking you to fix a day for your return?' said I.

'Why, no: I hardly can, under the circumstances; but be assured, love, I shall not be long away.'

'I don't wish to keep you a prisoner at home,' I replied: 'I should not grumble at your staying whole months away – if you can be happy so long without me – provided I knew you were safe; but I don't like the idea of your being there, among your friends, as you call them.'

'Pooh, pooh, you silly girl! Do you think I can't take care of myself?'

'You didn't last time. – But THIS time, Arthur,' I added, earnestly, 'show me that you can, and teach me that I need not fear to trust you!'

He promised fair, but in such a manner as we seek to soothe a child. And did he keep his promise? No; – and, henceforth, *I can never trust his word.* Bitter, bitter confession! Tears blind me while I write. It was early in March that he went, and he did not return till July. This time, he did not trouble himself to make excuses as before, and his letters were less frequent, and shorter and less affectionate, especially after the first few weeks: they came slower and slower, and more terse and careless every time. But still, when *I* omitted writing he complained of my neglect. When I wrote sternly and coldly, as I confess I frequently did at the last, he blamed my harshness, and said it was enough to scare him from his home; when I tried mild persuasion, he was a little more gentle in his replies, and promised to return; but I had learnt, at last, to disregard his promises.

Those were four miserable months, alternating between intense anxiety, despair, and indignation; pity for him, and pity for myself. And yet, through all, I was not wholly comfortless; I had my darling, sinless, inoffensive little one to console me, but even this consolation was embittered by the constantly recurring thought, 'How shall I teach him, hereafter, to respect his father, and yet to avoid his example?'

But I remembered that I had brought all these afflictions, in a manner wilfully, upon myself; and I determined to bear them without a murmur. At the same time I resolved not to give myself up to misery for the transgressions of another, and endeavoured to divert myself as much as I could; and besides the companionship of my child and my dear, faithful Rachel, who evidently guessed my sorrows and felt for them, though she was too discreet to allude to them, – I had my books and pencil, my domestic affairs, and the welfare and comfort of Arthur's poor tenants and labourers to attend to; and I sometimes sought and obtained amusement in the company of my young friend Esther Hargrave: occasionally, I rode over to see her, and once or twice I had her to spend the day with me at the manor. Mrs Hargrave did not visit London that season: having no daughter to marry, she thought it as well to stay at home and economize; and, for a wonder, Walter came down to join her in the beginning of June and stayed till near the close of August.

The first time I saw him was on a sweet, warm evening, when I was sauntering in the park with little Arthur and Rachel, who is head-nurse and lady's-maid in one – for, with my secluded life and tolerably active habits, I require but little attendance, and, as she had nursed me and coveted to nurse my child, and was moreover so very trustworthy, I preferred committing the important charge to her, with a young nursery-maid under her directions, to engaging anyone else: – besides it saves money; and since I have made acquaintance with Arthur's affairs, I have learnt to regard that as no trifling recommendation; for, by my own desire, nearly the whole of the income of my fortune is devoted, for years to come, to the paying off of his debts, and the money he contrives to squander away in London is incomprehensible. – But to return to Mr Hargrave: – I was standing with Rachel beside the water, amusing the laughing baby in her arms with a twig of willow laden with golden catkins, when greatly to my surprise, he entered the park, mounted on his costly black hunter, and crossed over the grass to meet me. He saluted me with a very fine compliment, delicately worded, and modestly delivered withal, which he had doubtless concocted as he rode along. He told me he had brought a message from his mother, who, as he was riding that way, had desired him to call at the manor and beg the pleasure of my company to a friendly, family dinner tomorrow.

'There is no one to meet but ourselves,' said he; 'but Esther is very anxious to see you; and my mother fears you will feel solitary in this great house so much alone, and wishes she could persuade you to give her the pleasure of your company more frequently, and make yourself at home in our more humble dwelling, till Mr Huntingdon's return shall render this a little more conducive to your comfort.'

'She is very kind,' I answered, 'but I am not alone, you see; – and those, whose time is fully occupied, seldom complain of solitude.'

'Will you not come tomorrow, then? She will be sadly disappointed if you refuse.'

I did not relish being thus compassionated for my loneliness; but, however, I promised to come.

'What a sweet evening this is!' observed he, looking round upon the sunny park, with its imposing swell and slope, its placid water, and majestic clumps of trees. 'And what a paradise you live in!'

'It is a lovely evening,' answered I; and I sighed to think how little I had felt its loveliness, and how little of a paradise sweet Grassdale was to me – how still less to the voluntary exile from its scenes. Whether Mr Hargrave divined my thoughts, I cannot tell, but, with a half-hesitating, sympathizing seriousness of tone and manner, he asked if I had lately heard from Mr Huntingdon.

'Not lately,' I replied.

'I thought not,' he muttered, as if to himself, looking thoughtfully on the ground.

'Are you not lately returned from London?' I asked.

'Only yesterday.'

'And did you see him there?'

'Yes – I saw him.'

'Was he well?'

'Yes – that is,' said he, with increasing hesitation and an appearance of suppressed indignation, 'he was as well as – as he deserved to be, but under circumstances I should have deemed incredible for a man so favoured as he is.' He here looked up and pointed the sentence with a serious bow to me. I suppose my face was crimson.

'Pardon me, Mrs Huntingdon,' he continued, 'but I cannot suppress my indignation when I behold such infatuated blindness and perversion of taste; – but, perhaps you are not aware –' He paused.

'I am aware of nothing sir – except that he delays his coming longer than I expected; and if at present, he prefers the society of his friends to that of his wife, and the dissipations of the town to the quiet of country life, I suppose I have those friends to thank for it. *Their* tastes and occupations are similar to his, and I don't see why his conduct should awaken either their indignation or surprise.'

'You wrong me cruelly,' answered he: 'I have shared but little of Mr Huntingdon's society, for the last few weeks; and as for his tastes and occupations, they are quite beyond me – lonely wanderer as I am. Where I have but sipped and tasted, he drains the cup to the dregs; and if ever for a moment I have sought to drown the voice of reflection in madness and folly, or if I have wasted too much of my time and talents among reckless and dissipated companions, God knows I would gladly renounce them entirely and for ever, if I had but *half* the blessings that man so thanklessly casts behind his back – but *half* the inducements to virtue and domestic orderly habits that he despises – but *such* a home, and *such* a partner to share it! – It is infamous!' he muttered between his teeth. 'And don't think, Mrs Huntingdon,' he added aloud, 'that I could be guilty of inciting him to persevere in his present pursuits: on the contrary, I have remonstrated with him again and again; I have frequently expressed my surprise at his conduct and reminded him of his duties and his privileges – but to no purpose; he only –'

'Enough, Mr Hargrave; you ought to be aware that whatever my husband's faults may be, it can only aggravate the evil for me to hear them from a stranger's lips.'

'*Am* I then a stranger?' said he in a sorrowful tone. 'I am your nearest neighbour, your son's godfather, and your husband's friend: may I not be yours also?'

'Intimate acquaintance must precede real friendship: I know but little of you, Mr Hargrave, except from report.'

'Have you then forgotten the six or seven weeks I spent under your roof last autumn? *I* have not forgotten them. And I know enough of *you*, Mrs Huntingdon, to think that your husband is the most enviable man in the world, and I should be the next if you would deem me worthy of your friendship.'

'If you knew more of me, you would not think it – or if you did, you would not say it, and expect me to be flattered by the compliment.'

I stepped backward as I spoke. He saw that I wished the conversation to end; and immediately taking the hint, he gravely bowed, wished me good evening, and turned his horse towards the road. He appeared grieved and hurt at my unkind reception of his sympathizing overtures. I was not sure that I had done right in speaking so harshly to him; but at the time, I had felt irritated – almost insulted by his conduct; it seemed as if he was presuming upon the absence and neglect of my husband, and insinuating even more than the truth against him.

Rachel had moved on, during our conversation, to some yards distance. He rode up to her, and asked to see the child. He took it carefully into his arms, looked upon it with an almost paternal smile, and I heard him say, as I approached –

'And this too, he has forsaken!'

He then tenderly kissed it, and restored it to the gratified nurse.

'Are you fond of children, Mr Hargrave?' said I, a little softened towards him.

'Not in general,' he replied; 'but that is such a *sweet* child – and so like its mother,' he added in a lower tone.

'You are mistaken there; it is its father it resembles.'

'Am I not right, nurse?' said he, appealing to Rachel.

'I think, sir, there's a bit of both,' she replied.

He departed; and Rachel pronounced him a very nice gentleman. I had still my doubts on the subject.

When I met him on the morrow, under his own roof, he did not offend me with any more of his virtuous indignation against Arthur or unwelcome sympathy for me; and, indeed, when his mother began, in guarded terms, to intimate her sorrow and surprise at my husband's conduct, he, perceiving my annoyance, instantly came to the rescue, and delicately turned the conversation, at the same time warning her, by a sidelong glance, not to recur to the subject again. He seemed bent upon doing the honours of his house in the most unexceptionable manner, and exerting all his powers for the entertainment of his guest, and the display of his own qualifications as a host, a gentleman, and a companion; and actually succeeded in making himself very agreeable – only that he was too polite. – And yet, Mr Hargrave, I don't much like you; there is a certain want of openness about you that does not take my fancy, and a lurking selfishness, at the bottom of all your fine qualities, that I do not intend to lose sight of. No; for, instead of combating my slight prejudice against you as uncharitable, I mean to cherish it, until I am convinced that I have no reason to distrust this kind, insinuating friendship you are so anxious to push upon me.

In the course of the following six weeks, I met him several times, but always, save once, in company with his mother or his sister, or both. When I called on them, he always happened to be at home, and when they called on me, it was always he that drove them over in the phaeton. His mother, evidently, was quite delighted with his dutiful attentions and newly acquired domestic habits.

The time that I met him alone was on a bright but not oppressively hot day in the beginning of July: I had taken little Arthur into the wood that skirts the park, and there seated him on the moss-cushioned roots of an old oak; and, having gathered a handful of bluebells and wild roses, I was kneeling before him, and presenting them, one by one, to the grasp of his tiny fingers; enjoying the heavenly beauty of the flowers, through the medium of his smiling eyes; forgetting, for the moment, all my cares, laughing at his gleeful laughter, and delighting myself with his delight, – when a shadow suddenly eclipsed the little space of sunshine on the grass before us; and, looking up, I beheld Walter Hargrave standing and gazing upon us.

'Excuse me, Mrs Huntingdon,' said he, 'but I was spellbound; I had neither the power to come forward and interrupt you, nor to withdraw from the contemplation of such a scene. – How vigorous my little godson grows! and how merry he is this morning.' He approached the child and stooped to take his hand; but, on seeing that his caresses were likely to produce tears and lamentations instead of a reciprocation of friendly demonstrations, he prudently drew back.

'What a pleasure and comfort that little creature must be to you, Mrs Huntingdon!' he observed with a touch of sadness in his intonation, as he admiringly contemplated the infant.

'It is,' replied I; and then I asked after his mother and sister.

He politely answered my enquiries, and then returned again to the subject I wished to avoid; though with a degree of timidity that witnessed his fear to offend.

'You have not heard from Huntingdon lately?' he said.

'Not this week,' I replied. – Not these three weeks, I might have said.

'I had a letter from him this morning. I wish it were such a one as I could show to his lady.' He half drew from his waistcoat pocket a letter with Arthur's still beloved hand on the address, scowled at it, and put it back again, adding – 'But he tells me he is about to return next week.'

'He tells *me* so every time he writes.'

'Indeed! – Well it is like him. – But to *me* he always avowed it his intention to stay till the present month.'

It struck me like a blow, this proof of premeditated transgression and systematic disregard of truth.

'It is only of a piece with the rest of his conduct,' observed Mr Hargrave, thoughtfully regarding me, and reading, I suppose, my feelings in my face.

'Then he is really coming next week?' said I, after a pause.

'You may rely upon it – if the assurance can give you any pleasure. – And is it *possible*, Mrs Huntingdon, that you can rejoice at his return?' he exclaimed, attentively perusing my features again.

'Of course, Mr Hargrave; is he not my husband?'

'Oh, Huntingdon, you know not *what* you slight!' he passionately murmured.

I took up my baby and, wishing him good morning, departed, to indulge my thoughts unscrutinized, within the sanctum of my home.

And *was* I glad? – Yes, delighted; – though I was angered by Arthur's conduct, and though I felt that he had wronged me, and was determined he should feel it too.

CHAPTER 30

DOMESTIC SCENES

On the following morning, I received a few lines from him myself, confirming Hargrave's intimations respecting his approaching return. And he did come next week, but in a condition of body and mind even worse than before. I did not however intend to pass over his derelictions this time without a remark; – I found it would not do. But the first day, he was weary with his journey, and I was glad to get him back; I would not upbraid him then; I would wait till tomorrow. Next morning, he was weary still: I would wait a little longer. But at dinner, when, after breakfasting at twelve o'clock on a bottle of soda-water and a cup of strong coffee, and lunching at two on another bottle of soda-water mingled with brandy, he was finding fault with everything on the table and declaring we must change our cook – I thought the time was come.

'It is the same cook as we had before you went, Arthur,' said I. 'You were generally pretty well satisfied with her then.'

'You must have been letting her get into slovenly habits then, while I was away. It is enough to poison one – eating such a disgusting mess!' And he pettishly pushed away his plate, and leant back despairingly in his chair.

'I think it is you that are changed, not she,' said I, but with the utmost gentleness, for I did not wish to irritate him.

'It may be so,' he replied carelessly, as he seized a tumbler of wine and water, adding, when he had tossed it off – 'for I have an infernal fire in my veins, that all the waters of the ocean cannot quench!'

'What kindled it?' I was about to ask, but at that moment the butler entered and began to take away the things.

'Be quick Benson – do have done with that infernal clatter!' cried his master – 'And *don't* bring the cheese! – unless you want to make me sick outright.'

Benson, in some surprise, removed the cheese, and did his best to effect a quiet and speedy clearance of the rest, but, unfortunately, there was a rumple in the carpet, caused by the hasty pushing back of his master's chair, at which he tripped and stumbled, causing a rather alarming concussion with the trayful of crockery in his hands, but no positive damage, save the fall and breaking of a sauce-tureen; – but, to my unspeakable shame and dismay, Arthur turned furiously around upon him, and swore at him with savage coarseness. The poor man turned pale, and visibly trembled as he stooped to pick up the fragments.

'He couldn't help it, Arthur,' said I; 'the carpet caught his foot – and there's no great harm done. Never mind the pieces now, Benson, you can clear them away afterwards.'

Glad to be released, Benson expeditiously set out the dessert and withdrew.

'What *could* you mean, Helen, by taking the servant's part against me,' said Arthur, as soon as the door was closed, 'when you knew I was distracted?'

'I did not know you were distracted, Arthur, and the poor man was quite frightened and hurt at your sudden explosion.'

'Poor man indeed! and do you think I could stop to consider the feelings of an insensate brute like that, when my own nerves were racked and torn to pieces by his confounded blunders?'

'I never heard you complain of your nerves before.'

'And why shouldn't I have nerves as well as you?'

'Oh, I don't dispute your claim to their possession, but *I* never complain of mine.'

'No – how should you, when you never do anything to try them?'

'Then why do you try yours, Arthur?'

'Do you think I have nothing to do but to stay at home and take care of myself like a woman?'

'Is it impossible then, to take care of yourself like a man when you go abroad? You told me that you could – and would too; and you promised –'

'Come, come, Helen, don't begin with that nonsense now; I can't bear it.'

'Can't bear what? – to be reminded of the promises you have broken?'

'Helen, you are cruel. If you knew how my heart throbbed, and how every nerve thrilled through me while you spoke, you would spare me. You can pity a dolt of a servant for breaking a dish; but you have no compassion for *me*, when my head is split in two and all on fire with this consuming fever.'

He leant his head on his hand, and sighed. I went to him and put my hand on his forehead. It was burning indeed.

'Then come with me into the drawing-room, Arthur; and don't take any more wine; you have taken several glasses since dinner, and eaten next to nothing all the day. How can *that* make you better?'

With some coaxing and persuasion, I got him to leave the table. When the baby was brought I tried to amuse him with that; but poor little Arthur was cutting his teeth, and his father could not bear his complaints; sentence of immediate banishment was passed upon him on the first indication of fretfulness; and, because, in the course of the evening, I went to share his exile for a little while, I was reproached, on my return, for preferring my child to my husband. I found the latter reclining on the sofa just as I had left him.

'Well!' exclaimed the injured man, in a tone of pseudo-resignation. 'I thought I wouldn't send for you; I thought I'd just see – how long it would please you to leave me alone.'

'I have not been *very* long, have I, Arthur? I have not been an hour, I'm sure.'

'Oh, of course, an hour is nothing to you, so pleasantly employed; but to *me* –'

'It has not been pleasantly employed,' interrupted I. 'I have been nursing our poor little baby, who is very far from well, and I could not leave him till I got him to sleep.'

'Oh to be sure, you're overflowing with kindness and pity for everything but me.'

'And why should I pity *you*? what is the matter with you?'

'Well! that passes everything! After all the wear and tear that I've had, when I come home sick and weary, longing for comfort, and expecting to find attention and kindness, at least, from my wife, – she calmly asks what is the matter with me!'

'There is *nothing* the matter with you,' returned I, 'except what you have wilfully brought upon yourself against my earnest exhortation and entreaty.'

'Now, Helen,' said he, emphatically, half rising from his recumbent posture, 'if you bother me with another word, I'll ring the bell and order six bottles of wine – and, by Heaven, I'll drink them dry before I stir from this place!'

I said no more but sat down before the table and drew a book towards me.

'Do let me have quietness at least!' continued he, 'if you deny me every other comfort,' and sinking back into his former position, with an impatient expiration between a sigh and a groan, he languidly closed his eyes as if to sleep.

What the book was, that lay open on the table before me, I cannot tell, for I never looked at it. With an elbow on each side of it, and my hands clasped before my eyes, I delivered myself up to silent weeping. But Arthur was not asleep: at the first slight sob, he raised his head and looked round, impatiently exclaiming –

'What are you crying for, Helen? What the deuce is the matter *now*?'

'I'm crying for you Arthur,' I replied, speedily drying my tears; and starting up, I threw myself on my knees before him, and, clasping his nerveless hand between my own, continued: 'Don't you know that you are a part of myself? And do you think you can injure and degrade yourself,[1] and I not feel it?'

'*Degrade* myself, Helen?' · ·

'Yes, degrade! What have you been doing all this time?'

'You'd better not ask,' said he with a faint smile.

'And you had better not tell – but you cannot deny that you *have* degraded yourself miserably. You have shamefully wronged yourself, body and soul – and me too; and I can't endure it quietly – and I won't!'

'Well, don't squeeze my hand so frantically and don't agitate me so, for Heaven's sake! Oh, Hattersley! you were right; this woman will be the death of me, with her keen feelings and her interesting force of character – There, there, do spare me a little.'

'Arthur, you *must* repent!' cried I, in a frenzy of desperation, throwing my arms around him and burying my face in his bosom. 'You *shall* say you are sorry for what you have done!'

'Well, well, I am.'

'You are not! you'll do it again.'

'I shall never live to do it again, if you treat me so savagely,' replied he, pushing me from him. 'You've nearly squeezed the breath out of my body.' He pressed his hand to his heart, and looked really agitated and ill.

'Now get me a glass of wine,' said he, 'to remedy what you've done, you she-tiger! I'm almost ready to faint.'

I flew to get the required remedy. It seemed to revive him considerably.

'What a shame it is,' said I, as I took the empty glass from his hand, 'for a strong young man like you to reduce yourself to such a state!'

'If you knew all, my girl, you'd say rather, "What a wonder it is you can bear it so well as you do!" I've lived more in these four months, Helen, than you have in the whole course of your existence, or will to the end of your days, if they numbered a hundred years; – so I must expect to pay for it in some shape.'

'You will have to pay a higher price than you anticipate, if you don't take care – there will be the total loss of your own health, and of my affection too – if *that* is of any value to you.'

'What, you're at that game of threatening me with the loss of your affection again, are you? I think it couldn't have been very genuine stuff to begin with, if it's so easily demolished. If you don't mind, my pretty tyrant, you'll make me regret my choice in good earnest, and envy my friend Hattersley his meek little wife – she's quite a pattern to her sex, Helen: he had her with him in London all the season, and she was no trouble at all. He might amuse himself just as he pleased, in regular bachelor style, and she never complained of neglect; he might come home at any hour of the night or morning, or not come home at all; be sullen sober, or glorious drunk; and play the fool or the madman to his own heart's desire without any fear or botheration. She never gives him a word of reproach or complaint, do what he will. He says there's not such a jewel in all England, and swears he wouldn't take a kingdom for her.'

'But he makes her life a curse to her.'

'Not he! She has no will but his, and is always contented and happy as long as he is enjoying himself.'

'In that case, she is as great a fool as he is; but it is not so. I have several letters from her, expressing the greatest anxiety about his proceedings, and complaining that you incite him to commit those extravagances – one especially, in which she implores me to use my influence with you to get you away from London, and affirms that her husband never did such things before you came, and would certainly discontinue them as soon as you departed and left him to the guidance of his own good sense.'

'The detestable little traitor! Give me the letter, and he shall see it as sure as I'm a living man.'

'No, he shall not see it without her consent; but if he did, there is nothing there to anger him – nor in any of the others. She never speaks a word against him; it is only anxiety *for* him that she expresses. She only alludes to his conduct in the most delicate terms, and makes every excuse for him that she can possibly think of – and as for her own misery, I rather *feel* it than *see* it expressed in her letters.'

'But she abuses *me*; and no doubt you helped her.'

'No; I told her she overrated my influence with you, that I would gladly draw you away from the temptations of the town if I could, but had little hope of success, and that I thought she was wrong in supposing that you enticed Mr Hattersley or anyone else into error. I had, myself, held the *contrary* opinion at one time, but I now believed that you mutually corrupted each other; and, perhaps, if she used a little gentle but serious remonstrance with her husband, it might be of some service, as, though he was more rough-hewn than mine, I believed he was of a less impenetrable material.'

'And so *that* is the way you go on – heartening each other up to mutiny, and abusing each other's partners, and throwing out implications against your own, to the mutual gratification of both!'

'According to your own account,' said I, 'my evil counsel has had but little effect upon *her*. And as to abuse and aspersions, we are both of us far too deeply ashamed of the errors and vices of our other halves, to make them the common subject of our correspondence. Friends as we are, we would willingly keep your failings to ourselves – even *from* ourselves if we could, unless by knowing them we could deliver you from them.'

'Well, well! don't worry me about them: you'll never effect any good by that. Have patience with me, and bear with my languor and crossness a little while, till I get this cursed low fever out of my veins, and then you'll find me cheerful and kind as ever. Why can't you be gentle and good as you were last time? – I'm sure I was very grateful for it.'

'And what good did your gratitude do? I deluded myself with the idea that you were ashamed of your transgressions, and hoped you would never repeat them again; but now, you have left me nothing to hope!'

'My case is quite desperate, is it? A very blessed consideration, if it will only secure me from the pain and worry of my dear, anxious wife's efforts to convert me, and her from the toil and trouble of such exertions, and her sweet face and silver accents from the ruinous effects of the same. A burst of passion is a fine, rousing thing upon occasion, Helen, and a flood of tears is marvellously affecting, but, when indulged too often, they are both deuced plaguy things for spoiling one's beauty and tiring out one's friends.'

Thenceforth, I restrained my tears and passions as much as I could. I spared him my exhortations and fruitless efforts at conversion too, for I saw it was all in vain: God might awaken that heart supine and stupified with self-indulgence, and remove the film of sensual darkness from his eyes, but I could not. His injustice and ill humour towards his inferiors, who could not defend themselves, I still resented and withstood; but when I alone was their object, as was frequently the case, I endured it with calm forbearance, except at times when my temper, worn out by repeated annoyances, or stung to distraction by some new instance of irrationality, gave way in spite of myself, and exposed me to the imputations of fierceness, cruelty, and impatience. I attended carefully to his wants and amusements, but not, I own, with the same devoted fondness as before, because I could not feel it: besides, I had now another claimant on my time and care – my ailing infant, for whose sake I frequently braved and suffered the reproaches and complaints of his unreasonably exacting father.

But Arthur is not naturally a peevish or irritable man – so far from it that there was something almost ludicrous in the incongruity of this adventitious fretfulness and nervous irritability, rather calculated to excite laughter than anger, if it were not for the intensely painful considerations attendant upon those symptoms of a disordered frame, – and his temper gradually improved as his bodily health was restored, which was much sooner than would have been the case, but for my strenuous exertions; for there was still one thing about him that I did not give up in despair, and one effort for his preservation that I would not remit. His appetite for the stimulus of wine had increased upon him, as I had too well foreseen. It was now something more to him than an accessory to social enjoyment: it was an important source of enjoyment in itself. In this time of weakness and depression he would have made it his medicine and support, his comforter, his recreation, and his friend, – and thereby sunk deeper and deeper – and bound himself down for ever in the bathos whereinto he had fallen. But I determined this should never be, as long as I had any influence left; and though I could not prevent him from taking more than was good for him, still, by incessant perseverance, by kindness, and firmness, and vigilance, by coaxing, and daring, and determination, – I succeeded in preserving him from absolute bondage to that detestable propensity, so insidious in its advances, so inexorable in its tyranny, so disastrous in its effects.

And here, I must not forget that I am not a little indebted to his friend Mr Hargrave. About that time he frequently called at Grassdale, and often dined with us, on which occasions, I fear, Arthur would willingly have cast prudence and decorum to the winds and made 'a night of it,' as often as his friend would have consented to join him in that exalted pastime; and if the latter had chosen to comply, he might in a night or two have ruined the labour of weeks, and overthrown with a touch the frail bulwark it had cost me such trouble and toil to construct. I was so fearful of this at first, that I humbled myself to intimate to him in private my apprehensions of Arthur's proneness to these excesses and to express a hope that he would not encourage it. He was pleased with this mark of confidence, and certainly did not betray it. On that and every subsequent occasion, his presence served rather as a check upon his host, than an incitement to further acts of intemperance; and he always succeeded in bringing him from the dining-room in good time and in tolerably good condition; for if Arthur disregarded such intimations, as 'Well, I must not detain you from your lady,' or 'We must not forget that Mrs Huntingdon is alone,' he would insist upon leaving the table himself, to join me, and his host, however unwillingly, was obliged to follow.

Hence, I learnt to welcome Mr Hargrave, as a real friend to the family, a harmless companion for Arthur, to cheer his spirits and preserve him from the tedium of absolute idleness and a total isolation from all society but mine, and a useful ally to me. I could not but feel grateful to him under such circumstances; and I did not scruple to acknowledge my obligation on the first convenient opportunity; yet, as I did so, my heart whispered all was not right, and brought a glow to my face, which he heightened by his steady, serious gaze, while, by his manner of receiving those acknowledgements, he more than doubled my misgivings. His high delight at being able to serve me was chastened by sympathy for me and commiseration for himself – about I know not what, for I would not stay to enquire or suffer him to unburden his sorrows to me. His sighs and intimations of suppressed affliction seemed to come from a full heart; but either he must contrive to retain them within it, or breathe them forth in other ears than mine: there was enough of confidence between us already. It seemed wrong that there should exist a secret understanding between my husband's friend and me, unknown to him, of which he was the object. But my afterthought was, 'If it is wrong, surely Arthur's is the fault, not mine.'

And indeed, I know not whether at the time, it was not for *him* rather than myself that I blushed; for, since he and I are one, I so identify myself with him, that I feel his degradation, his failings, and transgressions as my own; I blush for him, I fear for him; I repent for him, weep, pray, and feel for him as for myself; but I cannot act for him; and hence, I must be and I am debased, contaminated by the union, both in my own eyes, and in the actual truth. I am so determined to love him – so intensely anxious to excuse his errors, that I am continually dwelling upon them, and labouring to extenuate the loosest of his principles and the worst of his practices, till I am familiarized with vice and almost a partaker in his sins.[2] Things that formerly shocked and disgusted me now seem only natural. I know them to be wrong, because reason and God's word declare them to be so; but I am gradually losing that instinctive horror and repulsion which was given me by nature, or instilled into me by the precepts and example of my aunt. Perhaps, then, I was too severe in my judgments, for I abhorred the sinner as well as the sin; now, I flatter myself I am more charitable and considerate; but am I not becoming more indifferent and insensate too? Fool that I was to dream that I had strength and purity enough to save myself and him! Such vain presumption would be rightly served, if I should perish with him in the gulf[3] from which I sought to save him! Yet, God preserve me from it! – and him too. Yes, poor Arthur, I will still hope and pray for you; and, though I write as if you were some abandoned wretch, past hope and past reprieve, it is only my anxious fears – my strong desires – that make me do so; one who loved you less would be less bitter – less dissatisfied.

His conduct has of late been what the world calls irreproachable; but then I know his heart is still unchanged; – and I know that spring is approaching, and deeply dread the consequences.

As he began to recover the tone and vigour of his exhausted frame, and with it something of his former impatience of retirement and repose, I suggested a short residence by the seaside, for his recreation and further restoration, and for the benefit of our little one as well. But no; watering-places were so intolerably dull – besides, he had been invited by one of his friends to spend a month or two in Scotland for the better recreation of grouse-shooting and deer-stalking, and had promised to go.

'Then you will leave me again, Arthur?' said I.

'Yes, dearest, but only to love you the better when I come back, and make up for all past offences and shortcomings; and you needn't fear me this time: there are no temptations on the mountains. And during my absence you may pay a visit to Staningley, if you like: your uncle and aunt have long been wanting us to go there, you know; but somehow, there's such a repulsion between the good lady and me, that I never could bring myself up to the scratch.'

I was perfectly willing to avail myself of this permission, though not a little apprehensive of my aunt's questions and comments concerning my matrimonial experience, regarding which I had been very reserved in my letters, for I had not much that was pleasant to communicate.

About the third week in August, Arthur set out for Scotland, and Mr Hargrave accompanied him thither, to my private satisfaction. Shortly after, I, with little Arthur and Rachel, went to Staningley, my dear old home, which, as well as my dear old friends its inhabitants, I saw again with mingled feelings of pleasure and pain so intimately blended that I could scarcely distinguish the one from the other, or tell to which to attribute the various tears, and smiles, and sighs awakened by those old familiar scenes, and tones, and faces. Not quite two years had passed since I had seen and heard them last; but it seemed a far, far longer time; and well it might, for how immeasurably changed was I! how many things had I not seen, and felt, and learnt since then! My uncle too appeared perceptibly more aged and infirm, my aunt more sad and grave. I believe she thought I had repented of my rashness, though she did not openly express her conviction, or triumphantly remind me of her slighted counsels, as I had partly feared she would; but she observed me narrowly – more narrowly than I liked to be observed – and seemed to mistrust my cheerfulness and unduly mark each little indication of sadness or serious thought, to notice all my casual observations, and silently draw her own inferences from them; while, by a system of quiet cross-questioning renewed from time to time, she drew from me many things I should not otherwise have told her, and laying this and that together, obtained, I fear, a pretty clear conception of my husband's faults and my afflictions, though not of my remaining sources of comfort and hope, for though I endeavoured to impress her strongly with the notion of Arthur's redeeming qualities, of our mutual affection, and the many causes I had for thankfulness and self-congratulation, she received all such intimations coldly and calmly as if mentally making her own deductions – which deductions, I am persuaded, were generally far beyond the truth; though I certainly did exaggerate a little in attempting to picture the bright side of my position. Was it pride that made me so extremely anxious to appear satisfied with my lot, – or merely a just determination to bear my self-imposed burden alone, and preserve my best friend from the slightest participation in those sorrows from which she had striven so hard to save me? It might have been something of each, but I am sure the latter motive was predominant.

I did not much prolong my visit, for, not only did I feel my aunt's relentless watchfulness and incredulity to be a restraint upon me, and a silent reproach that oppressed me more than she could well imagine, but I was sensible that my little Arthur was an annoyance to his uncle, though the latter wished him well, and no great amusement to his aunt, though an object of her earnest affection and anxious solicitude.

Dear aunt! have you so tenderly reared me from infancy, so carefully guided and instructed me in childhood and youth; and could I give you no return but this – to disappoint your hopes, oppose your wishes, scorn your warnings and advice, and darken your latter years with anxious fears and sorrow for the sufferings you cannot relieve? – It almost broke my heart to think of it; and again and again I endeavoured to convince her that I was happy and contented with my lot; but her last words, as she embraced me and kissed the child in my arms, before I entered the carriage, were, –

'Take care of your son, Helen, and there may be happy days in store for you, yet. How great a comfort and treasure he is to you now I can well imagine; but if you spoil him to gratify your present feelings, it will be too late to repent it when your heart is broken.'

Arthur did not come home till several weeks after my return to Grassdale; but I did not feel so anxious about him now: to think of him engaged in active sports among the wild hills of Scotland was very different from knowing him to be immersed amid the corruptions and temptations of London. His letters, now, though neither long nor lover-like, were more regular than ever they had been before; and, when he did return, to my great joy, instead of being worse than when he went, he was more cheerful and vigorous, and better in every respect. Since that time, I have had little cause to complain. He still has an unfortunate predilection for the pleasures of the table, against which I have to struggle and watch; but he has begun to notice his boy, and that is an increasing source of amusement to him within doors; while his fox-hunting and coursing are a sufficient occupation for him without, when the ground is not hardened by frost; so that he is not wholly dependent on me for entertainment. But it is now January: spring is approaching; and, I repeat, I dread the consequences of its arrival. That sweet season I once so joyously welcomed as the time of hope and gladness, awakens, now, far other anticipations by its return.

CHAPTER 31

SOCIAL VIRTUES

March 20th, 1824. The dreaded time is come, and Arthur is gone, as I expected. This time he announced it his intention to make but a short stay in London, and pass over to the continent, where he should probably stay a few weeks; but I shall not expect him till after the lapse of many weeks: I now know that, with him, days signify weeks, and weeks months.

I was to have accompanied him, but, a little before the time arranged for our departure, he allowed – and even urged me, with an appearance of wonderful self-sacrifice, to go and see my unfortunate father, who is very ill, and my brother, who is very unhappy in consequence of both the illness and its cause, and whom I had not seen since the day our child was christened, when he stood sponsor along with Mr Hargrave and my aunt. Not willing to impose upon my husband's good-nature in thus allowing me to leave him, I made but a very short stay; but when I returned to Grassdale – he was gone.

He left a note to explain his so hasty departure, pretending that some sudden emergency had demanded his immediate presence in London, and rendered it impossible to await my return; adding that I had better not trouble myself to follow him, as he intended to make such a short stay, that it would hardly be worthwhile; and as, of course, he could travel alone at less than half the expense than if I accompanied him, it would perhaps be better to defer the excursion to another year, when he should have got our affairs into a rather more settled state, as he was now endeavouring to do.

Was it really so? – or was the whole a contrivance to ensure his going forth upon his pleasure-seeking excursion, without my presence to restrain him? It is painful to doubt the sincerity of those we love, but after so many proofs of falsity and utter disregard to principle how can I believe so improbable a story?

I have this one source of consolation left: – he had told me some time previously, that if ever he went to London or Paris again, he should observe more moderation in his indulgences than before, lest he should destroy his capacity for enjoyment altogether: he had no ambition to live to a prodigious old age, but he should like to have his share of life, and above all, to relish its pleasures to the last – to which end, he found it necessary to economize, for already, he feared, he was not so handsome a fellow as he had been, and young as he was, he had lately detected some grey hairs among his beloved chestnut locks; he suspected he was getting a trifle fatter too, than was quite desirable – but that was with good living and idleness; and for the rest, he trusted he was as strong and hearty as ever: only there was no saying what *another* such a season of unlimited madness and devilment, as the last, might not do towards bringing him down. Yes; he said this to *me* – with unblushing effrontery, and that same blithe, roguish twinkle of the eyes I once so loved to see, and that low, joyous laugh it used to warm my heart to hear.

Well! such considerations will doubtless have more weight with him than any that I could urge. We shall see what *they* can do towards his preservation, since no better hope remains.

July 30th. – He returned about three weeks ago, rather better in health, certainly, than before, but still worse in temper. And yet, perhaps, I am wrong: it is *I* that am less patient and forbearing. I am tired out with his injustice, his selfishness and hopeless *depravity* – I wish a milder word would do –; I am no angel and my corruption rises against it.[1] My poor father died last week: Arthur was vexed to hear of it, because he saw that I was shocked and grieved, and he feared the circumstance would mar his comfort. When I spoke of ordering my mourning, he exclaimed –

'Oh, I hate black! But however, I suppose you must wear it awhile, for form's sake; but I hope, Helen, you won't think it your bounden duty to compose your face and manners into conformity with your funereal garb. Why should you sigh and groan, and I be made uncomfortable because an old gentelman in —shire, a perfect stranger to us both, has thought proper to drink himself to death? – There now, I declare you're crying! Well, it must be affectation.'

He would not hear of my attending the funeral, or going for a day or two, to cheer poor Frederick's solitude. It was quite unnecessary, he said, and I was unreasonable to wish it. What was my father to me? I had never seen him, but once since I was a baby, and I well knew he had never cared a stiver about me; – and my brother too, was little better than a stranger. 'Besides, dear Helen,' said he, embracing me with flattering fondness, 'I cannot spare you for a single day.'

'Then how have you managed without me, these *many* days?' said I.

'Ah! then I was knocking about the world, now I am at home; and home without you, my household deity, would be intolerable.'

'Yes, as long as I am necessary to your comfort; but you did not say so before, when you urged me to leave you, in order that you might get away from your home without me,' retorted I; but before the words were well out of my mouth, I regretted having uttered them. It seemed so heavy a charge: if false, too gross an insult; if true, too humiliating a fact to be thus openly cast in his teeth. But I might have spared myself that momentary pang of self-reproach. The accusation awoke neither shame nor indignation in him: he attempted neither denial nor excuse, but only answered with a long, low, chuckling laugh as if he viewed the whole transaction as a clever, merry jest from beginning to end. Surely that man will make me dislike him at last!

> 'Sine as ye brew, my maiden fair,
> Keep mind that ye maun drink the yill?'[2]

Yes; and I *will* drink it to the very dregs: and none but myself shall know how bitter I find it!

August 20th. – We are shaken down again to about our usual position. Arthur has returned to nearly his former condition and habits; and I have found it my wisest plan to shut my eyes against the past and future, as far as *he* at least is concerned, and live only for the present; to love him when I can; to smile (if possible) when he smiles, be cheerful when he is cheerful, and pleased when he is agreeable; and when he is not, to try to make him so – and if that won't answer, to bear with him, to excuse him, and forgive him, as well as I can, and restrain my own evil passions from aggravating his; and yet, while I thus yield and minister to his more harmless propensities to self-indulgence, to do all in my power to save him from the worse.[3]

But we shall not be long alone together. I shall shortly be called upon to entertain the same select body of friends as we had the autumn before last, with the addition of Mr Hattersley and, at my special request, his wife and child. I long to see Milicent – and her little girl too. The latter is now above a year old; she will be a charming playmate for my little Arthur.

September 30th. – Our guests have been here a week or two; but I have had no leisure to pass any comments upon them till now. I cannot get over my dislike to Lady Lowborough. It is not founded on mere personal pique; it is the woman herself that I dislike, because I so thoroughly disapprove of her. I always avoid her company as much as I can without violating the laws of hospitality; but when we do speak or converse together, it is with the utmost civility – even apparent cordiality on her part; but preserve me from such cordiality! It is like handling briar-roses and may-blossoms – bright enough to the eye, and outwardly soft to the touch, but you know there are thorns beneath, and every now and then you feel them too; and perhaps resent the injury by crushing them in till you have destroyed their power, though somewhat to the detriment of your own fingers.

Of late, however, I have seen nothing in her conduct towards Arthur to anger or alarm me. During the first few days I thought she seemed very solicitous to win his admiration. Her efforts were not unnoticed by him: I frequently saw him smiling to himself at her artful manoeuvres; but, to his praise be it spoken, her shafts fell powerless by his side. Her most bewitching smiles, her haughtiest frowns, were ever received with the same immutable, careless good-humour; till, finding he was indeed impenetrable, she suddenly remitted her efforts, and became, to all appearance, as perfectly indifferent as himself. Nor have I since witnessed any symptom of pique on his part, or renewed attempts at conquest upon hers.

This is as it should be; but Arthur never will let me be satisfied with him. I have never, for a single hour since I married him, known what it is to realize that sweet idea, 'In quietness and confidence shall be your rest.'[4] Those two detestable men Grimsby and Hattersley have destroyed all my labour against his love of wine. They encourage him daily to overstep the bounds of moderation, and, not unfrequently, to disgrace himself by positive excess. I shall not soon forget the second night after their arrival. Just as I had retired from the dining-room, with the ladies, before the door was closed upon us, Arthur exclaimed –

'Now then, my lads, what say you to a regular jollification?'

Milicent glanced at me with a half reproachful look, as if *I* could hinder it; but her countenance changed when she heard Hattersley's voice shouting through door and wall.

'*I'm* your man! Send for more wine: here isn't *half* enough!'

We had scarcely entered the drawing-room before we were joined by Lord Lowborough.

'What *can* induce you to come so soon?' exclaimed his lady, with a most ungracious air of dissatisfaction.

'You know I never drink, Annabella,' replied he, seriously.

'Well, but you might stay with them a little: it looks so silly to be always dangling after the women – I wonder you can!'

He reproached her with a look of mingled bitterness and surprise, and sinking into a chair, suppressed a heavy sigh, bit his pale lips, and fixed his eyes upon the floor.

'You did right to leave them, Lord Lowborough,' said I. 'I trust you will always continue to honour us so early with your company. And if Annabella knew the value of true wisdom, and the misery of folly and – and intemperance, she would not talk such nonsense – even in jest.'

He raised his eyes while I spoke, and gravely turned them upon me with a half surprised, half abstracted look, and then bent them on his wife.

'At least,' said she, 'I know the value of a warm heart and a bold, manly spirit!'

And she pointed her words with a glance of triumph at me, which seemed to say, 'And that is more than *you* do,' and a look of scorn at her husband, that entered into his soul. I was intensely exasperated; but it was not for me to reprove her, or, as it seemed, to express my sympathy with her husband without insulting his feelings. All I could do, to obey my inward impulse, was to hand him a cup of coffee, bringing it to him myself, and before I served either of the ladies, by way of balancing her contempt by my exceeding deference. He took it mechanically from my hand, with a slight inclination, and, next minute, rose and placed it untasted on the table, looking, not at it, but at her.

'Well, Annabella,' said he, in a deep and hollow tone, 'since my presence is disagreeable to you, I will relieve you of it.'

'Are you going back to them, then?' said she, carelessly.

'No,' exclaimed he, with harsh and startling emphasis; 'I will NOT go back to them! And I will never stay with them one moment longer than I think right, for you or any other tempter! But you needn't mind that – I shall never trouble you again, by intruding my company upon you so unseasonably.'

He left the room, I heard the hall door open and shut, and immediately after, on putting aside the curtain, I saw him pacing down the park, in the comfortless gloom of the damp, cloudy twilight.

Such scenes as this are always disagreeable to witness. Our little party was completely silenced for a moment. Milicent played with her teaspoon, and looked confounded and uncomfortable. If Annabella felt any shame or uneasiness, she attempted to hide it by a short, reckless laugh, and calmly betook herself to her coffee.

'It would serve you right, Annabella,' said I at length, 'if Lord Lowborough were to return to his old habits, which had so nearly effected his ruin, and which it cost him such an effort to break. You would then see cause to repent such conduct as this.'

'Not at all, my dear! I should not mind if his Lordship were to see fit to intoxicate himself every day: I should only the sooner be rid of him.'

'Oh, Annabella!' cried Milicent. 'How *can* you say such wicked things! It would indeed be a just punishment, as far as you are concerned, if providence should take you at your word, and make you feel what others feel that –' She paused as a sudden burst of loud talking and laughter reached us from the dining-room, in which the voice of Hattersley was pre-eminently conspicuous, even to my unpractised ear.

'What *you* feel at this moment, I suppose?' said Lady Lowborough, with a malicious smile, fixing her eyes upon her cousin's distressed countenance.

The latter offered no reply, but averted her face and brushed away a tear. At that moment the door opened and admitted Mr Hargrave; just a little flushed, his dark eyes sparkling with unwonted vivacity.

'Oh, I'm glad you're come, Walter!' cried his sister – 'But I wish you could have got Ralph to come too.'

'Utterly impossible, dear Milicent,' replied he, gaily. 'I had much ado to get away myself. Ralph attempted to keep me by violence; Huntingdon threatened me with the eternal loss of his friendship; and Grimsby, worse than all, endeavoured to make me ashamed of my virtue, by such galling sarcasms and innuendoes as he knew would wound me the most. So you see, ladies, you ought to make me welcome when I have braved and suffered so much for the favour of your sweet society.' He smilingly turned to me and bowed as he finished the sentence.

'Isn't he *handsome* now Helen?' whispered Milicent, her sisterly pride overcoming, for the moment, all other considerations.

'He would be,' I returned, 'if that brilliance of eye, and lip, and cheek were natural to him; but look again, a few hours hence.'

Here the gentleman took a seat near me at the table, and petitioned for a cup of coffee.

'I consider this an apt illustration of Heaven taken by storm,' said he, as I handed one to him. 'I am in paradise now; but I have fought my way through flood and fire to win it. Ralph Hattersley's last resource was to set his back against the door, and swear I should find no passage but through his body (a pretty substantial one too).

Happily, however, that was not the only door, and I effected my escape by the side entrance, through the butler's pantry, to the infinite amazement of Benson, who was cleaning the plate.'

Mr Hargrave laughed, and so did his cousin; but his sister and I remained silent and grave.

'Pardon my levity, Mrs Huntingdon,' murmured he, more seriously, as he raised his eyes to my face. 'You are not used to these things: you suffer them to affect your delicate mind too sensibly.[5] But I thought of you in the midst of those lawless roisterers: and I endeavoured to persuade Mr Huntingdon to think of you too; but to no purpose: I fear he is fully determined to enjoy himself this night; and it will be no use keeping the coffee waiting for him or his companions: it will be much if they join us at tea. Meantime, I earnestly wish I could banish the thoughts of them from your mind – and my own too, for I hate to think of them – yes – even of my dear friend Huntingdon, when I consider the power he possesses over the happiness of one so immeasurably superior to himself, and the use he makes of it – I positively *detest* the man!'

'You had better not say so to me, then,' said I; 'for, bad as he is, he is part of myself, and you cannot abuse him without offending me.'

'Pardon me, then, for I would sooner die than offend you – But let us say no more of him for the present if you please.'

He then entirely changed the subject of discourse, and exerting all his powers to entertain our little circle, conversed on different topics with more than his usual brilliance and fluency, addressing himself, sometimes, exclusively to me, sometimes to the whole trio of ladies. Annabella cheerfully bore her part in the conversation; but I was sick at heart, – especially when loud bursts of laughter and incoherent songs, pealing through the triple doors of hall and ante-room, startled my ear and pierced my aching temples; – and Milicent partly shared my feelings; so that, to us, the evening appeared a very long one, in spite of Hargrave's apparently good-natured exertions to give it a contrary effect.

At last, they came; but not till after ten, when tea, which had been delayed for more than half an hour, was nearly over. Much as I had longed for their coming, my heart failed me at the riotous uproar of their approach; and Milicent turned pale and almost started from her seat as Mr Hattersley burst into the room with a clamorous volley of oaths in his mouth, which Hargrave endeavoured to check by entreating him to remember the ladies.

'Ah! you do well to remind me of the ladies, you dastardly deserter,' cried he, shaking his formidable fist at his brother-in-law; 'if it were not for them, you well know, I'd demolish you in the twinkling of an eye, and give your body to the fowls of heaven and the lilies of the field!'[6] Then, planting a chair by Lady Lowborough's side, he stationed himself in it, and began to talk to her, with a mixture of absurdity and rascally impudence that seemed rather to amuse than to offend her; though she affected to resent his insolence, and to keep him at bay with sallies of smart and spirited repartee.

Meantime, Mr Grimsby seated himself by me, in the chair vacated by Hargrave as they entered, and gravely stated that he would thank me for a cup of tea: and Arthur placed himself beside poor Milicent, confidentially pushing his head into her face, and drawing in closer to her as she shrank away from him. He was not so noisy as Hattersley, but his face was exceedingly flushed, he laughed incessantly, and, while I blushed for all I saw and heard of him, I was glad that he chose to talk to his companion in so low a tone that no one could hear what he said but herself. It must have been intolerable nonsense at best, for she looked excessively annoyed, and first went red in the face, then indignantly pushed back her chair, and finally took refuge behind me on the sofa. Arthur's sole intention seemed to have been to produce some such disagreeable effects: he laughed immoderately on finding he had driven her away – drawing in his chair to the table, he leant his folded arms upon it, and delivered himself up to a paroxysm of weak, low, foolish laughter. When he was tired of this exercise he lifted his head and called aloud to Hattersley, and there ensued a clamorous contest between them about I know not what.

'What fools they are!' drawled Mr Grimsby, who had been talking away, at my elbow, with sententious gravity all the time; but I had been too much absorbed in contemplating the deplorable state of the other two – especially Arthur – to attend to him.

'Did you ever hear such nonsense as they talk, Mrs Huntingdon?' he continued. 'I'm quite ashamed of them for my part: they can't take so much as a bottle between them without its getting into their heads –'

'You are pouring the cream into your saucer, Mr Grimsby.'

'Ah! yes, I see, but we're almost in darkness here. Hargrave, snuff those candles, will you?'

'They're wax; they don't require snuffing,' said I.

'"The light of the body is the eye,"' observed Hargrave, with a sarcastic smile. '"If thine eye be *single* thy whole body shall be full of light."'[7]

Grimsby repulsed him with a solemn wave of the hand, and then, turning to me, continued, with the same drawling tones, and strange uncertainty of utterance and heavy gravity of aspect as before, 'But as I was saying, Mrs Huntingdon, – they have no head at all: they can't take half a bottle without being affected some way; whereas I – well, I've taken three times as much as they have tonight, and you see I'm perfectly steady. Now that may strike you as very singular, but I think I can explain it: – you see *their* brains – I mention no names, but you'll understand to whom I allude – *their* brains are light to begin with, and the fumes of the fermented liquor render them lighter still, and produce an entire light-headed-ness, or giddiness, resulting in intoxication; whereas *my* brains being composed of more solid materials will absorb a considerable quantity of this alcoholic vapour without the production of any sensible result –'

'I think you will find a sensible result produced on that tea,' interrupted Mr Hargrave, 'by the quantity of sugar you have put into it. Instead of your usual complement of one lump you have put in six.'

'Have I so?' replied the philosopher, diving with his spoon into the cup and bringing up several half-dissolved pieces in confirmation of the assertion. 'Um! I perceive. Thus, madam, you see the evil of absence of mind – of thinking too much while engaged in the common concerns of life. Now if I had had my wits about me, like ordinary men, instead of within me like a philosopher, I should not have spoiled this cup of tea, and been constrained to trouble you for another. – With your permission, I'll turn this into the slop-basin.'

'That is the sugar-basin, Mr Grimsby. Now you have spoiled the sugar too; and I'll thank you to ring for some more – for here is Lord Lowborough, at last; and I hope his lordship will condescend to sit down with us, such as we are, and allow me to give him some tea.'

His lordship gravely bowed in answer to my appeal, but said nothing. Meantime, Hargrave volunteered to ring for the sugar, while Grimsby lamented his mistake, and attempted to prove that it was owing to the shadow of the urn and the badness of the lights.

Lord Lowborough had entered a minute or two before, unobserved by anyone but me, and been standing before the door, grimly surveying the company. He now stepped up to Annabella, who sat with her back towards him, with Hattersley still beside her, though not now attending to her, being occupied in vociferously abusing and bullying his host.

'Well, Annabella,' said her husband, as he leant over the back of her chair, 'which of these three "bold, manly spirits" would you have me to resemble?'

'By heaven and earth, you shall resemble us all!' cried Hattersley, starting up and rudely seizing him by the arm. 'Hallo Huntingdon!' he shouted – '*I've* got him! Come, man, and help me! And d—n me body and soul if I don't make him blind drunk before I let him go! He shall make up for all past delinquencies as sure as I'm a living soul!'

There followed a disgraceful contest; Lord Lowborough, in desperate earnest, and pale with anger, silently struggling to release himself from the powerful madman that was striving to drag him from the room. I attempted to urge Arthur to interfere in behalf of his outraged guest, but he could do nothing but laugh.

'Huntingdon, you fool, come and help me, can't you!' cried Hattersley, himself somewhat weakened by his excesses.

'I'm wishing you God-speed, Hattersley,' cried Arthur, 'and aiding you with my prayers: I can't do anything else if my life depended on it! I'm quite used up. Oh, ho!' and leaning back in his seat, he clapped his hands on his sides and groaned aloud.

'Annabella, give me a candle!' said Lowborough whose antagonist had now got him round the waist and was endeavouring to root him from the doorpost to which he madly clung with all the energy of desperation.

'*I* shall take no part in your rude sports!' replied the lady, coldly drawing back, 'I wonder you can expect it.'

But I snatched up a candle and brought it to him. He took it and held the flame to Hattersley's hands till, roaring like a wild beast, the latter unclasped them and let him go. He vanished, I suppose to his own apartment, for nothing more was seen of him till the morning. Swearing and cursing like a maniac, Hattersley threw himself on to the ottoman beside the window. The door being now free, Milicent attempted to make her escape from the scene of her husband's disgrace; but he called her back, and insisted upon her coming to him.

'What do you want Ralph?' murmured she, reluctantly approaching him.

'I want to know what's the matter with you,' said he, pulling her on to his knee like a child. 'What are you crying for Milicent? – Tell me!'

'I'm not crying.'

'You are,' persisted he, rudely pulling her hands from her face. 'How dare you tell such a lie?'

'I'm not crying now,' pleaded she.

'But you have been – and just this minute too; and I *will* know what for. Come now, you *shall* tell me!'

'Do let me alone Ralph! remember we are not at home.'

'No matter: you *shall* answer my question!' exclaimed her tormentor; and he attempted to extort the confession by shaking her and remorselessly crushing her slight arms in the gripe of his powerful fingers.

'Don't let him treat your sister in that way,' said I to Mr Hargrave.

'Come now, Hattersley, I can't allow that,' said that gentleman, stepping up to the ill-assorted couple. 'You let my sister alone, if you please.' And he made an effort to unclasp the ruffian's fingers from her arm, but was suddenly driven backward and nearly laid upon the floor by a violent blow in the chest accompanied with the admonition,

'Take that for your insolence! – and learn not to interfere between me and mine again.'

'If you were not beastly drunk, I'd have satisfaction for that!' gasped Hargrave, white and breathless as much from passion as from the immediate effects of the blow.

'Go to the devil!' responded his brother-in-law. 'Now Milicent, tell me what you were crying for.'

'I'll tell you some other time,' murmured she, 'when we are alone.'

'Tell me now!' said he with another shake and a squeeze that made her draw in her breath and bite her lip to suppress a cry of pain.

'*I'll* tell you, Mr Hattersley,' said I. 'She was crying from pure shame and humiliation for you; because she could not bear to see you conduct yourself so disgracefully.'

'Confound you, madam!' muttered he, with a stare of stupid amazement at my 'impudence,' 'It was *not* that – was it Milicent?'

She was silent.

'Come, speak up child!'

'I can't tell now,' sobbed she.

'But you can say "yes" or "no" as well as "I can't tell" – Come!'

'Yes,' she whispered, hanging her head and blushing at the awful acknowledgement.

'Curse you for an impertinent huzzy then!' cried he, throwing her from him with such violence that she fell on her side; but she was up again before either I or her brother could come to her assistance, and made the best of her way out of the room and, I suppose, upstairs, without loss of time.

The next object of assault was Arthur, who sat opposite, and had no doubt richly enjoyed the whole scene.

'Now Huntingdon,' exclaimed his irascible friend, 'I WILL NOT have you sitting there and laughing like an idiot!'

'Oh, Hattersley!' cried he, wiping his swimming eyes – 'you'll be the death of me.'

'Yes I will, but not as you suppose: I'll have the heart out of your body, man, if you irritate me with any more of that imbecile laughter! – What! are you at it yet? – There! see if that'll settle you!' cried Hattersley, snatching up a footstool and hurling it at the head of his host; but he missed his aim and the latter still sat collapsed and quaking with feeble laughter, with the tears running down his face; a deplorable spectacle indeed.

Hattersley tried cursing and swearing, but it would not do; he then took a number of books from the table beside him and threw them, one by one, at the object of his wrath, but Arthur only laughed the more; and, finally, Hattersley rushed upon him in a frenzy, and, seizing him by the shoulders, gave him a violent shaking, under which he laughed and shrieked alarmingly. But I saw no more: I thought I had witnessed enough of my husband's degradation; and, leaving Annabella and the rest to follow when they pleased, I withdrew – but not to bed. Dismissing Rachel to her rest, I walked up and down my room, in an agony of misery, for what had been done, and suspense, not knowing what might further happen or how or when that unhappy creature would come up to bed.

At last he came, slowly and stumblingly, ascending the stairs, supported by Grimsby and Hattersley, who neither of them walked quite steadily themselves, but were both laughing and joking at him, and making noise enough for all the servants to hear. He himself was no longer laughing now, but sick and stupid – I will write no more about *that*.

Such disgraceful scenes (or nearly such) have been repeated more than once. I don't say much to Arthur about it, for if I did, it would do more harm than good; but I let him know that I intensely dislike such exhibitions; and each time he has promised they should never again be repeated; but I fear he is losing the little self-command and self-respect he once possessed: formerly, he would have been ashamed to act thus – at least, before any other witnesses than his boon companions, or such as they. His friend, Hargrave, with a prudence and self-government that I envy for *him*, never disgraces himself by taking more than sufficient to render him a little 'elevated,' and is always the first to leave the table, after Lord Lowborough, who, wiser still, perseveres in vacating the dining-room immediately after us; but never once, since Annabella offended him so deeply, has he entered the drawing-room before the rest; always spending the interim in the library, which I take care to have lighted for his accommodation – or, on fine moonlight nights, in roaming about the grounds. But I think she regrets her misconduct, for she has never repeated it since, and of late she has comported herself with wonderful propriety towards him, treating him with more uniform kindness and consideration than ever I have observed her to do before. I date the time of this improvement from the period when she ceased to hope and strive for Arthur's admiration.

CHAPTER 32

COMPARISONS: INFORMATION REJECTED

October 5th. – Esther Hargrave[1] is getting a fine girl. She is not out of the school-room yet, but her mother frequently brings her over to call in the mornings when the gentlemen are out, and sometimes she spends an hour or two in company with her sister, and me, and the children; and when we go to the Grove, I always contrive to see her, and talk more to her than to anyone else, for I am very much attached to my little friend, and so is she to me. I wonder what she can see to like in me though, for I am no longer the happy, lively girl I used to be; but she has no other society – save that of her uncongenial mother, and her governess (as artificial and conventional a person as that prudent mother could procure to rectify the pupil's natural qualities), and, now and then, her subdued, quiet sister. I often wonder what will be *her* lot in life – and so does she; but *her* speculations on the future are full of buoyant hope – so were mine once. I shudder to think of her being awakened like me to a sense of their delusive vanity. It seems as if I should feel her disappointment even more deeply than my own: I feel, almost, as if I were born for such a fate, but *she* is so joyous and fresh, so light of heart and free of spirit, and so guileless and unsuspecting too – Oh, it would be cruel to make her feel as I feel now, and know what I have known!

Her sister trembles for her too. Yesterday morning, one of October's brightest loveliest days, Milicent and I were in the garden enjoying a brief half hour together with our children, while Annabella was lying on the drawing-room sofa, deep in the last new novel. We had been romping with the little creatures, almost as merry and wild as themselves, and now paused in the shade of the tall copper beech, to recover breath and rectify our hair, disordered by the rough play and the frolicsome breeze – while they toddled together along the broad, sunny walk; my Arthur supporting the feebler steps of her little Helen, and sagaciously pointing out to her the brightest beauties of the border as they passed, with semi-articulate prattle that did as well for her as any other mode of discourse. From laughing at the pretty sight, we began to talk of the children's future life; and that made us thoughtful. We both relapsed into silent musing as we slowly proceeded up the walk; and I suppose Milicent by a train of associations was led to think of her sister.

'Helen,' said she, 'you often see Esther, don't you?'

'Not very often.'

'But you have more frequent opportunities of meeting her than I have: and she loves you, I know, and reverences you too: there is nobody's opinion she thinks so much of; and she says you have more sense than mamma.'

'That is because she is self-willed, and my opinions more generally coincide with her own than your mamma's. But what then, Milicent?'

'Well, since you have so much influence with her, I wish you would seriously impress it upon her, never, on any account, or for anybody's persuasion, to marry for the sake of money, or rank, or establishment, or any earthly thing, but true affection and well-grounded esteem.'

'There is no necessity for that,' said I: 'for we have had some discourse on that subject already, and I assure you her ideas of love and matrimony are as romantic as anyone could desire.'

'But romantic notions will not do: I want her to have true notions.'

'Very right, but in my judgment, what the world stigmatizes as romantic, is often more nearly allied to the truth than is commonly supposed; for, if the generous ideas of youth are too often over-clouded by the sordid views of after-life, that scarcely proves them to be false.'

'Well, but if you think her ideas are what they ought to be, strengthen them, will you? and confirm them, as far as you can; for *I* had romantic notions once, and – I don't mean to say that I regret my lot, for I am quite sure I don't – but –'

'I understand you,' said I; 'you are contented for yourself, but you would not have your sister to suffer the same as you.'

'No – or worse. She might have far worse to suffer than I – for I *am really* contented, Helen, though you mayn't think it: I speak the solemn truth in saying that I would not exchange my husband for any man on earth, if I might do it by the plucking of this leaf.'

'Well, I believe you: now that you have him, you would not exchange *him* for another; but then you would gladly exchange some of his qualities for those of better men.'

'Yes; just as I would gladly exchange some of my own qualities for those of better women; for neither he nor I are perfect, and I desire his improvement as earnestly as my own. And he will improve – don't you think so Helen? – he's only six and twenty yet.'

'He may,' I answered.

'He will – he WILL!' repeated she.

'Excuse the faintness of my acquiescence, Milicent; I would not discourage your hopes for the world, but mine have been so often disappointed, that I am become as cold and doubtful in my expectations as the flattest of octogenarians.'

'And yet you do hope, still – even for Mr Huntingdon?'

'I do, I confess – "even" for *him*; for it seems as if life and hope must cease together. And is he so *much* worse, Milicent, than Mr Hattersley?'

'Well, to give you my candid opinion, I think there is no comparison between them. But you mustn't be offended, Helen, for you know I always speak my mind; and you may speak yours too; I shan't care.'

'I am not offended, love; and *my* opinion is that if there *be* a comparison made between the two, the difference, for the most part, is certainly in Hattersley's favour.'

Milicent's own heart told her how much it cost me to make this acknowledgment; and, with a childlike impulse, she expressed her sympathy by suddenly kissing my cheek, without a word of reply, and then turning quickly away caught up her baby, and hid her face in its frock. How odd it is that we so often weep for each other's distresses, when we shed not a tear for our own! Her heart had been full enough of her own sorrows, but it overflowed at the idea of mine; – and I too shed tears at the sight of her sympathetic emotion, though I had not wept for myself for many a week.

But Milicent's satisfaction in her choice is not entirely feigned: she really loves her husband; and it is too true that he loses nothing by comparison with mine. Either he is less unbridled in his excesses, or, owing to his stronger, hardier frame, they produce a much less deleterious effect upon him; for he never reduces himself to a state in any degree bordering on imbecility, and with him the worst effect of a night's debauch is a slight increase of irascibility, or it may be a season of sullen ferocity on the following morning: there is nothing of that lost, depressing appearance – that peevish, ignoble fretfulness, that wears one out with very shame for the transgressor. But then, it was not formerly so with Arthur: he can bear less now than he could at Hattersley's age; and if the latter does not reform, his powers of endurance may be equally impaired when he has tried them as long. He has five years the advantage of his friend, and his vices have not mastered him yet: he has not folded them to him and made them a part of himself. They seem to sit loose upon him, like a cloak[2] that he could throw aside at any moment if he would – but how long will that option be left him? – Though a creature of passion and sense, regardless of the duties and the higher privileges of intelligent beings, he is no voluptuary: he prefers the more active and invigorating animal enjoyments, to those of a more relaxing, enervating kind. He does not make a *science* of the gratification of his appetites either in the pleasures of the table or anything else; he eats heartily what is set before him, without demeaning himself by any of that abandonment to the palate and the eye – that unbecoming particularity in approval or disapproval which it is so hateful to witness in those we would esteem. Arthur, I fear, would give himself up to luxury as the chief good, and might ultimately plunge into the grossest excesses, but for the fear of irremediably blunting his appetites, and destroying his powers of further enjoyment. For Hattersley, graceless ruffian as he is, I believe there is more reasonable ground of hope; and – far be it from me to blame poor Milicent for his delinquencies – but I do think that if she had the courage or the will to speak her mind about them, and maintain her point unflinchingly, there would be more chance of his reclamation, and he would be likely to treat her better, and love her more, in the end. I am partly led to think so by what he said to me himself, not many days ago – I purpose to give her a little advice on the subject sometime; but still, I hesitate from the consciousness that her ideas and disposition are both against it, and if my counsels failed to do good, they would do harm by making her more unhappy.

It was one rainy day last week: most of the company were killing time in the billiard-room, but Milicent and I were with little Arthur and Helen in the library, and between our books, our children, and each other, we expected to make out a very agreeable morning. We had not been thus secluded above two hours, however, when Mr Hattersley came in, attracted, I suppose, by the voice of his child as he was crossing the hall, for he is prodigiously fond of her, and she of him.

He was redolent of the stables, where he had been regaling himself with the company of his fellow-creatures, the horses, ever since breakfast. But that was no matter to my little namesake: as soon as the colossal person of her father darkened the door, she uttered a shrill scream of delight, and, quitting her mother's side, ran crowing towards him – balancing her course with out-stretched arms, – and, embracing his knee, threw back her head and laughed in his face. He might well look smilingly down upon those small, fair features radiant with innocent mirth, those clear, blue, shining eyes, and that soft flaxen hair cast back upon the little ivory neck and shoulders. Did he not think how unworthy he was of such a possession? I fear no such idea crossed his mind. He caught her up, and there followed some minutes of very rough play, during which it is difficult to say whether the father or the daughter laughed and shouted the loudest. At length, however, the boisterous pastime terminated – suddenly, as might be expected: the little one was hurt and began to cry; and its ungentle playfellow tossed it into its mother's lap, bidding her 'make all straight.' As happy to return to that gentle comforter as it had been to leave her, the child nestled in her arms and hushed its cries in a moment; and, sinking its little weary head on her bosom, soon dropped asleep.

Meantime, Mr Hattersley strode up to the fire, and, interposing his height and breadth between us and it, stood, with arms akimbo, expanding his chest, and gazing round him as if the house and all its appurtenances and contents were his own undisputed possessions.

'Deuced bad weather this!' he began. 'There'll be no shooting today, I guess.' Then, suddenly lifting up his voice, he regaled us with a few bars of a rollicking song, which abruptly ceasing, he finished the tune with a whistle, and then continued, – 'I say Mrs Huntingdon, what a fine stud your husband has! – not large but good. – I've been looking at them a bit this morning; and upon my word, Black Bess, and Grey Tom, and that young Nimrod are the finest animals I've seen for many a day!' Then followed a particular discussion of their various merits, succeeded by a sketch of the great things *he* intended to do in the horse-jockey line[3] when his old governor thought proper to quit the stage – 'Not that I wish him to close his accounts,' added he; 'the old Trojan is welcome to keep his books open as long as he pleases for me.'

'I hope so, *indeed*, Mr Hattersley!'

'Oh yes! It's only my way of talking. The event must come, sometime, and so I look to the bright side of it – that's the right plan, isn't it, Mrs H.? – What are you two doing here, by the by – where's Lady Lowborough?'

'In the billiard room.'

'What a splendid creature she *is*!' continued he, fixing his eyes on his wife, who changed colour, and looked more and more disconcerted as he proceeded. 'What a noble figure she has! and what magnificent black eyes; and what a fine spirit of her own; – and what a tongue of her own, too, when she likes to use it – I perfectly adore her! – But never mind, Milicent: I wouldn't have her for my wife – not if she'd a kingdom for her dowry! I'm better satisfied with the one I have. – Now *then*! what do you look so sulky for? don't you believe me?'

'Yes, I believe you,' murmured she, in a tone of half sad, half sullen resignation, as she turned away to stroke the hair of her sleeping infant, that she had laid on the sofa beside her.

'Well *then*, what makes you so cross? Come here Milly, and tell me why you can't be satisfied with my assurance.'

She went, and, putting her little hand within his arm, looked up in his face, and said softly, –

'What does it amount to Ralph? Only to this, that though you admire Annabella so much, and for qualities that I don't possess, you would still rather have me than her for your wife which merely proves that you don't think it necessary to love your wife: you are satisfied if she can keep your house and take care of your child. But I'm not cross; I'm only sorry; for,' added she in a low, tremulous accent, withdrawing her hand from his arm, and bending her looks on the rug, 'if you don't love me, you don't, and it can't be helped.'

'Very true: but who told you I didn't? Did I say I loved Annabella?'

'You said you adored her.'

'True, but adoration isn't love. I adore Annabella, but I don't love her; and I love thee Milicent, but I don't adore thee.' In proof of his affection, he clutched a handful of her light brown ringlets and appeared to twist them unmercifully.

'Do you really, Ralph?' murmured she with a faint smile beaming through her tears, just putting up her hand to his, in token that he pulled *rather* too hard.

'To be sure I do,' responded he: 'only you bother me rather, sometimes.'

'*I* bother you!' cried she in very natural surprise.

'Yes, *you* – but only by your exceeding goodness – when a boy has been cramming raisins and sugar-plums all day, he longs for a squeeze of sour orange by way of a change. And did you never, Milly, observe the sands on the sea-shore; how nice and smooth they look, and how soft and easy they feel to the foot? But if you plod along, for half an hour, over this soft, easy carpet – giving way at every step, yielding the more the harder you press, – you'll find it rather wearisome work, and be glad enough to come to a bit of good, firm rock, that won't budge an inch whether you stand, walk, or stamp upon it; and, though it be hard as the nether millstone, you'll find it the easier footing after all.'

'I know what you mean, Ralph,' said she, nervously playing with her watch-guard and tracing the figure on the rug with the point of her tiny foot, 'I know what you mean, but I thought you always liked to be yielded to; and I can't alter now.'

'I do like it,' replied he, bringing her to him by another tug at her hair. 'You mustn't mind my talk Milly. A man must have something to grumble about; and if he can't complain that his wife harries him to death with her perversity and ill-humour, he must complain that she wears him out with her kindness and gentleness.'

'But why complain at all, unless, because you are tired and dissatisfied?'

'To excuse my own failings, to be sure. Do you think I'll bear all the burden of my sins on my own shoulders, as long as there's another ready to help me, with none of her own to carry?'

'There is no such one on earth,' said she seriously; and then, taking his hand from her head, she kissed it with an air of genuine devotion, and tripped away to the door.

'What now?' said he. 'Where are you going?'

'To tidy my hair,' she answered, smiling through her disordered locks: 'you've made it all come down.'

'Off with you then! – An excellent little woman,' he remarked when she was gone, 'but a thought too soft[4] – she almost melts in one's hands. I positively think I ill-use her sometimes, when I've taken too much – but I can't help it, for she never complains, either at the time or after. I suppose she doesn't mind it.'

'I can enlighten you on that subject, Mr Hattersley,' said I: 'she *does* mind it; and some other things she minds still more, which, yet, you may never hear her complain of.'

'How do you know? – does she complain to you?' demanded he, with a sudden spark of fury ready to burst into a flame if I should answer 'Yes.'

'No,' I replied; 'but I have known her longer and studied her more closely than you have done. – And I can tell you, Mr Hattersley, that Milicent loves you more than you deserve, and that you have it in your power to make her very happy, instead of which you are her evil genius, and, I will venture to say, there is not a single day passes in which you do not inflict upon her some pang that you might spare her if you would.'

'Well – it's not *my* fault,' said he, gazing carelessly up at the ceiling and plunging his hands into his pockets: 'if my ongoings don't suit her, she should tell me so.'

'Is she not exactly the wife you wanted? Did you not tell Mr Huntingdon you must have one that would submit to anything without a murmur, and never blame you, whatever you did?'

'True, but we shouldn't always have what we want: it spoils the best of us, doesn't it?[5] How can I help playing the deuce when I see it's all one to her whether I behave like a Christian or like a scoundrel such as nature made me? – and how can I help teasing her when she's so invitingly meek and mim – when she lies down like a spaniel at my feet[6] and never so much as squeaks to tell me that's enough?'

'If you are a tyrant by nature, the temptation is strong, I allow; but no generous mind delights to oppress the weak, but rather to cherish and protect.'

'I *don't* oppress her; but it's so confounded flat to be always cherishing and protecting; – and then how can I tell that I *am* oppressing her when she "melts away and makes no sign?"[7] I sometimes think she has no feeling at all; and then I go on till she cries – and that satisfies me.'

'Then you *do* delight to oppress her.'

'I don't, I tell you! – only when I'm in a bad humour – or a particularly good one, and want to afflict for the pleasure of comforting; or when she looks flat and wants shaking up a bit. And sometimes, she provokes me by crying for nothing, and won't tell me what it's for; and then, I allow, it enrages me past bearing – especially, when I'm not my own man.'

'As is no doubt generally the case on such occasions,' said I. 'But in future, Mr Hattersley, when you see her looking flat or crying for "nothing" (as you call it), ascribe it all to yourself: be assured it is something you have done amiss, or your general misconduct that distresses her.'

'I don't believe it. If it were, she should tell me so: I don't like that way of moping and fretting in silence, and saying nothing – it's not honest. How can she expect me to mend my ways at that rate?'

'Perhaps she gives you credit for having more sense than you possess, and deludes herself with the hope that you will one day see your own errors and repair them, if left to your own reflection.'

'None of your sneers, Mrs Huntingdon! I *have* the sense to see that I'm not always quite correct – but sometimes I think that's no great matter, as long as I injure nobody but myself –'

'It *is* a great matter,' interrupted I, 'both to yourself (as you will hereafter find to your cost) and to all connected with you – most especially your wife – but indeed, it is nonsense to talk about injuring no one but yourself; it is impossible to injure yourself – especially by such acts as we allude to – without injuring hundreds, if not thousands, besides, in a greater or less degree, either by the evil you do or the good you leave undone.'

'And as I was saying,' continued he – 'or would have said if you hadn't taken me up so short – I sometimes think I should do better if I were joined to one that would always remind me when I was wrong, and give me a motive for doing good and eschewing evil by decidedly showing her approval of the one, and disapproval of the other.'

'If you had no higher motive than the approval of your fellow mortal, it would do you little good.'

'Well, but if I had a mate that would not always be yielding, and always equally kind, but that would have the spirit to stand at bay now and then, and honestly tell me her mind at all times – such a one as yourself for instance – Now if I went on with you as I do with her when I'm in London, you'd make the house too hot to hold me at times, I'll be sworn.'

'You mistake me: I'm no termagant.'

'Well, all the better for that, for I can't stand contradiction – in a general way – and I'm as fond of my own will as another: only I think too much of it doesn't answer for any man.'

'Well, I would never contradict you without a cause, but certainly I would always let you know what I thought of your conduct; and if you oppressed me, in body, mind, or estate, you should at least have no reason to suppose "I didn't mind it."'

'I know that my lady; and I think if my little wife were to follow the same plan it would be better for us both.'

'I'll tell her.'

'No, no, let her be; there's much to be said on both sides – and, now I think upon it, Huntingdon often regrets that you are not more like her – scoundrelly dog that he is – and you see, after all, you can't reform *him*: he's *ten* times worse than I – He's afraid of you, to be sure – that is, he's always on his best behaviour in your presence – but –'

'I wonder what his worst behaviour is like, then?' I could not forbear observing.

'Why, to tell you the truth, it's very bad indeed – isn't it, Hargrave?' said he, addressing that gentleman, who had entered the room unperceived by me, for I was now standing near the fire with my back to the door. 'Isn't Huntingdon,' he continued, 'as great a reprobate as ever was d—d?'

'His lady will not hear him censured with impunity,' replied Mr Hargrave, coming forward, 'but I must say, I thank God I am not such another.'

'Perhaps it would become you better,' said I, 'to look at what you are, and say, "God be merciful to me a sinner."'[8]

'You are severe,' returned he, bowing slightly and drawing himself up with a proud yet injured air. Hattersley laughed, and clapped him on the shoulder. Moving from under his hand with a gesture of insulted dignity, Mr Hargrave took himself away to the other end of the rug.

'Isn't it a shame, Mrs Huntingdon?' cried his brother-in-law – 'I struck Walter Hargrave when I was drunk, the second night after we came, and he's turned a cold shoulder on me ever since; though I asked his pardon the very morning after it was done!'

'Your manner of asking it,' returned the other, 'and the clearness with which you remembered the whole transaction, showed you were not too drunk to be fully conscious of what you were about, and quite responsible for the deed.'

'You wanted to interfere between me and my wife,' grumbled Hattersley, 'and that is enough to provoke any man.'

'You justify it then?' said his opponent, darting upon him a most vindictive glance.

'No, I tell you I wouldn't have done it if I hadn't been under excitement; and if you choose to bear malice for it, after all the handsome things I've said – do so and be damned!'

'I *would* refrain from such language in a *lady's* presence, at least,' said Mr Hargrave, hiding his anger under a mask of disgust.

'What have I said?' returned Hattersley. 'Nothing but Heaven's truth – he will be damned, won't he, Mrs Huntingdon, if he doesn't forgive his brother's trespasses?'

'You ought to forgive him, Mr Hargrave, since he asks you,' said I.

'Do you say so? Then I will!' And, smiling almost frankly, he stepped forward and offered his hand. It was immediately clasped in that of his relative, and the reconciliation was apparently cordial on both sides.

'The affront,' continued Hargrave, turning to me, 'owed half its bitterness to the fact of its being offered in your presence; and since you bid me forgive it, I will – and forget it too.'

'I guess the best return I can make, will be to take myself off,' muttered Hattersley, with a broad grin. His companion smiled; and he left the room. This put me on my guard. Mr Hargrave turned seriously to me, and earnestly began –

'Dear Mrs Huntingdon, how I have longed for, yet dreaded this hour! Do not be alarmed,' he added, for my face was crimson with anger; 'I am not about to offend you with any useless entreaties or complaints. I am not going to presume to trouble you with the mention of my own feelings or your perfections, but I have something to reveal to you which you ought to know, and which, yet, it pains me inexpressibly –'

'Then don't trouble yourself to reveal it!'

'But it is of importance –'

'If so, I shall hear it soon enough – especially if it is bad news, as you seem to consider it. At present, I am going to take the children to the nursery.'

'But can't you ring, and send them?'

'No; I want the exercise of a run to the top of the house – Come Arthur.'

'But you will return?'

'Not yet; don't wait.'

'Then, when may I see you again?'

'At lunch,' said I, departing with little Helen in one arm, and leading Arthur by the hand.

He turned away, muttering some sentence of impatient censure or complaint, in which 'heartless' was the only distinguishable word.

'What nonsense is this Mr Hargrave?' said I, pausing in the doorway. 'What do you mean?'

'Oh, nothing – I did not intend you should hear my soliloquy. But the fact is, Mrs Huntingdon, I have a disclosure to make – painful for me to offer as for you to hear – and I want you to give me a few minutes of your attention in private, at any time and place you like to appoint. It is from no selfish motive that I ask it, and not for any cause that could alarm your superhuman purity; therefore, you need not kill me with that look of cold and pitiless disdain. I know too well the feelings with which the bearers of bad tidings are commonly regarded, not to –'

'What *is* this wonderful piece of intelligence?' said I, impatiently interrupting him. 'If it is anything of real importance, speak it in three words before I go.'

'In three words I cannot. Send those children away, and stay with me.'

'No; keep your bad tidings to yourself. I know it is something I don't want to hear, and something you would displease me by telling.'

'You have divined too truly, I fear; but still since I know it, I feel it my duty to disclose it to you.'

'Oh, spare us both the infliction – and I will exonerate you from the duty. You have offered to tell; I have refused to hear: my ignorance will not be charged on you.'

'Be it so – you shall not hear it from me. But if the blow fall too suddenly upon you when it comes, remember – I wished to soften it!'

I left him. I was determined his words should not alarm me. What could *he* of all men, have to reveal that was of importance for *me* to hear? It was, no doubt some exaggerated tale about my unfortunate husband, that he wished to make the most of to serve his own bad purposes.

6th. He has not alluded to this momentous mystery since; and I have seen no reason to repent of my unwillingness to hear it. The threatened blow has not been struck yet; and I do not greatly fear it. At present I am pleased with Arthur: he has not positively disgraced himself for upwards of a fortnight, and all this last week, has been so very moderate in his indulgence at table, that I can perceive a marked difference in his general temper and appearance. Dare I hope this will continue?

CHAPTER 33

TWO EVENINGS

Seventh. Yes, I *will* hope! Tonight, I heard Grimsby and Hattersley grumbling together, about the inhospitality of their host. They did not know I was near, for I happened to be standing behind the curtain, in the bow of the window, watching the moon rising over the clump of tall, dark elm-trees below the lawn and wondering why Arthur was so sentimental as to stand without, leaning against the outer pillar of the portico, apparently watching it too.

'So, I suppose we've seen the last of our merry carousals in this house,' said Mr Hattersley, 'I *thought* his good-fellowship wouldn't last long. – But,' added he, laughing, 'I didn't expect it would meet its end this way. I rather thought our pretty hostess would be setting up her porcupine quills, and threatening to turn us out of the house, if we didn't mind[1] our manners.'

'You didn't foresee *this*, then?' answered Grimsby with a guttural chuckle. 'But he'll change again when he's sick of her. If we come here a year or two hence, we shall have all our own way, you'll see.'

'I don't know,' replied the other: 'she's not the style of woman you soon tire of – but be that as it may, it's devilish provoking now, that we can't be jolly, because he chooses to be on his good behaviour.'

'It's all these cursed women!' muttered Grimsby. 'They're the very bane of the world! They bring trouble and discomfort wherever they come, with their false, fair faces and their d—d deceitful tongues.'

At this juncture, I issued from my retreat, and smiling on Mr Grimsby as I passed, left the room and went out in search of Arthur. Having seen him bend his course towards the shrubbery, I followed him thither, and found him just entering the shadowy walk. I was so light of heart, so overflowing with affection, that I sprang upon him and clasped him in my arms. This startling conduct had a singular effect upon him: first, he murmured, 'Bless you darling!' and returned my close embrace with a fervour like old times, and *then* he started, and in a tone of absolute terror, exclaimed –

'Helen! – What the devil is this!' and I saw, by the faint light gleaming through the overshadowing tree, that he was positively pale with the shock.

How strange that the instinctive impulse of affection should come first, and then the shock of the surprise! It shows, at least, that the affection is genuine: he is not sick of me yet.

'I startled you, Arthur,' said I, laughing in my glee. 'How nervous you are!'

'What the deuce did you do it for?' cried he, quite testily, extricating himself from my arms, and wiping his forehead with his handkerchief. 'Go back, Helen – go back directly! You'll get your death of cold!'

'I won't – till I've told you what I came for. They are blaming you, Arthur, for your temperance and sobriety, and I'm come to thank you for it. They say it is all "these cursed women," and that we are the bane of the world; but don't let them laugh, or grumble you out of your good resolutions, or your affection for me.'

He laughed. I squeezed him in my arms again, and cried in tearful earnest –

'Do – do persevere! – and I'll love you better than ever I did before!'

'Well, well, I will!' said he, hastily kissing me. 'There now, go. – You mad creature, how *could* you come out in your light evening dress, this chill autumn night?'

'It is a glorious night,' said I.

'It is a night that will give you your death, in another minute. Run away, do!'

'Do you see my death among those trees, Arthur?' said I, for he was gazing intently at the shrubs, as if he saw it coming, and I was reluctant to leave him, in my new-found happiness and revival of hope and love. But he grew angry at my delay, so I kissed him and ran back to the house.

I was in such a good humour that night: Milicent told me I was the life of the party, and whispered she had never seen me so brilliant. Certainly, I talked enough for twenty, and smiled upon them all. Grimsby, Hattersley, Hargrave, Lady Lowborough – all shared my sisterly kindness. Grimsby stared and wondered; Hattersley laughed and jested (in spite of the little wine he had been suffered to imbibe), but still, behaved as well as he knew how; Hargrave and Annabella, from different motives and in different ways, emulated me, and doubtless both surpassed me, the former in his discursive versatility and eloquence, the latter in boldness and animation at least. Milicent, delighted to see her husband, her brother and her over-estimated friend acquitting themselves so well, was lively and gay too, in her quiet way. Even Lord Lowborough caught the general contagion: his dark, greenish eyes were lighted up beneath their moody brows; his sombre countenance was beautified by smiles; all traces of gloom, and proud or cold reserve, had vanished for the time; and he astonished us all, not only by his general cheerfulness and animation, but by the positive flashes of true force and brilliance he emitted from time to time. Arthur did not talk much, but he laughed, and listened to the rest, and was in perfect good-humour, though not excited by wine. So that, altogether, we made a very merry, innocent and entertaining party.

9th. Yesterday, when Rachel came to dress me for dinner, I saw that she had been crying. I wanted to know the cause of it, but she seemed reluctant to tell. Was she unwell? No. Had she heard bad news from her friends? No. Had any of the servants vexed her?

'Oh, no ma'am!' she answered – 'It's not for myself.'

'What then, Rachel? Have you been reading novels?'

'Bless you, no!' said she with a sorrowful shake of the head; and then she sighed and continued, 'But to tell you the truth, ma'am, I don't like master's ways of going on.'

'What do you mean Rachel? – He's going on very properly – at present.'

'Well ma'am, if you think so, it's right.'

And she went on dressing my hair, in a hurried way, quite unlike her usual calm, collected manner, – murmuring, half to herself, she was sure it was beautiful hair, she 'could like to see 'em match it.' When it was done, she fondly stroked it and gently patted my head.

'Is that affectionate ebullition intended for my hair, or myself, nurse?' said I, laughingly turning round upon her; – but a tear was even now in her eye.

'What *do* you mean, Rachel?' I exclaimed.

'Well, ma'am, I don't know, – but if –'

'If what?'

'Well, if I was you, I wouldn't have that Lady Lowborough in the house another minute – not another *minute* I wouldn't!'

I was thunderstruck; but before I could recover from the shock sufficiently to demand an explanation, Milicent entered my room – as she frequently does, when she is dressed before me; and she stayed with me till it was time to go down. She must have found me a very unsociable companion this time, for Rachel's last words rung in my ears. But still, I hoped – I trusted they had no foundation but in some idle rumour of the servants from what they had seen in Lady Lowborough's manner last month; or, perhaps, from something that had passed between their master and her during her former visit. At dinner, I narrowly observed both her and Arthur, and saw nothing extraordinary in the conduct of either – nothing calculated to excite suspicion, except in distrustful minds – which mine was not, and therefore I would not suspect.

Almost immediately after dinner, Annabella went out with her husband to share his moonlight ramble, for it was a splendid evening like the last. Mr Hargrave entered the drawing-room a little before the others, and challenged me to a game of chess.[2] He did it without any of that sad but proud humility he usually assumes in addressing me, unless he is excited with wine. I looked at his face to see if that was the case now. His eye met mine keenly, but steadily: there was something about him I did not understand, but he seemed sober enough. Not choosing to engage with him, I referred him to Milicent.

'She plays badly,' said he: 'I want to match my skill with yours.

Come now! – you can't pretend you are reluctant to lay down your work – I know you never take it up except to pass an idle hour, when there is nothing better you can do.'

'But chess players are so unsociable,' I objected; 'they are no company for any but themselves.'

'There is no one here – but Milicent, and she –'

'Oh, I shall be delighted to watch you!' cried our mutual friend – 'Two *such* players – it will be quite a treat! I wonder which will conquer.'

I consented.

'Now Mrs Huntingdon,' said Hargrave, as he arranged the men on the board, speaking distinctly, and with a peculiar emphasis as if he had a double meaning to all his words, 'you are a good player, – but I am a better: we shall have a long game, and you will give me some trouble; but I can be as patient as you, and, in the end, I shall certainly win.' He fixed his eyes upon me with a glance I did not like – keen, crafty, bold, and almost impudent; already half triumphant in his anticipated success.

'I hope not, Mr Hargrave!' returned I, with vehemence that must have startled Milicent at least; but *he* only smiled and murmured, –

'Time will show.'

We set to work; he, sufficiently interested in the game, but calm and fearless in the consciousness of superior skill; I, intensely eager to disappoint his expectations, for I considered this the type of a more serious contest – as I imagined he did – and I felt an almost superstitious dread of being beaten: at all events, I could ill endure that present success should add one title to his conscious power (his insolent self-confidence, I ought to say), or encourage, for a moment, his dream of future conquest. His play was cautious and deep, but I struggled hard against him. For some time the combat was doubtful, at length, to my joy, the victory seemed inclining to my side: I had taken several of his best pieces, and manifestly baffled his projects. He put his hand to his brow and paused, in evident perplexity. I rejoiced in my advantage, but dared not glory in it yet. At length, he lifted his head, and, quietly making his move, looked at me and said, calmly, –

'Now, you think you will win, don't you.'

'I hope so,' replied I, taking his pawn that he had pushed into the way of my bishop[3] with so careless an air that I thought it was an oversight, but was not generous enough, under the circumstances, to direct his attention to it, and too heedless, at the moment, to foresee the after consequences of my move.

'It is those bishops that trouble me,' said he; 'but the bold knight can overleap the reverend gentleman,' taking my last bishop with his knight; – 'and now, those sacred persons once removed, I shall carry all before me.'

'Oh Walter, how you talk!' cried Milicent – 'She has far more pieces than you still.'

'I intend to give you some trouble yet,' said I; 'and perhaps, sir, you will find yourself checkmated before you are aware. Look to your queen.'

The combat deepened. The game *was* a long one, and I *did* give him some trouble: but he *was* a better player than I.

'What keen gamesters you are!' said Mr Hattersley, who had now entered, and been watching us for some time. 'Why, Mrs Huntingdon, your hand trembles as if you had staked your all upon it! and Walter – you dog – you look as deep and cool as if you were certain of success, – and as keen and cruel as if you would drain her heart's blood! – But if I were you, I wouldn't beat her, for very fear: she'll hate you if you do – she will, by Heaven! – I see it in her eye.'

'Hold your tongue, will you?' said I – his talk distracted me, for I was driven to extremities. A few more moves and I was inextricably entangled in the snare of my antagonist.

'Check,' – cried he: I sought in agony some means of escape – 'mate!' he added, quietly but with evident delight. He had suspended the utterance of that last fatal syllable the better to enjoy my dismay. I was foolishly disconcerted by the event. Hattersley laughed; Milicent was troubled to see me so disturbed. Hargrave placed his hand on mine that rested on the table, and, squeezing it with a firm but gentle pressure, murmured 'Beaten – beaten!' and gazed into my face with a look where exultation was blended with an expression of ardour and tenderness yet more insulting.

'*No, never*, Mr Hargrave!' exclaimed I, quickly withdrawing my hand.

'Do you deny?' replied he, smilingly pointing to the board.

'No, no,' I answered, recollecting how strange my conduct must appear; 'you have beaten me in that game.'

'Will you try another, then?'

'No.'

'You acknowledge my superiority?'

'Yes – as a chess-player.'

I rose to resume my work.

'Where is Annabella?' said Hargrave, gravely, after glancing round the room.

'Gone out with Lord Lowborough,' answered I, for he looked at me for a reply.

'And not yet returned!' he said seriously.

'I suppose not.'

'Where is Huntingdon?' looking round again.

'Gone out with Grimsby – as you know,' said Hattersley suppressing a laugh, which broke forth as he concluded the sentence.

Why did he laugh? Why did Hargrave connect them thus together? Was it true, then? – And was this the dreadful secret he had wished to reveal to me? I must know – and that quickly. I instantly rose and left the room to go in search of Rachel, and demand an explanation of her words; but Mr Hargrave followed me into the ante-room, and before I could open its outer door, gently laid his hand upon the lock.

'May I tell you something, Mrs Huntingdon?' said he, in a subdued tone, with serious, downcast eyes.

'If it be anything worth hearing,' replied I, struggling to be composed, for I trembled in every limb.

He quietly pushed a chair towards me. I merely leant my hand upon it, and bid him go on.

'Do not be alarmed,' said he: 'what I wish to say is nothing in itself; and I will leave you to draw your own inferences from it. You say that Annabella is not yet returned?'

'Yes, yes – go on!' said I, impatiently, for I feared my forced calmness would leave me before the end of his disclosure, whatever it might be.

'And you hear,' continued he, 'that Huntingdon is gone out with Grimsby?'

'Well?'

'I heard the latter say to your husband – or the man who calls himself so –'

'Go on, sir!'

He bowed submissively, and continued, 'I heard him say, – "I shall manage it, you'll see! They're gone down by the water; I shall meet them there, and tell him I want a bit of talk with him about some things that we needn't trouble the lady with; and she'll say she can be walking back to the house; and then I shall apologize, you know, and all that, and tip her a wink to take the way of the shrubbery. I'll keep him talking there, about those matters I mentioned, and anything else I can think of, as long as I can, and then bring him round the other way, stopping to look at the trees, the fields, and anything else I can find to discourse of."' Mr Hargrave paused, and looked at me.

Without a word of comment or further questioning, I rose, and darted from the room and out of the house. The torment of suspense was not to be endured: I would not suspect my husband falsely, on this man's accusation, and I would not trust him unworthily – I must know the truth at once. I flew to the shrubbery. Scarcely had I reached it, when a sound of voices arrested my breathless speed.

'We have lingered too long; he will be back,' said Lady Lowborough's voice.

'Surely not, dearest!' was *his* reply, 'but you can run across the lawn, and get in as quietly as you can: I'll follow in a while.'

My knees trembled under me; my brain swam round: I was ready to faint. She must not see me thus. I shrunk among the bushes, and leant against the trunk of a tree to let her pass.

'Ah, Huntingdon!' said she reproachfully, pausing where I had stood with him the night before – 'it was here you kissed that woman!' she looked back into the leafy shade. Advancing thence, he answered, with a careless laugh –

'Well, dearest, I couldn't help it. You know I must keep straight with her as long as I can. Haven't I seen you kiss your dolt of a husband, scores of times? – and do *I* ever complain?'

'But tell me, don't you love her still – a *little*?' said she placing her hand on his arm looking earnestly in his face – for I could see them plainly, the moon shining full upon them from between the branches of the tree that sheltered me.

'Not *one bit*, by all that's sacred!' he replied, kissing her glowing cheek.

'Good heavens, I *must* be gone!' cried she, suddenly breaking from him, and away she flew.

There he stood before me; but I had not strength to confront him now; my tongue cleaved to the roof of my mouth,[4] I was well-nigh sinking to the earth, and I almost wondered he did not hear the beating of my heart above the low sighing of the wind, and the fitful rustle of the falling leaves. My senses seemed to fail me, but still I saw his shadowy form pass before me, and through the rushing sound in my ears, I distinctly heard him say, as he stood looking up the lawn –

'There goes the fool! Run Annabella, run! There – in with you! Ah, he didn't see! That's right Grimsby, keep him back!' And even his low laugh reached me as he walked away.

'God help me now!' I murmured, sinking on my knees among the damp weeds and brushwood that surrounded me, and looking up at the moonlit sky, through the scant foliage above. It seemed all dim and quivering now to my darkened sight. My burning, bursting heart strove to pour forth its agony to God, but could not frame its anguish into prayer; until a gust of wind swept over me,[5] which, while it scattered the dead leaves, like blighted hopes, around, cooled my forehead, and seemed a little to revive my sinking frame. Then, while I lifted up my soul in speechless, earnest supplication, some heavenly influence seemed to strengthen me within:[6] I breathed more freely; my vision cleared; I saw distinctly the pure moon shining on, and the light clouds skimming the clear, dark sky; and then, I saw the eternal stars twinkling down upon me; I knew their God was mine, and He was strong to save and swift to hear.[7] 'I will never leave thee, nor forsake thee,'[8] seemed whispered from above their myriad orbs. No, no; I felt He would not leave me comfortless:[9] in spite of earth and hell I should have strength for all my trials, and win a glorious rest at last!

Refreshed, invigorated if not composed, I rose and returned to the house. Much of my newborn strength and courage forsook me,[10] I confess, as I entered it, and shut out the fresh wind and the glorious sky: everything I saw and heard seemed to sicken my heart – the hall, the lamp, the staircase, the doors of the different apartments, the social sound of talk and laughter from the drawing-room. How could I bear my future life? In this house, among those people – Oh, how could I endure to live! John just then entered the hall, and seeing me, told me he had been sent in search of me, adding that he had taken in the tea, and master wished to know if I were coming.

'Ask Mrs Hattersley to be so kind as to make the tea, John,' said I. 'Say I am not well tonight, and wish to be excused.'

I retired into the large, empty dining-room, where all was silence and darkness, but for the soft sighing of the wind without, and the faint gleam of moonlight that pierced the blinds and curtains; and there I walked rapidly up and down, thinking of my bitter thoughts alone. How different was this from the evening of yesterday! *That*, it seems, was the last expiring flash of my life's happiness. Poor, blinded fool that I was, to be so happy! I could now see the reason of Arthur's strange reception of me in the shrubbery: the burst of kindness was for his paramour, the start of horror for his wife. Now, too, I could better understand the conversation between Hattersley and Grimsby: it was doubtless of his love for *her* they spoke, not for me.

I heard the drawing-room door open: a light quick step came out of the ante-room, crossed the hall, and ascended the stairs. It was Milicent, poor Milicent, gone to see how I was – no one else cared for me; but *she* still was kind. I shed no tears before, but now they came – fast and free. Thus she did me good, without approaching me. Disappointed in her search, I heard her come down – more slowly than she had ascended. Would she come in there, and find me out? No; she turned in the opposite direction and re-entered the drawing-room. I was glad, for I knew not how to meet her, or what to say. I wanted no confidant in my distress. I deserved none – and I wanted none. I had taken the burden[11] upon myself: let me bear it alone.

As the usual hour of retirement approached, I dried my eyes, and tried to clear my voice and calm my mind. I must see Arthur tonight, and speak to him; but I would do it calmly: there should be no scene – nothing to complain or to boast of to his companions – nothing to laugh at with his lady love. When the company were retiring to their chambers, I gently opened the door, and just as he passed, I beckoned him in.

'What's to do with *you*, Helen?' said he. 'Why couldn't you come to make tea for us? and what the deuce are you here for, in the dark? What ails you, young woman – you look like a ghost?' he continued, surveying me by the light of his candle.

'No matter,' I answered – 'to you – you have no longer any regard for me, it appears; and I have no longer any for you.'

'Hal-low! what the devil is this?' he muttered.

'I would leave you tomorrow,' continued I, 'and never again come under this roof, but for my child' – I paused a moment to steady my voice.

'What in the devil's name *is* this, Helen?' cried he. 'What can you be driving at?'

'You know, perfectly well. Let us waste no time in useless explanation, but tell me, will you –'

He vehemently swore he knew nothing about it, and insisted upon hearing what poisonous old woman had been blackening his name, and what infamous lies I had been fool enough to believe.

'Spare yourself the trouble of forswearing yourself and racking your brains to stifle truth with falsehood,' I coldly replied. 'I have trusted to the testimony of no third person. I was in the shrubbery this evening, and I saw and heard for myself.'

This was enough. He uttered a suppressed exclamation[12] of consternation and dismay, and muttering, 'I *shall* catch it now!' set down his candle on the nearest chair, and, rearing his back against the wall, stood confronting me with folded arms.

'Well! – what then?' said he, with the calm insolence of mingled shamelessness and desperation.

'Only this,' returned I: 'will you let me take our child and what remains of my fortune, and go?'

'Go where?'

'Anywhere, where he will be safe from your contaminating influence, and I shall be delivered from your presence – and you from mine.'

'No – by *Jove* I won't!'

'Will you let me have the child then, without the money?'

'No – nor yourself without the child. Do you think I'm going to be made the talk of the country, for your fastidious caprices?'

'Then I must stay here, to be hated and despised – But henceforth, we are husband and wife only in the name.'[13]

'Very good.'

'I am your child's mother, and *your* housekeeper – nothing more. So you need not trouble yourself any longer, to feign the love you cannot feel: I will exact no more heartless caresses from you – nor offer – nor endure them either – I will not be mocked with the empty husk of conjugal endearments, when you have given the substance to another!'

'Very good – if *you* please. We shall see who will tire first, my lady.'

'If I tire, it will be of living in the world with you; not of living without your mockery of love. When *you* tire of your sinful ways, and show yourself truly repentant, I will forgive you – and, perhaps, try to love you again, though that will be hard indeed.'

'Humph! – and meantime, you will go and talk me over to Mrs Hargrave, and write long letters to aunt Maxwell to complain of the wicked wretch you have married?'

'I shall complain to no one. Hitherto, I have struggled hard to hide your vices from every eye, and invest you with virtues you never possessed – but now you must look to yourself.'

I left him – muttering bad language to himself, and went upstairs.

'You are poorly ma'am,' said Rachel, surveying me with deep anxiety.

'It is too true, Rachel!' said I, answering her sad looks rather than her words.

'I knew it – or I wouldn't have mentioned such a thing.'

'But don't *you* trouble yourself about it,' said I, kissing her pale, time-wasted cheek – 'I can bear it – better than you imagine.'

'Yes, you were always for "bearing" – But if I was you I wouldn't bear it – I'd give way to it, and cry right hard! – and I'd talk too, I just *would* – I'd let him know what it was to –'

'I have talked,' said I: 'I've said enough.'

'Then I'd cry,' persisted she. 'I wouldn't look so white and so calm, and burst my heart with keeping it in!'

'I *have* cried,' said I, smiling in spite of my misery; 'and I *am* calm now, really, so don't discompose me again, nurse: let us say no more about it – and *don't* mention it to the servants. – There, you may go now. Goodnight; – and don't disturb your rest for me: I shall sleep well – if I can.'

Notwithstanding this resolution, I found my bed so intolerable that, before two o'clock, I rose, and, lighting my candle by the rushlight that was still burning, I got my desk and sat down in my dressing-gown to recount the events of the past evening. It was better to be so occupied than to be lying in bed torturing my brain with recollections of the far past and anticipations of the dreadful future. I have found relief in describing the very circumstances that have destroyed my peace, as well as the little trivial details attendant upon their discovery. No sleep I could have got this night would have done so much towards composing my mind, and preparing me to meet the trials of the day – I fancy so, at least; – and yet, when I cease writing, I find my head aches terribly; and when I look into the glass I am startled at my haggard, worn appearance.

Rachel has been to dress me, and says I have had a sad night of it she can see. Milicent has just looked in to ask me how I was. I told her I was better, but to excuse my appearance admitted I had had a restless night. – I wish this day were over! I shudder at the thought of going down to breakfast – How shall I encounter them all? – Yet let me remember it is not *I* that am guilty: *I* have no cause to fear; and if *they* scorn me as the victim of their guilt, I can pity their folly and despise their scorn.[14]

CHAPTER 34

CONCEALMENT

Evening. Breakfast passed well over, I was calm and cool throughout. I answered composedly all enquiries respecting my health; and whatever was unusual in my look or manner was generally attributed to the trifling indisposition that had occasioned my early retirement last night. But how am I to get over the ten or twelve days that must yet elapse before they go? Yet why so long for their departure? When they *are* gone how shall I get through the months or years of my future life, in company with that man – my greatest enemy – for none could injure me as he has done? Oh! when I think how fondly, how foolishly I have loved him, how madly I have trusted him, how constantly I have laboured, and studied, and prayed, and struggled for his advantage; and how cruelly he has trampled on my love, betrayed my trust, scorned my prayers and tears, and efforts for his preservation – crushed my hopes, destroyed my youth's best feelings, and doomed me to a life of hopeless misery – as far as man can do it – it is not enough to say that I no longer love my husband – I HATE him! The word stares me in the face like a guilty confession, but it is true: I hate him – I hate him! – But God have mercy on his miserable soul! – and make him see and feel his guilt – I ask no other vengeance! if he could but fully know and truly feel my wrongs, I should be well avenged; and I could freely pardon all; but he is so lost, so hardened in his heartless depravity that, in this life, I believe he never will. But it is useless dwelling on this theme: let me seek once more to dissipate reflection in the minor details of passing events.

Mr Hargrave has annoyed me all day long with his serious

sympathizing, and (as *he* thinks) unobtrusive politeness — if it were more obtrusive it would trouble me less, for then I could snub him; but, as it is, he contrives to appear so really kind and thoughful that I cannot do so without rudeness and seeming ingratitude. I sometimes think I ought to give him credit for the good feeling he simulates so well; and then again, I think it is my *duty* to suspect him under the peculiar circumstances in which I am placed. His kindness may not all be feigned, but still, let not the purest impulse of gratitude to him induce me to forget myself; let me remember the game of chess, the expressions he used on the occasion, and those indescribable looks of his, that so justly roused my indignation, and I think I shall be safe enough. I have done well to record them so minutely.

I think he wishes to find an opportunity of speaking to me alone: he has seemed to be on the watch all day! but I have taken care to disappoint him; not that I fear anything he could say, but I have trouble enough without the addition of his insulting consolations, condolences, or whatever else he might attempt; and, for Milicent's sake, I do not wish to quarrel with him. He excused himself from going out to shoot with the other gentlemen in the morning, under the pretext of having letters to write; and instead of retiring for that purpose into the library, he sent for his desk into the morning-room where I was seated with Milicent and Lady Lowborough. They had betaken themselves to their work; I, less to divert my mind than to deprecate conversation, had provided myself with a book. Milicent saw that I wished to be quiet, and accordingly let me alone. Annabella, doubtless, saw it too; but that was no reason why she should restrain her tongue, or curb her cheerful spirits: *she* accordingly chatted away, addressing herself almost exclusively to me, and with the utmost assurance and familiarity, growing the more animated and friendly, the colder and briefer my answers became. Mr Hargrave saw that I could ill endure it; and, looking up from his desk, he answered her questions and observations for me, as far as he could, and attempted to transfer her social attentions from me to himself; but it would not do. Perhaps, she thought I had a headache and could not bear to talk — at any rate, she saw that her loquacious vivacity annoyed me as I could tell by the malicious pertinacity with which she persisted. But I checked it, effectually, by putting into her hand the book I had been trying to read, on the fly leaf of which I had hastily scribbled, –

'I am too well acquainted with your character and conduct to feel any real friendship for you, and, as I am without your talent for dissimulation, I cannot assume the appearance of it. I must, therefore, beg that hereafter, all familiar intercourse may cease between us; and if I still continue to treat you with civility, as if you were a woman worthy of consideration and respect, understand that it is out of regard for your cousin Milicent's feelings, not for yours.'

Upon perusing this, she turned scarlet and bit her lip. Covertly tearing away the leaf, she crumpled it up and put it in the fire, and then employed herself in turning over the pages of the book and, really or apparently, perusing its contents. In a little while Milicent announced it her intention to repair to the nursery, and asked if I would accompany her.

'Annabella will excuse us,' said she, 'she's busy reading.'

'No, I won't,' cried Annabella, suddenly looking up and throwing her book on the table. 'I want to speak to Helen a minute. You may go Milicent, and she'll follow in a while.' (Milicent went.) 'Will you oblige me, Helen?' continued she.

Her impudence astounded me; but I complied, and followed her into the library. She closed the door, and walked up to the fire.

'Who told you this?' said she.

'No one: I am not incapable of seeing for myself.'

'Ah, you are suspicious!' cried she, smiling with a gleam of hope – hitherto, there had been a kind of desperation in her hardihood; now she was evidently relieved.

'If I *were* suspicious,' I replied, 'I should have discovered your infamy long before. No, Lady Lowborough, I do not found my charge upon suspicion.'

'On what *do* you found it then?' said she, throwing herself into an arm chair, and stretching out her feet to the fender, with an obvious effort to appear composed.

'I enjoy a moonlight ramble as well as you,' I answered, steadily fixing my eyes upon her: 'and the shrubbery happens to be one of my favourite resorts.'

She coloured again, excessively, and remained silent, pressing her finger against her teeth, and gazing into the fire. I watched her a few moments with a feeling of malevolent gratification;[1] then, moving towards the door, I calmly asked if she had anything more to say.

'Yes, yes!' cried she eagerly, starting up from her reclining posture. 'I want to know if you will tell Lord Lowborough?'

'Suppose I do?'

'Well, if you are disposed to publish the matter, *I* cannot dissuade you, of course – but there will be terrible work if you do – and if you don't, I shall think you the most generous of mortal beings – and if there is anything in the world I can do for you – anything short of –' she hesitated.

'Short of renouncing your guilty connection with my husband, I suppose you mean,' said I.

She paused, in evident disconcertion and perplexity, mingled with anger she dared not show.

'I cannot renounce what is dearer than life,' she muttered in a low, hurried tone. Then, suddenly raising her head and fixing her gleaming eyes upon me, she continued earnestly, 'But Helen – or Mrs Huntingdon, or whatever you would have me call you – *will* you tell him? If you are generous, here is a fitting opportunity for the exercise of your magnanimity: if you are proud, here am I – your rival – ready to acknowledge myself your debtor for an act of the most noble forbearance.'

'I shall not tell him.'

'You will not!' cried she delightedly. 'Accept my sincere thanks, then!'

She sprang up, and offered me her hand. I drew back.

'Give me no thanks; it is not for *your* sake that I refrain. Neither is it an act of any forbearance: I have no wish to publish your shame. I should be sorry to distress your husband with the knowledge of it.'

'And Milicent? will you tell her?'

'No, on the contrary I shall do my utmost to conceal it from her. I would not for much that she should know the infamy and disgrace of her relation!'

'You use hard words, Mrs Huntingdon – but I can pardon you.'

'And now Lady Lowborough,' continued I, 'let me counsel you to leave this house as soon as *possible*. You must be aware that your continuance here is excessively disagreeable to me – not for Mr Huntingdon's sake,' said I, observing the dawn of a malicious smile of triumph on her face – 'You are welcome to him, if you like him, as far as *I* am concerned – but because it is painful to be always disguising my true sentiments respecting you, and straining to keep up an appearance of civility and respect towards one for whom I have not the most distant shadow of esteem; and because, if you stay, your conduct cannot possibly remain concealed much longer from the only two persons in the house who do not know it already. And, for your husband's sake, Annabella, and even for your own, I wish – I earnestly advise and *entreat* you to break off this unlawful connection at once, and return to your duty while you may, before the dreadful consequences –'

'Yes, yes, of course,' said she, interrupting me with a gesture of impatience. – 'But I cannot go, Helen, before the time appointed for our departure. What possible pretext could I frame for such a thing? Whether I proposed going back alone – which Lowborough would not hear of – or taking him with me, the very circumstance itself would be certain to excite suspicion – and when our visit is so *nearly* at an end too – little more than a week – surely, you can endure my presence *so* long! I will not annoy you with any more of my friendly impertinences.'

'Well! I have nothing more to say to you.'

'Have you mentioned this affair to Huntingdon?' asked she, as I was leaving the room.

'How dare you mention his name to me!' was the only answer I gave.

No words have passed between us since, but such as outward decency or pure necessity demanded.

CHAPTER 35

PROVOCATIONS

Nineteenth. – In proportion as Lady Lowborough finds she has nothing to fear from me, and as the time of departure draws nigh, the more audacious and insolent she becomes. She does not scruple to speak to my husband with affectionate familiarity in my presence, when no one else is by, and is particularly fond of displaying her interest in his health and welfare, or in anything that concerns him, as if for the purpose of contrasting her kind solicitude with my cold indifference. And he rewards her by such smiles and glances, such whispered words, or boldly spoken insinuations, indicative of his sense of her goodness and my neglect, as makes the blood rush into my face, in spite of myself – for I would be utterly regardless of it all – deaf and blind to everything that passes between them, since the more I show myself sensible of their wickedness, the more she triumphs in her victory, and the more he flatters himself that I love him devotedly still, in spite of my pretended indifference. On such occasions I have sometimes been startled by a subtle, fiendish suggestion inciting me to show him the contrary by a seeming encouragement of Hargrave's advances; but such ideas are banished in a moment with horror and self-abasement; and then I hate him tenfold more than ever, for having brought me to this! – God pardon me for it – and all my sinful thoughts! Instead of being humbled and purified by my afflictions, I feel that they are turning my nature into gall. This must be my fault as much as theirs that wrong me. No true Christian could cherish such bitter feelings as I do against him and her – especially the latter: him, I still feel that I could pardon – freely, gladly – on the slightest token of repentance; but *she* – words cannot utter my abhorrence. Reason forbids, but passion urges strongly; and I must pray and struggle long ere I subdue it.

It is well that she is leaving tomorrow, for I could not well endure her presence for another day. This morning, she rose earlier than usual. I found her in the room alone, when I went down to breakfast.

'Oh Helen! is it you?' said she, turning as I entered.

I gave an involuntary start back on seeing her, at which she uttered a short laugh, observing, –

'I think we are *both* disappointed.'

I came forward and busied myself with the breakfast-things.

'This is the last day I shall burden your hospitality,' said she, as she seated herself at the table. 'Ah, here comes one that will not rejoice at it!' she murmured, half to herself, as Arthur entered the room.

He shook hands with her and wished her good morning: then, looking lovingly in her face, and still retaining her hand in his, murmured pathetically, –

'The last – last day!'

'Yes,' said she with some asperity; 'and I rose early to make the best of it – I have been here alone this half hour, and *you*, you lazy creature –'

'Well, I thought I was early too,' said he – 'but,' dropping his voice almost to a whisper, 'you see we are not alone.'

'We never are,' returned she. But they were almost as good as alone, for I was now standing at the window, watching the clouds, and struggling to suppress my wrath.

Some more words passed between them, which, happily, I did not overhear; but Annabella had the audacity to come and place herself beside me, and even to put her hand upon my shoulder and say softly, –

'You need not grudge him to me, Helen, for I love him more than ever you could do.'

This put me beside myself. I took her hand and violently dashed it from me, with an expression of abhorrence and indignation that could not be suppressed. Startled, almost appalled, by this sudden outbreak, she recoiled in silence. I would have given way to my fury and said more, but Arthur's low laugh recalled me to myself. I checked the half-uttered invective, and scornfully turned away, regretting that I had given him so much amusement. He was still laughing when Mr Hargrave made his appearance. How much of the scene he had witnessed I do not know, for the door was ajar when he entered. He greeted his host and his cousin both coldly, and me with a glance intended to express the deepest sympathy mingled with high admiration and esteem.

'How much allegiance do you owe to that man?' he asked below his breath, as he stood beside me at the window, affecting to be making observations on the weather.

'None,' I answered. And immediately returning to the table, I employed myself in making the tea. He followed, and would have entered into some kind of conversation with me, but the other guests were now beginning to assemble and I took no more notice of him, except to give him his coffee.

After breakfast, determined to pass as little of the day as possible in company with Lady Lowborough, I quietly stole away from the company and retired to the library. Mr Hargrave followed me thither, under pretence of coming for a book; and first, turning to the shelves, he selected a volume; and then, quietly, but by no means timidly, approaching me, he stood beside me, resting his hand on the back of my chair, and said softly, –

'And so you consider yourself free, at last?'

'Yes,' said I, without moving, or raising my eyes from my book, – 'free to do anything but offend God and my conscience.'

There was a momentary pause.

'Very right,' said he; 'provided your conscience be not too morbidly tender, and your ideas of God not too erroneously severe; but can you suppose it would offend that benevolent Being to make ·the happiness of one who would die for yours? – to raise a devoted heart from purgatorial torments to a state of heavenly bliss when you could do it without the slightest injury to yourself or any other?'

This was spoken in a low, earnest, melting tone as he bent over me. I now raised my head; and, steadily confronting his gaze, I answered calmly, –

'Mr Hargrave, do you mean to insult me?'

He was not prepared for this. He paused a moment to recover the shock;[1] then, drawing himself up and removing his hand from my chair, he answered, with proud sadness, –

'That was not my intention.'

I just glanced towards the door, with a slight movement of the head, and then returned to my book. He immediately withdrew. This was better than if I had answered with more words, and in the passionate spirit to which my first impulse would have prompted. What a good thing it is to be able to command one's temper! I must labour to cultivate this inestimable quality: God, only, knows how often I shall need it in this rough, dark road that lies before me.

In the course of the morning, I drove over to the Grove with the two ladies, to give Milicent an opportunity for bidding farewell to her mother and sister. They persuaded her to stay with them the rest of the day, Mrs Hargrave promising to bring her back in the evening and remain till the party broke up on the morrow. Consequently, Lady Lowborough and I had the pleasure of returning tête-à-tête in the carriage together. For the first mile or two, we kept silence, I looking out of my window, and she leaning back in her corner. But I was not going to restrict myself to any particular position for her: when I was tired of leaning forward with the cold, raw wind in my face; and surveying the russet hedges, and the damp, tangled grass of their banks, I gave it up, and leant back too. With her usual impudence, my companion then made some attempts to get up a conversation; but the monosyllables 'yes,' or 'no,' or 'humph,' were the utmost her several remarks could elicit from me. At last, on her asking my opinion upon some immaterial point of discussion, I answered, –

'Why do you wish to talk to me, Lady Lowborough? – you must know what I think of you.'

'Well, if you *will* be so bitter against me,' replied she, 'I can't help it; – but *I'm* not going to sulk for anybody.'

Our short drive was now at an end. As soon as the carriage door was opened, she sprang out, and went down the park to meet the gentlemen, who were just returning from the woods. Of course I did not follow.

But I had not done with her impudence yet: – after dinner, I retired to the drawing-room, as usual, and she accompanied me, but I had the two children with me, and I gave them my whole attention, and determined to keep them till the gentlemen came, or till Milicent arrived with her mother. Little Helen, however, was soon tired of playing, and insisted upon going to sleep; and while I sat on the sofa with her on my knee, and Arthur seated beside me, gently playing with her soft, flaxen hair, – Lady Lowborough composedly came and placed herself on the other side.

'Tomorrow, Mrs Huntingdon,' said she, 'you will be delivered from my presence, which, no doubt, you will be very glad of – it is natural you should; – but do you know I have rendered you a great service? – Shall I tell you what it is?'

'I shall be glad to hear of any service you have rendered me,' said I, determined to be calm, for I knew by the tone of her voice she wanted to provoke me.

'Well,' resumed she, 'have you not observed this salutary change in Mr Huntingdon? Don't you see what a sober, temperate man he is become? You saw with regret the sad habits he was contracting, I know; and I know you did your utmost to deliver him from them, – but without success, until I came to your assistance. I told him, in few words, that I could not bear to see him degrade himself so, and that I should cease to – no matter what I told him, – but you see the reformation I have wrought; and you ought to thank me for it.'

I rose, and rang for the nurse.

'But I desire no thanks,' she continued, 'all the return I ask is, that you will take care of him when I am gone, and not, by harshness and neglect, drive him back to his old courses.'

I was almost sick with passion, but Rachel was now at the door: I pointed to the children, for I could not trust myself to speak: she took them away, and I followed.

'Will you, Helen?' continued the speaker.

I gave her a look that blighted the malicious smile on her face – or checked it, at least for a moment – and departed. In the ante-room

I met Mr Hargrave. He saw I was in no humour to be spoken to, and suffered me to pass without a word; but when, after a few minutes' seclusion in the library, I had regained my composure, and was returning, to join Mrs Hargrave and Milicent, whom I had just heard come downstairs and go into the drawing-room, – I found him there still, lingering in the dimly lighted apartment, and evidently waiting for me.

'Mrs Huntingdon,' said he as I passed, 'will you allow me one word?'

'What is it then? – be quick if you please.'

'I offended you this morning; and I cannot live under your displeasure.'

'Then, go, and sin no more,'[2] replied I, turning away.

'No, no!' said he hastily, setting himself before me – 'Pardon me, but I must have your forgiveness. I leave you tomorrow, and I may not have an opportunity of speaking to you again. I was wrong, to forget myself – and you, as I did; but let me implore you to forget and forgive my rash presumption, and think of me as if those words had never been spoken; for, believe me, I regret them deeply, and the loss of your esteem is too severe a penalty – I cannot bear it.'

'Forgetfulness is not to be purchased with a wish; and I cannot bestow my esteem on all who desire it, unless they deserve it too.'

'I shall think my life well spent in labouring to deserve it, if you will but pardon this offence – Will you?'

'Yes.'

'Yes? but that is coldly spoken. Give me your hand and I'll believe you. – You won't? Then, Mrs Huntingdon, you do *not* forgive me!'

'Yes – here it is, and my forgiveness with it: only – *sin no more.*'

He pressed my cold hand with sentimental fervour, but said nothing, and stood aside to let me pass into the room, where all the company were now assembled. Mr Grimsby was seated near the door: on seeing me enter almost immediately followed by Hargrave, he leered at me, with a glance of intolerable significance, as I passed. I looked him in the face, till he sullenly turned away, if not *ashamed*, at least *confounded* for the moment. Meantime, Hattersley had seized Hargrave by the arm, and was whispering something in his ear –

some coarse joke, no doubt, for the latter neither laughed nor spoke in answer, but, turning from him with a slight curl of the lip, disengaged himself and went to his mother, who was telling Lord Lowborough how many reasons she had to be proud of her son.

Thank Heaven, they are all going tomorrow.

CHAPTER 36

DUAL SOLITUDE

December 20th, 1824. – This is the third anniversary of our felicitous union. It is now two months since our guests left us to the enjoyment of each other's society; and I have had nine weeks' experience of this new phase of conjugal life – two persons living together, as master and mistress of the house, and father and mother of a winsome, merry little child, with the mutual understanding that there is no love, friendship, or sympathy between them. As far as in me lies, I endeavour to live peaceably with him: I treat him with unimpeachable civility, give up my convenience to his, wherever it may reasonably be done, and consult him in a business-like way on household affairs, deferring to his pleasure and judgment, even when I know the latter to be inferior to my own.

As for him: for the first week or two, he was peevish and low – fretting, I suppose, over his dear Annabella's departure – and particularly ill-tempered to me: everything I did was wrong; I was cold-hearted, hard, insensate; my sour, pale face was perfectly repulsive; my voice made him shudder; he knew not how he could live through the winter with me; I should kill him by inches. Again I proposed a separation, but it would not do: he was not going to be the talk of all the old gossips in the neighbourhood: he would not have it said that he was such a brute his wife could not live with him; – no; he must contrive to bear with me.

'I must contrive to bear with *you* you mean,' said I, 'for as long as I discharge my functions of steward and housekeeper, so conscientiously and well, without pay and without thanks, you cannot afford to part with me. I shall therefore remit these duties when my bondage becomes intolerable.' This threat, I thought, would serve to keep him in check, if anything would.

I believe he was much disappointed that I did not feel his offensive sayings more acutely, for when he had said anything particularly well calculated to hurt my feelings, he would stare me searchingly in the face, and then grumble against my 'marble heart,' or my 'brutal insensibility.' If I had bitterly wept, and deplored his lost affection, he would, perhaps, have condescended to pity me, and taken me into favour for a while, just to comfort his solitude and console him for the absence of his beloved Annabella, until he could meet her again, or some more fitting substitute. Thank heaven, I am not so weak as that! I was infatuated once, with a foolish, besotted affection, that clung to him in spite of his unworthiness, but it is fairly gone now – wholly crushed and withered away; and he has none but himself and his vices to thank for it.

At first (in compliance with his sweet lady's injunctions, I suppose) he abstained wonderfully well from seeking to solace his cares in wine; but at length he began to relax his virtuous efforts, and now and then exceeded a little, and still continues to do so – nay, sometimes, *not* a little. When he is under the exciting influence of these excesses, he sometimes fires up and attempts to play the brute; and then I take little pains to suppress my scorn and disgust: when he is under the *depressing* influence of the after consequences, he bemoans his sufferings and his errors, and charges them both upon me; he knows such indulgence injures his health, and does him more harm than good; but he says I drive him to it by my unnatural, unwomanly conduct; it will be the ruin of him in the end, but it is all my fault; – and *then* I am roused to defend myself – sometimes, with bitter recrimination. This is a kind of injustice I cannot patiently endure. Have I not laboured long and hard to save him from this very vice? would I not labour still, to deliver him from it, if I could? But could I do so by fawning upon him and caressing him when I know that he scorns me? Is it *my* fault that I have lost my influence with him, or that he has forfeited every claim to my regard? And should I seek a reconciliation with him, when I feel that I abhor him, and that he despises me? – and while he continues still to correspond with Lady Lowborough, as I know he does? No, never, never, never! – he may drink himself dead, but it is NOT my fault!

Yet I do my part to save him still: I give him to understand that drinking makes his eyes dull, and his face red and bloated; and that it tends to render him imbecile in body and mind; and if Annabella were to see him as often as I do, she would speedily be disenchanted; and that she certainly will withdraw her favour from him, if he continues such courses. Such a mode of admonition wins only coarse abuse for me – and indeed I almost feel as if I deserved it, for I hate to use such arguments, but they sink into his stupified heart, and make him pause, and ponder, and abstain, more than anything else I could say.

At present, I am enjoying a temporary relief from his presence: he is gone with Hargrave to join a distant hunt, and will probably not be back before tomorrow evening. How differently I used to feel his absence!

Mr Hargrave is still at the Grove. He and Arthur frequently meet to pursue their rural sports together: he often calls upon us here, and Arthur not unfrequently rides over to him. I do not think either of these *soi-disant* friends is overflowing with love for the other; but such intercourse serves to get the time on, and I am very willing it should continue, as it saves me some hours of discomfort in Arthur's society, and gives him some better employment than the sottish indulgence of his sensual appetites. The only objection I have to Mr Hargrave's being in the neighbourhood, is that the fear of meeting him at the Grove prevents me from seeing his sister so often as I otherwise should; for of late he has conducted himself towards me with such unerring propriety that I have almost forgotten his former conduct. I suppose he is striving to 'win my esteem.' If he continue to act in this way, he *may* win it; – but what then? the moment he attempts to demand anything more, he will lose it again.

February 10th. – It is a hard, embittering thing to have one's kind feelings and good intentions cast back in one's teeth. I was beginning to relent towards my wretched partner – to pity his forlorn, comfortless condition, unalleviated as it is by the consolations of intellectual resources and the answer of a good conscience towards God – and to think I ought to sacrifice my pride, and renew my efforts once again to make his home agreeable and lead him back to the path of virtue; not by false professions of love, and not by pretended remorse, but by mitigating my habitual coldness of manner, and commuting my frigid civility into kindness wherever an opportunity occurred; and not only was I beginning to think so, but I had already begun to act upon the thought – and what was the result? No answering spark of kindness – no awakening penitence, but an unappeasable ill-humour and a spirit of tyrannous exaction that increased with indulgence, and a lurking gleam of self-complacent triumph, at every detection of relenting softness in my manner, that congealed me to marble again as often as it recurred; and this morning he finished the business: – I think the petrifaction[1] is so completely effected at last, that nothing can melt me again. Among his letters was one which he perused with symptoms of unusual gratification, and then threw across the table to me, with the admonition, –

'There! read that, and take a lesson by it!'

It was in the free, dashing hand of Lady Lowborough. I glanced at the first page; it seemed full of extravagant protestations of affection; impetuous longings for a speedy reunion; and impious defiance of God's mandates, and railings against His Providence for having cast their lot asunder, and doomed them both to the hateful bondage of alliance with those they could not love. He gave a slight titter on seeing me change colour.[2] I folded up the letter, rose, and returned it to him, with no remark but, –

'Thank you – I *will* take a lesson by it!'

My little Arthur was standing between his knees, delightedly playing with the bright, ruby ring on his finger. Urged by a sudden, imperative impulse to deliver my son from that contaminating influence, I caught him up in my arms and carried him with me out of the room. Not liking this abrupt removal, the child began to pout and cry. This was a new stab to my already tortured heart. I would not let him go; but, taking him with me into the library, I shut the door, and, kneeling on the floor beside him, I embraced him, kissed him, wept over him with passionate fondness. Rather frightened than consoled by this, he turned struggling from me and cried out aloud for his papa. I released him from my arms, and never were more bitter tears than those that now concealed him from my blinded, burning eyes. Hearing his cries, the father came to the room. I instantly turned away lest he should see and misconstrue my emotion. He swore at me, and took the now pacified child away.

It is hard that my little darling should love him more than me; and that, when the well-being and culture of my son is all I have to live for, I should see my influence destroyed by one whose selfish affection is more injurious than the coldest indifference or the harshest tyranny could be. If I, for his good, deny him some trifling indulgence, he goes to his father, and the latter, in spite of his selfish indolence, will even give himself some trouble to meet the child's desires: if I attempt to curb his will, or look gravely on him for some act of childish disobedience, he knows his other parent will smile and take his part against me. Thus, not only have I the father's spirit in the son to contend against, the germs of his evil tendencies to search out and eradicate, and his corrupting intercourse and example in after life to counteract, but already *he* counteracts my arduous labour for the child's advantage, destroys my influence over his tender mind, and robs me of his very love; – I had no earthly hope but this, and he seems to take a diabolical delight in tearing it away.

But it is wrong to despair; I will remember the counsel of the inspired writer to him 'that feareth the Lord and obeyeth the voice of his servant, that *sitteth in darkness and hath no light*; – let him trust in the name of the Lord, and stay upon his God!'[3]

CHAPTER 37

THE NEIGHBOUR AGAIN

December 20th, 1825. – Another year is past; and I am weary of this life. And yet, I cannot wish to leave it: whatever afflictions assail me here, I cannot wish to go and leave my darling in this dark and wicked world alone, without a friend to guide him through its weary mazes, to warn him of its thousand snares, and guard him from the perils that beset him on every hand.[1] I am not well fitted to be his only companion, I know; but there is no other to supply my place. I am too grave to minister to his amusements and enter into his infantile sports as a nurse or a mother ought to do, and often his bursts of gleeful merriment trouble and alarm me; I see in them his father's spirit and temperament, and I tremble for the consequences; and, too often, damp the innocent mirth I ought to share. That father on the contrary has no weight of sadness on his mind – is troubled with no fears, no scruples concerning his son's future welfare; and at evenings especially, the times when the child sees him the most and the oftenest, he is always particularly jocund and open-hearted: ready to laugh and to jest with anything or anybody – but me – and I am particularly silent and sad: therefore, of course, the child dotes upon his seemingly joyous, amusing, ever-indulgent papa, and will at any time gladly exchange my company for his. This disturbs me greatly; not so much for the sake of my son's affection (though I do prize that highly, and though I feel it is my right, and know I have done much to earn it), as for that influence over him which, for his own advantage, I would strive to purchase and retain, and which for very spite his father delights to rob me of, and, from motives of mere idle egotism, is pleased to win to himself; making no use of it but to torment me, and ruin the child. My only consolation is that he spends comparatively little of his time at home, and, during the months he passes in London or elsewhere, I have a chance of recovering the ground I had lost, and overcoming with good the evil he has wrought by his wilful mismanagement. But then it is a bitter trial to behold him, on his return, doing his utmost to subvert my labours and transform my innocent, affectionate, tractable darling into a selfish, disobedient, and mischievous boy; thereby preparing the soil for those vices he has so successfully cultivated in his own perverted nature.

Happily, there were none of Arthur's 'friends' invited to Grassdale last autumn: he took himself off to visit some of them instead. I wish he would always do so, and I wish his friends were numerous and loving enough to keep him amongst them all the year round. Mr Hargrave, considerably to my annoyance, did not go with him; but I think I have done with that gentleman at last.

For seven or eight months, he behaved so remarkably well, and managed so skilfully too, that I was almost completely off my guard, and was really beginning to look upon him as a friend, and even to treat him as such, with certain prudent restrictions (which I deemed scarcely necessary); when, presuming upon my unsuspecting kindness, he thought he might venture to overstep the bounds of decent moderation and propriety that had so long retained him. It was on a pleasant evening at the close of May: I was wandering in the park, and he, on seeing me there as he rode past, made bold to enter and approach me, dismounting and leaving his horse at the gate. This was the first time he had ventured to come within its enclosure since I had been left alone, without the sanction of his mother's or sister's company, or at least the excuse of a message from them. But he managed to appear so calm and easy, so respectful and self-possessed in his friendliness, that, though a little surprised, I was neither alarmed nor offended at the unusual liberty, and he walked with me under the ash trees and by the waterside, and talked, with considerable animation, good taste, and intelligence, on many subjects, before I began to think about getting rid of him. Then, after a pause, during which we both stood gazing on the calm, blue water; I revolving in my mind the best means of politely dismissing my companion, he, no doubt, pondering other matters equally alien to the sweet sights and sounds that alone were present to his senses, – he suddenly electrified me by beginning, in a peculiar tone, low, soft, but perfectly distinct, to pour forth the most unequivocal expressions of earnest and passionate love; pleading his cause with all the bold yet artful eloquence he could summon to his aid. But I cut short his appeal, and repulsed him so determinately, so decidedly, and with such a mixture of scornful indignation tempered with cool, dispassionate sorrow and pity for his benighted mind, that he withdrew, astonished, mortified, and discomforted; and, a few days after, I heard that he had departed for London. He returned however in eight or nine weeks – and, did not entirely keep aloof from me, but comported himself in so remarkable a manner that his quick-sighted sister could not fail to notice the change.

'What have you done to Walter, Mrs Huntingdon?' said she one morning, when I had called at the Grove, and he had just left the room after exchanging a few words of the coldest civility. 'He has been so extremely ceremonious and stately of late, I can't imagine what it is all about, unless you have desperately offended him. Tell me what it is, that I may be your mediator, and make you friends again.'

'I have done nothing willingly to offend him,' said I. 'If he is offended, he can best tell you himself what it is about.'

'I'll ask him,' cried the giddy girl, springing up and putting her head out of the window; 'he's only in the garden – Walter!'

'No, no, Esther! you will seriously displease me if you do; and I shall leave you immediately, and not come again for months – perhaps years.'

'Did you call, Esther?' said her brother, approaching the window from without.

'Yes; I wanted to ask you –'

'Good morning, Esther,' said I, taking her hand and giving it a severe squeeze.

'To ask you,' continued she, 'to get me a rose for Mrs Huntingdon.' He departed. 'Mrs Huntingdon,' she exclaimed, turning to me and still holding me fast by the hand, 'I'm quite shocked at you – you're just as angry, and distant, and cold as he is: and I'm determined you shall be as good friends as ever, before you go.'

'Esther, how can you be so rude!' cried Mrs Hargrave, who was seated gravely knitting in her easy chair. 'Surely, you never *will* learn to conduct yourself like a lady!'

'Well mamma, you said, yourself –' But the young lady was silenced by the uplifted finger of her mamma, accompanied with a very stern shake of the head.

'Isn't she cross?' whispered she to me; but, before I could add my share of reproof, Mr Hargrave reappeared at the window with a beautiful moss rose in his hand.

'Here, Esther, I've brought you the rose,' said he, extending it towards her.

'Give it her yourself, you blockhead!' cried she, recoiling with a spring from between us.

'Mrs Huntingdon would rather receive it from you,' replied he in a very serious tone, but lowering his voice that his mother might not hear. His sister took the rose and gave it to me.

'My brother's compliments, Mrs Huntingdon, and he hopes you and he will come to a better understanding by and by. – Will that do, Walter?' added the saucy girl, turning to him and putting her arm round his neck, as he stood leaning upon the sill of the window – 'or should I have said that you are sorry you were so touchy? or that you hope she will pardon your offence?'

'You silly girl! you don't know what you are talking about,' replied he gravely.

'Indeed I don't; for I'm quite in the dark.'

'Now Esther,' interposed Mrs Hargrave, who, if equally benighted on the subject of our estrangement, saw at least that her daughter was behaving very improperly, 'I must insist upon your leaving the room!'

'Pray don't, Mrs Hargrave, for I'm going to leave it myself,' said I, and immediately made my adieux.

About a week after, Mr Hargrave brought his sister to see me. He conducted himself, at first, with his usual cold, distant, half-stately, half-melancholy, altogether injured air; but Esther made no remark upon it this time; she had evidently been schooled into better manners. She talked to me, and laughed and romped with little Arthur, her loved and loving playmate. He, somewhat to my discomfort, enticed her from the room to have a run in the hall; and, thence, into the garden. I got up to stir the fire. Mr Hargrave asked if I felt cold, and shut the door – a very unseasonable piece of officiousness, for I had meditated following the noisy playfellows, if they did not speedily return. He then took the liberty of walking up to the fire himself, and asking me if I were aware that Mr Huntingdon was now at the seat of Lord Lowborough, and likely to continue there some time.

'No; but it's no matter,' I answered carelessly; and if my cheek glowed like fire, it was rather at the question than the information it conveyed.

'You don't object to it?' he said.

'Not at all, if Lord Lowborough likes his company.'

'You have no love left for him, then?'

'Not the least.'

'I knew that – I knew you were too high-minded and pure in your own nature to continue to regard one so utterly false and polluted, with any feelings but those of indignation and scornful abhorrence!'

'Is he not your friend?' said I, turning my eyes from the fire to his face, with perhaps a slight touch of those feelings he assigned to another.

'He *was*,' replied he, with the same calm gravity as before, 'but do not wrong me by supposing that I could continue my friendship and esteem to a man who could so infamously – so impiously forsake and injure one so transcendently – well, I won't speak of it. But tell me, do you never think of revenge?'

'Revenge! No – what good would that do – it would make him no better, and me no happier.'

'I don't know how to talk to you, Mrs Huntingdon,' said he smiling; 'you are only half a woman – your nature must be half human, half angelic. Such goodness overawes me;[2] I don't know what to make of it.'

'Then sir, I fear you must be very much worse than you should be, if I, a mere ordinary mortal, am by your own confession, so vastly your superior; – and since there exists so little sympathy between us, I think we had better each look out for some more congenial companion.' And forthwith moving to the window, I began to look out for my little son and his gay young friend.

'No, *I* am the ordinary mortal, I maintain,' replied Mr Hargrave. 'I will not allow myself to be worse than my fellows; but *you* madame – I equally maintain there is nobody like you. But are you happy?' he asked in a serious tone.

'As happy as some others, I suppose.'

'Are you as happy as you desire to be?'

'No one is so blest as that comes to, on this side eternity.'

'One thing I know,' returned he, with a deep, sad sigh; 'you are immeasurably happier than I am.'

'I am very sorry for you, then,' I could not help replying.

'Are you *indeed*? – No – for if you were, you would be glad to relieve me.'

'And so I should, if I could do so, without injuring myself or any other.'

'And can you suppose that I should wish you to injure yourself? – No; on the contrary, it is your own happiness I long for more than mine. You are miserable now, Mrs Huntingdon,' continued he, looking me boldly in the face. 'You do not complain, but I see – and feel – and know that you are miserable – and must remain so, as long as you keep those walls of impenetrable ice about your still warm and palpitating heart; – and I am miserable too. Deign to smile on me, and I am happy: trust me, and you shall be happy also, for if you *are* a woman, I can make you so – and I *will* do it in spite of yourself!' he muttered between his teeth, 'and as for others, the question is between ourselves alone: you cannot injure your husband, you know; and no one else has any concern in the matter.'

'I have a son, Mr Hargrave, and you have a mother,' said I, retiring from the window, whither he had followed me.

'They need not know,' he began, but before anything more could be said on either side, Esther and Arthur re-entered the room. The former glanced at Walter's flushed, excited countenance, and then at mine – a little flushed and excited too, I dare say, though from far different causes. She must have thought we had been quarrelling desperately, and was evidently perplexed and disturbed at the circumstance; but she was too polite, or too much afraid of her brother's anger to refer to it. She seated herself on the sofa, and putting back her bright, golden ringlets, that were scattered in wild profusion over her face, she immediately began to talk about the garden and her little playfellow, and continued to chatter away in her usual strain till her brother summoned her to depart.

'If I have spoken too warmly, forgive me,' he murmured on taking his leave, 'or I shall never forgive myself.'

Esther smiled and glanced at me: I merely bowed, and her countenance fell. She thought it a poor return for Walter's generous concession, and was disappointed in her friend. Poor child, she little knows the world she lives in!

Mr Hargrave had not an opportunity of meeting me again in private for several weeks after this; but when he did meet me, there was less of pride and more of touching melancholy in his manner than before. Oh, *how* he annoyed me! I was obliged, at last almost entirely to remit my visits to the Grove, at the expense of deeply offending Mrs Hargrave and seriously afflicting poor Esther, who really values my society – for want of better, and who ought not to suffer for the fault of her brother. But that indefatigable foe[3] was not yet vanquished: he seemed to be always on the watch. I frequently saw him riding lingeringly past the premises, looking searchingly round him as he went – or if *I* did not, Rachel did. That sharp-sighted woman soon guessed how matters stood between us, and descrying the enemy's movements from her elevation at the nursery window, she would give me a quiet intimation, if she saw me preparing for a walk when she had reason to believe he was about, or to think it likely that he would meet or overtake me in the way I meant to traverse. I would then defer my ramble, or confine myself for that day to the park and gardens – or if the proposed excursion was a matter of importance, such as a visit to the sick or afflicted, I would take Rachel with me, and then I was never molested.

But one mild, sunshiny day, early in November, I had ventured forth alone, to visit the village school and a few of the poor tenants, and on my return, I was alarmed at the clatter of a horse's feet behind me approaching at a rapid, steady trot. There was no stile or gap at hand, by which I could escape into the fields: so I walked quietly on, saying to myself –

'It may not be he after all; and if it is, and if he *do* annoy me – it shall be for the last time – I am determined, if there be power in words and looks against cool impudence and mawkish sentimentality so inexhaustible as his.'

The horse soon overtook me, and was reined up close beside me. It *was* Mr Hargrave. He greeted me with a smile intended to be soft and melancholy, but his triumphant satisfaction at having caught me at last so shone through, that it was quite a failure. After briefly answering his salutation and enquiring after the ladies at the Grove, I turned away and walked on; but he followed, and kept his horse at my side: it was evident he intended to be my companion all the way.

'Well! I don't much care. If you want another rebuff, take it – and welcome,' was my inward remark. 'Now sir, what next?'

This question, though unspoken, was not long unanswered: after a few passing observations upon indifferent subjects, he began, in solemn tones, the following appeal to my humanity: –

'It will be four years next April since I first saw you, Mrs Huntingdon, – *you* may have forgotten the circumstance, but *I* never can – I admired you then, most deeply, but I dared not love you: in the following autumn, I saw so much of your perfections that I could not fail to love you, though I dared not show it. For upwards of three years, I have endured a perfect martyrdom. From the anguish of suppressed emotions, intense and fruitless longings, silent sorrow, crushed hopes, and trampled affections, – I have suffered more than I can tell, or you imagine – and you were the cause of it – and not, altogether, the innocent cause. My youth is wasting away; my prospects are darkened; my life is a desolate blank; I have no rest day or night:[4] I am become a burden to myself and others; – and you might save me by a word – a glance, and will not do it – Is this right?'

'In the first place, I don't believe you,' answered I: 'in the second, if you will be such a fool, I can't hinder it.'

'If you affect,' replied he earnestly, 'to regard as folly the best, the strongest, the most godlike impulses of our nature, – *I* don't believe *you* – I know you are not the heartless, icy being you pretend to be – you had a heart once, and you gave it to your husband. When you found him utterly unworthy of the treasure you reclaimed it; – and you will not *pretend* that you loved that sensual, earthly minded profligate so deeply, so devotedly that you can never love another? – I know that there are feelings in your nature that have never yet been called forth – I know, too, that in your present neglected, lonely state you are, and *must* be miserable. You have it in your power to raise two human beings from a state of actual suffering to such unspeakable beatitude as only generous, noble self-forgetting love can give (for you *can* love me if you will; you may tell me that you scorn and detest me, but – since you have set me the example of plain speaking – I will answer that *I do not believe you!*) but you will not do it! you choose rather to leave us miserable; and you coolly tell me it is the will of God that we should remain so. *You* may call this religion, but *I* call it wild fanaticism!'

'There is another life both for you and for me,' said I. 'If it be the will of God that we should sow in tears, now, it is only that we may reap in joy, hereafter.[5] It is his will that we should not injure others by the gratification of our own earthly passions; and you have a mother, and sisters, and friends, who would be seriously injured by your disgrace; and I too have friends, whose peace of mind shall never be sacrificed to my enjoyment – or yours either, with my consent – and if I were alone in the world, I have still my God and my religion, 'and I would sooner die than disgrace my calling and break my faith with Heaven to obtain a few brief years of false and fleeting happiness – happiness sure to end in misery, even here – for myself or any other!'

'There need be no disgrace – no misery or sacrifice in any quarter,' persisted he. 'I do not ask you to leave your home or defy the world's opinion.' – But I need not repeat all his arguments. I refuted them to the best of my power; but that power was provokingly small, at the moment, for I was too much flurried with indignation – and even shame – that he should thus dare to address me, to retain sufficient command of thought and language to enable me adequately to contend against his powerful sophistries. Finding, however, that he could not be silenced by reason, and even covertly exulted in his seeming advantage, and ventured to deride those assertions I had not the coolness to prove, I changed my course and tried another plan.

'Do you really love me?' said I seriously, pausing and looking him calmly in the face.

'Do I love you!' cried he.

'*Truly?*' I demanded.

His countenance brightened; he thought his triumph was at hand. He commenced a passionate protestation of the truth and fervour of his attachment which I cut short by another question: –

'But is it not a selfish love? – have you enough disinterested affection to enable you to sacrifice your own pleasure to mine?'

'I would give my life to serve you.'

'I don't want your life – but have you enough real sympathy for my afflictions to induce you to make an effort to relieve them, at the risk of a little discomfort to yourself?'

'Try me, and see!'

'If you have – *never mention this subject again.* You cannot recur to it in any way, without doubling the weight of those sufferings you so feelingly deplore. I have nothing left me but the solace of a good conscience and a hopeful trust in Heaven, and you labour continually to rob me of these. If you persist, I must regard you as my deadliest foe.'

'But hear me a moment –'

'No, sir! you said you would give your life to serve me: I only ask your *silence* on one particular point. I have spoken plainly; and what I say I mean. If you torment me in this way any more, I must conclude that your protestations are entirely false, and that you hate me in your heart as fervently as you profess to love me!'

He bit his lip and bent his eyes upon the ground in silence for a while.

'Then I must leave you,' said he at length, looking steadily upon me, as if with the last hope of detecting some token of irrepressible anguish or dismay awakened by those solemn words. 'I must leave you. I cannot live here, and be forever silent on the all-absorbing subject of my thoughts and wishes.'

'Formerly, I believe, you spent but little of your time at home,' I answered: 'it will do you no harm to absent yourself again, for a while – if that be really necessary.'

'If that be really *possible*,' he muttered – 'and can you bid me go so coolly! Do you really wish it?'

'Most certainly I do. If you cannot see me without tormenting me as you have lately done, I would gladly say farewell and never see you more.'

He made no answer, but, bending from his horse, held out his hand towards me. I looked up at his face, and saw, therein, such a look of genuine agony of soul that, whether bitter disappointment, or wounded pride, or lingering love, or burning wrath were uppermost, I could not hesitate to put my hand in his as frankly as if I bade a friend farewell. He grasped it very hard, and immediately put spurs to his horse and galloped away. Very soon after, I learned that he was gone to Paris, where he still is, and the longer he stays there the better for me.

I thank God for this deliverance![7]

END OF VOLUME II

VOLUME III

CHAPTER 38

THE INJURED MAN

December 20th, 1826. – The fifth anniversary of my wedding day, and I trust, the last I shall spend under this roof. My resolution is formed, my plan concocted, and already partly put in execution. My conscience does not blame me, but while the purpose ripens, let me beguile a few of these long winter evenings in stating the case for my own satisfaction – a dreary amusement enough, but having the air of a useful occupation, and being pursued as a task, it will suit me better than a lighter one.

In September, quiet Grassdale was again alive with a party of ladies and gentlemen (so called) consisting of the same individuals as those invited the year before last, with the addition of two or three others, among whom were Mrs Hargrave and her younger daughter. The gentlemen and Lady Lowborough were invited for the pleasure and convenience of the host, the other ladies, I suppose for the sake of appearances; and to keep me in check and make me discreet and civil in my demeanour. But the ladies stayed only three weeks, the gentlemen, with two exceptions, above two months, for their hospitable entertainer was loath to part with them and be left alone with his bright intellect, his stainless conscience, and his loved and loving wife.

On the day of Lady Lowborough's arrival, I followed her into her chamber, and plainly told her that, if I found reason to believe that she still continued her criminal connection with Mr Huntingdon, I should think it my absolute duty to inform her husband of the circumstance – or awaken his suspicions at least – however painful it might be, or however dreadful the consequences. She was startled at first, by the declaration, so unexpected, and so determinately yet calmly delivered; but rallying in a moment, she coolly replied that if I saw anything at all reprehensible or suspicious in her conduct, she would freely give me leave to tell his lordship all about it. Willing to be satisfied with this, I left her; and certainly I saw nothing thenceforth particularly reprehensible or suspicious in her demeanour towards her host; but then I had the other guests to attend to, and I did not watch them narrowly – for to confess the truth, I *feared* to see anything between them. I no longer regarded it as any concern of mine, and if it was my duty to enlighten Lord Lowborough, it was a painful duty, and I dreaded to be called to perform it.

But my fears were brought to an end, in a manner I had not anticipated. One evening, about a fortnight after the visitors' arrival, I had retired into the library to snatch a few minutes' respite from forced cheerfulness and wearisome discourse – for after so long a period of seclusion, dreary indeed, as I had often found it, I could not always bear to be doing violence to my feelings, and goading my powers to talk, and smile and listen, and play the attentive hostess – or even the cheerful friend: – I had just ensconced myself within the bow of the window, and was looking out upon the west where the darkening hills rose sharply defined against the clear amber light of evening, that gradually blended and faded away into the pure, pale blue of the upper sky, where one bright star[1] was shining through, as if to promise – 'When that dying light is gone, the world will not be left in darkness, and they who trust in God – whose minds are unbeclouded by the mists of unbelief and sin, are never wholly comfortless,'[2] – when I heard a hurried step approaching, and Lord Lowborough entered – this room was still his favourite resort. He flung the door to with unusual violence, and cast his hat aside regardless where it fell. What could be the matter with him? His face was ghastly pale; his eyes were fixed upon the ground; his teeth clenched; his forehead glistened with the dews of agony. It was plain he knew his wrongs at last!

Unconscious of my presence, he began to pace the room in a state of fearful agitation, violently wringing his hands and uttering low groans or incoherent ejaculations. I made a movement to let him know that he was not alone; but he was too preoccupied to notice it. Perhaps, while his back was towards me, I might cross the room and slip away unobserved. I rose to make the attempt, but then he perceived me. He started and stood still a moment; then wiped his streaming forehead, and advancing towards me, with a kind of unnatural composure, said in a deep, almost sepulchral tone —

'Mrs Huntingdon, I must leave you tomorrow.'

'Tomorrow!' I repeated. 'I do not ask the cause.'

'You know it then – and you can be so calm!' said he, surveying me with profound astonishment, not unmingled with a kind of resentful bitterness, as it appeared to me.

'I have so long been aware of –' I paused in time, and added, 'of my husband's character, that nothing shocks me.'

'But *this* – how long have you been aware of this?' demanded he, laying his clenched hand on the table beside him, and looking me keenly and fixedly in the face.

I felt like a criminal.

'Not long,' I answered.

'You knew it!' cried he with bitter vehemence – 'and you did not tell me! You helped to deceive me!'

'My lord, I did *not* help to deceive you.'

'Then why did you not tell me?'

'Because I knew it would be painful to you – I hoped she would return to her duty, and then there would be no need to harrow your feelings with such –'

'O God! how long has this been going on? how long has it been, Mrs Huntingdon? – Tell me – I MUST know!' he exclaimed with intense and fearful eagerness.

'Two years, I believe.'

'Great Heaven! and she has duped me all this time!' He turned away with a suppressed groan of agony, and paced the room again, in a paroxysm of renewed agitation. My heart smote me; but I would try to console him, though I knew not how to attempt it.

'She is a wicked woman,' I said. 'She has basely deceived and betrayed you. She is as little worthy of your regret as she was of your affection. Let her injure you no farther:[3] abstract yourself from her, and stand alone.'

'And you, madam,' said he sternly, arresting his walk and turning round upon me – 'you have injured me too, by this ungenerous concealment!'

There was a sudden revulsion in my feelings. Something rose within me, and urged me to resent this harsh return for my heartfelt sympathy, and defend myself with answering severity. Happily, I did not yield to the impulse. I saw his anguish as, suddenly smiting his forehead, he turned abruptly to the window, and, looking upward at the placid sky, murmured passionately, 'O God, that I might die!' – and felt that to add one drop of bitterness to that already overflowing cup, would be ungenerous indeed. And yet, I fear there was more coldness than gentleness in the quiet tone of my reply: –

'I might offer many excuses that some would admit to be valid, but I will not attempt to enumerate them –'

'I know them,' said he hastily, 'you would say that it was no business of yours – that I ought to have taken care of myself – that if my own blindness has led me into this pit of hell, I have no right to blame another for giving me credit for a larger amount of sagacity than I possessed –'

'I confess I was wrong,' continued I, without regarding this bitter interruption; 'but whether want of courage or mistaken kindness was the cause of my error, I think you blame me too severely. I told Lady Lowborough two weeks ago, the very hour she came, that I should certainly think it my duty to inform you if she continued to deceive you: she gave me full liberty to do so if I should see anything reprehensible or suspicious in her conduct – I have seen nothing; and I trusted she had altered her course.'

He continued gazing from the window while I spoke, and did not answer, but, stung by the recollections my words awakened, stamped his foot upon the floor, ground his teeth, and corrugated his brow, like one under the influence of acute physical pain.[4]

'It was wrong – it was wrong!' he muttered, at length. 'Nothing can excuse it – nothing can atone for it, – for nothing can recall those years of cursed credulity – nothing obliterate them! – nothing,

nothing!' he repeated in a whisper whose despairing bitterness precluded all resentment.

'When I put the case to myself, I own it *was* wrong,' I answered; 'but I can only now regret that I did not see it in this light before, and that, as you say, nothing can recall the past.'

Something in my voice or in the spirit of this answer seemed to alter his mood. Turning towards me and attentively surveying my face by the dim light, he said in a milder tone than he had yet employed, –

'You too have suffered, I suppose.'

'I suffered much, at first.'

'When was that?'

'Two years ago; and two years hence you will be as calm as I am now, – and far, far happier, I trust, for you are a man, and free to act as you please.'⁵

Something like a smile, but a *very* bitter one, crossed his face for a moment.

'You have not been happy lately?' he said with a kind of effort to regain composure, and a determination to waive the further discussion of his own calamity.

'Happy!' I repeated, almost provoked at such a question – 'Could I be so, with such a husband?'

'I have noticed a change in your appearance since the first years of your marriage,' pursued he: 'I observed it to – to that infernal demon,' he muttered between his teeth – 'and he said it was your own sour temper that was eating away your bloom: it was making you old and ugly before your time, and had already made his fireside as comfortless as a convent cell – You smile Mrs Huntingdon – nothing moves you. I wish my nature were as calm as yours!'

'My nature was not originally calm,' said I: 'I have learned to appear so by dint of hard lessons, and many repeated efforts.'

At this juncture Mr Hattersley burst into the room.

'Hallow, Lowborough!' he began – 'Oh! I beg your pardon,' he exclaimed on seeing me; 'I didn't know it was a tête-à-tête. Cheer up, man!' he continued, giving Lord Lowborough a thump on the back, which caused the latter to recoil from him with looks of ineffable disgust and irritation. 'Come, I want to speak with you a bit.'

'Speak, then.'

'But I'm not sure it would be quite agreeable to the lady, what I have to say.'

'Then it would not be agreeable to me,' said his lordship, turning to leave the room.

'Yes, it would,' cried the other, following him into the hall. 'If you've the heart of a man it would be the very ticket for you. It's just this, my lad,' he continued, rather lowering his voice, but not enough to prevent me from hearing every word he said, though the half-closed door stood between us: 'I think you're an ill-used man – nay, now, don't flare up – I don't want to offend you: it's only my rough way of talking. I must speak right out you *know*, or else not at all; – and I'm come – stop now! let me explain – I'm come to offer you my services, for though Huntingdon is my friend, he's a devilish scamp as we all know, and I'll be *your* friend for the nonce. I know what it is you want, to make matters straight: it's just to exchange a shot with him, and then you'll feel yourself all right again; and if an accident happens – why, that'll be all right too, I dare say, to a desperate fellow like you. – Come now! give me your hand, and don't look so black upon it. Name time and place, and I'll manage the rest.'

'That,' answered the more low, deliberate voice of Lord Low-borough, 'is just the remedy my own heart – or the devil within it, suggested – to meet him, and *not to sever without blood*. Whether I or he should fall – or both, it would be an *inexpressible* relief to me, if –'

'Just so! Well then –'

'No!' exclaimed his lordship with deep, determined emphasis. 'Though I hate him from my heart, and should rejoice at any calamity that could befall him – I'll leave him to God; and though I abhor my own life, I'll leave that too, to Him that gave it.'

'But you see in this case,' pleaded Hattersley –

'I'll not hear you!' exclaimed his companion, hastily turning away. 'Not another word! I've enough to do against the fiend within me.'

'Then you're a white livered fool, and I wash my hands of you,' grumbled the tempter as he swung himself round and departed.

'Right, right, Lord Lowborough!' cried I, darting out and clasping his burning hand, as he was moving away to the stairs. 'I begin to think the world is not worthy of you!'

Not understanding this sudden ebullition, he turned upon me with a stare of gloomy, bewildered amazement that made me ashamed of the impulse to which I had yielded; but soon a more humanized expression dawned upon his countenance, and, before I could withdraw my hand, he pressed it kindly, while a gleam of genuine feeling flashed from his eyes as he murmured, –

'God help us both!'

'Amen!' responded I; and we parted.

I returned to the drawing-room, where, doubtless, my presence would be expected by most, desired by one or two. In the ante-room was Mr Hattersley, railing against Lord Lowborough's poltroonery before a select audience, viz. Mr Huntingdon, who was lounging against the table exulting in his own treacherous villainy and laughing his victim to scorn, and Mr Grimsby, standing by, quietly rubbing his hands and chuckling with fiendish satisfaction. At the glance I gave them in passing, Hattersley stopped short in his animadversions and stared like a bull calf, Grimsby glowered upon me with a leer of malignant ferocity, and my husband muttered a coarse and brutal malediction.

In the drawing-room I found Lady Lowborough, evidently in no very enviable state of mind, and struggling hard to conceal her discomposure by an overstrained affectation of unusual cheerfulness and vivacity, very uncalled-for under the circumstances, for she had herself given the company to understand that her husband had received unpleasant intelligence from home, which necessitated his immediate departure, and that he had suffered it so to bother his mind that it had brought on a bilious headache, owing to which and the preparations he judged necessary to hasten his departure, she believed they would not have the pleasure of seeing him tonight. However, she asserted, it was only a business concern, and so she did not intend it should trouble *her*. She was just saying this as I entered, and she darted upon me such a glance of hardihood and defiance as at once astonished and revolted me.

'But I *am* troubled,' continued she, 'and vexed too, for I think it my duty to accompany his lordship, and of course I am very sorry to part with all my kind friends, so unexpectedly and so soon.'

'And yet, Annabella,' said Esther, who was sitting beside her, 'I never saw you in better spirits in my life.'

'Precisely so, my love; because I wish to make the best of your society, since it appears this is to be the last night I am to enjoy it, till Heaven knows when; and I wish to leave a good impression on you all,' – she glanced round, and seeing her aunt's eye fixed upon her, rather too scrutinizingly, as she probably thought, she started up and continued, – 'to which end I'll give you a song – Shall I, aunt? shall I, Mrs Huntingdon? shall I, ladies and gentlemen – all? – Very well, I'll do my best to amuse you.'

She and Lord Lowborough occupied the apartments next to mine. I know not how *she* passed the night, but I lay awake the greater part of it listening to his heavy step pacing monotonously up and down his dressing-room, which was nearest my chamber. Once I heard him pause and throw something out of the window, with a passionate ejaculation; and in the morning, after they were gone, a keen-bladed clasp-knife was found on the grass-plot below; a razor, likewise, was snapped in two and thrust deep into the cinders of the grate, but partially corroded by the decaying embers. So strong had been the temptation to end his miserable life, so determined his resolution to resist it.

My heart bled for him as I lay listening to that ceaseless tread. Hitherto, I had thought too much of myself, too little of him: now I forgot my own afflictions, and thought only of his – of the ardent affection so miserably wasted, the fond faith so cruelly betrayed, the – no, I will not attempt to enumerate his wrongs, – but I hated his wife and my husband more intensely than ever, and not for my sake, but for his.

'That man,' I thought, 'is an object of scorn to his friends and the nice-judging world. The false wife and the treacherous friend who have wronged him are not so despised and degraded as he; and his refusal to avenge his wrongs has removed him yet farther beyond the range of sympathy, and blackened his name with a deeper disgrace.[6] He knows this; and it doubles his burden of woe. He sees the injustice of it, but he cannot bear up against it; he lacks that sustaining power of self-esteem which leads a man, exulting in his own integrity, to defy the malice of traducing foes and give them scorn for scorn – or, better still, which raises him above earth's foul and turbulent vapours, to repose in Heaven's eternal sunshine. He knows that God is just, but cannot see his justice now: he knows this life is short, and yet death seems insufferably far away; he believes there is a future state, but so absorbing is the agony of this that he cannot realize its rapturous repose. He can but bow his head to the storm, and cling, blindly, despairingly, to what he knows to be right. Like the shipwrecked mariner cleaving to a raft, blinded, deafened, bewildered, he feels the waves sweep over him, and sees no prospect of escape; and yet he knows he has no hope but this, and still, while life and sense remain, concentrates all his energies to keep it. Oh, that I had a friend's right to comfort him, and tell him that I never esteemed him so highly as I do this night!'

They departed early in the morning before anyone else was down, except myself, and just as I was leaving my room, Lord Lowborough was descending to take his place in the carriage where his lady was already ensconced; and Arthur (or Mr Huntingdon as I prefer calling him, for the other is my child's name) had the gratuitous insolence to come out in his dressing-gown to bid his 'friend' goodbye.

'What, going already, Lowborough!' said he. 'Well, good morning.' He smilingly offered his hand.

I think the other would have knocked him down, had he not instinctively started back before that bony fist quivering with rage and clenched till the knuckles gleamed white and glistening through the skin. Looking upon him with a countenance livid with furious hate, Lord Lowborough muttered between his closed teeth a deadly execration he would not have uttered had he been calm enough to choose his words, and departed.

'I call that an unchristian spirit now,' said the villain. 'But I'd never give up an old friend for the sake of a wife. You may have mine if you like, and I call that handsome – I *can* do no more than offer restitution, can I?'

But Lowborough had gained the bottom of the stairs, and was now crossing the hall; and Mr Huntingdon, leaning over the banisters, called out, – 'Give my love to Annabella! – and I wish you both a happy journey,' and withdrew laughing to his chamber.

He subsequently expressed himself rather glad she was gone: 'She was so deuced imperious and exacting,' said he: 'now I shall be my own man again, and feel rather more at my ease.'

I know nothing more of Lord Lowborough's subsequent proceedings but what I have heard from Milicent, who, though she is ignorant of the cause of his separation from her cousin, has informed me that such is the case; that they keep entirely separate establishments; that she leads a gay, dashing life in town and country, while he lives in strict seclusion at his old castle in the north. There are two children, both of whom he keeps under his own protection. The son and heir is a promising child nearly the age of my Arthur, and no doubt a source of some hope and comfort to his father; but the other, a little girl between one and two,[7] with blue eyes and light auburn hair, he probably keeps from conscientious motives alone, thinking it wrong to abandon her to the teaching and example of such a woman as her mother. That mother never loved children, and has so little natural affection for her own that I question whether she will not regard it as a relief to be thus entirely separated from them, and delivered from the trouble and responsibility of their charge.

Not many days after the departure of Lord and Lady Lowborough, the rest of the ladies withdrew the light of their presence from Grassdale. Perhaps they might have stayed longer, but neither host nor hostess pressed them to prolong their visit – in fact, the former showed too plainly that he should be glad to get rid of them; – and Mrs Hargrave retired with her daughters and her grandchildren (there are three of them now) to the Grove. But the gentlemen remained: Mr Huntingdon, as I intimated before, was determined to keep them as long as he could; and, being thus delivered from restraint, they gave a loose to all their innate madness, folly, and brutality, and made the house night after night one scene of riot, uproar, and confusion. Who among them behaved the worst, or who the best, I cannot distinctly say; for, from the moment I discovered how things would be, I formed the resolution of retreating upstairs or locking myself into the library the instant I withdrew from the dining-room, and not coming near them again till breakfast; – but this I must say for Mr Hargrave, that from all *I* could see of him, he was a model of decency, sobriety, and gentlemanly manners *in comparison* with the rest.

He did not join the party till a week or ten days after the arrival of the other guests; for he was still on the continent when they came, and I cherished the hope that he would not accept the invitation. Accept it he did, however, but his conduct towards me, for the first few weeks, was exactly what I should have wished it to be – perfectly civil and respectful without any affectation of despondency or dejection, and sufficiently distant without haughtiness, or any of such remarkable stiffness or iciness of demeanour as might be calculated to disturb or puzzle his sister, or call forth the investigation of his mother.

CHAPTER 39

A SCHEME OF ESCAPE

My greatest source of uneasiness, in this time of trial, was my son, whom his father and his father's friends delighted to encourage in all the embryo vices a little child can show, and to instruct in all the evil habits he could acquire – in a word, to 'make a man of him'[1] was one of their staple amusements; and I need say no more to justify my alarm on his account, and my determination to deliver him at any hazard from the hands of such instructors. I first attempted to keep him always with me or in the nursery, and gave Rachel particular injunctions never to let him come down to dessert as long as these 'gentlemen' stayed; but it was no use; these orders were immediately countermanded and overruled by his father: he was not going to have the little fellow moped to death between an old nurse and a cursed fool of a mother.[2] So the little fellow came down every evening, in spite of his cross mamma, and learnt to tipple wine like papa, to swear like Mr Hattersley, and to have his own way like a man, and sent mamma to the devil when she tried to prevent him. To see such things done with the roguish naïveté of that pretty little child and hear such things spoken by that small infantile voice, was as peculiarly piquant and irresistibly droll to them as it was inexpressibly distressing and painful to me; and when he had set the table in a roar,[3] he would look round delightedly upon them all, and add his shrill laugh to theirs. But if that beaming blue eye rested on me, its light would vanish for a moment, and he would say, in some concern, – 'Mamma, why don't *you* laugh? Make her laugh, papa – she never will.'

Hence was I obliged to stay among these human brutes, watching an opportunity to get my child away from them, instead of leaving them immediately after the removal of the cloth, as I should always otherwise have done. He was never willing to go, and I frequently had to carry him away by force; for which he thought me very cruel and unjust; and sometimes his father would insist upon my letting him remain; – and then, I would leave him to his kind friends, and retire to indulge my bitterness and despair alone or to rack my brains for a remedy to this great evil.

But here again, I must do Mr Hargrave the justice to acknowledge that I never saw *him* laugh at the child's misdemeanours, nor heard him utter a word of encouragement to his aspirations after manly accomplishments. But when anything very extraordinary was said or done by the infant profligate,[4] I noticed, at times, a peculiar expression in his face, that I could neither interpret nor define – a slight twitching about the muscles of the mouth – a sudden flash in the eye, as he darted a sudden glance at the child and then at me; and then, I could fancy there arose a gleam of hard, keen, sombre satisfaction in his countenance at the look of impotent wrath and anguish he was too certain to behold in mine. But on one occasion, when Arthur had been behaving particularly ill, and Mr Huntingdon and his guests had been particularly provoking and insulting to me in their encouragement of him, and I particularly anxious to get him out of the room, and on the very point of demeaning myself by a burst of uncontrollable passion – Mr Hargrave suddenly rose from his seat, with an aspect of stern determination, lifted the child from his father's knee, where he was sitting half tipsy, cocking his head and laughing at me, and execrating me with words he little knew the meaning of, – handed him out of the room, and setting him down in the hall, held the door open for me, gravely bowed as I withdrew, and closed it after me. I heard high words exchanged between him and his already half-inebriated host as I departed, leading away my bewildered and disconcerted boy.

But this should not continue; my child must not be abandoned to this corruption: better far that he should live in poverty and obscurity with a fugitive mother, than in luxury and affluence with such a father. These guests might not be with us long, but they would return again; and he, the most injurious of the whole, his child's worst enemy, would still remain. I could endure it for myself, but for my son it must be borne no longer: the world's opinion and the feelings of my friends must be alike unheeded here, at least, alike unable to deter me from my duty. But where should I find an asylum, and how obtain subsistence for us both? Oh, I would take my precious charge at early dawn, take the coach to M—, flee to the port of —, cross the Atlantic, and seek a quiet, humble home in New England, where I would support myself and him by the labour of my hands. The palette and the easel, my darling playmates once, must be my sober toil-fellows now.[5] But was I sufficiently skilful as an artist to obtain my livelihood in a strange land, without friends and without recommendation? No; I must wait a little; I must labour hard to improve my talent and to produce something worthwhile as a specimen of my powers, something to speak favourably for me, whether as an actual painter or a teacher. Brilliant success, of course, I did not look for, but some degree of security from positive failure was indispensable – I must not take my son to starve. And then I must have money for the journey, the passage, and some little to support us in our retreat in case I should be unsuccessful at first; and not too little either, for who could tell how long I might have to struggle with the indifference or neglect of others, or my own inexperience, or inability to suit their tastes?

What should I do then? Apply to my brother, and explain my circumstances and my resolves to him? No, no; even if I told him *all* my grievances, which I should be very reluctant to do, he would be certain to disapprove of the step: it would seem like madness to him, as it would to my uncle and aunt, or to Milicent. No; I must have patience and gather a hoard of my own. Rachel should be my only confidant – I thought I could persuade her into the scheme; and she should help me, first to find out a picture-dealer in some distant town; then, through her means, I would privately sell what pictures I had on hand that would do for such a purpose, and some of those I should thereafter paint. Besides this, I would contrive to dispose of my jewels – not the family jewels, but the few I brought with me from home, and those my uncle gave me on my marriage. A few months' arduous toil might well be borne by me, with such an end in view; and in the interim, my son could not be much more injured than he was already.

Having formed this resolution, I immediately set to work to accomplish it. I might possibly have been induced to wax cool upon it afterwards, or perhaps, to keep weighing the pros and cons in my mind till the latter overbalanced the former, and I was driven to relinquish the project altogether, or delay the execution of it to an indefinite period, – had not something occurred to confirm me in that determination to which I still adhere, which I still think I did well to form, and shall do better to execute.

Since Lord Lowborough's departure, I had regarded the library as entirely my own, a secure retreat at all hours of the day. None of our gentlemen had the smallest pretensions to a literary taste, except Mr Hargrave; and he, at present, was quite contented with the newspapers and periodicals of the day. And if, by any chance, he should look in here, I felt assured he would soon depart on seeing me, for, instead of becoming less cool and distant towards me, he had become decidedly more so since the departure of his mother and sisters, which was just what I wished. Here, then, I set up my easel, and here I worked at my canvas from daylight till dusk, with very little intermission saving when pure necessity, or my duties to little Arthur called me away – for I still thought proper to devote some portion of every day exclusively to his instruction and amusement. But contrary to my expectation, on the third morning, while I was thus employed, Mr Hargrave *did* look in, and did *not* immediately withdraw on seeing me. He apologized for his intrusion, and said he was only come for a book; but when he had got it, he condescended to cast a glance over my picture. Being a man of taste, he had something to say on this subject as well as another, and having modestly commented on it, without much encouragement from me, he proceeded to expatiate on the art in general. Receiving no encouragement in that either, he dropped it, but did not depart.

'You don't give us much of your company, Mrs Huntingdon,' observed he, after a brief pause, during which I went on coolly mixing and tempering my colours; 'and I cannot wonder at it, for you must be heartily sick of us all. I myself am so thoroughly ashamed of my companions, and so weary of their irrational conversation and pursuits – now that there is no one to humanize them and keep them in check, since you have justly abandoned us to our own devices – that I think I shall presently withdraw from amongst them – probably within this week – and I cannot suppose you will regret my departure.'

He paused. I did not answer.

'Probably,' he added, with a smile, 'your only regret on the subject will be, that I do not take all my companions along with me. I flatter myself, at times, that though among them, I am not of them; but it is natural that you should be glad to get rid of me. I may regret this, but I cannot blame you for it.'

'I shall not rejoice at *your* departure, for you *can* conduct yourself like a gentleman,' said I, thinking it but right to make some acknowledgment for his good behaviour, 'but I must confess I shall rejoice to bid adieu to the rest, inhospitable as it may appear.'

'No one can blame you for such an avowal,' replied he gravely; 'not even the gentlemen themselves, I imagine. I'll just tell you,' he continued, as if actuated by a sudden resolution, 'what was said last night in the dining-room, after you left us – perhaps you will not mind it as you're so *very* philosophical on certain points,' he added with a slight sneer. 'They were talking about Lord Lowborough and his delectable lady, the cause of whose sudden departure is no secret amongst them; and her character is so well known to them all, that, nearly related to me as she is, I could not attempt to defend it. – God curse me,' he muttered, *par parenthèse*,[6] 'if I don't have vengeance for this! If the villain *must* disgrace the family, must he blazon it abroad to every lowbred knave of his acquaintance? – I beg your pardon, Mrs Huntingdon. Well, they were talking of these things, and some of them remarked that, as she was separated from her husband, he might see her again when he pleased.'

'"Thank you," said he; "I've had enough of her for the present: I'll not trouble to see her, unless she comes to me."

'"Then what do you mean to do, Huntingdon, when we're gone?" said Ralph Hattersley. "Do you mean to turn from the error of your ways, and be a good husband, a good father, and so forth – as I do, when I get shut of you and all these rollicking devils you call your friends? I think it's time; and your wife is fifty times too good for you, you *know* –"

'And he added some praise of you, which you would not thank me for repeating – nor him for uttering; proclaiming it aloud, as he did, without delicacy or discrimination, in an audience where it seemed profanation to utter your name – himself utterly incapable of understanding or appreciating your real excellencies. Huntingdon meanwhile, sat quietly drinking his wine, or looking smilingly into his glass and offering no interruption or reply, till Hattersley shouted out, –

'"Do you hear me, man?"

'"Yes, go on," said he.

'"Nay, I've done," replied the other: "I only want to know if you intend to take my advice."

'"What advice?"

'"To turn over a new leaf, you double-dyed scoundrel," shouted Ralph, "and beg your wife's pardon, and be a good boy for the future."

'"My wife! what wife? I have no wife," replied Huntingdon, looking innocently up from his glass – "or if I have, look you gentlemen, I value her so highly that any one among you, that can fancy her, may have her and welcome – you may, by Jove and my blessing into the bargain!"

'I – hem – someone asked if he really meant what he said, upon which, he solemnly swore he did, and no mistake. – What do you think of that, Mrs Huntingdon?' asked Mr Hargrave, after a short pause, during which I had felt he was keenly examining my half-averted face.

'I say,' replied I, calmly, 'that what he prizes so lightly, will not be long in his possession.'

'You cannot mean that you will break your heart and die for the detestable conduct of an infamous villain like that!'

'By no means: my heart is too thoroughly dried to be broken in a hurry, and I mean to live as long as I can.'

'Will you leave him then!'

'Yes.'

'When – and how?' asked he, eagerly.

'*When* I am ready, and *how* I can manage it most effectually.'

'But your child?'

'My child goes with me.'

'He will not allow it.'

'I shall not ask him.'

'Ah, then, it is a secret flight you meditate! – but with whom, Mrs Huntingdon?'

'With my son – and, possibly, his nurse.'

'Alone – and unprotected! But where can you go? what can you do? He will follow you and bring you back.'

'I have laid my plans too well for that. Let me once get clear of Grassdale, and I shall consider myself safe.'

Mr Hargrave advanced one step towards me, looked me in the face, and drew in his breath to speak; but that look, that heightened colour, that sudden sparkle of the eye made my blood rise in wrath: I abruptly turned away, and, snatching up my brush, began to dash away at my canvas with rather too much energy for the good of the picture.

'Mrs Huntingdon,' said he with bitter solemnity, 'you are cruel – cruel to me – cruel to yourself.'

'Mr Hargrave, remember your promise.'

'I *must* speak – my heart will burst if I don't! I have been silent long enough – and you *must* hear me!' cried he boldly intercepting my retreat to the door. 'You tell me you owe no allegiance to your husband; he openly declares himself weary of you, and calmly gives you up to anybody that will take you; you are about to leave him; no one will believe that you go alone – all the world will say, "She has left him at last, and who can wonder at it? Few can blame her, fewer still can pity him; but who is the companion of her flight?" Thus you will have no credit for your virtue (if you call it such): even your best friends will not believe in it; because it is monstrous, and not to be credited – but by those who suffer from the effects of it, such cruel torments that they know it to be indeed reality – But what can you do in the cold, rough world alone? you, a young and inexperienced woman, delicately nurtured, and utterly –'

'In a word, you would advise me to stay where I am,' interrupted I. 'Well, I'll see about it.'

'By *all means*, leave him!' cried he earnestly, 'but NOT alone! Helen! let *me* protect you!'

'Never! – while heaven spares my reason,' replied I, snatching away the hand he had presumed to seize and press between his own. But he was in for it now; he had fairly broken the barrier: he was completely roused, and determined to hazard all for victory.

'I must not be denied!' exclaimed he vehemently; and seizing both my hands, he held them very tight, but dropped upon his knee, and looked up in my face with a half-imploring, half-imperious gaze. 'You have no reason now: you are flying in the face of heaven's decrees. God has designed me to be your comfort and protector – I feel it – I know it as certainly as if a voice from heaven declared "Ye twain shall be one flesh"[7] – and you spurn me from you –'

'Let me go, Mr Hargrave!' said I sternly. But he only tightened his grasp.

'Let me go!' I repeated, quivering with indignation.

His face was almost opposite the window as he knelt. With a slight start, I saw him glance towards it; and then a gleam of malicious triumph lit up his countenance. Looking over my shoulder, I beheld a shadow just retiring round the corner.

'That is Grimsby,' said he deliberately. 'He will report what he has seen to Huntingdon and all the rest, with such embellishments as he thinks proper. He has no love for you, Mrs Huntingdon – no reverence for your sex – no belief in virtue – no admiration for its image. He will give such a version of this story as will leave no doubt at all, about your character, in the minds of those who hear it. Your fair fame is gone; and nothing that I or you can say can ever retrieve it. But give me the power to protect you, and show me the villain that dares to insult!'

'No one has ever dared to insult me as you are doing now!' said I, at length releasing my hands, and recoiling from him.

'I do not insult you,' cried he: 'I worship you. You are my angel –

my divinity! I lay my powers at your feet – and you must and shall accept them!' he exclaimed impetuously, starting to his feet – 'I *will* be your consoler and defender! and if your conscience upbraid you for it, say I overcame you and you could not choose but yield!'[8]

I never saw a man so terribly excited. He precipitated himself towards me. I snatched up my palette-knife and held it against him. This startled him: he stood and gazed at me in astonishment; I dare say I looked as fierce and resolute as he. I moved to the bell and put my hand upon the cord. This tamed him still more. With a half-authoritative, half-deprecating wave of the hand, he sought to deter me from ringing.

'Stand off, then!' said I. He stepped back – 'And listen to me. – I don't like you,' I continued, as deliberately and emphatically as I could, to give the greater efficacy to my words; 'and if I were divorced from my husband – or if he were dead, I would not marry you. There now! I hope you're satisfied.'

His face grew blanched with anger.

'I am satisfied,' he replied with bitter emphasis, 'that you are the most cold-hearted, unnatural, ungrateful woman I ever yet beheld!'

'Ungrateful sir?'

'Ungrateful.'

'No, Mr Hargrave; I am not. For all the good you ever did me, or ever wished to do, I most sincerely thank you: for all the evil you have done me, and all you would have done, I pray God to pardon you, and make you of a better mind.'

Here the door was thrown open, and Messrs Huntingdon and Hattersley appeared without. The latter remained in the hall, busy with his ramrod and his gun;[9] the former walked in, and stood with his back to the fire, surveying Mr Hargrave and me, particularly the former, with a smile of insupportable meaning, accompanied as it was, by the impudence of his brazen brow and the sly, malicious twinkle of his eye.

'Well, sir?' said Hargrave interrogatively, and with the air of one prepared to stand on the defensive.

'Well, sir,' returned his host.

'We want to know if you're at liberty to join us in a go at the pheasants, Walter,' interposed Hattersley from without. 'Come! there shall be nothing shot besides, except a puss or two;[10] *I'll* vouch for that.'

Walter did not answer, but walked to the window to collect his faculties. Arthur uttered a low whistle, and followed him with his eyes. A slight flush of anger rose to Hargrave's cheek; but in a moment, he turned calmly round, and said carelessly –

'I came here to bid farewell to Mrs Huntingdon, and tell her I must go tomorrow.'

'Humph! You're mighty sudden in your resolution. What takes you off so soon, may I ask?'

'Business,' returned he, repelling the other's incredulous sneer with a glance of scornful defiance.

'Very good,' was the reply; and Hargrave walked away. Thereupon, Mr Huntingdon, gathering his coat laps under his arms, and setting his shoulder against the mantelpiece, turned to me, and, addressing me in a low voice, scarcely above his breath, poured forth a volley of the vilest and grossest abuse it was possible for the imagination to conceive or the tongue to utter. I did not attempt to interrupt him; but my spirit kindled within me, and when he had done, I replied –

'If your accusation were true, Mr Huntingdon, how *dare you* blame me?'

'She's hit it, by Jove!' cried Hattersley, rearing his gun against the wall; and, stepping into the room, he took his precious friend by the arm, and attempted to drag him away. 'Come, my lad,' he muttered; 'true or false, *you've* no right to blame her, you *know* – nor him either; after what you said last night. So come along.'

There was something implied here that I could not endure.

'Dare you suspect me, Mr Hattersley?' said I, almost beside myself with fury.

'Nay, nay, I suspect nobody. It's all right – it's all right. So come along Huntingdon, you blackguard.'

'She can't deny it!' cried the gentleman thus addressed, grinning in mingled rage and triumph. 'She can't deny it if her life depended on it!' and muttering some more abusive language, he walked into the hall, and took up his hat and gun from the table.

'I scorn to justify myself to you!' said I. 'But you,' turning to Hattersley, 'if you presume to have any doubts on the subject, ask Mr Hargrave.'

At this, they simultaneously burst into a rude laugh that made my whole frame tingle to the finger's ends.

'Where is he? I'll ask him myself!' said I, advancing towards them.

Suppressing a new burst of merriment, Hattersley pointed to the outer door. It was half open. His brother-in-law was standing on the front without.

'Mr Hargrave, will you please to step this way?' said I.

He turned and looked at me in grave surprise.

'Step this way, if you please!' I repeated, in so determined a manner that he could not, or did not choose to resist its authority. Somewhat reluctantly he ascended the steps and advanced a pace or two into the hall.

'And tell those gentlemen,' I continued – 'these *men* whether or not I yielded to your solicitations.'

'I don't understand you, Mrs Huntingdon.'

'You *do* understand me, sir; and I charge you upon your honour as a gentleman (if you have any), to answer truly. Did I, or did I not?'

'No,' muttered he turning away.

'Speak up sir; they can't hear you. Did I grant your request?'

'You did not.'

'No, I'll be sworn she didn't,' said Hattersley, 'or he'd never look so black.'

'I'm willing to grant you the satisfaction of a gentleman,[11] Huntingdon,' said Mr Hargrave, calmly addressing his host, but with a bitter sneer upon his countenance.

'Go to the deuce!' replied the latter, with an impatient jerk of the head. Hargrave withdrew with a look of cold disdain, saying, –

'You know where to find me, should you feel disposed to send a friend.'

Muttered oaths and curses were all the answer this intimation obtained.

'Now Huntingdon, you see!' said Hattersley, 'clear as the day.'

'I don't care *what* he sees,' said I, 'or what he imagines; but you, Mr Hattersley, when you hear my name belied and slandered, will you defend it?'

'I will. Blast me if I don't!'

I instantly departed, and shut myself into the library. What could possess me to make such a request of such a man? I cannot tell, but drowning men catch at straws: they had driven me desperate between them; I hardly knew what I said. There was no other to preserve my name from being blackened and aspersed among this nest of boon companions, and through them, perhaps into the world; and beside my abandoned wretch of a husband, the base, malignant Grimsby, and the false villain Hargrave, this boarish ruffian, coarse and brutal as he was, shone like a glow-worm in the dark, among its fellow worms.

What a scene was this! Could I ever have imagined that I should be doomed to bear such insults under my own roof – to hear such things spoken in my presence – nay spoken *to* me and *of* me – and by those who arrogated to themselves the name of gentlemen? And could I have imagined that I should have been able to endure it as calmly, and to repel their insults as firmly and as boldly as I had done? A hardness such as this is taught by rough experience and despair alone.

Such thoughts as these chased one another through my mind, as I paced to and fro the room, and longed – oh, *how* I longed to take my child and leave them now, without an hour's delay! But it could not be: there was work before me – hard work, that must be done.

'Then let me do it,' said I, 'and lose not a moment in vain repinings, and idle chafings against my fate, and those who influence it.'

And conquering my agitation with a powerful effort, I immediately resumed my task, and laboured hard all day.

Mr Hargrave did depart on the morrow; and I have never seen him since. The others stayed on for two or three weeks longer; but I kept aloof from them as much as possible, and still continued my labour, and have continued it, with almost unabated ardour, to the present day. I soon acquainted Rachel with my design, confiding all my motives and intentions to her ear, and much to my agreeable surprise, found little difficulty in persuading her to enter into my views. She is a sober, cautious woman, but she so hates her master, and so loves her mistress and her nursling, that after several ejaculations, a few faint objections, and many tears and lamentations that I should be brought to such a pass, she applauded my resolution and consented to aid me with all her might – on one condition, only – that she might share my exile: otherwise, she was utterly inexorable, regarding it as perfect madness for me and Arthur to go alone. With touching generosity, she modestly offered to aid me with her little hoard of savings, hoping I would 'excuse her for the liberty, but really if I would do her the favour to accept it as a loan, she should be very happy.' Of course I could not think of such a thing; – but now, thank Heaven, I have gathered a little hoard of my own, and my preparations are so far advanced, that I am looking forward to a speedy emancipation. Only let the stormy severity of this winter weather be somewhat abated, and then, some morning, Mr Huntingdon will come down to a solitary breakfast-table, and perhaps be clamouring through the house for his invisible wife and child, when they are some fifty miles on their way to the western world – or it may be more, for we shall leave him hours before the dawn, and it is not probable he will discover the loss of both, until the day is far advanced.

I am fully alive to the evils that may and must result upon the step I am about to take; but I never waver in my resolution, because I never forget my son. It was only this morning – while I pursued my usual employment, he was sitting at my feet, quietly playing with the shreds of canvas I had thrown upon the carpet – but his mind was otherwise occupied, for, in a while, he looked up wistfully in my face, and gravely asked –

'Mamma, why are you wicked?'

'Who told you I was wicked, love?'

'Rachel.'

'No Arthur, Rachel never said so, I am certain.'

'Well then, it was papa,' replied he thoughtfully. Then, after a reflective pause, he added, 'At least, I'll tell you how it was I got to know: when I'm with papa, if I say mamma wants me, or mamma says I'm not to do something that he tells me to do – he always says, "Mamma be damned," – and Rachel says it's only wicked people that are damned. So mamma, that's why I think you must be wicked – and I wish you wouldn't.'

'My dear child, I am not. Those are bad words, and wicked people often say them of others better than themselves. Those words cannot make people be damned, nor show that they deserve it. God will judge us by our own thoughts and deeds, not by what others say about us. And when you hear such words spoken, Arthur, remember never to repeat them: it is wicked to say such things of others, not to have them said against you.'

'Then it's papa that's wicked,' said he, ruefully.

'Papa is wrong to say such things, and you will be very wrong to imitate him, now that you know better.'

'What *is* imitate?'

'To do as he does.'

'Does *he* know better?'

'Perhaps he does; but that is nothing to you.'

'If he doesn't, you ought to tell him, mamma.'

'I *have* told him.'

The little moralist paused and pondered. I tried in vain to divert his mind from the subject.

'I'm sorry papa's wicked,' said he mournfully, at length, 'for I don't want him to go to hell.' And so saying he burst into tears.

I consoled him with the hope that perhaps his papa would alter and become good before he died – but is it not time to deliver him from such a parent?

CHAPTER 40

A MISADVENTURE

Jan. 10th, 1827. While writing the above, yesterday evening, I sat in the drawing-room. Mr Huntingdon was present, but, as I thought, asleep on the sofa behind me. He had risen however, unknown to me, and, actuated by some base spirit of curiosity, been looking over my shoulder for I know not how long; for when I had laid aside my pen, and was about to close the book, he suddenly placed his hand upon it, and saying – 'With your leave, my dear, I'll have a look at this,'[1] forcibly wrested it from me, and, drawing a chair to the table, composedly sat down to examine it – turning back leaf after leaf to find an explanation of what he had read. Unluckily for me, he was more sober that night than he usually is at such an hour.

Of course I did not leave him to pursue this occupation in quiet: I made several attempts to snatch the book from his hands, but he held it too firmly for that; I upbraided him in bitterness and scorn for his mean and dishonourable conduct, but that had no effect upon him; and, finally, I extinguished both the candles, but he only wheeled round to the fire, and raising a blaze sufficient for his purposes, calmly continued the investigation. I had serious thoughts of getting a pitcher of water and extinguishing that light too; but it was evident his curiosity was too keenly excited to be quenched by that, and the more I manifested my anxiety to baffle his scrutiny, the greater would be his determination to persist in it – besides it was too late.

'It seems very interesting, love,' said he, lifting his head and turning to where I stood wringing my hands in silent rage and anguish; 'but it's rather long; I'll look at it some other time; – and meanwhile, I'll trouble you for your keys, my dear.'

'What keys?'

'The keys of your cabinet, desk, drawers, and whatever else you possess,' said he, rising and holding out his hand.

'I've not got them,' I replied. The key of my desk in fact was, at that moment, in the lock, and the others were attached to it.

'Then you must send for them,' said he; 'and if that old bitch, Rachel, doesn't immediately deliver them up, she tramps bag and baggage tomorrow.'

'She doesn't know where they are,' I answered, quietly placing my hand upon them, and taking them from the desk, as I thought, unobserved. 'I know, but I shall not give them up without a reason.'

'And *I* know, too,' said he, suddenly seizing my closed hand and rudely abstracting them from it. He then took up one of the candles and relighted it by thrusting it into the fire.

'Now then,' sneered he, 'we must have a confiscation of property. But first, let us take a peep into the studio.'

And putting the keys into his pocket, he walked into the library. I followed, whether with the dim idea of preventing mischief or only to know the worst, I can hardly tell. My painting materials were laid together on the corner table, ready for tomorrow's use, and only covered with a cloth. He soon spied them out, and putting down the candle, deliberately proceeded to cast them into the fire – palette, paints, bladders,[2] pencils, brushes, varnish – I saw them all consumed – the palette knives snapped in two – the oil and turpentine sent hissing and roaring up the chimney. He then rang the bell.

'Benson, take those things away,' said he, pointing to the easel, canvas, and stretcher;[3] 'and tell the housemaid she may kindle the fire with them: your mistress won't want them any more.'

Benson paused aghast and looked at me.

'Take them away, Benson,' said I; and his master muttered an oath.

'And this and all, sir?' said the astonished servant referring to the half-finished picture.

'That and all,' replied the master; and the things were cleared away.

Mr Huntingdon then went upstairs. I did not attempt to follow him; but remained seated in the arm chair, speechless, tearless, and almost motionless, till he returned about half an hour after, and walking up to me, held the candle in my face and peered into my eyes with looks and laughter too insulting to be borne. With a sudden stroke of my hand, I dashed the candle to the floor.

'Hal-lo!' muttered he, starting back – 'She's the very devil for spite! Did *ever* any mortal see such eyes? – they shine in the dark like a cat's. *Oh*, you're a sweet one!' so saying, he gathered up the candle and the candle-stick. The former being broken as well as extinguished, he rang for another.

'Benson, your mistress has broken the candle: bring another.'

'You expose yourself finely,' observed I as the man departed.

'I didn't say *I'd* broken it, did I?' returned he. He then threw my keys into my lap, saying, – 'There! you'll find nothing gone but your money, and the jewels – and a few little trifles I thought it advisable to take into my own possession, lest your mercantile spirit should be tempted to turn them into gold. I've left you a few sovereigns in your purse, which I expect to last you through the month – at all events, when you want more you will be so good as to give me an account of how that's spent. I shall put you upon a small monthly allowance, in future, for your own private expenses; and you needn't trouble yourself any more about my concerns; I shall look out for a steward, my dear; I won't expose you to the temptation. And as for the household matters, Mrs Greaves must be very particular in keeping her accounts: we must go upon an entirely new plan –'

'What great discovery have you made *now*, Mr Huntingdon? Have I attempted to defraud you?'

'Not in money matters, exactly, it seems, but it's best to keep out of the way of temptation.'

Here Benson entered with the candles, and there followed a brief interval of silence – I sitting still in my chair, and he standing with his back to the fire, silently triumphing in my despair.

'And so,' said he at length, 'you thought to disgrace me, did you, by running away and turning artist, and supporting yourself by the labour of your hands, forsooth? And you thought to rob me of my son too, and bring him up to be a dirty Yankee tradesman, or a low, beggarly painter?'

'Yes, to obviate his becoming such a gentleman as his father.'

'It's well you couldn't keep your own secret – ha, ha! It's well these women must be blabbing – if they haven't a friend to talk to, they must whisper their secrets to the fishes, or write them on the sand or something; and it's well too I wasn't overfull tonight, now I think of it, or I might have snoozed away and never dreamt of looking what my sweet lady was about – or I might have lacked the sense or the power to carry my point like a man, as I have done.'

Leaving him to his self-congratulations, I rose to secure my manuscript, for I now remembered it had been left upon the drawing-room table, and I determined, if possible, to save myself the humiliation of seeing it in his hands again. I could not bear the idea of his amusing himself over my secret thoughts and recollections; though, to be sure, he would find little good of himself therein indited, except in the former part – and oh, I would sooner burn it all than he should read what I had written when I was such a fool as to love him!

'And by the by,' cried he as I was leaving the room, 'you'd better tell that d—d old sneak of a nurse to keep out of my way for a day or two – I'd pay her her wages and send her packing tomorrow, but I know she'd do more mischief out of the house than in it.'

And as I departed, he went on cursing and abusing my faithful friend and servant with epithets I will not defile this paper with repeating. I went to her as soon as I had put away my book, and told her how our project was defeated. She was as much distressed and horrified as I was – and more so than I was that night, for I was partly stunned by the blow, and partly excited and supported against it by the bitterness of my wrath. But in the morning, when I woke without that cheering hope that had been my secret comfort and support so long, and all this day, when I have wandered about restless and objectless, shunning my husband, shrinking even from my child – knowing that I am unfit to be his teacher or companion, hoping nothing for his future life, and fervently wishing he had never been born – I felt the full extent of my calamity – and I feel it now. I know that day after day such feelings will return upon me: I am a slave, a prisoner – but that is nothing; if it were myself alone, I would not complain, but I am forbidden to rescue my son from ruin, and what was once my only consolation, is become the crowning source of my despair.

Have I no faith in God? I try to look to him and raise my heart to Heaven, but it will cleave to the dust:[4] I can only say – 'He hath hedged me about, that I cannot get out: he hath made my chain heavy. He hath filled me with bitterness, he hath made me drunken with wormwood:' – I forget to add – 'But though he cause grief, yet will he have compassion according to the multitude of his mercies. For he doth not afflict willingly nor grieve the children of men.'[5] I ought to think of this; and if there be nothing but sorrow for me in this world, what is the longest life of misery to a whole eternity of peace? And for my little Arthur – has he no friend but me? Who was it said, 'It is not the will of your Father which is in Heaven that one of these little ones should perish'?[6]

CHAPTER 41

'HOPE SPRINGS ETERNAL IN THE HUMAN BREAST'[1]

March 20th. – Having now got rid of Mr Huntingdon for a season, my spirits begin to revive. He left me early in February; and the moment he was gone, I breathed again, and felt my vital energy return; not with the hope of escape – he has taken care to leave me no visible chance of that – but with a determination to make the best of existing circumstances. Here was Arthur left to me at last; and rousing from my despondent apathy, I exerted all my powers to eradicate the weeds that had been fostered in his infant mind, and sow again the good seed they had rendered unproductive. Thank Heaven, it is not a barren or a stony soil; if weeds spring fast there, so do better plants.[2] His apprehensions are more quick, his heart more overflowing with affection than ever his father's could have been; and it is no hopeless task to bend him to obedience and win him to love and know his own true friend, as long as there is no one to counteract my efforts.

I had much trouble at first in breaking him of those evil habits his father had taught him to acquire, but already that difficulty is nearly vanquished now: bad language seldom defiles his mouth, and I have succeeded in giving him an absolute disgust for all intoxicating liquors, which I hope not even his father or his father's friends will be able to overcome. He was inordinately fond of them for so young a creature, and, remembering my unfortunate father as well as his, I dreaded the consequences of such a taste. But if I had stinted him in his usual quantity of wine or forbidden him to taste it altogether, that would only have increased his partiality for it, and made him regard it as a greater treat than ever. I therefore gave him quite as much as his father was accustomed to allow him – as much indeed, as he desired to have, but into every glass I surreptitiously introduced a small quantity of tartar-emetic – just enough to produce inevitable nausea and depression without positive sickness. Finding such disagreeable consequences invariably to result from this indulgence, he soon grew weary of it, but the more he shrank from the daily treat the more I pressed it upon him, till his reluctance was strengthened to perfect abhorrence. When he was thoroughly disgusted with every kind of wine, I allowed him, at his own request, to try brandy and water and then gin and water; for the little toper was familiar with them all, and I was determined that all should be equally hateful to him. This I have now effected; and since he declares that the taste, the smell, the sight of any one of them is sufficient to make him sick, I have given up teasing him about them, except now and then as objects of terror in cases of misbehaviour: 'Arthur, if you're not a good boy I shall give you a glass of wine,' or 'Now Arthur, if you say that again you shall have some brandy and water,' is as good as any other threat; and, once or twice, when he was sick, I have obliged the poor child to swallow a little wine and water *without* the tartar-emetic, by way of medicine; and this practice I intend to continue for some time to come; not that I think it of any real service in a physical sense, but because I am determined to enlist all the powers of association in my service:[3] I wish this aversion to be so deeply grounded in his nature that nothing in after life may be able to overcome it.

Thus, I flatter myself, I shall secure him from this one vice; and for the rest, if on his father's return I find reason to apprehend that my good lessons will be all destroyed – if Mr Huntingdon commence again the game of teaching the child to hate and despise his mother and emulate his father's wickedness, I will yet deliver my son from his hands. I have devised another scheme that might be resorted to in such a case, and if I could but obtain my brother's consent and assistance, I should not doubt of its success. The old hall where he and I were born and where our mother died, is not now inhabited, nor yet quite sunk into decay, as I believe. Now if I could persuade him to have one or two rooms made habitable and to let them to me as a stranger, I might live there, with my child, under an assumed name, and still support myself by my favourite art. He should lend me the money to begin with, and I would pay him back, and live in lowly independence and strict seclusion, for the house stands in a lonely place, and the neighbourhood is thinly inhabited, and he himself should negotiate the sale of my pictures for me. I have arranged the whole plan in my head; and all I want, is to persuade Frederick to be of the same mind as myself. He is coming to see me soon, and then I will make the proposal to him, having first enlightened him upon my circumstances sufficiently to excuse the project.

Already, I believe, he knows much more of my situation than I have told him. I can tell this by the air of tender sadness pervading his letters; and by the fact of his so seldom mentioning my husband, and generally evincing a kind of covert bitterness when he does refer to him; as well as by the circumstances of his never coming to see me when Mr Huntingdon is at home. But he has never openly expressed any disapprobation of him or sympathy for me; he has never asked any questions, or said anything to invite my confidence. Had he done so, I should probably have had but few concealments from him. Perhaps, he feels hurt at my reserve. He is a strange being – I wish we knew each other better. He used to spend a month at Staningley every year, before I was married; but, since our father's death, I have only seen him once, when he came for a few days while Mr Huntingdon was away. He shall stay many days this time, and there shall be more candour and cordiality between us than ever there was before, since our early childhood: my heart clings to him more than ever; and my soul is sick of solitude.

April 16th. – He is come and gone. He would not stay above a fortnight. The time passed quickly, but very, very happily, and it has done me good. I must have a bad disposition, for my misfortunes have soured and embittered me exceedingly: I was beginning insensibly to cherish very unamiable feelings against my fellow mortals – the male part of them especially; but it is a comfort to see there is at least one among them worthy to be trusted and esteemed; and doutbless there are more, though I have never known them – unless I accept poor Lord Lowborough, and he was bad enough in his day;

but what would Frederick have been, if he had lived in the world, and mingled from his childhood with such men as these of my acquaintance? and what *will* Arthur be, with all his natural sweetness of disposition, if I do not save him from that world and those companions? I mentioned my fears to Frederick and introduced the subject of my plan of rescue on the evening after his arrival, when I presented my little son to his uncle.

'He is like you, Frederick,' said I, 'in some of his moods: I sometimes think he resembles you more than his father; and I am glad of it.'

'You flatter me, Helen,' replied he, stroking the child's soft, wavy locks.

'No, – you will think it no compliment when I tell you I would rather have him to resemble *Benson* than his father.'

He slightly elevated his eyebrows, but said nothing.

'Do you know what sort of man Mr Huntingdon is?' said I.

'I think I have an idea.'

'Have you so clear an idea that you can hear, without surprise or disapproval, that I meditate escaping with that child to some secret asylum where we can live in peace and never see him again?'

'Is it really so?'

'If you have not,' continued I, 'I'll tell you something more about him' – and I gave a sketch of his general conduct, and a more particular account of his behaviour with regard to his child, and explained my apprehensions on the latter's account, and my determination to deliver him from his father's influence.

Frederick was exceedingly indignant against Mr Huntingdon, and very much grieved for me; but still, he looked upon my project as wild and impracticable; he deemed my fears for Arthur disproportioned to the circumstances, and opposed so many objections to my plan, and devised so many milder methods for ameliorating my condition, that I was obliged to enter into further details to convince him that my husband was utterly incorrigible, and that nothing could persuade him to give up his son whatever became of me, he being as fully determined the child should not leave him, as I was not to leave the child; and that, in fact, nothing would answer but this, unless I fled the country as I had intended before. To obviate that, he at length consented to have one wing of the old Hall put into a habitable condition, as a place of refuge against a time of need; but hoped I would not take advantage of it, unless circumstances should render it really necessary, which I was ready enough to promise; for, though, for my own sake, such a hermitage appears like paradise itself compared with my present situation, yet for my friends' sakes – for Milicent and Esther, my sisters in heart and affection, for the poor tenants of Grassdale, and above all for my aunt – I will stay if I possibly can.

July 29th. – Mrs Hargrave and her daughter are come back from London. Esther is full of her first season in town; but she is still heartwhole and unengaged. Her mother sought out an excellent match for her, and even brought the gentleman to lay his heart and fortune at her feet; but Esther had the audacity to refuse the noble gifts. He was a man of good family and large possessions, but the naughty girl maintained he was old as Adam, ugly as sin, and hateful as – one who shall be nameless.

'But indeed, I had a hard time of it,' said she: 'mamma was very greatly disappointed at the failure of her darling project, and very, very angry at my obstinate resistance to her will, – and is so still; but I can't help it. And Walter, too, is so seriously displeased at my perversity and absurd caprice, as he calls it, that I fear he will never forgive me – I did not think he *could* be so unkind as he has lately shown himself. But Milicent begged me not to yield, and I'm sure, Mrs Huntingdon, if you had seen the man they wanted to palm upon me, you would have advised me not to take him too.'

'I should have done so whether I had seen him or not,' said I. 'It is enough that you dislike him.'

'I knew you would say so; though mamma affirmed you would be quite shocked at my undutiful conduct – you can't imagine how she lectures me – I am disobedient and ungrateful; I am thwarting her wishes, wronging my brother, and making myself a burden on her hands – I sometimes fear she'll overcome me after all. I have a strong will, but so has she, and when she says such bitter things, it provokes me to such a pass that I feel inclined to do as she bids me, and then break my heart and say "There, mamma, it's all your fault!"'

'Pray don't!' said I. 'Obedience from such a motive would be positive wickedness, and certain to bring the punishment it deserved. Stand firm, and your mamma will soon relinquish her persecution; – and the gentleman himself will cease to pester you with his addresses if he finds them steadily rejected.'

'Oh, no! mamma will weary all about her before she tires herself with her exertions; and as for Mr Oldfield, she has given him to understand that I have refused his offer, not from any dislike of his person, but merely because I am giddy and young, and cannot at present reconcile myself to the thought of marriage under any circumstances: but, by next season, she has no doubt, I shall have more sense, and hopes my girlish fancies will be worn away. So she has brought me home, to school me into a proper sense of my duty, against[4] the time comes round again – indeed, I believe she will not put herself to the expense of taking me up to London again, unless I surrender: she cannot afford to take me to town for pleasure and nonsense, she says, and it is not *every* rich gentleman that will consent to take me without a fortune, whatever exalted ideas I may have of my own attractions.'

'Well Esther, I pity you; but still, I repeat, stand firm. You might as well sell yourself to slavery at once, as marry a man you dislike. If your mother and brother are unkind to you, you may leave them, but remember you are bound to your husband for life.'

'But I cannot leave them unless I get married, and I cannot get married if nobody sees me. I saw one or two gentlemen in London, that I might have liked, but they were younger sons,[5] and mamma would not let me get to know them – one especially, who I believe rather liked me, but she threw every possible obstacle in the way of our better acquaintance – wasn't it provoking?'

'I have no doubt you would feel it so, but it is possible that if you married him, you might have more reason to regret it hereafter, than if you married Mr Oldfield. When I tell you not to marry *without* love, I do not advise you to marry for love alone – there are many, many other things to be considered. Keep both heart and hand in your own possession, till you see good reason to part with them; and if such an occasion should never present itself, comfort your mind with this reflection: that, though in single life your joys may not be very many, your sorrows, at least will not be more than you can bear. Marriage *may* change your circumstances for the better, but in my private opinion, it is far more likely to produce a contrary result.'

'So thinks Milicent, but allow me to say, *I* think otherwise. If I thought myself doomed to old-maidenhood, I should cease to value my life. The thought of living on, year after year at the Grove – a hanger-on upon mamma and Walter – a mere cumberer of the ground[6] (now that I know in what light they would regard it), is perfectly intolerable – I would rather run away with the butler.'

'Your circumstances are peculiar I allow; but have patience, love; do nothing rashly. Remember you are not yet nineteen, and many years are yet to pass before anyone can set you down as an old maid: you cannot tell what Providence may have in store for you. And meantime, remember you have a *right* to the protection and support of your mother and brother, however they may seem to grudge it.'

'You are so grave, Mrs Huntingdon,' said Esther after a pause. 'When Milicent uttered the same discouraging sentiments concerning marriage, I asked if she was happy: she said she was; but I only half believed her; and now I must put the same question to you.'

'It is a very impertinent question,' laughed I, 'from a young girl to a married woman so many years her senior – and I shall not answer it.'

'Pardon me, dear *madam*,' said she, laughingly throwing herself into my arms, and kissing me with playful affection; but I felt a tear on my neck, as she dropped her head on my bosom and continued, with an odd mixture of sadness and levity, timidity and audacity, – 'I know you are not so happy as I mean to be, for you spend half your life alone at Grassdale, while Mr Huntingdon goes about enjoying himself where, and how he pleases – I shall expect *my* husband to have no pleasures but what he shares with me; and if his greatest pleasure of all is not the enjoyment of my company – why – it will be the worse for him – that's all.'

'If such are your expectations of matrimony, Esther, you must indeed, be careful whom you marry – or rather, you must avoid it altogether.'

CHAPTER 42

A REFORMATION

Sept. 1st. – No Mr Huntingdon yet. Perhaps he will stay among his friends till Christmas; and then, next spring, he will be off again. If he continue this plan, I shall be able to stay at Grassdale well enough – that is, I *shall* be able to stay, and that is enough; even an occasional bevy of friends at the shooting season may be borne if Arthur get so firmly attached to me – so well established in good sense and principles, before they come, that I shall be able, by reason and affection, to keep him pure from their contaminations. Vain hope, I fear! but still, till such a time of trial comes, I will forbear to think of my quiet asylum in the beloved old hall.

Mr and Mrs Hattersley have been staying at the Grove a fortnight; and as Mr Hargrave is still absent, and the weather was remarkably fine, I never passed a day without seeing my two friends, Milicent and Esther, either there or here. On one occasion, when Mr Hattersley had driven them over to Grassdale in the phaeton, with little Helen and Ralph, and we were all enjoying ourselves in the garden – I had a few minutes' conversation with that gentleman, while the ladies were amusing themselves with the children.

'Do you want to hear anything of your husband, Mrs Huntingdon?' said he.

'No, unless you can tell me when to expect him home.'

'I can't. – You don't want him, do you?' said he with a broad grin.

'No.'

'Well, I think you're better without him, sure enough – for my part, I'm downright weary of him. I told him I'd leave him if he didn't mend his manners – and he wouldn't; so I left him – you see

I'm a better man than you think me; – and what's more, I have serious thoughts of washing my hands of him entirely, and the whole set of 'em, and comporting myself from this day forward, with all decency and sobriety as a Christian and the father of a family should do. – What do you think of that?'

'It is a resolution you ought to have formed long ago.'

'Well, I'm not thirty yet: it isn't too late, is it?'

'No; it is never too late to reform, as long as you have the sense to desire it, and the strength to execute your purpose.'

'Well, to tell you the truth, I've thought of it often and often before, but he's such devilish good company is Huntingdon, after all – you can't imagine what a jovial good fellow he is when he's not fairly drunk, only just primed or half-seas-over – we all have a bit of a liking for him at the bottom of our hearts, though we can't respect him.'

'But should you wish yourself to be like him?'

'No, I'd rather be like myself, bad as I am.'

'You can't continue as bad as you are without getting worse – and more brutalized every day – and therefore more like him.'

I could not help smiling at the comical, half angry, half confounded look he put on at this rather unusual mode of address.

'Never mind my plain speaking,' said I; 'it is from the best of motives. But tell me, should you wish your sons to be like Mr Huntingdon – or even like yourself?'

'Hang it, no.'

'Should you wish your daughter to despise you – or, at least, to feel no vestige of respect for you, and no affection but what is mingled with the bitterest regret?'

'Oh, blast it, no! I couldn't stand that.'

'And finally, should you wish your wife to be ready to sink into the earth when she hears you mentioned; and to loathe the very sound of your voice, and shudder at your approach?'

'She never will; she likes me all the same, whatever I do.'

'Impossible, Mr Hattersley! you mistake her quiet submission for affection.'

'Fire and fury –'

'Now don't burst into a tempest at that – I don't mean to say she does not love you – she does, I know, a great deal better than you deserve – but I am quite sure, that if you behave better, she will love you more, and if you behave worse, she will love you less and less till all is lost in fear, aversion, and bitterness of soul, if not in secret hatred and contempt. But, dropping the subject of affection, should you wish to be the tyrant of her life – to take away all the sunshine from her existence, and make her thoroughly miserable?'

'Of course not; and I don't, and I'm not going to.'

'You have done more towards it than you suppose.'

'Pooh, pooh! she's not the susceptible, anxious, worriting[1] creature you imagine: she's a little meek, peaceable, affectionate body; apt to be rather sulky at times, but quiet and cool in the main, and ready to take things as they come.'

'Think of what she was five years ago, when you married her, and what she is now.'

'I know – she was a little plump lassie then, with a pretty pink and white face: now, she's a poor little bit of a creature, fading and melting away like a snow-wreath – but hang it! – by Jupiter, that's not my fault!'

'What is the cause of it then? Not years, for she's only five and twenty.'

'It's her own delicate health, and – confound it, madam! what would you make of me? – and the children, to be sure, that worry her to death between them.'

'No, Mr Hattersley, the children give her more pleasure than pain: they are fine well dispositioned children –'

'I know they are – bless 'em!'

'Then why lay the blame on them? – I'll tell you what it is: it's silent fretting and constant anxiety on your account, mingled I suspect, with something of bodily fear on her own. When you behave well, she can only rejoice with trembling; she has no security, no confidence in your judgment or principles; but is continually dreading the close of such short-lived felicity: when you behave ill, her causes of terror and misery are more than anyone can tell but herself. In patient endurance of evil, she forgets it is our duty to admonish our neighbours of their transgressions.[2] – Since you *will* mistake her silence for indifference, come with me, and I'll show you one or two of her letters – no breach of confidence, I hope, since you are her other half.'

He followed me into the library. I sought out and put into his hands two of Milicent's letters; one dated from London and written during one of his wildest seasons of reckless dissipation; the other in the country during a lucid interval. The former was full of trouble and anguish; not accusing *him*, but deeply regretting his connection with his profligate companions, abusing Mr Grimsby and others, insinuating bitter things against Mr Huntingdon, and most ingeniously throwing the blame of her husband's misconduct on to other men's shoulders. The latter was full of hope and joy, yet with a trembling consciousness that this happiness would not last; praising his goodness to the skies, but with an evident, though but half-expressed wish that it were based on a surer foundation than the natural impulses of the heart, and a half prophetic dread of the fall of that house so founded on the sand,[3] – which fall had shortly after taken place, as Hattersley must have been conscious while he read.

Almost at the commencement of the first letter, I had the unexpected pleasure of seeing him blush; but he immediately turned his back to me and finished the perusal at the window. At the second, I saw him, once or twice, raise his hand and hurriedly pass it across his face. Could it be to dash away a tear?[4] When he had done, there was an interval spent in clearing his throat and staring out of the window, and then, after whistling a few bars of a favourite air, he turned round, gave me back the letters and silently shook me by the hand.

'I've been a cursed rascal, God knows,' said he as he gave it a hearty squeeze, 'but you see if I don't make amends for it – G—d d—n me if I don't!'

'Don't curse yourself, Mr Hattersley; if God had heard half your invocations of that kind, you would have been in hell long before now – and you *cannot* make amends for the past by doing your duty for the future, in as much as your duty is only what you *owe* to your Maker, and you cannot do *more* than fulfil it – another must make amends for your past delinquencies. If you intend to reform, invoke God's blessing, his mercy, and his aid; not his curse.'

'God help me, then – for I'm sure I need it – Where's Milicent?'

'She's there, just coming in with her sister.'

He stepped out at the glass door, and went to meet them. I followed at a little distance. Somewhat to his wife's astonishment, he lifted her off from the ground and saluted her with a hearty kiss and a strong embrace; then, placing his two hands on her shoulders, he gave her, I suppose, a sketch of the great things he meant to do, for she suddenly threw her arms round him and burst into tears, exclaiming, –

'Do, do, Ralph – we shall be so happy! How very, very good you are!'

'Nay, not I,' said he, turning her round and pushing her towards me. 'Thank *her*; it's her doing.'

Milicent flew to thank me, overflowing with gratitude. I disclaimed all title to it, telling her her husband was predisposed to amendment before I added my mite[5] of exhortation and encouragement, and that I had only done what she might – and ought to – have done herself.

'Oh, no!' cried she, 'I couldn't have influenced him, I'm sure, by anything that I could have said. I should only have bothered him by my clumsy efforts at persuasion, if I had made the attempt.'

'You never tried me, Milly,' said he.

Shortly after, they took their leave. They are now gone on a visit to Hattersley's father. After that, they will repair to their country home. I hope his good resolutions will not fall through, and poor Milicent will not be again disappointed. Her last letter was full of present bliss and pleasing anticipations for the future; but no particular temptation has yet occurred to put his virtue to the test. Henceforth, however, she will doubtless be somewhat less timid and reserved, and he more kind and thoughtful – Surely, then, her hopes are not unfounded; and I have one bright spot, at least, whereon to rest my thoughts.[6]

CHAPTER 43

October 10th. – Mr Huntingdon returned about three weeks ago. His appearance, his demeanour and conversation, and my feelings with regard to him, I shall not trouble myself to describe. The day after his arrival, however, he surprised me by the announcement of an intention to procure a governess for little Arthur: I told him it was quite unnecessary, not to say ridiculous, at the present season: I thought I was fully competent to the task of teaching him myself – for some years to come, at least: the child's education was the only pleasure and business of my life; and since he had deprived me of every other occupation, he might surely leave me that.

He said I was not fit to teach children, or to be with them: I had already reduced the boy to little better than an automaton, I had broken his fine spirit with my rigid severity; and I should freeze all the sunshine out of his heart, and make him as gloomy an ascetic as myself, if I had the handling of him much longer. And poor Rachel, too, came in for her share of abuse, as usual; he cannot endure Rachel, because he knows she has a proper appreciation of him.

I calmly defended our several qualifications as nurse and governess, and still resisted the proposed addition to our family; but he cut me short by saying it was no use bothering about the matter, for he had engaged a governess already, and she was coming next week; so that all I had to do was to get things ready for her reception. This was a rather startling piece of intelligence. I ventured to enquire her name and address, by whom she had been recommended, or how he had been led to make choice of her.

'She is a very estimable, pious young person,' said he; 'you needn't be afraid. Her name is Myers, I believe; and she was recommended to me by a respectable old dowager – a lady of high repute in the religious world. I have not seen her myself, and therefore cannot give you a particular account of her person and conversation, and so forth; but, if the old lady's eulogies are correct, you will find her to possess all desirable qualifications for her position – an inordinate love of children among the rest.'

All this was gravely and quietly spoken, but there was a laughing demon in his half-averted eye that boded no good I imagined. However, I thought of my asylum in —shire, and made no further objections.

When Miss Myers arrived, I was not prepared to give her a very cordial reception. Her appearance was not particularly calculated to produce a favourable impression at first sight, nor did her manners and subsequent conduct, in any degree, remove the prejudice I had already conceived against her. Her attainments were limited, her intellect noways above mediocrity. She had a fine voice, and could sing like a nightingale, and accompany herself sufficiently well on the piano; but these were her only accomplishments. There was a look of guile and subtlety in her face, a sound of it in her voice. She seemed afraid of me, and would start if I suddenly approached her. In her behaviour, she was respectful and complaisant even to servility: she attempted to flatter and fawn upon me at first, but I soon checked that. Her fondness for her little pupil was over-strained, and I was obliged to remonstrate with her on the subject of over-indulgence and injudicious praise; but she could not gain his heart. Her piety consisted in an occasional heaving of sighs and uplifting of eyes to the ceiling, and the utterance of a few cant phrases. She told me she was a clergyman's daughter, and had been left an orphan from her childhood, but had had the good fortune to obtain a situation in a very pious family; and then she spoke so gratefully of the kindness she had experienced from its different members that I reproached myself for my uncharitable thoughts and unfriendly conduct, and relented for a time – but not for long; my causes of dislike were too rational, my suspicions too well founded for that; and I knew it was my duty to watch and scrutinize till those suspicions were either satisfactorily removed or confirmed.

I asked the name and residence of the kind and pious family. She mentioned a common name, and an unknown and distant place of abode, but told me they were now on the Continent, and their present address was unknown to her. I never saw her speak much to Mr Huntingdon; but he would frequently look into the schoolroom to see how little Arthur got on with his new companion, when I was not there. In the evening, she sat with us in the drawing-room, and would sing and play to amuse him – or *us*, as she pretended – and was very attentive to his wants, and watchful to anticipate them, though she only talked to me – indeed, he was seldom in a condition to be talked to. Had she been other than she was, I should have felt her presence a great relief to come between us thus, except, indeed, that I should have been thoroughly ashamed for any decent person to see him as he often was.

I did not mention my suspicions to Rachel; but she, having sojourned for half a century in this land of sin and sorrow, has learned to be suspicious herself. She told me from the first she was 'down of that new governess,'[2] and I soon found she watched her quite as narrowly as I did; and I was glad of it, for I longed to know the truth: the atmosphere of Grassdale seemed to stifle me, and I could only live by thinking of Wildfell Hall.

At last, one morning, she entered my chamber with such intelligence[3] that my resolution was taken before she had ceased to speak. While she dressed me, I explained to her my intentions and what assistance I should require from her, and told her which of my things she was to pack up, and what she was to leave behind for herself, as I had no other means of recompensing her for this sudden dismissal, after her long and faithful service – a circumstance I most deeply regretted but could not avoid.

'And what will you do, Rachel?' said I – 'will you go home, or seek another place?'

'I have no home, ma'm, but with you,' she replied; 'and if I leave you, I'll never go into place again as long as I live.'

'But I can't afford to live like a lady, now,' returned I: 'I must be my own maid and my child's nurse.'

'What *signifies*!' replied she in some excitement. 'You'll want somebody to clean and wash, and cook, won't you? I can do all that; and never mind the wages – I've my bits o' savings yet, and if you wouldn't take me, I should have to find my own board and lodging out of 'em somewhere, or else work among strangers – and it's what I'm not used to – so you can please yourself ma'm.' Her voice quavered as she spoke, and the tears stood in her eyes.

'I should like it above all things, Rachel, and I'd give you such wages as I could afford – such as I should give to any servant of all work I might employ; but don't you see I should be dragging you down with me, when you have done nothing to deserve it?'

'Oh, fiddle!' ejaculated she.

'And besides, my future way of living will be so widely different to the past – so different to all you have been accustomed to –'

'Do you think, ma'm, I can't bear what my missis can? – surely I'm not so proud and so dainty as that comes to – and my little master too, God bless him?'

'But I'm young, Rachel; I shan't mind it; and Arthur is young too – it will be nothing to him.'

'Nor me either: I'm not so old but what I can stand hard fare and hard work, if it's only to help and comfort them as I've loved like my own barns[4] – for all I'm too old to bide the thought o' leaving 'em in trouble and danger, and going amongst strangers myself.'

'Then you shan't, Rachel!' cried I, embracing my faithful friend. 'We'll all go together, and you shall see how the new life suits you.'

'Bless you, honey!' cried she affectionately returning my embrace. 'Only let us get shut of this wicked house and we'll do right enough, you'll see.'

'So think I,' was my answer; – and so that point was settled.

By that morning's post, I despatched a few hasty lines to Frederick, beseeching him to prepare my asylum for my immediate reception – for I should probably come to claim it within a day after the receipt of that note, – and telling him, in few words, the cause of my sudden resolution. I then wrote three letters of adieu: the first to Esther Hargrave, in which I told her that I found it impossible to stay any longer at Grassdale, or to leave my son under his father's protection; and, as it was of the last importance[5] that our future abode should be unknown to him and his acquaintance, I should disclose it to no one but my brother, through the medium of whom I hoped still to correspond with my friends. I then gave her his address, exhorted her to write frequently, reiterated some of my former admonitions regarding her own concerns, and bade her a fond farewell.

The second was to Milicent; much to the same effect, but a little more confidential, as befitted our longer intimacy, and her greater experience and better acquaintance with my circumstances.

The third was to my aunt – a much more difficult and painful undertaking, and therefore I had left it to the last; but I must give her some explanation of that extraordinary step I had taken, – and that quickly, for she and my uncle would no doubt hear of it within a day or two after my disappearance, as it was probable that Mr Huntingdon would speedily apply to them to know what was become of me. At last however, I told her I was sensible of my error: I did not complain of its punishment, and I was sorry to trouble my friends with its consequences; but in duty to my son, I must submit no longer; it was absolutely necessary that he should be delivered from his father's corrupting influence. I should not disclose my place of refuge even to her, in order that she and my uncle might be able, with truth, to deny all knowledge concerning it; but any communications addressed to me under cover to my brother, would be certain to reach me. I hoped she and my uncle would pardon the step I had taken, for if they knew all, I was sure they would not blame me; and I trusted they would not afflict themselves on my account, for if I could only reach my retreat in safety and keep it unmolested, I should be very happy, but for the thought of them; and should be quite contented to spend my life in obscurity, devoting myself to the training up of my child, and teaching him to avoid the errors of both his parents.

These things were done yesterday: I have given two whole days to the preparation for our departure, that Frederick may have more time to prepare the rooms, and Rachel to pack up the things – for the latter task must be done with the utmost caution and secrecy, and there is no one but me to assist her: I can help to get the articles together, but I do not understand the art of stowing them into the boxes, so as to take up the smallest possible space; and there are her own things to do, as well as mine and Arthur's. I can ill afford to leave anything behind, since I have no money, except a few guineas in my purse; – and besides, as Rachel observed, whatever I left would most likely become the property of Miss Myers, and I should not relish that.

But what trouble I have had throughout these two days struggling to appear calm and collected – to meet him and her as usual, when I was obliged to meet them, and forcing myself to leave my little Arthur in her hands for hours together! But I trust these trials are over now: I have laid him in my bed for better security, and never more, I trust, shall his innocent lips be defiled by their contaminating kisses, or his young ears polluted by their words. But shall we escape in safety? Oh, that the morning were come, and we were on our way at least! This evening, when I had given Rachel all the assistance I could, and had nothing left me but to wait, and wish and tremble, I became so greatly agitated, that I knew not what to do. I went down to dinner, but I could not force myself to eat. Mr Huntingdon remarked the circumstance.

'What's to do with you *now*?' said he, when the removal of the second course gave him time to look about him.

'I am not well,' I replied: 'I think I must lie down a little – you won't miss me much?'

'Not the least; if you leave your chair, it'll do just as well – better a trifle,' he muttered as I left the room, 'for I can fancy somebody else fills it.'

'Somebody else *may* fill it tomorrow,' I thought – but did not say. 'There! I've seen the last of *you*, I hope,' I muttered as I closed the door upon him.

Rachel urged me to seek repose, at once, to recruit my strength for tomorrow's journey, as we must be gone before the dawn, but in my present state of nervous excitement, that was entirely out of the question. It was equally out of the question to sit, or wander about my room, counting the hours and the minutes between me and the appointed time of action, straining my ears and trembling at every sound lest someone should discover and betray us after all. I took up a book and tried to read. My eyes wandered over the pages, but it was impossible to bind my thoughts to their contents. Why not have recourse to the old expedient, and add this last event to my chronicle? I opened its pages once more, and wrote the above account – with difficulty, at first, but gradually my mind became more calm and steady. Thus several hours have passed away: the time is drawing near; – and now my eyes feel heavy, and my frame exhausted: I will commend my cause to God, and then lie down and gain an hour or two of sleep; and *then*! –

Little Arthur sleeps soundly. All the house is still: there can be no one watching. The boxes were all corded by Benson, and quietly conveyed down the back stairs after dusk, and sent away in a cart to the M— coach-office. The name upon the cards was Mrs Graham, which appellation I mean henceforth to adopt. My mother's maiden name was Graham, and therefore I fancy I have some claim to it, and prefer it to any other, except my own, which I dare not resume.

CHAPTER 44

THE RETREAT

October 24th. – Thank Heaven, I am free and safe at last! – Early we rose, swiftly and quietly dressed, slowly and stealthily descended to the hall, where Benson stood ready with a light to open the door and fasten it after us. We were obliged to let one man into our secret on account of the boxes, etc. All the servants were but too well acquainted with their master's conduct, and either Benson or John would have been willing to serve me, but as the former was more staid and elderly, and a crony of Rachel's besides, I of course directed her to make choice of him as her assistant and confidant on the occasion, as far as necessity demanded. I only hope he may not be brought into trouble thereby, and only wish I could reward him for the perilous service he was so ready to undertake. I slipped two guineas into his hand, by way of remembrance, as he stood in the doorway, holding the candle to light our departure, with a tear in his honest grey eye and a host of good wishes depicted on his solemn countenance. Alas! I could offer no more: I had barely sufficient remaining for the probable expenses of the journey.

What trembling joy it was when the little wicket closed behind us, as we issued from the park! Then, for one moment, I paused, to inhale one draught of that cool, bracing air, and venture one look back upon the house. All was dark and still; no light glimmered in the windows; no wreath of smoke obscured the stars that sparkled above it in the frosty sky. As I bade farewell for ever to that place, the scene of so much guilt and misery, I felt glad that I had not left it before, for now there was no doubt about the propriety of such a step – no shadow of remorse for him I left behind: there was nothing to disturb my joy but the fear of detection; and every step removed us farther from the chance of that.

We had left Grassdale many miles behind us before the round, red sun arose to welcome our deliverance, and if any inhabitant of its vicinity had chanced to see us then, as we bowled along on the top of the coach, I scarcely think they would have suspected our identity. As I intend to be taken for a widow, I thought it advisable to enter my new abode in mourning: I was therefore attired in a plain black silk dress and mantle, a black veil (which I kept carefully over my face for the first twenty or thirty miles of the journey), and a black silk bonnet, which I had been constrained to borrow of Rachel for want of such an article myself – it was not in the newest fashion, of course; but none the worse for that, under present circumstances. Arthur was clad in his plainest clothes, and wrapped in a coarse woollen shawl; and Rachel was muffled in a grey cloak and hood that had seen better days, and gave her more the appearance of an ordinary, though decent old woman, than of a lady's maid.

Oh, what delight it was to be thus seated aloft, rumbling along the broad, sunshiny road, with the fresh morning breeze in my face, surrounded by an unknown country all smiling – cheerfully, gloriously, smiling in the yellow lustre of those early beams, – with my darling child in my arms, almost as happy as myself and my faithful friend beside me; a prison and despair behind me, receding farther, farther back at every clatter of the horses' feet, – and liberty and hope before! I could hardly refrain from praising God aloud for my deliverance, or astonishing my fellow passengers by some surprising outburst of hilarity.[1]

But the journey was a very long one, and we were all weary enough before the close of it. It was far into the night when we reached the town of L—, and still we were seven miles from our journey's end; and there was no more coaching – nor any conveyance to be had, except a common cart – and that with the greatest difficulty, for half the town was in bed. And a dreary ride we had of it that last stage of the journey, cold and weary as we were; sitting on our boxes, with nothing to cling to, nothing to lean against, slowly dragged and cruelly shaken over the rough, hilly roads. But

Arthur was asleep in Rachel's lap, and between us we managed pretty well to shield him from the cold night air.

At last we began to ascend a terribly steep and stony lane which, in spite of the darkness, Rachel said she remembered well: she had often walked there with me in her arms,[2] and little thought to come again so many years after, under such circumstances as the present. Arthur being now awakened by the jolting and the stoppages, we all got out and walked. We had not far to go; but what if Frederick should not have received my letter? or if he should not have had time to prepare the rooms for our reception; and we should find them all dark, damp, and comfortless; destitute of food, fire, and furniture, after all our toil?

At length the grim, dark pile appeared before us. The lane conducted us round by the back way. We entered the desolate court, and in breathless anxiety surveyed the ruinous mass. Was it all blackness and desolation? No; one faint red glimmer cheered us from a window where the lattice was in good repair. The door was fastened, but after due knocking and waiting and some parleying with a voice from an upper window, we were admitted, by an old woman who had been commissioned to air and keep the house till our arrival, – into a tolerably snug little apartment, formerly the scullery of the mansion, which Frederick had now fitted up as a kitchen. Here she procured us a light, roused the fire to a cheerful blaze, and soon prepared a simple repast for our refreshment; while we disencumbered ourselves of our travelling gear, and took a hasty survey of our new abode. Besides the kitchen there were two bedrooms, a good sized parlour, and another smaller one, which I destined for my studio, all well aired and seemingly in good repair, but only partly furnished with a few old articles, chiefly of ponderous black oak – the veritable ones that had been there before, and which had been kept as antiquarian relics in my brother's present residence, and now, in all haste, transported back again.

The old woman brought my supper and Arthur's into the parlour, and told me, with all due formality, that 'The master desired his compliments to Mrs Graham, and he had prepared the rooms as well as he could upon so short a notice, but he would do himself the pleasure of calling upon her tomorrow, to receive her further commands.'

I was glad to ascend the stern-looking stone staircase, and lie down in the gloomy old-fashioned bed, beside my little Arthur. He was asleep in a minute; but, weary as I was, my excited feelings and restless cogitations kept me awake till dawn began to struggle with the darkness; but sleep was sweet and refreshing when it came, and the waking was delightful beyond expression. It was little Arthur that roused me, with his gentle kisses: – He was here, then – safely clasped in my arms, and many leagues away from his unworthy father! – Broad daylight illumined the apartment, for the sun was high in heaven, though obscured by rolling masses of autumnal vapour.

The scene, indeed, was not remarkably cheerful in itself, either within or without. The large bare room with its grim old furniture, the narrow, latticed windows, revealing the dull, grey sky above and the desolate wilderness below, where the dark stone walls and iron gate, the rank growth of grass and weeds, and the hardy evergreens of preternatural forms, alone remained to tell that there had been once a garden, – and the bleak and barren fields beyond might have struck me as gloomy enough at another time, but now, each separate object seemed to echo back my own exhilarating sense of hope and freedom: indefinite dreams of the far past and bright anticipations of the future[3] seemed to greet me at every turn. I should rejoice with more security, to be sure, had the broad sea rolled between my present and my former homes, but surely in this lonely spot I might remain unknown; and then, I had my brother here to cheer my solitude with his occasional visits.

He came that morning; and I have had several interviews with him since; but he is obliged to be very cautious when and how he comes: not even his servants, or his best friends must know of his visits to Wildfell – except on such occasions as a landlord might be expected to call upon a stranger tenant – lest suspicion should be excited against me, whether of the truth or of some slanderous falsehood.

I have now been here nearly a fortnight, and but for one disturbing care, the haunting dread of discovery, I am comfortably settled in my new home: Frederick has supplied me with all requisite furniture and painting materials: Rachel has sold most of my clothes for me, in a distant town, and procured me a wardrobe more suitable to my present position: I have a second-hand piano, and a tolerably well-stocked bookcase in my parlour; and my other room has assumed quite a professional, business-like appearance already. I am working hard to repay my brother for all his expenses on my account; not that there is the slightest necessity for anything of the kind, but it pleases me to do so: I shall have so much more pleasure in my labour, my earnings, my frugal fare, and household economy, when I know that I am paying my way honestly, and that what little I possess is legitimately all my own; and that no one suffers for my folly – in a pecuniary way at least. – I shall make him take the last penny I owe him, if I can possibly effect it without offending him too deeply. I have a few pictures already done, for I told Rachel to pack up all I had; and she executed her commission but too well, for among the rest, she put up a portrait of Mr Huntingdon that I had painted in the first year of my marriage. It struck me with dismay, at the moment when I took it from the box and beheld those eyes fixed upon me in their mocking mirth, as if exulting, still, in his power to control my fate, and deriding my efforts to escape.

How widely different had been my feelings in painting that portrait to what they now were in looking upon it! How I had studied and toiled to produce something, as I thought, worthy of the original! what mingled pleasure and dissatisfaction I had had in the result of my labours! – pleasure for the likeness I had caught; dissatisfaction, because I had not made it handsome enough. Now, I see no beauty in it – nothing pleasing in any part of its expression; and yet it is far handsomer and far more agreeable – far less repulsive I should rather say – than he is now; for these six years have wrought almost as great a change upon himself as on my feelings regarding him. The frame, however, is handsome enough; it will serve for another painting. The picture itself I have not destroyed, as I had first intended; I have put it aside; not, I think, from any lurking tenderness for the memory of past affection, nor yet to remind me of my former folly, but chiefly that I may compare my son's features and countenance with this, as he grows up, and thus be enabled to judge how much or how little he resembles his father – if I may be allowed to keep him with me still, and never to behold that father's face again – a blessing I hardly dare reckon upon.

It seems Mr Huntingdon is making every exertion to discover the place of my retreat. He has been in person to Staningley, seeking redress for his grievances – expecting to hear of his victims, if not to find them there – and has told so many lies, and with such unblushing coolness, that my uncle more than half believes him, and strongly advocates my going back to him and being friends again; but my aunt knows better: she is too cool and cautious, and too well acquainted with both my husband's character and my own to be imposed upon by any specious falsehoods the former could invent. But he does not *want* me back; he wants my child; and gives my friends to understand that if I prefer living apart from him, he will indulge the whim and let me do so unmolested, and even settle a reasonable allowance on me, provided I will immediately deliver up his son. But, Heaven help me! I am not going to sell my child for gold, though it were to save both him and me from starving: it would be better that he should die with me, than that he should live with his father.

Frederick showed me a letter he had received from that gentleman, full of cool impudence such as would astonish anyone who did not know him, but such as, I am convinced, none would know better how to answer than my brother. He gave me no account of his reply, except to tell me that he had not acknowledged his acquaintance with my place of refuge, but rather left it to be inferred that it was quite unknown to him, by saying it was useless to apply to him or any other of my relations for information on the subject, as it appeared I had been driven to such extremity that I had concealed my retreat even from my best friends; but that if he *had* known it, or should at any time be made aware of it, most certainly Mr Huntingdon would be the last person to whom he should communicate the intelligence; and that he need not trouble himself to bargain for the child, for he (Frederick) fancied he knew enough of his sister to enable him to declare, that wherever she might be, or however situated, no consideration would induce her to deliver him up.

30th. – Alas! my kind neighbours will not let me alone. By some means they have ferreted me out, and I have had to sustain visits from three different families, all more or less bent upon discovering who and what I am, whence I came, and why I have chosen such a home as this. Their society is unnecessary to me, to say the least, and their curiosity annoys and alarms me: if I gratify it, it may lead to the ruin of my son, and if I am too mysterious, it will only excite their suspicions, invite conjecture, and rouse them to greater exertions – and perhaps be the means of spreading my fame from parish to parish, till it reach the ears of someone who will carry it to the lord of Grassdale Manor.

I shall be expected to return their calls, but if, upon enquiry, I find that any of them live too far away for Arthur to accompany me, they must expect in vain for a while, for I cannot bear to leave him, unless it be to go to church; and I have not attempted *that* yet, for – it may be foolish weakness, but I am under such constant dread of his being snatched away that I am never easy when he is not by my side; and I fear these nervous terrors would so entirely disturb my devotions, that I should obtain no benefit from the attendance. I mean, however, to make the experiment next Sunday, and oblige myself to leave him in charge of Rachel for a few hours. It will be a hard task, but surely no imprudence; and the vicar has been to scold me for my neglect of the ordinances of religion. I had no sufficient excuse to offer, and I promised, if all were well, he should see me in my pew next Sunday; for I do not wish to be set down as an infidel; and besides, I know I should derive great comfort and benefit from an occasional attendance at public worship, if I could only have faith and fortitude to compose my thoughts in conformity with the solemn occasion, and forbid them to be forever dwelling on my absent child, and on the dreadful possibility of finding him gone when I return; and surely God in His mercy will preserve me from so severe a trial: for my child's own sake, if not for mine, He will not suffer him to be torn away.

November 3rd. – I have made some further acquaintance with my neighbours. The fine gentleman and beau of the parish and its vicinity (in his own estimation, at least), is a young . . .

*   *   *

Here it ended. The rest was torn away. How cruel – just when she was going to mention me! for I could not doubt it *was* your humble servant she was about to mention, though not very favourably of course – I could tell that, as well by those few words as by the recollection of her whole aspect and demeanour towards me in the commencement of our acquaintance. Well! I could readily forgive her prejudice against me, and her hard thoughts of our sex in general, when I saw to what brilliant specimens her experience had been limited.

Respecting me, however, she had long since seen her error, and perhaps fallen into another in the opposite extreme; for if, at first, her opinion of me had been lower than I deserved I was convinced that now my deserts were lower than her opinion; and if the former part of this continuation had been torn away to avoid wounding my feelings, perhaps the latter portion had been removed for fear of ministering too much to my self-conceit. At any rate, I would have given much to have seen it all – to have witnessed the gradual change, and watched the progress of her esteem and friendship for me, – and whatever warmer feeling she might have – to have seen how much of love there was in her regard, and how it had grown upon her in spite of her virtuous resolutions and strenuous exertions to – but no, I had no right to see it: all this was too sacred for any eyes but her own, and she had done well to keep it from me.

CHAPTER 45

RECONCILIATION

Well Halford, what do you think of all this? and while you read it, did you ever picture to yourself what my feelings would probably be during its perusal? Most likely not; but I am not going to descant upon them now: I will only make this acknowledgement, little honourable as it may be to human nature, and especially to myself: – that the former half of the narrative was, to me, more painful than the latter; not that I was at all insensible to Mrs Huntingdon's wrongs or unmoved by her sufferings, but, I must confess, I felt a kind of selfish gratification in watching her husband's gradual decline in her good graces, and seeing how completely he extinguished all her affection at last. The effect of the whole, however, in spite of all my sympathy for her and my fury against him, was to relieve my mind of an intolerable burden and fill my heart with joy, as if some friend had roused me from a dreadful nightmare.

It was now near eight o'clock in the morning, for my candle had expired in the midst of my perusal, leaving me no alternative but to get another, at the expense of alarming the house, or to go to bed and wait the return of daylight. On my mother's account, I chose the latter; but how *willingly* I sought my pillow, and how much sleep it brought me, I leave you to imagine.

At the first appearance of dawn I rose, and brought the manuscript to the window, but it was impossible to read it yet. I devoted half an hour to dressing, and then returned to it again. Now, with a little difficulty, I could manage; and with intense and eager interest, I devoured the remainder of its contents. When it was ended, and my transient regret at its abrupt conclusion was over, I opened the window and put out my head to catch the cooling breeze, and imbibe deep draughts of the pure morning air. A splendid morning it was; the half-frozen dew lay thick on the grass, the swallows were twittering round me, the rooks cawing and cows lowing in the distance; and early frost and summer sunshine mingled their sweetness in the air. But I did not think of that: a confusion of countless thoughts and varied emotions crowded upon me while I gazed abstractedly on the lovely face of nature. Soon, however, this chaos of thoughts and passions cleared away, giving place to two distinct emotions; joy unspeakable that my adored Helen was all I wished to think her – that through the noisome vapours of the world's aspersions and my own fancied convictions, her character shone bright, and clear, and stainless as that sun I could not bear to look on; and shame and deep remorse for my own conduct.

Immediately after breakfast, I hurried over to Wildfell Hall. Rachel had risen many degrees in my estimation since yesterday. I was ready to greet her quite as an old friend; but every kindly impulse was checked by the look of cold distrust she cast upon me on opening the door. The old virgin had constituted herself the guardian of her lady's honour, I suppose, and doubtless she saw in me another Mr Hargrave, only the more dangerous in being more esteemed and trusted by her mistress.

'Missis can't see anyone today, sir – she's poorly,' said she in answer to my enquiry for Mrs Graham.

'But I must see her, Rachel,' said I, placing my hand on the door to prevent its being shut against me.

'Indeed, sir, you can't,' replied she, settling her countenance in still more iron frigidity than before.

'Be so good as to announce me.'

'It's no manner of use, Mr Markham; she's poorly, I tell you.'

Just in time to prevent me from committing the impropriety of taking the citadel by storm, and pushing forward unannounced, an inner door opened, and little Arthur appeared with his frolicsome playfellow the dog. He seized my hand between both his, and smilingly drew me forward.

'Mamma says you're to come in, Mr Markham,' said he, 'and I'm to go out and play with Rover.'

Rachel retired with a sigh, and I stepped into the parlour and shut the door. There, before the fireplace, stood the tall, graceful figure wasted with many sorrows.[1] I cast the manuscript on the table, and looked in her face. Anxious and pale, it was turned towards me; her clear, dark eyes were fixed on mine with a gaze so intensely earnest that they bound me like a spell.

'Have you looked it over?' she murmured. The spell was broken.

'I've read it through,' said I, advancing into the room, – 'and I want to know if you'll forgive me – if you *can* forgive me?'

She did not answer, but her eyes glistened, and a faint red mantled on her lip and cheek. As I approached, she abruptly turned away, and went to the window. It was not in anger, I was well assured, but only to conceal or control her emotion. I therefore ventured to follow and stand beside her there, – but not to speak. She gave me her hand, without turning her head, and murmured, in a voice she strove in vain to steady –

'Can *you* forgive *me?*'

It might be deemed a breach of trust, I thought, to convey that lily hand to my lips, so I only gently pressed it between my own, and smilingly replied, –

'I hardly can. You should have told me this before. It shows a want of confidence –'

'Oh, no,' cried she, eagerly interrupting me, 'it was not that! It was no want of confidence in you; but if I had told you anything of my history, I must have told you all, in order to excuse my conduct; and I might well shrink from such a disclosure, till necessity obliged me to make it. But you forgive me? – I have done very, very wrong, I know; but, as usual, I have reaped the bitter fruits of my own error, – and must reap them to the end.'

Bitter indeed was the tone of anguish, repressed by resolute firmness, in which this was spoken. Now, I raised her hand to my lips, and fervently kissed it again and again; for tears prevented any other reply. She suffered these wild caresses without resistance or resentment; then, suddenly turning from me, she paced twice or thrice through the room. I knew by the contraction of her brow, the tight compression of her lips, and wringing of her hands, that meantime a violent conflict between reason and passion was silently passing within. At length she paused before the empty fireplace, and turning to me, said calmly – if that might be called calmness, which was so evidently the result of a violent effort –

'Now Gilbert, you must leave me – not this moment, but soon – and you must *never come again.*'

'Never again, Helen? just when I love you more than ever!'

'For that very reason, if it be so, we should not meet again. I thought *this* interview was necessary – at least, I persuaded myself it was so – that we might severally ask and receive each other's pardon for the past; but there can be no excuse for another. I shall leave this place, as soon as I have means to seek another asylum; but our intercourse must end here.'

'End here!' echoed I; and approaching the high, carved chimney-piece, I leant my hand against its heavy mouldings, and dropped my forehead upon it in silent, sullen despondency.

'You must not come again,' continued she. There was a slight tremor in her voice, but I thought her whole manner was provokingly composed, considering the dreadful sentence she pronounced. 'You must know why I tell you so,' she resumed; 'and you must see that it is better to part at once: – if it be hard to say adieu for ever, you ought to help me.' She paused. I did not answer. 'Will you promise not to come? – If you won't, and if you do come here again, you will drive me away before I know where to find another place of refuge – or how to seek it.'

'Helen,' said I, turning impatiently towards her, 'I cannot discuss the matter of eternal separation, calmly and dispassionately as you can do. It is no question of mere expedience with *me*; it is a question of life and death!'

She was silent. Her pale lips quivered, and her fingers trembled with agitation, as she nervously entwined them in the hair chain to which was appended her small gold watch – the only thing of value she had permitted herself to keep. I had said an unjust and cruel thing; but I must needs follow it up with something worse.

'But Helen!' I began in a soft, low tone, not daring to raise my eyes to her face – 'that man is *not* your husband: in the sight of Heaven he has forfeited all claim to –' She seized my arm with a grasp of startling energy.

'*Gilbert, don't!*' she cried, in a tone that would have pierced a heart of adamant. 'For God's sake, don't *you* attempt these arguments! No *fiend* could torture me like this!'

'I won't, I won't!' said I, gently laying my hand on hers; almost as much alarmed at her vehemence, as ashamed of my own misconduct.

'Instead of acting like a true friend,' continued she, breaking from me and throwing herself into the old arm chair – 'and helping me with all your might – or rather taking your own part in the struggle of right against passion – you leave all the burden to me; – and not satisfied with that, you do your utmost to fight against me – when you know that I –' she paused, and hid her face in her handkerchief.

'Forgive me, Helen!' pleaded I, 'I will never utter another word on the subject. But may we not still meet as friends?'

'It will not do,' she replied, mournfully shaking her head; and then she raised her eyes to mine, with a mildly reproachful look that seemed to say, 'You must know that as well as I.'

'Then what *must* we do?' cried I, passionately. But immediately I added in a quieter tone – 'I'll do whatever you desire; – only *don't* say that this meeting is to be our last.'

'And why not? Don't you know that every time we meet, the thought of the final parting will become more painful? Don't you *feel* that every interview makes us dearer to each other than the last?'

The utterance of this last question was hurried and low, and the downcast eyes and burning blush too plainly showed that *she*, at least, had felt it. It was scarcely prudent to make such an admission, or to add – as she presently did – 'I have power to bid you go, now: another time it might be different,' – but I was not base enough to attempt to take advantage of her candour.

'But we may write,' I timidly suggested – 'You will not deny me that consolation?'

'We can hear of each other through my brother.'

'Your brother!' A pang of remorse and shame shot through me.

She had not heard of the injury he had sustained at my hands; and I had not the courage to tell her. 'Your brother will not help us,' I said: 'he would have all communion between us to be entirely at an end.'

'And he would be right, I suppose. As a friend of both, he would wish us both well; and every friend would tell us it was our interest, as well as our duty, to forget each other, though we might not see it ourselves. But don't be afraid, Gilbert,' she added, smiling sadly at my manifest discomposure, 'there is little chance of my forgetting you. But I did not mean that Frederick should be the means of transmitting messages between us, only that each might know, through him, of the other's welfare; – and more than this ought not to be; for you are young, Gilbert, and you ought to marry – and will sometime, though you may think it impossible now: – and though I hardly can say I wish you to forget me, I know it is right that you should, both for your own happiness and that of your future wife; – and therefore I must and will wish it,' she added resolutely.

'And you are young too, Helen,' I boldly replied, 'and when that profligate scoundrel has run through his career, you will give your hand to me – I'll wait till then.'

But she would not leave me this support. Independently of the moral evil of basing our hopes upon the death of another, who, if unfit for this world, was at least no less so for the next, and whose amelioration would thus become our bane and his greatest transgression our greatest benefit, – she maintained it to be madness: many men of Mr Huntingdon's habits had lived to a ripe though miserable old age; – 'and if I,' said she, 'am young in years I am old in sorrow; but even if trouble should fail to kill me before vice destroys him, think, if he reached but fifty years or so, would you wait twenty or fifteen – in vague uncertainty and suspense – through all the prime of youth and manhood – and marry at last a woman faded and worn as I shall be – without ever having seen me from this day to that? – You would not,' she continued interrupting my earnest protestations of unfailing constancy, – 'or if you would you should not. Trust me, Gilbert; in this matter I know better than you. You think me cold and stony hearted, and you may, but –'

'I don't Helen.'

'Well, never mind; you might if you would – but I have not spent my solitude in utter idleness, and I am not speaking now from the impulse of the moment as you do: I have thought of all these matters again and again; I have argued these questions with myself, and pondered well our past, and present, and future career; and, believe me, I have come to the right conclusion at last. Trust my words rather than your own feelings, now, and in a few years you will see that I was right – though at present I hardly can see it myself,' she murmured with a sigh as she rested her head on her hand. – 'And don't argue against me any more: all you can say has been already said by my own heart and refuted by my reason. It was hard enough to combat those suggestions as they were whispered within me; in your mouth they are ten times worse, and if you knew how much they pain me you would cease at once, I know. If you knew my present feelings, you would even try to relieve them at the expense of your own.'

'I will go – in a minute, if *that* can relieve you – and NEVER return!' said I with bitter emphasis – 'But, if we may never meet, and never hope to meet again, is it a crime to exchange our thoughts by letter? May not kindred spirits meet, and mingle in communion whatever be the fate and circumstances of their earthly tenements?'

'They may, they may!' cried she with a momentary burst of glad enthusiasm. 'I thought of that too, Gilbert, but I feared to mention it, because I feared you would not understand my views upon the subject – I fear it even now – I fear any kind friend would tell us we are *both* deluding ourselves with the idea of keeping up a spiritual intercourse without hope or prospect of anything further – without fostering vain regrets and hurtful aspirations, and feeding thoughts that should be sternly and pitilessly left to perish of inanition –'

'Never mind our kind friends: if they can part our bodies, it is enough; in God's name, let them not sunder our souls!' cried I, in terror lest she should deem it her duty to deny us this last remaining consolation.

'But no letters can pass between us here,' said she, 'without giving fresh food for scandal; and when I departed, I had intended that my new abode should be unknown to you as to the rest of the world; not that I should doubt your word if you promised not to visit me, but I thought you would be more tranquil in your own mind if you knew you could not do it; and likely to find less difficulty in abstracting yourself from me if you could not picture my situation to your mind. But listen,' said she, smilingly putting up her finger to check my impatient reply: 'in six months you shall hear from Frederick precisely where I am; and if you still retain your wish to write to me, and think you can maintain a correspondence all thought, all spirit – such as disembodied souls or unimpassioned friends, at least, might hold, – write, and I will answer you.'

'Six months!'

'Yes, to give your present ardour time to cool and try the truth and constancy of your soul's love for mine. And now, enough has been said between us. – Why can't we part at once!' exclaimed she almost wildly, after a moment's pause, as she suddenly rose from her chair with her hands resolutely clasped together. I thought it was my duty to go without delay; and I approached and half extended my hand as if to take leave; she grasped it in silence. But this thought of final separation was too intolerable: it seemed to squeeze the blood out of my heart; and my feet were glued to the floor.

'And must we never meet again?' I murmured in the anguish of my soul.

'We shall meet in Heaven. Let us think of that,' said she in a tone of desperate calmness; but her eyes glittered wildly, and her face was deadly pale.

'But not as we are now,'[2] I could not help replying. 'It gives me little consolation to think I shall next behold you as a disembodied spirit, or an altered being, with a frame perfect and glorious, but not like this! – and a heart, perhaps, entirely estranged from me.'

'No Gilbert, there is perfect love in Heaven!'

'*So* perfect, I suppose, that it soars above distinctions, and you will have no closer sympathy with me than with any one of the ten thousand thousand angels[3] and the innumerable multitude of happy spirits round us.'

'Whatever I am, you will be the same, and therefore, cannot

possibly regret it; and whatever that change may be, we know it must be for the better.'

'But if I am to be so changed that I shall cease to adore you with my whole heart and soul, and love you beyond every other creature, I shall not be myself; and, though, if ever I win Heaven at all, I must, I know, be infinitely better and happier than I am now, my earthly nature cannot rejoice in the anticipation of such beatitude, from which itself and its chief joy must be excluded.'

'Is your love *all* earthly then?'

'No, but I am supposing we shall have no more intimate communion with each other, than with the rest.'

'If so, it will be because we love them more and not each other less. Increase of love brings increase of happiness, when it is mutual, and pure as that will be.'

'But can *you*, Helen, contemplate with delight this prospect of losing me in a sea of glory?'[4]

'I own I cannot; but we know not that it will be so; – and I do know that to regret the exchange of earthly pleasures for the joys of Heaven, is as if the grovelling caterpillar[5] should lament that it must one day quit the nibbled leaf to soar aloft and flutter through the air, roving at will from flower to flower, sipping sweet honey from their cups or basking in their sunny petals. If these little creatures knew how great a change awaited them, no doubt they would regret it; but would not all such sorrow be misplaced? And if that illustration will not move you, here is another: – We are children now; we feel as children, and we understand as children;[6] and when we are told that men and women do not play with toys, and that our companions will one day weary of the trivial sports and occupations that interest them and us so deeply now, we cannot help being saddened at the thought of such an alteration, because we cannot conceive that as we grow up, our own minds will become so enlarged and elevated that we ourselves shall then regard as trifling those objects and pursuits we now so fondly cherish, and that, though our companions will no longer join us in those childish pastimes, they will drink with us at other fountains of delight, and mingle their souls with ours in higher aims and nobler occupations beyond our present comprehension, but not less deeply relished or less truly good for that, – while yet both we and they remain essentially the same individuals as before. But Gilbert, can you really derive no consolation from the thought that we may meet together where there is no more pain and sorrow, no more striving against sin, and struggling of the spirit against the flesh; where both will behold the same glorious truths, and drink exalted and supreme felicity from the same fountain of light and goodness – that Being whom both will worship with the same intensity of holy ardour, and where pure and happy creatures both will love with the same divine affection? If you cannot, never write to me!'

'Helen, I can! if faith would never fail.'[7]

'Now, then,' exclaimed she, 'while this hope is strong within us –'

'We will part,' I cried. 'You shall not have the pain of another effort to dismiss me: I will go at once; but –'

I did not put my request in words: she understood it instinctively and *this* time she yielded too – or rather, there was nothing so deliberate as requesting or yielding in the matter: there was a sudden impulse that neither could resist. One moment I stood and looked into her face, the next I held her to my heart, and we seemed to grow together in a close embrace from which no physical or mental force could rend us. A whispered 'God bless you!' and 'Go – go!' was all she said; but while she spoke, she held me so fast that, without violence, I could not have obeyed her. At length, however, by some heroic effort, we tore ourselves apart, and I rushed from the house.

I have a confused remembrance of seeing little Arthur running up the garden walk to meet me, and of bolting over the wall to avoid him – and subsequently running down the steep fields, clearing the stone fences and hedges as they came in my way, till I got completely out of sight of the old Hall and down to the bottom of the hill; and then of long hours spent in bitter tears and lamentations, and melancholy musings in the lonely valley, with the eternal music in my ears, of the west wind rushing through the over-shadowing trees, and the brook babbling and gurgling along its stony bed – my eyes, for the most part, vacantly fixed on the deep, checkered shades restlessly playing over the bright sunny grass at my feet, where now and then a withered leaf or two would come dancing to share the revelry, but my heart was away up the hill in that dark room where she was weeping desolate and alone – she whom I was not to comfort, not to see again, till years or suffering had overcome us both, and torn our spirits from their perishing abodes of clay.

There was little business done that day, you may be sure. The farm was abandoned to the labourers, and the labourers were left to their own devices. But one duty must be attended to: I had not forgotten my assault upon Frederick Lawrence; and I must see him to apologize for the unhappy deed. I would fain have put it off till the morrow; but what if he should denounce me to his sister in the meantime? No, no, I must ask his pardon today, and entreat him to be lenient in his accusation, if the revelation must be made. I deferred it however, till the evening, when my spirits were more composed and when – oh, wonderful perversity of human nature! – some faint germs of indefinite hopes were beginning to rise in my mind; not that I intended to cherish them after all that had been said on the subject, but there they must lie for a while, uncrushed though not encouraged, till I had learnt to live without them.

Arrived at Woodford, the young squire's abode, I found no little difficulty in obtaining admission to his presence. The servant that opened the door told me his master was very ill, and seemed to think it doubtful whether he would be able to see me. I was not going to be balked however. I waited calmly in the hall to be announced, but inwardly determined to take no denial. The message was such as I expected – a polite intimation that Mr Lawrence could see no one; he was feverish and must not be disturbed.

'I shall not disturb him long,' said I; 'but I must see him for a moment: it is on business of importance that I wish to speak to him.'

'I'll tell him sir,' said the man. And I advanced farther into the hall and followed him nearly to the door of the apartment where his master was – for it seemed he was not in bed. The answer returned was that Mr Lawrence hoped I would be so good as to leave a message or a note with the servant, as he could attend to no business at present.

'He may as well see me as you,' said I; and, stepping past the astonished footman, I boldly rapped at the door, entered, and closed it behind me. The room was spacious and handsomely furnished – very comfortably, too, for a bachelor. A clear, red fire was burning in the polished grate: a superannuated greyhound, given up to idleness and good living, lay basking before it on the thick, soft rug, on one corner of which, beside the sofa, sat a smart young springer, looking wistfully up in its master's face; perhaps, asking permission to share his couch, or, it might be, only soliciting a caress from his hand or a kind word from his lips. The invalid himself looked very interesting as he lay reclining there, in his elegant dressing-gown, with a silk handkerchief bound across his temples. His usually pale face was flushed and feverish; his eyes were half closed, until he became sensible of my presence – and then he opened them wide enough; – one hand was thrown listlessly over the back of the sofa, and held a small volume with which, apparently, he had been vainly attempting to beguile the weary hours. He dropped it, however, in his start of indignant surprise as I advanced into the room and stood before him on the rug. He raised himself on his pillows and gazed upon me with equal degrees of nervous horror, anger, and amazement depicted on his countenance.

'Mr Markham, I scarcely expected this!' he said; and the blood left his cheek as he spoke.

'I know you didn't,' answered I; 'but be quiet a minute, and I'll tell you what I came for.' Unthinkingly I advanced a step or two nearer. He winced at my approach, with an expression of aversion and instinctive physical fear anything but conciliatory to my feelings. I stepped back however.

'Make your story a short one,' said he, putting his hand on the small silver bell that stood on the table beside him, – 'or I shall be obliged to call for assistance. I am in no state to bear your brutalities now, or your presence either.' And in truth the moisture started from his pores and stood on his pale forehead like dew.

Such a reception was hardly calculated to diminish the difficulties of my unenviable task. It must be performed, however, in some fashion: and so I plunged into it at once, and floundered through it as I could.

'The truth is, Lawrence,' said I, 'I have not acted quite correctly towards you of late – especially on this last occasion; and I'm come to – in short, to express my regret for what has been done, and to beg your pardon. – If you don't choose to grant it,' I added hastily, not liking the aspect of his face, 'it's no matter – only, *I've* done *my* duty – that's all.'

'It's easily done,' replied he, with a faint smile bordering on a sneer: 'to abuse your friend and knock him on the head, without any assignable cause, and then tell him the deed was not quite correct, but it's no matter whether he pardons it or not.'

'I forgot to tell you that it was in consequence of a mistake,' muttered I. 'I should have made a very handsome apology, but you provoked me so confoundedly with your – Well, I suppose it's my fault. The fact is, I didn't know that you were Mrs Graham's brother, and I saw and heard some things respecting your conduct towards her, which were calculated to awaken unpleasant suspicions, that, allow me to say, a little candour and confidence on your part might have removed; and at last, I chanced to overhear a part of a conversation between you and her that made me think I had a right to hate you.'

'And how came you to know that I was her brother?' asked he in some anxiety.

'She told me herself. She told me all. *She* knew I might be trusted. But you needn't disturb yourself about *that*, Mr Lawrence, for I've seen the last of her!'

'The last! is she gone then?'

'No, but she has bid adieu to me; and I have promised never to go near that house again while she inhabits it.' I could have groaned aloud at the bitter thoughts awakened by this turn in the discourse. But I only clenched my hands, and stamped my foot upon the rug. My companion however, was evidently relieved.

'You have done right!' he said in a tone of unqualified approbation, while his face brightened into almost a sunny expression. 'And as for the mistake, I am sorry for both our sakes that it should have occurred. Perhaps you can forgive my want of candour, and, remember, as some partial mitigation of the offence, how little encouragement to friendly confidence you have given me of late.'

'Yes, yes, I remember it all: nobody can blame me more than I blame myself in my own heart – at any rate, nobody can regret more sincerely than I do the result of my *brutality* as you rightly term it.'

'Never mind that,' said he, faintly smiling; 'let us forget all unpleasant words on both sides, as well as deeds, and consign to oblivion everything that we have cause to regret. Have you any objection to take my hand – or you'd rather not?' It trembled through weakness, as he held it out, and dropped before I had time to catch it and give it a hearty squeeze, which he had not the strength to return.

'How dry and burning your hand is Lawrence,' said I. 'You are really ill, and I have made you worse by all this talk.'

'Oh, it is nothing: only a cold got by the rain.'

'My doing, too.'

'Never mind that – but tell me, did you mention this affair to my sister?'

'To confess the truth, I had not the courage to do so; but when you tell her, will you just say that I deeply regret it, and –'

'Oh, never fear! I shall say nothing against you, as long as you keep your good resolution of remaining aloof from her. She has not heard of my illness then, that you are aware of?'

'I think not.'

'I'm glad of that, for I have been all this time tormenting myself with the fear that somebody would tell her I was dying, or desperately ill, and she would be either distressing herself on account of her inability to hear from me or do me any good, or perhaps committing the madness of coming to see me. I must contrive to let her know something about it, if I can,' continued he reflectively, 'or she will be hearing some such story. Many would be glad to tell her such news, just to see how she would take it; and then she might expose herself to fresh scandal.'

'I wish I had told her,' said I. 'If it were not for my promise, I would tell her now.'

'By no means! I am not dreaming of that; – but if I were to write a short note, now – not mentioning you, Markham, but just giving a slight account of my illness, by way of excuse for my not coming to see her, and to put her on her guard against any exaggerated reports she may hear, – and address it in a disguised hand – would you do me the favour to slip it into the post-office as you pass? for I dare not trust any of the servants in such a case.'

Most willingly I consented, and immediately brought him his desk. There was little need to disguise his hand, for the poor fellow seemed to have considerable difficulty in writing at all, so as to be legible. When the note was done, I thought it time to retire, and took leave after asking if there was anything in the world I could do for him, little or great, in the way of alleviating his sufferings, and repairing the injury I had done.

'No,' said he; 'you have already done much towards it; you have done more for me than the most skilful physician could do; for you have relieved my mind of two great burdens – anxiety on my sister's account, and deep regret upon your own, for I do believe these two sources of torment have had more effect in working me up into a fever, than anything else; and I am persuaded I shall soon recover now. There is one more thing you can do for me, and that is, come and see me now and then – for you see I am very lonely here, and I promise your entrance shall not be disputed again.'

I engaged to do so, and departed with a cordial pressure of the hand. I posted the letter on my way home, most manfully resisting the temptation of dropping in a word from myself at the same time.

CHAPTER 46

I felt strongly tempted, at times, to enlighten my mother and sister on the real character and circumstances of the persecuted tenant of Wildfell Hall; and at first I greatly regretted having omitted to ask that lady's permission to do so; but, on due reflection, I considered that if it were known to them, it could not long remain a secret to the Millwards and Wilsons, and such was my present appreciation of Eliza Millward's disposition, that, if once she got a clue to the story, I should fear she would soon find means to enlighten Mr Huntingdon upon the place of his wife's retreat. I would therefore wait patiently till these weary six months were over, and then, when the fugitive had found another home, and I was permitted to write to her, I would beg to be allowed to clear her name from these vile calumnies: at present I must content myself with simply asserting that I knew them to be false, and would prove it some day, to the shame of those who slandered her. I don't think anybody believed me: but everybody soon learned to avoid insinuating a word against her, or even mentioning her name in my presence. They thought I was so madly infatuated by the seductions of that unhappy lady that I was determined to support her in the very face of reason; and meantime I grew insupportably morose and misanthropical from the idea that everyone I met was harbouring unworthy thoughts of the supposed Mrs Graham, and would express them if he dared. My poor mother was quite distressed about me; but I couldn't help it – at least I thought I could not; though sometimes I felt a pang of remorse for my undutiful conduct to her, and made an effort to amend, attended with some partial success – and indeed I was generally more humanized in my demeanour to her than to anyone else, Mr Lawrence excepted. Rose and Fergus usually shunned my presence; and it was well they did, for I was not fit company for them, nor they for me, under the present circumstances.

Mrs Huntingdon did not leave Wildfell Hall till above two months after our farewell interview. During that time she never appeared at church, and I never went near the house: I only knew she was still there by her brother's brief answers to my many and varied enquiries respecting her. I was a very constant and attentive visitor to him throughout the whole period of his illness and convalescence; not only from the interest I took in his recovery, and my desire to cheer him up and make the utmost possible amends for my former 'brutality,' but from my growing attachment to himself, and the increasing pleasure I found in his society – partly, from his increased cordiality to me, but chiefly on account of his close connection – both in blood and in affection – with my adored Helen. I loved him for it better than I liked to express; and I took a secret delight in pressing those slender, white fingers, so marvellously like her own, considering he was not a woman, and in watching the passing changes in his fair, pale features, and observing the intonations of his voice – detecting resemblances which I wondered had never struck me before. He provoked me at times, indeed, by his evident reluctance to talk to me about his sister, though I did not question the friendliness of his motives in wishing to discourage my remembrance of her.

His recovery was not quite so rapid as he had expected it to be: he was not able to mount his pony till a fortnight after the date of our reconciliation; and the first use he made of his returning strength, was to ride over by night to Wildfell Hall, to see his sister. It was a hazardous enterprise both for him and for her, but he thought it necessary to consult with her on the subject of her projected departure, if not to calm her apprehensions respecting his health, and the worst result was a slight relapse of his illness; for no one knew of the visit, but the inmates of the old Hall – except myself; and I believe it had not been his intention to mention it to me, for when I came to see him the next day, and observed he was not so well as he ought to have been, he merely said he had caught cold by being out too late in the evening.

'You'll *never* be able to see your sister, if you don't take care of yourself,' said I, a little provoked at the circumstance on her account, instead of commiserating him.

'I've seen her already,' said he, quietly.

'You've seen her!' cried I, in astonishment.

'Yes.' And then he told me what considerations had impelled him to make the venture, and with what precautions he had made it.

'And how was she?' I eagerly asked.

'As usual,' was the brief though sad reply.

'As usual – that is, far from happy and far from strong.'

'She is not positively ill,' returned he; 'and she will recover her spirits in a while I have no doubt – but so many trials have been almost too much for her. How threatening those clouds look!' continued he, turning towards the window. 'We shall have thunder showers before night, I imagine; and they are just in the midst of stacking my corn. Have you got yours all in yet?'

'No. – And Lawrence, did she – did your sister mention me?'

'She asked if I had seen you lately.'

'And what else did she say?'

'I cannot tell you all she said,' replied he with a slight smile, 'for we talked a good deal, though my stay was but short; but our conversation was chiefly on the subject of her intended departure, which I begged her to delay till I was better able to assist her in her search after another home.'

'But did she say no more about me?'

'She did not say much about you, Markham. I should not have encouraged her to do so, had she been inclined; but happily she was not: she only asked a few questions concerning you, and seemed satisfied with my brief answers; wherein she showed herself wiser than her friend – and I may tell you too, that she seemed to be far more anxious lest you should think too much of her, than lest you should forget her.'

'She was right.'

'But I fear *your* anxiety is quite the other way, respecting her.'

'No, it is not: I wish her to be happy; but I don't wish her to forget me altogether. She knows it is impossible that I should forget *her*; and she is right to wish me not to remember her too well. I should not desire her to regret me *too* deeply; but I can scarcely imagine she will make herself very unhappy about me, because I know I am not worthy of it, except in my appreciation of her.'

'You are neither of you worthy of a broken heart, – nor of all the sighs, and tears, and sorrowful thoughts that have been, and I fear will be wasted upon you both; but at present, each has a more exalted opinion of the other than, I fear, he or she deserves; and my sister's feelings are naturally full as keen as yours, and I believe *more* constant; but she has the good sense and fortitude to strive against them in this particular; and I trust she will not rest till she has entirely weaned her thoughts –' he hesitated.

'From me,' said I.

'And I wish you would make the like exertions,' continued he.

'Did she *tell* you that that was her intention?'

'No; the question was not broached between us: there was no necessity for it, for I had no doubt that such was her determination.'

'To forget me?'

'Yes Markham! Why not?'

'Oh! well,' was my only audible reply; but I internally answered, – 'No, Lawrence, you're wrong there, she is *not* determined to forget me. It would be *wrong* to forget one so deeply and fondly devoted to her, who can so thoroughly appreciate her excellencies and sympathize with all her thoughts as I can do, and it would be wrong in me to forget so excellent and divine a piece of God's creation as she, when I have once so truly loved and known her.' But I said no more to him on that subject. I instantly started a new topic of conversation, and soon took leave of my companion, with a feeling of less cordiality towards him than usual. Perhaps I had no right to be annoyed at him, but I was so nevertheless.

In little more than a week after this, I met him returning from a visit to the Wilsons; and I now resolved to do *him* a good turn, though at the expense of his feelings, and, perhaps, at the risk of incurring that displeasure which is so commonly the reward of those who give disagreeable information or tender their advice unasked. In this, believe me, I was actuated by no motives of revenge for the occasional annoyances I had lately sustained from him, – nor yet by any feeling of malevolent enmity towards Miss Wilson, but purely by the fact that I could not endure that such a woman should be Mrs Huntingdon's sister, and that, as well for his own sake as for hers, I could not bear to think of his being deceived into a union with one so unworthy of him, and so utterly unfitted to be the partner of his quiet home, and the companion of his life. He had had uncomfortable suspicions on that head himself, I imagined, but such was his inexperience, and such were the lady's powers of attraction and her skill in bringing them to bear upon his young imagination, that they had not disturbed him long, and I believe the only effectual causes of the vacillating indecision that had preserved him hitherto from making an actual declaration of love, was the consideration of her connections, and especially of her mother, whom he could not abide. Had they lived at a distance, he might have surmounted the objection, but within two or three miles of Woodford, it was really no light matter.

'You've been to call on the Wilsons, Lawrence,' said I as I walked beside his pony.

'Yes,' replied he, slightly averting his face: 'I thought it but civil to take the first opportunity of returning their kind attentions, since they have been so very particular and constant in their enquiries, throughout the whole course of my illness.'

'It's all Miss Wilson's doing.'

'And if it is,' returned he, with a very perceptible blush, 'is that any reason why I should not make a suitable acknowledgment?'

'It is a reason why you should not make the acknowledgment she looks for.'

'Let us drop that subject if you please,' said he in evident displeasure.

'No, Lawrence, with your leave we'll continue it a while longer; and I'll tell you something, now we're about it, which you may believe or not as you choose – only please to remember that it is not my custom to speak falsely, and that in this case, I can have no motive for misrepresenting the truth –'

'Well, Markham! what now?'

'*Miss Wilson hates your sister*. It may be natural enough that, in her ignorance of the relationship, she should feel some degree of enmity against her, but no good or amiable woman would be capable of evincing that bitter, cold-blooded, designing malice towards a fancied rival that I have observed in her.'

'Markham!!'

'Yes – and it is my belief that Eliza Millward and she, if not the very originators of the slanderous reports that have been propagated, were designedly the encouragers and chief disseminators of them. She was not desirous to mix up *your* name in the matter, of course, but her delight was, and still is, to blacken your sister's character to the utmost of her power without risking too greatly the exposure of her own malevolence!'

'I cannot believe it,' interrupted my companion, his face burning with indignation.

'Well, as I cannot prove it, I must content myself with asserting that it *is* so to the best of my belief; but as you would not willingly marry Miss Wilson if it *were* so, you will do well to be cautious, till you have proved it to be otherwise.'

'I never told you, Markham, that I *intended* to marry Miss Wilson,' said he proudly.

'No, but whether you do or not, she intends to marry you.'

'Did she tell you so?'

'No, but –'

'Then you have no right to make such an assertion respecting her.' He slightly quickened his pony's pace, but I laid my hand on its mane, determined he should not leave me yet.

'Wait a moment, Lawrence, and let me explain myself; and don't be so very – I don't know what to call it – *inaccessible* as you are. – I know what you think of Jane Wilson; and I believe I know how far you are mistaken in your opinion: you think she is singularly charming, elegant, sensible, and refined: you are not aware that she is selfish, cold-hearted, ambitious, artful, shallow-minded –'

'Enough, Markham, enough.'

'No; let me finish. – You don't know that, if you married her, your home would be rayless and comfortless; and it would break your heart at last to find yourself united to one so wholly incapable of sharing your tastes, feelings, and ideas – so utterly destitute of sensibility, good feeling, and true nobility of soul.'

'Have you done?' asked my companion quietly.

'Yes; – I know you hate me for my impertinence, but I don't care if it only conduces to preserve you from that fatal mistake.'

'Well!' returned he, with a rather wintry smile – 'I'm glad you have overcome, or forgotten, your own afflictions so far as to be able to study so deeply the affairs of others, and trouble your head, so unnecessarily, about the fancied or possible calamities of their future life.'

We parted – somewhat coldly again; but still we did not cease to be friends; and my well-meant warning, though it might have been more judiciously delivered, as well as more thankfully received, was not wholly unproductive of the desired effect: his visit to the Wilsons was not repeated, and though, in our subsequent interviews, he never mentioned her name to me, nor I to him, – I have reason to believe he pondered my words in his mind, eagerly though covertly sought information respecting the fair lady from other quarters, secretly compared my character of her with what he had himself observed and what he heard from others, and finally came to the conclusion that, all things considered, she had much better remain Miss Wilson of Ryecote Farm, than be transmuted into Mrs Lawrence of Woodford Hall. I believe, too, that he soon learned to contemplate with secret amazement his former predilection, and to congratulate himself on the lucky escape he had made; but he never confessed it to me, or hinted one word of acknowledgement for the part I had had in his deliverance – but this was not surprising to anyone that knew him as I did.

As for Jane Wilson, she, of course, was disappointed and embittered by the sudden cold neglect, and ultimate desertion of her former admirer. Had I done wrong to blight her cherished hopes? I think not; and certainly my conscience has never accused me, from that day to this, of any evil design in the matter.

CHAPTER 47

STARTLING INTELLIGENCE

One morning, about the beginning of November, while I was inditing some business letters, shortly after breakfast, Eliza Millward came to call upon my sister. Rose had neither the discrimination nor the virulence to regard the little demon as I did, and they still preserved their former intimacy. At the moment of her arrival, however, there was no one in the room but Fergus and myself, my mother and sister being both of them absent, 'on household cares intent;'[1] but *I* was not going to lay myself out for her amusement, whoever else might so incline: I merely honoured her with a careless salutation and a few words of course,[2] and then went on with my writing, leaving my brother to be more polite if he chose. But she wanted to tease me.

'What a pleasure it is to find you at home, Mr Markham!' said she, with a disingenuously malicious smile. 'I so seldom see you now, for you never come to the vicarage. Papa is quite offended I can tell you,' she added playfully, looking into my face with an impertinent laugh, as she seated herself, half beside and half before my desk, off the corner of the table.

'I have had a good deal to do of late,' said I, without looking up from my letter.

'Have you indeed! Somebody said you had been strangely neglecting your business these last few months.'

'Somebody said wrong, for, these last *two* months especially, I have been particularly plodding and diligent.'

'Ah! Well, there's nothing like active employment, I suppose, to console the afflicted; – and, excuse me, Mr Markham, but you look so very far from well, and have been, by all accounts, so moody and thoughtful of late, – I could almost think you have some secret care preying on your spirits. *Formerly,*' said she timidly, 'I could have ventured to ask you what it was, and what I could do to comfort you: I dare not do it now.'

'You're very kind, Miss Eliza. When I think you can do anything to comfort me, I'll make bold to tell you.'

'Pray do! – I suppose I mayn't guess what it is that troubles you?'

'There's no necessity, for I'll tell you plainly. The thing that troubles me the most at present, is a young lady sitting at my elbow and preventing me from finishing my letter, and thereafter, repairing to my daily business.'

Before she could reply to this ungallant speech, Rose entered the room; and Miss Eliza rising to greet her, they both seated themselves near the fire, where that idle lad, Fergus, was standing, leaning his shoulder against the corner of the chimney-piece, with his legs crossed and his hands in his breeches pockets.

'Now, Rose, I'll tell you a piece of news – I hope you've not heard it before, for good, bad or indifferent, one always likes to be the first to tell – It's about that sad Mrs Graham –'

'Hush-sh-sh!' whispered Fergus, in a tone of solemn import. '"We never mention her; her name is never heard."'[3] And glancing up, I caught him with his eye askance on me, and his finger pointed to his forehead; then, winking at the young lady with a doleful shake of the head, he whispered – 'a monomania – but don't mention it – all right but that.'

'I should be sorry to injure anyone's feelings,' returned she, speaking below her breath, 'another time, perhaps.'

'Speak out, Miss Eliza!' said I, not deigning to notice the other's buffooneries, 'you needn't fear to say anything in my presence – that is *true.*'

'Well,' answered she, 'perhaps you know already that Mrs Graham's husband is not really dead, and that she had run away from him?' I started, and felt my face glow; but I bent it over my letter, and went on folding it up as she proceeded; 'but perhaps you did *not* know that she is now gone back to him again, and that a perfect reconciliation has taken place between them? Only think,' she continued, turning to the confounded Rose, 'what a fool the man must be!'

'And who gave you this piece of intelligence, Miss Eliza?' said I, interrupting my sister's exclamations.

'I had it from a very authentic source, sir.'

'From whom, may I ask?'

'From one of the servants at Woodford.'

'Oh! I was not aware that you were on such intimate terms with Mr Lawrence's household.'

'It was not from the man himself, that I heard it; but he told it in confidence to our maid Sarah, and Sarah told it to me.'

'In confidence, I suppose; and you tell it in confidence to us; but *I* can tell *you* that it is but a lame story after all, and scarcely one half of it true.'

While I spoke, I completed the sealing and direction of my letters, with a somewhat unsteady hand, in spite of all my efforts to retain composure, and in spite of my firm conviction that the story *was* a lame one – that the supposed Mrs Graham, most certainly, had not *voluntarily* gone back to her husband, or dreamt of a reconciliation. Most likely, she was gone away, and the tale-bearing servant, not knowing what was become of her, had *conjectured* that such was the case, and our fair visitor had detailed it as a certainty, delighted with such an opportunity of tormenting me. But it was possible – barely possible, that someone might have betrayed her, and she had been taken away by force. Determined to know the worst, I hastily pocketed my two letters, and muttering something about being too late for the post, left the room, rushed into the yard and vociferously called for my horse. No one being there, I dragged him out of the stable myself, strapped the saddle on to his back and the bridle on to his head, mounted, and speedily galloped away to Woodford. I found its owner pensively strolling in the grounds.

'Is your sister gone?' were my first words as I grasped his hand, instead of the usual enquiry after his health.

'Yes; she's gone,' was his answer, so calmly spoken, that my terror was at once removed.

'I suppose I mayn't know where she is?' said I, as I dismounted and relinquished my horse to the gardener, who, being the only servant within call, had been summoned by his master, from his employment of raking up the dead leaves on the lawn, to take him to the stables.

My companion gravely took my arm, and leading me away to the garden, thus answered my question: –

'She is at Grassdale Manor, in —shire.'

'Where?' cried I, with a convulsive start.

'At Grassdale Manor.'

'How was it?' I gasped. 'Who betrayed her?'

'She went of her own accord.'

'Impossible, Lawrence!! She *could* not be so frantic!' exclaimed I, vehemently grasping his arm, as if to force him to unsay those hateful words.

'She did,' persisted he in the same grave, collected manner as before – 'and not without reason,' he continued, gently disengaging himself from my grasp: 'Mr Huntingdon is ill.'

'And so she went to nurse him?'

'Yes.'

'Fool!' I could not help exclaiming – and Lawrence looked up with a rather reproachful glance. 'Is he dying then?'

'I think not, Markham.'

'And how many more nurses has he? – how many ladies are there besides, to take care of him?'

'None: he was alone, or she would not have gone.'

'Oh, confound it! this is intolerable!'

'What is? that he should be alone?'

I attempted no reply, for I was not sure that this circumstance did not partly conduce to my distraction. I therefore continued to pace the walk in silent anguish, with my hand pressed to my forehead; then suddenly pausing and turning to my companion, I impatiently exclaimed,

'Why did she take this infatuated step? What fiend persuaded her to it?'

'Nothing persuaded her but her own sense of duty.'

'Humbug!'

'I was half inclined to say so myself, Markham, at first. I assure you it was not by my advice that she went, for I detest that man as fervently as you can do – except, indeed that his reformation would give me much greater pleasure than his death: – but all I did was to inform her of the circumstance of his illness (the consequence of a fall from his horse in hunting), and to tell her that that unhappy person, Miss Myers, had left him some time ago.'

'It was ill done! Now, when he finds the convenience of her presence, he will make all manner of lying speeches and false, fair promises for the future, and she will believe him, and then her condition will be ten times worse and ten times more irremediable than before.'

'There does not appear to be much ground for such apprehensions at present,' said he, producing a letter from his pocket: 'from the account I received this morning, I should say –'

It was *her* writing! By an irresistible impulse, I held out my hand, and the words – 'Let me see it,' involuntarily passed my lips. He was evidently reluctant to grant the request, but while he hesitated, I snatched it from his hand. Recollecting myself, however, the minute after, I offered to restore it.

'Here, take it,' said I, 'if you don't want me to read it.'

'No,' replied he, 'you may read it if you like.'

I read it and so may you.

GRASSDALE, NOV. 4th.

Dear Frederick,

I know you will be anxious to hear from me: and I will tell you all I can. Mr Huntingdon is very ill, but not dying, or in any immediate danger; and he is rather better at present than he was when I came. I found the house in sad confusion: Mrs Greaves, Benson, every decent servant had left, and those that were come to supply their places were a negligent, disorderly set, to say no worse – I must change them again if I stay. A professional nurse, a grim, hard old woman, had been hired to attend the wretched invalid. He suffers much, and has no fortitude to bear him through. The immediate injuries he sustained from the accident, however, were not very severe, and would, as the doctor says, have been but trifling to a man of temperate habits; but with *him* it is very different. On the night of my arrival, when I first entered his room, he was lying in a kind of half delirium. He did not notice me till I spoke; and then, he mistook me for another.

'Is it you, Alice, come again?' he murmured. 'What did you leave me for?'

'It is I, Arthur – it is Helen, your wife,' I replied.

'My wife!' said he, with a start. – 'For Heaven's sake, don't mention her! – I have none. – Devil take her,' he cried, a moment after, – 'and you too! What did you do it for?'

I said no more; but observing that he kept gazing towards the foot of the bed, I went and sat there, placing the light so as to shine full upon me; for I thought he might be dying, and I wanted him to know me. For a long time, he lay silently looking upon me, first with a vacant stare, then with a fixed gaze of strange, growing intensity. At last he startled me by suddenly raising himself on his elbow and demanding in a horrified whisper, with his eyes still fixed upon me, – 'Who is it?'

'It is Helen Huntingdon,' said I, quietly, rising at the same time, and removing to a less conspicuous position.

'I must be going mad,' cried he – 'or something – delirious perhaps – but leave me, whoever you are – I can't bear that white face, and those eyes – for God's sake go, and send me somebody else, that doesn't look like that!'

I went, at once, and sent the hired nurse. But next morning, I ventured to enter his chamber again; and, taking the nurse's place by his bedside, I watched him and waited on him for several hours, showing myself as little as possible, and only speaking when necessary, and then not above my breath. At first he addressed me as the nurse, but, on my crossing the room to draw up the window-blinds, in obedience to his directions, he said –

'No, it isn't nurse; it's Alice. Stay with me do! that old hag will be the death of me.'

'I mean to stay with you,' said I. And after that, he would call me Alice – or some other name almost equally repugnant to my feelings. I forced myself to endure it for a while, fearing a contradiction might disturb him too much: but when, having asked for a glass of water, while I held it to his lips, he murmured 'Thanks, dearest!' – I could not help distinctly observing – 'You would not say so if you knew me,' intending to follow that up with another declaration of my identity, but he merely muttered an incoherent reply, so I dropped it again, till some time after, when, as I was bathing his forehead and temples with vinegar and water to relieve the heat and pain in his head, he observed, after looking earnestly upon me for some minutes –

'I have such strange fancies – I can't get rid of them, and they won't let me rest; and the most singular and pertinacious of them all is your face and voice; they seem just like hers. I could swear at this moment, that she was by my side.'

'She is,' said I.

'That seems comfortable,' continued he, without noticing my words; 'and while you do it, the other fancies fade away – but *this* only strengthens. Go on – go on, till it vanishes too. I can't stand such a mania as this; it would kill me!'

'It never will vanish,' said I distinctly, 'for it is the truth.'

'The truth!' he cried, starting as if an asp had stung him. 'You don't mean to say that you are really she!'

'I do; but you needn't shrink away from me, as if I were your greatest enemy: I am come to take care of you, and do what none of *them* would do.'

'For God's sake, don't torment me now!' cried he in pitiable agitation; and then he began to mutter bitter curses against me, or the evil fortune that had brought me there; while I put down the sponge and basin, and resumed my seat at the bedside.

'Where are they?' said he – 'have they all left me – servants and all?'

'There are servants within call, if you want them; but you had better lie down now and be quiet: none of them could or would attend you as carefully as I shall do.'

'I can't understand it at all,' said he, in bewildered perplexity. 'Was it a dream that –' and he covered his eyes with his hand, as if trying to unravel the mystery.

'No Arthur, it was not a dream, that your conduct was such as to oblige me to leave you; but I heard that you were ill and alone, and I am come back to nurse you. You need not fear to trust me: tell me all your wants, and I will try to satisfy them. There is no one else to care for you; and I shall not upbraid you now.'

'Oh! I see,' said he with a bitter smile, 'it's an act of Christian charity, whereby you hope to gain a higher seat in Heaven for yourself, and scoop a deeper pit in hell for me.'

'No; I came to offer you that comfort and assistance your situation required; and if I could benefit your soul as well as your body, and awaken some sense of contrition and –'

'Oh, yes; if you could overwhelm me with remorse and confusion of face, now's the time. What have you done with my son?'

'He is well, and you may see him some time, if you will compose yourself, but not now.'

'Where is he?'

'He is safe.'

'Is he here?'

'Wherever he is, you will not see him till you have promised to leave him entirely under my care and protection, and to let me take him away whenever and wherever I please, if I should hereafter judge it necessary to remove him again. But we will talk of that tomorrow: you must be quiet now.'

'No, let me see him now. I promise, if it *must* be so.'

'No –'

'I swear it, as God is in Heaven! Now then, let me see him.'

'But I cannot trust your oaths and promises: I must have a written agreement,[4] and you must sign it in presence of a witness – but not today, tomorrow.'

'No, today – now,' persisted he: and he was in such a state of feverish excitement, and so bent upon the immediate gratification of his wish, that I thought it better to grant it at once, as I saw he would not rest till I did. But I was determined my son's interest should not be forgotten; and having clearly written out the promise I wished Mr Huntingdon to give upon a slip of paper, I deliberately read it over to him, and made him sign it in the presence of Rachel. He begged I would not insist upon this: it was a useless exposure of my want of faith in his word, to the servant. I told him I was sorry, but since he had forfeited my confidence, he must take the consequence. He next pleaded inability to hold the pen. 'Then we must wait until you can hold it,' said I. Upon which, he said he would try; but then, he could not see to write. I placed my finger where the signature was to be, and told him he might write his name in the dark, if he only knew where to put it. But he had not power to form the letters. 'In that case, you must be too ill to see the child,' said I; and finding me inexorable, he at length managed to ratify the agreement; and I bade Rachel send the boy.

All this may strike you as harsh, but I felt I must not lose my present advantage, and my son's future welfare should not be sacrificed to any mistaken tenderness for this man's feelings. Little Arthur had not forgotten his father, but thirteen months of absence, during which he had seldom been permitted to hear a word about him, or hardly to whisper his name, had rendered him somewhat shy; and when he was ushered into the darkened room where the sick man lay, so altered from his former self, with fiercely flushed face and wildly gleaming eyes – he instinctively clung to me, and stood looking on his father with a countenance expressive of far more awe than pleasure.

'Come here, Arthur,' said the latter, extending his hand towards him. The child went, and timidly touched that burning hand, but almost started in alarm, when his father suddenly clutched his arm and drew him nearer to his side.

'Do you know me?' asked Mr Huntingdon intently perusing his features.

'Yes.'

'Who am I?'

'Papa.'

'Are you glad to see me?'

'Yes.'

'You're *not*!' replied the disappointed parent, relaxing his hold, and darting a vindictive glance at me.

Arthur, thus released, crept back to me and put his hand in mine. His father swore I had made the child hate him, and abused and cursed me bitterly. The instant he began I sent our son out of the room; and when he paused to breathe, I calmly assured him that he was entirely mistaken; I had never once attempted to prejudice his child against him.

'I did indeed desire him to *forget* you,' I said, 'and especially to forget the lessons you taught him; and for that cause, and to lessen the danger of discovery, I own I have generally discouraged his inclination to talk about you; – but no one can blame me for that, I think.'

The invalid only replied by groaning aloud and rolling his head on a pillow in a paroxysm of impatience.

'I am in hell, already!' cried he. 'This cursed thirst is burning my heart to ashes! Will *nobody* –'

Before he could finish the sentence, I had poured out a glass of some acidulated,[5] cooling drink that was on the table, and brought it to him. He drank it greedily, but muttered, as I took away the glass, –

'I suppose you're heaping coals of fire on my head[6] – you think.'

Not noticing this speech, I asked if there was anything else I could do for him.

'Yes; I'll give you another opportunity of showing your Christian magnanimity,' sneered he: – 'set my pillow straight, – and these confounded bed-clothes.' I did so. 'There – now, get me another glass of that slop.' I complied. 'This is delightful! isn't it?' said he with a malicious grin, as I held it to his lips – 'you never hoped for such a glorious opportunity?'

'Now, shall I stay with you?' said I, as I replaced the glass on the table – 'or will you be more quiet if I go, and send the nurse?'

'Oh, yes, you're wondrous gentle and obliging! – But you've driven me mad with it all!' responded he, with an impatient toss.

'I'll leave you then,' said I, and I withdrew, and did not trouble him with my presence again that day, except for a minute or two at a time, just to see how he was and what he wanted.

Next morning, the doctor ordered him to be bled; and after that, he was more subdued and tranquil. I passed half the day in his room at different intervals. My presence did not appear to agitate or irritate him as before, and he accepted my services quietly, without any bitter remarks – indeed he scarcely spoke at all, except to make known his wants, and hardly then. But on the morrow – that is, today – in proportion as he recovered from the state of exhaustion and stupefaction – his ill-nature appeared to revive.

'Oh, this sweet revenge!' cried he, when I had been doing all I could to make him comfortable and to remedy the carelessness of his nurse. 'And you can enjoy it with such a quiet conscience too, because it's all in the way of duty.'

'It is well for me that I *am* doing my duty,' said I, with a bitterness I could not repress, 'for it is the only comfort I have; and the satisfaction of my own conscience, it seems, is the only reward I need look for!'

He looked rather surprised at the earnestness of my manner.

'What reward *did* you look for?' he asked.

'You will think me a liar if I tell you – but I *did* hope to benefit you: as well to better your mind, as to alleviate your present sufferings; but it appears I am to do neither – your own bad spirit will not let me. As far as *you* are concerned, I have sacrificed my own feelings, and all the little earthly comfort that was left me, to no purpose; – and every little thing I do for you is ascribed to self-righteous malice and refined revenge!'

'It's all very fine, I dare say,' said he, eyeing me with stupid amazement; 'and of course I ought to be melted to tears of penitence and admiration at the sight of so much generosity and superhuman goodness, – but you see I can't manage it. However, pray do me all the good you can, if you do really find any pleasure in it; for you perceive I am almost as miserable just now as you need wish to see me. Since you came, I confess, I have had better attendance than before, for these wretches neglected me shamefully, and all my old friends seem to have fairly forsaken me. I've had a dreadful time of it, I assure you: I sometimes thought I should have died – do you think there's any chance?'

'There's always a chance of death; and it is always well to live with such a chance in view.'

'Yes, yes – but do you think there's any likelihood that this illness will have a fatal termination?'

'I cannot tell; but, supposing it should, how are you prepared to meet the event?'

'Why the doctor told me I wasn't to think about it, for I was sure to get better, if I stuck to his regimen and prescriptions.'

'I hope you may, Arthur, but neither the doctor nor I can speak with certainty in such a case: there is internal injury, and it is difficult to know to what extent.'

'There now! you want to scare me to death.'

'No; but I don't want to lull you to false security. If a consciousness of the uncertainty of life can dispose you to serious and useful thoughts, I would not deprive you of the benefit of such reflections, whether you do eventually recover or not. Does the idea of death appal you *very* much?'

'It's just the only thing I can't bear to think of; so if you've any –'

'But it must come sometime,' interrupted I; 'and if it be years hence, it will as certainly overtake you as if it came today, – and no doubt be as unwelcome then as now, unless you –'

'Oh, hang it! don't torment me with your preachments now, unless you want to kill me outright – I can't stand it, I tell you – I've sufferings enough without that. If you think there's danger, save me from it; and then, in gratitude, I'll hear whatever you like to say.'

I accordingly dropped the unwelcome topic. And now, Frederick, I think I may bring my letter to a close. From these details, you may form your own judgment of the state of my patient, and of my own position and future prospects. Let me hear from you soon, and I will write again to tell you how we get on; but now that my presence is tolerated – and even required in the sick-room, I shall have but little time to spare between my husband and my son, – for I must not entirely neglect the latter: it would not do to keep him always with Rachel, and I dare not leave him for a moment with any of the other servants, or suffer him to be alone, lest he should meet them. If his father get worse, I shall ask Esther Hargrave to take charge of him for a time, till I have reorganized the household at least; but I greatly prefer keeping him under my own eye.

I find myself in rather a singular position: I am exerting my utmost endeavours to promote the recovery and reformation of my husband, and if I succeed what shall I do? My duty, of course, – but how? – No matter; I can perform the task that is before me now, and God will give me strength to do whatever he requires hereafter. – Goodbye, dear Frederick.

HELEN HUNTINGDON

'What do you think of it?' said Lawrence as I silently refolded the letter.

'It seems to me,' returned I, 'that she is casting her pearls before swine.[7] May they be satisfied with trampling them under their feet, and not turn again and rend her! But I shall say no more against her: I see that she was actuated by the best and noblest motives in what she has done; and if the act is not a wise one, may Heaven protect her from its consequences! May I keep this letter, Lawrence? – you see she has never once mentioned me throughout – or made the most distant allusion to me; therefore, there can be no impropriety or harm in it.'

'And therefore, why should you wish to keep it?'

'Were not these characters written by her hand? and were not these words conceived in her mind, and many of them spoken by her lips?'

'Well,' said he. And so I kept it; otherwise, Halford, you could never have become so thoroughly acquainted with its contents.

'And when you write,' said I, 'will you have the goodness to ask her if I may be permitted to enlighten my mother and sister on her real history and circumstance, just so far as is necessary to make the neighbourhood sensible of the shameful injustice they have done her? I want no tender messages, but just ask her that, and tell her it is the greatest favour she could do me; and tell her – no, nothing more. – You see I know the address, and I might write to her myself, but I am so virtuous as to refrain.'

'Well, I'll do this for you, Markham.'

'And as soon as you receive an answer, you'll let me know?'

'If all be well, I'll come myself and tell you, immediately.'

CHAPTER 48

FURTHER INTELLIGENCE

Five or six days after this, Mr Lawrence paid us the honour of a call; and when he and I were alone together – which I contrived as soon as possible, by bringing him out to look at my cornstacks – he showed me another letter from his sister. This one he was quite willing to submit to my longing gaze: he thought, I suppose, it would do me good. The only answer it gave to my message was this: –

'Mr Markham is at liberty to make such revelations concerning me as he judges necessary. He will know that I should wish but little to be said on the subject. I hope he is well; but tell him he must not think of me.'

I can give you a few extracts from the rest of the letter, for I was permitted to keep this also – perhaps, as an antidote to all pernicious hopes and fancies.

He is decidedly better, but very low from the depressing effects of his severe illness and the strict regimen he is obliged to observe – so opposite to all his previous habits. It is deplorable to see how completely his past life has degenerated his once noble constitution, and vitiated the whole system of his organization. But the doctor says he may now be considered out of danger, if he will only continue to observe the necessary restrictions. Some stimulating cordials he must have, but they should be judiciously diluted and sparingly used: and I find it very difficult to keep him to this. At first, his extreme dread of death rendered the task an easy one; but in proportion as he feels his acute suffering abating and sees the danger receding, the more intractable he becomes. Now also, his appetite for food is beginning to return; and here too, his long habits of self-indulgence are greatly against him. I watch and restrain him as well as I can, and often get bitterly abused for my rigid severity; and sometimes he contrives to elude[1] my vigilance, and sometimes acts in open opposition to my will. But he is now so completely reconciled to my attendance in general that he is never satisfied when I am not by his side. I am obliged to be a little stiff with him sometimes, or he would make a complete slave of me: and I know it would be unpardonable weakness to give up all other interests for him. I have the servants to overlook and my little Arthur to attend to, – and my own health too, all of which would be entirely neglected were I to satisfy his exorbitant demands. I do not generally sit up at nights, for I think the nurse, who has made it her business, is better qualified for such undertakings than I am; but still, an unbroken night's rest is what I but seldom enjoy, and never can venture to reckon upon; for my patient makes no scruple of calling me up at any hour when his wants or his fancies require my presence. But he is manifestly afraid of my displeasure; and if at one time he tries my patience by his unreasonable exactions, and fretful complaints and reproaches, at another, he depresses me by his abject submission and deprecatory self-abasement when he fears he has gone too far. But all this I can readily pardon; I know it is chiefly the result of his enfeebled frame and disordered nerves – what annoys me the most is his occasional attempts at affectionate fondness that I can neither credit nor return; not that I hate him: his sufferings and my own laborious care have given him some claim to my regard – to my affection even, if he would only be quiet and sincere, and content to let things remain as they are, but the more he tries to conciliate me the more I shrink from him and from the future.

'Helen, what do you mean to do when I get well?' he asked this morning. 'Will you run away again?'

'It entirely depends upon your own conduct.'

'Oh, I'll be very good.'

'But if I find it necessary to leave you, Arthur, I shall not "run away:" you know I have your own promise that I may go whenever I please, and take my son with me.'

'Oh, but you shall have no cause.' And then followed a variety of professions, which I rather coldly checked.

'Will you not forgive me then?' said he.

'Yes, – I *have* forgiven you; but I know you cannot love me as you once did – and I should be very sorry if you were to, for I could not pretend to return it: so let us drop the subject, and never recur to it again. By what I *have* done for you, you may judge of what I *will* do – if it be not incompatible with the higher duty I owe to my son (higher, because he never forfeited his claims, and because I hope to do more good to him than I can ever do to you); and if you wish me to feel kindly towards you, it is *deeds* not *words* that must purchase my affection and esteem.'

His sole reply to this was a slight grimace, and a scarcely perceptible shrug. Alas unhappy man! words, with him, are so much cheaper than deeds; it was as if I had said, 'Pounds, not pence, must buy the article you want.' And then he sighed a querulous, self-commiserating sigh, as if in pure regret that he, the loved and courted of so many worshippers, should be now abandoned to the mercy of a harsh, exacting, cold-hearted woman like that, and even glad of what kindness she chose to bestow.

'It's a pity, isn't it?' said I; and whether I rightly divined his musings or not, the observation chimed in with his thoughts, for he answered – 'It can't be helped,' with a rueful smile at my penetration.

I have seen Esther Hargrave twice. She is a charming creature, but her blithe spirit is almost broken, and her sweet temper almost spoiled, by the still unremitting persecutions of her mother, in behalf of her rejected suitor – not violent, but wearisome and unremitting like a continual dropping. The unnatural parent seems determined to make her daughter's life a burden if she will not yield to her desires.

'Mamma does all she can,' said she, 'to make me feel myself a burden and encumbrance to the family, and the most ungrateful, selfish, and undutiful daughter that ever was born; and Walter, too, is as stern and cold, and haughty as if he hated me outright. I believe I should have yielded at once if I had known, from the beginning, how much resistance would have cost me; but now, for very obstinacy's sake, I *will* stand out!'

'A bad motive for a good resolve,' I answered. 'But however, I know you have better motives, really, for your perseverance: and I counsel you to keep them still in view.'

'Trust me, I will. I threaten mamma sometimes, that I'll run away, and disgrace the family by earning my own livelihood, if she torments me any more; and then that frightens her a little. But I *will* do it, in good earnest, if they don't mind.'

'Be quiet and patient awhile,' said I, 'and better times will come.'

Poor girl! I wish somebody that was worthy to possess her would come and take her away – don't you, Frederick?

If the perusal of this letter filled me with dismay for Helen's future life and mine, there was one great source of consolation: it was now in my power to clear her name from every foul aspersion. The Millwards and the Wilsons should see, with their own eyes, the bright sun bursting from the cloud – and they should be scorched and dazzled by its beams; – and my own friends too should see it – they whose suspicions had been such gall and wormwood[2] to my soul. To effect this, I had only to drop the seed into the ground, and it would soon become a stately, branching herb:[3] a few words to my mother and sister, I knew, would suffice to spread the news throughout the whole neighbourhood, without any further exertion on my part.

Rose was delighted; and as soon as I had told her all I thought proper – which was all I affected to know – she flew with alacrity to put on her bonnet and shawl, and hasten to carry the glad tidings to the Millwards and Wilsons – glad tidings I suspect, to none but herself and Mary Millward – that steady, sensible girl, whose sterling worth had been so quickly perceived and duly valued by the supposed Mrs Graham, in spite of her plain outside; and who, on her part, had been better able to see and appreciate that lady's true character and qualities than the brightest genius among them.

As I may never have occasion to mention her again, I may as well tell you here, that she was at this time privately engaged to Richard Wilson – a secret, I believe to everyone but their two selves. That worthy student was now at Cambridge, where his most exemplary conduct and his diligent perseverance in the pursuit of learning carried him safely through, and eventually brought him with hard-earned honours and an untarnished reputation, to the close of his collegiate career.[4] In due time, he became Mr Millward's first and only curate – for that gentleman's declining years forced

him at last to acknowledge that the duties of his extensive parish
were a little too much for those vaunted energies which he was
wont to boast over his younger and less active brethren of the
cloth. This was what the patient, faithful lovers had privately
planned, and quietly waited for years ago; and in due time they
were united, to the astonishment of the little world they lived in,
that had long since declared them both born to single blessedness;
affirming it impossible that the pale, retiring bookworm should
ever summon courage to seek a wife, or be able to obtain one if
he did, and equally impossible that the plain-looking, plain-dealing,
unattractive, unconciliating Miss Millward should ever find a
husband.

They still continued to live at the vicarage, the lady dividing her
time between her father, her husband, and their poor parishioners, –
and subsequently, her rising family; and now that the Reverend
Michael Millward has been gathered to his fathers, full of years and
honours,[5] the Reverend Richard Wilson[6] has succeeded him to the
vicarage of Lindenhope, greatly to the satisfaction of its inhabitants,
who had so long tried and fully proved his merits, and those of his
excellent and well-loved partner.

If you are interested in the after-fate of that lady's sister, I can
only tell you – what perhaps you have heard from another quarter –
that some twelve or thirteen years ago, she relieved the happy
couple of her presence by marrying a wealthy tradesman of L—; and
I don't envy him his bargain. I fear she leads him a rather uncomfortable life, though happily he is too dull to perceive the extent of his
misfortune. I have little enough to do with her myself: we have not
met for many years; but, I am well assured, she has not yet forgotten
or forgiven either her former lover or the lady whose superior
qualities first opened his eyes to the folly of his boyish attachment.

As for Richard Wilson's sister, she, having been wholly unable to
recapture Mr Lawrence or obtain any partner rich and elegant
enough to suit her ideas of what the husband of Jane Wilson ought
to be, is yet in single blessedness. Shortly after the death of her
mother, she withdrew the light of her presence from Ryecote Farm,
finding it impossible any longer to endure the rough manners and

unsophisticated habits of her honest brother Robert and his worthy wife, or the idea of being identified with such vulgar people in the eyes of the world, – and took lodgings in — the county town, where she lived, and still lives, I suppose, in a kind of close-fisted, cold, uncomfortable gentility, doing no good to others and but little to herself; spending her days in fancy-work and scandal; referring frequently to her 'brother the vicar' and her 'sister the vicar's lady,' but never to her brother the farmer and her sister the farmer's wife; seeing as much company as she can without too much expense, but loving no one and beloved by none – a cold-hearted, supercilious, keenly, insidiously censorious old maid.

CHAPTER 49

'The rain descended, and the floods came, and the winds blew, and beat upon that house; and it fell: and great was the fall of it.'[1]

Though Mr Lawrence's health was now quite re-established, my visits to Woodford were as unremitting as ever; though often less protracted than before. We seldom *talked* about Mrs Huntingdon; but yet we never met without mentioning her, for I never sought his company but with the hope of hearing something about her, and he never sought mine at all, because he saw me often enough without. But I always began to talk of other things, and waited first to see if *he* would introduce the subject. If he did not, I would casually ask, 'Have you heard from your sister lately?' If he said, 'No,' the matter was dropped: if he said 'Yes,' I would venture to enquire, 'How is she?' but never 'How is her husband?' though I might be burning to know; because I had not the hypocrisy to profess any anxiety for his recovery, and I had not the face to express any desire for a contrary result. Had I any such desire? – I fear I must plead guilty: but since you have heard my confession, you must hear my justification as well – a few of the excuses, at least, wherewith I sought to pacify my own accusing conscience: –

In the first place, you see, his life did harm to others, and evidently no good to himself; and though I wished it to terminate, I would not have hastened its close if, by the lifting of a finger, I could have done so, or if a spirit had whispered in my ear that a single effort of the will would be enough, – unless, indeed, I had the power to exchange him for some other victim of the grave, whose life might be of service to his race, and whose death would be lamented by his friends. But was there any harm in wishing that, among the many thousands whose souls would certainly be required of them before the year was over, this wretched mortal might be one? I thought not; and therefore I wished with all my heart that it might please Heaven to remove him to a better world, or if that might not be, still, to take him out of this, for if he were unfit to answer the summons now, after a warning sickness, and with such an angel by his side, it seemed but too certain that he never would be – that, on the contrary, returning health would bring returning lust and villainy, and as he grew more certain of recovery, more accustomed to her generous goodness, his feelings would become more callous, his heart more flinty and impervious to her persuasive arguments – but God knew best. Meantime, however, I could not but be anxious for the result of His decrees; knowing, as I did, that (leaving myself entirely out of the question), however Helen might feel interested in her husband's welfare, however she might deplore his fate, still, while he lived, she *must* be miserable.

A fortnight passed away, and my enquiries were always answered in the negative. At length a welcome 'yes' drew from me the second question. Lawrence divined my anxious thoughts, and appreciated my reserve. I feared at first, he was going to torture me by unsatisfactory replies, and either leave me quite in the dark concerning what I wanted to know, or force me to drag the information out of him, morsel by morsel, by direct enquiries – 'and serve you right,' you will say; but he was more merciful; and in a little while, he put his sister's letter into my hand. I silently read it, and restored it to him without comment or remark. This mode of procedure suited him so well that thereafter he always pursued the plan of showing me her letters at once, when I enquired after her, if there were any to show: it was so much less trouble than to tell me their contents; and I received such confidences so quietly and discreetly that he was never induced to discontinue them.

But I devoured those precious letters with my eyes, and never let them go till their contents were stamped upon my mind; and when I got home, the most important passages were entered in my diary among the remarkable events of the day.

The first of these communications brought intelligence of a serious relapse in Mr Huntingdon's illness, entirely the result of his own infatuation in persisting in the indulgence of his appetite for stimulating drink. In vain had she remonstrated, in vain she had mingled his wine with water: her arguments and entreaties were a nuisance, her interference was an insult so intolerable that at length, on finding she had covertly diluted the pale port that was brought him, he threw the bottle out of the window, swearing he would not be cheated like a baby, ordered the butler, on pain of instant dismissal, to bring a bottle of the strongest wine in the cellar, and, affirming that he should have been well long ago if he had been let to have his own way, but she wanted to keep him weak in order that she might have him under her thumb – but by the Lord Harry, he would have no more humbug – seized a glass in one hand and the bottle in the other, and never rested till he had drunk it dry. Alarming symptoms were the immediate result of this 'imprudence' as she mildly termed it – symptoms which had rather increased than diminished since; and this was the cause of her delay in writing to her brother. Every former feature of his malady had returned with augmented virulence: the slight external wound, half-healed, had broken out afresh; internal inflammation had taken place, which might terminate fatally if not soon removed. Of course, the wretched sufferer's temper was not improved by this calamity – in fact, I suspect it was wellnigh insupportable, though his kind nurse did not complain; but she said she had been obliged, at last, to give her son in charge to Esther Hargrave, as her presence was so constantly required in the sick room that she could not possibly attend to him herself; and though the child had begged to be allowed to continue with her there, and to help her to nurse his papa, and though she had no doubt he would have been very good and quiet, – she could not think of subjecting his young and tender feelings to the sight of so much suffering, or of allowing him to witness his father's impatience, or hear the dreadful language he was wont to use in his paroxysms of pain or irritation.

'The latter,' continued she, 'most deeply regrets the step that has occasioned his relapse, – but, as usual, he throws the blame upon me. If I had reasoned with him like a rational creature, he says, it never would have happened; but to be treated like a baby or a fool, was enough to put any man past his patience, and drive him to assert his independence even at the sacrifice of his own interest – he forgets how often I had *reasoned* him "past his patience" before. He appears to be sensible of his danger; but nothing can induce him to behold it in the proper light. The other night while I was waiting on him, and just as I had brought him a draught to assuage his burning thirst – he observed, with a return of his former sarcastic bitterness, –

'"Yes, you're mighty attentive *now*! – I suppose there's *nothing* you wouldn't do for me now?"

'"You know," said I, a little surprised at his manner, "that I am willing to do anything I can to relieve you."

'"Yes, *now*, my immaculate angel; but when once you have secured your reward, and find yourself safe in Heaven, and me howling in hell-fire, catch you lifting a finger to serve me *then*! – No, you'll look complacently on, and not so much as dip the tip of your finger in water to cool my tongue!"[2]

'"If so, it will be because of the great gulf over which I cannot pass;[3] and if I *could* look complacently on in such a case,[4] it would be only from the assurance that you were being purified from your sins, and fitted to enjoy the happiness I felt. – But are you *determined*, Arthur, that I shall not meet you in Heaven?"

'"Humph! What should I do there, I should like to know?"

'"Indeed, I cannot tell; and I fear it is too certain that your tastes and feelings must be widely altered before you can have any enjoyment there. But do you prefer sinking, without an effort, into the state of torment you picture to yourself?"

'"Oh, it's all a fable;"[5] said he, contemptuously.

'"Are you sure, Arthur? are you *quite* sure? Because if there is any doubt, and if you *should* find yourself mistaken after all, when it is too late to turn –"

' "It would be rather awkward, to be sure," said he; "but don't bother me now – I'm not going to die yet. – I can't and won't," he added vehemently, as if suddenly struck with the appalling aspect of that terrible event, "Helen, you *must* save me!" And he earnestly seized my hand, and looked into my face with such imploring eagerness that my heart bled for him, and I could not speak for tears.'

*

The next letter brought intelligence that the malady was fast increasing; and the poor sufferer's horror of death was still more distressing than his impatience of bodily pain. *All* his friends had not forsaken him, for Mr Hattersley, hearing of his danger, had come to see him from his distant home in the north. His wife had accompanied him, as much for the pleasure of seeing her dear friend, from whom she had been parted so long, as to visit her mother and sister.

Mrs Huntingdon expressed herself glad to see Milicent once more, and pleased to behold her so happy and well. 'She is now at the Grove,' continued the letter, 'but she often calls to see me. Mr Hattersley spends much of his time at Arthur's bedside. With more good feeling than I gave him credit for, he evinces considerable sympathy for his unhappy friend, and is far more willing than able to comfort him. Sometimes he tries to joke and laugh with him, but that will not do: sometimes he endeavours to cheer him with talk about old times; and this, at one time, may serve to divert the sufferer from his own sad thoughts; at another, it will only plunge him into deeper melancholy than before; and then Hattersley is confounded, and knows not what to say, – unless it be a timid suggestion that the clergyman might be sent for. But Arthur will never consent to that: he knows he has rejected the clergyman's well-meant admonitions with scoffing levity at other times, and cannot dream of turning to him for consolation now.

'Mr Hattersley sometimes offers his services instead of mine, but Arthur will not let me go: that strange whim still increases, as his strength declines – the fancy to have me always by his side. I hardly ever leave him, except to go into the next room, where I sometimes snatch an hour or so of sleep when he is quiet; but even then, the door is left ajar that he may know me to be within call. I am with him now, while I write; and I fear my occupation annoys him; though I frequently break off to attend to him, and though Mr Hattersley is also by his side. That gentleman came, as he said, to beg a holiday for me, that I might have a run in the park, this fine, frosty morning, with Milicent, and Esther, and little Arthur, whom he had driven over to see me. Our poor invalid evidently felt it a heartless proposition, and would have felt it still more heartless in me to accede to it. I therefore said I would only go and speak to them a minute, and then come back. I did but exchange a few words with them, just outside the portico – inhaling the fresh, bracing air as I stood – and then, resisting the earnest and eloquent entreaties of all three to stay a little longer, and join them in a walk round the garden, – I tore myself away and returned to my patient. I had not been absent five minutes, but he reproached me bitterly for my levity and neglect. His friend espoused my cause: –

' "Nay, nay, Huntingdon," said he, "you're too hard upon her – she must have food and sleep, and a mouthful of fresh air now and then, or she can't stand it I tell you. Look at her, man, she's worn to a shadow already."

' "What are her sufferings to mine?" said the poor invalid. "You don't grudge me these attentions, do you, Helen?"

' "No, Arthur, if I could really serve you by them. I would give my life to save you, if I might."

' "Would you *indeed*? – No!"

' "Most willingly, I would."

' "Ah! that's because you think yourself more fit to die!"

'There was a painful pause. He was evidently plunged in gloomy reflections, but while I pondered for something to say, that might benefit without alarming him, Hattersley, whose mind had been pursuing almost the same course, broke silence with, –

' "I say, Huntingdon, I *would* send for a parson, of some sort – If you didn't like the vicar, you know, you could have his curate, or somebody else."

' "No; none of them can benefit me if *she* can't," was the answer. And the tears gushed from his eyes as he earnestly exclaimed, – "Oh, Helen, if I had listened to you, it never would have come to this! And if I had heard you long ago – Oh, God! how different it would have been!"

' "Hear me now, then, Arthur," said I, gently pressing his hand.

' "It's too late now," said he despondently. And after that another paroxysm of pain came on; and then his mind began to wander, and we feared his death was approaching; but an opiate was administered, his sufferings began to abate, he gradually became more composed, and at length sank into a kind of slumber. He has been quieter since; and now Hattersley has left him, expressing a hope that he shall find him better when he calls tomorrow.

' "Perhaps, I *may* recover," he replied, "who knows? – this may have been the crisis. What do *you* think, Helen?"

'Unwilling to depress him, I gave the most cheering answer I could, but still recommended him to prepare for the possibility of what I inly feared was but too certain. But he was determined to hope. Shortly after, he relapsed into a kind of doze – but now he groans again.

'There is a change. Suddenly he called me to his side, with such a strange, excited manner that I feared he was delirious – but he was not. "That *was* the crisis, Helen!" said he delightedly – "I had an infernal pain here – it is quite gone now; I never was so easy since the fall – Quite gone, by Heaven!" and he clasped and kissed my hand in the very fulness of his heart; but, finding I did not participate his joy, he quickly flung it from him, and bitterly cursed my coldness and insensibility. How could I reply? Kneeling beside him, I took his hand and fondly pressed it to my lips – for the first time since our separation – and told him as well as tears would let me speak, that it was not *that* that kept me silent; it was the fear that this sudden cessation of pain was not so favourable a symptom as he supposed. – I immediately sent for the doctor. We are now anxiously awaiting him: I will tell you what he says. There is still the same freedom from pain – the same deadness to all sensation where the suffering was most acute.

'My worst fears are realized – mortification has commenced. The doctor has told him there is no hope – no words can describe his anguish – I can write no more.'

The next was still more distressing in the tenor of its contents. The sufferer was fast approaching dissolution – dragged almost to the verge of that awful chasm he trembled to contemplate, from which no agony of prayers or tears could save him. Nothing could comfort him now: Hattersley's rough attempts at consolation were utterly in vain. The world was nothing to him: life and all its interests, its petty cares and transient pleasures were a cruel mockery. To talk of the past was to torture him with vain remorse; to refer to the future was to increase his anguish; and yet to be silent was to leave him a prey to his own regrets and apprehensions. Often he dwelt with shuddering minuteness on the fate of his perishing clay – the slow, piecemeal dissolution already invading his frame; the shroud, the coffin, the dark, lonely grave, and all the horrors of corruption.

'If I try,' said his afflicted wife, 'to divert him from these things – to raise his thoughts to higher themes, it is no better: – "Worse and worse!" he groans. "If there be really life beyond the tomb, and judgment after death, how *can* I face it?" – I cannot do him any good; he will neither be enlightened, nor roused, nor comforted by anything I say; and yet he clings to me with unrelenting pertinacity – with a kind a childish desperation, as if *I* could save him from the fate he dreads. He keeps me night and day beside him. He is holding my left hand now, while I write; he has held it thus for hours: sometimes quietly, with his pale face upturned to mine: sometimes clutching my arm with violence – the big drops starting from his forehead, at the thought of what he sees, or thinks he sees before him. If I withdraw my hand for a moment, it distresses him: –

'"Stay with me, Helen," he says; "let me hold you so: it seems as if harm could not reach me while you are here. But death *will* come – it is coming now – fast, fast![6] – and – Oh, if I *could* believe there was nothing after!"

'"Don't try to believe it, Arthur; there is joy and glory after, if you will but try to reach it!"

'"What, for *me*?" he said, with something like a laugh. "Are we not to be judged according to the deeds done in the body? Where's the use of a probationary existence, if a man may spend it as he pleases, just contrary to God's decrees, and then go to Heaven with the best – if the vilest sinner may win the reward of the holiest saint, by merely saying, 'I repent?'"

'"But if you *sincerely* repent –"

'"I *can't* repent; I only fear."[7]

'"You only regret the past for its consequences to yourself?"

'"Just so – except that I'm sorry to have wronged you Nell, because you're so good to me."

'"Think of the goodness of God, and you cannot but be grieved to have offended Him?"

'"What *is* God – I cannot see him or hear Him? – God is only an idea."

'"God is Infinite Wisdom, and Power, and Goodness – and LOVE;[8] but if this idea is too vast for your human faculties – if your mind loses itself in its overwhelming infinitude, fix it on Him who condescended to take our nature upon Him, who was raised to Heaven even in his glorified human body, in whom the fulness of the godhead shines."[9]

'But he only shook his head and sighed. Then, in another paroxysm of shuddering horror, he tightened his grasp on my hand and arm, and groaning and lamenting, still clung to me with that wild, desperate earnestness so harrowing to my soul, because I know I cannot help him. I did my best to soothe and comfort him.

'"Death is so terrible," he cried, "I cannot bear it! *You* don't know, Helen – you can't imagine what it is, because you haven't it before you; and when I'm buried, you'll return to your old ways and be as happy as ever, and all the world will go on just as busy and merry as if I had never been; while I –"[10] He burst into tears.

'"You needn't let *that* distress you," I said; "we shall all follow you soon enough."

'"I wish to God I could take you with me now!" he exclaimed, "you should plead for me."

'"No man can deliver his brother, nor make agreement unto God for him,"[11] I replied: "it cost more to redeem their souls – it cost the blood of an incarnate God, perfect and sinless in himself, to redeem us from the bondage of the evil one; – let *Him* plead for you."

'But I seem to speak in vain. He does not now, as formerly, laugh these blessed truths to scorn: but still he cannot trust, or will not comprehend them. He cannot linger long. He suffers dreadfully, and so do those that wait upon him – but I will not harass you with further details: I have said enough, I think, to convince you that I did well to go to him.'

*

Poor, poor Helen! dreadful indeed her trials must have been! And I could do nothing to lessen them – nay, it almost seemed as if I had brought them upon her myself, by my own secret desires; and whether I looked at her husband's sufferings or her own, it seemed almost like a judgment upon myself for having cherished such a wish.

The next day but one, there came another letter. That too was put into my hands without a remark, and these are its contents: –

DEC. 5th

He is gone at last. I sat beside him all night, with my hand fast locked in his, watching the changes of his features and listening to his failing breath. He had been silent a long time, and I thought he would never speak again, when he murmured, faintly but distinctly –

'Pray for me, Helen!'

'I do pray for you – every hour and every minute, Arthur; but you must pray for yourself.'

His lips moved but emitted no sound; – then his looks became unsettled; and, from the incoherent half-uttered words that escaped him from time to time, supposing him to be now unconscious, I gently disengaged my hand from his, intending to steal away for a breath of air, for I was almost ready to faint; but a convulsive movement of the fingers, and a faintly whispered 'Don't leave me!' immediately recalled me: I took his hand again, and held it till he was no more – and then I fainted; it was not grief; it was exhaustion that, till then, I had been enabled successfully to combat. Oh Frederick! none can imagine the miseries, bodily and mental, of that death bed! How could I endure to think that that poor trembling soul was hurried away to everlasting torment? it would drive me mad! But thank God I have hope – not only from a vague dependence on the possibility that penitence and pardon might have reached him at the last, but from the blessed confidence that, through whatever purging fires the erring spirit may be doomed to pass – whatever fate awaits it, still, it is not lost, and God, who hateth nothing that he hath made,[12] *will* bless it in the end!

His body will be consigned on Thursday to that dark grave he so much dreaded; but the coffin must be closed as soon as possible. If you will attend the funeral come quickly, for I need help.

HELEN HUNTINGDON

CHAPTER 50

DOUBTS AND DISAPPOINTMENTS

On reading this, I had no reason to disguise my joy and hope from Frederick Lawrence, for I had none to be ashamed of. I felt no joy but that his sister was at length released from her afflictive, overwhelming toil – no hope but that she would in time recover from the effects of it, and be suffered to rest in peace and quietness, at least, for the remainder of her life. I experienced a painful commiseration for her unhappy husband (though fully aware that he had brought every particle of his sufferings upon himself, and but too well deserved them all), and a profound sympathy for her own afflictions, and deep anxiety for the consequences of those harassing cares, those dreadful vigils, that incessant and deleterious confinement beside a living corpse – for I was persuaded she had not hinted half the sufferings she had had to endure.

'You will go to her, Lawrence?' said I, as I put the letter into his hand.

'Yes, immediately.'

'That's right! I'll leave you, then, to prepare for your departure.'

'I've done that, already, while you were reading the letter, and before you came; and the carriage is now coming round to the door.'

Inly approving his promptitude, I bade him good morning, and withdrew. He gave me a searching glance as we pressed each other's hands at parting; but whatever he sought in my countenance, he saw there nothing but the most becoming gravity, it might be, mingled with a little sternness in momentary resentment at what I suspected to be passing in his mind.

Had I forgotten my own prospects, my ardent love, my

pertinacious hopes? It seemed like sacrilege to revert to them now, but I had not forgotten them. It was, however, with a gloomy sense of the darkness of those prospects, the fallacy of those hopes, and the vanity of that affection, that I reflected on those things as I remounted my horse and slowly journeyed homewards. Mrs Huntingdon was free now; it was no longer a crime to think of her – but did she ever think of *me*? – not *now* – of course it was not to be expected – but would she, when this shock was over? – In all the course of her correspondence with her brother (our mutual friend, as she herself had called him), she had never mentioned me but once – and that was from necessity. This, alone, afforded strong presumption that I was already forgotten; yet this was not the worst: it might have been her sense of duty that had kept her silent, she might be only *trying* to forget; but in addition to this, I had a gloomy conviction that the awful realities she had seen and felt, her reconciliation with the man she had once loved, his dreadful sufferings and death, must eventually efface from her mind all traces of her passing love for me. She might recover from these horrors so far as to be restored to her former health, her tranquillity, her cheerfulness even – but never to those feelings which would appear to her, henceforth, as a fleeting fancy, a vain, illusive dream; especially as there was no one to remind her of my existence – no means of assuring her of my fervent constancy, now that we were so far apart, and delicacy forbade me to see her or to write to her, for months to come at least. And how could I engage her brother in my behalf? how could I break that icy crust of shy reserve? Perhaps he would disapprove of my attachment now, as highly as before; perhaps he would think me too poor – too lowly born, to match with his sister. Yes, there was another barrier: doubtless there was a wide distinction between the rank and circum-stances[1] of Mrs Huntingdon, the lady of Grassdale Manor, and those of Mrs Graham the artist, the tenant of Wildfell Hall; and it might be deemed presumption in me to offer my hand to the former – by the world, by her friends – if not by herself – a penalty I might brave, if I were certain she loved me; but otherwise, how could I? And, finally, her deceased husband, with his usual selfishness, might have so constructed his will as to place restrictions upon her marrying again. So that you see I had reasons enough for despair if I chose to indulge it.

Nevertheless, it was with no small degree of impatience that I looked forward to Mr Lawrence's return from Grassdale – impatience that increased in proportion as his absence was prolonged. He stayed away some ten or twelve days. All very right that he should remain to comfort and help his sister, but he might have written to tell me how she was, – or at least to tell me when to expect his return; for he might have known I was suffering tortures of anxiety for her, and uncertainty for my own future prospects. And when he did return, all he told me about her was that she had been greatly exhausted and worn by her unremitting exertions in behalf of that man who had been the scourge of her life, and had dragged her with him nearly to the portals of the grave, – and was still much shaken and depressed by his melancholy end and the circumstances attendant upon it; but no word in reference to me – no intimation that my name had ever passed her lips, or even been spoken in her presence. To be sure, I asked no questions on the subject: I could not bring my mind to do so, believing, as I did, that Lawrence was indeed averse to the idea of my union with his sister.

I saw that he expected to be further questioned concerning his visit, and I saw too, with the keen perception of awakened jealousy, or alarmed self-esteem – or by whatever name I ought to call it – that he rather shrank from that impending scrutiny, and was no less pleased than surprised to find it did not come. Of course, I was burning with anger, but pride obliged me to suppress my feelings, and preserve a smooth face – or at least, a stoic calmness throughout the interview. It was well it did, for, reviewing the matter in my sober judgment, I must say it would have been highly absurd and improper to have quarrelled with him on such an occasion: I must confess too that I wronged him in my heart: the truth was, he liked me very well, but he was fully aware that a union between Mrs Huntingdon and me would be what the world calls a *mésalliance*; and it was not in his nature to set the world at defiance; – especially in such a case as this, for its dread laugh, or ill opinion, would be far more terrible to him directed against his sister than himself. Had he believed that a union was necessary to the happiness of both, or of either, or had he known how fervently I loved her, he would have acted differently; but seeing me so calm and cool, he would not for the world disturb my philosophy;[2] and though refraining entirely from any active opposition to the match, he would yet do nothing to bring it about, and would much rather take the part of prudence, in aiding us to overcome our mutual predilections, than that of feeling, to encourage them. 'And he was in the right of it,' you will say. Perhaps he was – at any rate, I had no business to feel so bitterly against him as I did; but I could not then regard the matter in such a moderate light; and, after a brief conversation upon indifferent topics, I went away, suffering all the pangs of wounded pride and injured friendship, in addition to those resulting from the fear that I was indeed forgotten, and the knowledge that she I loved was alone and afflicted, suffering from injured health and dejected spirits, and I was forbidden to console or assist her, forbidden even to assure her of my sympathy, for the transmission of any such message through Mr Lawrence was now completely out of the question.

But what should I do? I would wait, and see if she would notice me – which of course she would not, unless by some kind message entrusted to her brother, that, in all probability, he would not deliver, and then – dreadful thought! – she would think me cooled and changed for not returning it – or perhaps, he had already given her to understand that I had ceased to think of her! I would wait, however, till the six months after our parting were fairly passed (which would be about the close of February), and then I would send her a letter modestly reminding her of her former permission to write to her at the close of that period, and hoping I might avail myself of it, at least to express my heart-felt sorrow for her late afflictions, my just appreciation of her generous conduct, and my hope that her health was now completely re-established, and that she would, sometime, be permitted to enjoy those blessings of a peaceful, happy life, which had been denied her so long, but which none could more truly be said to merit than herself, – adding a few words of kind remembrance to my little friend Arthur, with a hope that he had not forgotten me, and, perhaps, a few more in reference to bygone times – to the delightful hours I had passed in her society, and my unfading recollection of them, which was the salt and solace of my life, – and a hope that her recent troubles had not entirely banished me from her mind. – If she did not answer this, of course I should write no more: if she did (as surely she would, in *some* fashion) my future proceedings should be regulated by her reply.

Ten weeks was long to wait in such a miserable state of uncertainty, but courage! it must be endured; – and meantime I would continue to see Lawrence now and then, though not so often as before, and I would still pursue my habitual enquiries after his sister – if he had lately heard from her, and how she was, but nothing more.

I did so, and the answers I received were always provokingly limited to the letter of the enquiry: She was much as usual: She made no complaints, but the tone of her last letter evinced great depression of mind: – She said she was better: – and, finally; – She said she was well, and very busy with her son's education, and with the management of her late husband's property and the regulation of his affairs. The rascal had never told me how that property was disposed, or whether Mr Huntingdon had died intestate or not; and I would sooner die than ask him, lest he should misconstrue into covetousness my desire to know. He never offered to show me his sister's letters now; and I never hinted a wish to see them. February, however, was approaching; December was past, January, at length, was almost over – a few more weeks, and then, certain despair or renewal of hope would put an end to this long agony of suspense.

But alas! it was just about that time she was called to sustain another blow in the death of her uncle – a worthless old fellow enough, in himself, I dare say, but he had always shown more kindness and affection to her than to any other creature, and she had always been accustomed to regard him as a parent. She was with him when he died, and had assisted her aunt to nurse him during the last stage of his illness. Her brother went to Staningley to attend the funeral, and told me, upon his return, that she was still there, endeavouring to cheer her aunt with her presence, and likely to remain some time. This was bad news for me, for while she continued there, I could not write to her, as I did not know the address, and would not ask it of him. But week followed week, and every time I enquired about her she was still at Staningley.

'Where *is* Staningley?' I asked at last.

'In —shire,' was the brief reply: and there was something so cold and dry in the manner of it, that I was effectually deterred from requesting a more definite account.

'When will she return to Grassdale?' was my next question.

'I don't know.'

'Confound it!' I muttered.

'Why, Markham?' asked my companion, with an air of innocent surprise. But I did not deign to answer him, save by a look of silent, sullen contempt, at which he turned away, and contemplated the carpet with a slight smile, half pensive, half amused; but quickly looking up, he began to talk of other subjects, trying to draw me into a cheerful and friendly conversation; but I was too much irritated to discourse with him, and soon took leave.

You see Lawrence and I somehow could not manage to get on very well together. The fact is, I believe, we were both of us a little too touchy. It is a troublesome thing Halford, this susceptibility to affronts where none are intended. I am no martyr to it now, as you can bear me witness: I have learned to be merry and wise, to be more easy with myself and more indulgent to my neighbours, and I can afford to laugh at both Lawrence and you.

Partly from accident, partly from wilful negligence on my part (for I was really beginning to dislike him), several weeks elapsed before I saw my friend again. When we did meet, it was *he* that sought *me* out. One bright morning early in June, he came into the field where I was just commencing my hay harvest.

'It is long since I saw you, Markham,' said he after the first few words had passed between us. 'Do you never mean to come to Woodford again?'

'I called once, and you were out.'

'I was sorry: but that was long since; I hoped you would call again; and now, *I* have called, and *you* were out – which you generally are, or I would do myself the pleasure of calling more frequently – but being determined to see you this time, I have left my pony in the lane, and come over hedge and ditch to join you; for I am about to leave Woodford for a while, and may not have the pleasure of seeing you again for a month or two.'

'Where are you going?'

'To Grassdale first,' said he, with a half-smile he would willingly have suppressed if he could.

'To Grassdale! Is she there, then?'

'Yes, but in a day or two she will leave it to accompany Mrs Maxwell to F— for the benefit of the sea air; and I shall go with them.' (F— was at that time a quiet but respectable watering place: it is considerably more frequented now).

Lawrence seemed to expect me to take advantage of this circumstance to entrust him with some sort of a message to his sister; and I believe he would have undertaken to deliver it without any material objections, if I had had the sense to ask him; though of course he would not *offer* to do so, if I was content to let it alone. But I could not bring myself to make the request; and it was not till after he was gone, that I saw how fair an opportunity I had lost; – and then, indeed, I deeply regretted my stupidity and my foolish pride; but it was now too late to remedy the evil.

He did not return till towards the latter end of August. He wrote to me twice or thrice from F—; but his letters were most provokingly unsatisfactory, dealing in generalities or in trifles that I cared nothing about, or replete with fancies and reflections equally unwelcome to me at the time, – saying next to nothing about his sister, and little more about himself. I would wait, however, till he came back: perhaps I could get something more out of him then. At all events, I would not write to her now, while she was with him and her aunt, who doubtless would be still more hostile to my presumptuous aspirations than himself. When she was returned to the silence and solitude of her own home it would be my fittest opportunity.

When Lawrence came, however, he was as reserved as ever on the subject of my keen anxiety. He told me that his sister had derived considerable benefit from her stay at F—, that her son was quite well, and – alas! that both of them were gone, with Mrs Maxwell, back to Staningley; – and there they stayed at least three months. But instead of boring you with my chagrin, my expectations and disappointments, my fluctuations of dull despondency and flickering hope, my varying resolutions, now to drop it, and now to persevere – now to make a bold push, and now to let things pass and patiently abide my time, – I will employ myself in settling the business of one or two of the characters, introduced in the course of this narrative, whom I may not have occasion to mention again.

Sometime before Mr Huntingdon's death, Lady Lowborough eloped with another gallant to the continent, where, having lived awhile in reckless gaiety and dissipation, they quarrelled and parted. She went dashing on for a season, but years came and money went: she sunk, at length, in difficulty and debt, disgrace and misery; and died at last, as I have heard, in penury, neglect, and utter wretchedness. But this might be only a report: she may be living yet for anything I, or any of her relatives or former acquaintances, can tell; for they have all lost sight of her long years ago, and would as thoroughly forget her if they could. Her husband, however, upon this second misdemeanour, immediately sought and obtained a divorce, and, not long after, married again. It was well he did, for Lord Lowborough, morose and moody as he seemed, was not the man for a bachelor's life. No public interests, no ambitious projects, or active pursuits, – or ties of friendship even (if he had had any friends), could compensate to him for the absence of domestic comforts and endearments. He had a son and a nominal daughter, it is true, but they too painfully reminded him of their mother, and the unfortunate little Annabella was a source of perpetual bitterness to his soul. He had obliged himself to treat her with paternal kindness: he had forced himself not to hate her, and even, perhaps, to feel some degree of kindly regard for her, at last, in return for her artless and unsuspecting attachment to himself; but the bitterness of his self-condemnation for his inward feelings towards that innocent being, his constant struggles to subdue the evil promptings of his nature (for it was not a generous one), though partly guessed at by those who knew him, could be known to God and his own heart alone; – so also was the hardness of his conflicts with the temptation to return to the vice of his youth, and seek oblivion for past calamities, and deadness to the present misery of a blighted heart, a joyless, friendless life, and a morbidly disconsolate mind, by yielding again to that insidious foe to health, and sense, and virtue, which had so deplorably enslaved and degraded him before.

The second object of his choice was widely different from the first. Some wondered at his taste; some even ridiculed it – but in this their folly was more apparent than his. The lady was about his own age – i.e. between thirty and forty – remarkable neither for beauty nor wealth, nor brilliant accomplishments; nor any other thing that I ever heard of, except genuine good sense, unswerving integrity, active piety, warm-hearted benevolence, and a fund of cheerful spirits. These qualities however, as you may readily imagine, combined to render her an excellent mother to the children, and an invaluable wife to his lordship. *He*, with his usual self-depreciation (or *ap*preciation?) thought her a world too good for him, and while he wondered at the kindness of Providence in conferring such a gift upon him, and even at her taste in preferring him to other men, he did his best to reciprocate the good she did him, and so far succeeded that she was, and I believe still is, one of the happiest and fondest wives in England; and all who question the good taste of either partner may be thankful if *their* respective selections afford them half the genuine satisfaction in the end, or repay their preference with affection half as lasting and sincere.

If you are at all interested in the fate of that low scoundrel, Grimsby, I can only tell you that he went from bad to worse, sinking from bathos to bathos of vice and villainy, consorting only with the worst members of his club and the lowest dregs of society – happily for the rest of the world – and at last met his end in a drunken brawl from the hands, it is said, of some brother scoundrel he had cheated at play.

As for Mr Hattersley, he had never wholly forgotten his resolution to 'come out from among them,'[3] and behave like a man and a Christian, and the last illness and death of his once jolly friend Huntingdon so deeply and seriously impressed him with the evil of their former practices that he never needed another lesson of the kind. Avoiding the temptations of the town, he continued to pass his life in the country immersed in the usual pursuits of a hearty, active country gentleman; his occupations being those of farming, and breeding horses and cattle, diversified with a little hunting and shooting, and enlivened by the occasional companionship of his friends (better friends than those of his youth), and the society of his happy little wife (now cheerful and confiding as heart could wish) and his fine family of stalwart sons and blooming daughters. His father, the banker, having died some years ago and left him all his riches, he has now full scope for the exercise of his prevailing tastes, and I need not tell you that Ralph Hattersley, Esqr., is celebrated throughout the country for his noble breed of horses.

CHAPTER 51

AN UNEXPECTED OCCURRENCE

We will now turn to a certain still, cold, cloudy afternoon about the commencement of December, when the first fall of snow lay thinly scattered over the blighted fields and frozen roads, or stored more thickly in the hollows of the deep cart ruts and footsteps of men and horses, impressed in the now petrified mire of last month's drenching rains. I remember it well, for I was walking home from the vicarage, with no less remarkable a personage than Miss Eliza Millward by my side. I had been to call upon her father, – a sacrifice to civility undertaken entirely to please my mother, not myself, for I hated to go near the house; not merely on account of my antipathy to the once so bewitching Eliza, but because I had not half forgiven the old gentleman himself for his ill opinion of Mrs Huntingdon; for though now constrained to acknowledge himself mistaken in his former judgment, he still maintained that she had done wrong to leave her husband; it was a violation of her sacred duties as a wife, and a tempting of Providence by laying herself open to temptation; and nothing short of bodily ill-usage (and that of no trifling nature) could excuse such a step – nor even that, for in such a case she ought to appeal to the laws for protection.[1] But it was not of him I intended to speak; it was of his daughter Eliza. Just as I was taking leave of the vicar, she entered the room, ready equipped for a walk.

'I was just coming to see your sister, Mr Markham,' said she; 'and so if you have no objection, I'll accompany you home. I like company when I'm walking out – don't you?'

'Yes, when it's agreeable.'

'That of course,' rejoined the young lady, smiling archly. So we proceeded together.

'Shall I find Rose at home, do you think?' said she, as we closed the garden gate, and set our faces towards Linden-Car.

'I believe so.'

'I trust I shall, for I've a little bit of news for her – if you haven't forestalled me.'

'I?'

'Yes: do you know what Mr Lawrence is gone for?' She looked up anxiously for my reply.

'*Is* he gone?' said I, and her face brightened.

'Ah! then he hasn't told you about his sister?'

'What of *her*?' I demanded, in terror lest some evil should have befallen her.

'Oh, Mr Markham, how you blush!' cried she with a tormenting laugh. 'Ha, ha, you have not forgotten her yet! But you had better be quick about it, I can tell you, for – alas, alas! – she's going to be married next Thursday!'

'No, Miss Eliza! that's false.'

'Do you charge me with a falsehood, sir?'

'You are misinformed.'

'Am I? Do you know better then?'

'I think I do.'

'What makes you look so pale then?' said she, smiling with delight at my emotion. 'Is it anger at poor me for telling such a fib? Well, I only "tell the tale as 'twas told to me:"[2] I don't vouch for the truth of it; but at the same time, I don't see what reason Sarah should have for deceiving me, or her informant for deceiving her; and that was what she told me the footman told her: – that Mrs Huntingdon was going to be married on Thursday, and Mr Lawrence was gone to the wedding. She did tell me the name of the gentleman, but I've forgotten that. Perhaps you can assist me to remember it. Is there not someone that lives near – or frequently visits the neighbourhood, that has long been attached to her? a Mr — oh dear! – Mr —'

'Hargrave?' suggested I, with a bitter smile.

'You're right!' cried she, 'that was the very name.'

'Impossible, Miss Eliza!!' I exclaimed in a tone that made her start.

'Well, you know, that's what they told me,' said she, composedly staring me in the face. And then she broke out into a long shrill laugh that put me to my wits' end with fury.

'Really, you must excuse me,' cried she: 'I know it's very rude, but ha, ha, ha! – did you think to marry her yourself? Dear, dear, what a pity! ha, ha, ha! – Gracious, Mr Markham! are you going to faint? O mercy! shall I call this man? Here, Jacob –' But checking the word on her lips, I seized her arm and gave it, I think, a pretty severe squeeze, for she shrank into herself with a faint cry of pain or terror; but the spirit within her was not subdued: instantly rallying, she continued, with well feigned concern –

'What can I do for you? Will you have some water – some brandy? – I dare say they have some in the public house down there, if you'll let me run.'

'Have done with this nonsense!' cried I sternly. She looked confounded – almost frightened again, for a moment. 'You know I hate such jests,' I continued.

'*Jests* indeed! I wasn't *jesting*!'

'You were laughing, at all events; and I don't like to be laughed at,' returned I, making violent efforts to speak with proper dignity and composure, and to say nothing but what was coherent and sensible. 'And since you are in such a merry mood, Miss Eliza, you must be good enough company for yourself; and therefore I shall leave you to finish your walk alone – for, now I think of it, I have business elsewhere; so good evening.'

With that I left her (smothering her malicious laughter) and turned aside into the fields, springing up the bank, and pushing through the nearest gap in the hedge. Determined at once to prove the truth – or rather the falsehood of her story, I hastened to Woodford as fast as my legs could carry me – first, veering round by a circuitous course, but the moment I was out of sight of my fair tormentor, cutting away across the country, just as a bird might fly – over pasture-land and fallow, and stubble, and lane – clearing hedges and ditches, and hurdles, till I came to the young squire's gates. Never till now had I known the full fervour of my love – the full strength of my hopes, not wholly crushed even in my hours of deepest despondency, always tenaciously clinging to the thought that one day she might be mine – or if not that, at least that something of my memory, some slight remembrance of our friendship and our love would be forever cherished in her heart. I marched up to the door, determined if I saw the master, to question him boldly concerning his sister, to wait and hesitate no longer, but cast false delicacy and stupid pride behind my back, and know my fate at once.

'Is Mr Lawrence at home?' I eagerly asked of the servant that opened the door.

'No sir, master went yesterday,' replied he, looking very alert.

'Went where?'

'To Grassdale, sir – wasn't you aware, sir? He's very close, is master,' said the fellow with a foolish, simpering grin. 'I suppose, sir –'

But I turned and left him, without waiting to hear what he supposed. I was not going to stand there to expose my tortured feelings to the insolent laughter and impertinent curiosity of a fellow like that.

But what was to be done now? Could it be possible that she had left me for *that* man? I could not believe it. Me she might forsake, but *not* to give herself to him! Well, I would know the truth – to no concerns of daily life could I attend, while this tempest of doubt and dread, of jealousy and rage distracted me. I would take the morning coach from L— (the evening one would be already gone), and fly to Grassdale, I *must* be there before the marriage. And why? Because a thought struck me, that *perhaps* I might prevent it – that if I did not, she and I might both lament it to the latest moment of our lives. It struck me that someone might have belied me to her: perhaps her brother – yes, no doubt her brother had persuaded her that I was false and faithless, and taking advantage of her natural indignation, and perhaps her desponding carelessness about her future life, had urged her, artfully, cruelly on, to this other marriage in order to secure her from me. If this *was* the case, and if she should only discover her mistake when too late to repair it – to what a life of misery and vain regret might she be doomed as well as me! and what remorse for me, to think my foolish scruples had induced it all! Oh, I *must* see her – she must know my truth, even if I told it at the church door! I might pass for a madman or an impertinent fool – even she might be offended at such an interruption, or at least might tell me it was now too late – but if I *could* save her! if she *might* be mine – it was too rapturous a thought!

Winged by this hope, and goaded by these fears, I hurried homewards to prepare for my departure on the morrow. I told my mother that urgent business which admitted no delay, but which I could not then explain, called me away to — (the last large town through which I had to pass). My deep anxiety and serious preoccupation, could not be concealed from her maternal eyes; and I had much ado to calm her apprehensions of some disastrous mystery.

That night there came a heavy fall of snow, which so retarded the progress of the coaches on the following day, that I was almost driven to distraction. I travelled all night of course, for this was Wednesday: tomorrow morning, doubtless, the marriage would take place. But the night was long and dark; the snow heavily clogged the wheels and balled the horses' feet;[3] the animals were consumedly lazy, the coachmen most execrably cautious, the passengers confoundedly apathetic in their supine indifference to the rate of our progression. Instead of assisting me to bully the several coachmen and urge them forward, they merely stared and grinned at my impatience: one fellow even ventured to rally me upon it – but I silenced him with a look that quelled him for the rest of the journey; – and when, at the last stage, I would have taken the reins into my own hand, they all with one accord opposed it.

It was broad daylight when we entered M— and drew up at the Rose and Crown. I alighted and called aloud for a post-chaise[4] to Grassdale. There was none to be had: the only one in the town was under repair. 'A gig then – a fly – car[5] – anything – only be quick!' There was a gig but not a horse to spare. I sent into the town to seek one; but they were such an intolerable time about it that I could wait no longer: I thought my own feet could carry me sooner, and bidding them send the confounded conveyance after me, if it were ready within an hour, I set off as fast as I could walk. The distance was little more than six miles, but the road was strange, and I had to keep stopping to enquire my way – hallooing to carters and clod-hoppers,[6] and frequently invading the cottages, for there were few abroad that winter's morning, – sometimes knocking up the lazy people from their beds, for where so little work was to be done – perhaps so little food and fire to be had, they cared not to curtail their slumbers. I had no time to think of *them*, however: aching with weariness and desperation, I hurried on. The gig did not overtake me: it was well I had not waited for it – vexatious, rather, that I had been fool enough to wait so long.

At length however, I entered the neighbourhood of Grassdale. I approached the little rural church – but lo! there stood a train of carriages before it – it needed not the white favours bedecking the servants and horses, nor the merry voices of the village idlers assembled to witness the show, to apprise me that there was a wedding within. I ran in among them, demanding, with breathless eagerness, had the ceremony long commenced? They only gaped and stared. In my desperation I pushed past them, and was about to enter the churchyard gate, when a group of ragged urchins, that had been hanging like bees to the windows, suddenly dropped off and made a rush for the porch, vociferating in the uncouth dialect of their country, something which signified, 'It's over – they're coming out!'

If Eliza Millward had seen me then, she might indeed have been delighted. I grasped the gate-post for support, and stood intently gazing towards the door to take my last look on my soul's delight, my first on that detested mortal who had torn her from my heart, and doomed her, I was certain, to a life of misery and hollow, vain repining – for what happiness could she enjoy with him? I did not wish to shock her with my presence now, but I had not power to move away. Forth came the bride and bridegroom. Him I saw not; I had eyes for none but her. A long veil shrouded half her graceful form, but did not hide it; I could see that while she carried her head erect, her eyes were bent upon the ground, and her face and neck were suffused with a crimson blush; but every feature was radiant with smiles, and, gleaming through the misty whiteness of her veil, were clusters of golden ringlets! O Heavens! it was *not* my Helen! The first glimpse made me start – but my eyes were darkened with exhaustion and despair – dare I trust them? Yes – it *is* not she! It was a younger, slighter, rosier beauty – lovely, indeed, but with far less dignity and depth of soul – without that indefinable grace, that keenly *spirituel* yet gentle charm, that ineffable power to attract and subjugate the heart – *my* heart at least. I looked at the bridegroom – it was Frederick Lawrence! I wiped away the cold drops that were trickling down my forehead, and stepped back as he approached; but his eye fell upon me, and he knew me, altered as my appearance must have been.

'Is that you Markham?' said he, startled and confounded at the apparition – perhaps, too, at the wildness of my looks.

'Yes, Lawrence – is that you?' I mustered the presence of mind to reply.

He smiled and coloured, as if half-proud and half-ashamed of his identity; and if he had reason to be proud of the sweet lady on his arm, he had no less cause to be ashamed of having concealed his good fortune so long.

'Allow me to introduce you to my bride,' said he, endeavouring to hide his embarrassment by an assumption of careless gaiety. 'Esther, this is Mr Markham, my friend Markham, Mrs Lawrence, late Miss Hargrave.'

I bowed to the bride, and vehemently wrung the bridegroom's hand.

'Why did you not tell me of this?' I said reproachfully, pretending a resentment I did not feel (for in truth I was almost wild with joy to find myself so happily mistaken, and overflowing with affection to him for this and for the base injustice I felt that I had done him in my mind – he might have wronged me, but not to *that* extent; and as I had hated him like a demon for the last forty hours, the reaction from such a feeling was so great that I could pardon all offences for the moment – and love him in spite of them too).

'I *did* tell you,' said he, with an air of guilty confusion, 'you received my letter?'

'What letter?'

'The one announcing my intended marriage.'

'I never received the most distant hint of such an intention.'

'It must have crossed you on your way then – it should have reached you yesterday morning – it was rather late, I acknowledge. But what brought you here then, if you received no information?'

It was now *my* turn to be confounded; but the young lady, who had been busily patting the snow with her foot during our short, *sotto voce*[7] colloquy, very opportunely came to my assistance by pinching her companion's arm and whispering a suggestion that his friend should be invited to step into the carriage and go with them; it being scarcely agreeable to stand there among so many gazers, and keeping their friends waiting, into the bargain.

'And so cold as it is too!' said he, glancing with dismay at her slight drapery, and immediately handing her into the carriage. 'Markham, will you come? We are going to Paris, but we can drop you anywhere between this and Dover.'

'No thank you. Goodbye – I needn't wish you a pleasant journey; but I shall expect a very handsome apology, sometime, mind, and scores of letters, before we meet again.'

He shook my hand and hastened to take his place beside his lady. This was no time or place for explanation or discourse: we had already stood long enough to excite the wonder of the village sightseers, and perhaps the wrath of the attendant bridal party; though, of course, all this passed in a much shorter time than I have taken to relate or even than you will take to read it. I stood beside the carriage, and, the window being down, I saw my happy friend fondly encircle his companion's waist with his arm, while she rested her glowing cheek on his shoulder, looking the very impersonation of loving, trusting bliss. In the interval between the footman's closing the door and taking his place behind, she raised her smiling brown eyes to his face, observing playfully –

'I fear you must think me very insensible, Frederick: I know it is the custom for ladies to cry on these occasions, but I couldn't squeeze a tear for my life.'

He only answered with a kiss, and pressed her still closer to his bosom.

'But what is this?' he murmured. 'Why, Esther, you're crying now!'

'Oh, it's nothing – it's only too much happiness – and the wish,' sobbed she, 'that our dear Helen were as happy as ourselves.'

'Bless you for that wish!' I inwardly responded as the carriage rolled away – 'and Heaven grant it be not wholly vain!'

I thought a cloud had suddenly darkened her husband's face as she spoke. What did *he* think? Could he grudge such happiness to his dear sister and his friend as he now felt himself? At *such* a moment it was impossible. The contrast between her fate and his *must* darken his bliss for a time. Perhaps too he thought of me: perhaps he regretted the part he had had in preventing our union, by omitting to help us, if not by actually plotting against us – I exonerated him from *that* charge, now, and deeply lamented my former ungenerous suspicions; but he *had* wronged us, still – I hoped, I trusted that he had. He had not attempted to check the course of our love by actually damming up the streams in their passage, but he had passively watched the two currents wandering through life's arid wilderness, declining to clear away the obstructions that divided them, and secretly hoping that both would lose themselves in the sand before they could be joined in one. And meantime, he had been quietly proceeding with his own affairs: perhaps his heart and head had been so full of his fair lady that he had had but little thought to spare for others. Doubtless he had made his first acquaintance with her – his first intimate acquaintance at least – during his three months' sojourn at F—, for I now recollected that he had once casually let fall an intimation that his aunt and sister had a young friend staying with them at the time, and this accounted for at least one half his silence about all transactions there. Now too I saw a reason for many little things that had slightly puzzled me before; among the rest, for sundry departures from Woodford, and absences more or less prolonged, for which he never satisfactorily accounted, and concerning which he hated to be questioned on his return. Well might the servant say his master was 'very close.' But why this strange reserve to *me*? Partly, from that remarkable idiosyncrasy to which I have before alluded; partly, perhaps, from tenderness to my feelings, or fear to disturb my philosophy by touching upon the infectious theme of love.

CHAPTER 52

FLUCTUATIONS

The tardy gig had overtaken me at last. I entered it, and bade the man who brought it drive to Grassdale Manor – I was too busy with my own thoughts to care to drive it myself. I would see Mrs Huntingdon – there could be no impropriety in that now that her husband had been dead above a year – and by her indifference or her joy at my unexpected arrival, I could soon tell whether her heart was truly mine. But my companion, a loquacious, forward fellow, was not disposed to leave me to the indulgence of my private cogitations.

'There they go!' said he as the carriages filed away before us. 'There'll be brave doings on yonder *today*, as what come tomorra. – Know anything of that family, sir? or you're a stranger in these parts?'

'I know them by report.'

'Humph! – There's the best of 'em gone anyhow. And I suppose the old misses is agoing to leave after this stir's gotten overed, and take herself off, somewhere, to live on her bit of a jointure; and the young 'un – at least the new 'un (she's none so very young) is coming down to live at the Grove.'

'Is Mr Hargrave married, then?'

'Aye sir, a few months since. He should a been wed afore, to a widow lady, but they couldn't agree over the money: she'd a rare long purse, and Mr Hargrave wanted it all to his-self; but she wouldn't let it go, and so then they fell out. This one isn't quite as rich – nor as handsome either, but she hasn't been married before. She's very plain they say, and getting on to forty or past, and so, you know, if she didn't jump at this hopportunity, she thought she'd never get a better. I guess she thought such a handsome young husband was worth all 'at ever she had, and he might take it and welcome; but I lay she'll rue her bargain 'afore long. They say she begins already to see 'at he isn't not altogether that nice, generous, perlite, delightful gentleman 'at she thought him afore marriage – he begins a being careless, and masterful already. Aye, and she'll find him harder and carelesser nor she thinks on.'

'You seem to be well acquainted with him,' I observed.

'I am, sir; I've known him since he was quite a young gentleman; and a proud 'un he was, and a wilful. I was servant yonder for several years; but I couldn't stand their niggardly ways – she got ever longer and worse did Missis, with her nipping and screwing, and watching and grudging; so I thought I'd find another place as *what* came.'

And then he discoursed upon his present position as ostler at the Rose and Crown, and how greatly superior it was to his former one, in comfort and freedom, though inferior in outward respectability; and entered into various details respecting the domestic economy at the Grove, and the characters of Mrs Hargrave and her son, – to which I gave no heed, being too much occupied with my own anxious, fluttering anticipations and with the character of the country through which we passed, that, in spite of the leafless trees and snowy ground, had for some time begun to manifest unequivocal signs of the approach to a gentleman's country seat.

'Are we not near the house?' said I, interrupting him in the middle of his discourse.

'Yes, sir; yond's the park.'

My heart sank within me to behold that stately mansion in the midst of its expansive grounds – the park as beautiful now, in its wintry garb, as it could be in its summer glory; the majestic sweep, the undulating swell and fall, displayed to full advantage in that robe of dazzling purity, stainless and printless – save one long, winding track left by the trooping deer – the stately timber-trees with their heavy laden branches gleaming white against the dull, grey sky; the deep, encircling woods; the broad expanse of water sleeping in frozen quiet; and the weeping ash and willow drooping their snowclad boughs above it – all presented a picture, striking, indeed, and pleasing to an unencumbered mind, but by no means encouraging to me. There was one comfort however, – all this was entailed upon little Arthur, and could not under any circumstances, strictly speaking, be his mother's. But how was she situated? Overcoming with a sudden effort my repugnance to mention her name to my garrulous companion, I asked him if he knew whether her late husband had left a will, and how the property had been disposed of. Oh, yes, he knew all about it; and I was quickly informed that to her had been left the full control and management of the estate during her son's minority, besides the absolute, unconditional possession of her own fortune (but I knew her father had not given her much), and the small additional sum that had been settled upon her before marriage.

Before the close of the explanation, we drew up at the park gates. Now for the trial – if I should find her within – but alas! she might be still at Staningley: her brother had given me no intimation to the contrary. I enquired at the porter's lodge if Mrs Huntingdon were at home. No, she was with her aunt in —shire, but was expected to return before Christmas. She usually spent most of her time at Staningley, only coming to Grassdale occasionally, when the management of affairs, or the interest of her tenants and dependants required her presence.

'Near what town is Staningley situated?' I asked. The requisite information was soon obtained. 'Now then, my man, give me the reins, and we'll return to M—. I must have some breakfast at the Rose and Crown, and then away to Staningley by the first coach for —'

'You'll not get there today, sir.'

'No matter, I don't want to get there today; I want to get there tomorrow, and pass the night on the road.'

'At an inn, sir? You'd better by half stay at *our* house; and then start fresh tomorrow, and have the whole day for your journey.'

'What, and lose twelve hours? not I.'

'Perhaps, sir, you're *related* to Mrs Huntingdon?' said he, seeking to indulge his curiosity since his cupidity was not to be gratified.

'I have not that honour.'

'Ah! well,' returned he with a dubious, sidelong glance at my splashed, grey trousers and rough pea-jacket.[1] 'But,' he added, encouragingly, 'there's many a fine lady like that 'at has kinsfolks poorer nor what you are, sir, I should think.'

'No doubt, – and there's many a fine gentleman could esteem himself vastly honoured to be able to claim kindred with the lady you mention.'

He now cunningly glanced at my face. 'Perhaps, sir, you *mean* to –'

I guessed what was coming, and checked the impertinent conjecture with, – 'Perhaps you'll be so good as to be quiet a moment. I'm busy.'

'Busy, sir?'

'Yes, in my mind, and don't want to have my cogitations disturbed.'

'Indeed, sir!'

You will see that my disappointment had not *very* greatly affected me, or I should not have been able so quietly to bear with the fellow's impertinence. The fact is I thought it as well – nay better, all things considered, that I should not see her today, – that I should have time to compose my mind for the interview – to prepare it for a heavier disappointment, after the intoxicating delight experienced by this sudden removal of my former apprehensions; not to mention that, after travelling a night and a day without intermission, and rushing in hot haste through six miles of new-fallen snow, I could not possibly be in a very presentable condition.

At M— I had time before the coach started to replenish my forces with a hearty breakfast, and to obtain the refreshment of my usual morning's ablutions, and the amelioration of some slight change in my toilet, – and also to dispatch a short note to my mother (excellent son that I was) to assure her that I was still in existence and to excuse my non-appearance at the expected time. It was a long journey to Staningley for those slow travelling days; but I did not deny myself needful refreshment on the road, nor even a night's rest at a wayside inn; choosing rather to brook a little delay than to present myself worn, wild, and weatherbeaten before my mistress and her aunt, who would be astonished enough to see me without that. Next morning, therefore, I not only fortified myself with as substantial a breakfast as my excited feelings would allow me to swallow, but I bestowed a little more than usual time and care upon my toilet; and, furnished with a change of linen from my small carpet-bag, well-brushed clothes, well-polished boots, and neat new gloves, – I mounted 'the Lightning,' and resumed my journey. I had nearly two stages yet before me, but the coach, I was informed, passed through the neighbourhood of Staningley, and, having desired to be set down as near the Hall as possible, I had nothing to do but to sit with folded arms and speculate upon the coming hour.

It was a clear, frosty morning. The very fact of sitting exalted aloft, surveying the snowy landscape and sweet, sunny sky, inhaling the pure, bracing air, and crunching away over the crisp, frozen snow, was exhilarating enough in itself; but add to this the idea of to what goal I was hastening, and whom I expected to meet, and you may have some faint conception of my frame of mind at the time – only a *faint* one though, for my heart swelled with unspeakable delight, and my spirits rose almost to madness – in spite of my prudent endeavours to bind them down to a reasonable platitude[2] by thinking of the undeniable difference between Helen's rank and mine; of all that she had passed through since our parting; of her long, unbroken silence; and, above all, of her cool, cautious aunt, whose counsels she would doubtless be careful not to slight again. These considerations made my heart flutter with anxiety, and my chest heave with impatience to get the crisis over, but they could not dim her image in my mind, or mar the vivid recollection of what had been said and felt between us – or destroy the keen anticipation of what was to be – in fact, I could not realize their terrors now. Towards the close of the journey, however, a couple of my fellow passengers kindly came to my assistance, and brought me low enough.

'Fine land this,' said one of them, pointing with his umbrella to the wide fields on the right, conspicuous for their compact hedge-rows, deep, well-cut ditches, and fine timber-trees, growing some-times on the borders, sometimes in the midst of the enclosure; – '*very* fine land, if you saw it in the summer or spring.'

'Aye,' responded the other – a gruff elderly man, with a drab great coat buttoned up to the chin and a cotton umbrella between his knees. 'It's old Maxwell's I suppose.'

'It *was* his, sir, but he's dead now, you're aware, and has left it all to his niece.'

'All!'

'Every rood of it, – and the mansion-house and all, – every hatom of his worldly goods! – except just a trifle, by way of remembrance to his nephew down in —shire and an annuity to his wife.'

'It's strange, sir!'

'It is sir. And she wasn't his own niece neither; but he had no near relations of his own – none but a nephew he'd quarrelled with – and he always had a partiality for this one. And then his wife advised him to it, they say: she'd brought most of the property, and it was her wish that this lady should have it.'

'Humph! – She'll be a fine catch for somebody.'

'She will so. She's a widow, but quite young yet, and uncommon handsome – a fortune of her own, besides, and only one child – and she's nursing a fine estate for him in — There'll be lots to speak for her! – 'fraid there's no chance for uz' – (facetiously jogging me with his elbow, as well as his companion) – 'ha, ha, ha! No offence, sir, I hope?' (to me) 'Ahem! – I should think she'll marry none but a nobleman, myself. Look ye sir,' resumed he, turning to his other neighbour, and pointing past me with his umbrella, 'that's the hall – grand park, you see – and all them woods – plenty of timber there, and lots of game – hallo! what now?'

This exclamation was occasioned by the sudden stoppage of the coach at the park gates.

'Gen'leman for Staningley Hall?' cried the coachman; and I rose and threw my carpet-bag on to the ground, preparatory to dropping myself down after it.

'Sickly, sir?' asked my talkative neighbour, staring me in the face (I dare say it was white enough).

'No. Here, coachman.'

'Thank'ee sir. – All right!'

The coachman pocketed his fee and drove away, leaving me not walking up the park, but pacing to and fro before its gates, with folded arms and eyes fixed upon the ground – an overwhelming force of images, thoughts, impressions crowding on my mind, and nothing tangibly distinct but this: – My love had been cherished in vain; my hope was gone for ever; I must tear myself away at once, and banish or suppress all thoughts of her like the remembrance of a wild, mad dream. Gladly would I have lingered round the place for hours, in the hope of catching at least one distant glimpse of her before I went, but it must not be: I must not suffer her to see me; for what could have brought me hither but the hope of reviving her attachment, with a view hereafter to obtain her hand? And could I bear that she should think me capable of such a thing? – of presuming upon the acquaintance – the *love* if you will – accidentally contracted, or rather forced upon her against her will, when she was an unknown fugitive, toiling for her own support, apparently without fortune, family or connections – to come upon her now, when she was reinstated in her proper sphere, and claim a share in her prosperity, which, had it never failed her, would most certainly have kept her unknown to me for ever? and this too, when we had parted sixteen months ago, and she had expressly forbidden me to hope for a reunion in this world – and never sent me a line or a message from that day to this? No! The very idea was intolerable.

And even, if she should have a lingering affection for me still, ought I to disturb her peace by awakening those feelings? to subject her to the struggles of conflicting duty and inclination – to whichsoever side the latter might allure, or the former imperatively call her – whether she should deem it her duty to risk the slights and censures of the world, the sorrow and displeasure of those she loved, for a romantic idea of truth and constancy to me, or to sacrifice her individual wishes to the feelings of her friends and her own sense of prudence and the fitness of things? No – and I would not! I would go at once, and she should never know that I had approached the place of her abode; for though I might disclaim all idea of ever aspiring to her hand, or even of soliciting a place in her friendly regard, her peace should not be broken by my presence, nor her heart afflicted by the sight of my fidelity.

'Adieu then, dear Helen, for ever! – Forever adieu!'

So said I – and yet I could not tear myself away. I moved a few paces, and then looked back, for one last view of her stately home, that I might have its outward form, at least, impressed upon my mind as indelibly as her own image, which alas! I must not see again – then, walked a few steps farther; and then lost in melancholy musings, paused again and leant my back against a rough old tree that grew beside the road.

CHAPTER 53

CONCLUSION

While standing thus, absorbed in my gloomy reverie, a gentleman's carriage came round the corner of the road. I did not look at it; and had it rolled quietly by me, I should not have remembered the fact of its appearance at all; but a tiny voice from within it roused me by exclaiming –

'Mamma, mamma, here's Mr Markham!'

I did not hear the reply, but presently the same voice answered –

'It is indeed, mamma – look for yourself.'

I did not raise my eyes, but I suppose mamma looked, for a clear, melodious voice, whose tones thrilled through my nerves, exclaimed –

'Oh, aunt! here's Mr Markham – Arthur's friend! – Stop, Richard!'

There was such evidence of joyous though suppressed excitement in the utterance of those few words – especially that tremulous, 'Oh, aunt –' that it threw me almost off my guard. The carriage stopped immediately, and I looked up and met the eye of a pale, grave, elderly lady surveying me from the open window. She bowed and so did I, and then she withdrew her head, while Arthur screamed to the footman to let him out; but before that functionary could descend from his box, a hand was silently put forth from the carriage window. I knew that hand, though a black glove concealed its delicate whiteness and half its fair proportions, and quickly seizing it, I pressed it in my own – ardently for a moment, but instantly recollecting myself, I dropped it, and it was immediately withdrawn.

'Were you coming to see us, or only passing by?' asked the low voice of its owner, who, I felt, was attentively surveying my countenance from behind the thick, black veil which with the shadowing panels, entirely concealed her own from me.

'I – I came to see the place,' faltered I.

'The *place*,' repeated she, in a tone which betokened more displeasure or disappointment than surprise.

'Will you not enter it then?'

'If you wish it.'

'Can you doubt?'

'Yes, yes! he *must* enter,' cried Arthur running round from the other door; and seizing my hand in both his, he shook it heartily.

'Do you remember me, sir?' said he.

'Yes, full well, my little man, altered though you are,' replied I, surveying the comparatively tall, slim young gentleman with his mother's image visibly stamped upon his fair, intelligent features, in spite of the blue eyes beaming with gladness, and the bright locks clustering beneath his cap.

'Am I not grown?' said he, stretching himself up to his full height.

'Grown! three inches upon my word?'

'I was *seven* last birthday,' was the proud rejoinder. 'In seven years more, I shall be as tall as you, nearly.'

'Arthur,' said his mother, 'tell him to come in. Go on Richard.'

There was a touch of sadness as well as coldness in her voice, but I knew not to what to ascribe it. The carriage drove on and entered the gates before us. My little companion led me up the park, discoursing merrily all the way. Arrived at the hall door, I paused on the steps and looked round me, waiting to recover my composure, if possible – or at any rate, to remember my new formed resolutions and the principles on which they were founded; and it was not till Arthur had been for some time gently pulling my coat, and repeating his invitations to enter, that I at length consented to accompany him into the apartment where the ladies awaited us.

Helen eyed me as I entered with a kind of gentle, serious scrutiny and politely asked after Mrs Markham and Rose. I respectfully answered her enquiries. Mrs Maxwell begged me to be seated, observing it was rather cold, but she supposed I had not travelled far that morning.

'Not quite twenty miles,' I answered.

'Not on foot!'

'No, madam, by coach.'

'Here's Rachel, sir,' said Arthur, the only truly happy one amongst us, directing my attention to that worthy individual, who had just entered to take her mistress's things. She vouchsafed me an almost friendly smile of recognition – a favour that demanded, at least, a civil salutation on my part, which was accordingly given and respectively returned[1] – she had seen the error of her former estimation of my character.

When Helen was divested of her lugubrious bonnet and veil, her heavy winter cloak etc., she looked so like herself that I knew not how to bear it. I was particularly glad to see her beautiful black hair unstinted still and unconcealed in its glossy luxuriance.

'Mamma has left off her widow's cap in honour of uncle's marriage,' observed Arthur, reading my looks with a child's mingled simplicity and quickness of observation. Mamma looked grave and Mrs Maxwell shook her head. 'And aunt Maxwell is never going to leave off hers,' persisted the naughty boy; but when he saw that his pertness was seriously displeasing and painful to his aunt, he went and silently put his arm round her neck, kissed her cheek, and withdrew to the recess of one of the great bay windows, where he quietly amused himself with his dog while Mrs Maxwell gravely discussed with me the interesting topics of the weather, the season, and the roads. I considered her presence very useful as a check upon my natural impulses – an antidote to those emotions of tumultuous excitement which would otherwise have carried me away against my reason and my will, but *just then* I felt the restraint almost intolerable, and I had the greatest difficulty in forcing myself to attend to her remarks and answer them with ordinary politeness; for I was sensible that Helen was standing within a few feet of me beside the fire. I dared not look at her, but I felt her eye was upon me, and from one hasty, furtive glance, I thought her cheek was slightly flushed, and that her fingers, as she played with her watch chain, were agitated with that restless, trembling motion which betokens high excitement.

'Tell me,' said she, availing herself of the first pause in the attempted conversation between her aunt and me, and speaking fast and low with her eyes bent on the gold chain – for I now ventured another glance – 'Tell me how you all are at Lindenhope? – has nothing happened since I left you?'

'I believe not.'

'Nobody dead? nobody married?'

'No.'

'Or – or expecting to marry? – No old ties dissolved or new ones formed? no old friends forgotten or supplanted?'

She dropped her voice so low in the last sentence that no one could have caught the concluding words but myself, and at the same time turned her eyes upon me with a dawning smile, most sweetly melancholy, and a look of timid though keen enquiry that made my cheeks tingle with inexpressible emotions.

'I believe not,' I answered – 'Certainly not, if others are as little changed as I.' Her face glowed in sympathy with mine.

'And you really did not mean to call?' she exclaimed.

'I feared to intrude.'

'To intrude!' cried she with an impatient gesture. – 'What' – but as if suddenly recollecting her aunt's presence, she checked herself and turning to that lady continued – 'Why aunt, this man is my brother's close friend and was my own intimate acquaintance (for a few short months at least), and professed a great attachment to my boy – and when he passes the house, so many scores of miles from his home, he declines to look in for fear of intruding!'

'Mr Markham is over modest,' observed Mrs Maxwell.

'Over ceremonious rather,' said her niece – 'over – well, it's no matter.' And turning from me, she seated herself in a chair beside the table, and pulling a book to her by the cover, began to turn over the leaves in an energetic kind of abstraction.

'If I had known,' said I, 'that you would have honoured me by remembering me as an intimate acquaintance, I most likely should not have denied myself the pleasure of calling upon you, but I thought you had forgotten me long ago.'

'You judged of others by yourself,' muttered she without raising her eyes from the book, but reddening as she spoke and hastily turning over a dozen leaves at once.

There was a pause of which Arthur thought he might venture to avail himself to introduce his handsome young setter and show me how wonderfully it was grown and improved, and to ask after the welfare of its father Sancho. Mrs Maxwell then withdrew to take off her things. Helen immediately pushed the book from her and after silently surveying her son, his friend, and his dog for a few moments, she dismissed the former from the room under pretence of wishing him to fetch his last new book to show me. The child obeyed with alacrity; but I continued caressing the dog. The silence might have lasted till its master's return had it depended on me to break it, but, in half a minute or less, my hostess impatiently rose, and taking her former station on the rug between me and the chimney corner, earnestly exclaimed –

'Gilbert, what *is* the matter with you? – why are you so changed? – It is a very indiscreet question I know,' she hastened to add: 'perhaps, a very rude one – don't answer it if you think so – but I hate mysteries and concealments.'

'I am not changed, Helen – unfortunately I am as keen and passionate as ever – it is not I, it is circumstances that are changed.'

'What circumstances? *Do* tell me!' Her cheek was blanched with the very anguish of anxiety – could it be with the fear that I had rashly pledged my faith to another?

'I'll tell you at once,' said I. 'I will confess that I came here for the purpose of seeing you (not without some monitory misgivings at my own presumption, and fears that I should be as little welcome as expected when I came), but I did not know that this estate was yours, until enlightened on the subject of your inheritance by the conversation of two fellow passengers in the last stage of my journey; and then, I saw at once the folly of the hopes I had cherished and the madness of retaining them a moment longer; and though I alighted at your gates, I determined not to enter within them; I lingered a few minutes to see the place, but was fully resolved to return to M— without seeing its mistress.'

'And if my aunt and I had not been just returning from our

morning drive, I should have seen and heard no more of you?'

'I thought it would be better for both that we should not meet,' replied I as calmly as I could, but not daring to speak above my breath from conscious inability to steady my voice, and not daring to look in her face lest my firmness should forsake me altogether: 'I thought an interview would only disturb your peace and madden me. But I am glad, now, of this opportunity of seeing you once more and knowing that you have not forgotten me, and of assuring you that I shall never cease to remember you.'

There was a moment's pause. Mrs Huntingdon moved away, and stood in the recess of the window. Did she regard this as an intimation that modesty alone prevented me from asking her hand? and was she considering how to repulse me with the smallest injury to my feelings? Before I could speak to relieve her from such a perplexity, she broke the silence herself by suddenly turning towards me and observing –

'You might have had such an opportunity before – as far I mean as regards assuring me of your kindly recollections, and yourself of mine, if you had written to me.'

'I would have done so, but I did not know your address, and did not like to ask your brother, because I thought he would object to my writing – but this would not have deterred me for a moment, if I could have ventured to believe that you expected to hear from me, or even wasted a thought upon your unhappy friend; but your silence naturally led me to conclude myself forgotten.'

'Did you expect me to write to *you* then?'

'No, Helen – Mrs Huntingdon,' said I, blushing at the implied imputation, 'Certainly not; but if you had sent me a message through your brother, or even asked him about me now and then –'

'I did ask about you, frequently. I was not going to do more,' continued she, smiling, 'so long as you continued to restrict yourself to a few polite enquiries about my health.'

'Your brother never told me that you had mentioned my name.'

'Did you ever ask him?'

'No; for I saw he did not wish to be questioned about you, or to afford the slightest encouragement or assistance to my too obstinate attachment.' Helen did not reply. 'And he was perfectly right,' added I. But she remained in silence looking out upon the snowy lawn. 'Oh, I will relieve her of my presence!' thought I; and immediately I rose and advanced to take leave, with a most heroic resolution – but pride was at the bottom of it, or it could not have carried me through.

'Are you going already?' said she, taking the hand I offered, and not immediately letting it go.

'Why should I stay any longer?'

'Wait till Arthur comes, at least.'

Only too glad to obey, I stood and leant against the opposite side of the window.

'You told me you were not changed,' said my companion: 'you *are* – very much so.'

'No, Mrs Huntingdon, I only *ought* to be.'

'Do you mean to maintain that you have the same regard for me that you had when last we met?'

'I have, but it would be wrong to talk of it now.'

'It was wrong to talk of it *then*, Gilbert; it would *not* now – unless to do so would be to violate the truth.'

I was too much agitated to speak; but, without waiting for an answer, she turned away her glistening eye and crimson cheek, and threw up the window and looked out, whether to calm her own excited feelings or to relieve her embarrassment, – or only to pluck that beautiful half-blown Christmas rose that grew upon the little shrub without, just peeping from the snow, that had hitherto, no doubt, defended it from the frost, and was now melting away in the sun. Pluck it however, she did, and having gently dashed the glittering powder from its leaves, approached it to her lips and said, –

'This rose is not so fragrant as a summer flower, but it has stood through hardships none of *them* could bear: the cold rain of winter has sufficed to nourish it, and its faint sun to warm it; the bleak winds have not blanched it, or broken its stem, and the keen frost has not blighted it. Look, Gilbert, it is still fresh and blooming as a flower can be, with the cold snow even now on its petals. – Will you have it?'

I held out my hand: I dared not speak lest my emotion should over-master me. She laid the rose across my palm, but I scarcely closed my fingers upon it, so deeply was I absorbed in thinking what might be the meaning of her words, and what I ought to do or say upon the occasion; whether to give way to my feelings or restrain them still. Misconstruing this hesitation into indifference – or reluctance even – to accept her gift, Helen suddenly snatched it from my hand, threw it out on to the snow, shut down the window with an emphasis, and withdrew to the fire.

'Helen! what means this?' I cried, electrified at this startling change in her demeanour.

'You did not understand my gift,' said she, – 'or, what is worse, you despised it: I'm sorry I gave it you; but since I did make such a mistake, the only remedy I could think of, was to take it away.'

'You misunderstood me, cruelly,' I replied, and in a minute I had opened the window again, leaped out, picked up the flower, brought it in, and presented it to her, imploring her to give it me again, and I would keep it for ever for her sake, and prize it more highly than anything in the world I possessed.

'And will this content you?' said she as she took it in her hand.

'It shall,' I answered.

'There, then; take it.'

I pressed it earnestly to my lips, and put it in my bosom, Mrs Huntingdon looking on with a half sarcastic smile.

'Now, are you going?' said she.

'I will if – if I must.'

'You *are* changed,' persisted she – 'you are grown either very proud or very indifferent.'

'I am neither, Helen – Mrs Huntingdon. If you could see my heart –'

'You *must* be one, – if not both. And why Mrs Huntingdon? – why not Helen, as before?'

'Helen, then – dear Helen!' I murmured. I was in an agony of mingled love, hope, delight, uncertainty, and suspense.

'The rose I gave you was an emblem of my heart,' said she; 'would you take it away and leave me here alone?'

'Would you give me your hand too, if I asked it?'

'Have I not said enough?' she answered with a most enchanting smile. I snatched her hand and would have fervently kissed it, but suddenly checked myself and said, –

'But have you considered the consequences?'

'Hardly, I think, or I should not have offered myself to one too proud to take me, or too indifferent to make his affection outweigh my worldly goods.'

Stupid blockhead that I was! – I trembled to clasp her in my arms, but dared not believe in so much joy,[2] and yet restrained myself to say, –

'But if you *should* repent!'

'It would be your fault,' she replied: 'I never shall, unless you bitterly disappoint me. If you have not sufficient confidence in my affection to believe this, let me alone.'

'My darling angel – my *own* Helen,' cried I, now passionately kissing the hand I still retained, and throwing my left arm around her, 'you never shall repent, if it depend on me alone. – But have you thought of your aunt?' I trembled for the answer and clasped her closer to my heart in the instinctive dread of losing my new-found treasure.

'My aunt must not know of it yet,' said she. 'She would think it a rash, wild step, because she could not imagine how well I know you; but she must know you herself, and learn to like you. You must leave us now, after lunch, and come again in spring, and make a longer stay, and cultivate her acquaintance; and I know you will like each other.'

'And then you will be mine,' said I printing a kiss upon her lips, and another, and another – for I was as daring and impetuous now as I had been backward and constrained before.

'No – in another year,' replied she, gently disengaging herself from my embrace, but still fondly clasping my hand.

'Another year! Oh, Helen, I could not wait so long!'

'Where is your fidelity?'

'I mean I could not endure the misery of so long a separation.'

'It would not be a separation: we will write every day; my spirit shall be always with you; and sometimes you shall see me with your bodily eye. I will not be such a hypocrite as to pretend that I desire to wait so long myself, but as my marriage is to please myself alone, I ought to consult my friends about the time of it.'

'Your friends will disapprove.'

'They will not greatly disapprove, dear Gilbert,' said she, earnestly kissing my hand – 'they cannot, when they know you – or if they could, they would not be true friends; I should not care for their estrangement. – Now are you satisfied?' She looked up in my face with a smile of ineffable tenderness.

'Can I be otherwise, with your love? And you *do* love me, Helen?' said I, not doubting the fact, but wishing to hear it confirmed by her own acknowledgement.

'If you loved as *I* do,' she earnestly replied, 'you would not have so nearly lost me – these scruples of false delicacy and pride would never thus have troubled you – you would have seen that the greatest worldly distinctions and discrepancies of rank, birth, and fortune are as dust in the balance compared with the unity of accordant thoughts and feelings, and truly loving, sympathizing hearts and souls.'

'But this is too much happiness,' said I, embracing her again; 'I have not deserved it Helen – I dare not believe in such felicity: and the longer I have to wait, the greater will be my dread that something will intervene to snatch you from me – and think, a thousand things may happen in a year! – I shall be in one long fever of restless terror and impatience all the time. And besides, winter is such a dreary season.'

'I thought so too,' replied she gravely: 'I would not be married in winter – in December, at least,' she added with a shudder – for in that month had occurred both the ill-starred marriage that had bound her to her former husband and the terrible death that released her – 'and therefore, I said another year in spring.'

'*Next* spring.'

'No, no – next autumn, perhaps.'

'Summer, then.'

'Well, the close of summer. There now! be satisfied.'

While she was speaking, Arthur re-entered the room – good boy for keeping out so long.

'Mamma, I couldn't find the book in either of the places you told me to look for it,' (there was a conscious something in mamma's smile that seemed to say, 'No, dear, I knew you could not,') 'but Rachel got it for me at last. Look, Mr Markham, a natural history with all kinds of birds and beasts in it, and the reading as nice as the pictures!'

In great good-humour, I sat down to examine the book and drew the little fellow between my knees. Had he come a minute before, I should have received him less graciously, but now I affectionately stroked his curling locks, and even kissed his ivory forehead: he was my own Helen's son, and therefore mine; and as such I have ever since regarded him. That pretty child is now a fine young man: he has realized his mother's brightest expectations, and is at present residing in Grassdale Manor with his young wife, the merry little Helen Hattersley, of yore.

I had not looked through half the book, before Mrs Maxwell appeared to invite me into the other room to lunch. That lady's cool, distant manners rather chilled me at first; but I did my best to propitiate her, and not entirely without success I think, even in that first short visit; for when I talked cheerfully to her, she gradually became more kind and cordial, and when I departed she bade me a gracious adieu, hoping erelong to have the pleasure of seeing me again.

'But you must not go till you have seen the conservatory, my aunt's winter garden,' said Helen, as I advanced to take leave of her, with as much philosophy and self-command as I could summon to my aid.

I gladly availed myself of such a respite, and followed her into a large and beautiful conservatory, plentifully furnished with flowers, considering the season – but of course, I had little attention to spare for *them*. It was not however for any tender colloquy that my companion had brought me there: –

'My aunt is particularly fond of flowers,' she observed, 'and she is fond of Staningley too: I brought you here to offer a petition in her behalf that this may be her home as long as she lives, and – if it be not our home likewise – that I may often see her and be with her; for I fear she will be sorry to lose me; and, though she leads a retired and contemplative life, she is apt to get low-spirited if left too much alone.'

'By all means, dearest Helen! – do what you will with your own. I should not dream of wishing your aunt to leave the place under any circumstances; and we will live either here or elsewhere as you and she may determine, and you shall see her as often as you like. I know she must be pained to part with you, and I am willing to make any reparation in my power. I love her for your sake, and her happiness shall be as dear to me as that of my own mother.'

'Thank you, darling! you shall have a kiss for that. Goodbye. There now – there Gilbert – let me go – here's Arthur, don't astonish his infantile brain with your madness.'

But it is time to bring my narrative to a close – anyone but you would say I had made it too long already; but for *your* satisfaction, I will add a few words more; because I know you will have a fellow-feeling for the old lady, and will wish to know the last of her history. I did come again in spring, and agreeably to Helen's injunctions, did my best to cultivate her acquaintance. She received me very kindly, having been doubtless already prepared to think highly of my character, by her niece's too favourable report. I turned my best side out of course, and we got along marvellously well together. When my ambitious intentions were made known to her, she took it more sensibly than I had ventured to hope. Her only remark on the subject, in my hearing, was –

'And so Mr Markham, you are going to rob me of my niece I understand. Well! I hope God will prosper your union, and make my dear girl happy at last. Could she have been contented to remain single, I own I should have been better satisfied; but if she must marry again, I know of no one, now living and of a suitable age, to whom I would more willingly resign her than yourself, or who would be more likely to appreciate her worth and make her truly happy, as far as I can tell.'

Of course I was delighted with the compliment, and hoped to show her she was not mistaken in her favourable judgment.

'I have, however one request to offer,' continued she. 'It seems I am still to look on Staningley as my home: I wish you to make it yours likewise, for Helen is attached to the place and to me – as I am to her. There are painful associations connected with Grassdale, which she cannot easily overcome; and I shall not molest you with my company or interference here: I am a very quiet person, and shall keep my own apartments and attend to my own concerns, and only see you now and then.'

Of course I most readily consented to this; and we lived in the greatest harmony with our dear aunt until the day of her death, which melancholy event took place a few years after – melancholy, not to herself (for it came quietly upon her, and she was glad to reach her journey's end), but only to the few loving friends and grateful dependants she left behind.

To return, however, to my own affairs: I was married in summer, on a glorious August morning. It took the whole eight months, and all Helen's kindness and goodness to boot, to overcome my mother's prejudices against my bride elect, and to reconcile her to the idea of my leaving Linden-Car[3] and living so far away. Yet she was gratified at her son's good fortune after all, and proudly attributed it all to his own superior merits and endowments. I bequeathed the farm to Fergus,[4] with better hopes of its prosperity than I should have had a year ago under similar circumstances; for he had lately fallen in love with the vicar of L—'s eldest daughter, a lady whose superiority had roused his latent virtues and stimulated him to the most surprising exertions, not only to gain her affection and esteem, and to obtain a fortune sufficient to enable him to aspire to her hand, but to render himself worthy of her, in his own eyes, as well as in those of her parents; and in the end he was successful, as you already know. As for myself, I need not tell you how happily my Helen and I have lived and loved together, and how blessed we still are in each other's society, and in the promising young scions that are growing up about us. We are just now looking forward to the advent of you and Rose, for the time of your annual visit draws nigh, when you must leave your dusty, smoky, noisy, toiling, striving city for a season of invigorating relaxation and social retirement with us.

Till then, farewell,

GILBERT MARKHAM

Staningley, June 10th, 1847.[5]

THE END

NOTES

All biblical references are to the Authorized Version (1611). Shakespeare references are to the Arden Shakespeare. References to novels are (unless otherwise indicated) made to Penguin editions. Anne Brontë's poetry is referred to in the edition, *The Poems of Anne Brontë*, ed. Edward Chitham (Macmillan, 1979); Emily Brontë's poetry is referred to in C. W. Hatfield's edition, *The Complete Poems of Emily Jane Brontë* (Columbia University Press, 1941). References to John Bunyan's *The Pilgrim's Progress* are to the edition by Roger Sharrock (Penguin, 1965); references to John Milton's *Paradise Lost* are to the edition by Alastair Fowler (Longman, 1968).

The following abbreviations have been used to frequently cited works:

CH: *The Brontës: The Critical Heritage*, ed. Miriam Allott (Routledge & Kegan Paul, 1974).

Hargreaves: *The Tenant of Wildfell Hall*, ed. G. D. Hargreaves and introduced by Winifred Gérin (Penguin, 1979).

OED: *The Oxford English Dictionary*, ed. Sir James Murray et al. (OUP, 1888–1928).

Life: Edward Chitham, *A Life of Anne Brontë* (Blackwell, 1991).

Rosengarten: *The Tenant of Wildfell Hall*, ed. Herbert Rosengarten and introduced by Margaret Smith (OUP, 1992).

SHLL: 'The Shakespeare Head Press Brontë': *The Brontës, Their Lives, Friendships and Correspondence*, 4 vols. (Blackwell, 1933, reissued 1980).

PREFACE TO THE SECOND EDITION

1. (p. 3) *success of the present work*: *The Tenant of Wildfell Hall* was a success by comparison with *Agnes Grey*, which had been published jointly as part of a three-volume work with Emily Brontë's *Wuthering Heights* in late 1847 by T. C. Newby. The authors had subsidized publication by £50. At

least 250 copies of 500 copies of the first edition of *Wildfell Hall* were sold: in all, Anne received £50 for the work. As three-volume novels sold at a retail price of £1. 11s. 6d. (perhaps £10 by today's rates), only circulating lending libraries and affluent private subscribers could afford to buy them. Unsold sheets of the first edition seem to have been sold as the 'second edition', with the addition of a Preface, perhaps in order to boost sales by implying demand.

2. (p. 3) *praises it has elicited ... it has been censured*: in fact praise and censure were often vehemently mingled, as critics struggled to assimilate their admiration for the 'power, effect, and ... nature' of Acton Bell's work with 'his' disposition to the savage, brutal and coarse (*Spectator*, 8 July 1848, 21, pp. 662–3; in *CH*, p. 250).

3. (p. 3) *it needs some courage to dive for it ... the clearance she effects*: the eccentric pair of comparisons for the novelist's liability to be abused by society for truth-telling is typically an androgynous pairing: a male diver, stirring up the mud from which he has salvaged the emblematic 'jewel', truth, is succeeded by an honest-to-goodness cleaning woman, whose dust-raising activities in the 'careless bachelor's apartment' are scorned because they reveal the filthy conditions in which privileged males live. This wittily preludes the major theme of male debauch. Chitham (*Life*, p. 168) notes that the Parsonage well had been cleansed in September 1847 of effluent, no doubt odoriferous.

4. (p. 4) *accused of extravagant over-colouring*: evidence of such an accusation is hard to find. Normally Anne Brontë's plain realism was praised, and the statement in *Atlas* (22 January 1948; *CH*, p. 232) cited by Hargreaves ('Preface', n. 3) that *Agnes Grey* is 'not wholly free from exaggeration' is obviously ironic, since it goes on '(there are some detestable young ladies in it)' and concludes by insisting that the novel 'does not offend by any startling improbabilities'.

5. (p. 4) *a morbid love of the coarse, if not of the brutal*: *Spectator*, 8 July 1848 (*CH*, p. 250).

6. (p. 4) *'Peace, peace,' when there is no peace*: this quotation from Jeremiah 8:11 is apocalyptic, denouncing those who 'have healed the hurt of the daughter of my people slightly, saying, Peace, peace; when there is no peace'. Anne Brontë, in accusing her society of wilfully exposing its daughters and sons to outrage, also invokes the prophet's wrath on society's silences.

7. (p. 5) *Such humble talents*: refers to the parable of the talents in Matthew 25 and Luke 19. Anne Brontë, fearful of hiding her gifts like the 'wicked and slothful servant' (Matthew 25:26) who wasted his talent (originally, a sum of

money), represents the writing of her narrative as a spiritual duty, which to have left undone would have incurred eternal consequences.

8. (p. 5) *Respecting the author's identity*: the Brontë sisters' male-sounding pseudonyms – Currer, Ellis and Acton Bell – were intended to secure a fair hearing against the double standard of criticism pertaining for male and female authors. The names also generated confusion. Emily's and Anne's publisher, T. C. Newby, attempted to cash in on the success of Charlotte's *Jane Eyre* by claiming that the three Bells were really one person. Charlotte and Anne accordingly visited the former's publisher, Smith, Elder, in London, during the month in which the Preface was written, to identify themselves. See the vivid account in Lyndall Gordon's *Charlotte Brontë: A Passionate Life* (Chatto & Windus, 1994), pp. 166–74.

VOLUME I

1. (p. 9) *TO J. HALFORD, ESQ.*: Halford, the first of the five 'H' characters in *Wildfell Hall* (Helen, Huntingdon, Hattersley, Hargrave), has no function other than to receive Markham's letters and never appears in person. His name is probably a relic of Anne's participation in the Brontës' childhood games, 'Sir Henry Halford', being one of the 'chief men' named as hers in the 'Play of the Islanders' of 1827, when she was seven (see Christine Alexander, *The Early Writings of Charlotte Brontë* (Blackwell, 1983), Ch. 5). Halford's imputed character, of grumpy reserve, however, meshes in with Anne Brontë's notion of a male norm.

CHAPTER I

1. (p. 11) *burying my talent . . . hiding my light under a bushel*: Matthew 25:25 and 5:15, and see Preface, n. 7. The parental dispute about Gilbert's profession is an authorial attempt to render a farmer culturally eligible for Helen's hand.

2. (p. 11) *looking neither to the right hand nor to the left*: Numbers 20:17, Deuteronomy 2:27, 5:32. Gilbert's background transmits conservative and patriarchal values, from which he, however, is shown to deviate.

3. (p. 12) *surtout*: a man's top-coat.

4. (p. 14) *Wildfell Hall*: Chitham describes Anne Brontë's house, Wildfell Hall, as 'mocking' Emily's Wuthering Heights by deromanticizing it and its mysterious inmate (*Life*, pp. 142–3); it may be more appropriate to think of it as a critical and rational alternative. Located five miles from the sea, which Anne especially loved, it seems to have been imagined as situated near her

personal terrain between Scarborough and Whitby, on the edge of the North Yorkshire moors. Winifred Gérin thought it based on Ponden Hall near Haworth (*Anne Brontë* (Nelson, 1976 edn.), p. 71). Such speculation is inconclusive. We note that Anne introduces the place in a spate of tea-table gossip rather than more portentously, thus domesticating our first view.

5. (p. 15) *every lady ought to be familiar with*: Mrs Markham's busybodying attempt to indoctrinate the newcomer with housewifely arts, which Helen resists, introduces the newcomer in a feminist light, as a strong and independent individual who stands against the norms spelt out, for instance, in the *Saturday Review*: 'Married life is woman's profession; and to this life her training – that of dependence – is modelled' ('Queen Bees or Working Bees?', *Saturday Review* 8 (November 1859), p. 576.)

6. (p. 17) *grim escutcheons*: shields with armorial bearings, indicative of an ancient Wildfell dynasty, now defunct. This family (as we learn later) may be Helen's maternal ancestry.

7. (p. 19) *shovel hat*: hard, broad-brimmed clerical hat.

8. (p. 19) *How doth the little busy bee*: first line of Isaac Watts's 'Against Idleness and Mischief', from *Divine Songs for ... the Use of Children* (1715), a traditional favourite amongst parents if not children, who had to learn it by heart in order to profit by the bee's example, so as to 'Improve each shining hour' through industrious enterprise. This furnishes the first allusion to the debate about education, in the comic key.

9. (p. 19) *old Eli, or David and Absalom*: Eli, judge and high priest in 1 Samuel 2–4, indulged his sons and forfeited his life; Absalom rebelled against David (2 Samuel 13–18), but at his death the father was inconsolable.

10. (p. 20) *were assured it was all fancy*: Mr Millward's dietary preoccupation seems a reversal of Jane Austen's Mr Woodhouse's nervous commendation of thin gruel and soft-boiled eggs in minute quantities in *Emma* (1815). The Markham narrative includes social comedy in the tradition of Austen, an author who was depreciated by Charlotte Brontë ('the Passions are perfectly unknown' (to Miss Austen), Letter to W. S. Williams, 12 April 1850, *SHLL*, Vol. 3, p. 99).

CHAPTER 2

1. (p. 22) *the light of your countenance*: Psalms 4:6, a flippant allusion. Markham's scriptural allusions tend to be glib and arbitrary until his narrative has been touched by Helen's influence.

2. (p. 22) *Linden-Car*: 'Linden' from lime-trees; 'car' (-'carr' or -'ker') in

northern dialect denotes marsh or bog (Kenneth Cameron, *English Place-Names* (Batsford, 1961), p. 214).

3. (p. 22) *Wildfell, the wildest and the loftiest eminence in our neighbourhood*: although Anne Brontë's style in describing Wildfell and the hall becomes itself rather wild, straining for effect in long, tortuous sentences connected by numerous dashes, it is notable that the narrative eye remains concerned with the agricultural properties and use of the land (or the lack); the prevalence of game; the territory as the property of farmer or land-owner: a perspective suited to Markham's calling.

4. (p. 22) *mansion of the Elizabethan era*: somewhat over half a century younger than Wuthering Heights, which bears the date 1500. For fuller consideration, see Introduction, pp. ix–xi.

5. (p. 23) *the shapes he chose to give them*: the topiary details add a unique twist to the theme of recidivism played out both by *Wildfell Hall* and *Wuthering Heights* (see S. Davies, *Emily Brontë* (Harvester Wheatsheaf, etc., 1988), pp. 130–54). Nature, 'tortured' to an art which represents nature (the boxwood swan, the lion) is in process of reverting to nature. However, swan and lion belong with laurel towers and fabricated warrior as armorial tributes to dynasty – a dynasty which has died out, subverted by nature. For Emily Brontë's mystery, Anne Brontë substitutes grotesquerie, in a chaotic vision in which human aspirations are in process of recrudescence, paralleling the disintegration in the ethical sphere of the novel: but the author fails to develop these implications.

6. (p. 23) *either in heaven or earth . . . under the earth*: Exodus 20:4. The source emphasizes the impiety of graven images, underlying the 'vanity' theme exemplified in the ruined garden.

7. (p. 23) *ghostly legends*: the first edition has 'legions'.

8. (p. 24) *the upper portion of a diminutive ivory nose*: the stylized but tender description of the gradually emergent child, preluding the arrival of his mother into the reader's ken, typifies Anne Brontë's affection for children and her longing for a baby of her own. The mother-child bond haunts the poetry, both Gondal and personal lyrics (e.g., 'Verses to a Child' (1838) in which the father has abandoned wife and child; 'Dreams' (1845): 'Then I may cherish at my breast / An infant's form beloved and fair . . .' (5–6)). In *Agnes Grey*, however, Anne Brontë showed an unsentimental awareness of original and conditioned sin in children.

9. (p. 24) *like Mahomet . . . since the mountain would not come to him*: proverbial. *OED* quotes Francis Bacon's essay, 'Of Boldness': 'If the hill will not come to Mahomet, Mahomet will go to the hill.'

10. (p. 24) *by the frock*: this detail points to the tender but transitional age of

the child. Boys were dressed as girls and belonged to the female world until initiation at five or six into the patriarchal hierarchy. Helen attempts to keep her son as a 'mother's boy' – condemned as effeminization and retardation by the community but in fact a radical attempt to save him from the evils of the men's world.

11. (p. 25) *roused my corruption*: i.e., the unregenerate 'old Adam' in Markham's male (and here, sexual) nature. The arousing 'proud, chilly look' seems to have been a feature of Gondal females, written into *Wuthering Heights* as the first Catherine's imperious manners and the second Catherine's scowls.

12. (p. 26) *the mania for Berlin wools*: 'a fine dyed wool used for knitting, tapestry, and the like' (*OED*). A perfunctory attempt to imply a historical period.

CHAPTER 3

1. (p. 29) *Ruin, Mrs Markham?*: Helen's emphasis on the word 'ruin' points up the ironic narrative mode in foregrounding key-words whose meaning will lie at the centre of the moral drama.

2. (p. 29) *the 'Farmer's Magazine'*: we must presume this to be an old copy of *The Farmer's Magazine ... Exclusively Devoted to Agriculture, and Rural Affairs*, published in Edinburgh but discontinued in 1825.

3. (p. 31) *done what I could to make him hate them*: Anne Brontë's novel is an early example of the 'temperance novel', whose best-known protagonist was Mrs Henry Wood, who won £100 for her novel *Danesbury House* in a Temperance League competition in 1860. Anne's presentation of the subject in a society where alcohol addiction was commonplace opens the subject to rational debate: Mrs Henry Wood argues that *all* who are not taught to abhor alcohol in childhood are due for damnation. A multitude of wine- and gin-lovers are shown dying horrible deaths or being saved by water-loving wives, or the factory-owner, who opens a coffee-shop to wean his workers from liquor. *Wildfell Hall* is exclusively concerned with abuse amongst the 'genteel' classes.

4. (p. 31) *What is it that constitutes virtue, Mrs Graham?*: Markham recites the essence of the doctrine of experience and choice famously expounded in Milton's *Areopagitica* (1644): 'If every action which is good, or evill in man at ripe years, were to be under pittance, and prescription, and compulsion, what were vertue but a name ... when God gave him reason, he gave him freedom to choose, for reason is but choosing' (*Complete Prose Works*, Vol. 2, ed. Ernest Sirluck (Yale University Press, 1959), p. 527). Anne Brontë's position was a modified version of this; but her experience of the corruption

latent in human nature taught her caution, and *Wildfell Hall* multiplies instances of men incapable of resisting temptation, however privileged their position. This is why Helen attempts behavioural immunization of her son.

5. (p. 32) *hitherto been able to muster against them*: Helen's confession of personal fallibility stokes the reader's curiosity (what is her history?) and reflects Anne Brontë's own practice of rigorous self-questioning and self-criticism, as revealed in the poetry ('Despondency': 'how many times / My feet have gone astray' (25–6)). Her concern for the young in a world of betrayal is most powerfully stated in 'Self–Communion': 'How shall it centre so much trust / Where truth maintains so little sway . . .?' (61–2).

6. (p. 33) *a mere Miss Nancy*: in West Riding dialect, an effeminate man, still current in 'nancy-boy', with homosexual aspersion. Anne Brontë highlights the function of ridicule in social control, especially in the construction of 'male' attitudes and behaviour by making a fool of men's so-called 'female' characteristics.

7. (p. 33) *get Mr Millward to talk to you about it*: Anne Brontë, herself a clergyman's daughter, satirically refuses the authority of the church in adjudicating for the individual conscience – a strongly Protestant attitude held in common with her sisters.

8. (p. 33) *though one rose from the dead*: Luke 16:31.

9. (p. 33) *the same argument with regard to a girl*: the chapter now becomes a full-scale debate on the double standard for male and female education, conducted as a dialectic, with Helen challenging Markham with the logical (and insulting) implications of his assumptions.

10. (p. 34) *to teach her how to sin is at once*: The first edition has 'to teach her how to sin, is it at once'. I accept Hargreaves's emendation of this convoluted, angry speech, in which either Anne Brontë or the compositor had become hopelessly entangled.

11. (p. 35) *incomprehensible discourse*: the excess manifested in Helen's attitude may imply her departure from reason and authorial backing, despite the fact that Helen's project to warn the young of snares is identical with that of the novelist in the Preface.

12. (p. 36) *spoiled by my mother and sister, and some other ladies of my acquaintance*: the narrator undermines the validity of the norms maintained by his own household against the stranger's feminism in a final ironic *coup* for the author and the newcomer.

CHAPTER 4

1. (p. 37) *to do what their soul abhorred*: a characteristically frivolous allusion to

Scripture by Markham (Psalms 107:18), which, however, carries an ironic resonance of the debate on aversion-therapy from the previous chapter.

2. (p. 38) *a crack*: brisk chat, or jest.

3. (p. 42) *the oracle with a Jove-like nod*: Jove (Zeus, or Jupiter) was the authoritarian father-god of classical mythology, not without bibulous and socializing tendencies (hence, 'jovial'). Mr Millward comically pontificates over the gathering, his prejudices and inclinations all dignified to oracular status by virtue of his priestly office.

4. (p. 42) (... *Mr Lawrence's father had shortened his days by intemperance*): the significance of this fact, slipped in parenthetically, becomes clear later when we learn of Arthur's father's alcoholism: if the condition is hereditary, he stands to inherit the tendency on both sides, accounting for the intensity of Helen's anxiety. George Eliot alludes to 'hereditary constitutional craving' for drugs and laudanum in *Middlemarch* (1871–2), Ch. 66.

5. (p. 43) *laudanum*: a derivative of opium used for medical purposes, freely available from pharmacies. Branwell Brontë's addiction to laudanum put him in the company of the great Romantic addicts, Coleridge and De Quincey, whose *Confessions of an English Opium-Eater* (1822) was a favourite book of the four children. See Daphne du Maurier, *The Infernal World of Branwell Brontë* (Gollancz, 1960), pp. 179–80. Although alcohol then as now was socially acceptable, Lawrence is able to gain credit for his argument by paralleling alcohol with opium, whose dangerous and antisocial properties were recognized. His decline of a second glass quietly reinforces the distrust of alcohol he shares with Helen.

6. (p. 44) *evolutions*: 'a wheeling about, a movement in dancing' (*OED*).

7. (p. 44) *I don't allow that!*: Mr Millward displays a provincial and puritanical antagonism to the waltz, a late eighteenth-century dance in triple time, of German origin, which swept Europe in the early nineteenth century. Its movements and the embrace of partners were considered sensual.

8. (p. 44) *Let your moderation be known unto all men!*: Philippians 4:5.

CHAPTER 5

1. (p. 46) *a painter's easel*: Anne Brontë's heroine is a professional artist, a painter in a period where women painters were rare, for they could acquire no training. Branwell Brontë had attempted to enter the Royal Academy Schools and had set up as a portrait painter in Bradford, neither of which was a possibility for a young woman: Anne here usurps this privilege for her heroine. However, although Anne Brontë makes her *alter ego* practise a different art from her own as novelist, she herself was competent at drawing

in pencil and ink and water-colour: her sketches survive from the age of nine (see Chitham, *Life*, p. 29). She tended to prettify her subjects, which, like Helen's, were chiefly portraits, landscapes and buildings, both representational and imagined. She had a light, soft touch with the pencil, and a classicizing tendency. In her novels, she is fond of word-painting descriptions of localities and seasons. Helen, as an artist on a larger scale than anything to which Anne could aspire, uses the 'male' oils in which Branwell had received training. See Gérin, *Branwell Brontë*, p. 58.

2. (p. 45) *the portrait of a gentleman*: the method of disclosure through a portrait to which the narrator responds is analogous with Lockwood's viewing of Edgar Linton's portrait in *Wuthering Heights*, Ch. 8: 'a soft-featured face ... The long light hair curled slightly on the temples; the eyes were large and serious; the figure almost too graceful'. The description of the representation of Arthur Huntingdon is revealing of the levity, narcissicism, lively sensuality and personal beauty of its as yet unknown subject.

3. (p. 49) *trespassed too much upon the forehead*: the phrasing hints subtly towards the trespasses committed by the sexually attractive and irresponsible Huntingdon.

4. (p. 50) *Let not the sun go down upon your wrath*: Ephesians 4:26.

CHAPTER 6

1. (p. 51) *Miss Millward*: Mary Millward, since 'Miss' with surname signifies the precedence of the eldest daughter. Hence, Charlotte was 'Miss Brontë', Anne merely 'Miss Anne Brontë'.

2. (p. 53) *to cure a greater evil by a less*: Markham's thought processes are made to betray a shallowness and manipulativeness which render it difficult for the reader to consider him as seriously eligible for the strong-minded heroine. Here he proposes to flirt with Helen on homoeopathic principles, curing himself of one source of malaise (Eliza) by taking it in a smaller dose (Helen). While this attitude is essentially misogynistic, and Anne Brontë is caustic about male manipulation of women's affections, it is also in this case psychologically unconvincing, sitting ill with his supposed sterling qualities, culture and feminist consciousness.

3. (p. 55) *'the clear, cold, eve' was fast 'declining'*: not traced.

4. (p. 55) *the gibbous moon*: between half and full moon.

5. (p. 56) *the last atom that breaks the camel's back*: variation of the proverbial 'last straw that breaks the camel's back'.

6. (p. 58) *never know how much I owe you*: by using the male character to present a serious objection to the family's pampering of sons and the

undervaluation of womenfolk, Anne Brontë manoeuvres the reader to consider the harm occasioned to both sexes by the double standard. The good-humoured conservatism of the mother, evidently herself never more than a chattel, is a realistic appraisal of the status quo, and Markham ends the letter by opening out the question to the reader's (Halford's – but also our) experience.

CHAPTER 7

1. (p. 60) *snooking about*: *OED* under snoke: dialect 'to snuff or smell; to go snuffing or smelling (at)'.

2. (p. 60) *with wonderful fluency*: Arthur's prodigious literacy is a tribute to Helen's educational methods.

3. (p. 63) – *Cliffs, full five miles distant*: Chitham (*Life*, p. 145) locates the source in cliffs north of Scarborough which Anne Brontë would have visited whilst accompanying her employers, the Robinsons, on their summer holidays.

4. (p. 65) *the blue sea burst upon our sight*: these passages, as Helen and Markham reach the sea, to which Helen rhapsodically responds, reflect Anne Brontë's own ecstasy at the vision of the sea. *Agnes Grey* ends with a comparable vision of union 'at the edge of the precipice where we stood together watching the splendid sunset mirrored on the restless world of waters at our feet' (Ch. 25). A drawing dated 13 November 1839 shows a young woman looking out to sea against the sunlight which is either fiercely rising or setting. Anne Brontë went to Scarborough in her terminal illness, to die within sight of the sea, which she associated with revival and (twice repeated in the description of Helen's response) 'exhilaration'.

5. (p. 67) *an electric start*: Helen's galvanized reaction expresses her traumatized fear of the penetration of her cover by her husband (though we do not know this yet). Her chosen position at the cliff-edge expresses the danger of her situation and her outstanding courage in meeting it. The two signs (of alarm and strength) are superficially contradictory, heightening the suspense of her as yet untold story.

6. (p. 68) *Miss Millward has many estimable qualities*: Anne Brontë, like George Eliot in the portrait of Mary Garth in *Middlemarch*, reclaims the unglamorous 'Marys' of literature and life, as the salt of the earth, undervalued and exploited by society for their plain usefulness. Markham's recurrently slighting remarks in this chapter reflect poorly on the narrator's taste and judgement.

CHAPTER 8

1. (p. 71) *Marmion*: Sir Walter Scott's *Marmion: A Tale of Flodden Field* (1808), a long balladic narrative poem, beloved by the Brontës as children, which is read and quoted by Jane in Ch. 33 of *Jane Eyre*, and competes with St John Rivers for Jane's attention. Its romantic appeal is anodyne against bad weather: 'I soon forgot storm in music'. Pocket editions were not in fact available in 1828, pointing up Anne Brontë's lack of real concern for historical verisimilitude.

2. (p. 72) *old buck*: 'gay, dashing fellow', from the male of any species, especially deer. This jocose back-slapping idiom represents Anne Brontë's idea of how gentlemen address one another. The author awakens intermittently to the memory of the epistolary device.

CHAPTER 9

1. (p. 81) *like bricks*: with gusto and attack.

2. (p. 81) *don't leave her one stone upon another*: superficially frivolous allusion to Jesus' prediction of the destruction of the Temple in Mark 13:2, extending the brick-hurling metaphor. However, Eliza's stoning of her rival's reputation, which is read as a serious attack upon Helen's honour, is satirically placed by the Gospel text, which insists on the integrity of the temple not built with hands – the faith of the individual.

3. (p. 84) *as it was*: confusingly placed clause, indicating 'even so' (i.e., despite the fact that Markham manifests himself at the last minute).

4. (p. 85) *over head and ears*: the first and second editions have 'head of ears': amended here in conformity with standard usage (*OED*: 'completely immersed').

5. (p. 85) *no good given or received*: the extended objection to 'small talk' and scandal is not simply related to Helen's role as victim of tittle-tattle but the expression of a profound Brontë aversion to vapid small talk without subject-matter. This is satirized in Lockwood's tea-party treat on his first visit to Wuthering Heights (Ch. 1), where surly bad manners are the norm and his attempts to observe etiquette and make polite conversation are violently repulsed.

6. (p. 86) *mere vanity and vexation of spirit*: trivial reference to Ecclesiastes 1:14. However, the 'vanity' theme in relation to social activities and values is central to the novel and to Anne Brontë's didactic poetry (see 'Vanitas Vanitatis' (1845)).

7. (p. 86) *so much pleasure in their toil as I do*: Helen speaks in a very modern-sounding way, as an independent person who expects to have to work for her living, to another working person – against the bias of a society in which women's work was socially suspect for anyone with pretensions to gentility.

CHAPTER 11

1. (p. 94) *I was not indifferent to her*: not as novelistic a circumlocution as Markham implies. The straightforward heroine-narrator of the realistic *Agnes Grey* uses it of Rosalie Murray: 'she is not so indifferent to him as she believes herself to be' (Ch. 14).

2. (p. 95) *she would not be living there by herself*: Anne Brontë exposes the social prejudice against women living independently: the presence of a male 'head of household', whether father, brother or husband, legitimates the woman, placing her in a position of legal or informal 'coverture'.

3. (p. 96) *in the bitterness of my soul*: casual reference to Job 7:11, 10:1.

CHAPTER 12

1. (p. 107) *a torrent of tears*: Markham is unlike the conventional male represented by Halford and Lawrence, in having his emotions very close to the surface. In his present paroxysms he echoes Heathcliff in *Wuthering Heights*, reacting emotionally on what Lyndall Gordon calls 'the Brontë scale' (*Charlotte Brontë: A Passionate Life*, (Chatto & Windus) p. 281).

2. (p. 109) *my angel not my angel, and my friend a fiend incarnate*: this religious phrasing, produced by Markham's inflamed brain under the influence of misconstruction, opens the hellfire theme pursued with bitter irony by the diary section of the novel.

CHAPTER 13

1. (p. 111) *'Shall I because a woman's fair,' etc*: a version of George Wither's seventeenth-century lyric, 'Shall I, wasting in despair, / Die, because a woman's fair?'

2. (p. 113) *vengeably*: 'vengibly' in the first edition. Rare archaic word, used in *Agnes Grey*: 'Miss Matilda, having ... vengeably thumped the piano for an hour' (Ch. 14) – the only instance recorded by *OED* after 1586.

CHAPTER 14

1. (p. 115) *chewing the cud of – bitter fancies*: a rueful variant on Shakespeare's *As You Like It*, IV. iii. 102, 'chewing the food of sweet and bitter fancy'.

2. (p. 116) *savage satisfaction*: the preposterous violence characterizing Markham's behaviour and language to his imagined rival is analogous to the violence staple to *Wuthering Heights*, and the source of the objection taken by reviewers to *Wildfell Hall*'s narrator as one who 'would serve as the ruffian of any other novelist' (E. P. Whipple, 'Novels of the Season', *American Review* 66, October 1848, in *CH*, p. 262), to whose 'brutal temper' Charles Kingsley objected ('Recent Novels', *Fraser's Magazine* 39, April 1849, in *CH*, p. 272).

3. (p. 118) *execrations not loud but deep*: *Macbeth*, V. iii. 27: 'Curses, not loud, but deep'.

4. (p. 118) *taking his rest on the sofa at home*: Markham's emotionally neutral attitude to his deed has a quality of mindless and infantile sadism in common with, e.g., Ch. 17 of *Wuthering Heights*, where, having slit Hindley's artery, Heathcliff kicks, tramples and dashes his enemy's head against the flagstones and then binds his wound 'with brutal roughness, spitting and cursing'. I conjecture a common Gondal source for such material.

CHAPTER 15

1. (p. 123) *bluebells*: Anne Brontë used this word for 'harebells'.

2. (p. 123) *Because, I happened ... I imagine*: this sentence represents an extreme instance of Anne Brontë's idiosyncratic excess and defect in the use of commas. I have not deleted the formally intrusive comma after 'Because', because I have chosen to read it as an emotional notation indicating the staccato breathlessness of speech under high stress; neither have I inserted a comma between 'a trifle more' and 'I imagine', which may therefore represent the outpouring of indignation Anne Brontë intended.

3. (p. 125) *Sir Humphrey Davy's 'Last days of a Philosopher'*: anachronistic, for Humphry Davy's *Consolations in Travel: or The Last Days of a Philosopher* was not published until 1830 – after this fictional event in *Wildfell Hall* (August, 1828).

4. (p. 129) *tore away a few leaves from the end*: i.e., the portion of the diary that would have revealed her feelings for Markham.

CHAPTER 16

1. (p. 130) *June 1st, 1821*: Anne Brontë takes the primary events of the inset diary back to a period within eighteen months of her own birth on 17 January 1820, and within three months of her mother's death on 15 September 1821. This epoch-making period of Anne's entrance into the world of loss becomes the period of her heroine's initiation into the tumult of a world of

corruption. In her late twenties, Anne Brontë is looking back to origins from the position of experience.

2. (p. 131) *till you were asked*: Helen's aunt's statements of the social pieties represent the extreme of conservative dogma concerning female passivity and acquiescence. She is a well-meaning member of the thought-police whose cautionary remarks cannot govern her niece, in part because the prudent good sense they offer is presented in terms bordering on the absurd.

3. (p. 132) *Remember Peter, Helen! Don't boast, but watch*: a reminder of the disciple Peter's frailty, unable to follow Christ's counsel at Gethsemane: 'Watch and pray, that ye enter not into temptation: the spirit indeed is willing, but the flesh is weak' (Matthew 26:41). The sermonical manner of Helen's aunt's speech, touched off by Helen's pert answers, is least calculated to appeal to an eighteen year old. But it is implicitly recognized as a serious and important piece of instruction in which marriage is considered as a spiritual life-or-death issue – as it turns out to be for Helen. This is pointed up by the chapter-title, 'The Warnings of Experience', which focuses on the immemorial incapacity of the young to profit by the experience of the older generation, and the older either to communicate sympathetically with the young or to choose appropriately for them: witness the aunt's pushing of the deadly bore, Mr Boarham.

4. (p. 132) *a worthless reprobate*: a key-word in *Wildfell Hall*, with a double implication, both worldly (a rake, a high-living scoundrel) and spiritual (rejected by God, hardened in sin). From the outset the diary shows itself as a spiritual testament, in which moral and social concerns are also theological issues, of eternal consequence. Helen's light-hearted response shows her to be unaware of the serious drama in which she participates, in which nothing less than the immortal soul is at stake: 'But what are all the poor fools and reprobates to do, aunt?'

5. (p. 134) *Mr Boarham, by name*: it is important to register the low quality of the rival suitors against whose repulsiveness (rendered in Dickensian carica-ture) Arthur Huntingdon's beguiling youth and light-heartedness must seem to Helen irresistible. The loathsome Solmes to whom the Harlowes attempt to marry the heroine of *Clarissa* is a comparable figure, supplied to demonstrate the motivation of virtuous young women drawn to such frivol-ous but attractive males as Huntingdon and Lovelace. Solmes is 'a very narrow mind, and no great capacity ... coarse and indelicate ... rough in his manners ... covetous' (*Clarissa*, Letter 32).

6. (p. 136) *I am an excellent physiognomist*: the Brontës were familiar with theories of physiognomy and phrenology, methods of reading character by study of facial features and head shape. See Ian Jack, 'Phrenology, Physi-

ognomy, and Characterisation in the Novels of Charlotte Brontë', *Brontë Society Transactions* 15, Part 80 (1970), pp. 377–91. Anne Brontë shows small respect for such 'scientific' methods of interpretation, considering them as a sophisticated way of judging by appearances.

7. (p. 136) *Mr Wilmot*: another 'reprobate', perhaps suggested, as was Charlotte's Mr Rochester, by the Restoration libertine poet, John Wilmot, second Earl of Rochester.

8. (p. 139) *grow, live and die in single blessedness*: remembers Theseus's insistence in Shakespeare's *A Midsummer Night's Dream* that Hermia marry Demetrius or enter a cloister, like the rose which 'withering on the virgin thorn, / Grows, lives, and dies, in single blessedness' (I. i. 77–8). Like Hermia, Helen prefers such privation to her detested wooers, and as with Hermia the reader is entirely in sympathy with the girl in her dilemma.

CHAPTER 17

1. (p. 143) *I could not away with*: elliptical use of 'away' as a verb representing a plain-spoken idiom corresponding with the modern 'I could not be doing with him'.

2. (p. 144) *Oh! well, let's have a look at them*: Arthur Huntingdon's speech-patterns are one with his brattishly careless and insolent behaviour-patterns (he slings Milicent's sketches one by one on to the table, without comment) and are symptoms legible to the reader of a contemptible character to which Helen is never wholly blinded. She allows his sexual charm to gild his impudence and levity.

3. (p. 144) *quizzing*: mockery of.

4. (p. 146) *from some purgatorial fiend to an angel of light*: savagely ironical, since this profane 'angel' is destined to lead Helen to hell-on-earth.

5. (p. 146) *a splendid painting of Vandyke's*: the ownership of such a picture by the great Flemish artist, Sir Anthony Vandyke (1599–1641), court-painter to King Charles I, makes Wilmot a fabulously wealthy member of the patrician classes. Helen is moving amongst the 'best' circles of her time.

6. (p. 146) *How do you regard me?*: In fishing for a declaration of feeling from an unattached young woman, Huntingdon is violating the social code and inviting Helen to do likewise. Manoeuvring her into dangerous positions, outside the social proprieties, he evidently enjoys the power of exposing her to struggle between feeling and duty.

7. (p. 147) *maledictions against his evil angel*: the ironic 'morality' framework in Ch. 17, pointed up by the predominance of unmediated dialogue, is brought into blackly comic relief by the interposition of the evil angel's evil angel

(i.e., the good angel, Helen's aunt). Huntingdon's 'maledictions', which could not have been minted in Heaven, exemplify the 'bad speech' he has learnt in a depraved society and which will issue in whole dictionaries of curses later in the novel.

8. (p. 147) *that shocking colour*: the blush of sexual arousal, complicated by rage. Huntingdon has marked Helen out from the assembly and her aunt ironically only reinforces the effect.

9. (p. 148) *someone to advise him, and remind him of what is right*: Anne Brontë begins the work of debunking the myth of woman as redemptive agent, empowered by her 'purity' to improve the morals of her menfolk, as celebrated in many novels of the period, e.g., in Charlotte Yonge's *Heartsease: or The Brother's Wife* (1854), whose heroine Violet goes about 'softening, healing, guarding, stirring up the saving part of each one's disposition' (Ch. 17).

10. (p. 150) *if I hate the sins I love the sinner*: theological commonplace, susceptible of casuistical interpretation. See Shakespeare, *Measure for Measure*, II. ii. 35–41: 'Condemn the fault, and not the actor of it?' (37). Charlotte Brontë had drawn this distinction in her early prose work, *Captain Henry Hastings* (1839), in relation to Elizabeth's degenerate brother, Henry: 'Her glance, more than her words, said: "Your faults and yourself are separate existences in my mind"' (*Five Novelettes*, ed. Winifred Gérin (Folio Press, 1971)). But see also Irene Tayler's astute analysis of Charlotte's complex expression of aggressive and compassionate feeling for her fictionalized brother, in *Holy Ghosts. The Male Muses of Emily and Charlotte Brontë* (Columbia University Press, 1990), pp. 142–50 – an analysis which could be extended to Anne's treatment of Huntingdon in *Wildfell Hall*.

11. (p. 150) *who can run fastest and farthest down the headlong road*: this vivid charge to perdition bears clear allusion to Matthew 7:13, 'for wide is the gate, and broad is the way, that leadeth to destruction', with conscious or unconscious analogy in the author's mind to Joseph's colourful account in *Wuthering Heights* of Heathcliff's urging Hindley 'dahn t'Broad road, while he flees afore tuh oppen t' pikes' (Ch. 10).

12. (p. 150) *the place prepared for the devil and his angels*: Matthew 25: 41.

13. (p. 150) *recall him to the path of virtue*: cf. Richardson's *Clarissa*, Introduction, p. xiii above.

CHAPTER 18

1. (p. 153) *to spare the partridges*: partridge-shooting was prohibited from 1 February to 1 September under the Game Reform Act of 1831. Gentlemen were permitted to 'devastate the moors', in Emily Brontë's scathing phrase (*Wuthering Heights*, Ch. 18), within limits that conserved the stock. Pheasants were conserved from 1 February to 1 October and grouse from 10 December to 12 August (named 'the glorious twelfth' amongst the slaughtering fraternity). Branwell Brontë was proud of his hunting prowess which is exhibited in a now lost picture entitled 'The Gun Group'. Emily Brontë too was a crack shot but regarded this 'manly' sport with contempt as a sign of human damage (see her Brussels essay, 'Le Chat', translated S. Davies, *Emily Brontë: Heretic* (Women's Press, 1994), pp. 248–9). In *Agnes Grey* Anne Brontë equates hunting men with the morally lowest of the low in the figure of the brutal Uncle Robson who encourages Tom in his sadism to the baby birds, leaning on his gun and commending the boy's depravity as 'spunk' (Ch. 5).

2. (p. 154) *at work*: on genteel sewing or embroidery.

3. (p. 154) *chariot*: small enclosed carriage with a coach box: the passengers sit facing the horses.

4. (p. 154) *barouche*: four-wheeled carriage with folding top for four passengers and a driver.

5. (p. 154) *phaeton*: light four-wheeled open carriage driven by owner. The different carriages suit their owners' temperaments and values rather as modern cars display pretensions: Huntingdon's fast phaeton may be thought of as the early nineteenth-century equivalent of a sports car.

6. (p. 156) *like the postscripts of their letters*: proverbial. Compare *Agnes Grey*, Ch. 22: 'I had enquiries to make, and, like the substances of a lady's postscript, the most important must come last.'

7. (p. 157) *put his arm round my neck and kiss me*: Huntingdon's manipulations of Helen's person show disrespect for her dignity which, by the standards of the day, constituted not just exploitation but a calculated attempt to compromise her. He derives his chief pleasure from the struggles of the victim of this orchestrated harassment. At this stage it is not clear whether the cocksure 'sportsman' is doing much more than seeking to make a 'kill'.

8. (p. 159) *too deeply absorbed in each other to notice her*: *Jane Eyre* also uses Jane's paintings to disclose her deepest fears and desires, in the visionary water-colours of Ch. 13. Helen's allegorical picture seems to resemble Anne Brontë's own style of painting symbolic scenes of conventionally pretty girls with significant trees, e.g., 'What you please' of 1840 (Chitham, *Life*, plate 10).

9. (p. 160) *a very Hebe*: daughter of Zeus and Hera, goddess of youth and cupbearer to the gods on Mount Olympus. Personification of nubile freshness.

10. (p. 160) *Let me have its bowels then*: the coarse suggestiveness of this

penetration and evisceration of Helen's innermost privacy (represented by the personal pictures) gestures forward to Huntingdon's rape-like assault on her diary and the vandalizing of her painting equipment in Ch. 40.

11. (p. 161) *ivory paper*: artist's heavy paper with fine glossed surface.

12. (p. 161) *stained with the blood of his prey*: this repellent image implies his exploitation of the human as well as the animal prey he hunts.

13. (p. 163) *Oh, why can't I hate him?*: recalls Richardson's *Pamela*: 'What is the matter, that, with all his ill usage of me, I cannot hate him?' (ed. P. Sabor (Penguin, 1980), p. 218). Anne Brontë is exploring a masochistic aspect of female psychology which cleaves to its abuser, thus reinforcing the abusive behaviour.

CHAPTER 19

1. (p. 166) *Farewell to thee!*: this 'song', with its emphasis on 'sunny' brightness, is a personal lyric composed by Anne Brontë, possibly related to the poetry she wrote to William Weightman who died in 1842 (see *Poems*, pp. 16–17, 171–2). Chitham believes, however, that 'there is no question of the beloved's death: '"Contempt" and "coldness" are given as the cause of the estrangement' (p. 171). However, the source of the contempt and coldness is indeterminate, and, despite the hope expressed by the last stanza, the lyric has a distinctly elegiac tone. It seems to me possible that the lyric may have been adapted from a personal poem to fit the circumstances of the novel, and not impossible that it may have been written especially for the novel.

2. (p. 166) *mortal language*: like Shorter, Chitham prints 'language', which is certainly preferable to 'languish' used as a noun, glossed by the *OED* as 'a tender look or glance', and accepted by both Rosengarten and Hargreaves. However, the rational Anne Brontë did not go in for 'languishes': and 'language' fits indisputably with 'mortal', in designating the heavenly character of the lost brightness. The sense depends on the fact that there exists an (unavailable) *immortal* language – an immortal 'languish' is inconceivable.

3. (p. 169) *I would sacrifice my body and soul*: the Faustian theme of glib bargains with the immortal soul, which is nothing more than a name to Huntingdon, tolls out in dark farce.

4. (p. 170) *tired nature's sweet restorer*: a circumlocution derived from the first line of Edward Young's 'The Complaint, or Night Thoughts on Life, Death, and Immortality' (1742): 'Tired Nature's sweet restorer, balmy Sleep!'

VOLUME II

CHAPTER 20

1. (p. 174) *a man of 'decided piety'*: the phrase which temporarily sticks in Huntingdon's throat derives from Virgil's *Aeneid*, I. 151: *'vir pietate gravis'* (a man confirmed in piety).

2. (p. 174) *a brand plucked from the burning*: Zechariah 3:2, Amos 4:11. The phrase has a long history in relation to Dissent and Methodism as a symbol of salvation, frequently used by Wesley concerning his 'providential' escape from the fire at Epworth Rectory in his youth. Huntingdon's comic fantasies playfully reconstruct Helen's aunt as a religious zealot of the sort the Brontë children themselves enjoyed caricaturing (see Valentine Cunningham, *Everywhere Spoken Against: Dissent in the Victorian Novel* (Clarendon Press, 1975)). It seems to have been a standing joke with Branwell Brontë (see Introduction, p. xxvi).

3. (p. 174) a *'sweet preacher'* . . . *a 'dear, delightful, heavenly-minded man'*: not identified.

4. (p. 175) *I don't think he cares enough about me*: a telling comment, which deepens our understanding of Helen's psychology. Because of her aunt's sterling influence, her background has left Helen principled, thoughtful and independent-spirited but, because of her uncle's laxness and her father's abdication of care, her self-esteem is complicated by a neediness which attaches her fatally to Huntingdon.

5. (p. 176) *a little lower than the angels*: Psalms 8:5, Hebrews 2:7, 9.

6. (p. 177) *his wife shall undo what his mother did!*: the cry of hubris for whose blind arrogance Helen will have to pay in the tragic knowledge not only of failure but also a sensation of being herself contaminated. See Ch. 30, n. 2, Ch. 34, n. 1; and Richardson's *Clarissa*, quoted in the Introduction, p. xiii.

7. (p. 177) *What fellowship hath light with darkness; or he that believeth with an infidel?*: Anne Brontë conflates 2 Corinthians 6:14 and 15. Paul goes on to say that 'ye are the temple of the living God' (16): the reference is a reminder of the sexual bond of marriage which turns man and wife into 'one flesh' – a pollution, in Helen's strict aunt's view, of the 'temple' of the godly by the ungodly.

8. (p. 177) *If he hear not them, neither will he hear though one rose from the dead*: adapted from the end of the parable of Dives and Lazarus in Luke 16:31, a key biblical text for *Wildfell Hall*. See n. 10 below and Ch. 49, n. 2.

9. (p. 177) *The wicked shall be turned into hell . . . forget God*: from Psalms 9:17.

10. (p. 177) *When you see yourselves parted for ever*: taking up the parable of Dives and Lazarus, in which the pauper is taken into bliss in Abraham's bosom and the rich man who had rejected his claim to charity is excluded. Dives cries from hell, 'send Lazarus, that he may dip the tip of his finger in water, and cool my tongue' (Luke 16:24) but his plea is denied.

11. (p. 177) *cast into the lake that burneth with unquenchable fire*: Aunt Maxwell now turns apocalyptic in quoting Revelation 20: 10, conflated with Luke 3: 17.

12. (p. 178) *Not for ever*: this phrase is the important pivot upon which turns Anne Brontë's version of the Brontë antagonism to the Christian vision of eternal hell as the punishment of sinners. Whereas Emily Brontë denied the goodness of God in the light of his punitive morality, Anne Brontë denied the eternity of hell as inconsistent with a loving Father: 'even the wicked shall at last / Be fitted for the skies' ('A Word to the Calvinists', 37–8). In an early religious crisis, she had consulted a Moravian minister, Revd James la Trobe, who had consoled her with his church's emphasis on divine Grace; latterly she corresponded with Dr David Thom, the leader of the sect of Bereon Universalists, who believed in universal salvation. See Tom Winnifrith, *The Brontës and their Background: Romance and Reality* (Macmillan, 1977 edn.), p. 35, 56–62.

13. (p. 178) *only till he has paid to the uttermost farthing*: Matthew 5:26

14. (p. 178) *If any man's work . . . so as by fire*: 1 Corinthians 3:15.

15. (p. 178) *is able to subdue . . . all men to be saved*: conflates Philippians 3:21 with 1 Timothy 2:4.

16. (p. 178) *will in the fulness of time . . . things in heaven*: conflates Ephesians 1: 10, Hebrews 2:9, Colossians 1:20.

17. (p. 178) *might signify either 'endless' or 'long-enduring'*: Hargreaves identifies this as New Testament Greek αἰώνιος, Old Testament examples of which might be interpreted as 'lasting for a long time' but which, when used in relation to God, signifies a literal eternity (Ch. 20, n. 10). Anne Brontë here lays bare her own excruciated struggle to secure a face-saving formula for God, as well as the proudly Protestant self-assurance with which she plunges into a theological and philosophical debate for which she is not formally qualified, given her ignorance of Greek and Hebrew. The speech is not quite in character for Helen, who is never shown as a deep student or thinker.

18. (p. 178) *a glorious thought to cherish in one's own heart*: here Helen confronts the difficulty that had struck Anne Brontë that the fear of hell-fire acts as a deterrent, and that to withdraw it may remove a social and spiritual control. Helen therefore compromises by advancing her doctrine as essentially a private rather than public article of faith.

19. (p. 179) *ludicrous, if it had not been too provoking*: Huntingdon's pantomime seems to be a close representation of Branwell Brontë's travesty of church behaviour, e.g., his novel fragment, *And The Weary Are At Rest* (1845) records his irreverent view of Wesleyanism.

20. (p. 179) *a caricature of the preacher*: in *Wuthering Heights*, Cathy defaces her pious books with 'an excellent caricature of my friend Joseph' (Ch. 3) and rebellious marginalia. She and Heathcliff hurl their tracts 'into the dog-kennel, vowing I hated a good book'. What in *Wuthering Heights* is presented with detached amusement and sympathy is condemned in *Wildfell Hall* but *not without* transmitting a certain amusement to the reader.

21. (p. 179) *it's love that rules the roast*: this form of the expression was current from the sixteenth to the nineteenth centuries (*OED*). See Byron's letter of 1820 to Mr Murray, reminiscing about the male clubs at Cambridge: 'while he [William Bankes] stayed, he ruled the roast – or rather the *roasting* – and was father of all mischiefs' (Moore's *Byron*, p. 97).

CHAPTER 21

1. (p. 182) *all the Sir Herberts and Valentines*: Helen dismisses the fabricated ideal knights of courtly romance, e.g., in the French medieval romance *Valentine and Orson*.

2. (p. 184) *all for love or the world well lost*: title of John Dryden's play of 1678, which had passed into common usage as a romantic formula.

CHAPTER 22

1. (p. 186) *amused*: in the archaic sense of 'beguiled, deluded' (*OED*).

2. (p. 187) *blackleg*: swindlers at gambling (*OED*).

3. (p. 187) *bedlamites*: lunatics (from 'Bedlam', or Bethlehem Hospital, the first English lunatic asylum).

4. (p. 187) *felo-de-se*: suicide.

5. (p. 188) *the poor devil, with a ghastly smile*: Anne Brontë constantly salvages casual phrases such as 'poor devil' from the colourless neutrality into which common usage has trodden them, and awakens our consciousness of their original meanings. Lowborough is indeed in a 'hell' more appalling than a mere 'gambling hell'. His smile is 'ghastly' (from 'ghostly') because he is playing away his soul: he has diminished to the spectre of himself.

6. (p. 188) *home – that is, to our club*: another piercing irony. As ministering demon, Huntingdon leads his 'noble' fellow deeper into the den of degradation and despair, by feeding Lowborough's thirst with alcohol. The club may be reminiscent of the infamous Hell-fire Club at Medmenham Abbey, described in Charles Johnstone's *Chrysal: or the Adventures of a Guinea* (1760–65). Another source may be Moore's *Byron*, whose accounts of Regency club antics had enlivened the Brontës' childhood: e.g., 'We were a company of some seven or eight, and used to sit up late in our friars' dresses, drinking burgundy, claret, champagne, and what not, out of the *skull-cup* and all sorts of glasses, and buffooning around the house in our conventual garments … The harmony of these our symposia was somewhat interrupted … by Matthew's threatening to throw Hobhouse out of a *window*, in consequence of I know not what commerce of jokes' (p. 98). Nearer home, Anne Brontë had witnessed the orgies of Branwell and his cronies, with their self-dramatizing 'hellfire' camaraderie. In the Lowborough inset story she focuses on the poignancy of what may be spiritually lost when control and self-esteem are forfeited: he is essentially a Byronic figure, with the Calvinist dread which Byron saw as having darkened his childhood.

7. (p. 189) *because you're a peer*: hereditary peers were immune from arrest for debt, though their property could be confiscated.

8. (p. 189) *What can't be cured must be endured*: proverbial.

9. (p. 189) *Then, they were demons themselves*: Helen brings to the surface of attention the movement from buried metaphor ('demons of drink … as black as the demon of play') to literal morality drama. The mutually reinforcing behaviour of male bondings is emphasized: the group polices its individuals (here, the disaffected Lowborough) when it feels its narcissistic code threatened. Anne Brontë shows the infantile character of debauch, with its machismo dependent on a mass act of sucking on the equivalent of babies' bottles.

10. (p. 190) *Stop poor sinner, stop and think*: perhaps composed by Anne Brontë herself in emulation of Methodist or Baptist admonitory hymns – possibly a 'temperance' hymn.

11. (p. 192) *providentially*: the narcissistic Huntingdon presents his crowning glory as a parody of the biblical 'helmet of salvation' (Ephesians 6:17), with authorial irony on the word 'providentially' which equates him with the 'elect'.

12. (p. 192) *a skeleton at a feast*: proverbial, after the Ancient Egyptian tradition of the *memento mori* at a feast. Lowborough as a *memento mori* disturbs the group's capacity to surrender to its customary mindless mirth: there follows a discussion of club rules so as to protect the group against this intrusion of reality.

13. (p. 192) *glided in, like the ghost in Macbeth*: Shakespeare, *Macbeth* III. iv. Lowborough's very mode of locomotion appears sinister to the fraternity, since, like Banquo's ghost, he disrupts the complacency of the feast by threatening to arouse guilt and unease.

14. (p. 193) *a fearful looking for of judgment and fiery indignation!*: Hebrews 10:27. Inga-Stina Ewbank's suggested emendation of 'for' to 'forth' is not accurate (*Their Proper Sphere: A Study of the Brontë Sisters as Early-Victorian Female Novelists* (Edward Arnold, 1966), p. 73): but the fact that Anne Brontë's language can present difficulties to the modern reader points up the roots of her English in the Authorized Version of the Bible, i.e., in early seventeenth-century usage.

15. (p. 193) *followed by a rather severe brain fever*: the Lowborough episode allows Anne Brontë to plot the downward curve of drug-abuse, which is not an aspect of Huntingdon's psychology. She illustrates the manic-depressive fluctuations of the combination of opium and alcohol, which she had observed at close quarters, together with the physical breakdown such a combination can entail.

16. (p. 193) *I tenderly brought him back to the fold*: Huntingdon viciously parodies the solicitude of the Good Shepherd who restored the one sheep that was lost, in the parable ('he rejoiceth more of that sheep, than of the ninety and nine which went not astray' (Matthew 18:13)). The shepherd stands for Christ's love of the human soul.

17. (p. 194) *a little wine for his stomach's sake*: 1 Timothy 5:23.

18. (p. 194) *media-via, ni-jamais-ni-toujours*: 'the middle way' (Latin); 'neither never nor always' (French).

19. (p. 197) *castaway*: one of the most emotive words in Anne Brontë's vocabulary, this word represented the predicament of the reprobated soul, God's reject, in Calvinist theology. In her poem, 'To Cowper', Anne Brontë answers the famous last verse of the eighteenth-century poet's 'The Cast-Away' ('. . . we perish'd, each alone, / But I, beneath a rougher sea / And whelm'd in deeper gulfs than he' (64–6)) with her own self-doubt: 'Yet should thy darkest fears be true, / If Heaven be so severe / That such a soul as thine is lost, / O! how shall I appear?' (41–4). The 1850 version of her beautiful 'Prayer' reads 'Unless Thou hasten to relieve, / Thy suppliant is a castaway' (8–9). Fear of reprobation haunts Nancy Brown in *Agnes Grey*: she too fears to be abandoned (Ch. 11). The younger Cathy in *Wuthering Heights* mocks the Calvinistic Joseph by calling him 'reprobate! you are a castaway' (Ch. 2).

20. (p. 199) *flirting her gold-mounted whip*: flicking or waving the whip. Annabella, who has the whip-hand in the relationship with the deluded Lowborough, preens her own powerfully sexual image in the mirror. She is now for the second time admired as 'a magnificent creature', where 'creature' carries the sense of the alien and animal. She lacks the susceptibilities of Lowborough and of Helen, and it is this absence of human sympathy and moral sense that places her beneath the fully human.

21. (p. 201) *what shall I do with the serious part of myself?*: one of the most brilliant, sombre touches of apprehension, the more impressive for its placement at the end of a chapter – intimating the awareness that Helen's intended husband has something catastrophically missing from his nature.

CHAPTER 23

1. (p. 202) *Grassdale Manor*: Hargreaves emends to 'Grass-dale' on the grounds that this is the form 'in the vast majority of cases in the Newby edition'. This is true, but the first and second instances are given as 'Grassdale' and subsequently the name recurs broken between one line and the next, which I surmise gave currency to the 'Grass-dale' which latterly emerges. I therefore print 'Grassdale'.

2. (p. 202) *to love him and to cleave to him*: echoing the Marriage Service in the Book of Common Prayer.

3. (p. 204) *you don't love me with all your heart*: playing on Jesus' first commandment: 'Thou shalt love the Lord thy God with all thy heart, and with all thy soul, and with all thy mind' (Matthew 22:37).

4. (p. 205) *not one atom more of it to you than He allows*: the Christian-feminist insistence on the priority of the allegiance to God over one's husband is as forcefully expressed in Charlotte Brontë's *Jane Eyre*: 'I could not, in those days, see God for his creature – of whom I had made an idol' (Ch. 24). Huntingdon is tempting Helen to commit idolatry.

5. (p. 205) *a sweet enthusiast*: 'enthusiast' derives from the Greek, 'filled with the god': pejorative in the late seventeenth and eighteenth centuries, with the sense of 'religious fanatic'; reclaimed in the Romantic period and by Dissenters because of renewed esteem for divine inspiration. Gondal was a theatre of 'enthusiasm', e.g., Emily's poem of 1839, 'Sleep not, dream not' addresses a child as 'Darling enthusiast, holy child' (11), predicting his fall from grace; Anne's poem of 1838, 'The North Wind', addresses 'a young enthusiast', 'wild and free' as the mountains (12–13).

6. (p. 205) *organ of veneration*: in phrenology, the pseudo-science which equated shape of skull with an individual's moral, intellectual and emotional qualities, the area at the top centre of the skull was held to denote the capacity for reverence or worship.

7. (p. 205) *gathering where he had not strawed*: Matthew 25:24 'Strawed' means 'strewed' or 'scattered'.

8. (p. 206) *who can eat ... more than I?*: Ecclesiastes 2:25. Huntingdon's five-part parody discourse whacks his pious wife with a text pillaged from the book of human vanity, written reputedly by Solomon.

9. (p. 207) *and to be merry*: Ecclesiastes 8:15.
10. (p. 207) *Rejoice . . . into judgment*: Ecclesiastes 11:9.

CHAPTER 24

1. (p. 210) *locked myself up in my own chamber*: this gesture of angry exclusion of Helen's husband from her bedroom as having no moral right to her person defies the law which appropriated wife to husband as sexual property. See Introduction, p. xviii.

2. (p. 210) *dumbfoundered*: a variant of 'dumbfound' or 'dumbfounded' (*OED*).

3. (p. 212) *He struck it off with a smart blow*: behaviour toward animals was always a litmus test of character for Anne Brontë. In *Agnes Grey*, the curate Mr Weston's care for Nancy Brown's cat (Chs. 11, 12) stands in contrast to the minister Mr Hatfield's casual brutality as he 'kicked my poor cat right across th' floor' (Ch. 11) and hits the Murrays' dog 'a resounding thwack' upon its skull (Ch. 14).

4. (p. 215) *are you going to be a good girl*: the infantile male attempts to assert control by infantilizing in turn, bringing his grown-up wife into the dependent relationship custom expects. The verbal demotion of grown woman to 'good girl' is a mode of subjection through role-play, whose greatest literary exponent is Elizabeth von Arnim in her characterization of Everard Wemyss in *Vera* (1921): ' "Now what has the little thing got into its head this time?" ' (p. 180); ' "Sh-sh, now. Go to sleep again like a good little girl" . . . "Who's my very own baby?" ' (p. 319).

CHAPTER 25

1. (p. 218) *rakish*: haggard, off-colour (from 'rake') – an ironic description from the mouth of the rake, Huntingdon.

2. (p. 218) *that tender, delicate bloom*: 'bloom' was used in the eighteenth and nineteenth centuries to denote the youthful freshness and glow of a young woman's complexion which conduces to the impression of untouched freshness and the condition of her sexual value. Anne Elliot, in Jane Austen's *Persuasion* (1818), has lost hers (Ch. 1) and is judged undesirable until she recovers it.

3. (p. 220) *patience, 'that first of woman's virtues'*: the traditional type of the perfect (i.e., perfectly compliant) woman was Griselda, the prodigy of patience who conformed unquestioningly to her husband's irrational dictates, even to the extent of appearing naked in company.

4. (p. 220) *Absence makes the heart grow fonder*: proverbial.

5. (p. 221) *his old governor*: irreverent slang for his father.

6. (pp. 223–4) *But now ... abominable club*: at over 300 words in length, this meandering descriptive sentence is the longest in a novel which frequently moves into loose complex grammar of mutually subordinate clauses. Here the listless motion of the language mimes Helen's poignant, pointless comings and goings in the *locus amoenus* or pastoral paradise of Grassdale, with its fertile Wordsworthian nature that does no one any good, because Huntingdon is not there to benefit from it. His 'abominable club' is the roaming sentence's dead end.

7. (p. 224) *sweet regent of the sky*: from the ballad 'Cumnor Hall', attributed to William Julius Mickle (1735–88).

8. (p. 224) *black blue vault of heaven*: in William Wordsworth's 'A Night Piece', the lonely traveller sees 'The clear Moon, and the glory of the heavens. / There, in a black-blue vault she sails along, / Followed by multitudes of stars' (13–15).

9. (p. 227) *though they sought them carefully with tears*: Hebrews 12:17, referring to Esau and the defilement of sin.

CHAPTER 26

1. (p. 230) *a moon to mitigate the deprivation*: a possible allusion to Shelley's poem *Epipsychidion*, in which Shelley's wife is viewed as the moon and the desired lady as the sun (277–383). Shelley's poem, known to Emily and Anne Brontë (Edward Chitham, *A Life of Emily Brontë*, pp. 73, 99, 133–4) attacks conjugal possessiveness.

2. (p. 231) *everything handsome about him*: Shakespeare, *Much Ado about Nothing*, IV. ii. 78.

CHAPTER 27

1. (p. 235) *You are breaking your marriage vows yourself*: Anne Brontë highlights the asymmetry of the marriage contract in which the woman's undertaking to 'love, honour and obey' put her in a double bind if the spouse should turn out to be irresponsible.

2. (p. 236) *However we do praise ourselves ... Than women's are*: the self-indulging and ambivalent Orsino's speech to Viola in *Twelfth Night* II. iv. 31–5 is an apt precedent to be quoted by the far more mercurial, light-minded Huntingdon. Anne Brontë emphasizes the double standard of sexual fidelity current in the early nineteenth century.

3. (p. 237) *a curtain lecture*: *OED* quotes Dr Johnson: 'A reproof given by a wife to her husband in bed', i.e., in the privacy of the curtained conjugal couch where he is at her mercy.

CHAPTER 28

1. (p. 239) *He may be taken from me*: Helen's fear, in an age of high infant mortality, is not morbidly far-fetched; but its intensity reflects the need and insecurity which are Helen's lot in life. The theme of loss of mate and child occurs in Anne Brontë's poetry a decade before *Wildfell Hall* (e.g., 'A Voice from the Dungeon', 53–4).

2. (p. 239) *He may live to curse his own existence*: Anne Brontë's earnest awareness of the harshness and corruption of human life for the young and growing spirit is evidenced in the poems of this period, especially 'When sinks my heart in hopeless gloom' (1845), 37–48.

3. (p. 239) *flesh of my flesh and shrine of that pure spark*: weds allusion to Genesis 2:23 (which denotes, however, the 'one flesh' of man and woman) with the New Testament idea of the body as temple of the Spirit of God (1 Corinthians 3:16–17). In her tendance of her child, Helen discerns a sacred duty to foster the Platonistic 'spark' of the divine in her child. She views her motherhood in the light of eternity; and, in her aghast recognition of the depravity unfolding in the father, desperately seeks means to abort it in the son. The novel now recurs to the theme of education set forth in the early chapters.

4. (p. 240) *Little angel!*: not entirely metaphorical. Anne Brontë recalls Christ's preference for children: 'Take heed that ye despise not one of these little ones; for I say unto you, That in heaven their angels do always behold the face of my Father which is in heaven' (Matthew 18:10). Compare also the dual meditation over the cradle of Hareton in *Wuthering Heights*, Nelly's '"How sweetly he smiles in his sleep!"' succeeded by Cathy's prophetic, '"Yes; and how sweetly his father curses in his solitude! You remember him, I dare say, when he was just such another as that chubby thing – nearly as young and innocent"' (Ch. 9), deriving from Lord Byron's drama, *Cain*, with its lament over the disinherited future of Cain's sleeping baby: 'He smiles, and sleeps . . .' (III. i. 18ff.).

5. (p. 241) *You are absolutely infatuated about it*: Anne Brontë's understanding of the infantile basis of Huntingdon's despotic possessiveness is dramatically focused, with poignant comedy, in this scene witnessing the father's jealousy of his wife's attention to their baby.

CHAPTER 29

1. (p. 244) *worn out with the baby's restless nights*: Helen is evidently breast-feeding the baby herself, in defiance of the then norms for women of rank.

CHAPTER 30

1. (p. 256) *degrade yourself*: 'degrade', repeated here four times in close succession, is a key-word in the moral world of *Wildfell Hall* as it is in *Wuthering Heights*, where Hindley degrades Heathcliff, who in turn degrades Hindley's son Hareton.

2. (p. 262) *almost a partaker in his sins*: Anne Brontë had an unsentimentally realistic view of the contaminating effects of the corrupted upon the apparently innocent or principled. Agnes Grey feels herself undergoing a comparable process of pollution: 'Already, I seemed to feel my intellect deteriorating, my heart petrifying, my soul contracting, and I trembled lest my very moral perceptions should become deadened' (*Agnes Grey*, Ch. 12).

3. (p. 262) *the gulf*: corresponds with the Miltonic 'abyss' down which the presumptuous damned fell to hell. For Emily Brontë, the 'gulf' was for daring and defying: 'Measuring the gulf it stoops and dares the final bound' (From her poem, 'Julian M. and A. G. Rochelle', 84).

CHAPTER 31

1. (p. 267) *my corruption rises against it*: see Ch. 2, n. 11, where Markham's 'corruption' is aroused by Helen's proud beauty. It is because Helen has suffered the ascent of her own unregenerate nature in the novel's central panel that she carries the moral authority, based on experience and self-knowledge, in the outer panels.

2. (p. 268) *Sine as ye brew ... drink the yill*: ('Since as you brew, my fair maiden, bear in mind that you must drink the ale'). Anne Brontë quotes from Robert Burns's (1759–96) 'Country Lassie'.

3. (p. 269) *power to save him from the worse*: Helen is carrying out the rational programme for dealing with a degenerate husband proposed by Agnes in *Agnes Grey*, whose conclusion is 'if she still found him incorrigible, to endeavour to abstract herself from him – to wrap herself up in her own integrity, and trouble herself as little about him as possible' (Ch. 23). Helen is never able to reach this conclusive stage of distancing because of the dangers to her son and the impossibility in practice of maintaining one's 'integrity' in proximity to a pathological attention-seeker.

4. (p. 270) *In quietness and confidence shall be your rest*: from Isaiah 30:15. The context of the quotation is also one of righteous indignation: Israel is said to 'despise this word, and trust in oppression and perverseness' (30:12).

5. (p. 273) *sensibly*: 'acutely, intensely' (*OED*).

6. (p. 274) *the fowls of heaven and the lilies of the field*: a drunkenly blasphemous garbling of Matthew 6:26, 28.

7. (p. 275) *thy whole body shall be full of light*: another blasphemy of Matthew 6:22. The text goes on: 'But if thine eye be evil, thy whole body shall be full of darkness'. Chapter 31 of *Wildfell Hall* is concerned with incorruptible 'treasures in heaven' (6:20), profaned by the squalid roisterers at Grassdale.

CHAPTER 32

1. (p. 281) *Esther Hargrave*: Esther (named after the biblical queen whose influence with her husband liberated the Jews) is an important secondary character, a form of youthful *alter ego* for Helen, exemplifying Anne Brontë's concern for the tutelage of the younger generation of women, commodified on the marriage-market by unscrupulous mothers (see Chitham, *Life*, pp. 152–3: 'Anne begins to wrestle with a now recurrent problem: how to warn young people about the pitfalls of life without robbing them of their spontaneity'). Branwell Brontë depicted 'Queen Esther' (after Martin) in a water-colour of 1830: see Gérin, *Branwell Brontë*, Plate 1.

2. (p. 284) *loose upon him, like a cloak*: a verbal echo of *Macbeth*, V. ii. 21.

3. (p. 286) *in the horse-jockey line*: used here to signify one who owns or breeds horses.

4. (p. 288) *a thought too soft*: Milicent's excessive compliance is another object-lesson in this chapter. Anne Brontë uses Milicent's husband, not a despicable man though at once rough and weak, to voice her case against female pliability, which can act as an incitement to men to misbehave. The author's concern is for the dynamics of relationships.

5. (p. 289) *it spoils the best of us, doesn't it?*: Hattersley's observation echoes in a major key the theme introduced by Markham in the minor key in Ch. 6: 'I might sink into the grossest condition of self-indulgence and carelessness about the wants of others, from the mere habit of being constantly cared for myself' (pp. 57–8).

6. (p. 289) *she lies down like a spaniel at my feet*: Mary Wollstonecraft, in *A Vindication of the Rights of Woman* (1792), memorably compared women with spaniels: '"These dogs," observes a naturalist, "at first kept their ears erect; but custom has superceded nature, and a token of fear is become a beauty"' (ed. Miriam Brody (Penguin, 1992 edn.), Ch. 5, p. 179).

7. (p. 289) *melts away and makes no sign*: cf. *II Henry VI*, III. iii. 29.

8. (p. 291) *God be merciful to me a sinner*: Luke 18:13.

CHAPTER 33

1. (p. 295) *mind*: I see no reason to emend 'mind' to 'mend' as Hargreaves does: the phrase 'mind our manners' was current and makes enough sense in context.

2. (p. 298) *a game of chess*: Anne Brontë deploys a Renaissance motif, used, e.g., to ironic effect in Thomas Middleton's play *Women Beware Women* (c. 1620–24), Act II, where the game of chess mirrors a seduction scene. The chess game between Helen and Hargrave is replete with sinister *double entendre*: it figures the war between the sexes enacted in Hargrave's attempt to entrap and 'conquer' Helen.

3. (p. 300) *my bishop*: Helen attacks with the chess piece known as the 'bishop', signifying the integrity she hopes to retain unassailably. However, Hargrave's 'knight' (his male sexuality) finds her bishop undefended, leaving her 'queen' (her integrity as a woman) open to attack, so that ultimately she is checkmated.

4. (p. 303) *my tongue cleaved to the roof of my mouth*: citing Job 29:10, where Job recalls the days of his glory, in which the great of the earth were silenced 'and their tongue cleaved to the roof of their mouth', whereas now 'They abhor me, they flee far from me, and spare not to spit in my face' (30:10). At this crisis of recognition of her forsakenness, Helen's affliction represents itself in scriptural language which is structured as a mesh of texts, moving from an Old Testament language of trauma towards a New Testament promise and assurance.

5. (p. 303) *a gust of wind swept over me*: Helen has involuntarily prayed 'God help me now!' and fallen to her knees: God answers in the breath of wind, his quickening Spirit. This experience of being breathed upon is Helen's personal version of the Pentecostal wind received by the disciples in Acts 2:2.

6. (p. 303) *some heavenly influence ... within*: 'influence' means, originally, 'flowing in', and represents the second stage of Helen's experience of spiritual assurance. This derives from the Reformation tradition of the individual's receiving of prevenient Grace in the soul's dark night. *Jane Eyre* is steeped in this tradition, and in this climactic passage, *Wildfell Hall* shares the psalmic intensity of Jane's despair at the end of Ch. 26: ' "Be not far from me, for trouble is near: there is none to help." ... That bitter hour cannot be described: in truth, "the waters came into my soul; I sank in deep mire; I felt no standing ..." '.

7. (p. 303) *strong to save and swift to hear*: James 1:19. The night scene is close in feeling to *Jane Eyre*, Ch. 28, where, kneeling on the heath, Jane 'felt the might and strength of God. Sure was I of His efficiency to save what He had made ...'

8. (p. 304) *I will never leave thee, nor forsake thee*: Helen, in her need, lays hold of the promises of Scripture, in the tradition of Bunyan's *Grace Abounding to the Chief of Sinners* (1666): here, Hebrews 13:5. Anne Brontë may have remembered Christ's words as repeated in the Epistle rather than the Gospel because Paul places his quotation in proximity to a judgement on adulterers (13:4).

9. (p. 304) *he would not leave me comfortless*: John 14:18. Jesus is here promising his own presence within each believer, in the person of the Holy Spirit, 'another Comforter, that ... may abide with you for ever; Even the Spirit of truth' (14:16–17).

10. (p. 304) *Much of my newborn strength and courage forsook me*: this does not invalidate the reality of the 'Pentecostal' scene; rather it tests the assurance of the Christian spirit against the arduous conditions of the real world – as with Christian in *The Pilgrim's Progress*, one of the most important texts of the Brontës' childhood.

11. (p. 305) *the burden*: a resonance of Christian's lonely burden in *The Pilgrim's Progress*: 'I dreamed, and behold I saw a man ... [with] a great burden on his back' (p. 39).

12. (p. 305) *a suppressed exclamation*: emended from the first edition, 'explanation'.

13. (p. 306) *husband and wife only in the name*: Anne Brontë is explicit in establishing that at this point Helen quits her husband's bed.

14. (p. 307) *pity their folly and despise their scorn*: the chapter of Helen's humiliation ends on a proud note of self-assertion, a spirit of righteous anger that is at one with the feminist spirit of the novel and its fiercely Protestant theme of the individual's power and duty to resist a corrupt consensus.

CHAPTER 34

1. (p. 311) *with a feeling of malevolent gratification*: Anne Brontë does not shrink from a full portrayal of the gall which provides a blackly compensatory pleasure to a hurt or rejected person. In this chapter Helen characteristically channels her destructive feelings not toward depression but outwards as retaliatory anger.

CHAPTER 35

1. (p. 316) *to recover the shock*: 'recover' could be used transitively in the nineteenth century in cases where we would say 'recover from'.

2. (p. 318) *Then, go, and sin no more*: John 8:11. The irony of this riposte lies in its gender reversal. In the Gospel, this is Christ's admonition to the woman who 'was taken in adultery, in the very act' (8:4). Here a woman enjoins it upon a male committing the sin of sexual harassment.

CHAPTER 36

1. (p. 323) *petrifaction*: 'turning to stone', completing the process of emotional hardening implied in a chain of images: 'hard, embittering', 'habitual cold-ness', 'frigid civility', 'congealed me to marble'. For a warm-hearted person like Helen, the necessary hardening is a personal disaster, but not as great a danger as to remain sensitive and at her husband's mercy would be.

2. (p. 323) *a slight titter on seeing me turn colour*: the word 'titter' is exquisitely chosen. Helen is married to the moral equivalent of a baby who must crave and suck at all and any attention, and has no notion of piety or dignity save as threats to his insecure sense of self.

3. (p. 324) *and stay upon his God*: Isaiah 50:10. Rosengarten comments, 'Probably cited from memory', presumably because of the slight inaccuracy and the italicization – but it is far more likely that Anne Brontë cited *all* her biblical texts from memory and, like her father, knew much of the Bible by heart.

CHAPTER 37

1. (p. 325) *perils that beset him on every hand*: the language is Bunyanesque. Helen's child is a pilgrim at the vulnerable outset of his journey through the wilderness of this world, in need of cherishing guidance. The realistic battle of indulgent, feckless father against severe, grieving mother for the soul of the child enacts the cosmic battle between Good and Evil. The father, like the devil in the Morality plays, enjoys an inbuilt advantage since he is offering fun and games – but the equation is complicated by the fact that Helen, on the side of the angels, sees that play and light-heartedness (which she can no longer give) are necessary to her son's development. Ironically, she is replicating her aunt's behaviour towards herself. The child now becomes pivotal to the plot.

2. (p. 329) *Such goodness overawes me*: The characterization of the unctuously flattering Hargrave may owe something to the reptilian advances of Milton's Satan, here echoing *Paradise Lost*, IX: 'her every air / Of gesture or least action overawed / His malice ... and for the time remained / Stupidly good' (459–61, 464–5), and his insincere praise of Eve's virtue (IX. 538–9). 'So glozed the Tempter,' Milton says; and Anne Brontë's Hargrave also persistently 'glozes'. There are also shades of the contest between Comus and the Lady in Milton's *A Masque: Comus* (1634), 244–52, 659–813). Richardson translated the biblical and Miltonic contest of fiend and woman to the sexual arena: see *Clarissa*, Letters 31, 152 and 199: 'Surely this is an angel, Jack' (p. 642); Lovelace is 'ashamed of being awed by her majestic loveliness and apprehensive virtue' (p. 643). Ironically, Clarissa's and Helen's very virtue arouses the seducer.

3. (p. 331) *that indefatigable foe*: again, Miltonic. Satan (whose name means 'Enemy') is recurrently alluded to as 'our grand foe' 'their secret foe' (*Paradise Lost* IV. 7), with his 'indefatigable wings' (II. 408).

4. (p. 332) *I have no rest day or night*: Hargrave impudently ransacks Scripture to furnish an account of his afflictions as a latter-day Job (Job 30:17) and a lamenter of Lamentations ('we labour, and we have no rest' (Lamentations 5:5)).

5. (p. 333) *we may reap in joy, hereafter*: Psalms 126:5.

6. (p. 333) *I still have my God and my religion*: Compare Jane's manifesto in *Jane Eyre*: 'The more solitary, the more friendless, the more unsustained I am, the more I will respect myself. I will keep the law given by God, sanctioned by man' (Ch. 27). Helen, of course, does not feel tempted by Hargrave as Jane does by Rochester, being repelled rather than attracted.

7. (p. 335) *I thank God for this deliverance!*: Helen concludes the second volume in a style comparable with that of the Puritan spiritual autobiographies which influenced Bunyan's *The Pilgrim's Progress*, e.g., after the battle with Apollyon, 'So when the battle was over, Christian said, "I will here give thanks to him that hath delivered me out of the mouth of the lion, to him that did help me against Apollyon"' (p. 94).

VOLUME III

CHAPTER 38

1. (p. 340) *one bright star*: Hesper-Vesper, the evening and the morning star, associated with Christ's death and resurrection: cf. Milton, *Paradise Regained*:

'So spake our Morning Star then in his rise' (I. 294). Anne Brontë poignantly uses this sacred image to express the grace of Mr Weston's coming into Agnes's life in *Agnes Grey*: 'appearing like the morning star in my horizon, to save me from the fear of utter darkness' (Ch. 11).

2. (p. 340) *When that dying light ... wholly comfortless*: Rosengarten defines this as paraphrase of 'a recurring biblical sentiment', referring to Psalm 112.

3. (p. 342) *Let her injure you no farther*: the first and second editions omit 'no'.

4. (p. 342) *like one under the influence of acute physical pain*: Lord Lowborough's violent physical manifestations of grief resemble in less extreme form those of Emily Brontë's Heathcliff, who grinds and gnashes his teeth (*Wuthering Heights*, Ch. 15) and dashes his head against a tree (Ch. 16).

5. (p. 343) *for you are a man, and free to act as you please*: i.e., it is open to Lord Lowborough as an injured husband to obtain a divorce, a right not available at that period to the vast majority of women, whatever their grievance. Divorce, before the Marriage and Divorce Law of 1857, was only possible by Act of Parliament: even after that date, a woman was unlikely to obtain one.

6. (p. 347) *blackened his name with a deeper disgrace*: Anne Brontë here attacks the scapegoating of cuckolded husbands in a patriarchal culture that plays all males off against one another as rivals for the females and measures male success by sexual prowess and willingness to resort to violence if this is brought into question.

7. (p. 348) *a little girl between one and two*: i.e., Arthur Huntingdon's child by Annabella, conceived near the beginning of their adultery. The physiological details of blue eyes and auburn hair make clear that the child 'takes after' her father.

CHAPTER 39

1. (p. 350) *to make a man of him*: in *Agnes Grey* Uncle Robson inculcates similar principles into the heir, Tom, by encouraging him to drink wine and brandy and to equate high consumption of these with a 'bold and manly spirit' and superiority to his sisters (Ch. 5); also by egging him on to sporting endeavours requiring 'spunk'. Manliness is equated with self-indulgence and public gratification of power-lust, symbolized by Tom's whip and spurs (Ch. 2).

2. (p. 350) *moped to death between an old nurse and a cursed fool of a mother*: cf. *Agnes Grey*: '"He's beyond petticoat government already: – by G—, he defies mother, granny, governess, and all!"' Ch. 5). In *Wildfell Hall*, the fraternity is initiating Helen's son into tribal customs by teaching him to despise gentleness and self-control as effeminate. They thus pass their own contempt for women to the next generation, who will visit it on their wives and beget

it in their children. These events are only an extreme case of the control-system of patriarchy. In removing her son, Helen is attempting to put herself between the elder and younger generations of males in order to stop the damage being passed along the line.

3. (p. 350) *set the table in a roar*: like the jester, Yorick, in Shakespeare's *Hamlet*, V. i. 185. The allusion brings to mind the *memento mori* of Yorick's skull.

4. (p. 351) *the infant profligate*: Emily and Anne Brontë were both interested in the skin-deep character of 'civilization'. *Wuthering Heights* is also a fable of culture and degradation, in which a controlled experiment in conditioning is carried out. As Heathcliff says to Hareton, '"Now, my bonny lad, you are *mine*! And we'll see if one tree won't grow as crooked as another, with the same wind to twist it' (Ch. 17). Hareton, like 'the infant profligate' in *Wildfell Hall*, loves the man who has taught him to curse and is reclaimed when 'petticoat government' (in the form of the second Cathy) supervenes.

5. (p. 352) *my sober toil-fellows now*: the theme of the self-supporting working woman is important in both Anne Brontë's novels, and central to *Agnes Grey*, in which Agnes is a governess ('working as a hireling among strangers' (Ch. 21)), and her mother, though born like Helen into the leisured classes, is proud to support herself as a teacher – to 'earn her own livelihood, and be chargeable to no one' (Ch. 19). The profession of visual artist was rarely possible to women, since formal training was not available until the 1850s (see Germaine Greer on the ambivalence of Helen's attitude to her art in *The Obstacle Race: The Fortunes of Women Painters and their Work* (Pan with Secker & Warburg, 1979), pp. 310–12; see also Karen Petersen and J. J. Wilson, *Women Artists. Recognition and Reappraisal from the Early Middle Ages to the Twentieth Century* (Women's Press, 1994 edn.)).

6. (p. 354) *par parenthèse*: 'by way of parenthesis' (French).

7. (p. 357) *Ye twain shall be one flesh*: incorporated into the marriage service in the Book of Common Prayer, from Matthew 19:5, Mark 10:8. The quotation is ironically inserted into Hargrave's speech since he is offering Helen an adulterous liaison in which she would forfeit all personal dignity.

8. (p. 358) *you could not choose but yield*: Hargrave threatens rape, the logical conclusion of his long assault. Lovelace's rape in *Clarissa* finds an echo here.

9. (p. 358) *his ramrod and his gun*: the current muzzle-loading gun required a ramrod to drive home the charge. Males in *Wildfell Hall* are recurrently seen armed with weapons; for the first time, Helen has taken up a weapon to defend herself (significantly, her palette-knife, the tool of her trade, which will ultimately guarantee her independence). Anne Brontë queries male glorification of arms and violent activity as compensation for their absence

of a sense of wholeness: she had read in Moore's *Byron* of the young aristocrat's passion 'for arms of every description', slicing at the bed-hangings with a bedside sword as a morning recreation and terrifying young women with wild 'firing at a mark' (p. 72). Byron's pugilism, disastrously aped by Branwell Brontë, even down to the boxing gloves, was shown by Moore as a compensation for the weakening deformity of his club foot.

10. (p. 359) *a puss or two*: sporting idiom for hares.

11. (p. 360) *the satisfaction of a gentleman*: a duel, over a question of 'honour', according to the 'gentlemen's code'. Hargrave's acknowledgement has formally placed him in a position of having insulted Huntingdon by making sexual advances to his wife. Throughout this scene, there is irony on the word 'gentleman', a dignity to which the crew are only nominally entitled.

CHAPTER 40

1. (p. 364) *With your leave, my dear, I'll have a look at this*: 'With your leave, my dear', in keeping with the courteous phrasings and endearments which accompany Huntingdon's intrusion into Helen's personal space (the book of her life and her life's work), carries sombre irony, since Helen has neither power nor legal right to stop her husband asserting possession of all her nominal property and alienating or destroying it as he sees fit. This scene represents a rape of Helen's spiritual world in the form of her diary-testament, as well as the temporary demolition of her means of securing liberty.

2. (p. 365) *bladders*: containers for artist's paints, made of animal bladders.

3. (p. 365) *stretcher*: frame on which artist's canvas is stretched tight.

4. (p. 368) *it will cleave to the dust*: Psalms 119:25.

5. (p. 368) *He hath hedged me about ... children of men*: Lamentations 3:7, 3:15, 3:32–3. The third chapter of Lamentations is structured upon the man of affliction's search to accept God's apparent abandonment and to see it in a providential perspective.

6. (p. 368) *It is not the will ... should perish*: Matthew 18:14. Helen comforts herself by resigning her son to the tenderness of the Almighty Father.

CHAPTER 41

1. (p. 369) *Hope springs eternal in the human breast*: Alexander Pope, *An Essay on Man* (1733), I. 95. Pope's point in praising Hope is ironic: whereas its existence depends on our ignorance of the future, its presence is essential to make life bearable. William Cowper in a long poem entitled 'Hope' saw

Hope as the deepest resource of the Christian: 'Hope, as an anchor firm and sure, holds fast / The Christian vessel, and defies the blast' (167–8). Hope was an important motif in Victorian iconography, painted blindfold with rainbow-coloured wings. It is personified in Emily Brontë's poetry ('O thy bright eyes', 37; 'How beautiful the Earth is still', 37–48, identified with the 'Comforter' and 'Guide', Emily's heretical version of the Holy Spirit). Anne Brontë's poetry represents a ceaseless conflict between reasons to hope and a tendency to despair (sustained as dialogue in 'Self-Communion' (1847–8): see especially on Hope, lines 245–96).

2. (p. 369) *so do better plants*: referring to the parable of the sower: Matthew 13; Mark 4. The naturally fertile soil of Arthur's genetic inheritance resembles the 'wealthy soil that might yield luxuriant crops under other and favourable circumstances' of Hareton Earnshaw's nature in *Wuthering Heights*, Ch. 18. Anne Brontë like Emily insists on the dual importance of genetic inheritance and conditioning.

3. (p. 370) *enlist all the powers of association in my service*: Helen is able to use a basis of Lockean associationism on which to construct a programme of aversion-therapy prefiguring modern behavioural theory and techniques.

4. (p. 374) *against*: 'by the time that' (archaic).

5. (p. 374) *younger sons*: a younger son would not be seen as a good catch because under the system of primogeniture, the eldest son would inherit the whole estate.

6. (p. 375) *a mere cumberer of the ground*: cf. the parable of the barren fruit-tree in Luke 13 ('why cumbereth it the ground?' (13:7)). Anne Brontë reflects on the dismaying pressure brought upon surplus daughters to marry and quit the parental home. She had personal experience of this callousness in the behaviour of her employer, Lydia Robinson, forcing her daughters to marry against their inclinations. As Charlotte Brontë wrote, 'Mrs Robinson is anxious to get her daughters husbands of any kind, that they may be off her hands' (Letter to Ellen Nussey, August 18, 1848; *SHLL*, p. 247).

CHAPTER 42

1. (p. 379) *worriting*: worrying, brooding (colloquialism).

2. (p. 380) *our duty to admonish our neighbours of their transgressions*: 'speak every man truth with his neighbour: for we are members one of another' (Ephesians 4:25). Helen's audacious plain speaking, which violates the female decorum of dumb submission to the male masters, claims the authority of the early church for the duty (not merely the right) of intervention in another family's concerns.

3. (p. 380) *that house so founded on the sand*: in Jesus' parable (Matthew 7:24–7), the wise man built his house on a rock 'and it fell not' (7:25) but the foolish man built his on sand, and the house was destroyed in a storm (7:27). The allusion expresses the insecurity of the dependent state of wifehood, whose house is in a literal sense founded upon her husband's character and behaviour.

4. (p. 380) *dash away a tear*: while tears were not, in the mid-nineteenth century, as taboo for males as they later became, the males of Huntingdon's set would have scorned them as effeminate. Hattersley's tears, however, have a yet larger significance: in Christian iconography, tears are signs of contrition, denoting the melting of the heart so that the work of Grace and redemption can take place.

5. (p. 381) *mite*: 'might', erroneously, in the first edition.

6. (p. 381) *one bright spot, at least, whereon to rest my thoughts*: it is an index of the importance and value of female friendship in *Wildfell Hall* that Helen can take real comfort from the amelioration of her friend's lot, brought about by her forthrightness, despite the unremitting horror of her own situation.

CHAPTER 43

1. (p. 382) THE BOUNDARY PASSED: THE BOUNDARY PAST in the first edition.

2. (p. 384) *down of that new governess*: distrustful or suspicious of her (dialect).

3. (p. 384) *intelligence*: in the sense of 'information' (*OED*).

4. (p. 385) *barns*: Yorkshire dialect for 'children', cognate with Scottish 'bairns', cf. the ballad Nelly Dean sings in *Wuthering Heights*, Ch. 9: 'It was far in the night, and the bairnies grat'.

5. (p. 385) *of the last importance*: in the sense of 'of the ultimate importance'.

CHAPTER 44

1. (p. 390) *some surprising outburst of hilarity*: something of Gondal emotion bursts through here in the paeon to liberty Helen inwardly utters. Anne's and Emily's Gondal heroines typically spent much of their lives imprisoned and dreaming of liberty. They might also be, like Helen, outlaws, hunted and homeless – but elated and free, as in 'Song: "Come to the banquet"' (1845), 25–30:

> O happy life! To range the mountains wild,
> The waving woods – or Ocean's heaving breast,

With limbs unfettered, conscience undefiled,
And choosing where to wander, where to rest!
Hunted, oppressed, but ever strong to cope –
With toils, and perils – ever full of hope!

2. (p. 391) *walked there with me in her arms*: Wildfell Hall is focused as Helen's devastated maternal home: she is returning to the site of her babyhood, her mother-country, a refuge though in ruins. Rachel, who is named after 'the mother of Israel' in the Old Testament, is a vestige of the mother-world, perhaps as Tabitha Aykroyd (the Brontës' beloved servant) had seemed for Anne.

3. (p. 392) *indefinite dreams of the far past and bright anticipations of the future*: Helen can only conceive of a future when she has brought herself into relation with her origins.

CHAPTER 45

1. (p. 399) *wasted with many sorrows*: Hargreaves's reference to 1 Timothy 6:10, adopted uncritically by Rosengarten, is entirely inappropriate, since it concerns persons who have erred from the faith through love of money. In fact the phrase has only a general biblical resonance, associated for instance with 'a man of sorrows' of Isaiah 53:3, 'The sorrows of a travailing woman' of Hosea 13:13, etc.

2. (p. 404) *But not as we are now*: a clear reference to 1 Corinthians 15:51–2: 'We shall all be changed', read in association with the Pauline texts which deny distinction in heaven of gender, race, status (e.g., Galatians 3:28). These passages reflect Anne Brontë's deep scrutiny of the scriptural texts concerning Heaven, no doubt in dialogue and latterly dispute with Emily Brontë, and her awareness of the inhumanity of the traditional reading of the divine system of reward and punishment. Heaven is distrusted by Markham as a place of separation, a magnified and irreversible version of that experienced on earth, for in heaven personality is lost. This is Markham's version of Cathy's dream in which '"heaven did not seem to be my home"' (*Wuthering Heights*, Ch. 9).

3. (p. 404) *ten thousand thousand angels*: Revelation 5:11.

4. (p. 405) *losing me in a sea of glory*: some of the finest phrasing in the novel is devoted to the nightmare vision of heaven. In *Wuthering Heights*, Cathy and Heathcliff choose their own heretical antinomian heaven rather than encounter this threat to their exclusive bond, rejecting the sanctions of anything 'that God or Satan could inflict' (Ch. 15).

5. (p. 405) *the grovelling caterpillar*: compare Emily Brontë's use of the caterpillar/butterfly motif, an ancient emblem of the soul's immortality, in

her apocalyptic Brussels essay, 'The Butterfly' (1842): 'As the ugly caterpillar is the origin of the splendid butterfly, so this globe is the embryo of a new heaven and a new earth' (tr. S. Davies, in Stevie Davies, *Emily Brontë: Heretic* (Women's Press, 1994, p. 251). But Emily's vision of earth as 'a vast machine constructed solely to produce evil' (p. 250) gives this conclusion a satiric edge.

6. (p. 405) *we feel as children, and we understand as children*: echoes 1 Corinthians 13:11.

7. (p. 406) *if faith would never fail*: Anne Brontë had wrestled with strong religious doubts, to the extent of fearing that God was a 'vain delusion' ('A Hymn', 29). The faith she represents in Helen was formed on the basis of conflict with the doubt voiced by Markham in this important dialogue.

CHAPTER 47

1. (p. 419) *on household cares intent*: casual allusion to Eve in Milton's *Paradise Lost*, V. 332 ('on hospitable thoughts intent').

2. (p. 419) *a few words of course*: a few commonplace words.

3. (p. 420) *We never mention her; her name is never heard*: from 'Oh! no! we never mention her', by Thomas Haynes Bayly (1797–1839).

4. (p. 426) *I must have a written agreement*: Helen seeks to use her advantage to bind her husband to sign away his right to custody of his son. Such a contract could not in fact have been binding in law, since the husband could revoke it at will.

5. (p. 428) *acidulated*: rendered acid (considered, as in the case of lemon, to have thirst-quenching properties).

6. (p. 428) *heaping coals of fire on my head*: see Proverbs 25:21–2: 'If thine enemy be hungry, give him bread to eat; and if he be thirsty, give him water to drink: For thou shalt heap coals of fire upon his head, and the Lord shall reward thee'. Huntingdon is accusing his wife of vindictive virtue. It is a shrewd hit.

7. (p. 430) *casting her pearls before swine*: see Matthew 7:6.

CHAPTER 48

1. (p. 433) *elude*: the first edition has 'illude', an archaism.

2. (p. 435) *such gall and wormwood*: See Anne Brontë's favourite chapter of Lamentations, 3 (19). The biblical phrase had passed into common usage.

3. (p. 435) *a stately, branching herb*: like the mustard seed in Jesus' parable, the tiny grain which grows into 'the greatest among herbs, and becometh a tree'

(Matthew 13: 31–2). Charlotte Brontë uses this image to designate the Brontë children's creative life in a poem called 'Retrospection': 'The mustard-seed in distant land / Bends down a mighty tree' (29–30).

4. (p. 435) *That worthy student was now at Cambridge ... collegiate career*: following in Anne Brontë's father's footsteps, for Patrick Brontë had studied at St John's College, and was ordained in 1806.

5. (p. 436) *full of years and honours*: cf. Genesis 25:8, 1 Chronicles 29: 28.

6. (p. 436) *Reverend Richard Wilson*: the first edition has 'Edward' for 'Richard', perhaps an authorial confusion with Reverend Edward Weston in *Agnes Grey*.

CHAPTER 49

1. (p. 438) *The rain descended ... great was the fall of it*: Matthew 7:27: another, and this time apocalyptic, allusion to the parable of the house built upon sand (see Ch. 42, n. 3 above). The radical instability of Huntingdon cannot withstand the final stress of the terror of death.

2. (p.441) *dip the tip of your finger in water to cool my tongue*: Huntingdon plays on the parable of Dives and Lazarus (Luke 16:19–31) which had evidently gripped the imaginations of Anne and Emily Brontë as a focus of separation-anxiety, even under optimistic conditions of personal salvation. (See Ch. 20, n. 10 above). The parable reverses the status of oppressor and oppressed in the afterlife, stressing the absolute *pro rata* basis of punishment hereafter for sin now. The question arose in Emily's, Branwell's and Anne's minds: how lovable was such a God, and how heavenly could heaven be under such conditions?

3. (p. 441) *the great gulf over which I cannot pass*: a near-direct quotation from the parable of Dives and Lazarus (see n. 2 above), in which Father Abraham replies to Dives' entreaty that Lazarus 'may dip the tip of his finger in water, and cool my tongue' (Luke 16:24) that 'between us and you there is a great gulf fixed' (16: 26).

4. (p. 441) *if I could look complacently on in such a case*: Anne Brontë could not. Through Helen, she unfolds her hope of an intermediate state of purgatorial atonement between hell and heaven. Emily Brontë repudiated such a heaven as callous, in the light of earth's suffering: 'Heaven itself, so pure and blest / Could never give my spirit rest' ('I see around me tombstones grey' (1841), 13–14.

5. (p. 441) *Oh, it's all a fable*: the stated opinion of the Romantic sceptics, Byron and Shelley, and latterly of Branwell Brontë, e.g., in his poem 'Azrael'. The phrasing also recalls Christopher Marlowe's *Dr Faustus* (c. 1594): 'I think hell's a fable', answered by Mephostophilis with the grimly ironic, 'Ay, think

so still, till experience change thy mind' (*The Tragical History of the Life and Death of Dr Faustus*, ed. J. D. Jump (Manchester University Press, 1962), sc. v, 128–9).

6. (p. 445) *But death will come – it is coming now – fast, fast!*: cf. *Dr Faustus* again in the accelerating panic of his final soliloquy: 'The devil will come, and Faustus must be damn'd' (sc. xix, 144).

7. (p. 446) *I can't repent; I only fear*: cf. *Dr Faustus* again: 'My heart is harden'd, I cannot repent', sc. vi, 18.

8. (p. 446) *God is infinite Wisdom . . . and LOVE*: Psalms 147:5; 1 John 4:8, 4:16.

9. (p. 446) *in whom the fulness of the godhead shines*: Colossians 2:9. Helen tries to settle Huntingdon's panic-stricken mind upon the human and intercessive person of the Trinity, the atoning Son, who has already taken Huntingdon's sins upon himself.

10 (p. 446) *as if I had never been; while I–* : compare Catherine's speech beginning, "I wish I could hold you . . . till we were both dead"' (*Wuthering Heights*, Ch. 15).

11 (p. 446) *No man . . . agreement unto God for him*: Psalms 49:7–8.

12. (p. 447) *God, who hateth nothing that he hath made*: see Ezekiel 33:11, and the Book of Common Prayer (collect for Ash Wednesday). See Ch. 20, notes 10–18 above for Anne Brontë's belief in universal redemption.

CHAPTER 50

1. (p. 450) *rank and circumstances*: as 'Mrs Huntingdon of Grassdale Manor', Helen is a person of 'rank', i.e., of inherited property, unearned income and gentry status. As 'Mrs Graham the artist', a working person living in a tenancy, she was merely middle class and therefore might be considered eligible by a farmer. Anne Brontë makes much of this perhaps in order to extend the novel to the required three-volume length.

2. (p. 452) *my philosophy*: i.e., 'my philosophic state of mind'.

3. (p. 457) *come out from among them*: 2 Corinthians 6:17. The quotation goes on: 'and be separate, saith the Lord, and touch not the unclean thing.' The novel here circles back to Ch. 20, and regretfully concurs with Aunt Maxwell's opinion, which she had attached to the same chapter of 2 Corinthians, that the unbeliever and the believer must live in separation. See Ch. 20, n. 7.

CHAPTER 51

1. (p. 459) *appeal to the laws for protection*: Mr Millward, the voice of ecclesiastical authority in the area, speaks for the forces of reaction which decreed that

there were literally *no* circumstances under which a married woman could take autonomous action, apart from appeal to law. However, the law offered women no redress from abuse. Charlotte Brontë records this in the case of Caroline's mother, Mrs Helstone, in *Shirley*: 'The world's laws never came near us – never! They were powerless as a rotten bulrush to protect me – impotent as idiot babblings to restrain him!' (ch. 24).

2. (p. 460) *tell the tale as 'twas told to me*: cf. Sir Walter Scott, 'The Lay of the Last Minstrel' (1805), II. xxii.

3. (p. 463) *balled the horses' feet*: packed the hoofs with snow, thus hampering progress.

4. (p. 463) *post-chaise*: enclosed coach carrying four persons, hired from stage to stage.

5. (p. 463) *A gig then – a fly – car*: a 'gig' was a light two-wheeled vehicle; a 'fly' a small hired carriage (drawn by one horse); a 'car' a two-wheeled cart of various description.

6. (p. 464) *clod-hoppers*: dismissive term for rustic labourers.

7. (p. 466) *sotto voce*: low-voiced, on an undertone.

CHAPTER 52

1. (p. 471) *pea-jacket*: a short woollen overcoat.

2. (p. 472) *platitude*: level condition.

CHAPTER 53

1. (p. 478) *and respectively returned*: Hargreaves emends 'respectively' to 'respectfully', on the grounds that the former is 'at best extremely weak': I have retained it, on the grounds that it makes adequate sense and that Anne Brontë's writing *could* on occasion be 'extremely weak'.

2. (p. 484) *dared not believe in so much joy*: Hargreaves prints 'believe in such felicity', since the 1848 New York edition has 'hope for such felicity', a discrepancy which he hypothesizes may represent 'different stages of the transmission of the text through proofs and a change of mind by the author'. However, since the New York version may erroneously have picked up the phrase 'believe in such felicity' from the manuscript for the page (p. 485) succeeding, I have retained the original, stronger version.

3. (p. 488) *Linden-Car*: the first edition has, erroneously, 'Linden Grange'.

4. (p. 488) *I bequeathed the farm to Fergus*: marriage to Helen has emancipated Markham from the need to work for a living and translated him into a

landed gentleman who needs to do nothing but supervise his wife's estates. No regret is shown at this emancipation, and we are given no idea as to how he and Helen spend their lives.

5. (p. 489) *June 10th, 1847*: possibly the date on which Anne Brontë completed the draft of *The Tenant of Wildfell Hall* (see Chitham, *Life*, p. 152).

SELECT BIBLIOGRAPHY

Alexander, Christine, *The Early Writings of Charlotte Brontë* (Blackwell, 1983).

Allott, Miriam (ed.), *The Brontës: The Critical Heritage* (Routledge & Kegan Paul, 1974).

Brontë, Charlotte, *Five Novelettes*, ed. Winifred Gérin (Folio Press, 1971).

Bunyan, John, *The Pilgrim's Progress*, ed. Roger Sharrock (Penguin, 1965).

Chitham, Edward, *A Life of Anne Brontë* (Blackwell, 1991).

Chitham, Edward, *A Life of Emily Brontë* (Blackwell, 1987).

Chitham, Edward, (ed.), *The Poems of Anne Brontë* (Macmillan, 1979).

Cowper, William, *Poetry and Prose*, ed. Brian Spiller (Hart-Davis, 1968).

Davies, Stevie, *Emily Brontë* (Harvester Wheatsheaf, 1988).

Davies, Stevie, *Emily Brontë: Heretic* (Women's Press, 1994).

du Maurier, Daphne, *The Infernal World of Branwell Brontë* (Gollancz, 1972).

Eliot, George, *Middlemarch, A Study of Provincial Life*, ed. W. J. Harvey (Penguin, 1965 edn.).

Ewbank, Inga-Stina, '*The Tenant of Wildfell Hall* and *Women Beware Women*', in *Notes and Queries*, 10 (1963), pp. 449–50.

Ewbank, Inga-Stina, *Their Proper Sphere: A Study of the Brontë Sisters as Early-Victorian Female Novelists* (Edward Arnold, 1966).

Gérin, Winifred, *Anne Brontë* (second edition) (Nelson, 1974).

Gérin, Winifred, *Branwell Brontë* (Nelson, 1961).

Gilbert, Sandra M. and Gubar, Susan, *The Madwoman in the Attic: The Woman Writer and the Nineteenth-Century Literary Imagination* (Yale University Press, 1979).

Gordon, Jan B., 'Gossip, Diary, Letter, Text: Anne Brontë's Narrative Tenant and the Problematic of the Gothic Sequel', *English Literary History*, 51, 4 (Winter, 1984), pp. 719–45.

Gordon, Lyndall, *Charlotte Brontë: A Passionate Life* (Chatto & Windus, 1994).

Greer, Germaine, *The Obstacle Race: The Fortunes of Women Painters and their Work* (Pan with Secker & Warburg, 1979).

Grundy, Francis H., *Pictures of the Past* (Griffith & Farrers, 1879).

Hargreaves, G. D. (ed.), *The Tenant of Wildfell Hall* (Penguin, 1979).

Hargreaves, G. D., 'Incomplete Texts of *The Tenant of Wildfell Hall*', *Brontë Society Transactions*, 16, 2 (1972), pp. 113–18.

Hatfield, C. W. (ed.), *The Complete Poems of Emily Jane Brontë* (Columbia University Press, 1941).

Jacobs, Naomi M., 'Gender and Layered Narrative in *Wuthering Heights* and *The Tenant of Wildfell Hall*', *The Journal of Narrative Technique*, 16, 3 (Autumn, 1986), pp. 204–19.

Langland, Elizabeth, *Anne Brontë: The Other One* (Macmillan, 1989).

McMaster, Juliet, '"Imbecile Laughter" and "Desperate Earnest" in *The Tenant of Wildfell Hall*', *Modern Language Quarterly*, 43, 4 (December, 1982), pp. 542–68).

Mill, J. S., and Taylor, Harriet, *Essays on Sex Equality*, ed. Alice S. Rossi (Chicago University Press, 1970).

Milton, John, *Paradise Lost*, ed. Alastair Fowler (Longman, 1968).

Moore, Thomas, *The Letters and Journals of Lord Byron; With Notices of his Life* (Chatto & Windus, 1830).

Petersen, Karen, and Wilson, J. J., *Women Artists. Recognition and Reappraisal from the Early Middle Ages to the Twentieth Century* (Women's Press, 1994 edn.).

Richardson, Samuel, *Clarissa; or the History of a Young Lady*, ed. Angus Ross (Penguin, 1983).

Rosengarten, Herbert (ed.) and Smith, Margaret (introd.), *The Tenant of Wildfell Hall* (Oxford University Press, 1992).

Scott, P. J. M., *Anne Brontë: A New Critical Assessment* (Vision Press, 1983).

Showalter, Elaine, *A Literature of Their Own: British Women Novelists from Brontë to Lessing* (Princeton University Press, 1977).

Tayler, Irene, *Holy Ghosts: The Male Muses of Emily and Charlotte Brontë* (Columbia University Press, 1990).

Winnifrith, Tom, *The Brontës and their Background: Romance and Reality* (Macmillan, 1977).

Wise, T. J., and Symington, J. A., (eds.), 'The Shakespeare Head Press Brontë': *The Brontës: Their Lives, Friendships and Correspondence*, 4 vols, (Blackwell, 1933, reissued 1980).

Wollstonecraft, Mary, *A Vindication of the Rights of Woman*, ed. Miriam Brody (Penguin, 1992 edn.).

READ MORE IN PENGUIN

In every corner of the world, on every subject under the sun, Penguin represents quality and variety – the very best in publishing today.

For complete information about books available from Penguin – including Puffins, Penguin Classics and Arkana – and how to order them, write to us at the appropriate address below. Please note that for copyright reasons the selection of books varies from country to country.

In the United Kingdom: Please write to *Dept. EP, Penguin Books Ltd, Bath Road, Harmondsworth, West Drayton, Middlesex UB7 ODA*

In the United States: Please write to *Consumer Sales, Penguin USA, P.O. Box 999, Dept. 17109, Bergenfield, New Jersey 07621-0120.* VISA and MasterCard holders call 1-800-253-6476 to order Penguin titles

In Canada: Please write to *Penguin Books Canada Ltd, 10 Alcorn Avenue, Suite 300, Toronto, Ontario M4V 3B2*

In Australia: Please write to *Penguin Books Australia Ltd, P.O. Box 257, Ringwood, Victoria 3134*

In New Zealand: Please write to *Penguin Books (NZ) Ltd, Private Bag 102902, North Shore Mail Centre, Auckland 10*

In India: Please write to *Penguin Books India Pvt Ltd, 706 Eros Apartments, 56 Nehru Place, New Delhi 110 019*

In the Netherlands: Please write to *Penguin Books Netherlands bv, Postbus 3507, NL-1001 AH Amsterdam*

In Germany: Please write to *Penguin Books Deutschland GmbH, Metzlerstrasse 26, 60594 Frankfurt am Main*

In Spain: Please write to *Penguin Books S. A., Bravo Murillo 19, 1° B, 28015 Madrid*

In Italy: Please write to *Penguin Italia s.r.l., Via Felice Casati 20, I–20124 Milano*

In France: Please write to *Penguin France S. A., 17 rue Lejeune, F–31000 Toulouse*

In Japan: Please write to *Penguin Books Japan, Ishikiribashi Building, 2–5–4, Suido, Bunkyo-ku, Tokyo 112*

In South Africa: Please write to *Longman Penguin Southern Africa (Pty) Ltd, Private Bag X08, Bertsham 2013*

READ MORE IN PENGUIN

PENGUIN CLASSICS

Agnes Grey   Anne Brontë

Drawing on her own experiences, Anne Brontë wrote her first novel out of an urgent need to inform her contemporaries about the desperate position of unmarried, educated women, driven to take up the only 'respectable' career open to them – that of governess. Agnes tells a story that is at once a compelling inside view of Victorian chauvinism and ruthless materialism and, according to George Moore, 'the most perfect prose narrative in English literature'.

Jane Eyre   Charlotte Brontë

Immediately recognized as a work of genius, *Jane Eyre* portrays a woman's passionate search for a wider and richer life than that traditionally accorded to her sex in Victorian society. This new Penguin Classics edition has an introduction and notes by Michael Mason.

also by Charlotte Brontë in Penguin Classics:

Shirley
Villette
The Professor
Juvenilia 1829–1935

and by Emily Brontë:

Wuthering Heights
The Complete Poems

Wuthering Heights, Jane Eyre, Villette, Shirley, The Professor, The Tenant of Wildfell Hall *and* Agnes Grey, *all read by Juliet Stevenson,* Jane Eyre, *read by Joanna David, and* Wuthering Heights, *read by Samuel West and Prunella Scales, are also available as Penguin Audiobooks.*